Donemere's Music

Two Stood Together

(Book Three in the Series)

Two Stood Together

Something...or someone...is stealing magic.

As newly risen Ér Ainíl of the Ganlonds, Donemere Saunders pledged to protect the sacred magical lands under her care. When she swore this oath to the *Niunda Wakan*, she didn't realize there were other places she would be expected to defend. Heeding a new call for divine intervention, Donnie, Sylvester, Falwaïn and Diego travel west to the magical lands of the Mîrlonds, where an unknown dark entity is stealing magic from deep within Írtha itself.

Meanwhile, her other friends also go adventuring. What each discovers about themselves, their traveling companions, and the past is far more than they could ever have imagined possible. But whatever the danger, they stand together through it all.

First U.S. Printed Edition: April 2019.

Cover photo by Ms. Gross.

CAG Publishing, 2019
ISBN: 978-0-9978411-5-2
eBook ISBN: 978-0-9978411-4-5

Acknowledgements: My everlasting thanks to Sally Green and Maura O'Neill, who were brave enough to read this story in its very first incarnation and to kindly give me their valuable input. And my gratitude goes to Trista Tolles for her wonderful work on the covers for my books. She makes it all look great!

This book is dedicated to those who stand together through thick and thin. You inspire us all.

To my beloved father, who was taken too soon from us and is so sorely missed. May peace be with you, Papa.

And as always to Rex, my real-life Wonder Dog: Thank you for teaching me so much about life and love and family.

Register of Major Characters in the Series

Donemere Saunders is the Ér Ainíl of the Ganlonds. During Donnie's defeat of Valledai, she joined the *Niunda Wakan*, the Nine Guardians, and rose to the office of Ér Ainíl, becoming the protective goddess of the magical lands under her care. This doesn't mean she's lost her sense of humor or her willingness to listen to those around her.

Rex the Wonder Dog is Donnie's German Shepherd Dog. He is her heart and her love, a piece of home that keeps her sane.

Tanygrisiau yr Eglwys Wen is Donnie's dour feline familiar, who she immediately renames **Sylvester**. Occasionally, he allows her to see how impressed he is with her magical abilities, and even more occasionally shows his affection for her.

The boombox provides clues to what Donnie should do next in the form of songs and their lyrics. While it will listen to her requests and sometimes her remonstrances, she cannot touch it with her magic, nor can anyone else.

Other Major Characters (listed alphabetically)

Akanna is from the Zal'Dorek Vinca of Gainál and is the king's army commander. She finds Diana fascinating, for good reason.

Aldalis Munkinum is the presiding Bishop of the Førrens Order of Manûs Mages. He believes the order should be the guardians and keepers of the Forrieghness Tower. He, like most wizards in the order, hates witches. He takes a particular dislike to Donnie.

Belnesem is the King of Medregai, a friend of Falwaïn, and the enemy of Valledai. While he accepted Donnie's help in the Battle of the Branmar Plain, he does not trust her to bury the dead.

Ben Saunders is Donnie's father, a kindly man with oddly blue eyes.

Bórlem is the leader of the birds of prey and is a member of the Animal Council.

Bréagna is a daughter of Morrían. She's not particularly good at setting force fields.

Brindle is the leader of the six magical trees Donnie used to expand her house. He is also used for the stirrups on her cotton saddle, so he can travel with Donnie on her adventures.

Bronadulach, leader of the bears, is Kaerdír of the Ganlonds. As Kaerdír, he leads the Animal Council.

Brother Hectern Mire is known in the Førrens Order of Manûs Mages for fighting and stealing rather than comforting or healing. Brother Mire, like his order's bishop, insists on accompanying Donnie and her friends to the Mîrlonds.

Carly, the youngest of the house trees, is great friends with Rex and oftentimes plays word games with him in the bathroom.

The chickens on the Codlebærn farm are Donnie's affectionate prognosticators for expected visitors.

Cyllwyn Mérd is an old willow tree who gave his life, and his life essence, to Donnie when she requested it. His memories have more than one surprise in them. (appears in Books One and Two)

Dantheus is Malwé's grandfather. Sir Dantheus is greatly worried about his grandson, the land and its people, and the future of Faen Eárna.

Diana is Donnie's best friend on the Codlebærn farm. Recently given her choice of form by Donnie, she is a warrioress once more. While she fights it all the way, more and more of her secrets are revealed.

Don **Diego**, known in Medregai as the Black Rider and in his own lands as Galto, remembers more about the Iquakawi than he lets on.

Durreen is the estranged vincan son of Juree of the Marcons and half-brother to Akanna of the Zal'Dorek. Born into a race of warriors, he wishes only to live peacefully.

Emily Saunders is Donnie's sister. She is confused and hurt by the revelations her aunt throws at her family.

Falwaïn, former Prince of Faen Eárna, is a widower who has been traveling the northern lands in search of adventure and death; instead, he joins with Donnie and her friends and ends up coming full circle in life.

Feirth is a giant. He and his mother just want to make it home.

Fine Fellow is a curious, very talkative house tree who loves nothing more than to learn. Brindle is the only one who can reliably get him to shut up.

Gaia, beloved Earth Mother and the greatest goddess of all, welcomed Donnie warmly into the *Niunda Wakan*.

Gak is next in line to Nagba and is the commander of the Førrens Sea Eagles. The Sea Eagles are the rightful guardians and keepers of the Toren fi Førrens or Forrieghness Tower.

Galæron of the Woodland Álvar is the king's trusted advisor and friend. He commands the archery troops for the king's forces. He trusts Donnie even less than his king does.

Gullrick is the Lord Chancellor of Faen Eárna. Donnie discovers that Thyton Gullrick is a puppet being controlled by someone—but by who, though?

Gwillagan is a daughter of Morrían, whose history Donnie is first introduced to in a magical tapestry woven by Gwillagan herself.

Gwydion is a Welsh god of magic from Donnie's world. He is known as a master planner, although he tends to focus on his failures more than his successes, unlike his old friend Gaia.

Hadronica Perlusgo is the not very talented, yet greedy mage of Marn Dím who finds the hiding place of the White Jewel.

Herbert Flint and **Emery Gold** are sorcerers working with the professor to retrieve the clock-watch. They will stop at nothing to get it.

Ixifír Bíun of the Dræda sorcerers is elusive and demanding; his manipulations seem to be everywhere and affect everyone. But then, he's had a long time to make his plans.

Julia Campos misses her mom and is angry at everyone, which makes her an easy target for her father's manipulations.

Juree of the Marcons is the Vincan Ambassador to the Sarn. He was the vincan army commander in Morlant for many a long year before his ambassadorship.

Liz Campos is Donnie's dearest friend from her world, who was secretly held in Valledai's captivity for six months before being liberated by Donnie. Donnie realized that someone in Medregai wanted Liz dead, so she sent Liz to Catie for protection.

Lorraine Saunders is Donnie's mother, a powerful and fierce woman, who is very protective of both her daughters.

Ma'oma is an elderly giantess who wants to see her younger children and their home just one more time before she dies.

Maeve Rae Danaher, or Little Maeve Rae as she would famously become known later in life, just wants to be a regular little girl living with her mother, Florrie Danaher. In reality, she is a very talented little girl fascinated by magic.

Malwé, current Prince of Faen Eárna, an honorary title bestowed on the leader of the Province of Faen Eárna, is known to be the only surviving son of Falwaïn and Sémere. His troubled past diminishes his father.

Méath-Degnír is the leader of the wolves and is a member of the Animal Council.

Mickey T, whose real name is Mecholætera, is a sweet, old Noctule bat. He is good friends with Sylvester and is a member of the Animal Council. He loves to play board games with his friends at the farm.

Miramdahl is the elf queen and wife of Belnesem, King of the Sarn. She has a jealous streak in her a mile wide, just not for her husband.

Mórbaen is the leader of the ruminants and is a member of the Animal Council.

Mournful Jack is a very quiet house tree who seldom speaks. He is apparently quite depressed, as evidenced by the forlorn sough he emits whenever he converses with anyone.

Na'aven is a water spirit who torments her former giant brother.

Nagba is the High Convoke of the Førrens Sea Eagles and is an old, old friend of Morrían and her daughters.

Neddy Cloys, whose full name is Franklin Edward Cloys Brightman, has been a pirate for most of his life and wants nothing more than to sail the high seas with his crew of faithful comrades; except perhaps to experience another exciting adventure with his witchy love, Catie.

Niunda Wakan, or the Nine Guardians, is a divine association composed of the goddesses of several peoples of Írtha. Donnie filled the ninth position when she ascended as Ér Ainíl of the Ganlonds.

Otis the horse loves blues music. He is fiercely loyal to his bond mate and to his friends.

Parry, another house tree, is in love with Brindle.

Philînan is a daughter of Morrían, whose history Donnie is first introduced to in a magical tapestry woven by her sister, Gwillagan.

Plug is Donnie's over-eager SUV.

Professor Gottleib-Lange, the man responsible for designing most of Germany's zeppelins in World War One back in Donnie's world, recognizes Liz immediately for what she is. The professor also knows that she and Catie possess the clock-watch he and his sorcerer associates seek.

Quillirana is a kindly healer of Hörthanc. She seems to know more about Catie and Sylvester than the cat himself does.

Sophie is the oldest of the house trees and has known Brindle for thousands of years. She is tired; always, very tired.

Sephala, Queen of the Bats, venerates her father, Mickey T, but she never really believed his stories of times gone by until now, when living proof of them arrives on the doorstep of the Ganlonds.

Smitty, whose full name is James Smith, is the best boatswain a pirate could ask for.

Tather and his men are a contingent of soldiers of Faen Eárna who are loyal to the old leaders and their violent ways.

Ulma Marg, the de facto leader of the Mountain Peoples' council, asks Diana to remove two things from her city, both of which she considers to be deadly dangerous.

Uncle, whose real name was Ungôl, was a Badûran Vírat. Because of the badûr he got Donnie to make with him, she must find and free his people or die. (appears in Books One and Two)

Valley Guy, whose real name was Valledai, was an evil sorcerer who wanted to exact his revenge on his enemies of old in Medregai. He and his army were defeated by the *Niunda Wakan* in the Battle of the Branmar Plain. (appears in Books One and Two)

Warren, formerly Mynydd Uchaf, King of the Free Wolves, has chosen to live his life as a man and finds that he is in love with Liz Campos. He will do anything for her, which includes protecting her difficult daughter from herself.

Wiwila is Donnie and Rex's bond mate. Together they make up the A'Rontauk, a magical triad the mage in the mountain long ago predicted would arise one day. Other horses at the farm include Gallantry (a.k.a. Arthewyll), Ampago, Raleen, and Jora.

Table of Contents

Prologue

The witch on Fellowes Island has lived there so long, even she cannot recall how many centuries it has been her home. A woman of considerable magical power and a great craver of solitude, she'd usually rebuff visitors to her craggy abode, calling upon the sea around her little skerry to roil and heave tempestuously and toss any errant and suddenly hapless boats back to the shores of the Icebay of Nœthlinga from whence they came.

But on this morning, she seemed to be expecting company, for the island's small jetty was bare of snow and ice and the path to her cottage was unobstructed and lined with holly branches. And the wild north sea, from the mainland to the little isle, was as tame and welcoming as ever it could be.

Inside the island's sole cottage, this witchly woman turned from the roaring blaze in the fireplace hearth and straightened her back, unfolding herself to her full height. Her critical gaze swept the main room of the large cottage, inspecting everything in it. When she finished this examination, her head moved in a small, silent gesture, indicating she was pleased with what she saw.

She was a tall and imposing personage who had wide-set, shrewd blue eyes; a thick, blonde braid hanging down the length of her back that was entwined with holly to signal her truth-telling craft; and reddened, long-fingered hands that had seen many a full day's work. She was clothed in a bespoke midnight blue velvet and silk gown that had a king's ransom of pearls and gemstones sewn into its bodice and whose hem just grazed the floor at the soles of her knee-high leather boots. Her dress was covered by a thick robe of brilliant sapphire velvet that draped her in luxurious warmth and left just enough showing of the raiment beneath to hint of its opulence.

The woman stepped to the center of the room and looked pensively at the closed front door. She soon shivered with cold and began rubbing her roughened hands together briskly to warm them. Although there were two fires roaring in the matching hearths at opposite ends of the long and high room, it was chilly less than ten feet from either conflagration.

Lost deep in her thoughts she stood, and the usual astute aspect of her expression faded. The stately witch frowned, her gaze now troubled and unfocused. She seemed to be contemplating something that unsettled her, although she did not have the look of someone who often experienced such distressing reminiscences, for her fine, unlined features carried an almost beatifically serene quality about them that spoke of complete contentment with her lot in life.

With a sudden hiss of impatience, the woman strode to the far end of the room to where a loom of almost gargantuan proportions was installed. To fit the dimensions of this uncommonly massive machine, the witch's cottage had been built to a similar scale. The loom towered upward, easily taller than the height of three very tall men, and it ran just as long, if not somewhat longer, and was nearly as wide from front to back. Currently, it was strung with hundreds and hundreds of strings of spun silk on the warp, while a nearly finished tapestry curved around the front of the machine to the back. Its colorful and detailed image was reflected in the mirrors positioned above and behind the warp, allowing the weaver to view her tapestries' scenes develop as she wove them. The many bobbins and their corresponding colored and mixed-colored threads for the weft hung from the unfinished tapestry's warp, waiting for the *webbestra* to resume her work with her shuttle.

After a few moments' study of her already completed handiwork, the witch sat at the loom and began working on the image of what looked to become a female. This as-yet-to-be-woven woman was standing before a man who had entered the room in the tapestry through an open doorway. Through that opening was the view of a magnificent citadel made of stone and steel, its gleaming appointments lining the darkened outlines of the city's soaring towers.

The man was dressed in brilliant red robes and had ice-white hair that flowed over his shoulders. He held a staff of elder wood in his grip; a staff that stood nearly as tall as he and which bore a blood-red stone at its crown. This staff he extended before him, its tip leaning slightly forward. The man, a sorcerer of some skill, no doubt, was quite handsome—almost too much so. And his cold blue eyes were not the eyes of a trustworthy man, which was only to be expected of a sorcerer of any magical line. He seemed to be demanding something from the other figure in the tapestry.

During the following two hours, the *webbestra* drew the form of the young woman into the tapestry's tableau, weaving her threads as though possessed by demons. All the while the witch worked her art, her face was alive with emotion and sparks of amethyst-colored magic flew around her. At times, she wore saddened expressions and shed tears as she whispered to herself with what seemed to be forgotten sorrow. Alternately, she wore easy smiles and muttered a litany of names and places, laughing to herself and shaking her head with remembered joy.

And then suddenly, the flashing fingers of the skillful weaver stilled and the room was abruptly silenced except for the sounds of the crackling flames erupting from the two fireplaces. The weaver, looking anguished for a prolonged period, turned her head to stare unseeingly over her left shoulder, her memories apparently having overwhelmed her at last. She rose from her sitting position at her loom, her face now tired and drawn, and she began pacing back and forth between the fireplaces impatiently.

It was perhaps twenty minutes later that a light tap sounded upon the cottage door. The woman strode over to it eagerly and flung it open, calling out with gladness, "Dear Philînan, I hath longed for thy visitation, for it hath been too many moon cycles since last we saw each other!"

Philînan allowed herself to be swept into the other woman's embrace and to be pulled through the cottage doorway. Once inside, she unclasped her bright crimson-colored traveling cloak and shook out the ice drops that had accumulated upon it during her journey over the water, complaining good naturedly, "Sweet sister Gwillagan, I cannot think how ye abide in this long winter all thy days!" Philînan's short, dark curls accentuated her small, slight frame and shook a little as she spoke. Her creamy skin was perfection itself and her stunning features made for an arresting sight, for she was a beauty in any age or any land. "But, aye," she continued heartily, " 'tis wonderful to be with ye again! And our dear sisters' arrivals will be soon, for I feel them making their way here. Oh, did ye know? Darling Rian will be joining us this time," she announced with a cheery grin, "as will Margawse and Vessica."

When Gwillagan murmured her surprised pleasure, Philînan nodded, adding, "Yes, our young sister hath returned from her southern travels and it seems she hath spent several days with Margawse in anticipation of their communal sojourn to Fellowes Island. I predict there will be much for her to share regarding the Mehen'Adrîum and their wise ones."

By wordless agreement, the two sisters sat at the table to partake of the stew made by Gwillagan and to drink the wine Philînan had brought with her, their tongues loosened liberally after each imbibed three large glasses of the potent beverage.

Shyly at first, then more boldly and bawdily, Philînan shared stories of a most beautiful young man whom she had come upon in Morlant whilst she had visited there two summers before. She confessed to her sister that he had stayed with her several times since then upon her beloved Mîrlonds.

An hour later, after imparting titillating tales of these illicit trysts and laughing with satisfied ardor of each recalled meeting with the handsome youth as she wandered the room distractedly, touching things here and there, completely unaware she was doing so, Philînan finally settled upon a stool piled with heavy, thick rugs and beamed at her sister.

For the first time, she noticed the tapestry on the loom and jumped to her feet again, her light blue eyes lively and sparkling with mischief. "Ye hath begun a new augury!" she cried and as her rambling feet took her to the loom she added gaily, "I know ye do not like anyone to behold an unfinished one, but these colors thou art using are most striking and I simply cannot resist my urges!" She sent her sister an arch smile over her shoulder. "Ye will not mind if I take a small peek, will ye?" she asked.

Gwillagan sat back with a chuckle and waved her coquettish sister on. And so, the dark-haired beauty peered over the edge of the loom at the finished end of the tapestry and began to admire the scene depicted in it.

It was but a moment later that Philînan gasped and choked out in a thin, strangled voice, "No! No, it cannot be!" Her frantic gaze ranged over the tapestry and then she turned desperately to the front end of the loom and its newly woven threads, her expression haunted. With another stifled cry, she turned her head back to the completed end of the tapestry and stared mutely at the figure of the handsome man.

Gwillagan ran to her sister's side, exclaiming, "Tell me what it is that distresses ye so, dear sister!"

Shaking her head helplessly, Philînan turned to Gwillagan and pointed at the unfinished wall hanging, inquiring, "Was that born from one of thy visions?"

"Surely it was; they all are. Ye know this!" her sister replied tartly.

Philînan shuddered and squeezed her eyes shut, shoving herself away from the loom as though burned by it.

Gwillagan bent over the loom's frame to study the image, looking to her right at the front of the warp. She had progressed quite far earlier that morning and she could now see that she had woven what looked like the *Hèset fî Bâslen* falling from the hands of the woman on the weaving end of the tapestry. The woman's face was also completed and showed clearly in the strong light of the many candles Gwillagan kept lit around the room. The young woman's familiar features displayed faltering disbelief, most obviously because of the knife handle protruding from her bleeding breast.

Like her sister moments before, Gwillagan gasped in horror and stood away from the loom as though it had scorched her fingers, whirling upon her white-faced sibling in a worried frenzy. "B-but, that woman is ye!" she declared, spluttering as she pointed at the woman's countenance in the tapestry. She looked down at her cringing sister again and demanded, "Who is this man? Do ye know him?"

Philînan shuffled across the room to the chair by the roaring fire and fell into its depths in a miserable heap. Nodding and avoiding her sister's eye, she whispered bitterly, "He be my lover, the young man of whom I hath regaled ye regarding our trysts together. But he is not yet as old as ye hath depicted him in thy vile imagery." She drew a thick rug from the stool before her, buried her face in its soft wool, and began to weep.

Gwillagan straightened her shoulders and clasped her hands in front of her, looking sorry for her sister. "Ye can never meet him again, Philly!" she reproached the younger woman sharply. "For he means us all harm, as anyone can see from the tapestry's prediction. He means to have the *Hèset fi Bâslen*, the Jewels of Light we seven fought so hard to regain and protect, and ye know I cannot give them to him, nor will I let ye do so, as ye are offering in that, that *wicked* weaving." She pointed an indignant finger at the offending tapestry, heaving a string of heavy sighs fraught with fear and frustration. "Philly, ye must stay away from him!" she urged almost righteously when she finally got her breathing under control again.

Philînan, her shoulders bent, let out a wail and a sob before lifting her tear-stained face to the towering Gwillagan. "I know it, sister, I know it," she agreed woefully, her voice cracking with sorrow. "I only hope I can do it, for I love him with all my heart, ye see."

Chapter 1
Three Little Birds

It had gone four in the morning and Donemere Saunders tossed and turned in her sleep, this time rolling onto her back and letting out a groan of surrender as she opened her eyes to stare at the darkened ceiling above. Thousands of whispers disturbed her restive slumber, most of which were complaining with anger or worry about the king's men and the effects they were having on the magical flora and fauna of the Ganlonds. These types of plaints she ignored because she could do nothing about them until the day had begun in earnest.

Some of the remaining whispers were fervent wishes for better lives, while still others were simple prayers for respite from overwhelming grief. It was these last ones that were giving Donnie her hard night's sleep. Her sympathy for those whose sorrow was both immediate and immense made her want to do her very best to ease their burdens and her mind raced with ideas, none of which seemed all that viable, really.

The violent battle the previous night on the Branmar Plain had wreaked a heavy toll and hundreds of animal soldiers had lost their lives alongside the king's soldiers while fighting their common enemy, the mad sorcerer Valledai and his evil armies. His forces, perhaps more aptly described as vicious cohorts in his quest to rule Medregai and become the Master of Time, had been comprised of astonishingly brazen okûns and several other dark confederates such as trolls, werns, and even a malicious giant. These unfortunate, depraved creatures were now mostly dead by combat or transmuted at the end of the battle by the *Niunda Wakan*—known mostly as the Nine Guardians. The reach of the Nine had gone deep into the nearby Brumal Mountains, but no farther than that, so it was unknown how many of the enemy lived in places farther away or what threat they might still pose. All Donnie knew for sure was that she was determined they would never again impose their destructive conflicts on the Ganlonds or any of the multitudes of magical and non-magical citizenry living there.

Having risen to the office of Ér Ainíl of the Ganlonds only last night, Donnie was now privy to the most private prayers and fears of those she protected. These wretched pleas for comfort and assistance came to her automatically with each prayer either spoken or thought by the magical creatures and plants making their homes within the magical lands. Donnie had already forced these growing number of whispered appeals from her head four times tonight because she was unsure of how to respond to them as they sounded off one after the other in her head in a near-constant litany.

She would have to do the same thing again now or she would get no sleep at all. And so, she banished these despairing cries and cleared her mind of all but the desire to return to dreamland. Slowly, her breathing eased and deepened as she fell once more into the black pool of oblivion.

In another hour she would be awakened again by the plaintive calls of her constituents, and so it would go until other noises encroached on her dreams shortly after sunrise, noises she could not then just thrust away and ignore.

These new interruptions began with muffled voices coming near to this side of her cottage, their words too faint to discern from her bed, their tones slowly fading away to silence.

A poorly stifled laugh was the next intrusion from the king's army encampment, the edge of which was situated quite close to the house.

Soon after that, the door from Liz's room to the outside opened and shut carefully, and the sound of light footsteps could be heard crossing the back porch.

And then Falwaïn mumbled in his sleep and rolled over, taking most of the down comforter with him.

Donnie released a frustrated sigh, wondering if there was any sense in trying to go back to sleep seeing as she'd only had maybe a total of five hours of restless slumber after the previous day's exhausting battle. She rubbed her eyes wearily before opening them, as always admiring the morning sun's strong rays lighting the bedroom through the stained-glass of the window. She turned to her left and looked at Falwaïn, studying the way the sun's rays lit his handsome, chiseled features and gilded his hair, turning both golden. She felt a rush of love well up for him and she rested a hand on his arm, reveling in the strong connection she could feel between them. The sun's light brightened as it rose properly now and, for a few moments, she let herself just simply enjoy the rich, beautiful colors blazing all around her.

Momentarily contented, she yawned, arched her back in a cat-like stretch, ignored the bolts of blue magic that escaped from her extremities, and sat up in bed, tugging some of the comforter back from Falwaïn to cover her legs. Her body began to glow with a blue radiance, the divine goddess magic in her determined to make itself felt regardless of how much she ignored it. Donnie smiled at it, liking the way it made her skin tingle and the blood in her veins sing.

Realizing that she was letting it get too bright, she put one hand on her heart and the other on her belly, and concentrated on pulling the magic deep within herself, trying to coerce it into melding with her triune. She was somewhat successful at this and was glad when she felt her body, her soul, and her mind each assimilate portions of the new magic.

But then stark memories of the battle the night before flooded into her mind, just as they had dominated her dark dreams and had been the subject of the relentless prayers of so many denizens of her beloved Ganlonds. It was a slow and awful process of remembrance that ended in her looking down at her bare left shoulder at the mysterious wound gaping there from the dragon's laser hit. Its black nothingness freaked her out as much this morning as it had last night when she'd first gotten a good look at it. That was after she and Falwaïn had finally had a chance to be alone. He had immediately taken her to the bathroom so they could both grab a quick shower and wash off their respective wounds. The only one of any concern was the one in her shoulder, and that one, despite her best magical efforts, stubbornly refused to heal. It was like looking into a black hole—there was simply nothing there, no blood, no tissue, no bone, nothing. But it hurt like the devil! She had eventually managed to set a charm that would keep the wound's surrounding tissue in a deep freeze, maintaining a relatively pain-free state, which had allowed her to go on with things without having to periodically refreeze the entire area.

Falwaïn, grim faced while she healed his cuts and abrasions easily with her witch magic, told her he was convinced that Ungôl had purposely made her promise something she could never attain so that she would die from her failure, but Donnie staunchly disagreed with him.

The *Badûran Vírat*, as she now understood Ungôl to have been after Falwaïn explained to her what that meant, had deeply desired her to help his people. Donnie knew this with absolute certainty and nothing anyone could say would sway her from that belief. She had been quite near when the great snake-like dragon she had facetiously renamed 'Uncle,' who was dying and in extreme pain at the time, had extracted from her the promise to rescue his people and lead them to the sea and their subsequent freedom. Because of this proximity to him and his intense manner, she had felt the depth and the truth of his desire, its measure finding sympathetic purchase in her own heart.

She was, however, willing to concede that perhaps he had tricked her into agreeing to his *badûr* as incentive for her to succeed in finding his people, wherever they might be, because the agreement between them now meant that she *must* find and help his kith and kind, as Uncle had longed for, or the wound in her shoulder would end up consuming her. It turned out, after a little trial and error last night, she'd become convinced that no magic in this world could stop that process from happening if she did not save his people because, when she'd found that both her witch magic and her divine magic failed to set the freezing charm properly, she'd had to tap into the bit of cosmic magic she'd been granted from the cosmos in order to get the charm to work at all.

She'd also had to use the cosmic magic to heal the few abrasions she'd received during the night's events. It had taken what seemed like forever to heal them, and she'd felt the cosmic power keep trying to pull back into her core like a rubber band rebounding, which it did for real as soon as the last scratch disappeared. She was left with the definite impression that she would need to allow time for this magic to recuperate within her before attempting to re-access it anytime soon, at least in any major way. She supposed she could perform the same or similar spell as she'd done the other day in order to acquire more of that peculiar brand of magic, but her muscles and tendons revolted at this idea as they still ached from merely the memory of the many contortionist's positions she'd been forced into during that first dance with the cosmos. There was no way she would willingly go through that again any time soon.

All of this meant that she had no idea how long she'd bought herself by setting the freezing charm, but she suspected it was going to be best to wrap things up here in Medregai within the next month or two, if possible, so they could move on—preferably to Uncle's homeland. But then, it was yet to be discovered just where they would find Uncle's kin, so nothing was in any way certain in that regard.

Feeling quite discontented with her life following these perturbations, Donnie pushed the covers from her legs and climbed out of bed quietly so as not to waken Falwaïn. She took clothing from the wardrobe and grabbed her boots, tiptoeing into the bathroom soundlessly, where she made herself ready for the day. She left through Liz's room, which was empty just as she'd figured it would be after having heard Warren's footsteps earlier, and made her way to the kitchen, where her breakfast was just sliding onto a plate.

She grabbed the plate and her mug of hot tea and strode into her office in the library, sitting down at her desk after snapping her fingers to light several candles nearby. A couple of the house trees, Mournful Jack and Fine Fellow, were awake and greeted her cheerily. The others, they said, were resting.

Donnie acknowledged this with a smile and a nod, noting, "It was a busy night for all of us, wasn't it?"

Fine Fellow launched into a torrent of agreement, relaying details of events that had occurred in the house the previous night. Donnie listened patiently for about three or four minutes before Mournful Jack interrupted and reminded him that Donnie had already been told much of what he'd just said, so there really was no reason to repeat it. Plus, Mournful Jack said, there were the books right in front of her and she could read it all at her leisure.

Donnie raised a friendly hand and said, smiling widely, "Thanks, guys, for all you do to protect us here in the house. But, yes, if you'll give me some time alone, I'd really appreciate that."

The two books Mournful Jack had referenced were lying on the flat leather surface of the walnut desk. As they'd discovered last night, the books detailed the adventures of herself and her friends over the last week or so and chronicled many of Donnie's experiences in Medregai and with magic to date. She flipped through them as she ate, finding in them some additional answers to her many questions. Naturally, they did not provide all the information she needed, but she at least knew where they should probably start in their quest to fulfill her promise to Uncle: with the Great Serpents of the Bitterbend Marshes. After all, they must know something regarding where Uncle and his brothers originated, and she was determined to convince them to give her that information.

She finished her breakfast and sat quietly contemplating the two books and wondered idly if a third was to be written. Maybe it had already been started?

Who would have it this time? Julia's father, she supposed, as he seemed the most likely candidate since he must have been the one who gave the previous two to Valley Guy. If she could somehow get her hands on the current book, say in the next day or so, and lock it away, she might get ahead of him for once. She decided she would read the previous books fully to see if there were any clues to his identity in them. To that end, she got up and carried her used dishes, along with the books, back to the kitchen, where she'd been hearing voices talking for the past quarter hour or so.

Falwaïn and Warren were seated at the kitchen table chatting quietly with Sylvester. Donnie's somewhat pompous cat had just suggested that it might be safest for Warren to borrow a horse to ride for the duration of the army's encampment on the magical lands instead of transforming into a wolf whenever he had to travel anywhere of real distance, which would undoubtedly cause more trouble than not since it would remind the king's soldiers that he could also change into a werewolf. Before Warren could argue the point, as he looked about to do, Falwaïn interjected that he too thought this was a very good idea and offered to talk with Akanna of the Zal'Dorek Vinca first thing that morning as all equestrian-related matters for the king's army came under her command.

Donnie's dog, Rex the Wonder Dog, was lying on the floor next to Warren, snoring to the rafters. Sylvester, her magical familiar, was settled in his favorite position on the corner of the table, sitting upright with his tail wrapped tightly around his front paws, his ever-present locket dangling upon his chest. Rex and Sylvester had opted last night to sleep in the barn where wounded animals from the battle had been recuperating. Donnie had attended to these patients herself before going to bed, so most were already healed and gone home, with only a few needing another few hours for Donnie's magical potions and ointments to do their work before those brave soldiers could also go back to their families.

Falwaïn, Warren and Sylvester looked over when the door to the library opened and Donnie entered the room, bidding them good morning. Before they could return her greeting, the front door opened and their friends Diana and Diego stumbled into the house, one after the other. The sleep-tousled Diana lurched toward Donnie's room and mumbled something about wanting a shower, while bleary-eyed Diego headed for the coffee maker. He sank down into a chair with a full mug of the black elixir and gazed at it as if it were the finest treasure in all the land.

Rex, awake now, got up and wiggled his way over to say a proper good morning to his mama, who knelt and kissed him soundly right between his eyes, in what she thought of as the mama spot.

While all this was going on, two more eggs for Diego were added to those that were already cooking on the stovetop, and the bread knife cut several more pieces of bread, which thereafter dived for the toaster. By the time Diana returned to the kitchen, her food was also cooked and waiting for her on the table.

About halfway through the meal, Julia tramped out of the workroom doorway and poured herself some coffee, taking up a piece of toast before returning to her room without saying a word to anyone at all.

Not that she was really noticed, as the conversation was already quite intense while everyone relived some of the more harrowing moments from the night before. Donnie encouraged this talk, knowing that sharing these difficult experiences would help herself and her friends process them. She sat quietly and listened compassionately to the stories being told all around, smiling where appropriate and looking concerned when needed. While she sat there, she was twice bombarded with the insistent prayers of the Ganlonds' many inhabitants, which she again forced from her mind until she could determine a method of dealing with them effectively. She hoped something appropriate would be suggested at the Ganlonds' Animal Council meeting later today and was relieved to realize that she felt fairly confident it would, and so she refused to let it stress her now.

After a good hour had gone by, Julia came back into the kitchen, refreshed her coffee and took up a plate of leftover eggs, sitting down next to Donnie to eat them.

"And how did you sleep, Julia?" asked Donnie, studying the girl. Julia was painfully thin from her long, enforced captivity by Valledai and would have circles under her eyes for days to come, Donnie knew, but she had hoped to see more signs of recovery than what she could find right now.

Granted, Julia was also still upset that her mother Liz, who had long been Donnie's best friend from home, had been sent by Donnie to an entirely different world and different time period, handing her over to the previous owner of the Codlebærn cottage, Catie, to protect. During the battle last night, Donnie had come to realize that Valley Guy's so-called benefactors wanted Liz dead for what was, as yet, a totally unfathomable reason and so she had sent her friend to Catie to safeguard her life. Even after this was explained to Julia, the girl had yet to truly forgive Donnie for sending Liz away and leaving the young girl alone in a land she did not know and with a group of people she did not like one bit.

Julia gave an insolent shrug in response to Donnie's friendly question, then she turned to Donnie and inquired blandly, waving her fork in the air, "What happens now? I mean, what is there to do in this backward hole?"

Taken aback by the unexpected question, Donnie's face was a study in surprise. She blinked widely at the girl for a few moments, and her halting reply, when it came, consisted of, "Um, well…I…don't really know for the rest of you. I know the things I have to do—"

"Which are?" Julia demanded defiantly, sneering at Donnie as though daring her not to reply.

Donnie ignored the rude challenge and instead pointed to the books on the table in front of her, explaining, "I have to read these more fully, to start. I've already found a few further clues that I didn't have before, so I imagine there are more for me to learn. I thought I might go to Catie's salt works so I can begin that task somewhere away from the hordes camping on our doorstep and get some peace and quiet."

Diana, having finished her coffee in a big gulp, set her cup down with a refreshed air and suggested immediately, "How about I join you? I'd like to read them too."

Sylvester cleared his throat with a "harrumph" and said that he should be the next to read them after Donemere because he needed to know what was in them more than any of the others did—he was her familiar, after all. Rex raised his head long enough to throw in a comment about also wanting to read them, along with a reminder that he was just as important as Sylvester was, then he lowered his head to the floor again and promptly fell back to dozing. Warren and Diego added that they too wanted to read them, and soon, please. Donnie looked at the queerly silent Falwaïn, who showed her a cagey grin and admitted he'd gone into the library after she'd fallen asleep and read them in their entirety twice in about fifteen minutes, going back for more in-depth reviews of anything he'd found particularly interesting. Only Julia looked as though she could not have cared less about the books' content and continued to shovel cold eggs and toast into her mouth.

Donnie sent her gaze traveling around her friends' earnest faces and allowed herself to chuckle. "Maybe we should ask the library for more copies," she suggested.

"Already did that," replied Diana, who turned beet red when everyone looked at her. "Last night, before I went to bed," she hurried to add, her embarrassment growing. "I had a quick glance through the books and asked the library to give us a few more copies so I could take a set with me to Catie's workroom. That was so Diego and I could read them," she said, turning guiltily to Diego, who was eyeing her with amusement.

"Yes, I am certain that was your intent," he drawled, essentially saying he was not certain about that at all.

Diana flashed him a scowl, obviously not sure if he was joking or not.

And it came to Donnie suddenly that each of her friends had ulterior motives for wanting to read the books, which was to know exactly what had been written about themselves within the books and just what Donnie might learn regarding their individual secrets.

"Why didn't you just take this set?" she asked Diana, indicating the books sitting in front of her.

"Probably because she discovered the same thing I did," Falwaïn supplied before Diana could answer, "which is that I could not take the books from the library. I tried to carry them into our room, but the moment I opened the library door, they were torn from my hand and flew back to their shelf."

Donnie gaped at him in astonishment, then she turned to look at Diana, who was nodding with agreement.

"Well, yeah, there was that problem," the statuesque warrioress conceded somewhat diffidently, "and so I wasn't really sure whether any copies, even if they had appeared, which they did not, would've made it out of the room either."

"It seems you are the only one allowed to take them from the library," observed Sylvester and he looked impressed by this. But a moment later his grave solemnity disappeared when he rolled his eyes and remarked, "Well, Rex probably can too, since he seems able to do just about anything you can, if not more." The cat flashed the dog a disgruntled look, and when Rex, disturbed by the sound of his name such that he again lifted his head from the floor, caught the look, he replied to it with a sleepy grin.

Donnie chuckled along with some of the others, although she could feel a definite edge in the air now. The cat's statement made her wonder if he too had tried to remove the books from the library last night and failed. She wondered if perhaps it would be best to get the books out of the way as soon as possible. Deciding to head over to the salt works immediately, she stood up, holding the leather-bound tomes in the crook of her arm, and said, "On that note, I am going to leave. See you all in a few hours."

Surprised goodbyes were murmured back to her from around the table, with Falwaïn shooting her a loving smile and wink, and then the other two men and Rex got up to follow her outside. Once there, Warren and Diego strode off in the direction of Catie's workshop behind the stables, whereas Donnie and Rex headed toward the back of the house and up the hill. As they crested the top of the valley, Rex said he would be playing nearby but would be within earshot if she needed him for anything. He disappeared in a whoosh and left Donnie nodding her agreement.

When she emerged from the other side of the forest not long afterward, she stood still for a good five minutes admiring the view because it was, in her opinion, the most stunning of those afforded in the vicinity of the Codlebærn valley. Drinking in her fill of nature's beauty, she began to creep carefully down the steep and rough terrain, making sure to avoid the area where the young boy had been killed in front of the ancient tree, Cyllwyn Mérd, whose memories Donnie carried within her, because she did not wish to relive that painful tragedy ever again if she could but help it.

Donnie soon found exactly what she was hoping for: a nice flat spot for her to sit or lie upon as she wished, with lots of springy grass covering it, and no chunks of granite marring its surface. She materialized a wool blanket and a couple of throw pillows onto the ground and settled upon these in a sitting position, again looking toward the western horizon and feeling truly peaceful for the first time in a long while.

Even her concern regarding Liz and Catie did not interfere with her current bliss because she knew that Catie would take good care of her friend. While she did not know Catie personally, if there was one thing Donnie had learned from reading Catie's journals and from listening to Sylvester and other magical creatures who knew her best describe their interactions with her, the eccentric little witch was certainly honorable when pressed into a commitment and would therefore take her promise to protect Liz very seriously. Plus, she was also an accomplished Madra Witch, so Donnie felt more than confident that Liz and Catie were, by now, safely away from whatever harm had been threatening them last night.

***

"Hell's hags, girlie, did no one ever teach ye to wield yer magic? No one a't'all?" demanded Catie for the umpteenth time, much aggrieved judging by the tone of her voice. She was staring at Liz with what Liz thought might well be a stern frown—it was hard to tell in this dim light, but since Catie had been frowning at her sternly all morning, she was likely doing it again.

"As I have been telling you for hours now, I am not a witch, so I have no magic to wield!" Liz maintained wearily, tired of arguing with the little woman, tired of hearing her voice, tired of running after her, tired of hiding with her, tired of—in fact, she was tired of just about everything to do with Catie right now. They had had a harrowing escape the night before and had been on the run ever since, dodging from hiding place to hiding place until Liz thought she was going to drop from exhaustion. How they did not get caught was beyond Liz's reckoning. They were on an island, for Fortin's sake, and not a particularly large one at that, which meant there were only so many corners in which to hide. Liz suspected they were now in this particular one for the third time since their desperate run had begun.

"Well, I say ye are one o' us, 'cause I ken feel it in ye, so ye jest need to b'lieve and it will come to ye. Then we could mebbe do somethin' 'bout disguisin' ye proper like."

"You mean like you're disguised? No, thanks," Liz refused the idea acerbically, glancing over at the little witch's badly transmogrified face, which looked like a mangled cross between a woman and a rabbit, most especially around the mouth and nose. When she'd informed Catie of this earlier in the morning, that personage had staunchly maintained that she had modeled herself upon her dear, departed ma and she would thank Liz to not insult her own lovely mother.

"And I claimed her as me ma, not me sister, so there was no lie about it neither!" Catie argued snarkily, coming the closest thus far to returning Liz's bad mood.

"Well, bully for you, but I had to maintain that lie about Julia!" Liz had protested, although she'd also been determined not to justify herself to this annoying little witch who had managed somehow to anger the island people so much that they had been searching high and low for her for the past two weeks solid, or so Catie had informed Liz when she had arrived on the island around two a.m. the previous night.

"The thing about lies," Catie had gone on to drawl pedantically, rolling her eyes upward while somehow still managing to look down her nose at Liz, "is that they're not needed as often as people seem ta think they are. But when they *are* needed, 'tis best ta be more skillful at tellin' 'em than ye appear ta be."

"How astute of you!" Liz had spat, making it sound like a complaint because this supposed lesson she was being taught was a bit rich coming from someone who had, according to Donnie, very much *unskillfully* told a rather large number of great big whoppers back in Medregai. "I'll have to remember that the next time I decide to tell one."

Liz brought her thoughts back to the present, absentmindedly rubbing her distended tummy with both hands, a wave of mixed apprehension and awe passing over her because she could hardly believe that she was carrying a child within her. And not just any child, but a werewolf's child! The baby, now just days, maybe even hours away from being born, was certainly restless, kicking and punching every time the poor thing was subjected to yet another episode of vigorous activity on its mother's part. Somewhat scared and certainly doubtful about what it might look like, let alone behave like, Liz had decided to go with Catie's warm assessment of the situation, which she had imparted to Liz somewhere around their fifth or sixth hiding place last night.

"Yep, the time stream dunna like it when an expectant woman enters it, so it escalates the babe's development, see, keepin' the mother in a sort o' sleepin' state upon the bye. Then it sends them ta their destination when the child nears its birthin' day. I only know this 'cause o' me aunt. See, she was nary two months pregnant the first time she stepped through the amulet's doorway after becoming with child and her babby was born the very day she arrived at the farm. Well, I tell ye, we was all more'n a might surprised by that! But the time stream is a provident caretaker, I must say that for it, so yer young 'un will be born full o' good health, rest assured. Plus, with Mynydd Uchaf as its father—ah, I mean ta say, ye tell me his name is Warren now, is that right? Well, imagine that, if ye ken! Who'd'a thought it could 'appen, eh? A bit circular and what, and not by intention, or so I gather!" she'd cackled to herself with glee. "Almost beggars belief, don't it?"

When Liz had bestowed only a nonplussed stare upon the little witch at the end of these confused ramblings, Catie cackled again merrily and further informed Liz, "Er, that is ta say, with him as the father, ye can look forward ta birthing a right good babe, ye can. It be fair certain, there ain't no better soul in any century on this here Earth than the one that wolf carries within himself."

"He is a man, not a wolf!" Liz had reminded her in a cutting voice and a distracted Catie had nodded agreement with this perfectly arguable statement before chivvying Liz to a new hiding place.

And so it was that now, after more than nine hours on the constant run, Liz hoped with all her heart, not to mention her aching feet, legs and back, that they would be able to stop somewhere soon and settle for a good, long while. Unfortunately, she could tell from Catie's hurried glances out the one window of the small hut they were currently occupying that she would feel the need to move on again almost immediately.

As if to prove Liz's unspoken surmise to be correct, Catie opened the creaking door of what was little more than a lean-to and motioned for Liz to follow her outside. Liz did so with great reluctance, both of them having now to cross in broad daylight the crude road that ran toward town. They made their way to a small copse of trees and tried to blend into the shadows there.

"If ye'd just be a tree, we could stay here awhile."

This was not the first time this nonsensical directive had been issued to Liz from Catie. As with the previous instances, Liz eyed the other woman with disdain and snapped, "I have no idea what you're talking about!"

Catie sighed loud and long to show that she was aggrievedly convinced Liz was not trying hard enough. "Ye must think o' yerself as a tree and ye will become one—it's as simple as that, as I keep tryin' ta make ye comprehend! Or, ye can try this, if ye like." She turned outwardly to face the road, backed right up next to the fat bole of the closest tree, shut her eyes to concentrate, and suddenly she was fading from sight so that she almost completely blended into her background.

Liz gasped and her eyes flew wide open. She could see the outline of Catie's form only because she had watched the little witch practically disappear right before her eyes. "I-I don't know how to do that!" she cried defensively. "I can't even imagine doing that!"

"Well, there then, that's yer problem!" crowed Catie in excitement, evidently feeling she'd made an important discovery. "If ye can't even imagine doin' somethin' as simple as makin' yerself invisible next to a tree, then yer doomed, I say, doomed! So, ye've got no 'magination at all, eh? That'll stand ye no good stead in our world, girlie. Nuthin' fer it, ye're gonna have ta let go and cram the craziest thoughts inta yer head. Go on, let 'em crowd everthin' else out!"

She came over and waved her hands around Liz's head until Liz rolled her eyes and let her mouth hang wide open, after scoffing emphatically in annoyance first. Catie remained undeterred and continued to wave the air around Liz, as though she could somehow shoo any logical thoughts from Liz's brain.

"All the sane stuff's gotta go," she urged quite seriously, "and only the crazy stuff can come in. Go on then, think of yerself as a tree, whate'er kind ye be partial ta, it'll be fine. Go on, I say," Catie insisted firmly, "and do it!" She grabbed Liz by the arm and pulled her along so that they both stood against the bole of a tree.

Liz, tired enough by now to attempt anything, forced her mind to empty of its customary sanity and tried to do as Catie commanded her—and so she thought of herself becoming a tree. She focused solely on that goal and imagined her body turning into pale, raw, living wood, covered by a layer of grey bark, while overhead her hair would have to turn to leaves. She concentrated on this so long and so hard that she even decided that right now she'd like nothing more than to be a banyan tree, a big ol' round one that could provide lots of shade for anyone who wanted to stop under her branches and her very lush, thick canopy of greenery. She made herself see every detail of her branches and bark, even her leaves, not once letting herself feel ridiculous for allowing such silly thoughts into her head. She was so caught up in all that that she did not even realize it when Catie led her out from under the real trees under which they'd taken refuge earlier.

Liz felt the hot sun beating down upon her and she wished for more leaves, and in her mind she saw them sprout, whereby she felt a physical relief of increased cooling shade. Which made her wonder. And that made her open her wearied eyes, which really just wanted to stay shut for several hours. And for the next couple of seconds she saw with those eyes that she had indeed become a tree and that Catie was standing next to her nearly totally invisible and hidden beneath Liz's branches. But then her arboreal disguise disappeared the moment Liz's brain understood what she was seeing with her exhausted eyes and her mind finally apprehended what she had just done and, more importantly, what it meant on the larger scale.

She gasped, "Oh, damn, I *am* a witch!" That was the last thing Liz knew for quite some time, as she was so surprised she passed right out in shock, crumpling to the ground where she stood.

Catie slowed Liz's fall with a gentle wave of magic, then she took up the same disguise that the other woman had generated moments before, although she made sure to cover Liz's prone body with some errant branches from her own banyan tree. Proud that she'd been able to coerce Liz's magic out of its enforced hibernation without too much trouble, Catie decided to let the other woman sleep a good long while, especially since the mob that had been chasing them last night had given up hours ago, so all around the two women everything was peaceful and quiet and would remain so until this evening, for sure. She herself might even take a standing nap, Catie thought sleepily, and she therefore set her mind toward that most favorable mission. As she fell into slumber, she vaguely hoped that while they were both unconscious none of the townspeople would come to investigate the new tree that had been added to the little grove here on the eastern edge of the sleepy little island of Tortuga.

***

Donnie awoke with a start, a sense of something having gone wrong making her return to consciousness instantly. A little bewildered by the effect this had on her sense of awareness, she sat up and looked around a little bewilderedly, directing her gaze over the nearby hillside but finding nothing to account for her abrupt awakening.

The tray on which Falwaïn had delivered a snack to her earlier still held the teapot and cup she'd used, along with a plate of cookies—most of which she had already consumed. Her tummy rumbled, so she picked up another round of creamy shortbread and popped it into her mouth, savoring its sweetness as it seemed to melt down her throat.

She brushed her hair with her fingers while setting her thoughts to the events of the last couple of hours. After arriving at her little reading nook on the moors, she'd sat alone for a few minutes, barely beginning to read the first book detailing their adventures before Falwaïn brought her the tea and cookies. He casually informed her that he would be with the king for the foreseeable future as they had yet to discuss what Falwaïn had learned about the Mountain People and their intentions toward the realm while he had been wandering the north in search of adventure, before coming to the Codlebærn farm.

Shortly after he'd left Donnie alone, Warren had stopped by, wanting— as far as Donnie could ascertain—to be assured that Liz would be okay and to marvel at the thought of him being father to a human baby. He asked Donnie the candid question of whether she thought the baby would, in fact, be human. She had considered her answer carefully, then admitted that she did indeed believe it would be a human baby, with perhaps some wolfish characteristics, but nothing too terrifically fantastical. He had gone away relieved, while Donnie had figuratively wiped her brow, hoping against hope that she was right and his and Liz's baby really would be human.

Not five minutes after that, Diego and Diana passed by on their way for a walk. They apparently soon parted company because Diana was the first to return. She plopped down gracefully next to Donnie with the manner of someone who wanted to talk, but she remained silent and had merely stared out toward the distant moors. Donnie went back to reading the book in her hands and, after a short while, Diana had gotten up to leave, saying she needed to pee. Donnie gave a small wave of acknowledgement and goodbye and, when she no longer heard Diana's footsteps behind her, turned to watch her friend's distant figure disappear into the forest above where Donnie was sitting.

And then, as if having waited for Donnie to be alone again, along came Diego. When he sat down next to Donnie, he glanced nervously at her and announced, "I am still concerned, Donnie, about what happened to me last night."

Donnie closed the book she was holding and set it upon the grass beside her. She leaned back on her palms and nodded sagely. "Yes, I've been thinking about that as well. I've already read what is in the book about the incident, but what else can you tell me about it?"

"Ah, *si, si*, I read that part too," Diego admitted, his accent thick with emotion, "*anoche*. You all had left the room, but I stayed behind a few minutes so I could see what was written regarding my battle with the werewolves. It was accurate as far as events go, but it did not describe the encounter from my viewpoint. You see, I felt the monster's teeth sink into my flesh and I felt something stir within my heart, and suddenly I knew that I too was magical. I can feel that power still, a sort of humming in my veins that makes me jumpy and unable to settle to any one thing, you know?" He looked at her questioningly.

She gave him a reassuring smile and patted his knee a couple of times. "Yes, I know that feeling only too well," she said with meaning. "I've become quite accustomed to it over the last six months. It will quieten down, you know, as you accept your magic more fully. I gather you think the werewolf that bit you somehow imparted its magic to you, but I believe its bite may have simply kick-started your own magic, which was already existing in a latent state within you. I certainly don't sense anything evil about your power. By that I mean that all my senses, human, witchly, and divine alike, register you as being the same you that you were before the bite, only now you are more intensely you because of the awakening of your magic."

"But how can that be?" he asked incredulously. "I saw others who were bitten by werewolves and they either died or changed into a werewolf themselves. Yet I did not!" He shook his head wonderingly.

Donnie chewed her lip a minute, deep in thought. Finally rousing herself, she turned to him. "I think the spell your grandmother put on you protected you somehow from the effects of the werewolf bite," she mused. "She must have loved you a great deal for her spell to still be this effective so many years after she cast it on you. According to Sylvester, only a spell that's been set with either immense love or immense hatred can last such a long time after it's been cast." Donnie paused before asking, "Do you remember the last time you saw her? Maybe she cast it then, or maybe it was a spell she cast on you regularly, because that too will make a spell stronger."

"Ah, *si, si*, that makes sense to me," Diego murmured his agreement, his eyes lighting with fire because he was much intrigued by Donnie's suggestion. "*Mi abuela* was constantly blessing all of us. As a matter of fact, every day she would put a blessing onto us children. She told us it would help to make us safe out in the world."

"There you go, that's the most likely answer then," Donnie pointed out warmly, smiling at him again. "Her magic from these blessings she gave you managed to protect you, even all these years afterward. On the other hand, I have no idea why the werewolf bite would make your own magic wake up, but it seems to have done just that."

Diego had stayed with Donnie for a couple minutes more after this conversational exchange took place and then he too had moved on, striding much more confidently back toward the cottage than he had been before his talk with Donnie.

Julia flounced by nearly half an hour later, but she made no remark to Donnie or even acknowledged her presence. The young girl reached the salt works and headed south. Donnie suspected she was retracing her steps from yesterday morning and thought about following the girl, but she decided instead to listen to the earth to see if there was anyone nearby that Julia could meet with. Finding only animals and plants in that direction, Donnie let Julia walk in peace and again returned to her reading, but only after refilling and then immediately draining her teacup, the lukewarm brew tasting uncharacteristically sweet to her taste buds.

It was not long before Sylvester came by and reminded her that he would like to read the books next. Donnie, feeling suddenly sleepy, promised that he would indeed be the next in line after her. The last thing she could remember subsequent to that was watching the cat disappear over the top of the moor situated right in front of her.

After this brief reflection of the morning's event's, Donnie looked around her again, her head woolly and her thoughts disjointed, and it was only then that she realized the books were gone. She turned this way and that in alarm, but the books were nowhere to be found. And that was when she felt something even worse.

She scrambled to her feet and hurried back toward the house, a corresponding terror for whoever had cried out for her help echoing in her heart. When she rushed around the corner from the back of the house, she saw that all her friends except Rex and Julia were gathered at the front of the stables or near the well and appeared to be chatting equitably with the king and his officers. Donnie noticed that Warren was astride a tall grey horse, which did not appear thrilled with this situation as it was becoming quite agitated. She sent it a calming spell and it quieted down some, thereafter seeming to accept the odd and somewhat feral smell of its rider.

The scared voices called out for Donnie again. She paused for a moment and listened to the earth, finding Rex first, then Julia, both of whom were safe. Donnie extended her reach and finally found the frightened souls crying to her.

Made more than a little angry by her discoveries, Donnie strode up to the king, who turned to her with a smile on his face that soon faltered and fled when she demanded without ceremony, "Release my birds!"

Belnesem stepped backward, away from Donnie's fury and the blue bolts of magic that were escaping her twitching fingertips. "There is something wrong with your birds?" he asked, his eyes startled wide and wary. He glanced down at the ground in confusion when the boombox appeared at his feet and began belting out "Three Little Birds," although he thereafter ignored the modern contraption.

Donnie, on the other hand, took comfort from the song being played, drew a deep breath, pulled the escaping magic back into herself, and said to him more calmly, "Yes, there is definitely something wrong with my birds because your men have taken them. And that means you and your army must leave my lands as soon as possible."

Falwaïn stepped up to her and murmured reprovingly under his breath, "Donnie!"

She ignored him. "I mean it, you must leave. Most of your men are healed and those who aren't currently, will be so within the next hour or two. I will make certain of it. A couple hours should give you just enough time to pack up and be on your way."

Belnesem flashed her an angry, offended look. "You are most welcome for our aid last night, witch, but it seems we will—"

Donnie interrupted him with a snort. "Call me whatever names you want, but I will remind you that you didn't come to my aid, you came to defeat your enemy, which you did with my help! I welcomed you onto my lands because I knew the battle had to occur here, but after the actions of several of your men this morning, I'm now quite livid. To put it plainly, I want my birds back, and then I want you off my property!" Her chest was heaving again from her growing ire, even though the song kept reassuring her that all would be just fine with the birds.

The king was looking thoroughly startled and upset by her demands. He practically bellowed at her, "Birds? What are these birds you keep referring to? I do not know of what you are speaking!"

"Ask your men!" Donnie ground out between clenched teeth.

Belnesem turned around and faced those assembled. "Who has taken her birds?" No one moved. He stepped forward menacingly, but his tone was soft when he reiterated, "I want to know who has her birds."

One of the captains shuffled to the front and said, "My lord, I believe I know what this is about. We, er, several of us, that is, noticed that there were a rather large number of chickens here, and, well, we thought only to provide you a feast, so we helped ourselves to a few of them. We did not believe it would be a problem. I mean, after all, they are just chickens, and there seems to be more than plenty here."

"Where are these chickens?" Belnesem demanded.

"Well, milord, Feelie has taken them away to slaughter. I am not sure exactly where he is doing that. He went up there." The man pointed toward the eastern rim of the valley.

Belnesem swung back toward Donnie and offered, in what was close to but not quite an apologetic tone, "If they are already dead by my cook's hand, I will recompense you for them."

Donnie shook her head and with a snap of her fingers materialized the six hens and their stick cages to right in front of her. A flick of her index finger and the cages were opened, allowing the birds to escape and crowd around her feet with frightened squawks. Another flick sent the small, wooden prisons hurtling through the air to crash at terrific speed into the hillside on an outcropping of granite, where they were quite violently pulverized. "Nobody kills my chickens," she stated flatly.

The king nodded, this time with real apology in his manner. "Indeed. I will have my men punished for their transgression."

Before he could add anything more, which he looked about to do, Donnie interjected, "Oh, not yet, you won't. When I said I wanted my birds back, I didn't just mean the chickens."

Belnesem had clearly grown very tired of the situation. "Again, I do not know of what you speak!"

"I want the Sûlrím back too!" Donnie's eyes narrowed. "Three of them are missing, according to an old bat friend of mine. And they disappeared while a whole company of your men were in the area."

"Donnie, they may have wandered away on their own," Warren posited composedly from atop the grey horse. "The Sûlrím are notorious for being mysterious creatures. Just because the king's men were nearby, doesn't mean they took the birds. That does not make the king's men thieves."

Diana now entered the fray with, "But Donnie has already proven that some of his men *are* thieves, so I don't think it's a stretch to wonder if perhaps others aren't also!"

The king made an impatient movement with his hands and said, "Everyone will be searched before they exit your lands, whenever that is." He glanced over at Donnie, but she was staring intently at Galæron, who looked distinctly uncomfortable at her attention.

Akanna added stiffly, "You will find the Sûlrím nowhere amongst my soldiers, I am certain. We know better than to capture one of those birds, let alone three."

Donnie rounded on the vincan. "Why do you say that?"

Akanna eyed her firmly, noting the magic still crackling from Donnie's fingers, but she did not back down one iota. "Perhaps you are unaware of what Sûlrím do to those who attempt to cage them. As anyone born here would know, they are not birds with which one wishes to trifle, under any circumstances. That is why they were hunted almost to extinction nearly four score years ago. I have seen the devastation one small flock was able to wreak upon an entire battalion of soldiers when I was but a fresh recruit in the vincan army. Two vincans survived the experience and, once they had healed, neither ever spoke another word afterward to anyone about anything. It was only during the throes of their fever when we first found them that we learned who, or rather what, had attacked them and why."

Just then a king's soldier came along the upper rim of the valley on a dead run. He whistled a short series of notes, whistled them again, and all heads turned toward him. When he approached, he saluted both the king and his commanders, reporting breathlessly, "My king, word has come from the northern edge of the Branmar Plain that six elves have just been found newly dead. Their bodies lie within a league of the Annûar Path and they look to have been savaged by the Wind Wings we passed yesterday morning. Others heard their screams but arrived too late to rescue the elves. As I say, all six are confirmed dead."

Galæron stared at the man in shock before he turned to one of his archers and said something low. The elf captain shook his head. Galæron swung around, crossed his arms in front of him, and dug his heels in. "I am confident that none of my archers are missing."

The messenger stepped forward again and the king gave him leave to speak further.

"Thank you, your grace," he said, bowing. "That is not the only strange occurrence this morning to do with the elves. We have been arranging the bodies of the dead and have found one elf corpse too many."

"What do you mean, one too many?" Belnesem's widened gaze looked to Galæron for an answer, but the elf commander could only give him a bewildered shrug.

Instead, it was the messenger who replied. "Well," he began nervously, "according to the elf captain in charge at the battle site, two hundred and twenty-four of their archers were killed last night. And yet, milord, today they have found two hundred and twenty-*five* bodies." After relaying this, the soldier stepped backward and was dismissed by a wave of the king's hand, whereafter he disappeared to whence he'd come.

Donnie bent her head and put a hand over one ear. A moment later she said, "The missing Sûlrím have returned to the others, it seems. And I've found the six bodies your messenger mentioned near the Annûar Path. They do appear to be elves at first glance, but I don't think that's what they truly are. There's something not quite right about them. Now, what is it?" She studied the gruesomely torn and tattered bodies carefully with her mind's eye. Judging from the state of the corpses, if three little Sûlrím were responsible for these men's deaths, then Akanna was correct—you'd have to be a fool to try to capture even one.

It took Donnie several seconds of searching because she was having to inspect the wrecked bodies from a tree that was a few yards distant, but she eventually realized what was bothering her about the dead elves. She opened her eyes and raised her head to meet Galæron's blazing gaze. "They don't have pointed ears."

"Then they are not my brethren," the elf lord breathed with evident relief.

"No," Donnie conceded, pursing her lips in thought. "I believe they are some of Valley Guy's benefactors, which is what he called the Iceni Meræ. But what could they possibly want with the Sûlrím? And too, I guess this must mean that the Iceni Meræ aren't from Medregai, or they would've known better than to capture a Sûlrím," she ruminated, "wouldn't they?"

Falwaïn nodded his head in agreement, stopping her thought flow with, "Perhaps they wanted exactly what did happen—to cause a rift between us, I mean. They knew you'd accuse Belnesem's men for the theft and there would be no way for him to prove their innocence. But you're right, they aren't from here or they'd know the fierce reputation of the Sûlrím, although I imagine they've learned that lesson by now."

"Have any of you ever heard of the Iceni Meræ, or had dealings with them?" asked Donnie, looking to the king and his commanders.

Belnesem and Galæron shook their heads no immediately, but Akanna was slower to respond.

The vincan, towering over Donnie by a good four inches, gazed down at her steadily when she replied, "There is legend of the Iceni within vincan lore, but I do not recall it in detail. Much like what occurred with Orgos in his guise as Valledai, the Iceni, as they were called in my peoples' stories, appeared one day and worked diligently to bring the vincan race to a more advanced state. They apparently accomplished their goals with my people, because after less than a century, they disappeared and were never heard from again. I understand they also were seen in the south," she said, giving Diana an appraising sort of glance over Donnie's shoulder before adding, "but I cannot speak to their involvement with anyone there."

Donnie turned to ask Diana if she'd heard of the Iceni Meræ, but her friend was already walking away from them toward the barn. Donnie bit her lip and looked after the warrioress pensively.

Warren dismounted just as Falwaïn excused them all and moved over to take Donnie by the arm, leading her to the back porch, with Sylvester, Warren and Diego following close behind.

Falwaïn let go of Donnie once they'd climbed the steps, then he leant against the railing, crossed his arms in front of his chest, and informed her grimly, "Donnie, you can't order the king around like you just did."

She raised her chin and replied stubbornly, "On my lands, yes, I can. And I'm serious when I say that I want the king and his army off them as soon as possible. Early this afternoon would be perfect."

All around, surprised gasps were uttered in response to this demand, with Warren taking a step toward her and spluttering, "Wh-what?" in disbelief. "You cannot be serious!"

Donnie rounded on the former Wolf King and retorted forcefully, "You know full well they can't stay on the Ganlonds!"

Then she turned back to Falwaïn when he protested her inflexibility by noting, "But, Donnie, you insulated the land so your magic won't harm normal humans, right? Therefore, what is this rush to have them gone?"

"I am not worried about my magic making any of them *crazy*," Donnie replied, and she blew a harried breath. Pausing to collect her thoughts, she then pointed at herself and Sylvester and explained, "We have the Animal Council meeting this afternoon and I don't want anyone on my lands who hasn't a right to be here. I have a feeling I'm going to learn a lot about my little 'realm' today and that is not something that should be overheard by strangers. Plus, look at the mess they're making of the place! What was lovely thick grass yesterday is now trampled down mud. It's going to take weeks and weeks for this valley alone to recover. Seriously, this area has its own ecosystem, which is being destroyed rapidly by the king's army. I can hear thousands of complaints being laid by all sorts of creatures living in the Ganlonds—which is one of the, shall we say, weirder aspects of being their goddess and guardian, believe me. You have to remember, I pledged to protect them with my magic and my life just last night! Therefore, I am doing exactly that by having the king's men and horses and whatever and whoever else is part of his army leave here as soon as possible." She again jutted her chin out as if daring any of the guys to refute her.

It was left to Falwaïn to do so. Looking forlorn, he reminded her in a quiet voice, "Donnie, they must be given time to honor their dead. And please don't suggest they leave that entirely for you to do, for they will never agree to that. You can help them, yes, but they must participate themselves because they will owe the families of the dead the story of their loved one's *byrgen* when the army finally returns home. Nothing will make the king or any of his forces leave before the fallen have been sent on their journey to Canavar. Surely you can understand that?"

He regarded her intently until she relented with a long, heavy sigh.

"Yes, all right, of course, I can understand that," she conceded. "But we'll hold the funeral tonight on the Branmar Plain at just before sunset."

Warren scowled at her. "Donnie, you're being stubborn for no good reason! Truly, there are far too many fallen to be readied for the *byrgen* for it to be performed as soon as tonight. You must allow the king and his men a couple of days more for their preparations."

Donnie again stuck her chin out and countered stiffly, "All they need to do is ready the dead wherever they lie now. I will take care of moving them to the funeral pyres. I am, after all, a damn powerful witch, or did you forget that? And at the same time, we can perform the *byrgen* ritual for the fallen animal soldiers, whom you also appear to have forgotten, my friend, in your oh-so strenuous protests in favor of the Sarn king's dead!"

At first Warren looked stunned and infuriated by this accusation, but then he mastered himself and closed his eyes, hanging his head a moment later. "Of course we must also honor the dead of the animal army," he said quietly, but with feeling. "You are correct, I was not considering them in the plan for the king's soldiers, but as you imply, they too have every right to be included in the ritual as this is their land as much as it is yours. I can only apologize for my egregious oversight."

Donnie studied him a while in silence, frowning unhappily throughout the duration of her perusal of his distinctly human features. She noticed that all remaining vestiges of his time as either wolf or werewolf were absent now. While she suspected that Liz was right about him and that he had indeed started life as a human, she was surprised that he would shed his former animal life so willingly and so utterly. Taking her time about replying, she eventually reminded them all, "None of us should forget our origins or those who have traveled our paths with us, right? No matter who we become."

Upon this solemn suggestion, the three men nodded thoughtfully. Without further protest they went back to the encampment to relay the plan for the night and to assist in moving things along.

Donnie sat down in a rocker on the porch and looked questioningly at Sylvester, who was perched on the railing in front of her. He had been uncharacteristically silent and she wondered why.

He returned her regard for some time before observing, "You do not trust the king or his men."

"Nope."

"May I ask why? Is there a reason for this distrust that perhaps is detailed in the books regaling our adventures?"

Donnie pursed her lips, made a face, and looked around distractedly as she considered the question before answering it. "Well, yes and no. Let's just say there are a couple of things that don't make sense, and while they don't necessarily involve the king's men, I'm not sure exactly who they involve. Therefore, I'm going to trust no one."

"Ah, I see," the cat murmured, nodding with approval. "And just where are the books now?"

"I don't know, they seem to be missing."

The cat stared at her with incredulity for several seconds before his expression changed drastically and he noted dryly, "You do not appear at all upset by that."

"No, I guess I'm not, not really."

After a long pause, Sylvester inquired, "Did you have a chance to read through them to your satisfaction before they were lost?"

"Did I read through them—well, you know, that is a really good question, Sylvester. I wouldn't say it was to my satisfaction exactly, but I think it was sufficient for me to be getting on with, yes. And I am hopeful that everyone will come clean about whatever they're hiding from me."

This made the cat straighten up tall and look at her with increased curiosity. "Whatever do you mean by that?"

"Well, for instance, did you know that, back in Moên Flírbann, Valley Guy looked you over and found something about your triune that reminded him of his benefactors?"

"He what?" the cat squeaked, looking shocked and dismayed.

"Yep," Donnie nodded. "He also said you had a cloudiness within you. All that was why he couldn't connect with your triune."

"I swear to you, I know nothing of that!" the cat protested.

Donnie nodded and gave him a reassuring smile. "Yeah, so I can tell looking at you now. You really are not aware of anything dark within yourself, at least not consciously, that's for sure."

The cat, who had gotten up and begun to pace along the porch railing, stopped, hissed, shook himself, and resumed his pacing. His demeanor reeked of worry.

Donnie watched his actions and let her mind ponder the problem, which clearly the cat was also doing. At nearly the same time, they both came to a similar conclusion.

Sylvester stopped pacing and sat down again, while Donnie's eyes cleared and she leaned back in the rocker, meeting the cat's hopeful gaze.

"Could it be from one of the spells that have been cast upon me?" he asked, thinking back to the rather significant number of spells that circled his form which Donnie's use of the Silver Hand had revealed to them the other day.

Donnie flashed him an agreeable grin. "I kinda thought that too."

"Can you use the Silver Hand upon me again to see if we can find which spell might be the culprit?" Sylvester glanced at her nervously several times as he spoke, his eyes darting away momentarily between each look. He was obviously in dread of himself being shown to be a threat or even a potential traitor.

"Sure, but we'll have to do it sometime later. I still need to recover from yesterday."

"But, Donemere, what if I do something that…" the cat faltered, looking away from her.

Donnie leaned forward in her chair and reassured him, "While I may not trust strangers, Sylvester, I do trust you. I am not concerned by this, so you try not to be too, okay?"

He stared at her as though she were a loon and shook his head slowly, gazing off with an agonized expression at the possibilities presented in case of his own treachery, terrible possibilities that gained momentum in his mind as the seconds ticked by. Donnie could tell that he would soon convince himself that he must leave the Ganlonds for everyone's safety.

"I mean it, Sylvester, I trust you," Donnie repeated, but the cat wasn't listening to her. So she told him something that was chipping away at her own psyche. "All last night, as I'd known it would, my subconscious spent a great deal of time reliving the dragons' murders in excruciating detail."

It took a few seconds, but her words finally penetrated the cat's fog of self-absorption and he brought himself back to their conversation, much startled by her revelation. "But you did not murder them! It was not like that at all!" he argued loyally.

Donnie grimaced and scoffed in disdain, retorting, "Didn't I? 'Cause that's exactly how I think of their deaths, you know, with a surety I cannot seem to shake. I mean, just look at it objectively. Their lives were not given in service, there was no fair match between them and me, and they were mere pawns who'd played their parts well—too well—in the subterfuges of Valley Guy and his so-called benefactors." Donnie's features suddenly took on deep sorrow and she cried out to the cat, hot tears springing to her eyes, "Damn it, Sylvester, if only I'd been able to spend more time with Murlaín and her children...or if they'd managed to somehow be with Uncle at his death, where he could've explained to them what was really going on, then there could have been a very different outcome for them. Oh, if only I hadn't had to..." she murmured, letting her cracking voice tail away into silence.

Before the cat could break that silence, Donnie added bitterly, "I wish I could somehow gain the same calm acceptance of death that you and Falwaín and the others carry within yourselves. Maybe then I wouldn't feel as though I'd cheated those young dragons out of their lives."

Sylvester sighed, aware of what Donnie had just done, aware that she had deflected his worry of himself into concern for herself, and that she had done so for his sake, to pull him back onto a healthier path than he had been spiraling toward.

"You must never forget your trials and lessons from the gods," he reminded her gently. "By that, I do not mean solely that it was the gods who directed you to kill the *vírata* and therefore they must share this terrible burden with you, but also that you should remember what they taught you about death. Which is that not only should the dead be revered, but to remember that they may provide wise counsel to the living. I urge you, think of what the dragons' deaths mean to you now, for only you can ensure that their lives count for something more than them being mere pawns of your enemies. Only you can do this for them, Donemere, only you," he repeated solemnly, gazing at her with his full confidence in her shining nakedly from his eyes.

Unable to speak in the face of the cat's very unusual, yet whole-hearted show of emotional support for her, Donnie nodded her thanks jerkily. Deep in her heart, she made a resolution to do exactly as Sylvester had suggested: she would find a way to make sure that Murlaín and her two dragon children had neither lived nor died in vain.

Sylvester jumped down from the porch railing and started to walk toward the steps, throwing over his shoulder, "I will check with the other council members to see when they will be available to assemble and will return once we have set the hour of our meet."

Since no reply seemed necessary from Donnie, she did not give one.

Chapter 2
Love Machine

After sitting alone for a while staring blankly at the trampled grass in the back yard and beyond it to the vegetable garden, both of which Donnie acknowledged to herself she had been neglecting woefully for far too long, she rose to her feet. Undecided still for another half minute, she finally traipsed to the barn in search of Diana. There she found her majestic and glorious friend mundanely rubbing a curry comb over Otis's smooth white withers to his rump.

The horse was about to fall asleep from the rhythmic motion of the comb, his head drooping low while he slowly scuffed his feet and twitched his long tail to scare off flies. He was the first to realize that Donnie had entered the barn through the open door.

Otis rumbled deeply in his throat in greeting, tossed his head upward and smiled wide. Diana, on the other hand, turned away to hide her face, moving behind Otis to where the riding tack was kept. She replaced the curry comb to its drawer and tried to slip by Donnie, who by now had returned Otis's welcome and was rubbing his nose affectionately, without speaking.

But when Diana came closer, Donnie deliberately stepped into her path. "You are avoiding me," she observed, looking at her friend questioningly.

Diana dodged this remark by crowing facetiously, "No-no, not at all, of course not! You're just really busy and I don't want to take up your time when it's better spent on others. And so, ah, I think I'm gonna go read the books now, if you don't mind." She started to move off, but Donnie again stepped into her path.

"You can't. They're missing."

Diana's brown eyes flew wide in shock. "What?" she gulped.

Otis too evidenced great surprise at this news with a noticeable flaring of both his eyes and nostrils and by taking a small step backward.

"Yep, they're not to found anywhere around here anymore," Donnie reiterated brightly.

"The king's men must have stolen them," Diana suggested, looking stern.

"Oh no, I don't think so." Donnie hurriedly forestalled her friend from saying or doing more in that same vein, adding, "And it doesn't really matter anyway, because I managed to read what I needed to in them. And naturally, I now have some questions for you guys."

"Questions for us?" Diana all but spluttered in panic when she finally got over her shock and could speak.

Otis groaned at this feeble response. "Yeah, she means for us, all right," he muttered sarcastically. "You're gonna have to tell her the truth, Diana."

Donnie snorted in sardonic laughter. "Oh, I don't think she's the only one who needs to come clean, is she?"

Otis gave Donnie a wolfish grin. "Who, me? What did I do?" he joked in all seeming innocence.

Unamused this time, Donnie glared at him, her lips crimped together tightly. "You didn't just happen to come to this farm, did you? As a matter of fact, I'm almost certain that both you and Diana came here on purpose." Donnie crossed her arms in front of her before putting a hand up to her face and tapping her cheek a couple times pensively with a finger, small arcs of magic escaping from her with each tap. "You know it strikes me suddenly that I've never heard the story of exactly how you came to be here with Catie."

Otis guffawed and grinned at her question, exclaiming in a too-loud voice that underscored his nervousness, "Ha-ha, well, you know, that's funny. Um, so, er, well okay…er, I came here a long, long time ago, right? Er, but you know that already, don't ya?" he hemmed and hawed, starting and restarting his sentences. "Er, yeah, so, long time ago, like I said. Oh, yeah, yeah, that was, that was when Catie started up her salt works again after the war, don't ya know! And ah, well, my ah, my previous owner, a real stupid girl she was, well, we were here to buy some salt, see, and she hadn't tied me properly and I got away from the post 'cause I was eating grass and not paying attention to where I was going and I, er, I got lost. Catie found me over by the Glade and decided I'd be welcome to stay here on her magical lands, so she, er, she bartered the lady for me and this is where I've been ever since!"

Donnie stared at him vacantly throughout most of this nonsense and waited until his painful recitation was over before rolling her eyes toward the heavens. "Oh, puhleeze, who are you trying to kid with that lame-o lie? I mean, was it a girl or a lady with you? Did you wander off or did you get lost on purpose because you were looking for something?" She transferred her doubting gaze to Diana and rebuked her too. "I suppose you're gonna tell me something just as ridiculous as that as well, right? Or were you by chance the stupid girl in his tall tale?"

"No-no, that wasn't me, Donnie, I swear it," Diana said quietly. She looked guilty as hell, but also resolute. "Yes, okay, we have been lying to you and everyone else," she admitted with reluctance, "but I swear it was with good reason. And, no, we can't tell you the truth right now, but you have to believe that we would never mean any of you harm. You do know that, don't you?" she asked, her voice quavering with emotion.

Donnie considered them for what seemed a very, very long time to each before she nodded. "Yeah, I suppose I know that. But you must also see that your refusal to tell what you're hiding makes it impossible to trust either of you fully now. And may I point out, unless I know what it is you're not telling me, whatever that is may very well cause something terrible, perhaps even cataclysmic, to happen later. And no one is going to thank you for that if anything does occur." She paused again, this time gazing at them with disappointment because she could see that she was making no headway in convincing them to confess. "So, what's it gonna take to get you to tell me the truth? By that I mean, what needs to happen for you to come clean? Is it just time or some specific event?"

Diana and Otis exchanged a meaningful look and then Otis finally said, "Let's just say it has more to do with events than time, although time is a factor too. But the moment we can, we'll tell you everything we know."

"Yeah, right. I won't hold my breath." Donnie sighed discontentedly. "Well, what can you tell me now? There must be something." She crossed her arms in front of her again, leaned back on her hips, and generally took up a combative stance.

Repeating their exchange of long, silent looks at each other, Diana was the one who turned back to Donnie and said with a worried frown, "You know the okûns who came to the house, the ones Julia inadvertently let in last night?"

"Yes."

"They were looking for something, something in your office area, because they didn't even try to follow us into the library. It must have been something either on your desk or in the cabinet behind it. I think, maybe, they were going for the top cupboard where you have your more precious keepsakes stored."

"What makes you say that?"

Diana glanced at Donnie uncertainly and pursed her lips, casting her mind back to the previous night's jumbled events. After a few moment's consideration, she said, "Well, when the house trees started messing with them, you know, vibrating so that the okûns became mired in their wood? Well, it seemed to me that those monsters could have saved themselves by jumping onto the rug or the furniture, but they didn't, they jumped more toward the door. That brought them a lot closer to the cabinet, although not so close to your desk, now that I come to think of it."

"I think they might have been after the brass doorstopper, because you keep that kinda close to the cabinet," Otis put in knowingly. "The one that looks like Rex, I mean."

Donnie's right eyebrow raised higher and higher as she contemplated this suggestion. "Well, that's interesting, isn't it? But I doubt it can be the doorstopper they were after since that was commercially made back in my time, so unless someone's hidden something in it since I bought it…"

Her voice trailed away as she held her hands out. The doorstopper in question materialized onto her palms and she began to inspect it, running her fingers over the German Shepherd Dog's form. Diana stepped nearer to study the brass item intently with Donnie, while Otis moved to one side so he too could see. Even though Donnie pushed and prodded everywhere, there did not appear to be any sort of hidden compartment in the solid brass figure. She reached inside herself and asked her various types of magic to touch the doorstopper to see if they would respond in any way to it. Her hands glowed blue for a second, but that was all—her magic seemed to fall back into her as quickly as it had arisen and Donnie could only think that must mean there was nothing otherworldly about the doorstopper. She certainly could not sense any kind of magic attached to the thing, anyway.

"Nope, for all intents and purposes, this thing appears to be just a big lump of metal, perfect for a doorstopper," she finally said, and the statuette disappeared from her hands. She adopted her truculent manner again and studied her friends with a scowl.

Diana flashed Donnie an apologetic grimace and shook her head slowly from side to side. "I don't honestly know what they were after, but it had to be something very important."

"Yes," Donnie agreed crisply, "especially since the okûn king was with them. He was the one Otis killed in the back yard."

Otis and Diana looked at her aghast and exclaimed, "What?" in unison.

"Oh, yes," confirmed Donnie, purposefully continuing to exhibit only blatant mistrust toward them. "Did you really not know that?"

Diana touched Donnie on the arm and implored fervently, "Donnie, I swear, we are only holding back information about ourselves, not anyone else."

"I don't believe that," replied Donnie, giving a few quick shakes of her head, "because I think you know the Iceni Meræ."

Otis stepped backward, tossed his head, and spat angrily, "Them!"

Diana shot him a warning look. "We really can't talk about them right now!" she ordered, and she put her hand on his nearest shoulder to further restrain him. She turned back to Donnie and repeated in a small voice made sad with regret, "We really can't, Donnie."

Donnie whirled, turning her back on them, and strode toward the door. Halfway there she stopped of a sudden and turned on her heel again, looking back to demand, "Tell me what the okûn king used to break the charm so he could get out of the house."

Diana stared beseechingly at Donnie, tears forming in her dark brown eyes, but upon seeing nothing except steely anger in Donnie's gaze, she turned away in misery.

It was Otis who replied to Donnie. "I believe it's called a trengé stave," he said. "They are really rare and quite old and I've never seen one."

With a curt nod, Donnie left them alone in the barn. Diana turned to watch her go, then she punched the nearest stall post as hard as she could, pulverizing it into hundreds of splinters.

***

Falwaïn took a couple steps in the direction of the open flap of the king's reception tent, his gaze following the stiffened backside of his old friend, Belnesem. He watched while the king emerged from the tent into the blazing sunshine. Belnesem stopped just outside the tent and motioned for one of his pages to step forward. He told the boy to find his two high commanders and the servant took off at a full run up the hillside.

Belnesem turned back into the tent and resumed his seat at his desk. He leaned back in his chair and studied Falwaïn, Warren and Diego with an inscrutable stare which the three men returned, also without expression.

It took less than five minutes for both Akanna and Galæron to answer the summons given them. They joined Falwaïn and his friends in standing before the king, waiting silently for him to speak.

Belnesem wasted no time in doing so. He pointed toward his three guests and announced through clenched teeth, "Lord Falwaïn and his new friends tell me we have been granted a short reprieve from the witch's order that we vacate her lands immediately."

Not a soul in the tent was left wondering what the king's opinion of this news could be. Everything about him fairly screamed that he was on the cusp of losing his temper once again, as he had when first informed of Donnie's change of heart a few minutes ago, and as he had, to be honest, when she had first ordered his army to leave the Ganlonds a little over an hour and a half before.

He added coldly, "We have until tonight, as she now so generously decrees. After, of course, she herself presides over the *byrgen* rites for not just our dead, but also the dead of the animal army, it seems."

"I will not have my brave archers honored in death and buried by a faithless, vile witch!" Galæron declared, almost spitting the words while sneering angrily at what he reckoned were intruders in their midst. "Nor will I have their final rites sullied by having them shared with the rotting corpses of what should amount to nothing more than game for the king's table! The

Álvar have never consorted with witches and their kind and we will not do
so tonight."

Warren, his own ire flaring up because he and the others had already sat
through the king's many aspersions regarding Donnie without saying a word
in protest, addressed the Sarn king when he bit out a response to the elf's
fresh insults. "I'm sure that would be fine with Donnie. She can move your
dead to somewhere just outside her lands, where you may deal with *their*
rotting corpses at your leisure. Which means we can go back to the original
plan and you can leave now!"

Falwaïn, more practiced in statesmanship, held up a placating hand and
interjected in an even tone, "Your grace, there will be no need for that, just
as there is no need for enmity on any side here. While I too am aware of the
perfidy of witches throughout Medregai's history and understand any
reluctance toward letting one officiate a *byrgen*, I am more than confident
that Donemere will honor our dead fully and most reverentially. I would
request that you all keep in mind that she is not merely a witch, but rather, a
goddess—one who is in league with our very own Néhanna of the Sarn,
Amelda of the Valkérian Elves, and Bahiti of the Batathan Vinca. She could
be in no better company than they and I believe our dead could not be sent
to Canavar more auspiciously than with her intendance."

Akanna made a small movement as if to step forward and she said in a
blandly controlled voice, "If the Ér Ainíl of the Ganlonds wishes to perform
the *byrgen* for our soldiers, I have no argument to pit against that proposal.
Nor will I protest her desire to have the ceremony include her own fallen
soldiers, who fought as fiercely and died as courageously as any of ours did.
I speak for all my men when I make this declaration."

Galæron scoffed at this, but otherwise held his tongue, awaiting the
king's orders.

Belnesem waved a hand and stood up, meeting the hardened gazes of his
guests one by one and coming to settle upon Falwaïn. "What is to be our
part in the ceremony tonight?" he inquired.

"In the actual ceremony, I do not know," replied Falwaïn, quashing the
apprehension threatening to color his voice because of his own doubts.
"Donnie merely asked that you ready each fallen soldier where they lie on
the Branmar Plain and said that she will take care of moving them onto the
funeral pyres."

"Humph!" the king snorted unhappily. "And what then, what happens
after the ceremony? Are we not to have the customary feast?"

Falwaïn opened his mouth and closed it again, finally admitting, "I do
not know that either. But I am certain we will all be content with whatever
Donemere has planned. I trust in her implicitly."

Belnesem frowned with distain at, what to him, was an outrageous statement. "You do?" the king questioned seriously. "And I suppose that if I refuse to do as your witch asks, you will side with her, will you not?" he observed, a sudden undercurrent chilling the air between himself and his longtime friend.

Though Falwaïn may have previously found it difficult to make so obvious and bold a break between them, after receiving the message for him hidden within the king's question, he replied steadfastly and simply, "Yes, I will."

Belnesem nodded his head slowly before he conceded, "Then we must do as she asks, for I will not have anything come between us...for now."

"Thank you, your grace," Falwaïn said appreciatively while bowing to his king. "Your decision is most kind and wise for everyone concerned."

Ignoring the poorly stifled, disbelieving snort that emanated from Galæron, the king returned his attention to his two high commanders and ordered imperiously, "You know what to do. We have until sunset to ready both the dead and the living."

With a brusque wave, he indicated that he was granting leave to all to exit the tent and for Falwaïn, Warren and Diego to return to the farm.

After making a couple stops on the way, with one being to the barn, they found Donnie working in the garden, pulling weeds. She had not been at it long for she had only a small patch cleared. Instead it seemed she had spent a while cutting the long grass with an odd-looking contraption on wheels that had a cushioned seat, an engine, and a low platform that clearly served a purpose. The men noticed the machine but set to helping her with the garden without inquiry, each glad to be doing something physical and all needing time to themselves to process today's events, along with those of yesterday and the several days before.

The four of them worked hard for nearly two hours and, when finished, the entire garden was neat and tidy and there were several mounds of weeds that Warren and Diego volunteered to dump into the weed bin situated at the far end of the garden. This was just a big box in which the weeds could be dried so that Donnie could burn them later in the year, when the box was full.

Sylvester and Rex had come back during this time period and were both sunning themselves on the ground in front of the back porch. Sylvester purred lightly, enjoying the feel of the sunshine on his thick coat, while Rex lay beside him and snored with abandon. Diana had taken Otis for a ride to the north just after the men began helping Donnie with the garden and she and the horse had yet to return. Of Julia, there was no sign.

Donnie and Falwaïn climbed the steps to the back porch and sat down in a couple of the rockers there. Sylvester stirred from his lethargy and dragged himself up the stairs too, sitting at the top of them while he began to groom himself awake.

He paused in his endeavors long enough to say casually, "We should leave within the hour to meet with the Animal Council."

Donnie nodded and sank back in the chair, rocking herself gently as she relaxed her sore muscles.

After several minutes, Warren called out that he'd like to read the books about their adventures while she was meeting with the council and Diego seconded this same desire. When Donnie informed them that the books were missing, they both stopped transferring the latest batch of weeds from the wheelbarrow to the box and instead stared at Donnie in surprise.

"They're missing?" repeated Warren wonderingly.

"Yes," said Donnie, "and I think that's a good thing. There's no sense in all of us obsessing over them, so let's just forget about them and go on with life, such as it is. All right? I mean, do we necessarily need to read about everything that happened, after having lived through it already?"

Warren and Diego, after considering this pearl of wisdom, eventually shrugged their agreement with it before going back to their task. Donnie glanced over at Falwaïn and he also indicated that he was okay with what she'd said.

"You got a chance to read what you needed to, I suppose?" he inquired, and when she nodded, he dropped the subject.

When the other two were finished putting the weeds away, Falwaïn roused himself to ask, "How long will your meeting with the animals take; do you know?" He looked first at Donnie, then at Sylvester.

Donnie said she didn't know, and Sylvester added, "Nor do I. But we should undoubtedly begin our journey to the meeting place as soon as possible now."

"Can we walk to it or will I need to ride Otis?" asked Donnie curiously, glancing down at the boombox, which had just appeared at her feet and begun playing the funky classic "Love Machine."

"It would be best to ride, yes," answered Sylvester, also sparing the music box a quick look but otherwise ignoring it. "It will take far too long for you to walk there. But where can Diana be with Otis, and why would she take him out for so long, today of all days?" he noted peevishly.

Falwaïn stood up and offered Donnie his hand, grinning widely at her and then down at the boombox. "I think I know why Diana felt quite comfortable doing that. Come with me," he coaxed, drawing Donnie with him off the porch and toward the barn, leading her in a twirling dance to the hip-twisting song as the boombox belted it out at top volume. The other men, smiling secretively, followed them. Sylvester nodded to Rex and the two of them also went into the barn with the others, where the cat jumped onto the railing immediately and Rex wound his way through the men's legs until he was next to his mama, who was stopped in surprise in front of the stall Diana had used when she was the farm's cow.

And there, in the stall, stood a proud, slim horse, stamping its feet in a lively manner and looking for all the world as if it belonged there. This beautiful girl was nearly the exact color and shade of Donnie's honey-amber hair.

Donnie gaped at the horse in astonishment and turned to Falwaïn, speechless.

"Yes, she's yours," he said, answering the question in Donnie's eyes.

She let out a small squeal of excitement and sputtered, "How? Who? Where?" Not waiting for an answer, she began to approach the graceful creature, making sure to send soothing thoughts toward it, although there was probably no need for that since the horse appeared to be of calm and steady nature.

The three men chuckled together, watching Donnie with enjoyment.

It was Falwaïn who replied. "If you recall," he reminded her with an easy smile, "Diego and I left our horses with the army last night so that we could ride back to the cottage with you in Plug. Earlier this morning, we stopped by the mounted soldiers' encampment to retrieve our mounts and, while we were there, we asked Akanna if she had any horses she was willing to let us barter for since Diana would obviously be needing one now. Akanna said quite definitely that no, she did not have such a horse for Diana and that the only horse she would barter for was the grey that Warren was wanting to borrow and the price for him would be taken care of by Warren acting as the attendant for Raleen's previous rider at the *byrgen* tonight, who was Akanna's cousin, K'lan Tai. So Raleen now belongs to Warren. And then Akanna told us that she had the perfect horse for you, insisting it be a gift from her. She said she found the young filly wandering the fields alone more than six months ago, so she took the horse with her and trained it. She says, unlike Raleen, it's still young enough not to have bonded with anyone yet."

When Donnie turned for an explanation of what he meant by that, the horse surprised her by stepping forward and nudging her mischievously on the shoulder with its long nose. They all laughed in delight at the horse and at Donnie's pleased expression. She began to scratch the horse's cheek and cooed at it. The horse responded by again nudging Donnie with its nose.

"What name will you give her, Donnie?" asked Warren.

"Her name is Wiwila." Donnie and Diego said these same words almost in unison, which made them turn to stare at each other.

"You heard her!" Donnie cried incredulously.

Diego smiled widely, his whole aspect alight with joy. "Yes, I can hear her thoughts!" he exclaimed eagerly. "Perhaps that is because she speaks in a language I feared I would never hear again. You see, she knows my grandmother's tongue!"

"What?" This was said by almost everyone as their gazes darted from Diego to Donnie to young Wiwila and back again.

"Is that what she's speaking?" asked Donnie, marveling at the coincidence. "I wondered why I couldn't understand her, although she understood me when I asked for her name."

"*Si*," answered Diego, listening hard as the horse projected its thoughts and words into his mind. "She was trained by the vinca using Mannish commands, which is how she understood you. She does not speak it though, she says, because she does not have sufficient magic yet. Not like once she gets older. Until then, she will do her best to learn your language without magic, because she very much wants to bond with you, Donnie."

"Okay, but I still don't understand what you mean by bonding," she complained, "so someone's going to have to explain it to me."

She looked at Falwaïn expectantly, who chuckled again before telling her, "First you must look Wiwila directly in the eye until you feel she is ready, then you breathe into her nose, letting your life essence meet hers. From there, it all takes care of itself. Go on, try it," he urged, and Donnie nodded.

She faced Wiwila and their gazes locked. Without realizing what she was doing, Donnie leant down and breathed into Wiwila's nose, while Wiwila also exhaled her own breath. A faint blue cloud emanated from Donnie, while a faint yellow one blew from Wiwila. These two clouds came close together, flashed with sudden light, and seemed to merge and twist around each other into an intricate braid, which faded from sight. And for a few moments, Donnie felt Wiwila's heart beating and then she saw with Wiwila's eyes and she felt Wiwila's happiness at finally being bonded to someone, for she now had someone to love wholeheartedly and to love her back. This exchange of emotion and experience lasted only a few seconds, but it was powerful to them both. Donnie stepped forward and threw her arms around Wiwila's neck, planting a sound kiss upon the young horse's cheek.

Rex came up behind Donnie at that moment and bonked her on the back of her knees, so Donnie introduced him laughingly to Wiwila. The horse and dog touched noses and the same ritual was repeated, much to the astonishment of everyone present, horse and dog included. Rex was greatly excited by the bonding, as was Wiwila. They both hopped a little in Wiwila's stall, Rex sing-songing musically with happiness and Wiwila tossing her head and whinnying with joyous ecstasy.

Donnie looked questioningly at Sylvester, as though giving him the option to bond with Wiwila too, but he shook his head, his eyes wide and round.

"No-no, I shall pass on that opportunity. I do not believe it would work with me, anyway," the cat demurred hastily.

Donnie, scratching Wiwila's strong neck with her fingertips, glanced back at the men to ask, "Where did she come from? I mean, how did Akanna end up with her?"

"Akanna told us that she found the abandoned filly around Morlant, which is near the Mîrlonds," Warren replied, "and those are another patch of magical lands located in Gainál, quite a distance west of here. Akanna had no idea how the horse got there, because no one in the area had ever seen the young lass before."

When Donnie brought her gaze over to Diego, certain that Wiwila must be telling him something about her origins, he supplied, "She got here by magic, Donnie, apparently through what my mother's people called an *očhimeni thyópa*." He added with obvious reluctance, "It is how the Iquakawi walk through time. I believe the best interpretation for it would be 'traveler's gate'."

Sylvester sat down on the rail and noted with interest, "I have read of those and I believe they are also called the *giât y teithiwr*. They are nearly impossible to harness so one should never trust them because there is no guarantee they will land where you think they will. At least, that is what the *Havener Compendium* details regarding them. Did the Iquakawi find a way in which to steady them?" he inquired curiously, looking at Diego.

Diego nodded, admitting with feeling, "Oh yes, they made them quite reliable. We went through the *očhimeni thyópa* whenever our enemies would get too near, as they sometimes would, even with my grandmother checking their location every day. They would still come very close to us occasionally, and then we would have to escape through time, and not just move to another place."

"You time-walked yourself?"

"Yes," Diego replied, and he looked just as uncomfortable answering questions regarding the Iquakawi today as he had been a couple of days before when Donnie had questioned him about them. "At least five times that I can remember," Diego continued, "but it was probably many more. I am sorry I lied to you about this the other day, but I was not sure if I should share Iquakawi secrets with you. But now I know I must."

"Diego, just who were these enemies that you had to escape through time to avoid?" interjected Warren, looking as though he might already know the answer.

Diego leaned back against the wall and crossed his arms in front of him, very much aware he was about to drop a bombshell on them. He studied Donnie for a few seconds, then replied, "I could not say anything earlier when you asked about them because of who was present, but now that we are alone, I can tell you. *Mi abuela* called them the Iceni Meræ."

Shocked, Donnie took a step backward, her mouth hanging wide. Which was generally how the rest of the group also reacted, except for a grim-faced Warren, who was nodding to himself.

"The people chasing you were the Iceni Meræ?" reiterated Donnie in a croaking kind of voice.

"*Si*," Diego affirmed gravely. "I never saw any of them until that day in Moên Gjendeben, when they had visited with Valledai, and so I did not know their name then. But they caught one of us once, back in my world, when I was a child, I mean. It occasioned my first time-walk, or at least the first one I recall." He heaved a bitter sigh before going on. "I was seven years of age," he explained, his voice melancholic. "I remember that we had to abandon almost everything we carried with us, including our plans to meet up with other Iquakawi the following full moon. We were all very frightened when the alarm sounded to warn that our enemies would be upon us within minutes. *Mi abuela* and the other wise folk amongst us hurried to open the *očhimeni thyópa* and we were all sent through it immediately. Normally, we could pass through it at our leisure and the gateway would close itself in an hour or so, but this time we could not wait for it. So, one of the wise, a young girl called Šinte, stayed behind to make sure the gateway was closed the instant the last of us went through. She was supposed to kill herself with the venom of the rattlesnake, which each of the wise ones always kept with them in case of their being caught prisoner. The timing was so close that day, Šinte just barely got the *očhimeni thyópa* closed before the Iceni Meræ captured her and began to hurt her. *Mi abuela* said that she could feel the pain of her cunning sister for several days before her torture by the enemy was finally ended upon her death. Only then did we mourn her loss. And we never knew exactly how she died."

Diego paused, deeply saddened by the memories he was sharing. "My grandmother never forgave herself for her sister's torture and death. She said that she had gotten lazy and had not checked the enemy's location that wicked morning because they had been so far away the day before. She had not thought they would close the gap between us so quickly." He straightened from the wall and let his arms fall to his sides, adding with a sigh, "She would never again skip a day, not in all the years I traveled with her. And when she would take out her singing bowl to see where the enemy was at the start of each day, she would begin by singing to Šinte's spirit to ask for her forgiveness. *Mi abuela* swore that Šinte was still looking over us all, because our enemies never again came that close."

Donnie crooked a puzzled eyebrow at him. "Why were they after you in the first place?"

"I believe there were many reasons," Diego responded to this question thoughtfully, taking his time with it. "But I was not privy to most of them, of course, since I was still a very young man when my father took us to Mexico City to live with his people. I did not see my grandmother or the Iquakawi after that."

Falwaïn grunted a pensive "Hmm," before inquiring of Diego, "Have you ever heard of the Sôla?"

Donnie shot him an appreciative look, coupling it with an approving nod.

"*Si*," said Diego, returning Falwaïn's gaze with interest, "they are the Two who will find the One, the One who will lead the Iquakawi out of darkness and into light." Diego paused, dug through his memory a little more before adding, "I seem to recall that they were created by the ancient ones, the Sasdá Aĥon. If you remember, we call them the first gods, which is because they were the first Iquakawi—that we are told of anyway. We pass these stories to our children so that they are known throughout the generations, but we have no proof of any of it."

"Oh yeah, sure, that's understood," Donnie assured him. "Most ancient civilizations are the same. Um, tell me, do you happen to know what the Sôla look like? What form they take, I mean?"

Diego looked mystified for a moment, then suggested, "I would presume they must take animal form because of how closely my mother's people lived with wild creatures. Much like you, Donnie, they included animals of all kinds in their daily lives. They spoke to them and asked for their help in understanding the world or in making their rituals stronger, that kind of thing. Sometimes they treated them as gods and other times as friends when they would come upon one in the forest or the field—or in our camp." He added the last bit with a chuckle, obviously recalling some amusing event or other. "The wise ones would speak with the animal and it would answer back. *Mi abuela* said they tried to do this with plants and trees, but they would not listen to the Iquakawi's overtures, so she said her people stopped expecting responses from any plant. Still, though, she said they continued to talk to the plants just in case one day one decided to reply. But I believe that no trees or flowers—or weeds," Diego paused here, chuckling again before going on, "not even one had acknowledged the Iquakawi by the time I left them, so I doubt the Sôla would take that form."

Warren turned to Donnie and Falwaïn and questioned, "Why do you ask about these Sôla?"

Donnie smiled warmly at him, explaining readily, "The second book of our adventures mentions them, that's why. I really only know that they have something to do with Liz. It was an incident that occurred the day after Liz was born. Her birth mother Theris brought Liz to her adoptive mother and left her with Selma to raise, but Theris also gave Selma the Sôla at the same time. She described them pretty much the same way Diego did, you know, about the Two who will find the One. The book says they were wrapped in a bundle that Theris put on the table while still holding her baby, but the book didn't tell much more about them than that."

"That means they must be something relatively small, if Theris was able to hold them and Liz in her arms together," Warren observed, and Donnie nodded her agreement.

"Actually, I think I might know what they are," Donnie admitted, her face set in a pretty frown, "because Liz had a garage sale about a year after her mom died and I'm pretty sure I bought them that day. Liz said they'd been in the family forever, but she had no idea how they'd come to be in Selma's house."

"Oh, I know what they are then," piped up Rex excitedly and, when all faces were turned toward him, he explained, "they're the bronze statuettes of the condor and fox guarding that demented knife that tried to kill Mama. They're in the top cupboard of the cabinet in your office."

Donnie clapped her hands and grinned at him. "Yep, that's what I think too!" she exclaimed. She turned expectantly toward Diego and said, "Now, if we can just figure out what activates them and makes them go from statue to being real, we might actually learn something helpful about them. Do you know what could do that?"

Diego admitted with a slow shaking of his head that he did not know such a thing, so Donnie looked at Sylvester. "Got any ideas?"

But he appeared to be stumped also and mimicked Diego's expression and negative shake of his head. "There has been no sign of life to them— ever that you can recall?" he asked.

Donnie looked to Rex for confirmation first, and then she replied with confidence, "Nope, not to my knowledge. You ever see anything, honey?"

To which the dog said, "Uh-uh, me neither."

"Well, I can't be the One then. And, boy howdy, am I ever grateful for small mercies," Donnie drawled, sounding much relieved indeed.

"Why do you say that?"

She turned to Falwaïn and pointed out in response, "If I were, they most surely would've done something to show themselves by now, wouldn't you think? Especially since last night and everything that happened then. But there I was, sitting within three feet of them first thing this morning for over an hour and nary a peep came from either of them even once, and neither looked to have changed position in any way, no toe or claw out of place, nothing like that. Therefore, I am fairly confident I don't affect them at all."

Several heads nodded or murmured in either thoughtful agreement or quiet hesitation.

"I wonder who is the One, if it's not you?" queried Warren rhetorically. "And when will we meet them? Because we're sure to since Donnie has the Sôla in her possession."

This was pondered silently for a few moments by all before Donnie asked Diego, "Does Wiwila say if anyone was around her when she went through the, um, whatchamajiggy? The traveler's gate, I mean."

"The *očhimeni thyópa*? I do not know, but I can ask her," he offered.

But Falwaïn held up a hand to stop Diego and touched Donnie on the arm. "You try talking to her now. I think you'll find things a lot different since you bonded with her."

Surprised and excited by the implication of his words, Donnie reached out toward Wiwila with her mind and instantly they were connected in a way that made language superfluous. Both felt a thrill of true communion, which was made even deeper when Rex joined them in their psychical conversation.

Once Donnie had the answers she sought from Wiwila, she extracted her mind from this shared metaphysical discourse and said aloud, "She was alone and had wandered far from her herd when she saw a flash of light in front of her. That was when things got strange. She thinks of it as like looking at two lands at once. I believe she means that she could see her world, but superimposed on that was a window to this world. Before she knew it, her curiosity had gotten the better of her and she had stepped through the window and found herself in a sunny meadow instead of her native rocky hills. Not aware of the consequences of what she was doing, she walked away from the window back to her world and began to explore here. By the time she was ready to go home, she could no longer find the window, so she was stuck here. That was just a couple days before Akanna found her."

She beamed at Falwaïn and remarked happily, "That's what bonding does, huh? Gives you a kind of closeness you can't get with just talking to each other, I mean. I like it—er," she declared and then hesitated, glancing down at Rex who had just turned to her in haste with a huge grin plastered to his face. "*We* like it, all three of us!" she amended.

Even Wiwila seemed to somehow understand this sentiment as she tossed her head and whinnied, while the others chuckled together.

Sylvester, of course, had remained quite sober throughout all this and now reminded Donnie that they needed to leave for the council meeting. She acknowledged him with a short nod and went to find her saddle.

Warren beat her to it and carried it over, stopping in front of Donnie to say, "We," he nodded, indicating the other two men, "think you need to reconsider your demand that the king's army be off the Ganlonds right after the *byrgen* tonight. You see, the army and those traveling with it will expect to share one last feast tonight in honor of their departed friends and family." When Donnie opened her mouth to protest this, Warren implored her, "Please, just bring it up at the meeting and see what the council leaders suggest. That's all we ask." He turned away then to heft the saddle up and over Wiwila's back.

And so Wiwila, for the first time, got to experience Donnie's magical saddle, which, when cinched around the horse, felt soft and light. When Donnie climbed into it, the material of the saddle encased her legs and expanded around her to make for a very comfortable seat, which also felt quite pleasing on the horse's back. Wiwila pranced around in it proudly, making it clear that she was glad beyond measure to be going on a journey with her new bond mates and the funny little friend they called Sylvester, who jumped onto the saddle in front of Donnie. Since this seemed to be expected from the tiny creature, Wiwila did nothing to buck it off. And though it took her a while, the horse would eventually come to understand that there was another presence with them, one that emanated from the wooden parts of the saddle and which was apparently named Brindle.

Donnie, soft-handed with the silken bridle and reins she'd fashioned to match her saddle, directed Wiwila to head away from the farm and to the east. Rex trotted easily alongside the horse. Because she didn't want any of the king's people to be able to follow them, Donnie made sure to have the trees and other plants in her path move aside until the horse and dog had passed and then return to their original places.

It was quite an effective strategy, especially since the forest itself did even more against the two sets of prying eyes, and their owners, that had positioned themselves earlier that morning amongst the trees and which were cloaked from sight. But the trees and other plants in the area knew these invaders were there and made sure to raise obstacle after obstacle before them so that, within a couple minutes only, the horse and dog were so far ahead they were impossible to follow by anyone, even if that person was flying an agile spydercycle, as these two were. The two foreign scouts regrouped and flew over the treetops, looking downward, searching for but finally conceding that their quarry had truly given them the slip, greatly aided by the sentient forest stretching below. They gave up and flew their solar-powered and smoothly quiet machines back to the moors south of the cottage, where their captain impatiently awaited them and his other scouts. Of course there were six scouts who would never return to report anything, least of all that they had initially been successful in capturing three Sûlrím, but after that their plan had gone deadly wrong. The captain would find this out soon enough though, and neither he nor his scouts lingered in the Ganlonds unduly long thereafter.

Back on the ground, Wiwila managed a brisk trot for much of the journey, which took her over half an hour. Throughout this time, Donnie could feel herself being pulled from several directions, many of which were calls from animals praying for help or guidance, although others had no triune associated with them. These, she suspected, were some of the magical artifacts hidden on the Ganlonds, a theory bolstered by Sylvester when she described the sensations to him.

"The Ganlonds have never had an Ér Ainíl in all the time I have lived on them, so it does not surprise me in the least that many of the magical elements within the Ganlonds are now reaching out to you so that you may know and protect them. At least those which are well known to almost all of us, that is. Others, I am sure, are reacting in no way at all to you yet, for staying hidden may well mean their survival," the cat expounded.

He looked up at Donnie before commenting perspicaciously, "I hope you are not heeding the calls from the animals praying to you, for you must not answer every prayer they send."

Donnie, stung by his insightfulness, straightened tall in the saddle and muttered self-consciously, "What'd'ya mean?"

The cat was silent for a time, collecting his thoughts and choosing his words carefully. Finally, he pointed out succinctly, "If you fix their lives for them, they will lose all independence and that will serve no one well."

"Oh," Donnie sighed, relaxing into this truth. "You're right about that, thanks. I was beginning to be kinda frazzled trying to come up with ways to make them all happy."

"Yes, your frustrations have risen to the surface more than once today and I suspected their cause was due to your desire to assist everyone in your care. Do you not recall our lessons on this very subject during the past winter?"

"You mean, the ones about letting things happen naturally, that even though I can fix something, I probably shouldn't?"

"Yes," her familiar replied pedantically, "those are indeed the ones to which I reference." He lifted his right front paw to place it onto her hands, which were resting on the pommel of the saddle. He reminded her in a dry, stern voice, "Live and let live is one of the most important tenets of Wiccecræft and must not be abandoned simply because you have reached a higher level in your magical powers."

"You're right again," conceded Donnie, chewing her lip thoughtfully. "Gaia told me something similar about being a god—she said we gods mustn't choose the paths of those who look to us for protection and guidance. It's called the *kaeran bel hanan anmaet*, which is pretty much the same principle as live and let live."

"There is none wiser than Gaia," the cat murmured, pleased to have made his point so readily with Donnie.

Donnie chuckled down at him affectionately and said, "My friend, you certainly come close to her abilities at times, you know that? I thank you kindly for the timely reminder of just what my role really should be here. In the future, I am going to listen to the prayers called out in my name, hope for the best and wisest decision by the petitioner on how *they* deal with their problem, and otherwise let them live their lives in peace and by their will. I will also do what I can to ensure that the borders of the Ganlonds are made much more inviolable than they are right now, which I can't do until the king's army is off them." She took a deep, cleansing breath, before confessing, "It's not just the denizens of the Ganlonds I'm contending with, you know. Y'see, there're just too many soldiers here, I can't keep track of what they're all doing or saying and that only adds to my tensions of the morning. It's like I'm constantly being bombarded by this jumble of thousands of voices and feeling shot through with myriad emotions—all of which are not mine, most of which are not in any way connected with anyone who belongs here on the Ganlonds, and none of which I feel I can trust! So, I am on edge like you wouldn't believe! And maybe, just maybe, that has made me overreact to the king and his men a little bit," she confessed with a diffident shrug.

Sylvester considered this problem for a minute, admitting fairly, "That is understandable, certainly, and likely not imprudent of you to feel. And while I agree that the Ganlonds must be cleared of strangers as soon as possible, perhaps setting that for tomorrow morning might make a more courteous and opportune schedule for all concerned rather than demanding it occur tonight after the *byrgen* ceremony. I will argue the case for that with the council members and see how they respond. And now, I must welcome you to the Gahal Glæd," he informed her, raising his paw again to point to the path ahead of them.

And there, sun-kissed and wavering slightly to the naked eye, was a splendiferous clearing set within the deep greens and shadows of the forest where Donnie could see the animal leaders whom she'd met last night convened upon the series of pillars she had read about that morning in the second book of their adventures. Much like yesterday evening, the self-same magical creatures were in heated discussion about something, only today's argument ended abruptly at Donnie's arrival to the entrance of the beautiful Glimmering Glade.

Bronadulach, the Cave Bear who had borne the mantle of Kaerdír of the Ganlonds for the past decade, was the council's leader. Lumbering in his great bulk, he carefully lowered himself from his position on the highest of the pillars to the ground and motioned for the others to join him, which they did without protest. In the meanwhile, Donnie dismounted Wiwila and stood quietly before the assembled council.

The bear graciously bowed to Donnie, a move the others also copied. When they straightened, Donnie waved her hands wide and insisted, "Oh, there is no need for that, really. I would much prefer we meet as friends and partners in the future, and hail each other as such. You have bowed to no one before this and I would never expect you to do so to me now."

While this sat well with almost everyone and inspired a noticeable puffing up of shoulders or wings, it did not appear to do so with Méath-Degnír. The giant grey wolf sent Donnie a hooded look which she did not miss, but for which she was able to gauge its cause correctly.

Addressing just him, she elucidated her remarks by explaining, "You are my most trusted advisors now, and my request is meant to signalize my respect for each of you and the communities you represent. I would ask that you honor me always by providing me with your wisest and most fair-minded counsel in all our doings and meetings. As you are aware, judging from the, er, discussion we interrupted between you, the Ganlonds need all of us to protect them, not just me. As you yourself pointed out so rightly only a few moments ago, Méath-Degnír, I will have to be away at times, perhaps even for extended periods, so the defense of the Ganlonds will fall to you and your brethren and whoever else is best suited for that task. I will, naturally, ensure that you have whatever you need at your disposal on the occasions of my absence and will work with you to prepare the Ganlonds for whatever might come while I am gone. But that means we all must share in the responsibility for protecting the magical lands equally and I feel very strongly that if the responsibility for the Ganlonds' safety is equal, then so must the respect amongst us be."

The wolf listened to her closely and, by the time she finished talking, his expression had cleared. He gave her a nod of approval and thereafter regained his inherent demeanor of stillness and watchfulness.

Donnie faced the council calmly, clasped her hands in front of her and beamed at them, glad that she had such passionate leaders to help her govern and guide the magical communities of the Ganlonds. She looked over at Mickey T, the wise old bat who many a time had kept Donnie and the others company while they had been bound to the valley. Next came Bórlem, the Eagle Owl, and then the Giant Deer stag, Mórbaen. Lastly came Méath-Degnír, king of the Ettin Wolves, and Bronadulach, the mightiest Great Bear of Medregai. She regarded them all with affection and pride, then turned her bright gaze to Bronadulach to enquire, "Is this where we are to hold our meeting?"

As though in response to her inquiry, the Gahal Glæd quaked once, and then what could only be described as a brilliant rent in the fabric of space was torn vertically near the group of council leaders. This dazzling gash in the real world grew longer and wider, revealing another clearing behind it which was centered around a ring of birch trees unlike any other in the world. The trees and their branches had been trained to grow in such a convoluted, looping manner as to fashion a throne comprised of a wide seat and arms and a high back. The back stood at least twelve feet tall and sprayed out behind the throne in more loops, presumably making some sort of shape or shapes there, which were impossible to see because of the angle from which the onlookers were viewing it. Lining the more solid parts of the throne's seat and back was a bed of thick, dried moss, the green of the moss contrasting beautifully with the white of the birch bark behind it. And at the foot of the throne, the roots of the trees had risen to form a stool which was also covered in a thick layer of dried moss.

Around the sides and back of the clearing, flowers of all colors, hues, and varieties decorated the scene and, behind these, lush ferns towered and swayed. Beyond them stood a thick line of shrubs and trees, several species with which Donnie was heretofore unacquainted. Myriad insects buzzed around in the air there, alighting on flowers or leaves or branches, different parts of their bodies thick with pollen which they happily spread about. And while the sun could not be seen above, a radiant light nevertheless shone down upon the entire scene, gilding everything with sparkling gold highlights.

As more and more of this mystical wonderland was displayed to the onlookers and, as the door in the space wall opened ever farther to reveal the breadth of the floral hamlet on the other side, so too did Donnie's jaw drop until she was staring at it dead still, wholly and completely entranced by the richly incredible sights her eyes were barely taking in as being real.

Bronadulach sat down on his back legs and gestured his giant front paw at this burgeoning miracle while intoning in a low voice, "Whereas 'tis right and proper for the council to meet in the Gahal Glæd, Donemere of the Codlebærn, it would not do to establish your court here. The Ganlonds have therefore opened up the Imôríma for that purpose."

When Donnie could finally manage to draw her gaze from the magical wonderland that was the Imôríma, she threw him a questioning look.

He gave her a compliant nod and went on to explain, "The Imôríma, or Hidden Wing, was created many eons ago for the first Ér Ainíl, and this place has been preserved and protected, hidden away, if you will, by the Ganlonds. Throughout its ensuing ages, it has been tended by various magical animals, some of whom you see before you doing their best work to maintain the Imôríma's incomparable beauty. This place and its marvels are yours to do with as you see fit," the bear announced, and he looked quite pleased to be able to say this to Donnie.

She gulped, which meant she finally had to close her mouth and stop looking like a star-struck fish. Tentatively, she took a step through the door into the Imôríma and was instantly assailed by an olfactory concoction beyond compare. It was as if she could smell the fragrances of each and every flower individually, with indescribably alluring medleys tantalizing her senses in brief wisps that were too fleetingly lived and greatly mourned by their passing. She moved her head around on her neck somewhat like a bird, turning in this direction, then that, as another heavenly whiff drifted by her. She noticed too that she could see with startling clarity and her ears caught the buzz of bees and beetles and other insects and amplified these so that it all built to a loud crescendo before, all at once, it fell back down to a whisper and a semblance of normalcy was restored.

She took another step in and felt the warmth of the soil beneath her and that of the light shining above and immediately felt cozy between them. Then came the soft embrace of the air around her, and she wanted only to slump into its arms and let it hold her forever, such was the love that emanated back to her from the Imôríma through her skin. The hug lasted only a few seconds before it was gone, but it made Donnie stand still and close her eyes in awe, a small gasp escaping her parted lips.

She breathed deeply of the place and took another step. And with each step she made, the Imôríma welcomed her, proudly showing itself and opening wide its secret world to her. By the time she made it to the throne, her heart was light and bursting with love and joy and laughter and she felt like she might literally float into the air with very little provocation. She lowered herself to the moss-covered seat and sank back into the depths of the chair until her back rested solidly upon moss-covered wood. Once again, she felt a metaphysical hug that rejuvenated her soul and made her smile beatifically.

She motioned for the others, who were still waiting in the glade, to enter the Imôríma. Watching them closely, she took almost as much pleasure in their reactions to the place as what she herself had experienced during her first steps into this majestic sanctum.

When they were all inside the Imôríma, the opening to the glade disappeared and the small clearing around them reclaimed its perfectly circular form. In front of where the Animal Council members stood there appeared moss-covered platforms, each fashioned intricately from gnarled birch roots and modeled specifically for its respective animal's size and stature. The council members all climbed or flew atop these seats and settled onto their inviting cushioning with soft sighs.

By now, everyone present was smiling at each other with comradery and feeling happier than they had since they were very young. Donnie, having several seconds longer of exposure to the Imôríma than the others, waited until these initial reactions had faded and normal expressions returned to everyone's faces. But there was a relaxed air about them all that had not been there before entering the Imôríma, and for this Donnie was grateful. They had several issues to discuss, and not all of them would be without contention. Delaying no further, they got down to the business of managing the Ganlonds' needs, secure in the knowledge that no one on the outside could either intrude or overhear them.

Chapter 3
Do Not Weep at My Grave

Liz's water broke. She felt the release of it, its wetness and its warmth running down her legs, understood what it meant, and stared resignedly at the sand beneath her feet. She brought her gaze up to meet Catie's, whose face was shadowed and almost impossible to read because of the barrels of rum towering around them. Liz had inadvertently let out a soft moan at the moment of realization, which made Catie turn to her. Catie too looked down at Liz's feet, her eyes growing big once she spotted the dark stain there.

Her head shot up so she was looking at Liz's face again. "Naow?" she mouthed silently, and Liz nodded.

Catie glanced over at the sailship anchored in deep waters. She had told Liz earlier that she hoped to board it at nightfall when they wouldn't be so easily seen. But that was still several hours away, which was clearly out of the question, what with this new development. She swung her head back to peer nervously at the tree line behind them, seeming to be searching for someone, but then she frowned suddenly, a mumbled curse on her lips. Taking a small wand from the voluminous fabric of her orange skirts, she flicked it upward once. A soft yellow ball of light emerged from the wand tip and zoomed like a shot to the ship, where it was lost from sight.

After a few minutes' wait, a faint movement of something substantial showed faintly against the dark wood of the ship and some white splashes of spray could be seen where the bulkhead emerged from the otherwise peaceful water. Not long after that, a long rowboat came into view and the women saw that it was being crewed by two men who seemed inordinately winded by their efforts. Weirdly, two long ropes trailed behind the dinghy for no obviously apparent reason. The men landed the boat in the shallows just down from where the women were hiding, climbed out and pulled the dinghy farther onto the shore to beach it. They turned back toward dry land and waded through the foamy remnants of the gently crashing waves.

The barrels of flavorsome rum had been stacked there by the people of the basse terre. It was meant as a supposed offering to the captain and crew of the *Drunken Knave*, presumably in the hopes that the pirate ship would sail away without its entire complement of raucous crew members coming ashore to amuse themselves by tearing the nearby villages apart to procure, or more likely steal their own rum, as the *Knave's* crew was reputed to do when in certain ports.

But the town's fathers were feeling confrontational today and the rum was actually intended to draw some of the crew ashore so they could be used as a distraction. Albert Hilton, the magistrate of le Fort de la Roche, which was situated nearby, was a wily bailie of dubious character himself. He knew the sailship well enough to guess they had come for the witch, and he was therefore determined to thwart her escape, for the daft woman had stolen something of his and he would have it back or see her and the entire crew of the *Drunken Knave* murdered. His waiting men, hidden well from sight, were hoping for blood in the coming skirmish, looking forward to ridding the sea of the nasty scourge that had just landed on their shores.

The two sailors from the sailship strode toward the rum, rotating their heads like cautious cranes on their necks, searching warily for threats. The nearer of the two put his hands to his cheeks and gave a funny kind of whistle, and Catie stepped from behind the barrels, pulling Liz with her.

A series of events happened quickly then, one on top of the other, with the first being that the two approaching pirates fell into a large trap covered by flimsy boards and a dusting of sand that had been dug in front of the rum, where they plummeted several feet to the trap's bottom.

Three explosions sounded and bullets whizzed by the women's heads, with two landing in the rum barrels with loud *thwacks!* More pistols were immediately heard being shot, so Catie ducked and pushed Liz back into the space between the barrels where they'd been hiding moments before. She squeezed herself in after Liz while several more *thwacks* sounded all around them, along with the *glug-glug* of rum pouring out of the bullet holes either to the sand below or onto the crouching women's shoulders.

Then a squad of twenty soldiers ran grimly out of the nearby trees and advanced on a dead run at the women, the rum, and the captured pirates, who were yelling their heads off in the sand trap as though the gods in the heavens above would hear them.

This precipitated a strange sight to behold, for from the shallow depths of waves arose ten pirates, each with knife or cutlass in hand, and all with a devilishly dangerous look to them. These dripping thieves, cutthroats, and former soldiers or slaves, as befitted each, rushed onshore and met the soldiers with snarls, taunts, and deadly skill.

Catie reached out to grasp Liz's hand and pulled her out of their hiding place. Together they hurried to the rowboat, where Catie helped Liz over the bulwark and then ordered the pregnant woman to sit down.

Liz, soaking wet from the ocean waters they'd just dashed through and feeling faint from the distillery smell that clung to her clothing, found herself in the midst of her first labor pain. She hunched over and stared at the surreal scene taking place only yards away from her through narrowed eyelids. All she could think to do was to huff, "Be careful not to get shot," at the other woman between her short, hurried breaths.

Catie spared her a scornful glance while leaning over the boat's side to snatch a rope from the deck and retorted, "Not one of those dozy bastards could hit a barn with those dratted firesticks this far away, so there's no need ta worry 'bout ennything such as that!" After declaring this, she ran back to the men in the trap, threw one end of the rope to them, and tied the other end around one of the bottom barrels of rum. It was still full of the exotic brew and weighed more than enough for her purposes. She grabbed the rope, braced herself against the barrel and called to the men to climb. They were topside in moments and joined the fray going on around them.

Catie trudged back to the beached rowboat and, when she saw that Liz was no longer in the throes of a contraction, told Liz to get out and help her. Liz carefully climbed out of the boat and the two women pushed on its bow, trying to back it up to where it floated freely. They had no luck with this until Catie looked at Liz, took her by the hand and canted:

"Back we go,
Back ta the sea;
Push again, lo',
And then we're free!"

She said it once before indicating that Liz should join her, and the two women repeated the spell together. When that didn't seem to be working, she rounded on Liz and snapped, "Ye have ta *want* it when you say it, girl! Naow, let's cast it again!"

They repeated the spell once more, chanting it over and over until the boat moved backward enough so that it floated freely. Catie helped Liz inside it again, then clambered aboard herself, her breathing ragged and gulping because of the heaviness of her soaked skirts.

She scrambled around in the boat and found additional oars, setting them into their locks so that there were now three full sets of oars positioned and ready for use. She turned around to look back at the shore and barely heard when Liz screamed at her to watch out. A very large fist met her chin and she reeled backward into the boat, her feet flying upward.

The towering giant of a man who'd hit Catie launched himself into the boat and took her by the hair, thrusting her forward to her knees and up against the edge of the rowboat, where he held her squirming body, both of them panting with effort and rage. Liz screamed again and one of the men they'd freed from the trap leaped through the water toward the rowboat. The captain of the guard, who happened to be the nephew of the magistrate and an almost exact physical replica of his uncle, only thirty years younger, turned to meet the brigand halfway and shot him up close, leaving the magistrate standing alone at the side of the rowboat

Secure in the knowledge his soldiers had things well enough in hand behind him, the magistrate turned to the women and locked eyes with Catie menacingly, growling, "Give it back to me now, witch, and I might let yer precious captain and his crew live. Look around ye, hag. My men are about to slaughter yer friends, so ye best make up yer mind quick!"

And indeed, in moments it seemed the eight pirates who yet remained in the realm of the living were surrounded by an entire company of twenty soldiers, newly arrived. The pirates moved into a small circle, their backs to each other, weapons raised and readied to meet their deaths.

The hulk holding Catie twisted her arm behind her with one hand while using the other to twist the bun at the nape of her neck. She screamed in agony, and one of the pirates took a step toward her, but she shouted, "No!" at him and he stayed where he was.

Liz registered this vaguely in the fog of fear her brain had become and she too screamed, "No!" although she meant hers for the big man to stop hurting Catie. She added roughly, "Let her go, you bastard!" and this brought the magistrate's attention upon her.

Albert Hilton eyed Liz with distaste, taking her in from head to toe and making it clear he found nothing at all to his liking. He was a pampered, corpulent, middle-aged white man with two grizzled tufts of steel-grey hair sticking up over his ears on an otherwise bald, somewhat wizened head. He had small grey eyes that were soulless and that had the hatred of those not like him burned deep into them. He was married to the former governor's daughter, but she was old and hadn't been in his bed in thirty years, by mutual agreement. But that didn't mean he had ever abstained from relations with prisoners or slaves under his care. As a matter of fact, Albert Hilton liked his colored women slim and light-skinned, preferably shackled, and as young as he could get them, priding himself on being a young slave girl's first, even if she were no older than eight.

He noted Liz's swollen belly, her age, her crimson hair, and her darkly honeyed skin in one sweep of his mean gaze and sneered at her, "Cut it, ye filthy whorin' red flea, or I'll scalp ye!" He accompanied this threat with a wave of the long knife he pulled from the belt cinched around his thick waist. Ignoring Catie for the moment, he warned Liz, "That little tick inside of ye may not see the light of day if I so want. Ye make another noise and I can promise ye that's exactly what I'll want!"

Liz, angered beyond endurance by the threat itself and by the violence implicit in it and in the actions of the man holding Catie, and egged on by the beginning twinge of another labor pain, swore at him. "You greasy little cocksucker," she ground out between clenched teeth, "don't you dare threaten my child!"

The magistrate, who had turned momentarily from Liz back to Catie when he'd finished speaking, whirled around, enraged to be spoken to thusly by what he considered nothing more than a brown-skinned harlot of no value or consequence. Spittle flying from his mouth, he screamed at her, "I'll do more than threaten it now, ye darkie slut!" And with that he lunged toward Liz, knife thrust wickedly at her belly.

A flash of blackish-red raced around his hand and pushed his fist even harder at Liz. Catie noticed this wisp of magic, recognized it, and whipped around as best she could, searching the beach wildly with her eyes, just managing to catch sight of an ice-blond figure before it vanished into nothing. She turned back to look at Liz, dreading what she'd see, but Liz was unhurt, albeit mightily stunned, for the magistrate's hand was caught in what looked to be a wolf's jaw.

This supernatural wolf, having the appearance of a phantom, seeing as it was totally transparent, was nevertheless real enough to stop the hand of Albert Hilton in mid-thrust and crush down on it until the knife was forced from his fingers in agony. The magistrate gasped disbelievingly and tried to pull his hand from the mystical wolf's mouth. The wolf renewed its bite and thick, red blood oozed from where its teeth were now firmly embedded in the magistrate's flesh.

The moment the blooding began, the wolf became solid and Albert Hilton lost first his hand and then his throat to the wolf's forceful bite. The hulking bodyguard holding Catie fell to the wolf's fanged attack moments later.

Suddenly and inexplicably, there seemed to be a whole pack of wolves everywhere, some phantom, others only too real, and they were all going after the magistrate's men. Catie, reacting the quickest, shouted out to the pirates and they converged on the rowboat. It took two of them to dump into the water the maimed body of the large thug who'd attacked Catie. Then order somehow arose from chaos and they were heading toward the *Drunken Knave*, their own wounded and dead lodged haphazardly on the bottom of the rowboat.

What became of the wolves, Liz never knew because, by this time, another labor pain had her in its full grip. The men had to lift her up to waiting hands reaching down from the deck, which she was oblivious to thankfully as they bounced her this way and that while she was lifted. This new labor pain was long and intense, and Catie pushed a handkerchief into Liz's mouth to muffle her ear-splitting screams. Catie thereafter directed the men in forceful, angry commands on just how to handle properly a birthing woman.

They carried Liz into a cabin at the stern of the *Knave* and placed her on a long table in the middle of the room, holding her aloft until Catie had spread enough linens for a makeshift bed on the table. They put Liz down as gently as they could under the watchful, stern eye of Catie, who ordered the men out, adding that she wanted them to fetch the cook and several buckets of clean, hot water.

Two hours later, Liz, exhausted and sore, curled up around her baby in the hammock that was hung in the far corner of the room. It swayed gently with the ship's movement, which told Liz they had left the calmer waters of the harbor of Tortuga. She gazed down at her son and drank him in. The babe's dark eyes were open and peered up at her soulfully until they slowly drooped, little by little, and he fell into his first nap. Liz smiled with love and followed him into sleep.

It was nearly sunset when she awoke. She looked down, but her son was gone. Her gaze darted frantically around the darkening cabin until she saw Catie sitting in a chair, the baby boy swaddled in a blanket and resting quietly upon her lap.

Seeing that Liz was awake, Catie swiftly brought the babe back and together they worked on getting him to suckle from Liz's breast. Once their endeavors were successful, Catie left him lying on Liz, lit the lamps in the room with a snap of her fingers, and went in search of dinner for the adults. She returned with two plates of food, which she placed on the table, and helped Liz climb out of the hammock, an endeavor made easier by the thick, wide mattress laid atop the hammock's netting.

Grateful for Catie's kindnesses, Liz sank down into a chair at the table and adjusted her son so that she could have one hand free to eat her meal. She was starving and it showed by the rapidity with which she cleared her plate.

Catie ate more birdlike and barely dented the mounds on her own plate. She had somehow managed to convince the cook to boil up a pot of tea for Liz and she cautioned Liz to make it last. "Ye see, fresh water be mighty hard to come by on a sailship, so it don't get drunk much. Most o' us'll quench our thirsts with rum, 'specially since that little bairn of yers jest used up nearly half a barrel of good water what's on board. I'm sure ye'll not be wantin' to drink rum with us ta share with the babe later, will ye? So ye best drink that tea real slow, I say."

Liz shook her head and sent Catie an outraged glare, not sure if the other woman was being facetious or not.

Catie chuckled silently to herself, with her breast moving up and down as the only sign of her amusement.

"You know, he's not my first child," Liz reminded her.

"Aye, I gather ye've got a girl too—well, she'll be a woman naow, won't she? And I dunna think she's all that genteel, is she? Not for a lady of the future, I mean," observed Catie innocently.

Liz, about to snap an insult back at her, stopped herself with a sigh. "No," she said honestly, "Julia is not all that genteel. But how do you know that?"

" 'Cause I once had occasion to read me some of them books being writ about Donnie's adventures, that's how. Ta be fair, they seem ta talk about ye all, mebbe even me a bit here and there, ye know? So's I know what ta expeck from yer first child. And alls I can say is I'm a hopin' this bairn here will be a might smarter and kindlier than his sister, with any luck fer him."

Stung again by the other woman's observations, Liz sat up straight and narrowed her eyes at Catie, but before she could respond, Catie interjected, looking down at the baby boy resting on Liz's arm, "He sure is beautiful, ain't he? Jest perfeck, like I told ye he would be. Although, that wolf pack o' his is something special, eh? I dunno about ye, but I was not 'spectin' ennythin like that ta come out o' 'im and rescue us. How d'ye think he did it?" she inquired earnestly, looking from the baby to Liz, and back again. "He surely don't have his magic bound yet, do he?" she noted, then asked, "Got any idea who did yers?"

Liz too considered these very good questions to ask, but as she had no answers for them, she shrugged and looked mystified. "Are you sure my magic was bound? I mean, I'm still not convinced that, if I have any power at all, it's that strong. For all I know, that was you that made me look like a tree, not me."

Catie scoffed at this nonsense and took a large gulp of whatever was in her tankard. From the smell that drifted to Liz's nose a few moments later, it had to be rum.

"While I canna say how much power ye have in yer fingers, no, ye're certainly no Ísolé, trust me. Ye're a witch, right and proper, jest like me," Catie maintained stoutly.

Liz was not any happier to hear this now than she had been the previous times the little witch had said it to her, so she ignored the comment and instead focused on her child. He had fine black hair, watchful black eyes, and skin as honeyed as hers, if not a little darker. He was staring at her now as though mesmerized by everything about her, and when she smiled at him, she thought he tried to smile back.

She caressed his face with her fingers and saw an arc of turquoise blue magic reach from her right index finger to his soft cheek, and he closed his eyes and gurgled in ecstasy. Astonished by both the magic arc and her son's reaction to it, she gasped and looked up at a grinning Catie.

"Told ye," she said smartly.

"But I don't feel it buzzing in me, not like how Donnie says it makes her feel," Liz protested.

"Oh, I think that's mebbe 'cause the bairn was takin' it from ye while he was still in yer womb. I bet once ye've got yer strength back, ye'll feel it right enough. Jest don't go givin' it all ta him, 'cause babes canna control it, so they can be dangerous ta be around. Ye'll have ta learn how ta help him control his magic, even if it means bindin' him 'til he understands the consequences ta his spells."

"His spells? Pshaw! What spells could he possibly be setting at this age?"

"Ye mean besides that wolf pack o' his?" Catie muttered, right before she took another long pull on her tankard of rum.

"Oh, that had to be one of us conjuring them," Liz protested, further positing, "or maybe it's just a protection he has because of his father being a werewolf. That's possible, isn't it?"

"I s'pose it could be that," Catie conceded dryly. "Still, ye'll have ta be schoolin' him not ta use his magic much right now."

"I really can't believe he's able to do all that much in his current state," Liz argued stubbornly.

"Ha!" the little witch cackled, "ye might believe that, but it'd make ye no more than a colossal fool! I'm tellin' ye, witchy bairns know how ta set magic ta their every whim from their birthin' day, so their mothers better be ready ta offset that magic with boundaries, and the stricter they are with those limits, the better, as far as I'm concerned!"

Liz was much intrigued by the vehemence with which this last remark was made and she eyed Catie circumspectly because of it, musing, "Hmm, that sounds like the voice of experience talking. Do you happen to have children of your own?"

Catie did a double-take, then stammered, "Me-me? No-no, 'course not! Blinkin' frogs, there ain't been no bairns here!" and she pointed her thumb at her mid-section, glaring all the while at Liz.

Liz, amused, sat back in her chair and chortled, "They're not a disease, you know. They're just kids."

Nodding vigorously, Catie added, "And witchy ones are the worst, I tell ye true! Didn't yer first child, that Julia, cause any trouble when she was a mite?"

About to answer an absolute negative, Liz paused and thought more deeply about the answer. *Had* there been any issues with Julia having magical powers? Liz suddenly realized that she had not really spent all that much time around Julia until she'd come to live with Liz after Selma died. Selma had taken care of Julia from day one and had never asked Liz to do much of anything toward tending the child thereafter. Therefore, Liz had no idea whether Julia had exhibited any otherworldly characteristics at any time in her young life.

Liz's jaw dropped and, perhaps for the first time, she truly understood just how little she had been involved in Julia's early years and how much Selma had done for them both.

"I don't know," she confessed, looking wretched at having to admit that even to herself. "My mother took care of her because I was so young. And I would have to guess that my mom was the one to bind my magic, so maybe she did the same with Julia's—if Julia even has any magical powers, that is."

"Oh, she must have 'em, given that her da is one o' them Icenies and ye're a witch. If she ain't shown no sign of it up 'til naow, that must be 'cause she's bound. Ye may not know it, but I remember readin' that she met her da the morning of the Battle of the Branmar Plain back there in Medregai."

Liz's eyes nearly popped out of her head and she spluttered, "She did what?"

Catie nodded. "Yessiree, she certainly did. Well, as long as the book was telling me right, she did. See, I spent a fair time lookin' though them books, tryin' ta learn what was ta become of everyone. Granted, I only made it through the first two b'fore I grew bored. After all, there weren't not nearly enuff about me in 'em, ye know, and I thought that was rare and unfortunate of the author—an opportunity missed, if ye will!"

"I so don't care about any of that," Liz retorted sharply, then she caught her breath and said, "Well, wait a minute, yes, I do too care about that. Why did you travel to the future and make the movie directors for *Wolf Hunter*, *The Adventures of Galto*, and *Songs of the Earth* all use actors who look just like their counterparts in Írtha?"

"What convinces ye I did that?" Catie inquired slyly, gazing slant-eyed from the corners of her eyes at the other woman across the table, but Liz merely deadpanned back at her. "Well, yes, I did do that," Catie admitted after the short stare-down between them was finished.

"Why?" Liz repeated firmly.

Catie raised her chin and replied, "Mebbe I was jest tryin' ta make sure that Donnie would feel comfortable wi' 'em when she met 'em. Or mebbe, just mebbe," she added drolly, giving Liz an arch wink, "I wanted ta let women from the future know how 'andsome the men are back in Írtha!"

Rolling her eyes and shaking her head, Liz groaned exasperatedly, "Okay, don't tell me the truth. But let's get back to Julia meeting her father the morning of the battle."

"I dunna know much about it, like I told ye!" grumbled Catie, draining her tankard dry. "I was bored and didna finish all the books 'cause there were too many. Alls I know about yer daughter and her father was what Donnie tells everyone at the end of the battle that they met in the morning and he convinced Julia ta leave her door open in the back of the house once everybody'd left for the battlefield."

Liz drew her breath in at this news with a loud gasp. She allowed this new revelation to permeate her brain a bit before she began to nod slowly, all the while chewing on her lip. "Of course, that's why she did that," she murmured, more to herself than Catie. "Now it makes sense."

At this point, Catie stood up and announced that she was going to get more rum before bed. Liz, still lost in her own thoughts, registered Catie's intentions just as the little witch got to the door of the cabin.

"Wait a minute," she called to the other woman, "you haven't told me where we're going or really anything about our situation here!"

Catie turned back around as she began to slip through the door to reply, "Well, in a few days we'll be in Port o' Spain. After that, we'll head farther south. We'll talk more later." And with that, she was gone.

Frustrated by the inadequacy of this response, Liz grunted and growled, then picked up her son, who was sleeping again, and carried him over to the hammock, positioning him carefully upon it. She went around and searched the cabin, which was surprisingly furnished with ample writing materials, several nautical books as reading material, and a few dresses that were outlandish and garish and probably belonged to Catie.

Liz found a clean shift she could use for sleeping and changed into that. And for the first time in her life, she used a chamber pot. Feeling sore, stiff, and out of sorts, she climbed back into the hammock with her child and curled around him. Her last thought of the day was that she was going to have to name him tomorrow, and then sleep came at her like a freight train and she knew no more.

***

Donnie led Wiwila into her stall in the stables and chatted with Brindle after she put the saddle in its usual place and began grooming the horse. Brindle asked if she'd learned anything of importance from reading the books of their adventures and Donnie nodded thoughtfully as she stroked the curry comb over Wiwila's back.

"Yes, there were several things in them, actually. Not the least of which is the connection between Diana and Otis. I'm worried because they won't tell me the truth about themselves, even when I confronted them earlier today. But I think Diana read some of the same passages I did in the books, so she must have an idea of what I was trying to get her to reveal."

"Which is?" Brindle asked curiously.

"That Diana is much more than a slave girl of the Mehen'Adríum, for one. And Otis knew that. Besides, just watching them last night you could tell they had ridden into battle together many times before."

"Mm, yes, I thought the same when you sent me to them last night. They did not speak much at all throughout our maneuvers, and yet Otis was able to anticipate Diana's commands perfectly, much as Wiwila does yours," the old tree observed, which caused Donnie to still her movements and stare over at the saddle's stirrups, from which the tree's gravelly voice resonated.

"Are you serious? Wow, if that's true, then it must mean they've been bonded, right?"

"That would be my assessment as well, yes," Brindle concurred.

Donnie again moved the curry comb while she silently contemplated Brindle's theory. When she put the comb away and picked up the brush, she finally spoke again, musing, "I wonder who all went to the library to read the books last night while I was sleeping. Do you know, Brindle?"

"Yes, and I can tell you that everyone did, even Julia."

Once more Donnie paused her movements before she nodded slowly and murmured to herself, "That is quite intriguing, isn't it? And she acts like she's not interested at all."

"A ploy, obviously, to feign carelessness. As a correction to my earlier statement, I feel I should say that the only one who did not visit the library last night was Otis."

Confused, Donnie inquired after a moment's thought, "You mean Rex and Sylvester came and read some of the books too?"

"Yes, Donemere, they all came. None spent much more than half an hour, but each most certainly did come."

"Hmm, funny…and they were all nearby when the books went missing," Donnie observed.

"I thought those were hidden by you—are you saying you do not have them?"

"No, I do not. I stepped outside time for a bit and read through them," she admitted, "going back to mark certain events before I came back into real time and took a nap. When I awoke, they were gone. It's okay, but only because I'd already gotten what I needed from them. But it does make me wonder who wanted to keep me away from them, if that's what they were actually after. Maybe they just wanted to know what had been said about themselves. I dunno, I don't get why they were taken."

She finished with Wiwila and placed a blanket over the horse's back to keep her warmed up for their coming ride to the Branmar Plain tonight. Then she went to stand at the stables' door, looking into the building to study its layout, slowly figuring out how she could create enough stalls for all the horses they currently had plus two more, just in case they were ever needed. Happily, it would take only some minor modifications to do so and it would still leave plenty of room for her stores of oats and hay, and other paraphernalia stored in the stables. She got busy with her magic, transforming the interior within just a few minutes.

Afterward, as she was puttering around in the building, putting things away and generally tidying up, Falwaïn, Warren and Diego walked in, saying they had been looking for her for a while.

Falwaïn told her that the king and his troops were ready to move out from the valley and begin the trek to the Branmar Plain. "Have you decided about tonight and how long they can stay on the Ganlonds to celebrate their dead?" he asked her.

Donny correctly read the hesitation and doubt in the men's faces and, because of it, she crossed her arms in front of her, leaned back on her hips and sighed loudly, pursing her lips while she studied her friends. "Believe it or not," she said quietly, "I understand their pain. And so, I thought about it and finally came up with a way to give them what they want, but also do what's best for my magical lands. When we get there, you'll see." She let her arms fall to her sides and smiled reassuringly at the men. "I suppose we should leave soon ourselves, shouldn't we? I think I'll just nip in and take a shower, then we can all go in, say, half an hour or thereabouts?"

When the men nodded agreement, she left them in the stables and hurried into the bathroom, calling out to Julia that they would leave in a short while, in case she wanted to go with them to the funeral ceremony. After her shower, Donnie dressed in black leathers and boots, covering her clothing with a long, black cloak that was hanging in the wardrobe when she opened it. She'd never seen the cloak before, but when she put it on, it hung on her shoulders perfectly, and she got the feeling it was a gift from something or someone on the Ganlonds. It was thick and warm and would be most appropriate for tonight's somber events.

She was only mildly surprised that Julia had apparently declined to join them, as she was nowhere in sight when Donnie went back out to the barn. The men had the horses saddled, so Donnie climbed aboard Wiwila for their second trip that day. Sylvester joined her with a big leap from where he sat on the well and settled himself down in front of Donnie on the saddle. Rex trotted alongside Wiwila as they made their way out of the valley, with the guys bringing up the rear on their respective horses. Of Diana and Otis, there was no sign.

They were more than halfway to the Branmar Plain before they joined the rear guard of the king's army. Falwaïn took the lead and they pushed ahead so they could catch up to the king's retinue. Once there, Donnie hung back a little, not wanting another confrontation with the king or Galæron, although she did make sure to sidle over to Akanna, who flashed a smile at her and Wiwila.

Donnie returned the smile with a wide, joyous one of her own. "I really must thank you for gifting Wiwila to me," she enthused once she'd gotten closer to the vincan.

Akanna bowed her head and replied soberly, "It is my pleasure to so honor the Ér Ainíl of the Ganlonds. And young Wiwila needed someone worthy of her own bright spirit with whom to bond. I felt neither of you could find a better bond-mate than each other."

Rex, having followed Donnie to trot alongside the vincan commander, urged Donnie, "Tell her about me, Mama!"

Donnie agreed with an excited nod and corresponding widening of her eyes, saying to Akanna, "Have you ever heard of a horse bonding with a dog too? Because after Wiwila and I bonded, Rex walked up to her and the bonding ritual was repeated. So, it's like the three of us are bonded to each other now."

Akanna looked surprised, but nodded to herself slowly, clearly pleased with this news. "How wonderfully serendipitous. You see, I was born near the Mîrlonds, which are in the Gainál province. The Mîrlonds is the only other remaining location of magical lands here in Medregai, with even many of the elven forests now having fallen into less because of—"

"Into less?" Donnie interjected in confusion.

"Yes, it means the earth's magic can no longer reach the surface there, so it is less than it once was—you understand?" When Donnie nodded that she did, Akanna resumed what she was saying before she was interrupted. "This has been happening for centuries, you understand, and the myriad places that once were havens for all magical creatures have been reduced to a mere five within Írtha, although it could be fewer by now." Akanna shrugged, her voice grave as she continued. "To make a long story very short, the Ganlonds and Mîrlonds are two of these havens and were once ruled by two sisters whose magic was different but supreme. That was more than a millennium ago and no one now living knows their fate, for both simply disappeared from Írtha. And that marked the beginning of the lessening. As part of that beginning, the mage in the mountain died, but not before he prophesied that one day an Ér Ainíl would arise again and she would become part of a magical triad, or, as it is called in the old vincan language, an A'Rontauk." Akanna's eyes gleamed as she glanced over at Donnie appreciatively. "And so, it seems the mage in the mountain foresaw your ascension and knew that you would bond with two other magical creatures."

"Fascinating!" Donnie gushed, charmed with the idea of the three of them making a magical triad. "Did he say anything about what we'll do together?"

Akanna's features assumed an expression of regret as she answered, "To my knowledge, no. But I am made most content to have played my part in bringing your bond mate to you. May your association prove to be both fruitful and beneficial."

"Thanks, I bet it will!" called out Rex, who was listening closely to the conversation between the two women.

A soldier rode back to meet them and said that Akanna was needed ahead. She saluted a farewell and cantered away on her own horse, leaving Donnie to mull over what she had just related to Donnie.

They exited the forest a few minutes later with the king's army, which spread out onto the Branmar Plain in a much more disorderly fashion than it had the previous evening when the battle had begun between them and Valledai's evil forces. Donnie soon realized that she had lost sight of her friends in the fast-growing crowd that was becoming more raucous by the minute, so she asked Rex if he could find them. Her dog turned back to her and called, "Sure, follow me," and he took off to the right, with Wiwila trotting briskly after him.

True to his word, Rex brought them up behind the king's contingent not long thereafter, and Donnie had Wiwila walk beside Diego and his horse Ampago. Diego nodded to her when she moved up beside him, but did not say anything, nor did Donnie utter a word to him. It was a few minutes before anyone else realized that she had joined them, and it was the king himself who noticed her first. She felt Belnesem's cool glance, more than saw it, and when she lifted her eyes to meet the icy stare of the elf Galæron, she did so with overt defiance on her face.

Falwaïn rode between them, making sure to show Donnie a wide smile of welcome. He dropped back and asked in a low voice, "Where do you want to hold the *byrgen*? How much farther do we have to go?"

"Just until the new forest we created last night," she replied, her voice as quiet as his. "I moved all the bodies there earlier, after my meeting."

"Okay," he said slowly, "but I should tell you that there are reports of minor injuries occurring to anyone venturing too near the angry saplings and their evil okûn souls. Er, look, I know you're a bit peeved at the king and his men, but you're not going to have his army set up camp right there, are you?"

Donnie, noting that he looked slightly amused at this prospect, mugged facetiously back at him and chuckled. "No, you wise ass, of course not. They should keep heading north of the forest. They'll know where when they see it," she assured him.

He hesitated for just a moment, then shot her a loving smile and a wink before cantering back to the king.

Half an hour later, they came to a standstill on the northern edge of the plain, which now was bounded by a thin ridge of trees, through which was visible a large, flat area that would indeed be quite accommodating to the king's army. The king twisted back toward Donnie and sent her a slight bow of approval, to which she remained impassive.

Warren moved his horse over to Donnie and leaned close to ask in her ear, "How did you manage this? There's no field like this located here."

She beamed a very self-satisfied smile at him, answering in a pseudo-perky voice, "For your next lesson in the library, research what it means to fold space, and you shall have your answer!"

He rolled his eyes and scoffed at her. "Does it, perchance, mean what seems blaringly obvious from its description?"

Donnie looked at him slyly. "That would be cheating you out of a singularly compelling lesson, and you know how I'd hate to do that!"

He said no more, but his shoulders shook with laughter as he urged his horse forward to where Falwaïn was still conversing with the king.

While the bulk of the army continued to the camp site soon thereafter, Donnie and her friends turned back toward the new forest that Falwaïn had joked about. The forest had been created the night before by the goddesses of the *Niunda Wakan*, or the Nine Guardians. The *Fforest yr Anfodlonr*, which translated to the 'Forest of the Unwilling,' was made up of young saplings of various tree varieties. They had been birthed from the living bodies and souls of Valledai's forces who remained on the plain and in the surrounding forests and mountains at the end of the battle. These creatures were converted by the goddesses instead of killed, a judgment made by the grace of the almightiest of goddesses, Gaia herself, at Donnie's strenuous urgings. Gaia had later warned Donnie that the forest was sure to be unsafe for anyone to pass through, and Donnie was determined to use tonight's ceremony as a way to protect the Ganlonds from the forest's inherent and determined wickedness. This evil aura she could already sense emanating from the trees, seeping into the ground below and even permeating the air above. She hoped to at least mitigate its potential impact by adding a deep layer of love all around it.

The bodies of the king's dead had been laid out in front of the forest, their many long rows a sobering sight. A smaller, but no less wrenching number of animal corpses were laid out closer to the forest, their bodies tended to by animal and human caretakers alike.

Each of Donnie's little group dismounted their horses and walked forward to gaze around sadly, everyone feeling at a loss for words. The magnitude of the previous night's battle hit them all in that instant and they reached for their friends' hands, with Rex leaning up against Donnie's leg, while Sylvester jumped onto her shoulder. They stayed this way for some time until, one by one, they returned to their horses.

It was approaching sunset before the army finished setting up camp. The bereaved at first began to congregate around the area where the dead were assembled, but soon they were directed by the army's captains to encircle the forest with their numbers. Unbeknownst to all save her friends and the king and his high commanders, Donnie sent out a spell that would compel each mourner to draw near the place where their dead loved one or friend would be moved for the *byrgen*.

At a signal from the king for her to commence the ceremony because the circle of the bereaved had been completed, Donnie motioned for the attendants to take their places beside their assigned dead soldier. Donnie walked slowly between the bodies, her head bent in prayer as she moved down the middle row. Reaching the center section, she lifted her face and drew her power inward, letting it build until she began to glow faintly with it. She closed her eyes and reveled in the sun's kiss on her skin for a moment while her magic vibrated just beneath this solar osculation. She lifted her arms straight above her and let them fall to her sides, and from where she stood a network of her magic, a brilliant and dazzling blue in color, stretched underneath the dead and the living assembled around her.

A great sigh resounded throughout the masses gathered upon the Branmar Plain when the corpses of the dead and their attendants appeared before the mourners in a one-row formation that encircled the entirety of the new forest, just on its outer edge. For every two or three slain king's soldiers in this row, there was a least one slain animal soldier, and these were all interspaced such that the two crowds of mourners were well-mixed and everyone made welcome, for all were fellows in the gravity of their shared grief.

Donnie moved through a break in the thick circle of bereaved, a break created by the king's captains and their quiet commands. As she walked through this deep entrenchment of profound sorrow and greatest love, her magic still flowed into the ground, reaching out now to the very core of the Ganlonds, for the Ganlonds itself would take part in the ceremony tonight. Every step she took was emblazoned with her magic, just as every particle of air around her was energized with it. She slowly joined the king and his high commanders where they were stationed only feet away from the dead, standing just a little apart from the king's retinue.

Her friends had all been asked to participate as attendants, with Falwaïn attending an old friend of his named Sproghan of Harhall, whom he had known since his first real battle back when he was just a lad, and Diego attending another of Akanna's vincan warriors, a young orphaned female named Bazl'rit. Warren and the body of Akanna's cousin K'lan Tai were situated in front of where Donnie stood, but he was the only one of her human friends that she could see, although she felt Falwaïn's reassuring presence to her left and Diego's nervous one to her right.

Of her animal friends, Sylvester was attending Diali, the fierce Sparrow Queen, who had been a beloved fellow steward of the Gahal Glæd, and he too was on Donnie's left, but not as far from her as was Falwaïn.

Rex was attending Bauffaela of the Bau tribe of Ettin Wolves, daughter of Méath-Degnír, the King of the Free Wolves. She had been Warren's former mate in his wolven days, before he and Bauffaela and their wolf pups had been transformed into werewolves by Valledai. By a strange coincidence, or possibly just arranged by fate, Bauffaela's body and Rex were positioned right next to the body of K'lan Tai and a noticeably emotional Warren. For Warren, tonight meant not only a goodbye to loved ones such as Bauffaela, but it also brought an official close to his life as a wolf, for his future now lay in a very different direction. Donnie was glad her pup had agreed to attend the dead wolf, for Warren could barely look at her limp body without breaking down into racking sobs. She felt Rex push a small wave of love at his friend and watched as Warren received it, noting the strengthening of Warren's back and the deepening of his breath, until he was once again calm and composed.

Belnesem strode over to Donnie and took her hand. He too was in the throes of emotional turmoil and he tried twice to say something, but could not find his voice. When he finally did, he said, "Is there a way I can speak so that everyone can hear me? I mean, everyone on the plain, not just those surrounding us here? Can you help me with that?"

Donnie assured him she could, and he turned around to face the line of dead, composing his thoughts carefully. He indicated he was ready just as the setting sun touched the western horizon in the cloudless sky above and the landscape all around them was bathed in a rich, golden hue. Donnie put her hand on the king's shoulder and used her magic to project his voice into the minds of all sentient beings everywhere on the Ganlonds, even those not present upon the Branmar Plain.

"Tonight, we share our greatest grief," the king orated in his deep, strong voice. "Bound in battle, bonded in friendship, we honor the brave warriors who gave their lives last night so that we may all live free. Their journey to Canavar begins here on the Branmar Plain with us, and ends in the holy land in the company of those who have gone before them and who are just as dearly loved and sorely missed as our beloved here will be. Our prayers will guide our friends home, and the love in our hearts will initiate their paths. Fair friend Mændís will find no fault with our warriors or the good and useful lives they spent in Medregai. With the aid of our devoted benediction, he will certainly send them straight through the Chamber of Reckoning and on to Canavar accompanied by his highest blessings. For tonight, our mutual will can have no equal in the past or the future, and the Priest of the Dead must surely be moved by our great affection for our friends and our fellows."

To this point, no one else had moved or spoken, and all that could be heard was the flames of the many torches held by the king's men, which were being fanned in the slight wind that crossed the plain. But when Belnesem began the Benediction for the Dead, all heads bowed and many voices repeated the ancient words with him.

"In the name of all that is holy, we ask noble Mændís to hear our prayer for our fallen, for they cannot speak for themselves. In their every day, in their every battle, they strove to be honorable and courageous, decent and praiseworthy, fair and honest. And while they may be taken from our lives, they can never be removed from our hearts or our memories, for there they will live forever. There they will always be smiling, laughing, and loving. For that precious gift which may heal our wounded hearts, we kneel to the earth and send our love and gratitude out to all earthly creatures, so that eternity may be theirs as well as being gifted to the friends we commit to the elements tonight. Our prayer is resolute, our will is steadfast."

Donnie, having never heard nor read the benediction given here in Medregai, was caught off-guard when the king knelt near the end of his prayer, but she managed to keep her hand on him so that his words did not falter in anyone's hearing as she quickly knelt beside him, her own head bowed. When she looked up at the end of his words, she realized that every living soul in sight, including all birds, bees and such, had reached down to touch the ground, to send out the requested prayer of eternity to all living creatures. Her breath caught in her throat for a second, then she sighed, for she could feel enormous reserves of love pooling beneath her all around, a swell of emotion needing only a direction in which to send the souls of their loved ones on to the final journey of this life.

The king stood and turned from her so that her hand fell away from his back. He smiled more kindly at her than he had since this morning. "If you would continue the honors," he murmured, and she nodded.

The sun had just set and twilight was falling rapidly. Donnie stepped forward and said, using her magic to project into everyone's hearing again, "The trees and plants of the Ganlonds wish to assist in honoring the brave soldiers of the animal army and the king's army. To that end, they have graciously supplied all the makings for the funeral pyres."

She extended her arms upward, and with this movement great pyres appeared under every fallen soldier, pyres made of small tree trunks and thick branches, each topped with dense beds of leaves and other plants, all dried and ready to burn, but all still holding the essence of life, which would be released by the funeral fires' flames.

Donnie slowly walked forward so that she was standing only a few feet behind Rex and Warren and the bodies they attended. She stopped, looked around at the grieving onlookers and the stoic attendants, and said to all present on her magical lands, "The Ganlonds have reached out to other magical lands throughout Írtha and they have provided anointing oils of frankincense, myrrh, hyssop and rose, which will now be placed upon each of our dear friends whose souls we are commending tonight to their final journey from this life."

With another wave of Donnie's arms, all attendants were provided with a receptacle of consecrated oils with which to anoint the body next to them. When the attendants finished, any remaining oils were poured onto the waiting pyre underneath the fallen either by the attendant or with Donnie's magical assistance.

The fragrances around the funeral pyres were now overpowering and enthralling, with each attendant breathing deeply of them as the pleasing odors blended into a soothing balm for their souls.

Once again, Donnie waved her arms and projected her voice into everyone's hearing. "The attendants will now find before them herbs and flowers provided by the Ganlonds that should be scattered over the bodies of the fallen and their pyres."

She waited until the attendants began to spread the dried herbs and flower petals, again magically assisting those who needed it before she started to explicate the combination of plants and their purpose. "For the dead," she explained, "there is bay for honor and reward, sage for wisdom, and ivy for eternal life. For the living, for those much cherished by the dead and the friends who honor them tonight, so as to help them heal from this day forward, there are rose petals to symbolize the love and friendship between them that will never die. There is also rosemary for remembrance of times shared and zinnia to recall to us our missing friends' faces. And finally, for everyone, both living and dead, thyme is provided to give us courage and strength, while mugwort is there to bring tranquility to our troubled hearts and minds, and ghost flower will lend us perspective so that we may send our loved ones to Mændís free of encumbrances of the heart and soul which might somehow delay their journeys to Canavar."

The attendants, when done spreading the herbs and flower petals, took a few steps back from the pyres so that they were now in line with Donnie and bowed their heads.

The boombox appeared at Donnie's feet and played a funeral dirge of exquisite composition. The notes of the music seemed to come from the earth below them, they were so lush and full, and not from the tinny box from the future. Donnie had never heard the dirge before, could not recite its words before now, but she nevertheless knew exactly what to say in what was, really, a benediction for the living, and just when to say it. When the time came, she sent her prayer out to all mourners on the magical lands, her voice sad and serious as it reverberated over the plain.

> *"Do not weep o'er this grave,*
> *for it holds me no more.*
> *I am changed into light and air,*
> *and the west winds carry me afar.*
> *I am in the moon and the sun,*
> *in the sky and the stream.*
>
> *I am born of the earth,*
> *and am once again her happy child.*
> *I exist in the birds who fly above her,*
> *and the worms who gently probe her soils.*
> *My life before is but a memory,*
> *my death a shadow that slips away unseen.*
>
> *For I am all and I am nothing.*
>
> *I am at peace in my death,*
> *and rejoice that the living go on without me.*
> *This is how it has been for ages,*
> *and so shall it be for eons to come.*
>
> *So...do not weep at my grave,*
> *for I am here no more."*

The dirge ended and, for the last time that night, Donnie raised her arms above her head and projected her voice into the hearing of all. "The final gift from the Ganlonds tonight is the Flame of Ívers'Fa, which took refuge long ago upon these magical lands after the Red Warlock used it to forge the key to the hiding place of the Five Jewels of Light." When she named the mystical fire, it appeared in two balls of beautiful red flames upon the palms of her upraised hands. She felt a slight warmth on her skin there, but was otherwise unscathed by the brilliant fire. "The Sûlrím will use the Flame to light the pyres," she instructed, and marveled at the soft flutter of wings on her fingertips as the little birds flew through the fire in her hands, each bright with mystical flame when they soared away. After the last birds had gone, the Flame of Ívers'Fa returned to its secret home within the Ganlonds and was seen no more that night.

The lighting of the pyres was nothing less than sheer spectacle, and a breathtaking tracery of hot red light was woven that encircled the new forest in seemingly seconds by the thirty small birds whose flight was uncannily inspired and psychically coordinated to an absolute micro-second. This entrancing pattern of light remained visible in the air for nearly five minutes when, by that time, all pyres were roaring wildly with flames.

For the next hour or more, the crowd of mourners thinned slowly, with those who were too overcome with grief or were needed elsewhere for duty being the first to leave. The *byrgen* attendants were tasked with standing by their respective pyre until it burned itself out, and Donnie stood with them, as did the king and his high commanders. Because a magical flame had been used to light the fires, the pyres lasted not much longer than two hours, by which time there was little more than fine ash left of the brave soldiers who had given their lives the night before.

Donnie waited patiently for her friends in the same spot she'd stood throughout the ceremony, idly hoping that the spell she'd wound into the *byrgen* to contain the ire of the new forest would be successful. She supposed only time would tell on that score. But she had agreed earlier in the afternoon with the leaders of the Animal Council that she would cast the spell, while they would counsel their kin and kind to keep away from the forest for the foreseeable future, for it was known that the saplings were wanting violence. Some of the older trees had volunteered to make their way to the new forest tomorrow and would root themselves nearby, if only to keep watch on the angry young trees, and Donnie had not said no to that offer.

Diego found Donnie pretty much immediately after the funeral pyres subsided, while Rex and Warren went in search of Sylvester, with the three of them lending their commiserations to many of the animal families. This took some long while before they were able to make their way back to stand beside Donnie. When they returned, Warren looked absolutely miserable, so Donnie stepped up to him and embraced him gently. He put his head on her shoulder and she felt his whole body shaking. The night had certainly taken its emotional toll on him and Donnie let some of her power flow into him. He felt its comfort as it passed through his body and back into the ground, and he released some of his pain to it when Donnie advised him to do so.

Falwaïn was the last to join their huddle, lingering to say his farewells to the king. When Belnesem and his commanders strode toward their camp and disappeared into the thin line of trees edging the plain, meaning that the plain was now cleared of all the king's folk, Donnie waved her hand in their direction. A blue wall of light flashed for just a second, then was gone. And gone too was the encampment, with only the thick forest that rightfully stood there now showing.

Diego turned to her with a gasp. "What did you just do?" he asked.

Donnie chuckled and laid a reassuring hand on his forearm, turning him around so they could walk to their horses. "Nothing really, other than I unfolded space so that the camp is no longer connected to the Ganlonds. And now, no one from outside may enter the Ganlonds, not even the villagers to get salt from Catie's saltworks, nor any magical creatures who do not belong here. The magical lands need some time to recover, you see. As one of the results of the council meeting today, it was agreed that I would ensure the king's men would indeed leave tonight and have no further admittance until a much later date." She stopped and looked at both Warren and Falwaïn at this point, sighing heavily at their confused faces before resuming her footsteps. "Honestly, it was not just me who wanted them gone, but rather most of the magical lands' inhabitants wished for that quite fervently. So, in reality, I was only forcing what my constituents demanded to happen most of last night and all of today. And now the Ganlonds are safe from outside intruders until I turn off my blocking spell, which will be when the council agrees it to be."

"I suspected as much, which is why Jora and I did not go with the king," a crisp voice broke into the conversation. Donnie and her friends whirled as one to see a dark, cloaked figure walking toward them, quietly leading her sleek black horse behind her.

Everyone in their little group stared at this vision with open mouths and wide eyes. As Akanna of the Zal'Dorek Vinca of Gainál approached them, each of their stunned expressions were visible in the bright moonlight of the night except for the cat and dog, whose features were shrouded by their natural coloring. But they too were quite shocked by this unexpected turn of events.

So much so that it was Sylvester who croaked, "What do you think you are doing? You do not belong on the Ganlonds!"

Akanna looked down at him and nodded. "True," she admitted, "but I do belong on the Mîrlonds and they very much need your help. Therefore, I've come to persuade you to go there, to at least see if my suspicions about what is happening there are correct. And if the Mîrlonds are in real danger, I am hoping you can save them, or rather, that their Ér Ainíl can. Where is she?" The vincan looked searchingly through their number and reiterated her question. "Where is the one you call Diana?"

Chapter 4
Don't Take Your Guns to Town

The ride back to the cottage began without conversation while they all tried to fathom the bombshell Akanna had just dropped upon them.

Warren, who rode beside Falwaïn and led the way back, was the first to address the others, remarking gravely, "I never even had the sense that Diana was a witch, let alone a goddess."

"She is not a witch," Akanna refuted the claim, eyeing Donnie calmly from where she was riding abreast of the other woman. "Ghira Ma'Hai is an ovid," Akanna explained, keeping her dark-eyed gaze on Donnie. "She is a slave maiden of the Mehen'Adríum become warrior. That is the origin of the term, but it is now accepted as any maiden of any land who trains hard and walks the path of the ovids before her. Her power is in her fierce ability to fight and to brave any battle set before her. Unfortunately, this particular ovid deserted the Mîrlonds long ago, but why she did so is a mystery to all who know of her existence. I recognized her last night from my childhood. While she left the Mîrlonds when I was still quite young, I have never forgotten her. She is the reason I became the warrior I am now."

"You grew up on the Mîrlonds?" asked Donnie, who had Sylvester sitting in front of her on the saddle. He was staring at Akanna distrustfully.

"There and at nearby Morlant," the vincan replied. "My mother was Kaerdír for the Mîrlonds for a very long time. A couple of long years, or what I gather you call decades, after her death, I too earned that graced position and have held it ever since."

"You are currently the Kaerdír of the Mîrlonds?" inquired Sylvester, his haughty voice carrying a distinct note of affront. "If that is true, why have you left them? A Kaerdír belongs on their lands, living with the other inhabitants to ensure all are governed fairly."

Akanna spared him an amused glance, then returned a more serious regard to Donnie. "I can infer from his statement that your cat has very specific ideas of what a Kaerdír may or may not do, ideas that would never be successful on the Mîrlonds for there remain few inhabitants and they would not take kindly to my interfering in their ways of life. My position as Kaerdír mostly entails making sure that no one harms the magical lands in any way. And it is in that capacity that I seek your assistance, since I am quite certain that someone is doing exactly that and the magical lands are suffering greatly. Just who or how this harm is being committed eludes me; hence, the need for your assistance."

Donnie studied the other woman for a few moments without speaking. She sighed before inquiring, "Is that really all you want from us?"

Akanna's sharp jaw tightened and her eyes flashed in the moonlight. "No, that is not all I want," she admitted. "I wish also to convince our Ér Ainíl to return home with me."

Donnie shot her a discerning glance and said with a nod, "I thought that was probably what you were after, at least in part." She leaned back in her saddle and sighed again. "Diana is free to go where she pleases and no one has any right to expect more of her than she has already given."

"I disagree," Akanna protested firmly, while Sylvester shook his head vehemently, also in apparent disagreement with Donnie. Akanna went on, saying, "Ghira Ma'Hai is the Ér Ainíl of the Mîrlonds, and they need her now more than ever. They are her responsibility, a duty which she can no longer avoid."

"Perhaps," acknowledged Donnie, "but I want to know more about her situation before making a determination like that about her. I know her—she must've had a darn good reason for leaving the Mîrlonds and, if that reason still exists, I am not about to help you force her back there if she doesn't want to go."

Diego interjected loyally, "Nor will I, Donnie, because I too believe that Diana is free to do as she pleases!" He and Rex were bringing up the rear of the little troupe and had to strain some to hear the conversation.

Rex piped up, "Yeah, Mama, we can't make her go back there if she doesn't want to. That wouldn't be right!"

"Pay them no mind," Sylvester said to the vincan in his usual pedantic way, "for they do not understand what is needed to manage and protect magical lands. It must have been quite difficult for you to maintain the Mîrlonds with an absent Ér Ainíl."

"Whaddya mean?" Donnie protested, ready to argue the point. "The Ganlonds have done pretty well up to now without one, so why should it be any different for the Mîrlonds?" Her stubbornness was well and truly aroused now and it could be heard in the truculence of her voice.

Sylvester turned around on his perch and sat facing her, his expression aggrieved. "I simply mean that once one of the magical lands accepts an Ér Ainíl, things change, including how the lands regenerate magical power. The magic must now go through the Ér Ainíl and then back into the magical lands and its inhabitants, which serves to magnify the power greatly. If there is no Ér Ainíl or, as in this case they are missing, that very important step is bypassed and the magic will begin to die. While, yes, that will occur very slowly, it will nevertheless occur, for no magical lands can go for very long periods without at least a Madra witch helping them or an Ér Ainíl to regenerate and increase the magic. Without that assistance, there is no way for the magical lands to thrive. Rather, they can merely subsist, and that for only a relatively short period. Diana must have known that by leaving the Mîrlonds, she was sentencing it and its inhabitants to a slow death."

"Oh, now wait a minute!" Donnie cried, as did Diego and Rex. Warren turned and looked like he might say something too, but refrained from doing so in the end. Falwaïn wisely sat and listened.

"That's a really harsh way of looking at it, Sylvester, especially since we don't know the details!" Donnie protested, frowning at the cat. "I mean, I'm sure that was not at all in Diana's mind when she left. You know her, she wouldn't do something like that if she thought it would kill someone."

"But she must have realized it in the intervening years, yet she never returned," Akanna pointed out quietly. "It has been a very long time since she left, for we vincans live as long as elves do, so I can tell you it has been more than two centuries since she disappeared. At first, the Mîrlonds seemed to do just fine without her, but in the last fifty years, her absence has become more and more of an issue. Many of the original inhabitants made the long and difficult journey to here, where there was at least a witch of some repute who was helping to keep the Ganlonds alive."

"Catie," murmured the cat, and Donnie nodded.

"But in the last two years, I have made the sojourn to the Mîrlonds three times and, on each occasion, I have found them in increasingly desiccated states. I would not have left them the last time I went there but for the fact that it was known widely that Valledai was amassing his forces to attack all Free Peoples of Medregai. The king convinced me to remain in his service so that we could go after Valledai together here in the Annûar region before he made his way west."

"And what does the king think of you leaving him now?" Donnie asked curiously, and she noticed that Falwaïn turned his head and leaned back to make sure he caught Akanna's reply.

"My pledge to the king was to assist in defeating our common enemies of Valledai and his host of okûns. That victory is now realized," she said stiffly, her voice taut with suppressed emotion, giving an indication of just how uncomfortable she was discussing this particular subject. "I am therefore at liberty to resign my commission with the king's army. Which I have done with his—well, not with his blessing exactly, but he accepted my resignation and we have agreed that our immediate destinies are no longer conjoined."

"Ah, so you feel free to do as you please," Diego pointed out churlishly, "an advantage Diana is not to be afforded, *no es eso correcto*?" He was staring at the vincan's long back, his handsome features edged with outrage and his right hand gripping the handle of the knife on his hip.

Akanna turned right around in her saddle to glare back at him, ready to pounce ferociously upon him if needed. "No!" she spat back. "As I already explained, my duty now lies with the Mîrlonds, as does Ghira Ma'Hai's. She is responsible for the well-being of the magical lands and it is time for both of us to go home!"

Afraid the two warriors would come to blows, Donnie maneuvered Wiwila between them and frantically waved a hand, successfully breaking their heated and intense eye contact. "Whoa, time out, you two!" she exclaimed, relieved when Akanna turned to her distractedly, even though the vincan was clearly still furious. "Let's get back to the cottage and see what Diana has to say about all this. There's no sense in us being at loggerheads with each other until we hear her explanations. Right? I mean, doesn't that seem reasonable and rational?" When the other two both blew out heavy, fractious breaths and nodded, Donnie exhaled a small, tight breath herself and asked, "Does anyone know where Diana and Otis went today?"

"She said something about replacing an item, but I don't know what, because she mumbled it at me as I passed by her," Warren supplied.

Little else was said after that. The path soon narrowed so that they could ride only in single file, making any kind of discussion impractical. While Donnie could have widened the path with her magic, she decided not to, feeling that it might be best to give everyone some time alone with their thoughts. She was gladdened that Diego was standing up for Diana, but she did not want him alienating Akanna unnecessarily. She therefore made sure to have the vincan take the path ahead of her, while she stayed back so that she and Rex came before Diego.

When they reached the edge of the valley, Donnie snapped her fingers and the electric lights she'd hung on the buildings around the farm and on top of the well flickered to life to light the way to the stables more clearly. They dismounted at the well and led their horses into the barn, where they found Diana just finishing up with giving Otis a good rubdown. In the stall next to him stood a beautiful, fawn-colored cow, who was contentedly chewing some hay.

Donnie stopped in her tracks and grinned at the new addition, then at Diana. "Please tell me she's not magical," she said, and Diana chuckled in reply, "No, she's not."

Sighing gratefully, Donnie left Wiwila where she stood and went over to the cow's stall. "Does she have a name?"

"No, the previous owners just called her 'the new cow' and pretty much left her to her own devices," Diana explained, still running a couple of body brushes over Otis' gleaming white coat. "They'd gotten her a few weeks ago from the wife's aunt and uncle as a wedding gift, but they'd also received one from the husband's father. You can guess which cow they were set on keeping. So, you can name her whatever you want," Diana added, shooting Donnie a gleaming smile.

Donnie scratched the cow around the ears and down her nose, and the cow leaned into the stroke, her liquid brown eyes closing in happiness. "While it may be clichéd, I think I am going to call her Gertie. She looks like a Gertie, don't you think? Kinda calm and sweet?"

Donnie glanced around, but the only one who seemed to agree with her was Diana, who wore a wide grin and was nodding mutely. On the other hand, Falwaïn was having to bite his lip to keep from laughing out loud.

"What's so funny?" Donnie asked him suspiciously.

He really could no longer contain himself and he suddenly barked with glee, thereafter holding himself by the middle while continuing to chuckle vigorously to himself. Donnie shot him a reproving glare, which made him laugh even louder. Warren, who had been more successful at maintaining a straight face to this point, finally crumpled and began guffawing too. Diego shrugged and wore a mystified look, as did Rex. Sylvester just rolled his eyes to the ceiling, while Akanna, standing behind Diego, looked slightly amused herself.

Diana, taking pity on Donnie, finally enlightened her. "In Medregai," she explained, "Gertie literally means a witch's cow, or more generally, a woman who likes really big dicks."

Donnie sputtered with amazement, clapped her hands together, and shouted, "No! Really? Oh, then Gertie she has got to be!" which set them all to laughing even harder. Except for Sylvester, naturally, who shook his head from side to side, looking like the much tormented and grossly put-upon kitty cat who was invariably at his wits' end that he always loved to play. Which made Donnie reach down and ruffle the fur on his head before informing him, "You know I'm never really gonna change all that much; right, puddy-tat?"

He scoffed and mumbled something under his breath.

Rex, who was sitting right next to the cat, grinned slyly and quipped, "I dunno, why *did* you think she'd change? Just 'cause she's an Ér Ainíl now? That's not gonna do anything to her personality, you know. Not my mama," he added proudly, "she's got a mind all her own and she's not afraid to use it!"

"Yes, I know," drawled the cat haughtily. "I just wish she would use it for something other than seeing how far into the gutter she can drag us all!"

Donnie giggled and giggled at this, looking over at Diana and Otis, as usual, to share yet another joke at the cat's expense with them. It almost felt like old times.

But then Akanna stepped forward and caught Diana's laughing gaze, which sobered instantly. The vincan, emboldened, came even closer and demanded, "Speaking of Ér Ainíls, the Mîrlonds need you to return to them immediately, my lady. They are under attack in some way and are dying rapidly. You must come back and save them."

Diana looked at her aghast and exclaimed, "Oh, shit, you remember me?"

"Of course, I remember you," the vincan said, her eyes sparkling and vibrant, "you are unforgettable! You, and your exploits, inspired me and many other vincan girls to become warriors just like you. We even called ourselves the Ovids of Ma'Hai as we went through our training." She chuckled ruefully and sent Diana a shy look. "Last night, during the battle, we all recognized you, for you always had a distinctive and stylish way of fighting that no one else was ever able to quite mimic, although we all tried very hard to do just that. You were our dream, you see, our goal of who we should be."

Diana now looked utterly horrified and she backed up a couple steps before turning away to place the brushes in her hands onto the stall's top rail. When she turned back to reply to Akanna, her face was composed, but her voice was wooden, almost monotone in its caution. "I do not know why you are here, but I have nothing to give you. You should leave this place and forget about me. And no, I will never go back to the Mîrlonds."

A profound silence met this statement. For some time, the only noises made were of the horses moving their feet, the cow eating hay, and the barn creaking with age.

Akanna, whose body had somehow assumed an imperious stance, stood staring down her nose at Diana. Diana met her regard blandly, crossing her arms in front of her and leaning back on her hips.

Falwaïn caught Donnie's eye and he mimed that he and the others would leave. With an almost imperceptible nod, she agreed, and the men grabbed the reins of the horses and led them back outside. Warren called low to the dog and cat and they too left the barn.

"Akanna," Donnie began tentatively, but she was interrupted by the vincan holding up a hand to forestall her.

"You must speak with Ghira Ma'Hai privately, I see that," Akanna conceded stiffly. "I am not ready to give up on her, nor does her refusal mean that I still do not request your assistance with the Mîrlonds. I fear they are dying, and I will not abandon them to that fate." She heaved a great sigh and broke her gaze from Diana's so that she could look at Donnie. "I will set up camp in the woods at the top of the valley, if you do not mind, and we can resume our discussion in the morning. Is that acceptable to you?" she asked.

Donnie snapped her fingers and said, "I've just set up a tent for you. It has everything you will need. We'll eat our supper soon, so I suggest you keep company with the men for now. Diana and I will come out in a bit and we'll take care of the horses. Right, Di?" she inquired, looking over at her friend, who nodded reluctantly.

The vincan turned around and left without another word.

Donnie watched Akanna disappear out the door, then she leaned on the rail in front of her, placing her chin on her forearm, and said, "So, at least now I know one part of your secret. Oh, and I presume Otis and you are bonded, aren't you? And you probably have been for quite a while—like a few centuries maybe. Am I right?"

Otis tossed his head in agreement and replied, "Yes, we were both quite young when we bonded, and we've been together ever since. Well, except for the years she was with Kaledar and I was here with Catie. But after she was freed from Kaledar in the War of Unity, she found me here on the Codlebærn farm and we reunited."

"What's your real name?" Donnie asked him curiously, but before he could answer, she straightened up and stood tall, and said to Diana, her voice rough with emotion, "I know yours is Ghira Ma'Hai, and that you are an ovid and also an Ér Ainíl. That's about all I know of your past. Of your present, I know that you are two of my very best friends and I trust you both with my life and those of my friends and loved ones. I remind you of this simply because none of it has changed. And look, I obviously don't know why you left the Mîrlonds, but I know you two, who you are at heart, and I believe in you both. Therefore, I know that you must have left your magical lands for a really good reason. When you're ready to share that reason with me, I will listen to you and do my very best to understand exactly what happened, I promise. And I will not judge you."

She turned back to Otis and repeated, "Your name?"

He tossed his head again and replied, "Just call me Otis. Like Diana, I prefer to leave my former life behind. Who I was before no longer matters; only the future does."

Donnie nodded, a fleeting, sad expression crossing her features, as she noted, "That must be one hell of a story you've got to tell." She wet her lips and took a chance, adding, "And I bet it has everything to do with Julia's father, Ixifír Bíun of the Dræda sorcerers."

Diana's features changed immediately. Her jaw tightened, her eyes glittered, and her whole aspect hardened. "Him," she growled. "He took everything from me."

And then Otis interjected quietly, "He took everything from *us*."

Gratified that she had gotten this new, small piece of information out of them, Donnie admitted, "I suspected as much. He sure seems to have made himself very busy mucking around in our lives. And I don't guess he's anywhere near done with that."

Diana's eyes met Donnie's, and Donnie, seeing the torment in them, advised her friend softly, "You're gonna have to tell me one day, or else he will, I'm sure of it. He wants me to know about you and what happened, I can tell. See, when I read through the two books that Valley Guy had about our adventures, there were some very obvious hints that I think this Ixifir Bíun had a hand in engineering. And I think he's going to use this to try to drive a wedge between us. Therefore, I suggest you stop refusing to tell me what happened to you and start figuring out just how to get over whatever is keeping you *from* telling me your story, whether it's fear, anger, embarrassment, whatever, just try to overcome it, so we can maybe preempt his machinations. Honestly, the more I know, the better prepared I'll be when I finally meet that bastard, as I'm pretty sure will happen one day, and probably sooner rather than later. Help me, Diana," she said, a plea in her voice, "help me fight him."

Diana shook her head and replied, "You should stay away from him. Fighting him is what he wants. And that's because he never loses, so if you don't fight him, you won't lose everything like we did. I mean it, Donnie, just stay away from him."

Otis gave Diana a gentle nudge, saying quietly, but reprovingly, "You weren't listening to her. I think she's right, I think he's going to force her to meet him. And she's gonna have no choice but to fight him."

"Then we'll sacrifice ourselves," Diana told him defiantly. "I bet he wants us as badly as he does Donnie, so if we give ourselves up to him, I'm sure we can convince him to leave her alone."

"Is that what you did before, sacrifice yourselves?" Donnie asked, and the other two turned back to her with a jerk, as though they had forgotten she was there.

"What?" Diana spluttered. "No! No, of course not. Look, I-I don't want to talk about this anymore. Let's just get the other horses bedded for the night and then shovel some dinner into our bellies. Okay? Can we just do that and that's all?"

"Sure," Donnie assured her friend and the two women strode outside to collect the other horses. With Donnie using her magic to assist them, they had all horses unsaddled, brushed and fed in about twenty minutes.

When they went into the house, the food dishes were just being levitated to the dining room table. Julia was sitting next to Diego, but neither one was talking to the other. Warren was staring at Akanna, who was discussing some shared acquaintances in the king's army with Falwaïn. Sylvester watched them from the corner of the table at Warren's elbow. Rex was across the room and eating at his own dish, wolfing down the mixture of kibble and eggs that Donnie had set to frying for him a few minutes earlier. Donnie and Diana took their seats and the serving dishes began to float around the table so that food could be scooped out of them at will. Dinner was an uncomfortably quiet affair, and everybody pretty much scattered the moment it was done. The only ones who hung about afterward were Donnie, Falwaïn, Sylvester and Rex.

Sylvester wanted to know if Diana had relented and finally confessed to Donnie. Donnie filled him and the others in on just what she'd learned from Diana and Otis, and ended by saying, "But that's all I know."

Falwaïn leaned back in his chair and took a sip from the glass of whiskey set before him. He laced his fingers behind his head and chuckled ruefully. "Akanna's absolutely bent on convincing us all to go with her to the Mîrlonds, you know. I'm not sure we'll get her to leave without us, short of physically evicting her from the Ganlonds, that is."

"Oh, I have every intention of traveling to the Mîrlonds to help her," Donnie admitted, sending him a searching look. "I kind of feel like magic wants us to go, so that means we have to, don't we?" When he smiled and nodded in answer, she turned to the dog and cat, who both murmured, "We go where you go," and it was left at that.

"I doubt Diana will accompany us though," Donnie said, pursing her lips and frowning. "I'm pretty sure something terrible happened there, something she's either greatly afraid of or ashamed of...or maybe both." She turned her chair around so that she could lean back onto Falwaïn, who brought his arms down and put them around her, snuggling her into his shoulder and rubbing the top of her head with his chin and kissing her affectionately.

The cat watched this play out before groaning audibly, then made as though to leave until Donnie halted him by saying, "You have to get used to this, Sylvester. We're a family now, the four of us: you, me, Rex and Falwaïn, and soon enough we'll add a couple of kids to that list. There's going to be a lot of snuggling going on for many years to come. So, my advice to you is to accept it and, who knows, maybe you'll even get to liking it one day."

The cat scoffed at this sentiment, but he stayed where he was and gave no further indication that he found Donnie and Falwaïn's closeness anything but ordinary.

"Mama," began Rex, and all eyes rested upon him curiously, "how are we gonna get there? To the Mîrlonds, I mean. 'Cause if we ride like we normally do, it's gonna take us weeks and weeks to get there. It's really far away, you know."

Donnie considered this for a moment before suggesting, "Maybe I can fold space again, you know, to get us closer. I don't think I should do that all the way there though, 'cause I have no idea what the country is like in that area or who I might be disturbing. But I can maybe shave off most of our travel time by folding space in small increments, especially if you scout ahead and report back to me what you find. I would suggest we take Plug, because then we'd be there in a couple days, but I gather there are lots of settlements between here and there and she'd cause way too much of a stir, so I think we'll just have to ride the horses. Plus, I have to admit that I am very much looking forward to enjoying my first long journey with Wiwila," she added, smiling as she reached behind her and pulled Falwaïn's head down so their lips met in a wonderfully satisfying kiss. Afterward, she laid her arm across the table toward Sylvester, pointing a finger at him to ask, "Or is there something here on the Ganlonds that might help us get there sooner, some kind of magical artifact or some such? Do you know?"

"No-o-o," the cat replied after thinking it over for a minute. "Not really. There is supposed to be a connection between all of the magical lands, but if that is true, I do not know what it comprises or how it manifests itself, let alone where it is."

"Would Bronadulach or any of the others know, do you think?"

"Possibly Mickey T might, as he is the eldest of us all."

Donnie started with sudden astonishment, as did Falwaïn behind her. "Seriously?" Donnie squeaked. "Mickey T is older than you?"

"Yes, of course, by a number of years," Sylvester assured her. "He has lived through several Mannish ages, going back many centuries. As a matter of fact, nearly all bats here on the Ganlonds are his descendants, however many times removed, of course. He told me once that when he became more, or rather, when he became magical, there were five others with him. They have all died off now, or so he believes. He says they stayed together for a long time, then two of them went their own way west and were never heard from again. If still alive, they might even make their home on the Mîrlonds, as that would be the most likely place they could go and retain their magic to live out their long lives. The three who stayed here with Mickey T are already dead, with Maritelian being the last. I met her, you know. She was Sephala's mother and was really quite nice, as I recall. She died, oh, it must be nearly a hundred years ago now. Mickey T has never really been the same without her, even though Sephala does all she can to make his life enjoyable. Still, life is never quite as good without your mate, is it?" the cat added, muttering it absently.

"That," Falwaïn pointed out with great interest, "was spoken as though from hard and bitter experience." He turned a sympathetic frown to the cat, then raised a questioning eyebrow.

The cat confessed forlornly, "Yes, well, I once had a mate, or thought I did, but she apparently could not be true to me for more than a few weeks.

She has since birthed a litter of kittens with a tomcat who wandered onto the Ganlonds last spring when his villager mistress unthinkingly failed to secure him at home. He is now becoming magical and Meludya finds him fascinating." Sylvester admitted this with a sad sort of asperity, clearly flummoxed by the circumstances he'd just described.

Donnie gave him a commiserating moue and offered in a low voice, "Well, that just sucks."

Sylvester nodded in solemn agreement, as did Rex and Falwaïn.

"I suppose I can ask Mickey T tomorrow if he's aware of a faster method of transport between the magical lands," Donnie said, yawning widely. "Hoo boy, it's pretty much bedtime for me, I think."

"For all of us, is more like it," commented Falwaïn, although neither he nor Donnie moved.

Rex, on the other hand, stood up and shook himself hard, then crouched down in a bigger yawn than even Donnie had just given. He sang out, "Arrrufffff!" with the yawn, and gazed steadily at his mama as if to tell her he was more than ready to go to bed.

She and Falwaïn chuckled together and Falwaïn helped Donnie to her feet. The four of them retired to the master bedroom.

In the morning at just a little before dawn, Warren was again the first one to be up and out the door while the others still slept. He'd decided in the night that he wanted to know just where Julia had been all of yesterday, feeling that Liz would expect him to take care of the girl in her absence. He knew it was a little crazy of him, but he nevertheless intended to fulfill that unmade promise no matter what.

He reached the backyard, where he transformed into his wolven form and used his keen sense of smell to follow Julia's track. It led to a small outcropping of flat rock on the side of a high moor about a mile or so southwest of the cottage. He scanned the jagged rocks and steep inclines around him after noting that Julia had built a fire ring in the large slab's midst, which had a thick pile of ash and several small stubs of burned tree limbs within its carefully piled circle of stones. He looked to his left and saw at least ten large rocks and boulders that appeared to have been dragged several feet in various directions, with some of them seeming to have been freshly split into pieces. Continuing his perusal of the general area, he spotted what looked like little craters gouged out unnaturally in the turf for as far as he could see. After investigating a couple of these holes, he realized that they were not made by any animal he knew. It took him some while, but it finally came to him that they were practice holes.

Which meant Julia had magical powers and she was airing them out and getting to know them here on the moors by herself. Warren wondered vaguely why she hadn't gone to Donnie once she'd discovered she had magical powers; Donnie could have helped her and probably would have set up lessons for her. Thinking about this a minute, he shook his head, finally understanding that Julia wanted to keep her powers hidden from the others at the cottage. He thought that was quite silly of her. After all, she would learn much faster with a tutor, and there could be none better than either Donnie or Sylvester.

Nevertheless, he would do as he thought Liz would wish and would keep Julia's secret, not telling anyone about this new development. At least not yet.

He returned to the cottage, pausing on the doorstep when he heard raised voices inside. Julia, it seemed, was hurling an insult at Donnie, something about her being a troublesome meddler.

Warren opened the front door at the same moment Julia grabbed the handle and he felt a shock of red-hot anger course through his hand and into his body from the girl's touch. He stared at her in surprise when she pushed her hands at him and he felt himself being thrown backward, coming back to earth with a painful thud several yards away. She stepped out onto the porch and pushed at him again and he felt a great, crushing weight hit him, invisible though it was. Several of his ribs cracked loudly and he suddenly found it impossible to breathe.

And then Donnie was in front of Julia and had the girl encased in a shining shield of some making. Warren finally managed to gulp in some badly needed air and felt the full pain of his injuries assault his senses. Donnie ran to him, the others right behind her and crowding around him, which he registered in the back of his mind while he concentrated on drawing another breath into his severely injured body. Donnie passed her hands over his chest and he was released from the excruciating pain and could at last breathe a little better. He inhaled and exhaled slowly, taking a shuddering, thankful breath, and grabbed Donnie's hand.

"Don't blame her, she's just scared and alone," he muttered, and he passed out from the shock of what had been done to him.

Donnie peered down at him and gave a woeful smile. "Damn you, Warren, for being the voice of calm even now," she whispered wryly. She got up while Falwaïn, Diego and Akanna carefully gathered Warren in their arms and slowly carried him around the side of the house to his and Liz's room.

Diana stood next to Julia with her hand on her knife, watching the girl fight to remove the shield that was keeping her from leaving, ready to pounce in case Julia somehow managed to free herself.

Donnie walked up to Julia and the shield was gone, but before Julia could do anything, Donnie's hands were turning her around and propelling her firmly back inside and Julia found her muscles would do nothing but comply. "Sit," Donnie ordered when they were inside, leaving her to Diana's supervision with the angry warning of, "Don't fuck with me, Julia, or I will bind you to a chair and keep you there all goddamn day!"

The girl sank down onto the nearest chair sulkily and glared at the other two women with hatred.

Donnie ignored this and strode over to the stove, turning it on so the kettle would boil. She reached into her herb cupboard and pulled out various healing herbs and medicines. Arnica was poured into a glass of cold water from the fridge, which was placed onto a wide tray. Next, alfalfa, burdock, red raspberry, dandelion leaf, chickweed, and nettle went into the mortar and pestle and were ground up to be used as a tea, which Donnie dumped into the strainer of a small teapot, pouring the hot water from the kettle over the fragrant mixture to let it steep. The teapot also was placed onto the tray, along with a cup and saucer. Comfrey leaves and roots went into the mortar and were mashed into a thick paste with apple cider vinegar. Lastly, she got out a tincture of calendula and sat it down beside the comfrey paste. She opened a lower drawer in the sideboard and retrieved bandages and a couple of clean, white linen towels.

These too went onto the tray and Donnie carried the whole kit to the bedroom where the others had laid Warren out onto the bed. She put the tray on the bedside table and had Falwaïn help her cut off Warren's shirt so that she could inspect his injuries. His chest was misshapen and his skin red and blotchy. She put her ear to his breast and listened to his breathing, which was shallow and ragged. His lungs seemed to be filling with fluid.

"Damn it!" she swore aloud, gently placing her hands on his skin and looking with her mind's eye at his internal wounds. She found the puncture in his left lung and viewed the cells there in magnification, forcing them to repair the tear in the tissue. She did the same with a small puncture in his right lung. She also removed the fluid seeping in from blood vessels that had already made its way into the lungs. She took her time with all of this removal and repair, wanting to make sure she got it correct. When she was satisfied with these efforts, she began to knit the bones back together. There were several fractures on the top six ribs of both sides of his chest, and some hairlines on a few of the ribs below those first six. She knew she could never get to all of the breaks in the bones, but she could fix the worst of them.

Some three hours later, she stood back and surveyed her handiwork. The comfrey had been spread all over Warren's chest, front and back, and was covered by bandages. He was now breathing more freely on his own and was sleeping soundly due to the sleep spell she'd placed on him. She awakened him long enough to get both the arnica water and most of the tea into him, then charmed him to fall back to sleep and remain that way until tomorrow morning.

Falwaïn had stuck with her throughout her ministrations to their friend, assisting where he could and otherwise watching her for any indication that she needed something from him. The others drifted in and out during the long morning, each one gazing down at Warren with mixed emotions, all of them clearly struggling with having Julia in their midst. No one was ready to leave her alone though, and they all made sure that at least two of them stayed in the main room of the cottage to guard her.

She, for her part, laid her head down on her arms and refused to look at anyone. Sylvester attempted to get her to talk about how her powers had become unbound, as they clearly had, but she just hissed at him and made as though to send a push of power at him. He hissed back and raised the same kind of shield Donnie had used earlier, a trick she'd first taught him after she'd made the septic tank and then had given him further instruction on after she'd flown on the broomstick and had conjured a similar shield to protect herself.

The little push of power Julia had released toward the cat (whether that was inadvertent or on purpose only she knew for sure) rebounded back and hit her squarely in the face. She felt it slap her cheek and her head bounced backward. She tightened her lips, scowling at him.

"I can do that all day, if you insist," he informed her austerely, his eyes flashing with ire.

Thereafter, Julia refused to be drawn into any interactions with the others, and they all eventually settled in chairs around the room to wait for Donnie and Falwaïn to return. Rex made sure to guard the front door, his reproving glare never wavering from Julia.

It was nearly noon when Donnie finished and she and Falwaïn walked back into the main room of the cottage. With a wave of her hand, Donnie set various utensils to chopping and mixing and whatever else was needed to prepare a lunch of egg salad sandwiches. She went into her bedroom and changed her clothes, which had become somewhat soiled with the herbal remedies she'd used on Warren. She returned to the kitchen just as the platters of sandwiches floated to the table.

Everyone sat down and began to eat, with Sylvester asking first, "Will Warren recover?"

Donnie nodded and glanced at the cat when she replied, "Yes, I think he should be fine, but it'll take a while. There are so many fractures, small ones, I mean, that it will take me several hours more to heal even just some of them, but I'm too exhausted to do all that right now. Is there any place on the Ganlonds that's known for having healing properties?" She looked back in the direction of the cat and hooked an eyebrow at him.

He was eating his sandwich delicately, the mayonnaise sticking to his whiskers in a couple places. He finished chewing what he had in his mouth and licked his lips extensively before responding to Donnie's query.

"We could try imbuing him with the magic of the Gahal Glæd, as that most assuredly possesses healing qualities. While it would not have been able to accomplish what you have so far with his injuries, it might just complete the healing process at once."

"Let's hope so, otherwise he's going to be in a fair amount of pain for the next six to eight weeks," Donnie observed. She'd sat next to Julia near the end of the table, and with Sylvester situated in front of the girl, they had her effectively cut off from the others. They both had their backs to Julia and ignored her during the meal, but each was prepared to block any new efforts on her part to attack anyone else, if she were unwise enough to attempt that.

When the meal was over, Diana pushed back her chair and moved to stand behind the chair straight across from Julia, eyeing the girl with disfavor. "Why did you hurt Warren?" she demanded, and the atmosphere in the kitchen immediately tensed. "He's done nothing to you except try to befriend you."

Julia raised her chin and her eyes narrowed with Diana's accusal. She sneered at the warrioress, explaining contemptuously, "He got in my way. Anyone who does that around me from now on is going to find themselves in a world of pain."

In the blink of an eye, Diana went from standing still on the other side of the table with her arms crossed in front of her to crouching behind Julia with her right arm around the girl's neck and the girl's hands pinned behind her back. She began to squeeze Julia's throat in the crook of her arm and no one said a word in protest.

Silently, they all watched as Julia's expression changed from defiance to terror as it became harder and harder for her to breathe.

Just as she looked about to pass out, Donnie laid a hand on Diana's arm and ordered quietly, "That's enough, Di. If she gives us any more trouble, you can have at her. But for now, I want to talk to her."

Diana let Julia go and the girl coughed and choked, her white, shocked face turning deep red as she took huge, plunging breaths of the precious air that could once again fill her lungs. After a full minute of watching Julia hack away, Donnie poured a glass of water and handed it to her. The young woman downed it resentfully and banged the empty glass onto the table so hard that it broke into several pieces.

Donnie hissed at her angrily and waved a hand over the glass to repair it, then she turned in her chair to face Julia.

"I've told you before that I might not be able to stop these very dexterous and dangerous warriors from killing you," she reminded the young woman crossly. "Perhaps now you have a better grasp of just what I meant by that warning." She looked at Julia's neck with a raised eyebrow and Julia gave her a grudging nod.

But Donnie did not stop there. She expanded her warning, cautioning Julia further. "You will never be fast enough to stop them, you know," she pointed out. "If any one of them wants you dead, dead you will be. And that will happen before you have a chance to defend yourself, even with your magic. Have I made myself clear?" When Julia shot her a somewhat confused, disbelieving look, Donnie continued in a hard voice, adding, "Let me spell it out for you then. If you try to harm anyone else of our group or any creature here on the Ganlonds, all possible protection I might choose to afford you will be forfeited and one or more of these warriors, or maybe it will be my cat or possibly even my dog, will make sure you never breathe again. And that retribution will be as swift as it is final."

"Mom would kill you—"

"Your mother will understand completely because she is going to be told first thing what you did here today," Donnie exclaimed, talking over the girl's protest. "And if she doesn't understand it, it will be too late for her or anyone else to do anything about it because you will be dead," she added flatly, and Julia swallowed hard.

"I got it," she snarled. "Now, leave me alone." Defiance had returned to her eyes and she quivered with anger, her legs moving under her so that she could stand.

Diana placed her hands onto Julia's shoulders and held her firmly in her chair. "You'll stay put until Donnie's finished with you," she growled in Julia's ear.

Julia half-turned backward and sent Diana a searing glare, looking as though she was going to chew a hole in her cheek, she was so mad. But she kept quiet and settled down in her seat.

The boombox chose that moment to appear on the kitchen counter and begin to play the iconic "Don't Take Your Guns to Town."

Donnie glanced at it thoughtfully, but turned her attention back to the situation with Julia. She got up and went over to stand on the other side of the table from the young woman, exactly where Diana had stood a few minutes before. "Okay, you are going to answer some questions," she announced, and Sylvester nodded his head in agreement.

"Yes, gel," he said, pronouncing it the old way with a hard 'g'. "How did your powers become unbound? You will tell us this now." He stood and studied her earnestly, as if waiting to catch her in a lie.

"What does that matter?" Julia groused with a nasty smirk to her face. "You can't do anything about it!"

"You might be surprised at what I can do," the cat rejoined caustically.

"Ha!" she scoffed. "You're just another one of Donnie's pets!" She spat this with bravado at the cat, but she watched him closely when he began to mutter something under his breath. She couldn't take her eyes off him, it seemed, and soon she was staring at him slack-jawed and vacant-eyed.

"Tell me how your powers became unbound," Sylvester repeated, and Julia replied mechanically, "My father cast a spell on me to force them out."

Sylvester turned to Donnie. "I suspected as much," he stated gravely.

"Is that significant in some way?" she asked him.

"Yes, it certainly is. You see, when the magical powers of an initiate of any age are bound, there are limited circumstances under which they can become *un*bound. It could be that a specified time limit, date, or event has been reached, or perhaps the one who bound them will remove their spell and the initiate's powers will be set free, or they can be coaxed out by the initiate themselves if they are in a situation where certain defenses get dropped."

"But none of that is what happened with Julia."

"No," the cat agreed. "Her father cast a spell to release her powers, which probably means that only those skills he wanted her to access have been released. I noticed this yesterday when I tracked her to her practice spot and observed her exercise session with her powers. While they are strong, she exhibited a limited range of magical talents and her memorized lessons were all geared toward attacking others."

Donnie gazed at him a long time before she spoke, considering what he'd just said while also reflecting upon the song the boombox was still playing. When she understood their mutual point, she remarked in a soft, sad voice, "He taught her to attack but not defend."

"Precisely," the cat intoned ominously. "She will have no magical method of protecting herself *except* to harm others. Even if she wants not to harm them, that is all she will be able to do, is attack them, and that will likely manifest as lethal assaults, especially if she does not learn to control the amount of force she uses. For instance, I do not believe she truly meant to harm Warren so seriously, but she was agitated in the moment and he was indeed obstructing her path, so she lashed out at him the only way she could—magically speaking, that is. She even made as though to frighten me earlier by repeating the same movement she used to push her power at Warren. I would swear she was completely surprised when she expelled a fair amount of force with her pantomiming motion, which I then reduced by half and rebounded back to her. And that was enough to make my point that she was not skilled enough to best me in a magical fight."

"Is there any way Donnie can fix what her father did?" asked Falwaïn. While he and the others had been listening and watching silently until now, they were all much concerned with this surprising development regarding Julia.

The cat shook his head slowly from side to side. "No. As I have warned a thousand times over, it is not wise to lay a spell directly on top of another that has been set by a different witch or sorcerer, for there are certain to be ramifications affecting both spells, which will almost always be negative and tragic. No, there is no fixing a spell unless you are the one who cast it in the first place."

Donnie pulled out the chair in front of her and plopped down into it heavily. She buried her face in her hands and heaved a deep sigh of angst. When she finally looked up at the cat, she said, "This changes everything. I don't think we can keep her here—heck, what am I saying? I don't think we *should* keep her here! She's gonna harm someone else, and what if I'm not around to heal their injuries?"

"Can you not force her into lessons with you whereby she learns to control the force she expends with her attacks?" inquired Akanna. "I mean, can she not reduce her attacks to the point where they would be harmless unless she so chooses?"

"That would require her to control her temper, which is impossible for her to do on any given day." Diego commented sagely, an observation that had most of the others groaning in agreement. He shrugged, adding, "No, Donnie is correct; she will be harming others indiscriminately, whether she truly means to or not."

"Can't you re-bind her powers?" asked Rex from where he sat by the front door, his ears perked up straight and an alert expression on his face. He'd never liked Julia, true, but he felt very sorry for her now. Like his mama, the dog couldn't help feeling somewhat protective of Julia, like she was his and Donnie's responsibility, so they couldn't just abandon her.

All eyes turned to Sylvester, who was already shaking his head at Rex's question. "No, because we don't know the details of her father's spell, and what did I just warn about laying a spell on top of another's? That will not work, I say!" he insisted.

"Well, hell's harpies!" exclaimed Donnie, banging her fist on the table and letting out a few more choice epithets before asking, "What are we gonna do with her? Especially when we leave for the Mîrlonds? I mean, we can't leave her here and we can't take her with us!"

Two loud gasps resounded in the room at this news; one from Akanna and the other from Diana.

Donnie's regarded the women with a rueful expression and declared, "Oh, I forgot to tell you: we're gonna go save the Mîrlonds. We leave as soon as Warren can travel."

Chapter 5
Animal Farm

They had argued for nearly an hour about the trip to the Mîrlonds, and then about what to do with Julia. Neither argument ended with a welcomed plan of action.

Diana refused to go anywhere near the Mîrlonds, while Akanna refused to go there without her. Everyone else was eager to go and see how they could help, but the warrioresses stood their respective grounds stubbornly, each rebuffing all attempts at persuasion.

Donnie, frustrated with both women, ended that particular argument by asking Sylvester to test Julia's reactions so they could confirm the cat's speculation that the girl was able to perform only offensive magic and no defensive. After several attempts failed to get her to raise a shield, block a strike, or simply move out of the way using her magic, Donnie was convinced that Sylvester was right. This meant that Julia would only be able to destroy, not defend, and was unlikely to be good at creating anything that wasn't in some way connected with inflicting death or pain on others. Her father had essentially cursed her into being a killer. And that meant the immediate problem became what to do with her now, not just later. While everyone recognized that they could not evict her from the Ganlonds and leave her to wander Medregai, getting into all sorts of trouble, no one felt comfortable having her stay in the cottage with them, or letting her travel with them, if they did indeed go to the Mîrlonds.

There were suggestions of imprisoning her in her room, or perhaps constructing a separate building for her somewhere on the Ganlonds, but Donnie and Rex both rejected those ideas. Donnie finally agreed to limit her access inside the house to her room and bathroom, the workshop, and the kitchen. But Donnie insisted on letting the girl practice her magical skills at her chosen spot, if only to make sure Julia would not go into full attack mode on the cottage through sheer frustration.

The spell Donnie cast meant that if Julia ever tried to enter a forbidden room or stepped through the front door without Donnie's permission, she would be automatically transported to the porch outside her own bedroom. From the porch, she could access either her bedroom or her chosen practice spot, to which she was transported the moment she stepped off the porch. At her practice spot, whenever she went outside that area, she would be automatically transported back to the side porch outside her bedroom. She would not be allowed to venture elsewhere on the Ganlonds.

Naturally, this did not go down well with Julia. Donnie had to hastily dematerialize the young woman to her side porch when Julia readied herself to conduct a full-on attack on the others. Nor was the girl happy that Sylvester had cast a spell on her so easily, especially seeing as it was a spell that had caused her to confide her secrets. Julia managed to hurl a couple of chairs around before Donnie sent her to the porch, but these were caught handily by Falwaïn and Diana, so there was no damage done. But the incident made Donnie rethink the plan and she reluctantly blocked the girl's access to the kitchen, setting a charm so that all her meals would be served to her in her bedroom.

Donnie hated that she had to do this to Liz's daughter, mostly because she knew how hurt Liz was going to be about it. Despite what she'd told Julia earlier, Donnie had no desire to see anyone harm the girl in any way, no matter how awful she behaved. But she also recognized that Julia was choosing to follow the path her father had set her upon and that she would not leave it anytime soon without sufficient provocation. What could, or eventually would, entice Julia back to a better path was anybody's guess. But Donnie had to wonder if Julia would have been more amenable to that if Liz were here, and she felt guilty about not having come up with a better plan to protect Liz from Julia's father than simply sending her through the time portal to Catie. Granted, she'd had about a second or so to make the choice of how to keep Liz out of Ixifír Bíun's grasp, but it now seemed perhaps to have been an imprudent one. No one could control Julia like Liz could and Donnie should have foreseen there would be nothing but trouble from the girl with Liz out of the picture.

But then, she hadn't reckoned on Julia becoming magical too.

Nor had they figured on Julia meeting up with her father yet again the morning after the battle, before the king's army left and Donnie could seal off the Ganlonds from intruders. Julia had confessed, under Sylvester's mesmerization spell, that she'd spent most of the day with Ixifír Bíun of the dreaded Dræda line of sorcerers, as she grandly called him, and with her lover, who, it turned out, was named Meyondrun and not Rorschach or something like it, as Donnie had believed. And Julia admitted that her father had confirmed the planned pregnancies of herself and Liz, although he apparently refused to explain why they had been necessary

When Donnie interjected, "Which pregnancy of Liz's was planned? If it's the current one, why did he want her dead so badly? Or did he mean her pregnancy with you?", the girl had no answer to these questions and just shook her head in a confused manner. Interestingly, she also said that Ixifír Bíun was convinced that Donnie's pregnancy had been planned, but this time he did not know by whom or how that could have been possible.

Falwaïn was greatly surprised by this supposition and said that he'd not seen any dragon fruit or its tell-tale purple haze the night of their first date, nor had he experienced a time loss then, two certain characteristics needed for effecting a deliberate pregnancy, at least as far as they all knew. Having her own thoughts on her pregnancy, Donnie listened to him and tucked the rest of the information into the back of her mind, where several clues and other tidbits were still percolating, all waiting for further enlightenment before she could determine how they fit into the overall picture.

The afternoon wore on, with Donnie, Sylvester and Rex, once again accompanied by Wiwila, meeting for a second time with the Animal Council in the Imôríma, or Hidden Wing of the Ganlonds. When Donnie raised the probability of her and the others making the trek to the Mîrlonds, she was not surprised to find that each of the council members had some very definite opinions about it.

"Well, no, Donemere, I do not know how the magical landth are connected to each other or where, but I do believe they are. More importantly though, you mutht thtay here! Pleathe do not leave uth tho thoon; don't put yourthelf in danger like that right away!" cried Mickey T, and Bórlem nodded in vigorous agreement, adding a, "Hear, hear!" to Mickey T's plea.

The owl went on to say, "Your place, if you do not mind my saying so, is here with us. We are in dire need of your wise counsel, dear Ér Ainíl, for we have many disagreements amongst ourselves that need settling!"

Noting Bronadulach's jaw tightening, Donnie raised her eyebrows at the huge owl and demurred, "But those are issues for the Kaerdír to decide, surely? If you need my assistance in healing someone, or say creating or moving something, you know, that sort of task, I am most happy to serve. But the running of the Ganlonds' affairs must remain as it has previously been."

"Quite right," noted Mórbaen crisply. "No, Bórlem, we cannot prejudice the Ér Ainíl's time with us when she has other, more pressing adventures to experience such as this imminent journey to the Mîrlonds, which, I am sure you can see, has paramount importance to our petty squabbles."

Donnie was so astonished by this verbal roundabout, she could only stare at the giant deer stag with her mouth hanging open.

Sylvester, officious as ever, stepped forward and tut-tutted loudly, reminding the council, "If you will recall, my friends, we discussed this same subject only yesterday and I am sure it was understood by all that Donemere would be absent from the Ganlonds periodically, at her own discretion. And she decreed that the Kaerdír would remain as the managing head of the magical lands and that her role would be mainly that of spiritual leader and protector." When the others looked at him much aggrieved by what they seemed to feel was an unnecessary reprimand, he added superiorly, "May I also point out that we have rules of council that have served us quite well for some long while. If, with their aid, we cannot soothe our squabbles, be they petty or no, then perhaps we may bring some of the more contentious issues before Donemere later. Otherwise I must protest, because I firmly believe we should make several concerted efforts at deciding them ourselves before taking the long step of involving our beloved Ér Ainíl. What say you, Bronadulach?"

Donnie thought to herself that it was definitely a good thing he had not asked this question of Méath-Degnír, who was hunched over unhappily and appeared ready to howl his displeasure at his fellows.

Bronadulach, used as he was to the council members' ways, replied smoothly, "I agree there must be a process set up to petition our beloved Ér Ainíl's favor and I have, in fact, set aside four weeks a year, each centering around the solstices, for just such occasions. In addition, I have scheduled a discussion on this very subject at tomorrow morning's council meeting and I recommend we pool our collective experience to create a methodology that is both sustainable and fair-minded to all. But I agree with Sylvester that it would be premature to draw Donemere into the discussion at this stage, certainly."

Sylvester preened at this congruous opinion to his own, but he said nothing more, although, in truth, Bronadulach did not hesitate long enough for him or anyone else to respond before moving back to the original subject. "As for the proposed visit to the Mîrlonds," he said, eyeing Donnie circumspectly, "I believe it would also be in the Ganlonds' interests for her to go. I myself have noticed a distinct increase, for many years now, of magical creatures from there moving to live here. It was fortuitous for us that Catie was sufficiently capable to enlarge the Ganlonds by nearly five percent over the last century, which is the only way we could have accommodated everyone who immigrated here during that same period. To a one, they call themselves refugees, and they all eventually tell the same frightened tale, which is that the Mîrlonds are shrinking and its magic is falling away ever faster—quite drastically so in the last two years, if the reports are to be believed."

Méath-Degnír could hold himself back no longer and he suddenly joined the fray. "Those who have come here more recently say it is as if the magic is being eaten, or otherwise consumed in increasing quantities by some monster or monsters who are now lodged into the very heart of the Mîrlonds," the wolf interjected impatiently, his words spoken in a growl. "While there are still a significant number of magical creatures making their homes in the Mîrlonds, to survive much longer they must either come here, if they are able to do so, or they will have to choose between becoming less and eventually dying on their homeland as nonmagical creatures or leaving the Mîrlonds and facing almost certain death on the long and arduous journey to the Ganlonds. We know with certainty that many of them will never endure the trip between there and here. But we cannot, in good conscience, leave them to die such deaths. And there is another reason that I too believe it will be in the Ganlonds' best interests for Donemere to go to the Mîrlonds, and this is because of the other magical creatures from all around Medregai who are, as we speak, gathering outside the Ganlonds and who are seeking refuge from tyranny and strife, or so they all claim. If we add to their number many more from the Mîrlonds, we will assuredly encounter much more serious problems than these 'petty squabbles' with which our time today has thus far been wasted!" He gave a little snarl when he finished his complaint, punctuating his ill opinion of the meeting's progress.

Donnie was gaping again, then she shut her mouth when she realized it and said, "Wait a minute, are you telling me that there are magical creatures waiting outside the Ganlonds for admittance?"

The wolf nodded, while the others sighed or looked woeful.

"Oh, restless refugees!" exclaimed Donnie. She asked Bronadulach, "Is there a specific process for allowing them onto the Ganlonds, or can anyone settle here?"

The giant bear shrugged. "I am afraid that is, in a manner of speaking, a question that might be best for you to decide as Ér Ainíl of the Ganlonds. Previously, we have accepted the trickle of applicants over the years without much cause for concern. You see, the Ganlonds have specific methods of ensuring that only those who are sincerely seeking a safe and good home are allowed to remain here as a full and true citizen. But there are now more than four hundred magical creatures already assembled just beyond our borders, waiting to be let in, with several more reportedly making their way here. I imagine that within a week or two, that, er, shall we call it an exodus, should be complete. We," he paused and indicated himself and the other council members, "naturally, will establish a process for the applicants to make their individual cases for admittance and the Ganlonds themselves will dictate who stays, but you must determine how many we can possibly accommodate, for the Ganlonds will have to be expanded commensurately."

"Damn," swore Donnie softly, and she looked like a deer in headlights while her gaze swept the council members. "How do I do that? Expand the Ganlonds, I mean?"

"There is likely to be instruction in one of Catie's journals," Sylvester supplied helpfully. "If I recall correctly, I believe she first investigated it some eighty years ago and managed then and one other time afterward to successfully enlarge the area that her magic maintained. We should find that journal, as that would be the most expedient method of learning how to expand magical lands. Otherwise, I am afraid we will have to commit the same research she did, which took several months to accumulate."

"Oh, great joy!" Donnie drawled defensively. "The journals we have don't go back anywhere near that far, you know!"

"Well, that must mean she hid the previous ones," deduced Sylvester. "There has to be a clue in one of those we do have as to where she would be likely to conceal these previous journals of hers," he added confidently, a feeling Donnie did not share.

"I dunno," she reflected doubtfully, "I've read through all the ones we have pretty thoroughly, and I don't recall anything like that even being hinted at. I mean, I could tell she must have written more journals than just those that we have, sure, but she didn't say anything about where those might be." Donnie sat with her arms crossed in front of her and surveyed the others critically. "You know, if I can't figure out how to expand the magical lands, I don't think we can possibly take many newcomers, can we? Didn't you tell me yesterday that nonmagical food sources have been growing scarcer lately? Granted, we lost a high number of magical animals in the battle with Valley Guy, but it sounds like there are already a greater number waiting to get in than we have room for. Which means we have to find these other journals and expand the Ganlonds or turn those seeking refuge away." She paused and let that sink in for a minute before she turned back to Sylvester. "But where can these other journals be?" she asked pointedly, adding, "We know they're not in the library and that the library can't find them."

There was silence as they each contemplated potential hiding places that Catie was known to have utilized previously.

But then Sylvester, letting out a small gasp, suggested, "What about the ones you found in her workshop in those very large cauldrons at the back of the stables? You know the ones I mean, yes? Every time you ask for more of Catie's journals, these appear on the shelves instead," he reminded her.

"Well, yeah, but those are blank," Donnie pointed out, which left them all peering at each other with similar expressions of puzzlement.

Mickey T was the first to break the renewed silence. "But what if they are not blank?" he posited excitedly. "What if Catie uthed invithible ink on them? Theriouthly, think about it, Catie would love thomething like that! I remember reading that you can write with lemon juithe, you know. Tho it would be thimple for Catie to have done that!"

Donnie, about to pooh-pooh the idea, stopped herself and decided to give it more serious consideration. "Well, I suppose that's possible," she acknowledged, "but more likely, there must a spell to make ink invisible, isn't there?" She looked at Sylvester when she asked this, and he nodded and gave Mickey T a knowing and somewhat rueful shrug, which the bat returned after a moment of obvious disappointment. He'd apparently really wanted to see lemon juice in action.

Donnie snapped her fingers and what looked like hundreds of leather-bound books appeared in neat stacks at her feet. She picked up one and thumbed through its pages, not seeing impressions of lettering on any of the thick sheaves of paper, but she was game to try a spell to reveal whatever might possibly be written there in invisible ink. She thought a moment, then canted:

> "What was bidden by another,
> Long ago to be concealed.
> What was hidden from all others,
> Is now to be revealed.
> On these pages shall appear,
> Words displayed in stages.
> The letters showing clear,
> To be visible throughout the ages."

Several long seconds went by before anyone was ready to concede the effort had been a failure. Donnie's eyes traveled the discouraged faces around her, back and forth, until she finally asked, "Any other ideas?"

"Well," began Mickey T, stubbornly sticking to his original theory, "if Catie did uthe lemon juithe, heat would be juth the thing to make the letterth appear." He jutted his chin out and looked around him, daring the others to refute his suggestion.

Sylvester kept his expression neutral, although his reply came out with a hint of superciliousness to it. He looked at Donnie and intoned, "Perhaps it is best to attempt that, if only to content our bat friend here."

Mickey T scowled at him and Donnie laughed at them both.

"Well, it can't hurt and I think it's worth a try," she observed kindly, raising the book up and blowing a warming breath onto the open pages before her.

It took about three seconds for words to begin to form on the blank paper. While everybody else evinced surprise, Mickey T grinned smugly. "And you thought I wath crathy," he crowed, and there came apologetic chuckles from Donnie and all his fellow council members.

Donnie repeated the warming breath over the book, but this time set the pages to riffling from one side to the other automatically, so that all pages were heated sufficiently for the ink to be darkened and made readable. And soon she had a book that was chock full of Catie's childish scrawl and really bad, horribly inventive spelling, which she knew would give her multiple headaches before she had managed to glean everything she could from it.

With a sigh of resignation, Donnie floated the other seemingly blank books into the air and arranged them in rows of large circles around her before blowing long warming breaths over them, walking between them as she blew. And just like that, she now had several times as many journals to read as she had before. Far from overjoyed by this daunting prospect, she requested that the one she needed show itself now and a book from the bottom row zoomed up to her hands. She sent the others back to the library and set to reading the pages that were opened before her, while the council members discussed methods for determining some basic immigration and settlement processes to try.

A few minutes later, Donnie closed the book and sent it to the library, armed with a plan for increasing the Ganlonds' footprint. In summary, she would have to stand in the midst of the Gahal Glæd, which was, magically speaking, the heart of the Ganlonds. She was to call up the magic of the glade and allow it to pass through her body over and over again. With each iteration, she was to concentrate on increasing the magic, making it stronger and more abundant. She was to do this until she dropped from exhaustion, and if she was lucky, according to Catie's notes, she might have increased the lands by as much as a quarter mile all around.

According to Catie's research, these would be new lands, generated from the increased magic and not land that was commandeered by the spell, which was why they were so difficult to create. But this distinction was important to Donnie because she knew there were human settlements just past the current borders of the Ganlonds and there was no way she wanted to take over their lands—that would cause far too many problems of the political sort that she had no desire to encounter. Additionally, it would mean the king and his army would return and she definitely did not want that.

She conducted some quick math in her head with numbers she felt were conservative and calculated that, for the increased number of animals that were likely to be seeking asylum on the Ganlonds to be able to live and thrive, in addition to the nonmagical animals and plants needed for sufficient food sources, realistically they would require more like another ten miles in all directions. Which sounded impossible to do.

Not about to be defeated by such an obstacle, Donnie somehow knew, instinctively she supposed, that there were a couple of ways she could further increase the magic of the Ganlonds and thereby increase their size. She decided to try the first, which was to get Diana to help her with the spell. She figured that two Ér Ainíls just might be able to join their magic together and increase it to a much greater amount with relative ease. While they might have to run through the spell multiple times, she was positive they would be able to increase the Ganlonds by far more than a quarter mile each time.

Now, if she could only convince Diana to step back into her role of Ér Ainíl, even temporarily.

She had no desire to have to rely on the second method, which would be for her to perform another dance with the cosmos, only this time she would be dancing for more cosmic power, which she could then use to increase the magic of the Ganlonds. She could only imagine, heaving a great shudder at the painful memory of her previous dance, the gyrations she'd be put through to successfully petition the cosmic gods to grant her wish of sufficient power for their needs regarding enlarging the Ganlonds. She knew she would go there only as a last resort, even though it might help with the dragon wound on her shoulder.

No, she told herself, it had to be much easier to convince Diana to help her.

Later that afternoon, when they had returned from the council meeting, they found the four warriors sitting on the back porch drinking beer, with the two women sitting at opposite ends, as far away as Diana could make them, and the two men sitting beside each other in the middle. Falwaïn said that he had just checked on Warren, who was sleeping peacefully and had not even moved since the morning. Donnie thanked him with a kiss and a smile as she climbed onto his lap.

It was a hot day and they all looked to be quite thirsty, judging from the number of empty bottles each had standing around their chairs. Donnie immediately wondered if she could use this to her advantage, if Diana had drunk enough to make her more amenable. Initially, it seemed she had, for when Donnie explained what the problem was and how she wanted to fix it, Diana looked excited at the prospect of them combining their magic.

But then the warrioress sobered and said, "No, it's no good; I would be of little use to you, really. Do you have any idea how long it's been since I tried to tap into my goddess magic? I doubt there's much there anymore, and I'd end up just being a drag on you. I mean, what if you couldn't even do as well with me as you would alone? That would make me feel awful." She shook her head and said firmly, "Nope, you'll have to do it without me."

Donnie hung her head and adopted a forlorn expression. She honestly didn't know what to say to Diana.

But just then, Otis surprised them all by walking around the corner of the house to enjoin her in a voice full of what sounded most like regret. "I think you should give it a try, Diana," he said quietly, "because it will help Donnie out. And considering all she's done for us, I think we owe it to her." The horse came to a stop in front of where Diana was sitting and tossed his head. "From what I gather, there are a lot of magical animals, and even some trees and other plants that need to feel safe again, and they're gathering just outside the Ganlonds. Since there isn't room here for them, they're going to have to be turned away to fend for themselves. You and I know only too well what that's like, how frightening it is to be on your own like that without power to help yourself." He tossed his head again and added, "So, I think we have to help them too, if maybe just to help ourselves feel stronger." He said all this quite matter-of-factly and stood there staring at Diana until she groaned softly with acquiescence.

Donnie, never one to forego an opportunity, jumped up and grabbed Diana by the hand, pulling the taller woman out of her chair and to her feet. "No better time than the present, eh?" she suggested, grinning up at her startled friend. She put her arm around Diana's waist and shepherded her down the steps and over to Otis, where she practically hoisted Diana onto his back. Wiwila came trotting from the side yard too, the boombox affixed to her saddle and blaring "Animal Farm." Before the others were even really aware of what was happening, the two horses turned with their riders and loped back around the house and out of sight, with both women singing loudly along with the chorus of the song.

Akanna got up and strode to the edge of the porch, looking ready to follow, but she was halted by Falwaïn, who called out, "Oh, no, Akanna, we stay here. This is Ganlonds' business and that's nothing to do with any of us."

Diego nodded complacently and patted the arm of the chair Diana had just vacated beside him. He took another long swig of his beer, then invited the vincan to, "*Siéntese aquí, mi amiga.* Sit here next to me and I will tell you a tale from my boyhood that will make at least one of your blackest black hairs turn whitest white, *lo garantizo.*"

Akanna, amused by this 'guarantee' of his, came back and sat down in the proffered chair to be entertained by the darkly handsome—and quite drunk—raconteur.

By the time the two Ér Ainíls and their horses reached the Gahal Glæd, Donnie could tell that Diana was already regretting her decision to help. Mindful of the boombox's clue when they'd set out for the glade, Donnie had sent a request for assistance to all the magical secret keepers of the Ganlonds, warning them to not tarry even one minute so that Diana wouldn't have time to back out.

Rex and Sylvester met them at the entrance to the glade and ushered them inside immediately, neither of them giving Diana even a moment to protest.

Once in the glade, Donnie hopped off Wiwila and introduced Diana briefly to the members of the council. "They're here to help, 'cause I think we'll need it to be successful at this," Donnie explained, and Diana moved her shoulders with bemusement in reply.

Donnie's teeth gleamed as she flashed her friend a smile. "I figure we might as well use our entire mystical arsenal here in one go, so I've also invited any magical creature the Ganlonds have entrusted with one or more of its secrets. But here, how about we figure out the logistics of the spell together, okay?" And she made sure to keep Diana engaged up to the very last moment before the spell was to begin.

Within the next five minutes, close to a hundred animals shuffled, flew, or scampered into the glade. Donnie was taken aback by how many there were, each of whom signified some part of a hidden and mystical aspect of the Ganlonds. She watched them trickle in, sometimes chewing her lip and musing to herself about whether they represented magical artifacts and phenomena she already knew about, or were they privy to secrets that she, as Ér Ainíl, had not yet been told of?

As these magical citizens of the Ganlonds entered the glade, they were asked to settle around the edges of the clearing, whereas Donnie and Diana stood in its center, facing the back of the glade. Both women had in their lines of sight two very old, massive trees who had volunteered to be the spell's anchors, as the amount of force likely to be passing through them all, and the glade itself, was sure to be enormous. Other trees had already moved into place, agreeing to act as buffers to keep anyone not involved in the spell outside its influence. Donnie laid out the details of the spell and took one last, quick look around. It had worked out like she'd hoped and there was a magical creature situated approximately every two feet around the circumference of the glade.

Donnie turned in a circle as she gave instructions to her helpers. "Now, once we start, you will feel the magic enter your body and then leave it, so be sure to let it go as it needs to and to build in multiple directions if it so desires. Give it no obstacles or limits and, please, please, do not try to hold onto it," she cautioned them all. "We need you to act simply as conduits for the magic. Just so you know, the more connections we make between ourselves, the more magic we should be able to call up at one time, which I will then magnify and send through the process again. If we do this right, we should create an elaborate web of power that will grow around us. It might also be more in the general shape of a sphere, I'm not sure. Its beginning will be Diana and its end will be me, although that may not be apparent except at the beginning and the end of the spell. Please, if anyone feels too tired to go on at any point, tell me that before breaking your place in the chain so I have time to re-route the supply of magic around you." Once more, she looked around the circle at each of the magical creatures, who nodded that they understood.

Still slowly turning, Donnie added, "I don't want this to hurt anyone, but I don't honestly know what will happen. Seriously, no one should go any further than they are magically able to do, so no martyrs today, okay? I don't want anyone sacrificing themselves for the greater good. If you feel like it is too much for you to handle at any time, I really do want you to tell me that so I can help you. Furthermore, I want it understood that we will run this spell for as long as we can and no longer than I feel is necessary. After that, we'll see how far we've been able to expand the magical lands. If that's by ten miles, fabulous. If it's by ten feet, not so fabulous, but at least we'll know how effective we've been."

Sylvester piped up and added, "Essentially, we should all view this as a trial run. If we need to cast this spell on a regular basis, we may certainly do so. Our goal, of course, is to provide a home to any magical creature the Ganlonds grants refuge to over the next few weeks. That will be an ongoing effort, to be sure, so we should not feel as though this is the only opportunity we have. Naturally, we will not have two Ér Ainíls to help in the future," he pointed out, and Donnie saw Diana give a start of surprise, "for Diana will, I expect, wish to return to her own magical lands before long. But I am confident that Donemere will cast the spell quite expertly without her, when the time for that comes." He beamed at Donnie when he finished speaking and she gave him a fake smile in return, wishing he'd left well enough alone.

She then turned to wink at Diana and said in a voice barely more than a whisper, "Do not listen to him. You are welcome here for as long as you want to be here."

Diana, her brown eyes filled with misery, was looking as though she was about to withdraw totally. She spread her hands in a helpless gesture and whispered back, "Donnie, I can't do—"

She was interrupted by Mickey T's passionate cry of, "Here we go!" And this was followed by a great cheer from all around, with everyone exchanging excited glances of anticipation.

Donnie shrugged and grinned at Diana before repeating in a loud, firm voice, "That's right; here we go!"

Diana sighed, but straightened resolutely and made herself stand tall. When Donnie held out her hands, Diana clasped them tightly in her own strong fingers. Donnie stared at her friend, but without really focusing on her, and allowed her power to build up so that she was soon glowing with an aura of pure cobalt, and by extension, so was Diana.

The two stood together and whispered in unison the spell to incite the magic of the glade:

"We need Mother's love to grow,
as we all know.
And her power to thrive,
to ensure we survive.
We feel her magic in our bones,
hardening skin of stones.
And emboldening hearts brave,
to keep us from our graves."

These words they repeated three times in succession and then Diana was lit from within by the glade's all-powerful, intemerate white magic. Her dark eyes turned brilliant white and, when she reached her right hand toward the first anchor tree, a blaze of blindingly white magic hit it and began to travel the mystical circle, flowing into and through each of the magical creatures assembled. When the magic passed through the last anchor tree and into Donnie, she felt its surge, its welcome release into her triune and she felt it fold into itself and then expand. This folding and expanding went on continuously and she suddenly found herself riding an emotional "high" as the magic enhanced her own powers, leaving her giddy and feeling invincible. She directed these sensations toward further magnifying the magic of the glade, which was the lifeblood and power source of the Ganlonds.

As the minutes passed by, hundreds and then thousands of magical energy connections were made between the various beings gathered in the clearing. These multitudinous white strands of fulminating magic formed an intricate, pulsating web that had no real, discernible shape to it, being that it was neither spiral nor spherical as Donnie expected it would be, and it, in fact, did not conform to any sort of regularity or recognized polygonal shape. But it continued to build, continued to connect each magical being, directing it to all of those standing within the clearing. Even some of the trees guarding their circle were connected, the magic seeking kindred hearts to work the spell.

By the time the first animal called out that he could take no more, they had been working the spell for more than forty minutes. But when the young beaver called out to Donnie, she was so caught up in the euphoria she was experiencing, that it took Diana shaking her hand vigorously to awaken her to his cries.

Donnie hastily willed the magic of the glade to slow its racing speed, deciding it would be best to break the spell here and now in order to see how much they had accomplished with it thus far. She pulled back on the magic flowing through her and felt only relief when Diana's grasp on her fingers relaxed with just as much gratitude, as neither woman had realized until now just how tight their grip had been on each other. Donnie canted the words, "We are safe, Mother. Mother, we are safe," three times, and the magical strands connecting everyone retreated back to only Donnie and Diana, and then solely to Donnie. She pushed the magic down into the ground and out of her body, keeping only the same amount she'd had before the spell had been cast.

Donnie immediately knelt and touched the earth, sending her mind's eye out to the edges of the magical lands, and there she got an enormous surprise, for not only had they expanded to twice what she'd hoped for, more land was continuing to form. She could feel the perimeter moving back from where she had her consciousness centered and so she let it rise to the surface and watched as more several inches of land were added in seconds. Slowly, the new lands behind her began to be populated with the magical grasses, herbs, flowers and shrubs that were plentiful all over the Ganlonds. She sensed, more than saw, that many of the trees who lived on the outskirts of the old perimeter had started to migrate farther outward in order to explore the newly generated hills and valleys. She took her mind's eye to one such hill and watched with fascination as some trees ventured toward her, and she marveled, as always, at their slow, crab-like gait.

When she returned her consciousness to her body, she stood up and grinned at Diana and the others, who had closed around them.

"We did it!" she exclaimed, and the magical creatures cheered with both pride and exhaustion, for the long spell working had tired them all greatly. They congratulated each other with boisterous happiness when Donnie explained just how much new lands had been added and most began to leave in groups in order to collect their families so they could go get a proper look at their collective handiwork.

Finally, only Donnie, Diana and their two horses remained within the Gahal Glæd, for even Sylvester and Rex could not contain their excitement and had left along with several of their closest animal friends. Donnie, watching them go, noted with amusement that neither even thought to call out to her, but she knew where they were going anyway, and she did not blame them. What they had accomplished today as a cohesive group was nothing short of a miracle, and everyone involved had every right to bask in the afterglow.

She looked at Diana inquiringly, who responded with a shake of her head.

"No, that's okay. I'm sure we'll have plenty of time to get to know the new lands in the next few weeks," Diana said, maintaining a cool and calm demeanor as she jumped onto Otis's back.

Donnie climbed into her saddle and, after they were both settled on their respective steeds, offered, "How about I make you a saddle like mine?" She pointed down at the linen rig, which had just encased her legs and plumped up to give her a fabulously cushy seat. While it looked weird, it was the most comfortable saddle ever and she was happy to spread the wealth with her friend, if she wanted.

But Diana shot her a somewhat diffident look before replying, "No, thanks. I think I want to make my own, if you don't mind. I kind of like having a bit of magic in my fingertips again, so I might as well see what I can design for myself, you know?"

"Ah, so our spell awakened your goddess magic, did it?"

"Yeah, I guess so, because I can suddenly feel it again, something I haven't been able to do in a really, really long time," admitted Diana, a shy grin tugging at the corners of her mouth.

"I can feel it too!" declared Otis, his own wide smile more than a little smug. He even turned to give Donnie a wink. "I didn't realize how much I missed it, but it always made me feel stronger too," he explained, adding softly, "It feels good. It feels right."

When they got back to the stables, Donnie offered to take care of both horses and Diana, eager to make a start on her own hand-made saddle, agreed immediately and went around to Catie's workshop, where Donnie stored the pattern and materials she'd used for her saddle. Otis said he could wait until Donnie was finished with Wiwila and so it was about twenty minutes later that Donnie grabbed a couple of curry combs and began running them over the big horse's white coat. She also gave him some oats and he munched on them as she combed the dirt from his back.

"You know," she mused absentmindedly after several minutes of combing, "while I don't want to pressure you into telling me anything Diana wouldn't want you to, I have to say, you sure seem to want to go back to the Mîrlonds pretty bad. Or am I reading you wrong?"

The horse finished chewing and swallowed the oats in his mouth before responding, but when he did, it was in a forced, cheerful tone that just bordered on being defensive. "Yeah, well," he said, "without giving anything away, I guess I can tell ya that I think it's way past time we went back there and, now that we know something's wrong, it makes it even harder to stay away. I mean, that's our home. Frankly, I wanted to go back almost as soon as we left there."

Because he wasn't facing Donnie, she didn't see the fleeting expression of pain that passed over his features. "Man," he exclaimed when the pangs of regret were gone and his eyes were sparkling with fond memories, "was it beautiful back then, even more so than here because there's mountains, meadows, forests, and a long strip of rugged cliffs and smooth beaches. It has everything you could ever want, all kinds of terrain and all kinds of weather…everything." His voice tailed away wistfully. He moved his feet, his hooves heavy on the packed dirt of his stall. "There's even a patch of desert in the southern part that connects to the sea and the beaches. It reminded me of when I was a colt and my brother and I would race from the camp to the water, which was nearly twenty miles. I usually beat him because I was the oldest by about five minutes."

"You have a twin brother? Where is he, what happened to him?" Donnie inquired enthusiastically, struck by the thought of Otis maybe having family he could reconnect with one day.

Otis took a moment to answer before telling her sadly, "As far as I know, he's long gone, just like the rest of my family. There was a terrible battle a long time ago, and nearly my entire family was wiped out, as were those of our bond mates. We heard that pretty much no one in our families survived."

"Oh," Donnie remarked softly, "I'm sorry for that." She made a few more strokes on his back with the combs before asking, as nonchalantly as she could because she didn't want him to clam up on her now, "You grew up with the Mehen'Adríum too, didn't you?"

"Yes," he acknowledged, avowing gravely, "we didn't lie about that part, you know. Diana really was born a slave girl of the Mehen'Adríum and I was just another one of their horses. I grew up thinking I was going to belong to a warrior in the Army of the Night. That's what I was trained for anyway, not to carry a slave girl who would become the youngest concubine of Hoeris, the king back then. For her fifteenth birthday, she told him that she wanted her own horse and so he let her look us all over. That's when she found me and we bonded like you and Wiwila have. And the rest was history, as they say." He turned to smile at Donnie. "It's a nice feeling, huh? Being bonded, I mean."

"Yeah, it sure is," Donnie agreed, grinning back at him happily. She reminded herself to be careful with her questions and her answers as this was the most she'd gotten him to say about himself ever, seeing as before this he'd stuck to his lie about being a farm horse from the south. She knew he would never give away too much without Diana's consent, but she was glad that he trusted her with as much as he'd just revealed. She finished combing him and began brushing away the dirt and hair she'd lifted with the combs, deciding it was time to change the subject a little. "So, how big are the Mîrlonds?" she asked, curious because she was genuinely surprised to learn that they apparently consisted of such varied ecosystems.

Otis considered the question a few seconds before replying. "When we left," he explained, "they were physically about two hundred miles at their widest and about the same length. But on a mystical or supramundane level, they were about three times that size. They're not like the Ganlonds, you know, where the magical lands are all contained in a generally circular area that stretches outward pretty evenly from the cottage. The Mîrlonds, you see, are in a loosely rectangular shape, with all these extending tips and points wherever the terrain is too rough or contoured, or where the magic just decided not to go, I guess. You know how magic is—just when you think you can control it and make it do what you want, it goes all screwy on you."

Donnie snickered, recalling several times when magic had done just that to her, especially in her lessons with Sylvester this past winter. "Yeah, I know what you mean."

"But that doesn't happen with Ixifír Bíun," the horse said, growing serious again suddenly. "Watch out for him, Donnie. He gets people to do what he wants, even when they think they're not. And then he takes everything from them. He did that to us, and just look at what he did to Valledai, or rather, Orgos. If you hadn't insisted he not be put to death, he would have lost even his life this time. And I guarantee you, he thought he was the one in control, not Ixifír Bíun."

"You're right, he did think that." She chewed her lip thoughtfully, asking, "Um, what did you mean by 'this time'? Had he met this old Ixy dude before?"

Otis started with surprise, gave a little shake of his head, and joked, "Did I say that? Wow, I must be getting a bit soft in the head, 'cause I have no idea who Valledai did or didn't meet in his lifetime. I mean, how could I know something like that, right?"

Donnie chortled with him and dropped the subject, silently berating herself for asking what she had already sensed would be a loaded question for the horse to answer. She remained silent and soon finished going over the magnificent stallion with the dandy brush. She then set to rubbing some of her special liniment on him for his legs. Using her magic, she floated the bottle of medicine above her hands and had it tip over for it to pour a large quantity of the muscle salve into her palms. This she worked along Otis's flank and down each of the legs on his left side.

He craned his neck so he could see her better and noted, "You only put this on me when we're going to do a lot of exercise."

She looked up at him from where she was kneeling and shot him an innocent grin, chuckling to herself. "Well," she confessed, still grinning, "I'm really hoping we're gonna be taking that journey west together, aren't you?"

He chuckled too and tossed his head, showing his teeth. Before he took another mouthful of oats, he conceded, "You know I am. I guess it depends on what magic does to her when she makes that saddle."

"Oh, I think we'll find that magic is pretty happy to have her back and is going to play real nice with her," Donnie replied absently as she rubbed more liniment into his back leg. "While it was great having everybody help with that spell today—and I have to say, it wouldn't have been half as effective without you all—it was Diana who really pulled a full load along with me. She was real hesitant at first, but then the magic started flowing through her like water and soon she was directing it like the pro she is. It's really hard not to love the feeling of pure magical power running through your body like that, you know. It gets to be kind of addictive after a while."

"Oh, we all got quite a taste of that today, so I know exactly what you mean," the horse declared with feeling. "I've never had that kind of magic running through my bones before, let alone that much. It was like floating and galloping and swimming, all at the same time. By that I mean, it was rejuvenating and yet also enervating. I thought I was exhausted afterward, but now it's like I feel more whole, or something…full of life, maybe, than I've ever felt before."

Donnie smiled, hearing the awe in his voice. Finding a touch of that in herself, she confessed in a murmur, "Yeah, it was kind of like that for me as well."

"Then it must like that for Diana too, wouldn't you think? Oh, I know she misses magic!" he exclaimed heartily. "There were so many times I'd see her watching Catie or you, and I could tell she wanted that back, to be able to do what you do." He became confused at this point and backtracked by adding, "Well, not what you do, no, but what she used to be able to do. Honestly, I've never seen anyone do what you do, not with that much magic. Maybe Gaia could do more than you, I guess, but the only time I've seen her was the other night on the Branmar Plain. And, wow, she's really something, isn't she?" the horse added earnestly, clearly much impressed by the mother goddess.

Donnie, who was rubbing liniment on his other side now, gave a little gust of laughter. "That's the understatement of the year, my friend!" she said in a somewhat strangled, but amused voice. "She's mom, boss, and spiritual leader all in one, and she knows it too. I can only imagine how many voices she hears praying in her head all the time!"

"Huh?" asked the horse, dumbfounded. "Voices?"

Donnie snorted and gave a short nod while she rubbed vigorously on his front leg, the sharp scent of the liniment clearing out her sinuses quite effectively. "Yeah, see, every time someone makes a prayer or plea to me, I hear their voice in my head. It's not bad if it's only a few doing it, but when it gets to be thousands at once, it's pure hell. I hear one start, then another and another and another, and so on. And most of the time, there's not a thing I can do for them, not really. For now, I'm redirecting them to my office in the glade, er, well, I don't really know what else to call it, other than maybe a reception room," she explained candidly, moving to the back leg now. "Anyway, I have a desk there and some other stuff that Sylvester and Rex and I came up with to take everything down that's asked of me by the citizens of the Ganlonds—record it, I mean, and prioritize it automatically. All I can say is, it's a good thing I taught myself to multitask magically 'cause that is comin' in real handy nowadays. I've been having to compartmentalize a lot, it seems."

"Um, Donnie, did you not know that you can set a gûlig for that?" Otis asked hesitantly.

"Since I have no idea what one is, nope, I haven't done that," Donnie admitted. "So, what's a gûlig and how would I go about setting one?"

"Well, Diana's gonna have to tell you the how. But I remember she had that same problem too at first until Ištara Jakkar taught her about the gûlig. It basically does everything you just described, but it does it in your head instead of outside your head." The horse struggled to find a more detailed description, finally coming up with, "So, like, if you need to just send out your lovingkindness to a bunch of your faithful, it makes sure everyone who needs that, receives it. Or if somebody asks you for something unique to them, the gûlig separates those from the rest, and it lets you decide what to do and how to respond. Then it carries out whatever you want. And I gather that's all done without much effort or thinking on your part. Diana said it saved her from going mad when she set hers."

Donnie thought about this and looked pleased. "That's cool, because I was worried about what would happen whenever I was away from the Ganlonds with the current system. But if it all occurs in my head with a gûlig, I can go anywhere, can't I?"

"Yeah," agreed the stallion. "I think that's why the gods made 'em, so they could travel without worrying, because when your followers start to no longer believe in you, your goddess magic can kind of plummet, or so I was told."

Arching an eyebrow in surprise, Donnie said, "I did not know that, but it certainly makes sense. I mean, it makes sense that my goddess power basically comes from those who believe in me. It also tells me that we have to convince Diana to go back to the Mîrlonds, because if her magic is this strong right now, she must have a large number of faithful who still believe in her."

Otis gave a soft whinny, as he tossed his head, adding gravely, "And it sounds like they need her now more than ever."

Chapter 6
Alison

After leaving the stables, Donnie headed to the library and spent an hour reading up on the people and events Otis had mentioned to her. She wasn't sure if he'd intended to tell her all that he had, but she was definitely going to use this opportunity to glean more information regarding him and Diana, and potentially about her enemy, who she thought of stalwartly as the old, dreaded Ixy dude. Truth be told, she wanted to refer to him as the pixie dude just to get his goat if ever he should read the books being written about her and her friends, but she decided that might be an insult to pixies, whom she presumed existed somewhere in this magical world of Írtha.

As part of her reading, she found that Hoeris of Thelmos had been king of the Mehen'Adríum just a little over six hundred years ago and his much feared "Army of the Night" were considered the most fearless fighters of their native land, or pretty much any other land in Írtha. Hoeris embraced magic with gusto, as did his entire army, and therefore his soldiers—men, women and children alike—were infamous for their spell work as much as their horsemanship, swordsmanship and other fighting skills. They had conquered nearly the entire continent of Fal'Adîn and had moved to strike on Medregai when they were suddenly annihilated by an unknown disease, with tens of thousands falling ill and dying within the first month after it was first encountered. Donnie carefully read through the symptoms of this widespread scourge and thought they sounded somewhat like the bubonic plague of old from her world, but there were enough differences that she suspected it was something else, something even more insidious.

It must have been a spell, she decided, perhaps the blackest of all black spells one could cast. It killed somewhere close to three million people in one year, all of whom were in the southern nations. Donnie thought it was probably something old Ixy dude would have come up with, although on the surface it had been set in motion, perhaps even cast, by three sorcerers who had been aligned with the combined forces of men of the Sarn, elves of the Woodland Álvar, and vincans of Gainál. This alliance called themselves the Medregai Unified Forces, which made Donnie snort with derision when she noticed that most other species living in Medregai were not represented within these supposed unified forces. But, funnily enough, this deadly trifecta of united armies was comprised of exactly who she would have named as likely suspects to be working with or possibly even controlled by Ixy and his fellow Iceni Meræ.

The first cases of the horribly lethal disease let loose upon the southern peoples were reported during the Mehen'AdrÍum's siege of the Port of Halbis, which was laid for nearly a month. By the end of that time period, the forces of the Mehen'AdrÍum were in disarray and floundering, and most of them had withdrawn to their homelands, unfortunately taking the disease with them.

To be fair, the history books mentioned that the vinca left the vicinity of the port nearly two weeks before the spell had been released because of news of a threat that was to come from the Western Sea at the farthest edge of GainÁl, which was vincan territory. That turned out to be the army of the Zi'ahn Lo'ba, with whom the Mehen'AdrÍum shared many ancestors.

The Zi'ahn Lo'ba, who were even more mystical than their warlord cousins, wanted to establish new homes for themselves in the MÎrlonds, which for several centuries had been under the guidance and care of the Zal'Dorek vincans. The vincans managed to drive the Zi'ahn Lo'ba back to their ships, but it took five weeks for them to do so. By the time the vincans returned to KenadÍn, the Mehen'AdrÍum had already retreated in panic and the city was quarantined for the next two years.

Made immensely curious by all this new information, Donnie studied a map provided in one of the books she was reading and found that the Port of Halbis lay just outside the city of KenadÍn in Medregai's southern-most region of Trenethera. This was slightly east and far, far south of the cottage by several hundred miles. The port and its parent city were located at the western end of the Strait of GulbrÄn, which was the narrowest water body between the land masses of Medregai and Fal'AdÎn, with the SÔlom Ocean otherwise separating them to the west, and the Chalis Sea to the east.

Donnie sat back in her chair and let what she'd just read sink in fully. She knew that Hoeris had died in the year of the plague and that he had ruled for a little less than seventy years. His Army of the Night had been created twenty-five years before his death and was completely decimated by the plague and disbanded thereafter, which narrowed the timeframe for when Diana and Otis must have been born. While the most powerful magic of the Mehen'AdrÍum might have allowed Diana to double her minimum expected lifetime of a century and Otis's of a half century, it certainly could not account for their survival for almost six centuries.

This told her that Diana must have been made Ér AinÍl of the MÎrlonds in either the first or second decade after the plague ravished her people, a conclusion Donnie came to by judging Diana's appearance to be that of a thirty-five-year-old, give or take five years. Once she'd been accepted as goddess to the magical lands, she would have become both immortal and ageless, and so, apparently, would her bond-mate, Otis. Therefore, if she was right, Diana had been Ér AinÍl of the MÎrlonds for approximately four centuries before she'd been driven off them, presumably by the Iceni Meræ, with her whereabouts unknown until now.

Sighing, Donnie realized that she could ask neither Diana nor Otis if her deductions were anywhere near accurate, so she shoved them aside, letting them stew in the mix at the back of her mind, wondering if she could ask the gods to help her. Deciding it was worth a try, she took out pen and paper, writing a short note and folding it into quarters. This she materialized into the hidden recess of the fireplace mantel in her room, which she knew was a conduit to the gods. Barely had she emplaced the folded message into the recess when she realized she had already received an answer to it. Clicking her fingers, the note appeared on the table in front of her, rolled and tied with a thick string. At a touch of her finger, the string fell away and the paper opened to reveal a scrawled reply to her query that said shortly, "Not our business. Cannot help you."

"Well, that's a typical answer from a god, I s'pose," Donnie quipped to herself. Looking upward at the rafters, she added, "Fine, I won't expect help from you on this one."

Wondering where her friends were, she closed her eyes and listened to the happenings elsewhere on the farm. Diana was still in Catie's workshop at the back of the stables and mumbling to herself about what she wanted to do with her saddle, while Diego was passed out a few feet away from her, sprawled across his bed. Falwaïn too had fallen asleep, but he was in the chair at Warren's bedside and was snoring lightly. Akanna was sitting quietly in another chair in the corner of Warren's room, presumably watching the men sleep, unless she was in a light doze herself, something Donnie couldn't tell from the vincan's rhythmic breathing. Rex and Sylvester were not on the farm, which meant they were still exploring the newly created lands. Julia was sitting in her bedroom, but Donnie couldn't hear what she was doing.

Donnie got up from her desk and decided she would see for herself how Diana was faring with her saddle makings. When she walked into Catie's workshop, Diana turned to her and grunted with relief.

"I think I need your help after all," she admitted, a pink flush stealing over her perfect features.

Donnie waved off any embarrassment Diana was feeling and assured her friend, "That's why I'm here. Tell me what you need."

The two of them became engrossed in adjusting the saddle's pattern to suit Diana's wishes. When that was finally to their liking, they took their materials to Donnie's workshop because it had larger flat workspaces, and there they began the real work of tailoring the saddle to Diana's needs. It was some minutes before they realized they had an audience, and both women looked up at the same time.

"Oh, hey, Julia!" Donnie cried before Diana, who had stiffened, could say something rude to the girl. Donnie made sure she kept her tone friendly and interested when she asked, "How's your practicing coming along?"

Julia was standing in the open doorway to her room and leaning on the door jam, watching them as they worked. She took a moment to respond to Donnie's query, but she did so amiably enough. "It's good, I guess," she said with a shrug. "I just went through what my father taught me. Well, I tried some of the defensive and creation spells you and the cat told me to do, but I wasn't any good at them, so I gave up on those."

Donnie, intent on re-pinning a piece of the pattern to its matching linen material for the saddle, looked up at the girl and said evenly, "I wish you'd keep trying them. I mean, you're probably going to struggle with them for a really long while, granted. But I have faith in magic, and I think if you keep practicing, you'll eventually be able to do that stuff just as well as the attack stuff."

"Your cat didn't seem to think I would," Julia reminded her darkly.

"Well, this isn't the first issue he and I have disagreed upon," Donnie conceded, turning her attention back to what she was doing.

Julia moved up to the edge of the workbench and peered at the material curiously. "Does this mean you're making another saddle?" she asked.

Donnie waited a moment to see if Diana was going to reply, but she turned slightly and noticed the tightening of her friend's lips, so she took it upon herself to answer the question instead. "Yes," she said briskly, "but this one is for Diana. It's going to be a bit different from mine."

"I can see that. What's that thing at the back going to be?" Julia pointed to the large piece that was laid out behind the seat of the saddle. Beneath this fabric was a smooth, wide carved tongue of wood.

Again, Donnie paused before answering just to see if Diana wished to respond. When it again became clear that Diana was not going to talk, Donnie flashed a smile at Julia and explained brightly, "Diana's saddle is based on the traditional Mehen'Adríum design, which has very specific characteristics to it. Those pieces you're asking about comprise the kura, which is for back support. See here where the padded wood form will be? That's the support side of the kura, while the other side, which is the back or under side is used for storage of important items. The whole thing will attach to the cantle and have a thread lock on it that can only be opened by Diana."

"A thread lock?"

"Yes. Here, let me show you." Donnie took up a spare bit of linen and, with her finger, drew a line down its edge. A single thread came loose and began to unravel. Donnie grabbed the thread's end and wrapped it around a wooden bobbin and let the bobbin float freely above the cloth. It rotated quickly as more thread was curled around it. Whenever an edge was reached, another thread came loose and melded its end to the previous thread. This continued until all thread in the swatch of fabric was wound around the bobbin. Donnie then put all the pieces for the kura together and shoved them in front of Diana. She also sent the still-spinning bobbin through the air with a small wave of her hand and directed Diana to insert the linen thread from the bobbin into a sewing needle.

"I-I'm not good at that," Diana protested, and she moved back from the workbench. "Will you do it for me?" she asked, sending Donnie a look of pleading.

Donnie turned enquiringly to Julia, who shook her head. "No, not me," she said, holding her hands up as if to ward off the question.

Shaking her head at the pair of them, Donnie made a quick movement with her fingers and the needle was threaded. "This next part you'll have to do yourself," she instructed Diana, her tongue stuck firmly in her cheek. "Because otherwise it will only open for me."

Diana chuckled nervously and observed, "You're such a smart ass, Donnie. But all right, I guess it is for me to do, not you." She stepped back up to the workbench and straightened her shoulders, looking like she was about to dive into hot pudding or something just as undesirable. Her hands moved to just above the workbench and she started to set them in a certain motion, but she stopped, turned to Donnie, let her eyes flicker resentfully toward Julia, and asked in a strangled voice, "What do I do again?"

Donnie, taking pity on her, refrained from laughing outright. Instead, she gave her friend a knowing grin that Julia wouldn't be able to see from her vantage point, and replied serenely, "You are going to start with intent, remember? Then you will set the needle to sewing, having it close the gaps between the pieces of fabric. You will keep your intent strong, compelling the thread to act as a lock that will unravel only when necessary and only for you. It is of the utmost importance that you keep your focus on your intent. How tidy it all is when it's sewn doesn't matter, because all anyone is going to see is a piece of fabric that looks uncut and unsewn. That's why the lock is made of the same thread as the fabric."

"But someone could just cut the fabric and get at what's inside the kura, right?" interjected Julia.

"No," Donnie said with a quick shake of her head. "This is very special fabric that I spent an entire month fortifying," she explained, picking up a cut piece of linen. She held it in front of a lit candle, where it shimmered and glinted with myriad colors. "I learned so much from my first saddle, which somehow got destroyed. It was shredded by who knows what, and that was only possible because I hadn't put the correct enchantments on it when I made it. That's why I made sure this fabric is completely different.

So, trust me, once a piece is sewn into place on the pattern, nobody is going to be able to cut it, rip it, or damage it in any way that will keep it from its primary use, other than the one who sews it. Which in this case is Diana. That's not to say someone else can't mark it in some way with dirt or paint or whatnot. But they won't be able to destroy it. And whatever they put on it, Diana can lift away magically whenever she desires."

"Oh, that's cool," murmured Julia, touching the fabric admiringly.

Donnie replaced the piece in her hand back to the workbench and shot Diana another big grin, asking her, "Are you ready? It is time for you to cast your first spell in more than two hundred years." Donnie felt, more than saw Julia start with surprise, but the girl asked no questions.

Diana, setting herself squarely again, concentrated hard and not long afterward the needle began to move with a flash of silver, weaving in and out of the fabric. The completed needlework was solid, neither elaborate nor expressly pretty, but it would serve its purpose just fine. When the last stitch was made and the thread on the bobbin had run out, the newly sewn thread disappeared from view and Diana was left holding a small, stiff ball of seamless fabric and batting.

She grimaced at her handiwork, but said bravely, "And now for the rest of it." The new saddle quickly took form, with each part having a top and bottom or inside and outside layer. Between these was sandwiched a thick piece of cotton batting for comfort. The addition of the kura came at the end, its wood form lending it its desired shape.

"Okay, now we're ready for the stirrups," Donnie said, and she picked up the iron ones from the old leather saddle that Catie had used long ago on Otis. When she had these precisely positioned on the flat surface of the workbench, she turned to Julia and said, "I want you to try this time, if that's okay with Diana."

Donnie turned to Diana, who was looking dubious at this suggestion. But Donnie was determined to not let go of Julia, and she'd do what she could to reach her, get her to choose a different path from the one her father had laid out for her. If that meant teaching Julia magic skills and how to control the power in her fingertips, Donnie would keep her lessons positive and creative to draw the girl away from the darker skills her father wanted her to master.

Julia frowned uncertainly and said, "Y-you want me to sew it? I'm not really that good at sewing, you know."

Donnie gave her a warm smile and replied reassuringly, "Well, you're better than I am when I sew manually. I know your mom always said that your grandmother taught you to sew from an early age. And I remember that blue skirt you made when you were nineteen—that was very nice and looked great on you."

Julia blushed at this compliment and murmured, "Yeah, I still have that skirt back home."

Donnie again smiled. "Nowadays, I sew magically," she said, "and I'm pretty good at it, but I've practiced quite a bit. And that's what I want you to do here, is practice. Go on, levitate the needle and set it to sewing the strap that will attach one of the stirrups."

Julia and Diana both looked apprehensive about this idea, but Donnie ignored their expressions as she again encouraged the young woman to follow her instructions.

Julia did as asked and the needle floated in the air, thread trailing from it to the workbench. She concentrated hard and got the needle through the thick layers of the strap once, then twice. Perspiration stood out on her forehead, she was focusing so hard on her task. It took a lot longer than it would have either Donnie or Diana, but Julia finally had the first stirrup attached. When Donnie indicated the second stirrup, Julia looked like she would balk at the request, but she stayed silent while Donnie threaded the needle once again and set it floating in mid-air. Julia concentrated hard and the long needle was pushed through the thick layers of the strap. But she apparently tried to speed up her process, because she suddenly looked pleased with herself and flicked her fingers. The needle set to sewing, only it did it so fast that smoke was generated by the friction of the needle and thread passing through the fabric.

All three women yelled cries of, "Whoa, whoa, whoa!" and the needle came to a halt. It was glowing red with heat.

Julia glanced up, obviously scared Donnie was going to berate her.

While she might have done, Diana interjected cheerfully, "Well, you certainly got it done quickly!" She heaved a nervous breath and added, "Thanks, Julia. That's better work than I could've accomplished."

"But...I messed up," the girl pointed out, her voice trailing away.

"No, not really," Donnie told her kindly. "You just got a little hasty." She gave a merry chuckle and added, "Oh, you should have seen some of the mishaps I had, or nearly had, because I rushed. Honestly, it's nothing short of a friggin' miracle this cottage is still standing, believe me. I nearly burned it down twice, blew it up once, and flooded it another time, and pretty much all because I was in a hurry and let a spell get away from me." She patted Julia's arm and assured her, "You'll learn." With a wave of her hand, she had the needle finish its last movement before she cut the thread and tied a knot at its end. She picked up the stirrup and surveyed the strap's seam, pointing out to the young woman, "And, I am pleased to point out, you just did your first creative work with magic."

Julia looked almost shocked at this and stuttered, "I-I-I did, didn't I?"

Diana peered around Donnie's shoulder so she too could inspect the seam and said, "I think your mom would be proud. You did a good job on that, Julia, and I thank you for the assistance."

"Well, okay, but," the girl mumbled, obviously worried by something, "look, it's burnt there and there and that makes it look terrible. Can one of you fix it, Donnie?"

"Diana can," Donnie agreed, shrugging.

Diana shook her head. "Nope," she said, declaring firmly, "I'm leaving it like that. It will remind me that everyone deserves a second chance at doing good." Then she muttered so low that Donnie was the only one who could hear her clearly. "Except for Ixifir Bíun," she said, acid in her voice, "he doesn't deserve even a first chance. Seriously, Donnie, don't ever trust him to do the right thing."

Donnie turned slowly, her eyebrows raised high, and gave her friend a reassuring smile and nod. "Okay, I won't," she said.

Diana reached forward and hefted the saddle into her arms with a heartfelt, "Thanks, you two," and she strode with it toward the back door, which opened when she came near.

Donnie called out, "Let me know if you need any more help," and Diana nodded in acknowledgement before she disappeared out the door.

Donnie turned to Julia and inquired, "What about you, do you want to try more creative magic?"

Julia shook her head, replying, "No, but that was nice of you to include me, especially after what I did to, to—" She became silent and let her eyes fall.

"To Warren?" Donnie supplied.

Julia swallowed hard and said, "Yes, to him. I didn't really mean to hurt him so bad. I just wanted him out of my way."

Donnie studied her for a few moments, wondering how much truth was in that statement. She decided to stir the pot a little.

"You'll have to talk to him sooner or later, you know, because he's the father of your future half-sibling. So, you might as well accept that, Julia, and call him by his name."

Julia stared at Donnie unhappily and forced herself to say, "You're right." She took a deep breath and intoned, "W-Warren is the father of my half-brother and I must accept that." She gulped audibly and shot a wary smile in Donnie's direction before retreating toward her bedroom. "Well, I hope he recovers all right, and I promise to stay away from him and the others."

"That's best," Donnie agreed. "Unless I'm with them. I mean, I can't imagine making you staying all by yourself from now on, with only me for occasional company." She flashed Julia a winning smile, curious as to why the girl was suddenly so nervous around her.

"Oh, that's okay," Julia assured her too readily, "I'm good. Really, I don't need anyone's company, not even yours. But thanks for the offer!" She tacked on that last part as an obvious afterthought.

Donnie watched her door close thoughtfully. That had perhaps been the strangest encounter she'd ever had with Julia, and she'd had some mighty odd ones over the years. She again wished she'd done something different to protect Liz, because Liz would definitely have been able to make the girl feel less aggressive. At least, she'd always managed that in the past.

To her surprise, the boombox appeared on the workbench and softly played the last verse of "Alison."

Donnie listened until the music box turned itself off and then she said pensively, "Yeah, that's what I think too. She's sure working hard for all the pain she's got coming to her, isn't she?"

***

Liz awoke from her nap, the baby still at her breast, sleeping hard. She moved him so she could cover herself, then rose from her chair and carried him to the hammock, where she laid him gently in its middle.

She put on a long wrap that she'd found yesterday in the clothing trunk and walked to the cabin door, letting herself out and onto the main deck of the ship. As she'd discovered on previous forays for food or information, there were two cabins up top, one for the captain and the other occupied by herself and her son. As she had earlier, Liz now went in search of Catie and found the little witch in the captain's cabin, the two of them drinking rum and swapping reminiscences of their times together and those apart.

Despite the overall situation she found herself in, Liz liked what she'd seen of the captain thus far, so she did not hesitate to knock on his door. Before she entered in response to the called-out command to do so, she turned to the guard standing post outside the cabin and said, "Please have someone watch over my son while I am with the captain."

The guard looked her over with a disapproving scowl, but since she'd made the same request yesterday and the captain had barked at him to comply, he took himself off to the lady's cabin to ensure the babe was not left long without supervision.

Liz pushed the cabin door inward and waited for her eyes to adjust to the darkness inside the room, which was lit mostly by what little sunlight entered the room through the heavily paned cabin windows. The sailship was headed south, directly away from the sun, so the light in the dim cabin was being supplemented by two candelabras, each alight with four wax candles, for what little good they actually did.

When she could see well enough to walk in without tripping over her feet, Liz moved forward, the cabin door swinging shut behind her as the ship rolled to the port side with the waves.

The captain sat behind his eating table, his feet resting atop it, while Catie sprawled in a very unladylike position in a chair at one end. Neither said a word in greeting, but rather they both just stared at Liz a little bleary-eyed.

Liz ignored this somewhat cool reception and turned to the captain to ask brightly, "Can I see that map now? The one you said I could look at this morning," she clarified, beaming at the boyish-looking man.

Franklin Edward Cloys Brightman, or Neddy Cloys as he was known by the authorities and his friends, had been a pirate for the better part of his thirty-eight years. He was a small, spare man, handsome enough, and considered well-mannered for someone in his station of life. His bright blue eyes were his best feature and he used them to his advantage, having learned at a young age how to promote them as windows of emotion, even if that were imagined emotion. Many a maiden aunt, angry at him for one infraction or another, was soon melted by the deeply saddened periwinkle blue of those windows when he was a child, and nary a cross word was allowed to be said to him thereafter, not even when they were fully deserved. He was quite gifted at this, really, but he never abused the skill and employed it only when necessary, otherwise making sure to be a sharp, quick-witted fellow in all his dealings.

He turned these windows of the soul to Liz and gave her his sweetest of gazes. "Ye'll be wantin' to know when we hit land, are ye?" he asked, knowing full well that what she really wanted was to have a say on just where and when they were to hit land. He thought she looked the type to be too polite to ask for that sort of thing outright, though.

He was about to find out how wrong he was.

Catie, who did not share his illusion, looked on with interest.

Liz took a few more steps forward and returned his innocent gaze with a wide, calculating smile, showing her very white teeth off to their best advantage. "Oh, no," she said, keeping a predatory smile on her lips, which she had bitten before coming in to make sure they were as red as she could get them without lipstick, "your boatswain told me that you still plan to make land at Port of Spain the day after tomorrow. I'm just wondering what the land mass is that I can see quite plainly out my cabin window."

"Me bo'sun told ye that?" the captain repeated hollowly, and he shifted in his seat, glancing over at Catie, who was staring at the ceiling with no apparent concerns on her mind. Taking his cue from her, Neddy returned his attention to Liz after hastily regaining an impassive expression. "That, dear lady, is the wilderness of South America," he replied decisively, the lie falling blithely from his tongue.

Liz crossed her arms in front of her, her right eyebrow raised high. "Really, so soon?" she drawled, tapping her cheek with an irritated finger. "And wilderness, you say? How odd that I can see what looks like a port there. It's got ships and everything," she added sarcastically. "And you know what? I think we've been traveling due south, not southeast." She took another step closer and waved an impatient hand at him, demanding, "C'mon, give me the map. I want to see where we really are, because there's no way we're anywhere near Trinidad. And I also want to know why we're here and not where you say we are!" She turned on Catie at this juncture and huffed, "And then I want to know why we're doing any of this at all. And what the hell did you steal from that man back on Tortuga?"

Catie's arm shot upward and then came downward so she could point vigorously at Liz. She cackled gleefully, "And there it is! I knew that had ta be a comin'!"

Neddy Cloys could keep quiet no longer. He complained with a shout, "Now, look here, Miss Priss! Don't ye be goin' round menacin' me poor bo'sun! I mean that, ye know, 'cause 'e's a good lad, 'e is, and a mighty skilled bo'sun too, and that's very difficult to find these days, mind ye!" Poor Neddy was oddly stuck on the fact that Liz had just admitted to having a private conversation with his boatswain.

Liz's gaze traveled from outraged captain to laughing witch, and she chomped down on the words she really wanted to say to them both, instead staring at them like she'd just et something very disagreeable indeed. When she finally opened her mouth to speak, she was cut off by a sudden question from Catie.

"Have ye named the child yet? After all, it's been a whole week since the new mite came inta this world and we really should know what ta call 'im b'fore 'e turns seventeen!" A small smile played around Catie's lips, although she would have staunchly denied it if accused.

Liz rounded on the other woman, sparks almost literally flying from her dark eyes, while real turquoise-colored ones did fly from her twitching fingertips to the floor, which began to smoke a little where the sparks landed. "I will not be put off like this, Catie! And yes, I have named him. His name is Jessop Warren Campos and we're going to call him Jess or Jesse, got it?" she huffed at the fair-haired little witch. "And I mean it this time, I will not be sidetracked again! I want you to tell me what that damn thing is that you stole from that creep and why so many people were willing to die for it!"

Neddy Cloys sat very still and kind of shrunk down in his chair, eyeing the magical power shooting from Liz's fingertips with trepidation. He was grateful that her ire had turned to Catie, but he was also greatly concerned as to whether his ship would survive her temperament over the next several weeks. This was the third time she'd scorched the floor of his cabin, with seemingly no regard for having done so. Right now, of course, he had no wish to draw further attention to himself. He sat as still as he could, practically holding his breath because the air in the cabin was crackling with high tension and even higher magic.

This both fascinated and frightened poor Neddy because he had no magic himself and therefore no understanding of it, nor a way to combat it if needed. But he had learned to trust his old friend Catie, to trust that her witchy magic would get them through some very tight spots, which it generally always had. So now, all he could do was to wait and see how Catie would respond to this headstrong woman's passionate demands.

Catie, for her part, simply pursed her lips sternly and contemplated the excitable woman standing in front of her with a frown. She was well aware that Neddy was uncomfortable around magic and why, but she herself felt no qualms at Liz's erratic reactions. She was a Madra witch and a force to be reckoned with even on her very worst day and no Yfel witch was going to intimidate her. While she could feel the deep well of magic stirring within Liz, wanting to be released after having been held in check for nearly forty years, she was neither afraid nor apprehensive that Liz would do something she could not ward off easily. Nevertheless, she had to concede that it might well be time to inform the new mother of a few issues hanging over them all.

Begrudgingly, Catie waved her hand and sent another chair sliding forward so that it stood across the table from Neddy. She motioned for Liz to sit down, while at the same time, she had the cabin door open and a wooden bucket filled with water zoomed into the room. It flew to where Liz had stood moments before, conveniently slopping some of the water over the sides so as to douse the glowing embers of wood set alight by Liz's escaping magic.

After a low hiss sounded when the water hit the floor, Liz blushed slightly and murmured a low and embarrassed, "Sorry about that again," to Neddy, who gave her a forced grin, displaying a couple of gold teeth in his pained grimace of acknowledgement.

Liz, not to be deterred, settled into her chair and ordered, "Okay, go on," to Catie.

Catie chuckled to herself and shook her head, indulging the laugh and taking her time at getting over her amusement with Liz's high-handedness until Liz cleared her throat testily several times and Catie finally made herself sober. She liked Donnie's friend, this bossy, pushy newcomer to the world of magic, but she wasn't about to tell Liz that.

"All right, all right, hold yer horses, will ye? I gotta think about where ta start…" Catie let her voice fade away and again pursed her lips for a few moments. "Well, first of all, I'm not sure ye've thought about all the ramifications of what I've told ye so far."

"What do you mean by that?" Liz asked, somewhat thrown by Catie's chosen line of attack. She had expected something much different; just what, she wasn't sure, but not this.

"Well, when I told ye that yer daughter met with her father, did you no wonder what her father might be doin' there? Or who he might be?"

Defensively, Liz chortled, "Well, yeah, sure. I mean, sort of. You know, I've always wondered who he was, sure. But—oooohhhhh," she sighed, rolling her eyes upward, "now I see what you mean. Why was he there in Medregai, how did he get there, and what did he want with Julia?"

Nodding, Catie added, "And why did he want ye dead?"

Liz gulped audibly, and her eyes widened. "H-he wanted me dead?"

Still nodding, Catie replied crisply, "I b'lieve Donnie came ta that same conclusion, which is why she sent ye here ta me. Ixifir Bíun be his name, by the way, the father of yer daughter, I mean. He's one o' them Iceni Meræ folks what steals magic from udders and then does who knows what wi' it! I've had a couple o' run-ins widdem and, I tell ye, they dunna play nice, not never ta no one! So, what e're he wanted from yer daughter, it canna be nothin' good."

Dismayed by this last piece of news, Liz cried, "He's still there with Julia? Is he messing with her? Oh, she is just so impressionable—a-and impetuous, I bet he could get her to do anything and she wouldn't think twice about its impacts, not on herself or on others. But she wouldn't really mean to do anything bad, I know that. She's a good girl, deep down—" Liz paused at this point and heaved a long sigh redolent of regret. "Y'see, it's just that she's always wanted a mother and a father who were truly, truly proud of her. And this, this Ixifir, if he knows this about her, and he undoubtedly spotted it the moment he met her because she wears that desire like a crown for everyone to see, then he might be able to convince her to do something to harm Donnie or…" Liz swallowed hard at this juncture, forcing herself to finish the sentence by adding, "or Warren."

Catie shrugged her shoulders diffidently and adopted a sorrowful demeanor. "I got no way o' knowin' that," she admitted, genuinely grieved to see the deep worry now etched on the other woman's face. But it had to be done because this fiery witch needed to understand the situation, which she only partly did right now. Catie knew she'd have to clarify things a bit more so she added, "But I do know they won't leave ye alone, so I've been tryin' ta make sure I get ye safe, and that meant I needed what I stole from that toad back on Tortuga, that Albert Hilton fella."

Liz was so caught up by her worries that it took several seconds before she understood what Catie had just told her. She looked up to stare at the other woman with a confused scowl. "You think they'd come after me here?"

Catie snorted, "No, I *know* they'd come after ye here! Listen ta me, they want ye dead, and they likely want the same for yer wee bairn! Anyone helpin' ye will be fair game too, so ye better start thinkin' 'bout the rest o' us and what danger ye be puttin' us in!"

Liz gasped, the blood draining from her face and leaving her pale. "What do we do?" she exclaimed, looking from Catie to Neddy and back again.

"Well, we have a plan," Neddy answered, "and we dunna need ye to know it quite yet."

"Why not?" demanded Liz sharply.

"Because o' the books bein' writ about ye all, ye bawdy fool," Catie reminded her with exasperation. "Remember them things?"

Liz looked chagrined. "Well, yeah. Okay, I'd sort of forgotten about them until now."

"And because o' them, so far as anyone knows, we are on our way ta Port o' Spain and we'll land there the day after tomorrow. We're not gonna say anythin' diff'rent, at least not fer now." Catie's eyes gleamed in the darkness of the cabin. "And that's why I'm not gonna tell ye yet what it was ol' Albert Hilton was so desperate ta die for."

For a full minute, there was silence in the cabin. Liz chewed her lip thoughtfully, digesting what she'd just been told. Neddy Cloys and Catie both took some big gulps from their rum and silently congratulated themselves for having calmed Liz down without having to tell her everything they knew. They exchanged pleased smiles when they thought Liz was not looking at them and had her head bent.

But then Liz looked up and pointed out, "What makes you so sure the book hasn't already detailed your plan? Whoever has this next book, if there's even one being written—which we don't know for certain there is—then maybe it's with someone who won't care about me or even you. And therefore, they'd have no reason, or maybe even the ability to send the Iceni Meræ after us. Consequently," she announced importantly, "I am not going to accept your argument that you can't tell me more because of the possible existence of a book relaying the tales of our adventures." She shot the other two looks of triumph, making them wonder if she'd been able to read their unspoken communication moments before.

Neddy wisely sunk down farther in his chair and let his chin fall to his breast, a characteristic stance of his whenever faced with something he was determined to avoid.

Catie noted this and gave a wry snort. She looked him over and nodded with approbation. She supposed that if she could ever say that she'd loved someone, it would be Neddy Cloys. He was constant in his behavior, if nothing else. He, naturally, was quite smitten with her and had been from the day they'd first met, but she had taken some time to warm up to him. He was smallish, like her, although wiry and strong, and smarter than most men she'd encountered. But he was also a coward when it came to angry women and she knew full well that she was on her own with Liz.

She shifted her regard to Donnie's best friend and debated on just how much more she should tell the other witch. Sighing, she conceded that it might be a good time to show Liz the timepiece. She dug in her skirts and found her reticule, her fingers diving into its depths to pull out the very old metal clock-watch from Nuremburg. While each one like it that was still in existence was considered a rare find, this particular example was quite, quite special. It had innards of iron, while its outside was of ornately fashioned gold and silver. On its smooth back was engraved "*memento mori*," which meant simply, "remember you must die," effectively making mockery of man's desire to control life and, thereby, the time and nature of his death.

Catie placed the timepiece onto the table and, with a wave of her hand, slid it closer to Liz so she could inspect it. Liz held it in her palm and gave it close scrutiny in the dark room. Without thinking about it, she snapped her fingers and a turquoise-colored light ball appeared, which hovered above her outstretched hand so she could see the clock-watch more clearly.

Catie smiled at the action.

"This is really old," Liz observed, running her fingertips over the outer metal working with reverence. It had a weird vibration to it that intrigued her. She pressed the catch and the front grillwork popped open to reveal the face of the clock. It had a silver hour hand slowly moving around the dial, which had silver Roman numbers set within the gold facing. It was ticking loudly now that it was out of Catie's little handbag.

Liz noticed the small hole for the winding key, which Catie murmured was stored in the back compartment, adding that it was time to wind the clock. Liz carefully turned the piece over and opened its back, the smooth door swinging wide on a small hinge, the same as the front grillwork had. There, nestled in a cut-out, was the key. She used her fingernails to pluck it from this recess, went back to the front to insert the key and wound it several times. When done, she replaced the key and shut both the back and the front pieces, then she laid the clock-watch onto the table and turned to Catie expectantly.

"That piece there be called 'Kepler's clock-watch'," Catie replied in answer to Liz's unspoken question. " 'Twas crafted in the early years o' the sixteenth century and wonder-worked soon after by a very skilled and undeniably shrewd thaumaturge named Nicolaus Kepler. Now, ye must understand how bright Nicolaus was and what a strong witch he became. As a fact of long-standin', he was leader of a coven ta be rivaled by no udder in any age. He was the first I know ta determine that, wi' the correct resonance and a tightly woven spell, a piece such as this clock-watch could transport a body ta either the future or the past and do so with ease. He believed, quite rightly as it turned out, that all of time exists concurrently and time itself ent linear, as so many like ta believe it must be. Therefore, as Nicolaus often assured his fellow witches, shuttlin' 'twixt the past and future is merely a matter o' sharpened will and a turn of a watch stem."

"This thing can take us to the past or present?" queried Liz, disbelief coloring her voice. And then she remembered the amulet that Valledai had been so obsessed with, the one Donnie and Catie had used to send herself here to Catie.

"It most surely can," avowed Catie solemnly. "It were bein' held safe by me family 'til that scoundrel Albert Hilton commandeered it from me great auntie. She weren't usin' it ye see, 'cause she'd found the amulet, which she gave ta me after that. 'Course, the amulet works much better than this here timepiece, it do. The amulet gets ye right where ye want ta be and when, while this thing is pretty good with the wheres 'cause it dunna move ye at all. You stay in the same place when ye use it, but ye go ta a diff'rent time. Tho', it's not quite so precise with the whens 'cause it's only got an hour hand, ye see."

She said this last bit as if it explained the problem perfectly, which Liz supposed, in a way, that it did. Presumably, if the clock-watch had been crafted with a minute and a second hand as well as the hour hand, its precision would be as good as the amulet's.

"So, we're going to move through time with this, yes? Is that it, is that your plan?" asked Liz curiously.

"That be the mains'l o' it, yes," Neddy Cloys replied instead of Catie. Now that he was feeling more confident that his ship was not going to be burned to cinders today, at least not by Liz, he thought he might rejoin the conversation between the two witches.

"Where are we really headed?" Just as Liz finished asking her question, there came a series of shouts from outside that distracted them all.

Neddy Cloys jumped to his feet and strode around the table and to the door, pulling it open at the same time his much-revered boatswain grabbed hold of the outside door handle. James Smith, or Smitty as he was known on the ship, was nothing like the lad the captain had referred to him as. He was fifty if he was a day, and was a rotund, florid sailor with a keen eye and sharp breath. Smitty liked his rum even more than most, so he was nearly always pungent to be around. To give him credit where credit was due, no amount of alcohol ever seemed to affect him, so he was a sober drinker, if such an oxymoron ever lived.

He staggered into the cabin with the door, letting go of the handle in time to stop himself from careening into Neddy. He backed up and saluted his superior, who he knew hated such things, and gravely informed Neddy, "There be a crown's blagoon in our slag and 'tis draggin' the sea fro' us. 'Twould reckon ta be greetin' our grape shot by starshine."

Smitty talked in a special argot like this, and he always enunciated as if he had a mouthful of chewing tobacco, which he often did, admittedly. This combination made what he'd just said completely unintelligible to Liz, who stood behind Neddy and Catie. She held her breath and stared at the boatswain with confusion. He had flowered the room immediately with his unique odor the moment he'd stepped foot inside, and it was a sour fragrance that did not agree with Liz's olfactory senses. She exhaled carefully, brought her sleeve to her nose so she could inhale through that, then again held her breath, waiting to see what the captain had to say.

He clapped his hands together, turned to Catie and told her almost as arcanely as his boatswain would have, "Well, me girl, we're gonna need yer help wi' this. We canna outrun 'em outright, but a bit of yer special ministrations might be needed, so get yer holy cloth and whatnots out and get ta prayin'!" He looked back at Liz and intoned, "Time ta make yerself useful, Miss Priss, so ye can be helpin' Catie love 'ere do 'er prayin'." He pushed Smitty before him and they exited the cabin without a backward glance.

Liz blew out her breath again and repeated her inhalation process of before, knowing that Smitty's emissions would have lingered after him. She raised an enquiring eyebrow at Catie, who told her, "Get the child, dearie. Ye'll be wantin' 'im with ye." They too moved out of the cabin and into the fresh, sea air, where the little witch added in a low voice, "What Neddy likes ta call prayers are really spells, and we've got ta set a couple o' doozies b'fore nightfall."

Chapter 7
Thirty Days in the Hole

The morning after Julia attacked Warren, Donnie looked in on him. She found him looking unnaturally pale, with dark shadows deepening around his eyes. Bruises had begun to form on his chest and midsection—big, ugly purple ones. When she woke him temporarily from the sleeping spell she'd placed on him the day before, after much cajoling on her part he drank a small glass of water, although she was not able to get him to do anything else. His head kept lolling backward and his eyelids would not stay open for more than a few seconds before they drifted closed and he was again falling into an uneasy unconsciousness.

Feeling somewhat helpless, Donnie decided to give him a couple days to recover using his own magic, which she could sense doing what it could for him. She cast the sleeping spell over him again and was relieved when his chest began to rise and fall more evenly than it had when he was free of the spell. Not trusting that his innate magic would be enough, she canted another healing chant over him before she left. She would go on to repeat these same actions twice a day for the next two days.

At that point, she knew she had to wake him for a longer period because he needed more fluids than just two small glasses of water each day. While he was still sleeping soundly enough and his magic had risen higher in him than she'd ever felt it before, she had yet to see any real improvement in his injuries. And that worried her greatly. She needed to talk to him about his condition and his symptoms so she could figure out just how to help him best.

Laying her hands on his chest, she looked with her mind's eye at his lungs where they'd been punctured and saw that those were still healing, as she'd suspected would be the case because it was relatively easy for her to heal tissue. Bone was another matter entirely and she could see several small fractures inside his ribs. She had been "fixing" these smaller breaks each day as she found them.

She once again set to knitting more bone material together and searching for other small breaks. After another hour or so, she felt she was done for the present, knowing full well there were many more tiny breaks that still needed to heal and that she could never find them all no matter how many hours she spent at it.

Nevertheless, she waved a hand over Warren's still form to lift her sleeping spell. She sank down into the chair next to his bed and watched him closely as he awoke, listening particularly to his breathing, which had gotten progressively more ragged as he rose to consciousness.

Once fully awake, he was at least able to indicate with a movement of his throat that he needed to drink, so Donnie put a second pillow behind his head and helped him with a glass of water, holding it to his mouth and letting some of it dribble over his parched lips. By the time they were finished with that exercise, he'd managed to drink nearly half the liquid, but he looked utterly exhausted and almost worse than he had the day after Julia's attack.

"Can you talk?" she inquired, and he gave her a hesitant nod.

"I think so," he managed to croak, his voice gravelly.

She smiled at him and brushed his brow with affection. "Okay, but let's keep it to a minimum, shall we? Just blink once for no and twice for yes," she suggested, and he blinked twice with relief. Over the next two minutes, she asked him a series of yes/no questions that provided her with a clear picture of how he was doing. In a nutshell, he was feeling pretty rotten, as the myriad small breaks located throughout his ribs were painful and made breathing difficult, while movement was agony. So, she put the idea of taking him to the Gahal Glæd onto the back burner for now. If the glade's magic were ever to help him heal, it would not be today and probably not tomorrow. Right now, the trip there would be impossible for him to make, plus she had no idea how well his bones would be able to handle the force of the glade's magic coursing through his fragile body.

Reaching behind him, Donnie straightened the extra pillow so that it was vertical because she'd noticed his breathing had evened out more with it than it had been before when he was lying flat with just the one pillow. She was much heartened that his breathing eased immediately. With a snap of her fingers, she duplicated several more pillows and carefully placed them behind him until he was in a sitting position. His breathing was much better now, more relaxed and easy and he smiled at her gratefully.

"Oh, I am so sorry I didn't think of doing that sooner," she apologized with a sad groan and he sent her a reproving look. She gulped back the tears that had started to form in her eyes and said shakily, "Yeah, okay, I'll let that one go. I promise."

He shot her a beatific smile this time.

Donnie chuckled and touched his cheek with her finger. "Do you want me to put another sleeping spell on you?" she asked.

He considered this and whispered, "Not yet, no. I want to stay awake, eat something, maybe read for a while. I'd like to know more about where Liz—about your world, I mean." He looked embarrassed at the mention of Liz's name, so Donnie nodded, but said nothing.

She gave him several more sips of water, this time using a straw she conjured magically. She charmed the glass to never empty while he needed it, afterward setting the glass on a folding bed table she placed within his reach. She set another charm to have whatever books he wanted to read be sent to him here in bed. Immediately, six books appeared on the edge of the mattress, with a seventh opening in front of him, floating in a position that made it possible for him to read its text comfortably. Donnie left him contented for the moment and went into the kitchen, where she asked for plain scrambled eggs and soft toast to be prepared.

Diana was there with Diego and the two of them volunteered to take the food to Warren and help him eat it when it was finished cooking. This last comment was said by Diego with a mischievous grin.

Donnie shook with silent laughter, retorting, "Okay, but have him eat most of it, please."

"How's he doing today?" Diana inquired, turning as Falwaïn and then Akanna stumped into the house through the front door.

Donnie grimaced. "Not as well as I'd hoped, that's for sure," she replied, looking around at everybody in one sweeping glance. "The blows Julia landed with her magic essentially crushed his ribs, weakening them so they kind of keep fracturing as he breathes. I mended the bigger breaks the first day and a number of smaller ones every day since, but…I dunno. This morning I changed his position so that he's sitting up, which seems to relieve the weight and pressure on his ribs and lungs when he breathes. I am hoping that will stop new cracks from forming, or at least slow them down some." She shook her head slowly, her expression sad. "I'd feel so much better if Liz were here. Not only does she keep a pretty good handle on Julia, I think Warren would feel better having her around. He misses her, I can tell, but he thinks he's being weird because they didn't have that long together."

Falwaïn had walked over to her when he entered the room and now slid his arms around her, his hands sliding up her back as he nuzzled her neck tenderly. "How silly of him," he said against Donnie's smooth skin. "Love is love and it knows no time boundaries." He pulled back to kiss her lightly on the lips before releasing her to sit down in a chair between Diego and Akanna, who were sometimes still combatant toward each other if not chaperoned. While they were not currently exhibiting this tendency, it was something that seemed to come and go at the most unexpected moments, so he had learned it was easier to act as their buffer as much as possible.

Akanna had watched Falwaïn and Donnie's interaction with interest, afterward turning her regard to Diana, whom she had a habit of staring at with something akin to either awe or desire, Donnie wasn't sure which. Diana, as usual, ignored the vincan's existence.

Donnie sat down at the table across from Falwaïn and next to Diana, then waved her hand to bring the teapot and the coffeepot over, along with cups. While they had all eaten breakfast a couple hours before, coffee and tea never went amiss with this crowd.

When Donnie reached forward to pick up the teapot, Diana turned to her and gasped with surprise. "Donnie, you have a noticeable baby bump! How is that possible, when you're like what, a week pregnant?"

Donnie beamed across at Falwaïn, who gave her a lazy, loving smile in return. She pointed at him and then herself before explaining, "We've been stepping outside time at night during the witching hour and building ourselves a nice little home in that dimension. It's mirrored on this one, of course, and who knows how long we'll use it, but we kind of wanted to be alone with this pregnancy at times and just sort of...I dunno, revel in our relationship." She looked across at Falwaïn again.

He nodded back, his whole aspect alight with joy and love.

"Therefore," Donnie continued, stating with an important air, "I'm now three months along, or nearly that. The babies are doing really super well, the magical little rascals, the pair of 'em. They are quite a handful at times, what with their inadvertent lapses of magic control—which only seem to happen there, not here, thankfully." She rolled her eyes and made a face, while Falwaïn snickered softly. "And then there's their constant bickering with each other."

Falwaïn snickered even more loudly this time. "Donnie threatened to exchange bodies with me," he complained, a huge smile plastered on his face, "when I told her we could not name our children 'Always and Never,' and that she really should stop referring to them as 'freaks of nature.' As a result, she thought that perhaps I needed to experience the wonder of our children firsthand for myself."

Donnie chuckled with remembered amusement. "Yes, well, according to them, Calír, the boy, never gives Malisse, the girl, enough space, while Calír swears that he always does and that he moves the moment Malisse kicks him. So," Donnie shrugged, "you see where I get Never and Always. Their real names are, in full, Malisse Wiles and Calír Fen Saunders. I named the girl and Falwaïn named the boy. As you can tell, we decided to use my last name since those aren't really done here and consequently Falwaïn doesn't have one."

Falwaïn snorted loudest of all at this remark, pure delight and mischief dancing in his happy gaze. "Donnie thinks it's best to use something more than Calír, son of Falwaïn, and Malisse, daughter of Donemere, even though that system has worked perfectly well in the Sarn settlements of Medregai for thousands and thousands and thousands of years, but far be it from me to point that out," he muttered dolefully.

Once everyone had quit chortling at his expression, Diego asked good humoredly, "And just how did you work out the issue of experiencing the children's arguments firsthand?"

"Oh, that." Falwaïn turned to him and replied facetiously, "She made it so that I could hear them fighting—er, I mean talking—with each other, something I must admit they manage to do pretty much constantly, twenty-four hours a day, all day, every day." He looked back at Donnie and, with his shoulders shaking with mirth, added, "She kindly took that gift away after one very long month, at just around the time I was ready to commit suicide."

When the renewed chuckles subsided, Donnie corrected him dryly, "It was for less than a day, actually." This time, everyone laughed outright.

"So, you can do this, step outside time to another dimension, I mean?" Akanna inquired when the laughter settled down. She looked at Donnie, then at Diana, apparently asking them both the question.

Donnie nodded and turned to Diana, curious of her answer.

Diana gave a small smile and shook her head. "You are far stronger than I ever was, Donnie," she admitted wistfully. "I could never get to the Exos without help from Ištara Jakkar or Bahiti or one of the other—" She stopped abruptly and let out a nervous laugh.

"One of the other Nine," Donnie finished for her.

Diana's expression turned grim, while the others gaped at her in surprise—except for Akanna, that is, who nodded to herself thoughtfully.

"I wondered if maybe you weren't the reason there was a vacancy within the *Niunda Wakan*," Donnie told her friend, pleased her guess had been correct. "Our positions being so similar and all."

"Yes, well..." Diana mumbled.

Akanna, unable to contain herself any longer, eagerly leaned forward to ask, "What exactly is this Exos? I have heard of it, but I cannot recall where or why."

Donnie shook her head uncertainly and looked over at Diana, who somewhat grudgingly explained, "I believe Exos stands for Ex-Chrónos— you know, as in outside time? Gaia could tell you more about it because she was the one who first taught me of its existence. Ištara Jakkar called it the Fertile Realm and she said that anything could be made there and anything could be realized if you imagined it there. But the problem with the Exos is that you can't take what you create in it to the real world. I and several others attempted to do that, but nothing would work, no matter what we tried to bring back." She shrugged, adding, "Not even the smallest leaf would make it through."

"Hmm," murmured Donnie and she glanced at Falwaïn meaningfully before turning back to Diana, "We've been able to take Rex there with us, but not Sylvester. Do you have any idea why?"

Diana's finely chiseled features fell into a thoughtful expression and she was silent for several moments before replying. "If I recall my ancient Valkérian lore, only those touched in some way by divinity are allowed to go there."

Akanna drew a sharp breath in the midst of Diana's answer and, again unable to contain herself, exclaimed, "That is it, that is where I know the Exos—it is in a legend told by the elves! It is said that is where they hid their most precious artifacts from the Red Warlock. Although, whether what they sent to it was theirs to hide is another question. You see, the Valkérian elves are notorious for appropriating magical artifacts as their own, and whatever they hid in the Exos might well belong to others."

When Donnie looked at Falwaïn for confirmation of this assessment of the aforementioned elves, he nodded and admitted in a cheerful voice, "Akanna is quite correct and Valkérian elves have indeed acquired that deplorable habit, as have the Sarn. We are, in fact, notorious throughout the entirety of Írtha for re-appropriating all manner of belongings that seemingly should have ownership by others. That is true whether they are our enemies' possessions or those of friends who are about to become an enemy because of our light-fingered approach to friendship. Lest you believe all elves and all men are the same as us, conversely, the Midland elves and their kin are more prudent about pilfering such personal articles from their foes, as are, perhaps, most of the Free Peoples." He paused and pulled on his lower lip a moment, his eyes twinkling playfully. "But then, it has been my experience that those peoples fear magic quite rigidly, except for the Canelans, that is, and will heartily attempt to murder anyone they see wielding it. Which is why it's best to avoid those people entirely," he joked with an engaging grin, "and they are easily avoided because most of them live in Eastern Medregai. I myself have been avoiding them quite successfully for several years now."

Donnie threw a napkin at his face and let out a bark of laughter at his suddenly aggrieved expression.

"You wound me, woman," he murmured, and she laughed at him again.

Shaking his head while chuckling with amusement, Diego interrupted their hilarity by asking Akanna, "How did your people become aligned with the Sarn and the elves?"

The vincan considered how best to answer, then said, "Proximity and parity, I think describes it best. As regards proximity, the vincan home territory is adjacent to that of the Sarn. And what I mean by parity is that we are as strong physically as the Sarn and as the elves. Our brain capacity equals theirs, but we tend to live longer than they do, so we remember our history better and strive to never repeat it in the cases where it is dismal. We are more adept with magic than the Sarn, although the Valkérian are generally more skilled with it than the average vincan." She shrugged expressively, summing up by adding, "So, you see, there is parity between us. And we have some of the same goals, such as keeping dark magic away from our lands and our peoples."

Diego turned to Diana and, honestly curious to know more, asked her, "How did you become involved with the vinca if you are of an entirely different race?"

Donnie interjected, "Yeah, I've been wondering that kind of thing too, because I read that, while the Valkérian and the Sarn will sometimes mix their species together, the vinca never do that with anyone anymore, so the current vincan bloodline is much, much purer than either of the other two. Is that right?" she asked, turning to Akanna.

Akanna studied Donnie silently for a moment as if she were unsure of the motive of the question being asked. When Donnie kept gazing at her innocently, Akanna finally replied, "Until a little over a millennium ago, we had mainly allied ourselves with the southern people, as I suspect you are aware."

Donnie grinned and raised her right hand straight up, her elbow staying on the tabletop. "Guilty as charged," she admitted, looking anything but. "I find you all so fascinating, you know. But, forgive me," she apologized, returning her attention to Diana, "I think you were about to answer Diego's question before I so rudely interrupted."

Diana shot her a dark look, then shook her head at Diego. "I'd rather not talk about my past, if you don't mind."

"She intervened long ago between the Zal'Dorek and the Sarn, and became the re-unifier between us," announced Akanna, her eyes glinting with determination and a hint of arrogance. "We had fallen out with the rest of the Gossalyn Forces after the War of Sorrow, for our leaders felt our losses were too many for a war that was not of our making. They wanted nothing further to do with the Sarn, the Valkérian, or their allies because of their never-ending battles with dark sorcerers and their armies. Battles which we vincans too often won with our own blood." She glanced over at Falwaïn, who had abruptly turned his chair toward her, as he was clearly affronted by her claim. She raised a placating hand to him and said, "This is what I have been taught, not necessarily what I believe."

While Falwaïn was somewhat appeased by this statement, everyone could see that his ire was still up. The air in the room became tense because of it.

"I would just like to point out that a number of Sarn also died in those battles," he snapped, his voice sharp and his back ramrod straight and held stiff against his chair, "at least as many as either the vinca or the elves, and sometimes more than the other two combined. We've always felt that we won those battles fairly and with our own blood, not the blood of others."

Akanna regarded him without expression for a long pause before she acknowledged his claim. "I will concede the argument for our purposes here," she replied seriously, bowing her head in a gracious movement of what seemed to be mocking deference. She turned to Donnie and pointed out dryly, "Perhaps now you can see why there was need of intervention."

"Oh, yes, I think we can all see that," Donnie murmured to the vincan before she reached across the table to Falwaïn.

He sighed at the unspoken plea in her eyes and grasped her hand to squeeze it before releasing it. His usual reserve stole back over him so that his storm of sudden anger subsided into control and he sat back in his seat, composed once more.

Donnie shot him a grateful smile.

Then, as if Diana were not sitting right across from him, Diego asked Akanna, "And Diana brought you all together to become allies again?"

Diana huffed and scowled, drawing everyone's gazes back to her. She suddenly stood up and scraped her chair backward, her defiant expression openly daring Akanna to say more under threat of retaliation.

The vincan, her eyes flashing with a matching defiance, met Diana's challenge and she said with exaggerated care, "Yes, she did. But that was when she had courage in her heart, not cowardice!"

Rather wildly, Diego shot upward from his chair, hesitated a moment, and then lunged for the vincan, shouting, "*Demonia*, you have no right to speak to her like that! I have told you this before!"

Akanna jumped up too and braced herself for his blow.

Falwaïn surged to his feet and stepped between them directly into Diego's path, doing so just barely in time to stop the small mêlée that was about to occur right there in the kitchen. He grabbed Diego's shoulders and pinned him backward, with Diego struggling hard to get beyond his friend to the smirking vincan.

On the other side of the table, Diana hung her head low, hiding her face in her hands.

Donnie, alarmed by the instantly skyrocketing amounts of testosterone and other hormones flying every which way around her, stood up moments after the others, knocking her chair to the floor in the process. She ignored it and cried out, "Sit down right now, all of you, or I will make you sit! You may not brawl in my house!"

The only problem was that she forgot herself and used her goddess voice, which made the rafters above the table quiver and rattle, with long drifts of silt filtering down onto everything in the room.

The two men stopped scuffling with each other and all movement was stilled in the room for several seconds. Slowly, everyone turned to stare at Donnie. Seeing her set face, each of them sank back into their seats quietly, somewhat appalled at their behavior and at the implied threat of Donnie's response.

Donnie groaned under her breath with embarrassment, her cheeks pink and flushed, and she apologized to them in normal tone. "Sorry about how loud my words got there. Funny how that voice just seems to come out of me whenever I get upset."

"Then we should never upset her like that again, should we?" rejoined Falwaïn, as though schooling the others to behave.

Donnie glared at him half-seriously. "No, none of you should do that, should you?" she countered, and he looked slightly abashed.

But then he winked at her and assured glibly, "Yes, my honey woman, you are speaking very good words to us all now and in such a nice tone that we shall heed every one of them, shan't we?" He glanced around at the others, each of whom looked like they might start chortling again, but whether that laughter would be of the nervous variety or because they were genuinely amused was anyone's guess.

Nevertheless, the crisis had been averted and the air felt less thick all around them. The conversation, such as it was, continued once Donnie, after righting her chair and sitting down in it, said firmly, "Let's just leave opinions and accusations out of our talk for now and discuss some facts, shall we?" And she motioned imperiously for Akanna to speak.

"Very well," Akanna agreed, nodding in solemn acknowledgement of the directive. "Firstly, you should know that within Gaínál, the Zal'Dorek territory and that of the Sarn are separated by two natural barriers," she explained. "In the north of the region, the White Tower Mountains form a natural barrier that separates vincan settlements from the Sarn ones that are built around the capital city of Anûmanétus. The Donbragh'arík, which has its fresh-water feet in the southern-most peaks of the White Towers and its mouth at the Sôlom Ocean, isolates the western and southernmost reaches of Gaínál from Faen Eárna and the Sarn living there."

Donnie turned to Falwaïn. "Remember the cavern at Flírbann and those statues we discussed while eating lunch?"

He nodded.

"You told me then about a vincan fortress where the dwarves' Sacred Nine sacrificed themselves against the Red Warlock's—um, what was the name of his army again?"

"The Malacham An," Falwaïn supplied helpfully.

"Yes, that's it!" Donnie exclaimed, clapping her hands together before focusing again on Akanna. "So, that fortress must be on the vincan side of these barriers, correct?"

"Yes," confirmed Akanna and Falwaïn both.

"Does it still stand?"

Akanna nodded. "Yes, it remains as a stronghold of protection for the southwestern corner of all of Aldera, not just Gainál, and it also serves as the vincan military academy."

Donnie repeated this to herself, thinking hard before inquiring of the vincan, "Is it also what protects the Mîrlonds from the rest of Medregai?"

Surprised, Akanna nodded. "In part, yes. It is the only ingress through the Tegere Mountains and lies west of the Aldwuda."

"Aldwuda?" asked Donnie, intrigued.

Falwaïn murmured, "It translates to 'old wood' in ancient Mannish and is the oldest forest in Aldera, which is what the ancients called western Medregai. The forest covers nearly half of the Faen Eárna Province—er, the southern half, to be specific," he amended.

Donnie chewed her lip, her eyes unfocused while she considered this lesson in Medregai's geography. "Tell me, why did the Red Warlock, the goth guy I mean, attack Canta'Lem in the first place? That is the name of the fortress there, right?" she asked curiously, bouncing her gaze between Akanna and Falwaïn, and when they both nodded, she repeated, "Why did he attack there? Was there something in the fortress that he wanted, or did he really want to get to the Mîrlonds and maybe had to go through the fortress to reach them?"

This time, Akanna studied her for a singularly long time before responding. She said, in a voice that almost seemed to be chiding Donnie, "Again, I believe you know the answer to your question already. Of course, one must go by way of the fortress to get to the Mîrlonds. Attempting to reach the magical lands from either the north or south of the fortress is not advisable, as the Tegere Mountains are some of the steepest within Medregai and are always treacherous, no matter the time of year. Even if one went north of the Tegeres and then came south that way, there would be the great city of Morlant as the next obstacle, which cannot be avoided because of the steep terrain that, similar to the mountain formations leading to Canta'Lem, feeds all travelers directly into the city's gates. From the west, the magical lands are impossible to find unless one belongs on them because their border on the sea is enchanted. And accessing them from the south means crossing nearly two hundred miles of desert, a foolhardy venture which no one has ever survived, at least not in recorded history. Therefore, yes, the Red Warlock was indeed trying to reach the Mîrlonds by going through Canta'Lem. And yes, he would have succeeded in that endeavor if not for all those who stood their ground and held the fortress, be they dwarves, vinca, elves, men or any other peoples of the Gossalyn."

Donnie ignored the rebuke in Akanna's manner and asked crisply, "And what did he want on the Mîrlonds? He went there to get something, didn't he? Maybe to steal something?" Then, instead of looking at Akanna, she turned to Diana and said persuasively, "I think you're maybe the only one here who can answer that question, Di."

Diana let out a grunt, nodding her head and smiling sadly. "Yes, I probably am at that," she admitted. She added, in a glint of perspicacity, "Like Akanna, I suspect you already know the answer, or you've guessed it, haven't you?"

Donnie smiled at her but said nothing.

"All right," Diana muttered under her breath, as though surrendering. "The Red Warlock was there to steal the Five Jewels of Light, which were being kept on the Mîrlonds because their original hiding place was gone. Since that was before my time, I don't know why, really, they were there. Nor do I know where they should have been kept or why they had been moved." She paused, then said, "Okay, now you have to tell me how you knew I would be able to answer your question."

"Well, let me ask you another first—or well, two others," Donnie said, eyeing her friend circumspectly. "Who was Ér Ainíl of the Mîrlonds before you, and how did the Red Warlock get the jewels away from them?"

Diana's sharply indrawn breath told Donnie she'd hit on the truth.

"How did you know—" Diana started to say, then she stopped. "You really are good at this, aren't you?" she asked rhetorically. She hunched down in her chair and let out a forlorn sigh. After thinking back a bit, she explained, "I believe Sylvester told you about Catie's mother, Margawse, yes? And you've undoubtedly worked out for yourself that she was the Ér Ainíl of the Ganlonds for a very long time, which is why Catie was initially supposed to take her place, until you came along." She paused and, when Donnie nodded in the affirmative, she continued, "But Sylvester probably doesn't know about Margawse's sister, Philînan. She, like Margawse, was a Fægre witch, and was born of the gods. I'm not sure who her father was, although I know it was someone different from Arawn, Margawse's father. Anyway, Philînan fell in love with Malkôr, the Red Warlock, when he was a young man and was just coming into his power as a sorcerer. Whether he tricked her into giving him the Five Jewels of Light or she gave them to him willingly, I don't know. But she handed them over to him less than a month after the Gossalyn's stand at Canta'Lem."

"What happened to her after that?" asked Diego, and Diana shrugged at him.

"The legend was that Margawse went after her and killed her, and Margawse died sometime thereafter of a broken heart, but there was never anything in the scrolls left behind by either Philînan or Margawse to prove that theory, so who knows what's actually true? I've heard it said that Philînan was banished along with Nírgoth, or as she knew him, Malkôr, but I have no idea if that's any truer than her sister killing her."

"And now," said Donnie, trying not to appear too eager for the answer, "tell us how you came to take her place. Please?" She put her hand on Diana's forearm and lightly rubbed the smooth skin there, her smile warm and encouraging.

Diana, having had enough barriers broken down by now, conceded this part of her story. "Okay," she breathed softly. "But it's really nothing all that special. Otis and I set out to visit the Mîrlonds because I'd heard there was a cure found there for a terrible sickness that was killing my people by the hundreds of thousands. I had no idea what I needed to look for once I reached the magical lands, but I knew I had to find whatever it was. Back home, my king had died, what little family I had was gone, and most of my friends were already dead or dying too. When I reached Canta'Lem, I discovered that the vinca were sure it was something the Sarn had set loose upon my people, but I thought it might have been started by someone else. It took me a while, but I was finally able to prove that it originated with the Iceni Meræ, and the Sarn's mages who set it onto my people had no idea what it was going to do. They thought it would give everyone touched by it nightmares that would make them fear the Sarn and their allies so much, they would retreat without fight. I believed these wizards when they swore they had no idea it would let loose the Black Death, and I was able to convince the vinca, who have a very definite sense of right and wrong, that the rest of the Unified Forces had been duped, and that they too shared some of the guilt for the dreadful disease. I was taken to the heart of the Mîrlonds and given the Gift of the Glade, which cured me of the plague's effects, for I too had caught it and was near death by then. The Mîrlonds, for whatever reason, decided to make me their Ér Ainíl, and in exchange, the cure was given to my people and the plague came to an end." She shot Donnie a quick look. "That's the long and short of it, anyway. And that was the first time I learned not to trust Ixifír Bíun and the Iceni Meræ."

"How long were you Ér Ainíl of the Mîrlonds?" asked Falwaïn.

"Nearly four hundred years," she replied wistfully.

"You miss it," Diego stated, and Diana nodded.

"Yes, naturally, but I had to give it up because of Ixifír Bíun," she bit out harshly through gritted teeth. She turned to Donnie suddenly and cried, "Don't ever underestimate him, Donnie! I mean it, he's nothing but bad. It's like evil springs from his heart and from his every thought and action, and believe me when I say he has absolutely no concept of goodness or decency or anything healthy or warm or loving. He is the most depraved being I've ever had the great misfortune to meet!"

This bitter pronouncement was met by silence. This silence might have lingered if not for a sudden quaking of the ground. The cottage shook, as did everything inside it. It was just one, quick shake, but it certainly got everyone's attention.

Diego was the first to speak, looking around at the others with amazement and saying, "There it is again, a *temblor*, same as the last few days."

Donnie exclaimed at this in confusion, "What, what do you mean? Are you saying that's happened before?" She swung her inquiring gaze to meet Falwaïn's.

He nodded. "Yes, didn't I tell you? It's happened every day since you closed off access to the Ganlonds, and at right around this same hour each time. I think you're usually in a council meeting, so perhaps that's why you have not felt them before."

"Yeah, you're right," said Donnie, thinking back. "That's where Rex and Sylvester are now. I wanted to spend some extra time with Warren, so I begged off today's meeting."

"We all assumed it was something you had done," Akanna volunteered and the men nodded in agreement.

But Diana was shaking her head. "Not me, I didn't think that because I'm convinced it has something to do with Julia," she said. "But after each quake, I'd hurry to her room and she's been there every time. She says she doesn't know anything about the quakes. But then, she's pretty good at playacting, so I figure she's been lying to me." Diana frowned, muttering under her breath, "Or maybe I think that because I dislike her so much."

"Can you tell from where the shaking came?" Falwaïn asked Donnie.

"Unfortunately, no," she sighed. "I'll have to wait for it to happen again tomorrow morning. I'll be ready for it."

From the inner parts of the house, Warren's empty plate came zooming back into the kitchen. No one had even noticed it going in to him minutes before.

Donnie grinned at Diego and chuckled, "Looks like you're too late to help him with his meal."

"And it looks like Warren was very hungry," agreed Diego, grinning back at Donnie. "There is nothing but a few crumbs left."

Diana stood up and said, "Well, I'm done talking about all this, so I'm going to spend some time with Warren. Maybe I'll read to him so he can rest his eyes. See you all later." She left the room amid farewells from the others.

Diego turned to Falwaïn and enquired, "Shall we return to our practice session?" He included Akanna with a reluctant glance in her direction.

Falwaïn eyed Donnie questioningly and asked, "Do you mind?"

She waved them off with a thoughtful goodbye and watched the three of them stride outside, leaving her alone with her ruminations.

***

Liz awoke slowly and felt Jesse move within the curve of her arm. She looked down at him and smiled, a smile he returned. He had the blackest hair she'd ever seen on a baby and the most vivid blue eyes, just like his father's. She sighed with longing, for her dreams were haunted by the handsome warrior and the touch of his hands on her body, thrilling her skin and making her heart race.

"Warren," she whispered, just to say his name.

Then she looked down again at Jesse and told him, "You have a very gorgeous and wonderful father, you know that? And I can't wait until he sees your beautiful face. He's going to be so happy." She hugged the baby to her and vowed wistfully, "I don't know how we're gonna do it, but we will be with him again, and we'll do that before you grow too much more, I swear it!" She kissed the boy's forehead and heard him coo with delight.

They snuggled for another half hour before Liz heard her name being called just outside her cabin. She carefully climbed out of bed and padded across the wooden floor on bare feet. Opening the door, she admitted Catie into the room, who immediately went over to Jesse and picked him up into her arms. For all her complaints about "witchy bairns" being a pain in the ass, she certainly seemed to have a huge soft spot for Jesse and couldn't keep her hands off him if he was within twenty feet of her.

Liz dressed while Catie fawned over the baby, then she took him back into her arms and sat down in the chair at the desk to let him suckle from her breast.

A sailor knocked on the door and Catie received the tray of food and drink from him, closing the door again with her foot. She put the tray on the desk and pulled the other chair over so that she could eat her breakfast too. She rubbed the palms of her hands together in anticipation and looked over both plates hungrily. She, of course, was planning just what to take of Liz's allotment. The little blonde witch had an insatiable appetite and counted on Liz being too courteous to give her any grief about the pilfering of a couple bacon rashers. In this supposition, she was quite correct, so the two women ate without quarrel, with Catie relating the news from the night's watch while munching away on stolen slices of the heavily salted, cured pork.

"Our fog spell worked like a right middlin' beauty. An hour ago, though," she announced with a mix of pride and reticence, "the clipper ship houndin' us liked ta keel off our port side. But, while lingerin' lizards they may be, they still canna see us 'cause the mirror spell is doin' jest fine."

Some of this statement was difficult for Liz to understand because at mealtimes Catie tended to converse with her mouth full of food. She also managed somehow to do that ever so noisily, smacking her lips and chewing more loudly than most horses did while ingesting their oats and corn. Liz was glad, though, that Catie at least usually turned away when talking instead of looking straight at Liz.

"Well, that's good news," Liz noted with relief, having caught the gist of Catie's update. "Just how much farther do we have to go?" she asked, eating her porridge much more delicately than Catie ever seemed able to accomplish, feeling like she was in some way beholden to the universe to provide the better example of table manners between the two of them.

"Oh, not far, not far," Catie assured her, and her sky-blue eyes gleamed with satisfaction in the reflected dim light shining from the windows. "But I'm gonna need yer help agin, only this time, I need ta pick yer brains. I assume ye know yer hist'ry well enuff, eh?"

It took Liz a moment to realize there was a question in what Catie'd just said, and when she did, she scowled in hesitation. "Well, I'm usually pretty good with history, yes," she replied. "It was my minor in college, after all. I mostly concentrated on the Americas though, so if it's a question about somewhere else, I'll do my best, but I can't give you any guarantees. What do you want to know?"

Catie ran her tongue all over her lips and smacked them again before wiping them with the back of her hand and rubbing that onto her skirts. This was her ritual for signaling the end of her meal. She pushed back her chair a little and surveyed Liz and Jesse with fondness.

"We have come in sight of Brujas Point and what's commonly called in this era its limeny bay," she announced, her lively gaze bouncing from babe to mother and back.

Puzzled, Liz had to cast around in her mind for a thread of sense to what Catie had just stated, then her eyes widened when she thought she understood what was being asked. "Are we, by chance, trying to get to the Pacific Ocean?" she asked, pressing a small towel to her lips in lieu of an actual napkin.

"Not by chance, nor by luck, I'd say," Catie replied blithely. "Oh, no, we're a goin' there for a purpose. And the sooner we git there, the better off ye'll be."

"I see," said Liz, carefully folding the towel onto the tabletop. "Well, keeping in mind that there might well be a book out there detailing what we're doing and that those upon the ship following us may have it in their possession, I will supply you with this: a shortcut from the Atlantic Ocean to the Pacific Ocean was opened sometime in August of 1914."

Catie pursed her lips and nodded. "A boon to sailors, I'm sure it were," she observed tartly. "Would ye happen to know jest how long this shortcut might take ta cross?"

"It takes about half a day, I believe," Liz replied succinctly, "possibly less." She paused and added, "You say Brujas Point is nearby?"

" 'Tis indeed," confirmed Catie, "as is its isle."

"And we would be there in about an hour or so, I suspect? Supposing, of course, that we were to go there at all, I mean."

Catie eyed her with approval. "If we was ta visit that little isle, yes, I think it might take as much as an hour to arrive there."

"Ah, well. I think I'll take a slow promenade around the deck for a bit, perhaps ending at the bow so as to give myself a better view of the ocean in front of us and the limeny bay approaching."

Catie again beamed at Liz with approbation. "That sounds lovely, and who knows, I jest might meet ye up there at the prow," she said, clapping her hands together.

Half an hour later, the *Drunken Knave* had bypassed Brujas Point and was heading slightly northeast, toward where Limón Bay was situated. They'd caught a strong wind and were making good time, but there was a problem. The clipper that had been tracking them over the past week had also turned toward the bay and was sailing there fast, which seemed to confirm the supposition that those on board her did indeed know, or at least suspect, the *Knave's* destination.

"Who is on that ship, Catie?" Liz inquired curiously, studying the tall clipper critically before turning her gaze to the little witch beside her. Liz had Jesse swaddled in a thick, colorful shawl of Catie's, which was tightly looped around her small form so that she could carry him hands-free. Even still, Liz kept her arms wrapped around him and hugged him to her.

Catie shot her a hooded look and responded blandly, "There is no way I could know who would be on that boat."

Liz huffed with a hint of annoyance, hating that this woman, whom she sometimes truly liked and who, at other times, drove her positively batty, could get her goat like no one ever before.

"Generally, I mean," Liz clarified. "Are they the Iceni Meræ?"

Catie shrugged nonchalantly. "To my knowledge, which is based on the type o' ship it be and the flag 'tis flyin', I'd wager 'tis manned by British soldiers."

Liz stilled and stared at the other woman, aghast at this supposition. "Why would British soldiers be coming after us?"

Catie gave her a look as if she thought Liz a loon before pointing out dryly, "It might have somethin' ta do with the murders o' Albert Hilton and his retinue, dunt ye think? It has been my experience that the British Navy dunna take kindly ta anyone killin' their magistrates, nor, I imagine, ta havin' their officers' throats torn out by a pack o' phantasmic wolves, ye see."

Liz shook herself with frustration but refrained from retorting what she'd really like to say in reply to this nonsense. Instead, she asked more precisely, "So, you're telling me that they are not after us because we have Kepler's clock-watch?"

Catie's expression changed to a sorrowful one and she muttered cautiously, "Well, naow, that I canna say fer sure, can I? Their motivations are their own and thus far they've had no way o' sharin' 'em wi' the likes o' me, have they?" She chewed her lip a moment, then conceded, "But it's not such a far-fetched question ye ask, I'll grant ye that. And they mebbe do know about the clock-watch and they mebbe do want it back. But they canna have it yet, not while we still need it."

"Agreed," sighed Liz, and she and Catie both looked back at the ship following them with loud gasps and looks of fright, for the clipper was now closing the gap between themselves and the *Drunken Knave* at an alarming pace. The women turned toward the shore and realized that they had nearly ten more minutes before they'd be in the bay.

By silent consent, the two little witches joined hands and began to chant, the gold of Catie's magic and the turquoise of Liz's outlining their wind-struck forms up on the prow of the *Knave*.

The crew within sight of the women watched them for a short while before turning their attention back to their own tasks, some unconsciously crossing themselves in a religious manner. While they would not admit to the existence of magic, with many being either purely superstitious about that sort of thing or just lapsed Catholics on a heathen pirate ship, they didn't particularly care if magic were used because they would take all the help they could get in escaping that cursed clipper currently running them down. For they all knew that getting caught by the British meant certain death for the entire crew, with no questions asked aforehand.

Together, the women conjured a new wall of fog, thick and heavy, having it close behind them to obscure the bay from the other ship's view, knowing the British would have to slow down to ensure they didn't run aground.

As the *Drunken Knave* rounded the point and sailed into the bay's waters, Catie pulled out the clock-watch from her reticule and pressed a small button that was just slightly raised between the hinges for the back cover and front grillwork. She opened its back to get its winding key out and flipped it over to wind its inner workings six times, one turn for every forty feet of boat behind them. She replaced the key, opened the front grillwork and put one finger of her left hand onto the numeral one and another onto the nine and held them there, and then she put one finger of her right hand also onto the numeral one and another onto the five. Liz, facing Catie, put her hands over the other woman's and both witches concentrated hard on the year 1915.

***

Donnie was still sitting by herself at the table when the cat came in through the open front door. He leapt onto the table, sat down in front of her with his tail wrapped tightly around his front paws, and greeted her with a brisk, "You missed a productive meeting just now. We are getting very close to determining a process for immigration. I would gauge we should have one formulated within two more meetings."

"That's great news, Sylvester," Donnie replied, her voice overly bright and cheery. "Especially since there are now more than three thousand magical creatures seeking residency on the Ganlonds," she reminded him, fixing a forced, but still cheerful smile upon her face. They'd been told that number this morning when the deer twins, Bambi and Barbi, had come to gossip with Rex. The young does were the daughters of Mórbaen from the Animal Council. They had overheard their father discussing the crowds growing outside the Ganlonds with their mother when they'd awoken at sunrise and their parents hadn't realized their tender ears were listening.

The cat scoffed. "A lot you know. From what was said at the meeting, I'd say the total is growing exponentially by the hour."

Donnie gave him a genuine grin and exclaimed proudly, "Just listen to you, Sylvester, you're finally picking up my habit of hyperbole!"

The cat rolled his eyes heavenward and intoned sternly, "The number on the morrow, I fear, may well be far more than four thousand seeking refuge, for a falcon spotted several large groups of ruminants and ursines and who knows what else in the distance, all of whom appear to be headed our way. And, lest we forget, there are also trees gathering in several places too and their branches are all chock full of birds by now, I gather." He sighed. "It is going to take weeks to attend to them all. And what will we do with those who fail to meet our requirements?" He sighed again, this time with great worry.

Donnie took pity on him and said reassuringly, "My friend, we'll figure something out for them, no matter what. We won't just leave them high and dry, I promise."

He shot her a happier glance, then asked, "And how is Warren faring today?"

"Better than yesterday, but still not as well as I'd like," she admitted. "I'm not sure he'll be able to travel with us anytime soon, so we may have to go to the Mîrlonds without him."

The cat shook his head and shoulders in a small shrug. "Well," he said, "Diana is still insistent that she will not go with us either, so I suppose we can leave them here together, especially since Diana should now be able to handle whatever magical attacks Julia might possibly level upon her or Warren...or upon any other creature the foolish gel suddenly decides to hate here on the Ganlonds." He added the last phrase *sotto voce*.

"Oh, I don't know as there's anything sudden about her hatred, to be honest," Donnie replied, only half-joking. "She already pretty much hates anyone who isn't her father or her mother, or hadn't you noticed that yet?"

The cat shook his head wearily. "It would be impossible not to notice that, Donemere, although I believe we can add her lover to that short list also." He settled down more fully onto the table in a prone position, the locket around his neck clanking against the oak boards of the tabletop as he tucked his front paws underneath his chest. "Do you know the Ganlonds have been experiencing earthquakes?" he asked, gazing at her seriously.

"Yeah," Donnie nodded, adding, "I felt the one this morning. I don't think they can be natural, 'cause I guess they're happening around the same time every day. The one this morning took me off-guard, so I don't know where it originated, but I will be ready for the one tomorrow."

"There will likely not be another one now that you are aware of their existence."

"What, are you thinking the third book of our adventures will inform whoever is creating the quakes?" she asked curiously.

The cat frowned. "That is possible, of course, but only if the cause for them is indeed someone who has the third book in their possession. No, what I meant was that they are the talk of the magical lands and nearly everyone knows about them now and will be seeking to find their origin." The cat blinked at her solemnly. "They cannot continue, for they are upsetting many of the Ganlonds' residents."

Donnie thought that was possibly the understatement of the year considering how many strident voices she'd had to redirect to her gûlig when it became flooded with complaints after the quake occurred this morning. Her gûlig was quite strong and could handle several thousand messages at once, so for it to overflow back to her meant there had been a tremendous amount of terrified and angry objections sent to her all at once.

But all she said to the cat was a grave, "Agreed."

The boombox appeared on the opposite end of the table in mid-swing on the first chorus of the classic rock song, "Thirty Days in the Hole."

"Who do you believe is responsible for them and what will you do to her?" Sylvester asked, pointedly ignoring the music box as usual.

Donnie shook her head in response to his question. "Nope, I am not going down that road," she maintained staunchly, making a face at the boombox and its apparent message. "I will not speculate, and I am not going to accuse Julia either unnecessarily or prematurely. We don't know with any certainty that it's her or something she's doing."

"And yet she is the most likely candidate, as you are well aware," the cat insisted.

Donnie's shoulders drooped. "Yeah, I know that, Sylvester. But how am I ever going to explain all this to Liz? She loves her daughter, so I can't just turn my back on the girl. I don't like Julia, no, but she's not evil, or at least she never has been before coming here and meeting her father. Sure, she's selfish, rude, unthinking, self-serving—oh, the list goes on and on of her unattractive qualities and quirks. But, to my knowledge, she has never deliberately hurt anyone before. I swear, she was as shaken by what she did to Warren as the rest of us were." She was glaring at the cat by this time and he nodded his head grudgingly.

"She was, and that was plain to see," he conceded.

"I am so worried about her, Sylvester," Donnie admitted. "She is not the type to be able to control herself or her magic, which means it's probably going to take control of her. Maybe that's just what her father wanted to happen by only awakening her attack skills and leaving her other ones bound. I can't imagine being charged with such aggressive magic and *only* aggressive magic. Heavenly hags, that would turn a saint to the dark side, and Julia's no saint, so I'm sure it's completely messing up her mind, her decisions, her actions, everything!" Donnie stopped speaking abruptly and ran her fingers through her long hair, her brow furrowed and her eyes troubled. "I don't know what I can do to help her."

Donnie swallowed hard after this difficult admission. She stared at the cat, who said nothing, although he wore a sympathetic grimace.

So, Donnie added, "And that's just killin' me, because I don't want her to go bad. Nor does Liz. I can hear Liz's voice in my head, reminding me that she's just a girl, and that she doesn't truly understand the ramifications of her choices yet."

But Sylvester sat up now to firmly refute this declaration. "She is more than a girl, Donemere, so do not paint her otherwise." He paused, adding regretfully, "I suppose 'tis time for me to remind you that she must be held responsible for her actions."

Donnie blinked a few times, then stared at him in growing shock as full comprehension came to her. "What exactly are you saying, Sylvester?"

The boombox raised the volume on the song's chorus a tetch, just enough to make it intrude into Donnie's thoughts again.

"You know the answer to that," Sylvester insisted dryly. "Just as you know she must be punished for her deeds."

"B-but she *is* being punished!" Donnie protested, both to the cat and to the boombox. "I mean look, she's not allowed anywhere except her room, my workshop, and her practice area, and she has only me and Diana for some very occasional company!"

Sylvester stood suddenly, his tail swishing violently from side to side in agitation. "That is not punishment, Donemere, that is discipline!" he snapped. "Although the situation definitely calls for something more. She committed a deadly attack upon another magical being! Therefore, she must be held accountable. She is not a child to be confined to her room or sent to bed without supper; she is an adult who knew far better than to attack unprovoked someone else with her magic!"

Donnie sat back hard in her chair, unsure of just how to respond. It had honestly never occurred to her to sentence the girl to some sort of actual punishment for her attack on Warren. Donnie realized that she'd been naïvely hoping they would somehow get Liz back straight away, and she could then deal with her daughter without Donnie having to do anything at all. But, Donnie could see now that was both unrealistic and unfair.

These revelatory thoughts were unpleasantly interrupted by Sylvester continuing his chastisement of her.

"You must understand that everyone living upon the Ganlonds is aware of just what Julia did to Warren," he informed Donnie exasperatedly. "He is highly considered by all and there are many who are more than a little angry about his condition and his injuries. And they don't like that she is allowed to practice her magic unfettered by you or without sign of any sort of real confinement being placed upon her. And have you noticed how damaged her practice area has become? All sentient beings there have had to evacuate their homes, lest they be injured or killed by her savagery! Every single den, nest, and burrow in the area has been destroyed by her 'practice' and there are many who are ready to have her ousted from the Ganlonds permanently. Others wish her to be imprisoned in her room, with no access at all to the outside. And a few, those who had to evacuate their homes in haste, are calling for her to be sentenced to lessening!"

The cat was greatly upset by now, his voice rising to an almost shrieking kind of pitch. He had been pacing back and forth in front of Donnie while reciting his litany of charges against Julia and the desired retributions, but he now came to a full stop in front of Donnie and sat back down.

Noting the confusion on Donnie's face, he forced calm into his feverish voice and added, "Lessening is accomplished by taking the culprit to the glade, where the prisoner's magic is stripped from them. They are left with no memory of ever having been magical and escorted from the Ganlonds. Thereafter, they are considered acceptable prey for any magical creature with hunger. While that last consequence, naturally, would not be true with Julia, stripping her of magic entirely is not such a terrible idea, is it?"

Donnie stared at him wide-eyed for nearly a minute before she took a deep breath as she recovered from her shock. She had to admit that what he said was true and, deep down, she'd known all along that something more had to be done with Julia. She just had not wanted to face that fact, nor be the one to decide Julia's fate.

She ran her hands over her face, wishing with all her heart that Julia had never attacked Warren and forced this situation. When she finally looked at the cat again, she said quietly, "Okay, Sylvester, I understand. Give me another day or two to consider her punishment. And then I'll let you all know what I decide."

"Very good," the cat said, looking her bravely in the eye while he added a warning of, "otherwise, the council will decide and take action in your stead. And we will not ask for your consent. We cannot have such violence go unpunished, especially with the great influx of inhabitants we are facing currently. Rule of law must be maintained, even by you." He sighed, sad to see how stunned and pinched her face was. "I am sorry to be the one to inform you of this, Donemere, but it is better relayed by me than one of the other council members."

Donnie acknowledged his apology with a small nod and an unhappy expression. But she also murmured, "Yeah, I appreciate that, Sylvester. I was being stupid, I guess. But I see now that Julia's got to pay for her misdeeds, just like anyone else on the magical lands would."

The boombox seemed to agree with this pronouncement by skipping ahead to the last chorus of the song and turning up its volume.

Chapter 8
I'm Not Like Everybody Else

Julia lazed in bed, reading yet another book on magical theory from the library. She'd learned quite a bit over the last few days from the texts that Donnie had accumulated during her own studies of magic. While much of it was over Julia's head, and certainly beyond her talents, she had nothing else to do and it was something that at least kept her mind occupied.

One of the best things she'd learned from her reading was how to produce a layer of magic that blinded and deafened the house trees to whatever she did within her bedroom. It meant that here, in this room, she was safe from all prying eyes and ears, even Donnie's. She'd even learned how to extend it to the side porch so that nobody could tell if she was in the house or at her practice place at any given moment.

She glanced down at the book lying open beside her. It was the third book of Donnie's adventures and no one knew she had it except her father and Meyondrun, or Mey, as she liked to think of him. And she did like to think of him—he was dreamy, so handsome and muscular, with a body to die for. She thought he was a great lover, although she suspected that others might not because he was not all that touchy-feely, which was just fine with Julia. She was definitely not that touchy-feely herself.

She'd learned long ago that it did no good to show any kind of weakness, no matter what you might feel in your heart. Therefore, she made it a rule to never let anyone know what she felt. Well, except for her mom, and she somehow could never hide her feelings from Liz because her mom always saw right through her. And Liz was forever drawing Julia into a warm embrace to tell her that she was loved, forcing her daughter to endure that kind of closeness even though it did not come natural to Julia.

Her dad, though, was another story. Ixifír Bíun did not invite intimacy in any way, not with her, not with anyone. Meyondrun was probably the closest person to him and Mey had told her that he'd never received even so much as a real smile from Ixifír. Julia thought that an exaggeration considering that her dad seemed to smile a lot at Mey and even at herself. Of course, Julia didn't let that fool her. He was colder than anyone she'd ever known before and he wasn't afraid to show it. But he seemed to want her around, maybe even liked her, or wanted her to like him.

He had unbound her magic for her, telling her that Selma had done a poor job of binding it anyway, so he'd freed up her powers and taught her the proper exercises for practicing them. She knew that Donnie thought he'd only unbound certain magical skills on purpose, but Ixifír had assured her that he'd freed all those available and that she should just focus on feeling her full power within herself.

Next to her, the book's pages riffled as though in a light breeze. Julia knew what this meant. She swept some sheets over and found that a new chapter had been started and that it was about her and her thoughts. This she did not like at all. How did the damn thing get through her magic layer? Cripes, she'd set that up primarily because she didn't want Donnie in her head again, let alone some unknown author telling whatever about her. Her thoughts were her own and nobody had a right to know them but her. If magic wanted her to trust it, then it would leave her out of the books.

She waited for the text regarding herself to fade, to be obliterated out of sight, but after several minutes, it still stood on the page, accusingly. She swore aloud this time at it because she could not afford to have the book fall into anyone's possession but her own and she needed this new page to go away.

Julia thought a moment and figured out what she had to do. Her father had told her not to tear out any of the pages, but what could he know about it?

Her fingers lifted the offending page and, with a swift movement, ripped it out. She crumpled it into a ball in triumph and hurled it toward the corner, but it stopped in mid-air and zoomed back toward her as it flattened out. Its edges gleamed brightly for a second, then it whipped around her face, producing tiny cuts in her skin. Hastily, she raised her hands to ward off the suddenly dangerous sheaf and they were lacerated several times before the attack was over, stopping as abruptly as it had begun. She had barely had time even to cry out more than twice in pain.

Stunned, Julia shuddered in horror at her hands and forearms, little lines of cuts rising from her skin everywhere, some with enough blood to form actual droplets that began to run down her arms. She raced out of the bedroom and through Donnie's workroom to the bathroom, where she washed the cuts with water and then stared at her injured image in the mirror. She'd managed to get her arms up before too much damage was done to her face, but her hands were a mess.

With shaking limbs, she wrapped both hands in clean towels and slowly went back into her room, where she sank down onto the bed. She needed to heal these cuts, but the closest she'd be able to get to Donnie's medicinal supplies was the door of the workshop. Perhaps if she asked for them they would come to her, just like the books did from the library.

Julia calmly got up and walked back out to the workshop where she asked the house to bring her something to heal her cuts.

Sophie, the house tree she liked the least because she could hear the disdain for herself dripping in the tree's voice, responded by asking, "Just what did you do to get those injuries? We have to know so we can get you the right supplies."

Julia grimaced unhappily in the direction of the tree's voice. She made sure to keep her voice modulated and even because she didn't want the tree tattling on her to Donnie. "Um, I think I pissed off some bird or something while I was practicing with my magic, I don't know. I didn't really see it. Anyway, it gave me a bunch of cuts on my hands and arms, and a few on my face, which I'm sure you can see."

This was met by a long silence. Then, "Why would this 'bird or something' attack you like that?" questioned the same tree in a drawl. Sophie always found a way to make it evident that she liked Julia no more than Julia liked her.

Julia scoffed sneeringly. "Well, considering that every living creature in this freakin' place hates me and wants to see me dead, I don't have to do much to anyone anymore, do I? They'd all like the opportunity to attack me, which I'm pretty sure you know already."

The tree did not dispute this. Perhaps ten seconds went by before a small pile of bandages and a jar of ointment appeared on the floorboards in front of Julia. She picked them up and flounced back to her room without another word.

In her bedroom, she carefully applied the ointment to her face, neck and arms, feeling an immediate and significant reduction of pain from the stinging cuts. She hadn't even realized until now how much they were hurting her.

Once she'd covered all cuts with the salve, she wrapped first her right arm and then her left with long bandages. When she was finished, she sank back onto her pillows, a sense of relief washing over her. The magical ointment was working fast and she could feel some of the littler cuts already fading to nothing.

Julia picked up the book again and saw that the page had re-inserted itself back into place, with no sign whatsoever that it had been separated from the rest of the book, nor was there any show of her blood on its edges.

She also noted that not only had the text not disappeared, it had been expanded to more pages. She sighed, frustrated with her life. Why did everything she tried to do end up going wrong?

She missed her mom. She missed her mom a lot. Liz, at least, genuinely loved her and tried to understand her. Although, now that she had 'Jesse' she probably couldn't care less about her grown daughter. Julia felt a stab of jealousy shoot through her. That kid would have the childhood she should have had, knowing who his parents really were, even if one of them was a monster. And at least he'd be raised with their mom.

Her thoughts turned to her own childhood and the lies it was built upon. While Selma had always tried hard to love Julia, she had somehow never quite managed to do that and Julia had felt its lacking. Gary Wayne, on the other hand, had never hidden his hatred for her or any of the other Campos women. He had been a shadowy figure throughout most of Julia's young life because he'd stayed in Arizona when Selma had taken Liz and Julia to California with her. After that, Julia had seen Gary Wayne on maybe three occasions by the time she was a teenager. And that was when he started calling her, talking to her for hours and hinting at some secret that he wanted to reveal to her. She'd listened to him during these calls, growing to despise him and his denunciations of her and his constant proselytizing to her, but she'd also been fascinated by him and made curious about this secret of his.

And when she'd gone to visit him, he'd been even worse. But finally, he'd told her the truth, that he and Selma were not only not her parents, they weren't Liz's either, and that Liz was actually Julia's mother, while her father was some strange guy Liz had whored herself to on a one-night stand when she was fifteen years old. Gary Wayne had been cruel about the telling too, ridiculing Julia for believing that she might possibly be blood to him and Selma, what with her ice-blond hair and light skin. He'd laughed at her pain, and he'd made her see how her whole life was just one big lie and she was nothing but a joke between them all for believing she'd ever been wanted by anyone.

Julia turned her face to her pillow and felt the misery in her heart well up like it had so many other times in the years since that last visit with her "grandfather." Something was wrong in her, she knew this just as well as he had, and it was now driving her further and further away from the others here at the farm. Without her mother, without Liz's firm hand and loving heart, Julia felt untethered, convinced she had no place here.

Especially after her attack on that beast who'd slept once with her mom and impregnated her with his sickening child.

While a part of Julia felt contrition for what she'd done that day by attacking him so hard, she also thought too much was being made of it. It's not like she'd meant to kill him, for Fortin's sake, or even harm him as much as she had done.

She grunted with anger, remembering the exchange between Donnie and her supercilious cat that she'd read an hour or so ago, so she knew full well what they'd discussed about her. There was no way she was going to let them take her magic, and that meant it was time for her to leave this stupid place. Her father had warned her it might come to something like this. So, tonight, when Donnie and her boyfriend went to the Exos, that's when she'd do it. She'd get the Sôla that her father wanted so badly, and then open the portal to her father and Mey.

Julia reached into her pillowcase and withdrew the trengé stave her father had given her; she would need it tonight, for sure. She peered closely at the small metallic bar, feeling the strange warmth of it and marveling at the many iridescent colors contained in its depths. There were dark veins of varied colors, along with multi-colored flakes, which all seemed to sparkle and glitter as she moved the bar around in the light. The trengé was able to break through Donnie's protective shields and charms for a short while, but only from the inside of her spells. It was how the okûn king had broken out of the house the night of the big battle.

With it, Julia had been able to communicate with her father once a day, every day since Donnie had cast the blocking shield over the Ganlonds. The problem was, though, the stave created a small earthquake whenever she used it to break a hole in Donnie's shield. She gathered that was because the shield itself was so large and strong, effectively covering all of the magical lands in this area and preventing intruders from even seeing them. The trengé stave had to build up enough power to break through this wall so that Ixifír could open the portal to Julia, and the resonance waves the stave created would shoot back into the ground, creating the quakes. There was so much force in the resonance waves that Julia could see them depress the earth when they rebounded off the shield wall before breaking a hole in it that she could then keep open with her own magic, allowing her father to open a portal at her practice place and so that they could talk to each other. Unfortunately, because of these quakes, she had dared visit with her father just that one time each day at the scheduled hour.

She palmed the trengé stave now and turned over onto her back. For several minutes she stared up at the ceiling, contemplating what her life was going to be like away from this place with her father and lover. She couldn't wait for that to happen. While she knew her father wanted her to remain here as long as possible, he'd also told her that if she ever felt threatened, she was to escape as soon as she could.

She definitely felt threatened right now.

Without conscious thought, she began to finger the heavy necklace and pendant her father had also given her, calling it a panic button. He'd explained that, with a hole cut in Donnie's shields by the trengé stave, she could use it to call out to the towers they had hidden in Mount Gjendeben, and he would know within just a few minutes that he had to rescue her.

Julia savored the memory of the moment he'd spoken this promise to her because she'd liked it, and had felt a shiver run over her skin when he'd made the solemn vow to "rescue" her.

***

The *Drunken Knave* cleared the last lock of the newly built Panama Canal and headed out to the deep waters of the Pacific Ocean. Catie had had to do some fast talking and some even faster spell work to convince the authorities that the papers the ship used back in its day were good for use in 1915. It took her a while, but they'd been cleared to go through the canal at about eleven o'clock in the morning and it was now nearing sunset as the ship reached open water. Catie had explained their appearance to the canal officials as part of a celebration of tall ships that was to happen in San Francisco in just over two months' time. The men at the canal offices had stared at her blankly, clearly not caring why the crew of the *Knave* wanted to get to the western ocean.

Liz was again standing on the prow, watching for the coming sunset with anticipation. She had Jesse swaddled against her in the same shawl as she'd used earlier that morning to bind him to her. He was a quiet child and watchful of everything around him. He'd taken to staring up at his mother, his ear pressed against her heart, and would fall asleep in that position without fail. He was sleeping now, as a matter of fact. Liz glanced down at him and smiled with love. He was still too young to have any truly distinguishing features, but she thought he might have her facial structure, just like Julia did.

She heaved a sigh, worried about her young sister. Then, with an audible groan, she reminded herself that she needed to stop thinking of Julia as her sister. She could now openly claim her as a daughter and that was something she told herself she *must* do from now on. Too much damage had been done to Julia already by denying who she truly was and Liz was determined to somehow make that up to the fractious girl.

Idly, she wondered if Julia missed her and her periodic hugs, hugs that Julia always protested but never drew away from. She hoped so, because she sorely missed being able to give them to her daughter.

She looked at Jesse, love pouring from her heart to his. Fancifully, she thought that if she sent a wave of love out to her daughter, wherever, whenever Julia might be in the universe right then, she might be touched by it. Encouraged by this possibility, Liz pushed out a wave from her heart and willed it to reach Julia somehow. A moment later, and with a low chuckle, she chided herself for thinking such silly thoughts.

"That was nice of ye," a low, musical voice said, and Liz turned to find Catie standing behind her.

"What was nice of me?" Liz inquired, looking back at the other woman curiously.

Catie scoffed, stepping up so that she was standing even with Liz. "Ye might not be aware o' it, but when ye send out love ta someone, it leaves a sign. Bein' a witch o' the highest order and descended from the gods themselves, I can read that sign." She grinned at Liz with self-congratulation before asking brightly, "Missin' Warren again, are ye?"

"Always," Liz replied candidly, "although I was actually thinking of my daughter right then."

Catie's complacent expression changed to one of doubtfulness. "And ye was thinkin' lovey-dovey thoughts about 'er, were ye? Why? From what I gather, she's a singularly unlovable girl."

Liz shook her head, refuting this warmly. "No, she's not, not really," she assured Catie. "She's got enough of her father in her, I guess, to be difficult. But she's also got a lot of me in her too. And there are times when she reminds me so much of my mom that all I want to do is fold her into my embrace and hold her steady there for an hour or two!" She chuckled, remembering such times with real joy. "Not that she'd let me hug her for more than a minute or two before she'd start to protest, but I'm pretty sure she needed those long hugs just as much as I did."

"Ye're tellin' me that she is jest misunderstood, izzat right?" Clearly, the doubt was not erased from Catie's mind by Liz's convincing words.

Liz saw this and knew it was a battle not worth fighting. Instead, she asked, "Do you want me for something?"

"I do at that," Catie admitted, grinning cheerfully. "We've got ta turn this boat into something it's nowt."

"Oh, what's that?" Liz inquired, wondering what the quirky witch was intent on doing now.

"We-e-e-ell, we need ta become, er, stealth-like, ye see."

Liz's eyes narrowed. "Why?"

"We dunna want no one followin' us, o' course."

Liz shot the other woman a disbelieving glare and demanded, "And just who is going to follow us now? And why would they do that?"

"Ye never know, do ye?" Catie replied airily, waving her hands around for no apparent reason.

Deciding to forego the coming sunset because Jesse had just awoken and had become immediately fussy, Liz turned and led the way back toward her cabin, with Catie following her at a reluctant trot. Once inside, Liz lit the candles with a snap of her fingers, making Catie beamed proudly at her.

"Ye're comin' right along wi' yer magic lessons, I see," she said, her pert little face split with a big grin.

Liz ignored the compliment while she unbound Jesse and then placed him carefully on the big hammock, soothing him with soft words until he quieted and watched her silently. She turned back to Catie, clasped her hands in front of her, and declared firmly, "I want to know who could possibly be following us here in 1915 and why they would do that. And you're going to tell me the answers to those two questions without embellishing, prevaricating, or outright lying to me."

Catie, of course, chuckled merrily at this imperative. She really did like this little Native American witch who got bossy over the silliest issues. "There's no reason for ye ta know ennythin' udder than we might run inta a spot o' trouble if we dunna find a way ta make ourselves invisible or somethin' like it. Since ye've progressed so nicely with yer magic, I reckon we can do a bit more advanced spells now instead o' jest callin' up a big ol' bank o' fog. What d'ye say, are ye willin' ta try a spell like that wi' me?" The little blonde witch's blue eyes twinkled at Liz.

Liz hung her head and she exhaled heavily, her shoulders drooping in defeat. When she looked up, she gazed straight at Catie and replied, "No."

Catie's eyebrows shot upward and she faltered a bit in her humor. "Er, what d'ye mean, no?" she asked.

Liz studied her expectantly, explaining with exaggerated patience, "I mean what everyone means when they say no. In this specific case, no, I will not help you with whatever spell you want to cast on this ship."

Catie made a couple of faces that would have been funny in other circumstances, but now fell short of comical and served mostly to display how deeply shocked she was at Liz's adamantly negative response. She eyed Liz uncertainly.

Liz, disregarding Catie's consternation, added. "I will give you one caveat to that denial. If you tell me who is after us this time and why, and don't lie to me about it, I will reconsider my decision." She turned away and picked up Jesse because it was time to feed him. Calmly, and without speaking further, she sat with him in a chair, positioned them both, and gently rubbed the back of his head as he began to drink from her breast.

Catie stood contemplating her options. She looked down at her shoes, some very fine red ones that had the really pointy toes she loved so much to wear, then she glanced at Liz out of the sides of her eyes. Slyly, she protested, "Why, I'm a'takin' a dolloping umbrage ta yer attitude, Miss Priss. I canna, fer the life o' me, think why ye believe someone is after us, when I am jest bein' cautious-like and wantin' ta previde ye wi' a chance ta learn some high magic. But, if ye'd rather nowt stretch yerself ta somethin' so hard, then I s'pose the ship can muster along as it is all the way ta San Francisco City." She shuffled her feet toward the door, moving slowly, obviously waiting for Liz to relent and call her back.

This did not happen.

Catie got all the way out the door and was just about to have the latch click shut on it when she emitted a little yelp and hurried back inside the cabin. She frowned grimly at Liz, who was unbothered by any of what had just occurred and did not even look up from Jesse's sweet face.

The little blonde witch sighed as she sat down at the desk. She was beginning to think she might be slipping in her abilities to cajole and convince, and that was setting her heart to palpating a bit, because these talents had never before deserted her so thoroughly.

"All right," she admitted, "there be the possibility that someone here jest *might* show an interest in our whereabouts. And, yes, the Iceni Meræ may have alerted them ta our presence. But there's something else that might o' done that as well. See, when Nicolaus Kepler made his clock-watch, his brother, Urigen Kepler, made an orrery ta go wi' it, and the two pieces are connected 'cause that's what the brothers wanted. And they will signal each udder ever' so often when they are in the same time and such."

Liz, finally showing some interest, asked, "And the clock-watch you have in your possession has sent or received such a signal today, has it?"

Catie grinned at her in approval. "That's jest what it did!" she cried, marveling at Liz's perception. "And that means whoever has the orrery may have noticed the signal as well."

"What does this orrery do, other than tell where the planets in our solar system will be on a given day of the year?" Liz asked.

Here Catie bit her lip, obviously not wanting to answer the question too honestly.

Liz, knowing this to be the case, shot a finger at Catie and said, "Probitatis."

Stunned, Catie gaped at her and squawked indignantly, "Ye set a spell on me wi' dat, didn't ye? What be it, what spell did ye molest me wi'?"

Liz gazed back at her with an impassive expression. "Honesty," she said gravely, "it was an honesty spell. Although it's not likely to have much effect on you," she added in a low voice, "since it probably can't penetrate that thick layer of subterfuge you have around you all the time."

Catie, hearing this complaint, looked even more surprised, especially since the color had drained from her face. "Whaddye mean by that?" she demanded suspiciously.

Now it was Liz's turn to be taken aback. "Well, I didn't really mean anything by it," she retorted, looking askance at the other woman, "other than you always seem ready to lie about something as innocuous as what you had for breakfast, if you think you can get away with it. You seem to do that just for fun. But now you've got me curious about what you're *really* hiding." Liz concentrated her gaze on the other witch, wondering if there were indeed a layer of magic around her concealing something. To Liz's lasting astonishment, she caught a glimmer of a metaphysical layer of light green enshrouding Catie. Since Catie's magic always came out as gold in color, whatever spell was encasing her could not have been set by herself. "Omigod, you do have a thick layer of subterfuge around you, don't you?

And I can see that someone else cast the spell, whatever it is, because it's clearly not your own magic," she cried in amazement, leaning forward enough to disrupt Jesse. He squirmed and grunted, so Liz hastily changed breasts and set him to feeding again. When she looked up at Catie, she saw that the blonde witch was gazing at her darkly.

"Ye canna be sayin' such things as that, Miss Priss. There is nuthin' about me that ye need ta concern yerself wi', udder than helpin' me help you." Catie said this firmly, her tone brooking no argument on the matter.

Liz, after a moment's consideration, nodded, agreeing tightly, "All right. But I want you to stop lying to me about whatever it is you need me to help you do right now and all the stuff in the near future. You can lie about other things all you want, but when it comes to what we have to do to keep us all safe and get us to where we're planning to go, then you have to be open and honest with me." She stopped for a few seconds to let that sink in before adding, "After that, we'll just see what fate brings to us once Jesse and I are somewhere safe and you can part ways with us. Is that a deal?"

Catie narrowed her eyes, but she also nodded her head once.

Liz settled back a little more into her chair, relieved. "Fine," she said. "Now tell me what's so special about the orrery that Kepler's brother, Uri, Uni, whatever his name was, built."

"Well, it be one o' them cosmogony devices, don't it?"

Liz thought hard, using her linguistic skills to come up with, "That's got something to do with the origin of the universe, is that right?"

"Course it do," Catie replied with asperity, "seeing as they both be made with arccenium in their innards, or what ye might call star stuff. Ye place the clock-watch in the orrery and the dratted things'll do jest about the same thing as the amulet will."

Bewildered, Liz took a minute or two to parse through all this, finally positing, "Only they're still not as precise as the amulet, are they?"

"There ye go, ye got it in one. 'Tis 'bout time ye unnerstood somethin' I say." Catie made an unhappy face before continuing with, "Naow, iffen we had that orrery, we could pick any year in any of the original worlds ta visit, but wi'out it, we're stuck here jest travelin' through time in this one. And that means I canna get ye back to Donnie right now, nor yer babe to his da. Not wi'out that orrery. But, no matter what, I can get ye to San Francisco City and back to yer time wi' the clock-watch."

"Okay," Liz said slowly, thinking hard. "I guess that's better than nothing, because surely Donnie will travel there one day soon, right? I mean, as much as she loves her family, she's gonna want to visit them, so that means I should be able to see her and Warren and Julia before too much longer, don't you think?" she added, trying to keep her tone hopeful, although in truth her heart had sunk at Catie's confession that she could not take them back to Medregai.

It was a moment or two before Liz remembered more of what else had just been said and realization dawned upon her. "Are you telling me that Medregai is not on Earth?" she squeaked in disbelief.

Catie shrugged. "Well, not this Earth, ennyway, no. Did ye think it was?" she asked in surprise. "I mean, if ye consider it careful-like, ye'd have ta know," she added, looking at Liz doubtfully. "After all, there's no land mass here what corresponds ta Medregai, or din'ya look at a map whilst ye was there?"

Liz shook her head, blinking fast several times. "No," she choked out. "I had no reason to. I thought it was the same as England here."

"Oh, no, this Earth here is quite different from Írtha there," Catie assured her confidently, sending Liz a perky grin to bolster her spirits, presumably. "It's in another, er, whatchamacallit, a dimension, if ye know what that is? Although, it has been suggested that perhaps the planets the amulet goes ta all started out the same, ye know—as Earth, I mean, or whatever ye'd call it back then. Then they each developed however they would in their own dimension, makin' 'em all different in ever' sort o' way imaginable by the time people and such got ta walkin' on 'em."

Liz was absolutely floored by this news. While the many dimension theory had been kicked around by scientists for decades in her world, she had personally never thought it possible. "Does that mean the amulet, and the orrery too, I suppose, allow one to travel between these dimensions?" she inquired hesitantly.

"Well, sure, but the amulet can travel to udder ones too."

"Other ones? What do you mean by that?"

Catie, as she sometimes was wont to do, looked at Liz as if she were not being all that bright at the present moment. "Well, if ye reelly need me ta spell it out for ye, the original ones are what the orrery visits, aren't they?" she informed Liz in an impatient tone. "But there are plenty more than jest them what's shown on the orrery. I b'lieve they go on and on, never endin', if ye will. But I always made sure ta travel only to the first ones, 'cause I know those and know what I'll be gettin' when I visit there. And that's why I only go ta five o' them, 'cause the udders aren't always so nice ta be in, ye see."

Liz didn't know what to say to this. The concepts Catie was throwing around so blithely were too big for Liz to take in, most especially with the discovery that, not only was she being confronted with proof of the existence of different dimensions, it seemed she had been in two of them already!

Completely floundering by now, she cast around in her mind for a thread to hold onto, something to guide her out of the quagmire of scientific, spiritual, and philosophical revelations racing through her thoughts. "Ah, yeah," she muttered, her voice sounding stupidly awestruck to even her own ears. "So, um, so what is it again, ah, that you wanted us to do?" she asked, stumbling over which words to use to form her question because of the chaos occurring in her brain. "I mean, um—oh, it's a spell—yeah, yeah, that's it, you wanted to cast a spell of some sort, right?"

"O' course, I do," Catie said, rolling her eyes dramatically. "Are ye feelin' all right or are ye goin' daft, somethin' like that? Ye dunna look particularly well and yer actin' even more slow than ye usually do."

This insult worked pretty much like a good dousing of cold water or a sharp slap might have on Liz. She blinked her eyes wide, straightened in her chair, then took Jesse from her breast and put him on her shoulder to burp him, now suddenly alert and pissed off.

"Tell me about this spell you want to cast," she snapped, once she had Jesse situated comfortably.

"That's better," mumbled Catie under her breath, although Liz could hear her perfectly well. "I dunna need her takin' the dive ta deep water, do I?" She looked around the room like she was talking to someone else and blew a harried sigh.

Liz cleared her throat crossly and retorted, "Yes, yes, you've already established that you think I'm an idiot for being astounded that there are multiple universes and that we can visit at least some of them at will. But I wonder how you reacted when you were first told this same thing; hmm?" She eyed Catie knowingly and Catie suddenly looked sheepish.

"Could be I was a mite su'prised…could be at that," Catie admitted, her cheeks coloring pink. "Naow, I need ye ta get serious, Liz, 'cause we've got ta do somethin' ta hide the *Knave* from whoever has the orrery. And ye've got ta help me think o' jest what ta do!" She leaned forward imploringly, while Liz shook her head in frustration.

"Fine, I'll get serious," she bit out through clenched teeth, knowing it would do no good to argue with the stubborn little witch about just who needed to get serious. "What did you have in mind for us to do?" she repeated her question from earlier while she patted and rubbed Jesse's back, pleased when he burped a couple times.

"Well, as I said afore, we can mebbe make ourselves invisible-like, dunnya think?"

Liz, turning the problem over in her mind, looked out her windows absentmindedly and studied the tranquil marine scene set before her, still rubbing her child's back while he continued to expel gas in delicate little burps. Several steamships sailed across her view, both heading toward and away from the canal's waters, the setting sun's rays bright on their colorfully painted surfaces. With each one's appearance, an idea began to form in Liz's head and she finally turned to Catie with a pensive look on her face. "I don't think making ourselves invisible will work all that well for us; at least, not when we get closer to our destination, because we'll want to be able to dock there. Nope, I think we need to make a few modifications to the ship tonight under cover of darkness—not the least of which will be to acquire a boiler and some radio equipment."

"Acquire some what?" asked Catie, thoroughly dumbfounded. "And what was that first thing ye mentioned?"

Liz chuckled, grinning triumphantly at the little blonde witch sitting across the desk from her and Jesse. She really was amused at Catie's bewildered expression and the turning of the tables she'd just managed to pull off. Plus, she felt more in control of things than she had since Donnie had sent her through the time portal.

"It really sucks when you don't understand what the other person is talking about, doesn't it?" she asked archly, getting up with Jesse still on her shoulder. Without explaining a thing, she strode over to the window and began to study the general designs of the steamships passing within view.

***

Julia was ready. It was three o'clock in the morning, which was when the witching hour occurred and that meant Donnie and Falwaïn would be in the Exos, in the little dream world they'd been building in the "godly" dimension over the past week or so. There would be no better time for her to escape than now.

She looked around her room, making sure she'd packed everything she needed. Earlier, she'd asked her wardrobe for a duffle bag and had packed some clean clothes in it, along with some books she wanted to study later, including the third book of their adventures. While the bag was nearly full, she'd made sure to leave room for the Sôla figures that she had yet to steal.

After placing the open duffle bag on the chair next to the bedroom door, she gripped the trengé stave tightly in one hand and pulled on the latch for the outside door with the other. She stepped off the porch a moment later and was immediately transported to her practice area. Taking several deep breaths, she calmed her fast-beating heart, then looked up at the moon, which was full and shone down on the land around her, turning it silvery and haunting. The scars from her practice shots were deep and numerous all around, dotting the earth and rocks within range of where Donnie's spell dropped her each time she left the porch outside her room.

She would not be sorry to see the last of this place.

Excitement filled Julia's heart and she once again contemplated the future she'd imagined for herself and Mey with her father. She was going to learn everything Ixifir wanted to teach her and she was going to make sure she was the best partner and lover, maybe even wife, to Mey that she could be. Oh, and they'd have the child that was growing inside her even now. As a matter of fact, she had to remind herself of its existence because she kept forgetting about it.

Well, that would soon change. Her father, in his rescue of her, would have to take her through the time portal, which meant, according to what she'd read in the book when Catie had explained it to Liz, that she would be held in stasis until she was nearly ready to birth the baby. When she did finally arrive at the other end of the portal, presumably at the same time as her father, she would be heavily pregnant and ready to have the child. She had therefore dressed in her loosest clothing in preparation for the size and weight gain she would experience.

Yes, she was ready to do this. She was ready to say goodbye to her old life and embrace her new one.

So, why was she hesitating?

Julia bit her lip, knowing there was a voice inside her that was crying out that she was about to make the kind of mistake that Donnie was always warning her of, the kind that she could never recover from after she'd made it. What she was about to do would mean that she could never come back here, could never again be around Donnie or the others, and could never be with her mother either because Liz would not trust her once she knew what Julia had done to get away from this place and get to her father and Mey.

She suddenly sat down on her haunches and hung her head, almost as though in prayer. Somehow, she had to find the strength and courage within herself to cut the ties to her mom and Donnie so that she could move on to her new life with Ixifir and Meyondrun.

Lost in thought, she didn't realize how much time was passing and she would have lost her opportunity for escape entirely if not for an owl suddenly hooting somewhere nearby and another one answering the first. Brought out of her reverie by these sudden noises, Julia shuddered. Good gods, she hated this place, hated how primitive it was and how bucolic life here had to be. She wanted a modern life, one that she could really relate to, in a place where she felt like she belonged. And who knew how long it might be before she'd see her mom if she was stupid enough to stay here. It could be months or years, maybe even never. Was she supposed to stay here all that time, locked in her room at the cottage?

It was that distasteful thought more than anything else that decided her. She'd always hated confines and she'd had enough of them put on her lately. No, she had to go where she'd be free.

Steeling her reserve again, Julia stood tall and held the trengé stave up to the sky, making a circle with it. She quickly dropped it to the ground because when the resonance waves created from it bouncing off Donnie's shield rebounded to the stave they would be far too large for her to handle, something she'd learned the first time she'd used it. It took several seconds before the ground shook and, when it did, she crossed her arms, with her hands on the opposite shoulders, focused on the necklace her father had given her, and sent an urgent call out to him that she needed to be rescued right now and that she would be coming with the Sôla. Then she took a step backward so that she was again on the porch outside her room.

Julia ran to her bedroom door and yanked it open. Summoning all the magical power she could muster, she stood in the center of the workshop and stared at the wall facing her. Lifting her arms, she took aim and shot a dark green bolt of magic at the wooden boards. They broke apart and shattered, pieces flying everywhere as though they'd been hit with a bomb.

Julia eyed her handiwork with satisfaction, for the wall was completely destroyed. She slipped through the large hole she'd made in it and turned to the cupboard housing the Sôla, reaching for its doors. When she opened them, something flew at her and sank into the flesh of her left shoulder.

She sucked in her breath so that she wouldn't scream and grabbed the two statuettes she had come for from their shelf, determined to succeed where the okûn king had failed. Racing back to her bedroom, she dropped the Sôla into the waiting bag, slung its strap onto her right shoulder, and headed toward the outside door. Behind her, she heard the others gathering in the library to see what had happened. She didn't hear Donnie's voice, which gave her hope that she might make it to the portal in time.

She got to the porch and stepped off it, finally letting out a small cry of pain. Her feet hit the soft ground of her practice place and she looked to the spot where her father always opened the portal. It was empty, nothing there at all. She screamed now, screamed his and Mey's names, fearing they would abandon her and leave her to face the wrath of those she wanted to leave behind. Her fear burgeoned so fast that it overwhelmed her, and she found herself stamping around on the ground, crying and cursing for what seemed like several minutes, but was probably only a few seconds.

At precisely the same moment, two things happened. Donnie, Falwaïn, Rex, Sylvester, Diana, and Diego appeared behind her, while before her, the time portal was opened.

And then the boombox materialized on one of the nearby rocks, softly playing the classic, "I'm Not Like Everybody Else."

Donnie glanced at it forlornly before calling out to the young girl, pleading with her, "Julia, no, don't go! We'll find your mom soon, I promise, and we'll make this all okay somehow! I promise we can do that. Please, just trust me, Julia, please!"

Julia turned to her and saw the genuine concern on Donnie's face, and was shocked to see that same concern echoed on each of the others' faces too. She would have bet they thought of her with only hatred. Distracted by these thoughts, she looked back at the portal, waiting for her father or Mey to come, but they weren't there yet.

Rex said something about the knife and Julia felt it being pulled from her body, which she would have thought would be agony, but wasn't. Then she felt a sort of euphoria overtake her and realized that Donnie was healing her. She looked down at her shoulder and watched with a twinge of jealousy as the wound closed, leaving only a thin line to mark its place.

She then heard Diana remark, "Look, she's got the Sôla, you can see one of them sticking out of the bag. We can't let her take them, can we?"

Donnie shook her head and said, "I couldn't care less about them right now, it's Julia I'm worried about. Julia, I know you can hear us, so please listen to me. Whatever you think is going to happen here with us, is not true. Sylvester and I can work with you, and so can Diana, to transform your powers so they're more balanced. And we'll come up with something reasonable for you to do as recompense for your attack on Warren. Look, he doesn't want me to punish you at all, he said so this evening," she added desperately, seeing that her pleas were having no effect on the girl and that Julia kept turning toward the portal, apparently waiting for something to happen. Then it occurred to Donnie that Julia was waiting for someone to come through it.

Donnie regrouped her thoughts and pointed out in a calm, firm voice, "Julia, your father's not coming here tonight, that much he's already made clear, because otherwise he'd be here by now. Nor, apparently, is your lover. But *we're* here and we're all hoping you'll stay with us. We can help you, and I promise we'll find your mom as soon as we can. I'm hoping to be able to do that as soon as I figure out how to work the amulet, which, believe me, is going to be really soon! I'm almost there now, so just give me a few more days, okay? Then we can all work this out for the best and you can return to leading a positive life with your mom wherever you want to live, and we can all help you become the best version of yourself. You'll see, we'll all help you with that, I promise."

Each of the others with Donnie raised their voices in the same vow, calling out to Julia as if they were making a solemn pact with her.

She shook her head, trying to clear it of the renewed doubt filling it. No, she'd made her decision, more than once now, and she had to stick to it, didn't she? If she didn't, what would that say about her as an adult? She couldn't just keep relying on others to make things okay for her, she had to begin acting like an adult and working like one. Her father had said this to her earlier that week, when he thought she might have been slacking off on practicing with her magic, even though she'd assured him she had been working hard every day. But she'd seen by his expression that he hadn't believed her and that had spurred her to try even harder. She realized now that if he hadn't pushed her like that, she might not have been strong enough to break the wall tonight so she could get into the library.

Julia stood still and nodded to herself. She raised her gaze to the others and said quietly, "Donnie, look, I'm not like you or anybody else here. And you were right, I'm no saint, so quit trying so hard with me. I need to be pushed to get better, not bribed, like what you're trying now. Which is what Mom and Selma did all my life."

Startled by Julia's comment about not being a saint, Donnie studied her for a few moments, but found no artifice in either the girl's manner or expression. "Julia, like it or not, you're my responsibility," she said with a sigh, "so I am going to try as hard as I can with you. I am never going to give up on you, so you might as well just accept that now. I will always be around to help you and to hope for better for you. Always. No matter what happens."

"Well, that's pretty stupid of you," Julia noted stubbornly. "Because I'm gonna go live with my father now, and he is even more powerful than you, Donnie. I'm going to learn about magic from the best sorcerer that's ever lived and then I'm going to choose who I become and how I use my magic. And nobody but me will have any say over that. I am finally growing up and I am going to take responsibility for myself, so you don't have to feel at all like you need to do anything for me anymore. Nor does my mom."

She turned to go, taking a couple steps toward the portal, and then she stopped, looking back at Donnie. "Thanks for healing the wound from the knife. I hadn't expected you to have a trap set for me, so I wasn't ready for it when I opened the cupboard."

Donnie sent her an appraising look and nodded. "Yes, well, I figured that your father was after the Sôla, and he'd naturally use you to get them since his first try was thwarted by the house trees and Diana. I'd hoped I was wrong about you deciding to help him, but I made sure to modify the spell on the knife so it wouldn't go for my neck, but rather your shoulder in case you did open the doors to the cupboard."

Julia shrugged. "The scar will remind me of how powerful I am right now and how much I have to strive for yet. You'll see, I'll become more skilled than you one day—maybe even more than my dad, who knows? And then I'll really show you all what I can do."

As Julia moved closer to the portal so that she was nearly close enough to step into it, the zipper on her bag opened further and the books inside suddenly shot upward and flew back toward the cottage, apparently heeding the library's recall charm. In the process of their return home, they also dislodged the third book about their adventures, and it fell to the ground at her feet.

Julia reached down to pick it up, but it was no longer there. When she straightened, she looked up into Donnie's face, which was only inches away from hers now.

"Thanks," Donnie said politely. "I was wondering who had this. If you don't mind, I think I'll keep it for now."

Julia gave a jerky nod, fear rising inside her like a monster, making her heart pound in her ears. How had Donnie reached her so quickly, she wondered, waiting for the older woman to take hold of her arm or do something else to prevent her from leaving. She suddenly worried that Donnie would grab the duffle bag from her to get at the Sôla, and so she tightened her hold on it.

Donnie smiled faintly when she noticed this. "No problem," she said in a voice that was just above a whisper, "you can take them with you. They're more yours than mine, anyway. Besides, I have a feeling they'll keep you safe, or more precisely, they'll make your father happy and that should keep you safe for a little while at least."

Julia stepped away from Donnie in confusion. She thought hard for a moment, then tightened her lips resolutely and gave Donnie a farewell nod.

Donnie returned the gesture with a sad smile and reiterated what she'd said earlier to the girl just as Julia was readying herself to step into the time portal.

"I will always be around to help you, Julia," she reminded the girl with quiet passion, "no matter what happens. I want you to remember that. You can call on me anytime and I will be there as soon as I possibly can get to you. I promise you that."

Chapter 9
The Heart of the Matter

"You shouldn't have let her leave!" Warren repeated gruffly for what seemed to Donnie the hundredth time in the last half-hour. Because of the sleeping spell she had cast on him after the last time she had checked his injuries last night, he had slept through the incident with Julia and was angered when told this morning of her unforeseen departure.

"She's just a young girl," he reminded Donnie severely, "and now she's out there on her own, with no one to take care of her. She's going to get into trouble and that will be your fault!"

Donnie raised a challenging eyebrow at this unfair claim. He'd been berating her—albeit mildly because of the great pain he was still in—since she'd woken him and she had let him go on so he could get it out of his system, but she was done with that now.

"As was pointed out to me yesterday, Warren," Donnie began briskly, rising from where she'd been seated while she'd done more healing on his ribs before waking him, "Julia is a grown woman, not some errant child, and she must be held accountable for her deeds and misdeeds. As far as I can tell, she read the conversation in this dratted book between myself and Sylvester regarding what her punishment should be for her attack on you and she consequently decided it was time for her to leave." Donnie waved the third book of their adventures in her hand so that he could see it, noting how his eyes lit with interest. "There was no talking her out of it, that was plain to see by the time she headed for the time portal. And may I impress upon you how that was entirely her choice to make, not mine. While I know that you and Liz may not be thrilled about the situation, you both must understand that Julia is old enough to make her own decisions. And she will have to pay the consequences for her actions, whatever they may be, just like the rest of us do for ours. Which means her actions are neither my fault nor yours, so quit blaming me and yourself for them."

He gave a start of surprise at this small dig and blinked guiltily at her several times.

She placed the book on the bedside table. "I am going to leave this here with you for now so you can read about Liz and your child, which I think will set your mind at ease some. But I will want it back later. I'm not sure what I'm going to do with it after that, but I will certainly try my best to not become obsessed with it like Valley Guy and Julia did so that I don't end up relying on it to make my decisions. That would be quite, quite silly of me, don't you think? Therefore, I may end up chucking the thing in the fire later today, who knows?"

With that threat, the book seemed to shake and quiver a little. Donnie noticed this and groaned inwardly because she knew that meant the thing really was cursed in some way, as she'd suspected it was when she'd read of its reaction to Julia tearing out one of its pages. She'd have to discuss potential dispensation options for it with Sylvester later, she supposed. But for now it could serve the good and kindly purpose of letting Warren read about his newborn son, Jesse, and the adventures being experienced by Liz and Catie.

Donnie had read avidly through some of the book's chapters in order to glean all she could about her absent friend, as had Falwaïn and Rex, who had visited the Exos with Donnie after Julia left through the portal to join her father. They had delayed their trip to the Exos that night because, when they climbed into bed, Donnie had had a strong sense that something momentous was about to happen. Because of this feeling of something big impending, she had been close behind Julia the entire time the young girl had gone about enacting her father's commands to steal the Sôla from their cupboard. But she had neither done nor said anything to reveal herself until the others gathered in Julia's room and, as a group, they then followed the girl to her practice place.

She supposed a part of her had known for days that Julia would end up leaving the magical lands and would do so in a manner of her father's devising. Honestly, the more Donnie learned about him, the more her concern for Julia grew. She could only hope the girl would survive him long enough to see that her place was here and she'd therefore want to come back to the cottage, preferably with an adjusted attitude toward Warren and the magical creatures of the Ganlonds. Donnie was determined that, at a moment's notice, she would be ready to extricate Julia from whatever Ixifîr Bîun of the dreaded Dræda line of sorcerers had planned for the girl. She felt she owed that to Liz and to Julia as well.

Donnie left Warren and decided to go in search of Falwaïn, who had been behaving mysteriously for a while now, disappearing with Diego and Akanna for hours at a time each day. She had difficulty believing they were practicing with their swords and whatever other weapons they kept stored in Catie's workshop during these frequent absences, but was ready to have her mind changed on that, if that was indeed what they were doing.

Sylvester and Rex were waiting for her in the kitchen so they could go together to the next council meeting, which was a little less than two hours from now. Her dog and cat were sniping at each other because Rex had expressed a desire to play with his skunk buddies to pass the time until the meeting, but Sylvester was intent on lecturing him *ad nauseum* about his responsibilities, knowing full well that the dog would not remember to attend the meeting once he started playing with his friends.

"Well, if you're gonna preach to me about responsibilities," Rex huffed, annoyed by the cat's unrelenting superiority, "don't ya think it's time you told Mama what happened to her first saddle?"

Donnie, made curious by the sudden suggestion, looked calmly from Rex to Sylvester and murmured, "Hmm, yes, I wonder what did happen to my saddle. Do you know something about it that maybe I should be told?" The saddle in question had been the first one she'd sewn together, which had been inexplicably shredded this past winter. Nobody had owned up to its total annihilation thus far, although this was not the first time Rex had alluded to Sylvester's involvement in the poor saddle's demise.

Sylvester looked mighty uncomfortable for several moments, then gave Donnie a winning, toothsome smile. "Of course you'd want to know about that," he muttered under his breath, sending a sideways scowl towards Rex for bringing up the subject. "Well, it was just one of those days this past winter," he began affably, as though relating something of no consequence whatsoever, "you know, where it seemed nothing could go right. We had been for our walk in the Ternate Tunnel and you had all gone back into the house already, while I thought I had seen something near the barn, an owl, to be precise, and wondered how it came to be there." The cat cleared his throat, thought for a moment, then said in a bit of a rush, "So, I went to the barn, got startled by something that turned out to be Rex the Wonder dog here, and I then cut a few, unfortunate rents in the cloth of your saddle with my claws before I went back to the house. That was all that happened, nothing more, and-and…well, it was certainly nothing all that terrible, just a silly little misunderstanding."

He smirked at Rex defiantly, daring the dog to refute this story.

Which the dog did happily.

"Oh, he's just bein' modest, Mama," Rex explained in an earnest voice. "You saw the saddle, he really ripped it right apart—pretty much shredded it to ribbons, didn't he? Yeah, it happened on the first day when he and I both felt like something was following us throughout the tunnel when we were playing in it. You remember that day, right? You and Otis got upset with us 'cause Sylvester and I kept running back past you guys, screeching our lungs out, and you finally yelled at us to stop doin' that, sayin' we were behavin' like a couple of baby ninnies, and I said I was fine with that, just don't leave me alone again, then Sylvester said he was not a baby nuthin' and he wasn't scared, that I had surprised him and he reacted that way whenever he was surprised by anyone, but he said that last part just because he'd done his Nosferatu walk that you and Otis think is so funny. You know which walk I mean, right, Mama?" The dog, having run on and on throughout all this, paused now to take a big breath and added, "I think it was the first time he did that one in front of you guys. Anyway, it was *that* day; 'member?"

Donnie, shaking with suppressed giggles, nearly choked out her reply. "Oh, yes, I remember that day well, honey," she said, her eyes merry. "And I seem to recall that we had a blizzard right after that and none of us could go out much for the next week; isn't that right? Which is why I had no idea anything had happened to my saddle for quite some time."

"Yep, that's it, that's the day," the dog confirmed, nodding vigorously. He glanced over at the cat, who was now openly glaring at him, before he leaned toward his mama conspiratorially and went on in a low voice full of relished remembrance. "Well, we still don't know *what* was following us around the Ternate Tunnel that day, but something sure was, and it was no owl. When we got back to the house, we both thought it went to the barn, but I had more sense than to follow it there, unlike some who shall remain nameless."

He shot the cat a meaningful look, which had Sylvester spluttering in outrage, and then the dog turned back to Donnie. "So, *Sylvester* went to investigate 'cause I don't think he realized yet that it wasn't an owl out there," the dog continued, making it obvious that he had thought the cat's actions unwise indeed. "I couldn't leave him alone with it, though, could I? That meant I had to go back outside and, when I ran into the barn, I heard Sylvester snarlin' at it all low and mean-like, you know? But when I got in there, all I could see was its eyes, and they were glowing bright yellow over in the corner. Unfortunately, when I moved closer to Sylvester and told him to watch out for the monster, I knocked your saddle off the railing and it fell right on top of him, and, boy oh boy, did he ever have a screamin' match with that thing then! You shoulda heard it, Mama, there was so much screechin' and shriekin' goin' on under that thing, I wasn't sure it was ever gonna end! And you know what? It made me think that whatever had been chasing us had enchanted the saddle, made it wrap itself around Sylvester or something like that, 'cause he got all caught up in it and was rollin' around on the ground with it like it was a big ol' straitjacket or somethin', and then, all of a sudden, it was split in two—or, well, I guess it was three pieces; wasn't it? And then he got free from it and he disappeared like a shot back to the house. It was just amazin' to watch him erupt from it like that and then bolt like a bullet outta you know where! Man-oh-man, that was somethin' excitin' to see!" the dog recounted with wonder, shaking his head slowly from side to side. And then he grimaced ruefully, admitting, "But right after that the sun went behind a cloud 'cause the blizzard was comin' in, and I realized that what we'd thought were glowing eyes was really just the sun glinting off the bottom of the metal bowl that you kept out there to soak the linen for the saddle—you know, to make it all nice and white before you sewed it together? And that's all it was in that corner, was that bowl." The dog snapped at a fly buzzing near his snout and then he looked wide-eyed at his mama, for all the world a completely innocent pup. "Funny, huh, how the simplest things can trick your eyes like that, innit?" he added, somehow managing to maintain a straight face.

The cat, by this point, had turned around and was stalking out the front door, his long tail held high and stiff, his back arched and haughty. Donnie was not doing as well as the dog at suppressing her laughter, although she watched the cat go without breaking down completely, with just a couple snorts escaping her, but the moment he was out of sight, she howled with glee. It took a good three minutes before she was able to talk again and when she did, all she could manage to eke out was, "Thanks for clearin' that up, honey. Why don't you go outside now and play? I think it's gonna be just fine for you to miss the meeting today."

She made herself a travel cup of iced tea and carried it outside with her to the well, where Sylvester was sitting with his back to the house.

Donnie hauled herself up onto the well beside him and, admiring the view of the valley this afforded her, said, "I sent Rex off to play for the day. He needs that sometimes, you know, even though he has willingly taken on more duties and responsibilities now, what with being made an honorary member of the Animal Council—I know, it's not supposed to be just an honorary position, but it really kind of is, nevertheless. I mean, he's only got us here at the farm to represent, which is what you and I do anyway, so I think we can cut him slack occasionally about missing a few meetings here and there. Heavens knows we've had enough of 'em lately. I'm pretty sure there've been at least a score of 'em this week," she joked.

The cat sighed, tightened his lips, then hung his head. "I am sorry about your saddle," he said soberly. "I should have told you the truth of my part in its destruction long ago," he admitted, his forlorn voice barely above a low croak. "That was wrong of me."

Donnie put a finger under his chin and raised his face up so she could look him in the eye. "My friend, we all do stupid things like that, things that embarrass the hell out of us and that we're glad not everybody knows about. Your biggest mistake in this, as far as I can see, is goading Rex today into setting you up so perfectly."

The cat gulped audibly as his eyes flew wide. He stared up at Donnie disbelievingly.

"You've really gotta stop thinking he's all innocent and naïve and has no idea what he's doing," chuckled Donnie. "I'll grant you, he is my heart, my sweet, sweet boy, but he has a purely mischievous streak in him that's ten miles wide without anyone doing something to annoy him. So, imagine what he's like when somebody deliberately annoys him; say, like you were doing by not letting him play hooky today. You must understand the needs of your team, my friend, and sometimes you even have to cater to them."

The cat nodded in acknowledgement of this and said with feeling, "I will remember that in the future." Then he sighed again.

Donnie chuckled at him before slapping her hands on her knees. "Well, now that that's out of the way, I'm gonna go saddle Wiwila up so we can leave early for the meeting. I intend to find out what the others are up to. See, I can feel that Falwaïn is somewhere near the glade, and I thought I'd go find him. He, Akanna and Diego keep disappearing without explanation and that's made me very, very curious," she confessed, looking at the cat questioningly.

He shook his head and said, "I have no more idea than you what they are doing, but I am willing to travel with you when you are ready."

Five minutes later, they were on their way to the Gahal Glæd upon Wiwila. Wiwila knew the path so well to the glade by now that she was able to maintain a steady trot through the forest, which allowed them to reach their destination with plenty of time to spare before the meeting.

Donnie had asked Wiwila to go to Falwaïn and was surprised when the horse took them straight to the glade. Donnie dismounted and scooped Sylvester up onto her right shoulder, then led Wiwila by the reins to the glade's entrance, where the three of them halted, a surprising sight having stayed their movements.

For some time, no one noticed their presence. They stood quietly watching as Falwaïn, somehow having found a very large whiteboard and markers, was confidently teaching several young magical animals basic math fundamentals. These young creatures were sitting at long desktops that had low benches attached to them. Several math textbooks were opened all along the desks so that the students could follow along with their instructor. Diego was off to the left, where he had a small group of youngsters gathered round his whiteboard at similar desks, and they were apparently learning conversational Spanish; while Akanna was to the right and was teaching her small group defense techniques that were unique to each creature's physiology.

It was not until the alarm sounded on the watch Donnie had given to Falwaïn, which had been her grandfather's, that anyone even knew she was there. Once a couple of the students turned and cried out to her, the rest all came flooding toward her eagerly. Donnie had the presence of mind to take Sylvester off her shoulder and let him leap to the ground before any of the young animals reached her. She then caressed and cooed praise at those who vied for her attention and crowded closest to her, smiled with real pleasure at the rest, and enthusiastically complimented them all on applying themselves so assiduously to their lessons. They loved this and several of the younger ones began to spell "assiduously" out loud so that they had Donnie beaming at them with pride.

Falwaïn clapped his hands a few times to break this up and chivvied the students along, reminding them that afternoon classes would be held at the giant's cave at Mount Treyfal and they would all be expected to be there on time, even though it was a long distance away. They were going to spend the afternoon exploring the cave and finding out what wonders it held.

Unable to disguise her pleasure in him and the others, Donnie grinned widely as the last of the young animals departed, making sure to include Diego and Akanna in her overt show of approval of their actions.

Falwaïn strode up to her and put his arms 'round her waist, locking his hands together on the small of her back. He gazed down at her and grinned back. "You're early," he noted.

She nodded primly and replied, "Yes, and I'm being nosy. I was wondering where you three kept wandering off to without me, and now I know not only that, but also just how incredibly wonderful you all are. I can't believe you're teaching these kids like this!"

"Well," Falwaïn said, still grinning at her, "I figured you were unlikely to have time to do it any longer, and I felt that someone else should. Since we three were all pretty much at loose ends anyway, we decided to make ourselves useful. We started classes the day after the king and his army left, when you had another meeting with the Animal Council. We intended to hold the classes at the farm, but so many youngsters showed up that afternoon after I'd mentioned the idea to the deer twins, we knew immediately that we needed a larger space. Since the glade is one of the most magical places here on the Ganlonds, I wondered if it could help us out with supplies. When we came here, we asked the glade to provide what we needed and suddenly the whiteboards and desks and textbooks and all the other supplies appeared. We started teaching that very afternoon."

Diego moved to within a few feet of where Donnie and Falwaïn stood and cheerfully informed Donnie, "Most of the students can count to ten thousand in English, Spanish and Vincan already and they all know the alphabets and how to read and write their letters. Some students are even learning simple verb conjugations in Spanish. They are good pupils, quick to learn, and attentive."

"And we've made sure to make the afternoon lessons some sort of exploratory adventure," added Akanna. "That way the classes stay fun, but informative, and the children continue to enjoy them."

Donnie shook her head and marveled at her friends, with love swelling up in her heart for her man, in particular.

He somehow knew this and leaned forward to kiss her lightly on the bridge of her nose. "You can be nosy anytime you want with me," he murmured facetiously, letting his lips hover over hers a moment before claiming them for several seconds in a long, sweet kiss. When he pulled back away from her, he made a fuss of straightening her hair and her jacket before saluting her smartly and saying, "We must be off now, dearest, as we have a long trek ahead of us and we still have to swing by the cottage to get lunch and check to see just how bored Warren is today."

"Oh, I don't think he'll be too awfully bored," Donnie said, her mind on the book she was sure Warren must be devouring by now. She knew how worried he'd been about Liz and his child. And while Liz and Catie, and little Jesse too, were having quite the time, Donnie felt better about them now that she knew they were still together and moving toward a goal that should bring them a few steps closer to being in a place and time that Donnie and the others could more easily meet up with them. She hadn't had any real trust in Catie until she'd read the parts of the book regaling Catie and Liz's adventures, but now Donnie was fairly confident the little blonde witch was taking reasonably good care of Liz and Jesse, so she had no complaints to make there. And if they could make it to San Francisco in 2024, Liz would have Donnie's family to help her as well. Then Donnie might finally feel like she had perhaps done the right thing by sending Liz through the time portal to Catie to protect her from that dreadful old Ixy dude and his murderous intentions.

***

The *Drunken Knave* sailed about a mile or so behind a half dozen other steamships, with another three or four not far behind the *Knave*. During the night, Liz and Catie had worked their magic on converting the sailship to a combination steam- and sailship, materializing all the equipment and cladding they needed from other ships in dry dock at the Panama Canal or from those heading into the canal for crossing to the Atlantic Ocean. These ships were robbed with much regret on the part of the women, as it would surely make for an unsolvable mystery that would have to be investigated, and there was worry that someone on one of the boats or who worked at the canal might get blamed for the thefts. The two witches tried to make sure that they took only what was necessary and only in situations that would remain safe without the pilfered item. Nonetheless, all the ships in the vicinity were radioed urgently in the wee hours of the early morning to be on the lookout for the thieves and told that the authorities were hot on the trail of the craven criminals. Since this was patently untrue, nobody aboard the *Knave* worried all that much about it, but it did make them feel a little unsettled.

The good part of the arrangement, though, was that they blended in perfectly with the other ships in the waters around them now, and no one could possibly suspect their ship to be the sailship that had disappeared overnight.

The new name that appeared on their temporary hull was *Archimedes*, which was painted on one of the stolen panels. Liz updated their official papers with careful forgeries reflecting this new moniker and the crew was doing its best to familiarize themselves with the workings of a steam engine. It was good that both Catie and Liz were talented witches, seeing as they'd already had to thwart a couple of potential boiler explosions. As the day wore on, though, the crew felt more secure in what they were doing and the ship chugged along at a nice little rate of speed.

Liz was in her cabin with sweet little Jesse, while Catie was below keeping an eye on the boiler and those tending it when hue and cry were suddenly bellowed across the ship. Liz could tell it had nothing to do with the boiler, but she was in the midst of giving Jesse a bath and she could not leave him alone to find out what the source of the alarm was. She had just finished replacing the long dress she used to clothe him in when her door was pounded upon heavily. Hurrying across the room, she opened the door to find the captain standing there, looking quite agitated.

"Ye've got ta come 'ere," he ordered, pointing a dirty finger at her. He still wore his pirate clothes, which were a mishmash of breeches, filthy blouse and long coat, along with high, leather boots, all of which were of different colors and fabrics. His hair, as usual, was tied back in a queue, and looked to be dark brown in color, but that could be because he had likely not washed it in some time, or so Liz imagined.

She nodded, but held up her own finger and scurried back to pick up Jesse and swathe him in the shawl she used just for him.

The captain waited for her impatiently to shut her door, then she had to practically run to keep up with him as he strode toward the prow, where a small crowd was assembling. The crew there were mumbling and pointing at something in the distance. Catie was standing there too, and she turned as Neddy Cloys and Liz joined her.

"What in Fortin's ghost is that bloody thing?" Neddy pointed as he barked the question at Liz, jabbing a finger toward the horizon, where a big metallic balloon floated in the sky.

A sense of dread stole over Liz and she cleared her throat uneasily. "Well, that is what's called a dirigible," she explained. "It's an airship that usually has the balloon part, which is what you see now, and that's filled with hydrogen, I think. I just know it's highly flammable, so I'm pretty sure it uses hydrogen. And it has what's called a gondola slung underneath it and that's where its crew pilots the ship. There are cabins above, in the balloon itself, where the crew and any passengers sleep. These ships can cross really long distances, oceans even, so there's no telling where that one came from. It could be from anywhere in the world, is what I mean." She bit her lip nervously. "Do you think it has something to do with us?" she asked Catie in a low voice, hoping not to be overheard.

Catie shrugged, staring at the dirigible in the distance. "Who can tell? But I certainly dunna think we wimmen should be atop the ship when that thing comes near." She turned to look at Liz and said bluntly, "When it does, we'll see how well this costume o' yers is gonna work, won't we?" She pointed to the metal cladding they'd attached to the *Knave* to disguise it.

And so, a tense period of several hours ensued. The flying ship appeared to be taking its time, floating for long stretches above the ships in front of the *Knave*, inspecting them individually. Liz suspected that the dirigible would employ a high-powerful telescope, and therefore made sure that both she and Liz were below decks well before the airship got anywhere near their little steamship. She also made sure to scratch out the name painted on the boat's hull, just in case.

Much of the day was gone before the skies were clear again and the women were allowed back on deck. Liz set off immediately on a lengthy promenade to stretch her legs, planning to retire afterward to her cabin. She hoped that would be all they would see of the dirigible for the night. But it was not, for the airship returned no more than an hour later, forcing Liz to again hide. By now it was quite dark, so she'd had to be led by one of the crew members to the hold. The captain feared that the airship might be able to see into the windows of her cabin, so he'd decreed that she, Jesse and Catie must be hidden below decks.

In the morning, the airship remained high in the sky, following the little flotilla of ships sailing below it. All of these ships appeared to be going in the same direction: northwest.

During that morning, the two women would take a stroll around the top deck only whenever the airship was far enough away for them to feel comfortable being in the fresh air. Around lunchtime, Catie dressed herself in some clothes of Neddy Cloys and she remained above decks from then on, but there was no way Liz could pass for a man with Jesse swaddled to either her front or back. No, a child would not go unnoticed and therefore might cause the dirigible to forget following anyone else.

While no one knew who exactly was on that flying ship, there was no longer any doubt in anyone's mind about what its crew were after. All they could do was wait, hiding Liz and Jesse throughout most of the coming days, allowing them only a quick walk on the deck once night fell.

***

Donnie woke up with her head resting on Falwaïn's gently rising and falling chest, which was moving in a slow rhythm that meant he was still deeply asleep. She kissed him awake until he laughed at her to stop. Then they stretched together before wrapping their bodies around each other again, both sighing contentedly as they settled into position. They would have fallen back to sleep if Falwaïn had not remembered that they needed an early start that morning. He put her from him and sat up, shaking her until she got up and sat next to him.

Yawning, she ran her fingers through her sleep-tousled hair and asked why he had roused them so early.

"We need to explore Flat-Finger's cave, my beloved, my darling honey woman," he reminded her. "We have yet to discover what frightened those kids yesterday afternoon."

They both had gotten used to spending time in the Exos and then having to recall their places once they came back to the real world, so she was not surprised that he would recall the excursion to the cave first thing upon waking. And too, when they'd gone to the Exos earlier that morning, they had stayed for just a couple days because Donnie was concerned about the twins. She knew she had to make the trip to the Mîrlonds soon and she didn't want to be too big to travel comfortably or, worse yet, have to lug two newborns with her if she spent so much time in the Exos that she made it to the twins' due date. Nor did she want to be parted from them by having to leave them here if she birthed them before going, so she had discussed it with Falwaïn, and together they had decided to shorten their stays in the Exos, if not perhaps even eliminate them for a while. That way the twins would be born later, not until Donnie and the others had returned from the Mîrlonds.

Donnie, after reading what had been written in the third book of their adventures regarding what the time portal would do to her if she were still pregnant when she went through it, was determined to birth the kids here at the farm in Medregai at a time when she chose, vowing not to leave that important date to some magical portal to decide.

Unfortunately, she still did not know how to use the amulet to open a portal to anywhere. She was, at least, getting closer to finding the clue she needed to work it, she was sure of that. Every day, she was applying herself for a minimum of two hours to the newly found journals that Catie had filled with her haphazard and often bizarre thoughts, and Donnie felt she was definitely making headway in her search. There was so much in these old books though, that she'd had to set a charm to help her find only the parts that mentioned anything to do with the time portal or the amulet, otherwise, she'd only have been able to check a couple of the journals thus far. As it was, she was now nearly a third of the way through the more than three hundred journals that Catie had written unfailingly in lemon juice.

Discarding these thoughts, Donnie rose to her feet and followed the naked Falwaïn into the shower. Half an hour later they ambled into the kitchen together, where Rex and Sylvester were awaiting them. Before too much longer, nearly everyone else was at the table, in various stages of breakfasting. Donnie visited Warren in his room, did a half hour of healing on his ribs, happy that she was finding fewer and fewer breaks to fix each day, then lifted her sleeping spell and informed him of their plans for the morn. While she was talking to him, the kitchen sent a plate of food and full coffee cup zooming in to hover in front of him. Donnie told him the guys would help him to the bathroom in a few minutes and she left him nodding and chewing.

Half an hour later, they were ready to go. Rex had decided to stay home with Warren because he and Carly, the youngest of the house trees, were in the midst of their latest word game and Warren had offered to be their referee for scoring points whenever there was a dispute. Diana had also decided to remain at the farm, saying that she would keep Warren company while the game was being played.

Donnie and the others made it to the Branmar Plain while there were still a few tendrils of morning fog hanging about the lower reaches of the Brumal Mountains. The mountains soared above the land, majestic and rugged, as though standing guard over the plain.

They began to pass by the Forest of the Unwilling that was created at the end of the Battle of the Branmar Plain by the *Niunda Wakan*. Slowing their horses to a walk, they could clearly hear the menacing shaking of the new forest's leaves and branches, its thousands of transmuted saplings trembling at the travelers' presence.

A few older trees stood nearby, these being of natural origin. They had moved closer to the newly born, angry forest the morning after the *byrgen* for the dead to help contain the inherent malevolence of the transformed okûns and their evil army mates. Donnie noticed that these trees had since backed away quite a distance from the young forest.

That was moment when her gûlig relayed several jumbled prayers that were being sent to her, prayers that were regarding something that was happening within the new forest. Made very curious now, Donnie turned Wiwila to the direction of the nearest tree and asked with concern, when she neared it, "Janke, is there something wrong? Why have you and the others retreated so far from the new trees? Have they been attacking you, something like that?"

The tree took its time in responding, but assured her, "No, it is not us who have been attacked. Many of the young saplings have learned to walk already and have attempted to escape our conclave. Consequently, we have backed away to give ourselves time to catch them before they make it too far or before they snatch someone else."

"What do you mean, snatch someone else?" she and Sylvester asked together anxiously.

But the old tree merely replied, "Farther down, at the lake, Donemere of the Codlebærn, you will find answers to your questions."

Returning to her friends, Donnie gave them a brief rundown of what the tree had said and of the prayers she was continuing to receive. With unspoken agreement, they turned their horses toward the giant's lake and took off at a brisk canter. When they reached their destination, they saw a group of magical animals congregated there, their worried murmurs low and fervent.

Donnie and the others slipped off their horses and approached the little knot of concerned animal parents. Donnie zipped up her hoodie all the way to the top as she strode toward the animals because the air here by the water was far cooler than elsewhere.

Silky, the mother of two of Rex's closest skunk friends, came running toward Donnie the moment she saw her. "Oh, gracious Ér Ainíl, thank the goddess you have come! I don't know what to do! You see, the boys came here this morning because they wanted to accompany you into the giant's cave. But we've since learned they've been taken prisoner by some of the saplings and they've gone deep into the forest. We've attempted to rescue them ourselves, but several of us have been injured and we're afraid to try again because those wicked, *wicked* trees keep attacking us, preventing us from reaching the boys. But they're still in there and *who knows what is happening to them*!" the young mother wailed, her voice rising with fear.

Donnie looked around and realized that a number of the assembled animals did indeed have deep welts cut into their fur. Angry, she turned toward the trees and strode to the forest's edge, where she bit out through clenched teeth, "If any of you do anything to hurt those boys, you will pay even more dearly than you already have for your former misdeeds."

She felt Wiwila become concerned and sent a soothing caress to her horse, ordering her to stay where she was no matter what happened next. The horse agreed reluctantly and stamped her feet unhappily.

Kneeling, Donnie touched the ground and saw with her mind's eye that the two young skunks, whom Rex nicknamed Jimmy and Jonny because he could not pronounce their real names, were being held prisoner by two larger saplings at the center of the forest.

Donnie stood up tall, drew her power inwardly and let it rise within her, glad now that she had been spending so much time in the Exos because it had afforded her the opportunity to become very comfortable with both her goddess magic and that of the cosmos. It took her only seconds to build up to full strength and then she was stepping forward, her entire body aglow with the rich, deep cobalt of her magic. As had occurred before, whenever she called up this much power of late, the ground beneath her feet was infused by the light of that magic. The young trees she passed by were subdued by it, their furious shaking stilled.

Donnie slid these trees aside with a wave of her hand, creating a wide path upon which her friends followed her, their swords and knives at the ready. Sylvester had stayed with the other animal families, providing them with assurances that the boys would be returned unharmed. Donnie hoped he was right, but she could feel the forest's intentions were to kill the young skunks quite soon, and so she hastened her pace.

The closer Donnie and her friends got to the forest's center, the greater the number of trees surging toward them came. Many of these saplings lurched forward violently in their attempts to reach anyone in the group of rescuers. Their progress was effectively stymied by the protective wall of Donnie's power around herself and her friends.

But the combined magic from the many thousands of trees was strong, fueled by their collective rage, and each of the rescuers felt its evil working to infiltrate their own souls. The trees' magic was so strong that Donnie could not keep all the saplings at bay along their path and she had to release her hold on those at the edge of the forest so she could stop the ones that surrounded her and her friends. As they moved ever closer to the forest's center, to where the young skunks were being held, they could all hear the trees moving up behind them. The three warriors with Donnie stalked after her warily. Falwaïn and Diego each took a side to watch, while Akanna turned constantly to scan the rear.

It seemed ages, but they finally made it to the forest's heart. Donnie held off the trees around them in a wide circle, which her friends paced, each one ready to use the sharp edges of their blades against the stripling trees seeking to maim tender flesh.

Donnie approached the trees holding the young skunks, but stopped when she realized that they had started choking the animals. "Don't!" she cried out and backed off a couple steps.

The trees loosened their grip on the skunks' throats and the two young skunks coughed and gasped for air. Donnie could see only terror in their sweet eyes, but they never cried out.

Her heart breaking for them, she sent them a reassuring smile before returning her attention to the forest. "Why have you brought them here?"

she asked softly, looking around at the nearest trees. "Is there one among you who is your leader, and have they ordered you to bring these creatures to the center of your forest, to its heart? If so, I will speak with him or her, but to no other." She stated these words slowly and calmly, standing tall with her hands clasped in front of her.

Several trees fell away to reveal what had to be the largest of the young saplings, for it was nearly twice as thick and a couple feet taller than any of the others in the nearby area. It dragged itself forward and Donnie recognized its soul from a dream she'd had before they had rescued Liz and Julia. He was the okûn general who had grabbed first Liz and then Julia away from several voracious okûn who had been terrorizing them after the two women were brought to Medregai by Valledai, which had occurred at the same time Catie had brought Donnie to the little cottage.

This general was fiercely magical, and Donnie could see his former self glimmering over the shape of the beech sapling he had become. Too late, she realized his intention of turning himself back into an okûn using the collective pooling of magic he and his brethren were accomplishing.

One by one and in a matter of only a few seconds, the general and many of his soldier saplings transformed themselves into something that was halfway between their original bodies and their new tree forms. Their appendages remained branch-like, hard and wooden, while their bodies were covered in curling peels of rough bark, which made them look as though they were molting. Their long faces, never attractive, were lined and grey and carved into expressions of profound hatred and anger.

And suddenly, shockingly, Donnie could no longer hold any of them at bay and they were launching themselves at her and her friends.

Diego went down first under the weight of these monsters, his cries of astonishment cut short by the determined fingers of a hardened hand closing around his throat. Akanna fell next, and then it was just Donnie and Falwaïn, standing back to back, he with his broad sword flashing in all directions, and she shooting dark blue bolts of magical power designed to disable but not kill. She could feel the heartbeats of her two fallen friends and knew that they were still alive, but just barely because they were both being squeezed and choked mercilessly. She truly was not sure how she was going to end this without killing at least one of the changed saplings, an act she was not allowed to do without forfeiting her power to the next strongest in her line.

But then all of that didn't matter, because Falwaïn went down and he was calling to her, and Donnie could feel the rough arms of a couple of the changed okûns grab her from behind to press her arms to her side. Greatly angered by the pain being inflicted upon all of her friends now, and for the nightmarish terror the young skunks were experiencing, whom she could just see between the branch-like arms of the changelings in front of her, Donnie called upon the deepest depths of her physical and magical power and she shot it outward, flattening every creature within fifty feet of her.

Donnie screamed in rage, her voice echoing far over the land, because she could smell fresh blood and knew that the transformed okûns would go crazy on her friends since they had not fed for well over a week. She cursed the gods for limiting her ability to protect her friends and the magical creatures of the Ganlonds.

Just as the light of blood lust entered the sickly psychotic eyes of the changelings around her, there came a loud whinny, which was joined by another, and then two more called out, and the horses, led by Wiwila, were there and were kicking at and rearing up over the okûn monsters, beating them down, desperately making their way to their fallen riders.

Donnie was shooting lightning bolts at the changed okûns who had her friends pinned down, sending the monsters flying backward into the air. She managed to free Falwaïn and lifted him onto Gallantry, who took off with him toward the lake when Donnie slapped the horse's hindquarters. She did the same with Diego and Ampago, glad she'd freed her friend when she did because he was mere seconds from death.

Akanna was currently having more success at battling the changelings attacking her now and at least had not fallen victim to the vise-like grip of their hardened fingers for a second time. But they had wounded her in the side and her vincan blood was spurting onto her enemies, feeding their crazed desires.

Donnie sent another volley of lightning bolts shooting all around, trying to clear a path to the vincan, with Wiwila and Akanna's own horse, Jora, helping to fight the transformed okûns. It seemed that, by knocking out so many of their monstrous leaders, they had at least tipped the magical scales far enough so that no more saplings were transforming. That still left more than two hundred of the malevolent creatures to contend with, many of whom were now closing upon Donnie, Akanna, and their horses. She could feel Akanna faltering and she shouted for the vincan to hold on, but she didn't know if Akanna could hear her.

Donnie whipped around, sure that someone was stealing up on her, and found that she was right. The general was there, suddenly howling and gnashing his teeth at her, ready to claw her to the ground and rip at her skin. Donnie sent a wide push of her power at him and those right behind him, and they fell backwards. Then she saw two little streaks of black race past them all and head toward the lake. Good, that meant Jimmy and Jonny had been released. She feared they wouldn't make it back to their mom over the long path out of the forest, but she suddenly heard another loud whinny coming from that direction, and she sensed that the two young skunks had been lifted through the air onto something that was now racing them back to the edge of the lake and to safety.

Whirling, Donnie saw Otis approaching them, the huge white horse carrying Diana upon his back. And that glorious warrioress was slicing away at trees and changeling okûns with her sword on both sides of the horse, heedless of any cuts she herself was receiving. When the pair got close to where Donnie was, she jumped to the ground in a graceful arc and swung her blade hard at the changelings standing over Akanna, cutting three of them in half with that one blow. She reached down a hand to the vincan, who took it with relief, a brilliant flash of silver light passing between them.

Akanna got to her feet and looked down at where the cut in her skin had just been healed by Diana's magic. She shot a grateful look at Diana, who acknowledged it with a grim nod before turning away to hack at the limbs of another attacking monster with her magically sharpened sword.

Donnie's heart lifted when she saw Diana rescue Akanna and heal her, and then it soared because behind her warrior friends roared several Cave Bears, with Bronadulach at their fore. She understood now what Diana had used to send the little skunks away from the battle.

And then Falwaïn and Diego returned to the scene just minutes behind the bears. Both men looked much better than before because Falwaïn had realized that, by drinking the lake water, they would both be afforded the protection of the spirit of the lake, the giant known throughout Medregai as Flat-Finger. The lake's spirit was yet another transformation from the night of the battle with Valledai, only this one had been Donnie's work alone. Once they'd drunk some of the water, they had felt the giant's spirit working within their bodies to toughen their skins against any more attacks by the trees. They had re-entered the fray and fought their way back to the center of the forest.

Within just a few minutes of these fresh arrivals, the only changeling left alive was the general who had started it all. Diana held him by the point of her sword where he lay on the ground, snarling and growling at her with suppressed rage. She spat on him in response.

By now, the forest itself had calmed down, with many of the saplings retreating to the upper end of the forest, crowding together as they waited for what would happen next. Most had joined in on the attack due simply to their fear of the general, who they knew would gladly kill them all as soon as let any of them live. But he had needed their meager stores of magic to start the transformation process on himself and his preferred few, so he had bullied them all into helping him and promised them fresh blood and meat for dinner. That was impossible for any okûn to pass up, even after they'd been transmuted into trees.

Falwaïn, Diego and Akanna wrestled the okûn general to his feet and tied his arms behind his back, then also looped the rope around his feet. With their swords drawn to his back, they turned him so that he faced Donnie, who had been joined by Diana. Bronadulach and the other Cave Bears waited patiently in the background, including the one who had rescued the little skunk youngsters and taken them to their mother.

Donnie heaved a heavy, harried breath before murmuring to Diana, "Thanks for taking care of Jimmy and Jonny on your way here."

Diana shot Donnie a sly look and grinned humorously at her. "What else could I do? I sure wouldn't want Rex mad at me for letting something terrible happen to his little buddies," she joked. "Not when he's already completely pissed off at me because I made him stay at the cottage with Warren. We heard your call and we both wanted to answer it, but I got to the door first and made sure to lock it on my way out."

Laughing at the image conjured by Diana's words, Donnie nodded in agreement. "Yeah, he's probably mad as hell at you for that, but thanks for keeping him safe. I appreciate that and also your rescue of us—both were well-timed, my fearless sister. And anyway, I'm glad Rex was there to be with Warren, so he'll just have to get over any hurt feelings he might have toward you."

Diana tipped a couple fingers at her own forehead, as in salute to Donnie, and looked back at the okûn general. "What are we gonna do with him? Should I kill him? I know you're not allowed, but no such constraints have been placed on me, you know."

"I know," Donnie said, "and I don't think I'm really all that sorry about that circumstance. I mean, if I had started killing anyone, I was so mad I probably would have killed them all. And that I would never want to do." She sighed heavily and stepped closer to the okûn general held prisoner in front of her.

"Who taught you how to pool your magic like that?" she demanded. "It certainly wasn't Valley Guy—er, Valledai, I mean. Have you been hanging out with his benefactors somewhere without your boss knowing it?" she pressed, but the changeling okûn only sneered and grunted at her with disdain.

The boombox appeared at her feet and softly played "The Heart of the Matter." Donnie contemplated it and then the okûn general for a couple minutes, weighing her options silently in her head while unconsciously humming along with the song.

After much going back and forth in her opinions, she eventually declared, "You know, the only fair thing I can think to do is turn you into a tree again, but I'm not sure how that's going to stop you from repeating this whole mess a second time." She turned a questioning gaze to Diana, and then to Sylvester, who had just gotten there and was sitting beside the boombox.

Diana and the cat shrugged diffidently in response, leaving Donnie to muse, "I guess we'll just have to keep a really close eye on you from now on. Oh, well, here goes." She crossed her arms in front of her, palms to her shoulders, concentrated hard on what she wanted to do, and let her magic build up inside her until she was glowing brightly with it, then she pushed it slowly toward the okûn general. When it reached him, he was again changed into a beech sapling, his okûn features wiped away once more.

Donnie motioned for her friends to remove the rope from around his branches and trunk, and then she walked up to him, intending to give him a blessing in the hopes it might turn his dark heart toward the light. She pressed her left hand against his bark, while her right one she placed on her opposite shoulder again, and intoned, "Blessed be this dark soul, who is so filled with hate and anger. May the light of the mother goddess flood his heart and turn it into a vessel of goodness."

The moment she uttered the last syllable, there was a loud *CRACK!*

The bole of the tree split open and exploded into millions of pieces that were projected outwardly. Immediately, every one of these pieces stopped just as quickly as they'd shot away, coming to float serenely about six inches from where they'd originated. They remained in the air for several seconds before they dropped to the ground in a thick heap.

Donnie sucked in her breath, staring at the long stick clasped within the fingers of her left hand, its living warmth resonating with something deep inside her own heart. It was the only piece of wood left of the general that was bigger than a small splinter. She turned the heart wood over in her hands, marveling at it smoothness, and at the rich color of the light wood, its youth lending it a golden quality that was quite pleasing to the eye.

Still gaping incredulously, Donnie looked down at Sylvester, who, like everyone else, was gaping back at her. He recovered himself with a shake of his head and said with more than a little awe, "It appears your wand has finally found you, Donemere."

Chapter 10
The Payback

Donnie stood in front of the young, angry forest with her newly made wand clutched in her hand and considered what she was going to do about the grave situation facing them all. While she wanted to be fair to the many thousands of remaining trees, she also knew they could not be given the opportunity to attack anyone else ever again. Not sure of what else to do, she inquired of them what they wanted. This question, naturally, was met by the affronted stillness of absolute ridicule it quite deserved.

Donnie broke the silence with a groaning sort of chuckle that held no humor to it. "Besides being turned back into okûns, I mean," she clarified wearily. "I cannot do anything about that because the *Niunda Wakan* are the ones who made you as you are now, and only all of us together could reverse that spell. Considering the damage you've done to all sorts of magical creatures in just this past year, I don't see how any of us Nine would agree to return you to your former states. Sorry, but this was Gaia's call to make and she made it, so we all must live with it and make the best of it."

Sylvester cleared his throat and looked pointedly at Bronadulach when Donnie turned to the cat. She shifted her attention to the giant bear, who served as the Ganlonds' Kaerdír, and motioned him forward.

Bronadulach stepped closer and addressed Donnie more than anyone else when he explained, "The Ganlonds have exhibited great patience with the forest because of the protective boundary you placed upon the trees at the *byrgen*, Donemere. But I doubt, much the same as Sylvester plainly does, that the magical lands' forbearance will continue now that the trees have broken through your protections. As you are aware, any attacks upon other magical creatures without provocation are not tolerated here on the Ganlonds and the resultant punishment is often most severe."

Donnie made a face of thoughtful surprise. "Well, there you have it," she said to the trees with somewhat blithe relief. "I do believe this decision is out of my hands. Your futures, it seems, may already be decided for you because of your actions today. If the Ganlonds decide to take your magic, I imagine that will pretty much end your lives as you know them." She looked back at Bronadulach for confirmation of this and he nodded.

"Yes," he agreed gravely. "All memory of any former life will be wiped away and those trees who have this happen will then have no more than an ordinary soul. But this forest will be safe for other creatures to walk amongst, at least."

With an irresolute and vaguely sympathetic shrug, Donnie picked up her cat and put him on her shoulder. She looked around at her friends and announced with forced brightness, "It looks like we're done here. Are we ready to go spelunking?"

Several trees rustled their leaves and vibrated violently. Donnie used her wand, liking the way it focused her magic, and willed the closest trees to speak. Most were viciously denouncing the right of the magical lands to do anything to them, and these Donnie shut down with a quick flick of her wand.

Those few who spoke more reasonably kept their voices and they began to apologize obsequiously, making a veritable hodgepodge of outlandish promises of better behavior in gruff, gravelly voices, which no one was at all convinced they meant to keep.

Donnie used her magic to make sure her own clear voice was heard by all the thousands of saplings surrounding her. "Enough of your arguments, what's done is done; and I will remind you that it is your choices that have led us here. Now, for those who have no desire to remain as a magical tree here on the Ganlonds and would rather die, please move up the hill," she added, a little tongue in cheek. "Those who are fine with being a magical tree and will happily live in this forest by the Ganlonds' rules, move down here, toward the lake."

She raised an imperious hand when several voices shouted out in protest and most of the trees in the forest shook their leaves and branches at her, creating a slow, loud hissing sound that went on for some time without cessation.

"All right, all right," Donnie conceded once the hissing and shouting finally stopped. She crossed her arms in front of her and allowed her magic to rise until she glowed faintly with it, then turned in a circle, sending her wand in a sweeping gesture all around them once. A blue wall arose as the wand made its path around, which ended by enclosing them all within it, even overhead and presumably underfoot. "You can go wherever you want in this general area," Donnie said, pointing to the inside of the huge cylinder she'd just made. "This force field will keep you inside it and everyone else out. But you must understand that the Ganlonds will enforce the rules upon you and I will have no say in what is decided for you *by* the Ganlonds. You would be wise to remember that this is the one and only time any of you might be given a pass on your behavior, and that will occur only if the Ganlonds let it happen. I cannot stress to you enough that that may not happen at all, so you'd best be prepared for, to put it plainly, the ends of your magical selves. I imagine each of you will have an answer by tomorrow morning, if not sooner, as to what the Ganlonds have decided is to be your individual or perhaps collective fates. In the future, my dears, for those who might survive intact this day, you should know that I will encourage the Ganlonds to act upon you immediately if you again step out of line and harm any other magical creature living here on the Ganlonds without provocation, as Bronadulach says is done to all those who commit that crime." She looked around at the nearby trees and spread her palms in front of her before adding, "I guess the only thing left to say is, good luck with living a good life.'

It took nearly an hour, but eventually all the young trees were settled. Donnie made sure they were spread out as evenly as she could get them so they would not crowd each other as they grew if they remained where they were standing now. She even levitated herself off the ground high enough so she could get a good view of the entire forest from above, giving more directions about tree spacing until she was satisfied with everyone's efforts.

By then, her friends had exited the forest, with most moving gingerly through the force field. They had all gathered at the lake to wait for Donnie to be finished. When she had joined them, she and the others said goodbye to the bears, who trundled away in pairs.

The earlier attack by the young trees had given everyone a sense of anticlimax to the day, but Donnie was still determined to investigate the cave. She knelt beside the lake and felt for the giant's spirit. She tried to get him to talk to her about what could possibly be in there to frighten the children yesterday, but he refused to answer her entreaties. So, she drank of his waters and felt his reluctant spirit move within her to protect her from whatever might harm her in his old abode. She advised the others to do likewise if they hadn't already, and soon they were all standing at the cave's entrance, feeling rejuvenated and as though they were prepared to meet anything.

The entrance to the mammoth cave folded to the left, meaning there was no straightforward entry into it, and the giant must have had a tight squeeze whenever he went in and out of his home. This fold effectively cut off any direct sunlight, and the grey light that followed them into the cave was filtered and dim.

As the group moved inward, leaving the horses outside, darkness took over the scene and the explorers were met with an all-encompassing wall of inky blackness, with noises from their every movement echoing from several directions. Donnie conjured four blue light balls to light the cavern, making its walls and floor look strange in the eerie light. She split the light balls into fours and sent those out at full strength, so that now the cave was lit quite well.

To the left was the deepest darkness, while to the center and right were astonishingly well-furnished living areas. A bed stood in the corner which could easily fit their entire group, plus their horses, all lying prone, and still have room for a few more. In the center of the living space, a table at least ten times the size of Donnie's big oaken one took pride of place in front of a huge fireplace carved into the rock wall. Donnie touched the towering pile of roughly chopped wood next to the stone hearth and knew instinctively that it had not come from the Ganlonds, for there was no resonance from it that was at all familiar or magical. She guessed that, as part of Catie's spell to entrap the giant here so long ago, firewood from elsewhere would be provided, and she suspected the same would be true for water and food. The Codlebærns were not allowed to kill, after all, so their imprisonment spells must provide for sustaining whatever life they affected, she supposed.

There was also a very large, wooden chair and stool arranged at the edge of the hearth that were both covered thickly in massive rugs and blankets, dirty and dusty from many years of neglect. Upon the hearth stone lay a long smoking pipe that had to have been carved out of a mid-sized tree…Okay, maybe it was not quite *that* big, Donnie reproved her fanciful thoughts humorously.

They were all poking into corners and whatnot when the sound of pounding feet met their ears. As one, they whirled to watch Rex skidding toward them. He bowled into Akanna, who stood her ground and took hold of the pup so that he did not go careening off her steady stance. Donnie smiled at the vincan appreciatively.

"Diana, I am so mad at you!" the dog cried, scampering over to the warrioress in question. Then he hastily amended his plaint to, "Well, I'm not mad now, but I was a little while ago. But then Jimmy and Jonny came and told me and Warren what you did and then we read it in the new book Warren's got and we were like, whoa, that Diana is badass fer sure, you know? And we were sayin' how much we all like you and how sad it is that you don't wanna go home to your own magical lands, but that we hope Mama can help you get over that. And then that got us back to talkin' about you savin' everybody and I said I was gonna find you and tell you how we all feel and let you know just how grateful we are, and so I'm here to thank you for saving everybody!" Rex leaned against Diana's leg after finally stopping to catch his breath and stared up at her adoringly. "My friends said you were so brave and fierce, and that you fought off those mean old okûn changelings like they were weak little babies."

Diana, made severely uncomfortable by the dog's lavish praise and unfiltered observances, chuckled nervously and muttered, "Ah, yeah, well, it wasn't all that much, really. And I had the bears helping me, you know. And your mom, and all these guys," she added, waving her hands at the others.

But Rex would not be swayed as he avowed seriously, "Nope, you are the best and you should just own that, 'cause you are a real hero today. Everybody's sayin' so, ya know, all over the Ganlonds."

Donnie, grinning, clapped her hands and crowed to Diana, "Hear, hear! He's right; you are a real hero, my friend, and it's high time you accepted that about yourself."

Looking as though she was going to splutter in embarrassment, Diana spun around and strode over to the corner, where she began to search a large, crudely built bureau that stood next to the bed.

Falwaïn, chuckling along with Donnie, put his hands on his hips. He suddenly sobered and said, "I am confused. I distinctly remember reading in the first book of our adventures that, according to Rex, whenever one magical creature ate another here on the Ganlonds, their punishment was that they would get violently ill, not that they would lose their magic. Have things changed recently?"

She made a surprised face and turned to Sylvester, who was atop the table and studying something carved into its middle. "Sylvester, what about that? I know what he means; it was when Rex was thinking about the sparrow he'd eaten and how sick he'd been because of it."

The cat peered up at her and took a moment to understand her question because of how deep in thought he was. He shook himself, stood for a second, and sank back down to the tabletop. "The bird Rex ate was one who had been compromised by Valledai and turned against the Ganlonds. From what Bronadulach described of the incident—you see, he gets flashes of events that occur on the magical lands because he is the Kaerdír—he confirmed to me that, at just about the time the Ganlonds realized that the sparrow's spirit had been turned, Rex was hunting it. He was therefore allowed to kill and eat the bird without the most severe judgment being passed upon him. But if he had eaten a creature that had not been turned, then he very well might have been made less." The cat paused, frowned, and added, "That is, if anything can make him less. His powers really are nothing short of amazing, in so many ways, so it is possible that perhaps the Ganlonds would not have been able to do much other than make him sick, as did occur. When he came to me and told me about it, I was not allowed to give him the truth because of the binding spell on us all, so I had to invent the story about that being the punishment for eating another magical animal." The cat shrugged carelessly, then dismissed the entire subject with a peremptory, "Come here, Donemere. You must see this carving."

Rolling her eyes in resignation, Donnie stepped over to the table, which was shoulder height to her, and, employing a little boost of magic, climbed up onto the seat of the nearest chair so she could see what the cat was staring at. Intrigued, she placed her palms on the tabletop and leaned over the old and weathered carving, studying it from various angles by turning her head this way and that. "It looks familiar, but I don't know why," she finally admitted, after several long moments of perusal.

"It is the same design as the Ternate Tunnel you made this winter in the snow," the cat murmured, "and it is what you unconsciously draw whenever you are distracted and there is a flat surface in front of you."

Rex leapt onto the same chair as Donnie, and then bounded up to the table easily, where he too gazed over the carving. He nodded and said, "Sylvester's right, that's the same shape as the Ternate Tunnel. I didn't know that part about you doodling it, though. So, what d'ya think it means, Mama?" He sat down on his rump and looked over at her with curiosity.

Donnie moved her shoulders in bewilderment. "I dunno. That design does get stuck in my head sometimes, but I have no idea why or what it represents."

"More importantly, what is it doing here?" the cat pointed out. "I had simply assumed it was something you made up, but clearly that is not the case." He gazed up at Donnie, unblinking and grave.

But she had no answers for him and shook her head to indicate so. She turned around and Falwaïn helped her down off the chair, the dog and cat following her right after.

"Anyone else find anything of interest?" asked Falwaïn, but they all said no, so they looked over toward the darkness on the other side of the cavern, the side that pointed north, toward the long run of the Brumal Mountains.

Squaring her shoulders, Donnie walked to where several light balls were hovering in anticipation of moving into the blackness beyond. With a push of her hand, all but two of the light balls shot away. The other light balls moved to light the length of a tunnel that seemed to grow smaller as it progressed. Through this tunnel everyone followed Donnie and Falwaïn, who were in the lead. The tunnel, which continued for a hundred feet or so, led to another chamber that was much smaller than Flat-Finger's lair, although it and the tunnel were still big enough for the giant to have moved through comfortably.

They looked around this chamber, noting that hundreds of pictures were drawn on its surfaces, all crude and rudimentary, but many themed to represent a family, with a mother and father, and what appeared to be two small children, although a few of the crudest drawings showed three youngsters.

Diego found a way through this room to another tunnel, this one a little smaller than the previous one, which Flat-Finger would likely have had to crawl through in order to pass as it was too small for him to stand upright in. On the other side of this was another large cavern, over which a heavy, thick mist hung. From this massive cloud of mist dripped huge droplets of water, which made the floor of the chamber slippery and treacherous.

Taking great care with each step, the explorers moved farther into the cavern, gaping at its contents with consternation.

"I think we have found what frightened the young ones," Diego said as he stepped farther into the chamber, staring around him in growing horror.

Donnie split the light balls again and now there were more than thirty lights zooming around the cavern, throwing its gruesome decoration into nightmarish relief.

Everywhere they looked there were hundreds, maybe thousands of wet, sickly looking whitish-yellow stalagmites, all sculpted with the ghastly visage, and often along with his fully body, of Flat-Finger in the throes of what were obviously intense emotions. In most of these mini effigies (all of which were still as large or larger than any human-sized sculpture), the giant appeared angry to the point of being furious, and these surely must have seemed utterly terrifying to the young kits who had crowded mischievously into this cavern the day before, hoping to give their teachers a bit of a scare.

But the small students had not even been missed by the time the six of them, the two skunks Jimmy and Jonny and their ferret friends Fil, Cros, Hilan, and Teter, had come screeching back into the main cavern and then darted out into the sunshine and the safety of the meadow beyond, where the teachers had found them inconsolable and shaking like leaves caught in a strong wind. All six had refused to talk about what had occurred and just kept crying that they wanted to go home. And that was why Jimmy and Jonny had been so set on meeting up with Donnie and the others for their investigative excursion into the cavern this morning. They were determined to overcome their fears and stop their friends and family from the merciless teasing and name calling they'd been subjected to after the incident.

Closing her eyes and looking around instead with her mind's eye, Donnie realized what the young kits must have seen in the darkness. From their view so near the floor, the ghostly, misshapen faces carved within the stalagmites looked like enraged creatures caught in stone, struggling to their deaths. They unnerved Donnie now, even though she knew what they were, and she found she had to open her eyes.

She shivered, then caught her breath when Sylvester said in a hushed voice, "Oh, my heavens, no. Frightened does not even begin to describe it. Look," he urged, staring at something on the floor a little ahead of him. They all crowded forward to see what he was looking at.

Carved into six new, small stalagmites on the floor, standing amongst some of the more truly frightening versions of Flat-Finger, were sculpted figures of the kits, with all of them caught in the act of screaming in unholy terror.

Like Sylvester and Donnie, the others were completely unsettled by this bizarre sight. They each muttered to themselves and their friends in commiseration with the deserving fear etched upon the youngsters' faces in their statues.

And then it all got worse.

The mist above, unnoticed by any of them, had descended far enough that it hung just over their heads and now dropped over them in one swift movement. The light from the light balls was obliterated and darkness swallowed the explorers with the mist's descent.

The mist was creepy, thick and humid, stifling and invasive, pressing against the exposed skin of their faces and bodies, clinging to their clothing and weapons, until they felt almost violated.

Donnie, the first to understand that the mist was sentient, cried out, "Nobody move! I think it's just trying to see who we are, not hurt us."

"Agreed," said Falwaïn, who was standing right behind Donnie and now put a hand on her back when he felt for her in front of him. "But it is quite thorough in its touch, isn't it?" he added dryly, and this seemed to break the tension in the room and everybody once again breathed.

"It certainly is," remarked Akanna with a nervy chuckle. "My old mate, Briener, could have taken a few tips from this mist. If he had, we might still be mated," she joked, and the others laughed with her.

While it seemed the mist held them for a long time, it was, in reality, only seconds. The mist then lifted and retreated back to the ceiling, and the light balls illuminated the cavern once more. To add to the strangeness, when the mist receded, it left no moisture behind, so Donnie and the others were left bewilderingly dry after being fully engulfed by the mist only moments before.

They all looked upward at the gently billowing mist and were amazed when a finger protruded from its depths and pointed to a space farther back in the cavern. After looking around at each other, by silent agreement they set off in the wanted direction, coming to a stop only when they realized that they had come upon some statues of Flat-Finger when he was younger, and much happier.

Intrigued, they continued walking in this same direction, albeit much more slowly than before, and found other figures than just those of Flat-Finger. Here was likely the same mother, father and children depicted in the childishly drawn pictures in the other chamber. But wait, were there statues of three children or just two?

They discussed this question, moving along so that they arrived at what they all agreed looked to be the earliest sculptures made. Here was the only instance of what they knew for certain to be a girl, although her crafted features were not as sharp or precise as those on the other statues. By virtue of finding this lone girlish statue, it made it reasonably certain that the other two young giants represented in the sculptures were boys, and most likely brothers.

Donnie turned around toward the mist, which had lowered itself again back where they had been standing before, and called out to it, "This is you, isn't? You're the sister, and these other figures, they're your family, aren't they? You're Flat-Finger's sister."

The mist billowed toward them and a part of it extended down and draped itself around the youngest representations of the three siblings.

Diego, standing the closest to these sculptures, gasped in shock as he peered closely at the mist encompassing them. "Look!" he exclaimed. "Look at the water that gets dripped down—it rises back up in the air and returns to the mist! But with every drop, more mineral is deposited!"

And he was right. The drops that fell were heavy with minerals, while the drops that rose to rejoin the main cloud were clear and pure.

The mist drew back into a heavy cloud above them and billowed back to where it had been before. But now, at the feet of the three statues it had altered, were what must be names carved into the stone. Donnie willed herself to understand the hieroglyphs the mist had used, but it was Falwaïn who was able to read them first. He recounted quietly that the oldest boy, who could be identified because he had a much larger and more hooked nose than that of Flat-Finger, had apparently been called Feirth, while Flat-Finger was Garin and the girl's name was Na'aven.

Donnie, after reading this, turned back to the mist and said, "Na'aven? That's you, Na'aven, right?"

There was no response from the mist, but Donnie assumed that she must be correct in her surmise.

They all milled around the nearby statues, finding other figures, noting that there really was just the one of the young girl. But there were at least twenty statues each of the other members of the family as they grew older. The explorers discussed this oddity and concluded that the young girl must have died. So, Donnie posited this scenario to the mist.

"Na'aven, did you die when you were young? Is that what happened to you?" she asked, looking back at the mist, which was still lowered just above where Donnie and the others had been standing earlier.

The mist rose, billowing crazily, almost as if it were excited. It floated over to them and extended a thin finger at the statue of Flat-Finger, or Garin. This same finger then wrapped itself around the neck of the figure of Na'aven, swirling round and round it until there was a loud *Snap!*, and the statue's head fell to the floor.

"Your brother killed you?" asked Diana, her voice shocked, and the same finger of mist pointed again at the statue of Flat-Finger before the entire cloud returned to its previous location. "Wow," Diana breathed low, watching the mist go, "and I thought my childhood was terrible."

"Does no one else find it quite alarming that the mist could do that to a statue?" whispered Diego quietly, and Rex replied, "Oh, yeah, I'd say that was real scary! I mean, imagine what it could do to us if it wanted! And how would ya stop mist, huh?"

Akanna, who wore a pensive expression on her face, turned to Falwaïn and then to Sylvester, staring intently at both before venturing, "I seem to recall a story, more legend, really, of something happening to a young giantess around the Falls of Avendin. Do either of you recall that story?"

Falwaïn, about to shake his head no, suddenly grew astonished and cried eagerly, "Why, yes! Yes, I do remember something about that. Now, let me see," he said, searching his memory. "Ah, yes, that's what it was. The young giantess was supposedly playing on the falls by herself and fell to her death. The legend goes that she fell through the Mist of Avendin and was transformed into the soul of the mist. The Mist, which enshrouded pretty much the entire length of the falls, was long reported to grant immortality to anyone who breathed in its vapors." He stopped and turned to look at the mist behind them. "Can it be?" he asked with distraction, his mind racing ahead of his tongue. "I can't imagine anyone would have thought this is what became of the little girl, although it must be she, mustn't it? But I have no idea how she came to be here in this cave."

"How far away are the falls from here?" asked Donnie, looking down at the severed head curiously, and she felt Rex nod from where he stood leaning up against her leg.

"Oh, easily four hundred miles, I should think," Falwaïn replied, taken aback by that twist of the girl's tale. "That's a very long distance for a mist to travel, isn't it?" he pointed out.

"Unless it had assistance," posited Sylvester, "magical assistance, I mean."

"Are you thinking of Catie?" Donnie inquired, and the cat nodded.

"It could very well have been accomplished by her, yes."

Donnie returned his steady gaze and said, "Well, I might make that my next topic to research in her journals, see if she says anything about the mist or the giants. I mean, maybe they all lived here in these caves, not just Flat-Finger. After all, whoever drew the pictures in that other chamber must have been pretty young, and you wouldn't think even a giant that young would be left on his own."

Deciding to ask Na'aven, Donnie again called out to the mist and reiterated most of what they had just discussed.

In response, the mist once again extended a finger and beckoned them back to where they had been standing a few minutes ago. They wove their way through the phalanx of statues to their earlier location, only to find there were now life-sized sculptures of themselves where they had stood previously. Every one of them, other than Rex, had looks of controlled alarm on their features. Rex's figure, it should be noted, was wide-eyed and slack-jawed with apprehension.

Diana whistled in appreciation. "Damn, she's fast and she's good! She captured us all perfectly." Suddenly turning suspicious, she added in an urgent whisper to Donnie and Falwaïn, who were standing together, "I hope there's not something evil about this. You know, where she maybe *has* captured something of us, some piece of our soul or something like that?"

"That is unlikely," countered the cat decisively, jumping up onto the stone Donnie's shoulder. "Most of these statues are of Flat-Finger, which means Na'aven must have regularly touched him so that she could make these different statues. Even though she did this to him at least a thousand times, he still has his soul intact, even though he now exists only as the spirit of the lake."

The mist sent a spiral down, caressing the cat in a most inquiring way.

He looked up at it and replied, "Your brother chose to work for the side of evil when he was released from this cave and he was recently transmuted by the Ér Ainíl of the Ganlonds—er, that is the name of the magical lands that lie just outside this cave, in case you did not know that. Anyway, he was transformed into becoming the protective spirit of the lake that is located just up the hill from here."

The spiral finger left Sylvester and touched Donnie's shoulder.

Donnie straightened her back and nodded. "Yes, that was done by me. I'm Donnie, and these are my friends," she said, and quickly introduced them all to the spectral mist. "While I would never kill your brother, I did have to stop him killing others," she explained afterward, and the spiral retreated into the main cloud. "You are clearly aware, judging by the great number of statues here of him in the midst of an angry fit, that he has a recurring tendency to not control his actions, often brutally and fatally harming others, as he did to you. I couldn't let him continue doing that to those unfortunate enough to cross his path," she added matter-of-factly. "I did this to him during the battle that occurred just outside the cave a couple weeks ago, which you must have heard happening, right? Well, that was when I transformed him. He is now a citizen of the Ganlonds and is under my protection, although I'm not sure he realizes that yet, because he's still very angry with me."

Donnie paused here and made a face before continuing. "Well, he's angry with everyone and everything, isn't he? I'm guessing that's what happened with you, when you were a little girl. You weren't alone at the falls, were you? Did he get angry and strike out at you, causing your death?"

The mist had begun to billow as though greatly agitated because of Donnie's questions, so that Donnie finally pointed toward the exit tunnel, suggesting, "If you go through there, and then through the second tunnel into where he lived most of the time, you'll find the entrance to the cave is open. You could leave here, you know. Maybe go visit your brother out in the lake. Or just go somewhere else, so you need never see him again, if you like." She shrugged her shoulders diffidently before repeating, "If you like."

The mist moved hesitantly a few feet and then stopped, so Donnie and the others led the way back to the first chamber, the mist following behind them very slowly and at a fair distance. When they passed the table, Rex said, "I'll bet you're right, Mama, and the whole family lived here after Na'aven died. And that's why there's such a long table here, 'cause that one's too long for one giant, don't ya think?"

Donnie looked over at the table and considered what her dog had just said. Like Rex, she couldn't see a reason why a single giant would need such a long table, when there was just himself to feed. But if it had been a family table that had to seat five...well, its length made sense then.

"Yes, I think you're right, honey," she admitted, adding, "I just wish I knew why it has that old carving on it. And, I'd like to know if the carving is as old as the table or if it's something Flat-Finger carved himself, maybe after he was imprisoned here. Perhaps he'll be so happy to be reunited with his sister that he'll tell us."

When this was met by loud coughs and half-coughs from pretty much every one of her friends, Donnie acceded wryly, "Okay, perhaps not."

They walked out into the brilliant, warm afternoon sun, looked up at the clear sky, and all shook their heads together.

Diana was the first to say what everyone was thinking. "Na'aven shouldn't come out here right now. Maybe tonight at dusk or in the morning might be best, when she'll be less likely to lose her moisture, you know?"

Donnie swept her gaze around at her friends and suggested, "Why don't you all go back to the cottage, while I wait here with Na'aven? I'm going to have a frank conversation with Flat-Finger in the meantime, I think. There are some issues I want to discuss with him and he might be more inclined to talk to me if it's just the two of us instead of a whole crowd."

When the others started to protest this, Donnie waved them off and said, "No, seriously, you go ahead. Wiwila and I will stay here. I'll see you not long after dark, I promise. I've already told the kitchen to prepare a big pot of spaghetti."

"But Wiwila can't get you back to the house as quick as I can," argued Rex, who very much wanted to stay to protect his mama after what had happened earlier in the new forest.

"True," Donnie conceded, "but I can always just materialize us there, can't I? And I need to practice that with Wiwila anyway, just in case." She motioned for them to be away and even said, "Go on, shoo, you guys. I'm good here; I mean it."

When there looked to be more protests over her plan, she turned to Falwaïn for help and he took control, chivvying everyone onto their horses and starting to lead them toward home. He called out to a reluctant Rex, who was still refusing to leave Donnie's side, that he would give him half of Sylvester's pasta at dinner if he came with them straight away. This got everyone to laughing and they all made their exodus in a much better mood than they might have otherwise. Well, except for Sylvester, that is, who was clearly not certain if Falwaïn was joking about the pasta thing. Donnie sent her man a last, highly amused smile as the group retreated, and he tipped his head toward her, grinning at her in return.

Hugging herself and thinking about how lucky she was to have that wonderful man loving her every day of her life now, she turned to her right and walked slowly toward the lake. She sat down at its edge on a small boulder and contemplated the lake's clear, calm waters. Moving her gaze across the gorgeous vista before her, she noticed that there were places where a whitish glow lit the ground. Extending her senses toward one of these spots, she encountered the wonder of magic unadulterated by any creature's desires or needs. This was just simply magical power, and Donnie realized that this was the magic of the Ganlonds and that it was here to witness what would transpire between herself and Flat-Finger, perhaps even with Na'aven.

Taken aback by the realization that the Ganlonds were watching her to see how she would handle the coming contact with Flat-Finger, she let this revelation sink in and allowed herself to see the truth and the beauty of it. One of her deepest anxieties about being the Ér Ainíl of the Ganlonds was the great responsibility for the lives of all those living on the magical lands that she felt rested on her shoulders alone. But she now understood that she was here to direct and protect the Ganlonds and its inhabitants, while it was the magic within the Ganlonds that would have to make the final determination of what must be done and that she should trust in its choices and its wisdom. It knew its needs better than she ever would and it was not swayed by anything other than necessity.

She took a deep breath and felt some of the tightness that she carried within her body drain away. And, with a small burst of blue that shot from her midriff, she found that she was one step closer to the primal magic that sustained her own powers and the lives of the magical creatures of the Ganlonds. Again surprised, this time by the growth her powers had just experienced, she leaned back and chuckled warmly. She was grateful for the proof that she was still learning and growing, and that she was still meeting the approval of the gods and of magic itself.

She gave herself several minutes to order her thoughts and just enjoy the sunshine before beginning the showdown with Flat-Finger. While she had not expected him to, say, fully embrace his new role in life, she was disappointed that he remained so truculent and unhelpful even after several days of encounters with the gentle souls of the magical creatures of the Ganlonds.

She knew that many had been to his waters because she could see their tracks. Walking to the lake's shore and reaching down to touch one fresh, very small pawprint in the mud at her feet, she saw with her mind's eye that it had been created by little Jonny. A flash of memory came to her and she watched as Jonny and his brother played in the lake that very morning. They had apparently drunk some of the water, told themselves they were now protected from anything evil and then, feeling invincible, they moved off toward the new forest. After which, they had presumably got taken prisoner and nearly lost their lives.

Donnie stood up tall and surveyed the water. She cleared her throat and said, "I know you are there and can hear me, Flat-Finger. Show yourself."

The water in front of her rolled and swirled, rising in threatening mounds that looked as though they would crash onto the shore and sweep her away with them, and Donnie suspected that this was the lake's usual response when anyone came near. She reached down again and touched several more of the various prints in the mud at her feet and found this was indeed the case. It seemed the giant spent most of the time trying to scare the magical creatures away from its waters whenever they came to drink of it.

And, Donnie realized with sudden ire, the giant had found a way to separate his essence from the water at the lake's edges and had thereafter held back his essence so that almost all who had partaken of the lake's waters despite his menacing actions had drunk only plain, ordinary water, other than herself and her friends, with whom he had been too wary to try his usual tricks. She reached down to touch the grass to her side so she could tap into more of the Ganlonds' memories for this area and found that Julia's father had visited the lake in the early hours of the morning after the battle with Valledai and he had had a long talk with the giant's spirit. While the Ganlonds' memories did not detail their conversation, she watched as, just before Ixifir left, the waters moved in such a way that would cause this separation of waters.

Donnie stood up now, trembling with deep anger. "Show yourself!" she barked, and when the lake did the same thing as before, she blew a freezing breath that targeted just the water containing the giant's essence. That entire portion of the lake froze in seconds. With her magic, she made sure it was held suspended in the rest of the ordinary water and that all organisms living there were unharmed by what she was about to do.

She waited a few minutes, then unfroze the water with a hot, warming breath that quickly put the giant's waters into a rolling boil. She repeated this process for half an hour, alternating between freezing then boiling the giant's essence, until she finally let the lake's water come to ambient temperature. She allowed it to mix with the ordinary water surrounding it, and again demanded that Flat-Finger show himself.

This time, his figure rose unhappily and he made sneering faces as he towered over her, grunting with dislike.

"I met your sister, you know. In your cave," Donnie told him, inclining her head toward the cave's entrance. "She doesn't say much, does she? But she sure can tell a story!"

Flat-Finger looked at her, momentarily puzzled, then enlightenment dawned on his thick, dullard's features. "She took the 'ead offen her statue agin, didden she? Snapped it right off, I expeck."

Donnie merely narrowed her eyes at him in response.

The giant fell into what looked like a sitting position as he grumbled thickly, "She be setch a gool and a taddle-tail! Al'ays was! I was niver so glad ta be rid o' her as when she went tumblin' o'er them falls! Ye hear me? Glad I was, and glad I still am coz I niver liked 'er!"

"She was your little sister!" Donnie shouted back at him reprovingly. "That's what little sisters do, is annoy their older siblings! But you don't kill them for that, you nasty piece of offal! No wonder your entire family abandoned you!"

She had expected this to rile the giant; instead it seemed to amuse him.

"Better off wi'out 'em, I al'ays sed," he chuckled, and Donnie felt nothing except revulsion in her heart for him. "Ennyway," he continued ponderously, "I didden niver like any o' em, me bruther most spesh'lee. All 'igh and mighty, warn't 'e? Like 'e was somebuddy better'n me! I 'ope they's all dead, dead, dead, and they's bones rotten in the mire fer many a long year naow, jest whare they b'long! They turned they's backs on me and let that witch o' theirn trap me in me cave wi' that bitchee sissy o' mine fer 'undreds o' years. Ye got enny idee what that wass like, livin' wi' 'er al'ays 'uggin' me and makin' them cruddy statues?"

Thoroughly disgusted by now, Donnie took a couple steps back from the lake and deliberated on her options. Clearly, she could not let the giant go on with what he'd been doing for the last couple of weeks. And the Ganlonds seemed to feel the same way, seeing as the entire lake now had a white outline of magic around it, as though the magic of the Ganlonds was waiting for the right signal in order to pass its final judgment upon the giant's spirit.

The boombox materialized upon the rock she'd vacated a few minutes before and began to play the funk classic, "The Payback." Donnie frowned at it, chewed her lip for a minute or two, then nodded.

"Okay, if you insist, boombox," she said to the music machine. "Maybe she can talk some sense into him, or strong arm him into it if she must, considering they're both water spirits now. At least the sun is nearly down and it's finally cooled off some, so she'll be okay out here."

Donnie left the lake without saying another word to Flat-Finger, although he began to stutter that he had no desire to ever see his sister again. Donnie ignored him and went back into the cavern, where she found Na'aven's mist huddled at the back of the main cavern.

"You can come out now, Na'aven," Donnie said to the mist gently. "Your brother's being a real, well, to put it politely, a real jerk right now and doesn't wish to see you. But I'd appreciate it if you could somehow get him to understand that he must do as I tasked him in my spell on him, or else the Ganlonds will decide his fate, and I'm guessing they're not going to let his spirit live for much longer. I'm hoping you can influence him somehow—"

Donnie had barely gotten half of the last sentence out of her mouth before the mist began moving toward the outside. She followed it, a sense of foreboding suddenly overtaking her. She found herself running to keep up because the mist moved so swiftly, and still the mist had left the cavern long before she did.

Donnie gasped when she came into the open air, for the land all around was glowing with the Ganlonds' white magic, and Na'aven was nearly to the lake. Donnie used her own magic to materialize herself at the water's edge just as Na'aven's mist plunged into the lake. What happened next was an awesome sight to behold.

Two figures, that of Flat-Finger and the other of Na'aven, arose from the water's depths and met with a great clash on the surface of the lake, their fists swinging and legs kicking wildly, with great gushes of water spilling and spurting everywhere. Na'aven, though smaller and having the build of a child, and also having oddly undefined facial features just like her statue had before its head was severed, flashed with white and Donnie understood that the Ganlonds were helping her. Again and again, the two giants met, the outer "skin" of their forms slapping against each other and then splaying outward in great torrents of water, only to re-form moments later so it could all be repeated.

Wiwila, frightened by the noise and the spectacle of the battle, came to stand beside Donnie.

Noting Wiwila's concern, Donnie formed a protective shield around them both so they could stay dry and unharmed by the forcefulness of the water streams shooting all around them.

And then the two giants were fighting deep under the lake's water, and Donnie and Wiwila were forced backward as great waves came crashing over the shore and began to erode great chunks of soil from all around the lake's edges. The water within the lake rolled and bucked, Na'aven's form outlined in white magic and visible as she wrestled with her brother, both of them flinging huge sprays of water a hundred feet into the air. This went on for some while, then it all seemed to stop and everything went still.

The white glow of pure magic faded from around the lake and moved to the new forest, where it surfaced and, within moments, Donnie and Wiwila could hear the grunts and groans of pain and surprise of the thousands of trees being transformed by the sentence being passed upon them by the Ganlonds. Donnie felt their magical deaths in her heart, their lessening both ruthless and instant as the white magic of the Ganlonds rolled through the land. When it was done, not one changeling tree had anything more than a simple soul and their magic was gone, absorbed by the Ganlonds and fed back into the supernatural system that kept the magic flowing for all those who lived by the rules and principles developed by the Animal Council's leaders throughout millennia.

And then Donnie sensed a shifting in her heart, right where she'd felt Flat-Finger's protective magic lodge when she'd drank his waters a few hours before. A new spirit took its place and Donnie grasped that Flat-Finger too was no more.

Donnie could not actually mourn the passing of either the okûns or the giant, but she did recognize her part in all that was happening tonight. She had set most of this in motion herself and she felt that weigh upon her conscience, even though she reminded herself that it had not been her decision to take the lives that had been struck from the magical world this hour.

She hunched down in the grass where she stood and pressed her palms to the ground. As always, she could hear and feel the thudding of the Earth's core, it's heart, if you will, beating reassuringly and strongly. She reached down with her triune and found the magic lying beneath the Ganlonds. Touching it with a metaphysical finger, it resonated in her blood, making her heart sing, calmly affirming to her that fate had found its true way and she must accept what had just occurred and her part in it.

Donnie got to her feet, crossed her arms in front of her and pressed her hands to her opposite shoulders, canting a short blessing for the many souls that had just been sent on to the next life:

"Oh, Mother, I pray for the souls of those lost here tonight,
May they find their way to a new life full of goodness and light."

The earth around her glowed blue for a few seconds before that light faded. Donnie let her arms fall to her sides and she turned toward the lake so that she and Wiwila could walk to the lake's edge, where the young giantess's head and shoulders were beginning to form.

Woman and horse stood there, the sun starting to set, and waited for Na'aven to ready herself. When the water spirit did, her features were much clearer and crisper than previously. At first, they appeared too sharp and almost malicious, and then they softened so that she resembled more the child she had been at the time of her death, although then her face aged and she seemed several years older. Donnie watched this transformation in fascination and Na'aven smiled at her ruefully.

"I never really knew what I looked like all that well," she explained. "But the Ganlonds showed me how Garin thought of me, and that kind of jogged something within my memories of myself. Then I remembered that I was said to look just like my mother. So, I have fashioned myself after her somewhat now."

Donnie nodded appreciatively, but said nothing, and merely waited for Na'aven to clarify her presence.

"My brother is dead," Na'aven informed Donnie solemnly, her voice not quavering or faltering in any way, although she was clearly feeling emotional, "and his soul sent to Mændís to be judged. I have taken his place, most especially regarding his oath and burden toward the Ganlonds and the magical creatures living here."

Na'aven said all this quite matter-of-factly, still not wavering in her conviction of her message or her purpose. "The Ganlonds wish for me to stay, to remain here as the lake's spirit, and I have freely agreed to this. The many long years spent with my brother did not embitter me as they did him, although that may have been because I was able to release much of my resentment with every statue I created of him. He never had such an outlet and therefore kept it all inside him, where it grew and festered and made him uglier than ever. That being said, I was determined to have my revenge upon him tonight for my murder and that's why I left the cavern so quickly when you told me that the Ganlonds were prepared to kill him. I was not about to let someone else have that honor, not even such a preeminent magical entity as the Ganlonds itself."

Not knowing quite how to respond to this rather bald statement, Donnie studied the watery visage of the giantess thoughtfully. "Do you recall what happened at the falls?" she asked.

"Oh, yes, quite vividly, of course," Na'aven assured her. "We were not supposed to go there because of the elves, you see. They didn't like us much, even though we had lived on the Eotenmóras long before the Álvar moved to the lands south of us and renamed them Balwedané Feûr. The falls were known to the Ettins from the beginning of our history and I was curious about them. I would sometimes rush off after breakfast and run all the way there just so I could spend an hour in the water, letting it cascade over me and down upon the rocks. It made me feel alive to do that, to stand in that icy, torrential water. It made me feel like nothing else ever could, you know? It made me very happy, and we giants are not known for being an especially joyful lot. Garin knew this about me, knew that this was my secret joy, and he followed me there more than once to spy upon me. On this particular day, he decided to confront me and we argued. I suppose neither of us was really old enough to understand exactly what we were doing, but we'd seen others fight and it did not occur to us that one of us could actually die."

Na'aven seemed to sigh, although there was no wind in her lungs, let alone were there lungs to produce such a thing. Nevertheless, she made the sound and her expression saddened before she resumed her tale.

"He pushed me over the falls, of course, and I fell, not to my death so much as to my transformation. I watched my body being pummeled by the rushing water below me and I slowly realized that I was no longer in it. Rather, I was somehow hovering above it. How long I stayed there, I have no idea. But my mother and father eventually found me and they coaxed me away from the falls."

Na'aven paused, smiling a little. "They were friends with a most artful witch, and they brought her with them because she had put a tracking spell on me so that she could find me. It was she, more than anyone else, who realized I was not dead and who convinced me to leave the falls and to follow my parents' home. I have always thought that if she had still been around when Garin betrayed us all and had to be imprisoned, she would have found a way for me to remain with my parents rather than having to stay with Garin."

Donnie, somewhat startled by this news, interrupted Na'aven's story. "Wait, you mean it wasn't Catie who helped you at the falls?"

Na'aven shook her head, heavy droplets flying from her watery hair. "No, Catie was just a little girl back then, and not very skilled. This was long before she went away, you understand. No, it was Margawse who helped me, and she was wonderful and gracious, like you. I mean, you are both more divine than Catie ever was, for at least as long as I knew her. Margawse's other sister, Philînan, was a bit like you two, but even she was less, if you know what I mean."

"Her other sister?" Donnie gulped. "Wait, are you saying that Catie and Margawse were sisters? But I've been told that Catie was the daughter of Margawse and Gwydion."

"No, Margawse had a different child with him, a girl with reddish hair, if I recall her correctly," Na'aven averred, her eyes widening with surprise at Donnie's remark. "Frankly, even though Catie called her Mother, I always thought of Margawse and Catie as sisters and believed that to be their true relation. And yet, Margawse was certainly old enough to be Catie's mother…although I have it in my mind that they were all daughters of Morrían. But then, my mind is shadowy and fraught with confusion. There might have been a different sister. Perhaps Catie *was* her daughter. Or was Margawse not Margawse, but was she her other daughter? Well, that could be something I've made up in my memory, I'm afraid. It is so difficult to remember it properly. You see, Morrían died when I was little more than a babe, so I never knew her well." Na'aven smiled blandly, then she brightened and said confidently, "She too was a friend of the Ettins, especially the Eotens of Eotenmóras, who were my tribe. She was popular amongst our number and we added much of her history here in Medregai to ours."

Donnie decided to ignore Na'aven's confused ramblings and instead mused aloud, "Hmm, that must mean Catie was born here in Medregai, right? And maybe she lied to Sylvester about her parentage and what she was doing here. Well, no surprises there, I guess."

She focused back on Na'aven and inquired, "What did you mean when you said she went away? Where did she go and when? When did she come back?"

But Na'aven was shaking her head again. "That I do not know. My mother might know, if she's still alive, but I was too young to be told much about all that. I recall that Catie was sent away, but when Margawse and Philînan escaped, Catie was made to come back here and watch over the Ganlonds."

Donnie had to sit down after hearing this tidbit. She shuffled her feet to the same rock as before, noticing that the boombox had disappeared so she didn't have to move it to sit, and then she sank back against the hard surface.

"So, Catie took over after Margawse left?" Donnie reiterated, thinking aloud again. She reminded herself that Na'aven seemed almost completely confused about the past and, therefore, whatever she said couldn't be relied upon until proven by a second source. Nevertheless, it seemed likely that Catie had traveled at some point in her life, probably more than once, and had been made to return to watch over the Ganlonds. A task she finally ended by handing it to Donnie.

"But if that's true, that means she's been here far, far longer than she admitted to Sylvester," Donnie murmured, "which I already sort of knew. But I had no idea she was here *that* long. My goodness, this all does get curiouser and curiouser, doesn't it? So, do you remember from what or whom did Margawse and Philînan escape?" she asked Na'aven with resignation, once she'd regrouped her racing thoughts.

"Oh, dear, let me see," replied Na'aven, her face taking on a thoughtful expression. "Margawse had her child—as I said before she was a little girl with reddish blonde hair, as I recall, but I only saw her once so I can't be certain I am remembering her rightly. Or no, wait, might she have been Morrían's child, not Margawse's?" the young giantess questioned herself, looking unsure again. "You see, Morrían died but I would sometimes get her mixed up with Margawse because they looked and acted so much alike. Anyway, someone was hunting the two sisters, that much I know, so they escaped with the little girl, whoever she belonged to. My mother said they were in a different world after that, and that the little girl would have to grow up not knowing anything about who she really was.

"And within a few days of their leaving, Catie was called back here." Na'aven's expression became quizzical again and she admitted slowly, "There was something about a temporal aberration, something important. You see, the magical lands used to be somewhere else, then they were brought here, but that was by a really old Catie that nobody knew at that time. Then she went away and her mother, Morrían, came here and built her cottage on the Ganlonds. And Morrían's daughter, Margawse, replaced her as Ér Ainíl after Morrían died. I know this because there were others who came with the older Catie and sought refuge for their magical lands here too. And that's how all the magical lands came to be here in Írtha. I have no idea where they were before that, though.

"Now, when I was a little girl—this is around the time of the War of Sorrow, of course. Anyway, back then, there were eleven magical lands in all of Írtha and at leave five of them came to this world around the same time as the Ganlonds. But many of them had already died by the time Garin and I were imprisoned together in the cave, so I do not know which ones might remain."

Donnie sighed and hung her head for a moment. When she raised it back up, she inquired carefully, "How sure are you of all this, Na'aven? Because some of what you've told me is very different from what Catie admitted to and what a few other beings, like the trees in the Gahal Glæd, know of the past. Well, it's not completely different," she conceded, "it's just not clear to me who did what. Or when it was done."

Na'aven shrugged. "Well, I was a child when all this was going on, of course, so there is that to be considered. Plus my mind now exists only in a supramundane state and there is much gone from it after all this time. If my mother is still alive, she will know the truth to your queries."

Donnie clapped her hands to knees and stared at Na'aven in surprise, exclaiming, "Goodness, how long do you Ettins normally live, if much of this happened a couple millennia ago?"

It was Na'aven's turn to look taken aback. "You mean you don't know that we are one of the four immortal peoples of Írtha and only magic can kill us?"

"Four immortal peoples?" Donnie repeated hollowly.

The giantess water spirit stared at her expectantly. "Yes, of course," she said, "with the other three being Madra or higher witches and Munus or higher wizards, then the gods, and lastly there are the sorcerers, or magic thieves, as we called them. There are several other races that live a very long time, but none of them are immortal. I am, of course, thinking of the Álvar, who are not to be trusted, you know. They are infamous for their thieving too and have often been aligned with sorcerers throughout the ages. If you know any, be highly suspect of them, I beg you."

Donnie blinked several times and nodded at Na'aven with a faint smile haunting her lips. "Um, yes, I've met some already and can't say I was all that impressed. While beautiful and sparkly, they seemed to be hiding something and were quite defensive. And they hate dragons, apparently, which to me is just wrong."

Na'aven smiled back at her. "Oh, I knew I would like you! I used to love to play with the *vírata* of the Brumal Mountains. I was still small enough to ride them, you see. They were fun and full of mischief."

Donnie looked at the ground sadly and then back up at the water spirit, saying, "Well, we have to go in search of some soon, so you may get to meet more. Apparently, they're all gone from Medregai, so finding them is going to be a bit of a chore. And I—well, you should know that I was commanded by the gods to kill three of them a couple of weeks ago, during the battle we told you about earlier."

When Na'aven's features drew immediately into a stern frown, Donnie nodded, explaining forlornly, "The Iceni Meræ, the ones helping Valledai, or rather fooling him into thinking they were helping him, they implanted the dragons with all this weaponry from the future and so the gods directed me to kill them. It wasn't fair and it wasn't right, and I tried to convince the dragons to let me help them become something better because I so desperately wanted them to live, not die, but…" Donnie closed her eyes and swallowed her tears. "I failed and had to kill them because I couldn't let them destroy the king's army or my friends or the magical creatures from the Ganlonds who were fighting with the king," she admitted.

Na'aven was silent for quite a while before she pointed out carefully, "You know, if a debt is owed for their deaths, you will pay it. I remember my mother saying that about others in that kind of situation, and I think it will be true for you too."

"Yes, and I expect to pay dearly for them, Na'aven," Donnie admitted much more bravely than she felt. The mysterious wound in her shoulder still scared the bejeezus out of her and so she ignored it as if it wasn't really there. That was stupid of her maybe, but it got her through the day without obsessing about her potentially imminent death by black hole.

Dismissing these thoughts, she squared her shoulders and vowed, "For now, I am going to keep doing my best to help others as much as I can, whenever I can. Which," she intoned solemnly, spreading her hands wide, "is all any of us can ever do."

Na'aven appeared to agree with this because she let the subject drop, instead asking if Donnie had met any other giants or had news of them.

"No, all I know of them is what I learned from reading Flat-Finger's—er, your brother's mind, I mean." She shrugged and added, "I gather they went to Flírgai and settled there."

"Yes, that is what they intended when I was last with them," Na'aven replied. "Back in those days, I would stay with them in the main rooms of the cavern and even ventured outside sometimes when the weather suited me. My mother would read to me, you know, hoping to keep my mind active through all those many long years. It worked too and we were able to communicate quite well, but all that changed once Garin and I were left alone. I had nothing much to occupy my time and so I did what I could to torment him whenever possible and to keep my wits sharpened. I suppose I will have to pay for that one day, so I think we have that in common."

Donnie nodded sympathetically. "I can't blame you for wanting to make his life miserable after everything he did to you and your family. He managed to make me madder than a wet hen the few times I was forced to deal with him. But now that you've told me about your mother, I at least understand why you speak so eloquently and with real intellect, whereas he was—well, not to put too fine a point on it—quite the dullard."

For some reason, this seemed to amuse Na'aven greatly. It took Donnie nearly half a minute to realize that the water spirit was laughing because there was no sound to it, just a lot of water droplets flying in all directions. Na'aven apologized when she realized several of these droplets had landed in Donnie's direction.

"You will find," she explained to Donnie, "that if you meet other giants, they will act the same as Garin did. We giants made a pact long ago to never appear to be too intelligent to other peoples, but rather to maintain a staunch stubbornness and ignorance that seems impenetrable. That way, they leave us alone. My brother was actually quite brilliant and well read. I don't think you can have found his books and papers yet, but they should be assembled in a room that is accessed by standing upon the big table and pulling yourself up into the room."

She faltered a moment before pointing out wryly, "Well, if you are as tall as a grown giant you can do that. Otherwise, you will need to use the handholds carved into the wall to climb upward to the room…oh, even then…well, you're a witch, you can figure it out for yourself, I imagine."

Donnie, so bemused by the revelation regarding Flat-Finger's hidden intellect, had not really been listening to Na'aven go on about the giant's library. But she now suddenly remembered the carving in the middle of the big table and asked Na'aven about its origin.

Once again taken aback by a question from Donnie, Na'aven replied, "Why, that is the Sign of the Immortals, of course. Have you not yet read the Scroll of Talbula Halladd D'Orsti?" she inquired, her voice rising with what sounded a lot like impatience. "I believe all is explained in that about the Immortal peoples of Írtha. Granted, I have only ever read a copy of part of the scroll and I do not know if it was accurate, but it said that each of the lower sections of the symbol represent three magical branches of the four immortal peoples, while the jewel in the top end was for us, the Ettins. I'm not sure where the original scroll is now, but last I knew it was in the Forrieghness Tower in Anûmanétus, where the Sarn King makes his throne. If you have not yet visited there, I recommend you go, and soon. You can tell me about it when you return."

And to Donnie's immense surprise, the water spirit, after making this almost acerbically delivered suggestion, rolled her shoulders forward and her head disappeared in a great mound of water that smoothed out and vanished, leaving only a few waves to gently lap at Donnie's feet several seconds later.

With that, Donnie realized that she had been summarily dismissed by the giantess.

Chuckling to herself with amusement, Donnie took hold of Wiwila's neck and projected her next intentions to the horse in both pictures and words, sending the horse a calming wave of love. She took out her wand and, with a quick flick of it, materialized them both near the front porch of the cottage. She led Wiwila to the barn, gave her a quick rubdown and fed her some oats and hay, then made her way to the house, where dinner was just now being served and the conversation had apparently turned quite lively.

Chapter 11
Stairway to Heaven

When Donnie entered the cottage through the front door, her gaze went directly to Warren, whom, she was told, had insisted on joining them at the table for dinner. She noted the paleness beneath his naturally warm complexion and the grim set to his jaw denoting just how tightly he was holding himself against the pain he must surely be feeling throughout his entire torso.

She smiled sweetly and nodded hello at him, chirping, "It's very good to see you up and about a little bit, but we don't want you overdoing it, okay? Therefore, it's right back to bed with you after dinner, and we'll see how you're feeling in the morning. Now, that's me speaking as your doctor and I will brook no arguments from you or anyone else." She grinned at everyone and they all chuckled at her agreeably.

Warren nodded to her and the conversation continued its natural flow. It seemed they had collectively read of her interactions with the giants' spirits in this new book of their adventures, and had been discussing the need to visit the Forrieghness Tower in Anûmanétus all the while she had been in the stables preparing Wiwila for the night. The book was currently sitting open before Diego, who was glancing through it with interest, making his way slowly toward the front as the others talked.

Donnie soon gleaned that Sylvester thought the Talbula scroll, as he called it, should just simply be asked for in Donnie's library, but Falwaïn and Akanna did not like this idea because, if the scroll appeared, it would then reside here instead of at its rightful home of several millennia. This, naturally, meant that the two warriors were arguing for a visit to the capital city and its old tower, a detour that Sylvester and Diana thought unwise and unnecessary. Diego and Rex had yet to voice their opinions and both looked reluctant to do so, appearing quite glad to see Donnie and let her be the deciding vote.

Two large bowls of spaghetti, each liberally doused with cheesy tomato sauce, got passed around and emptied not long afterward, as everyone ate hungrily and cleared their plates quickly. Donnie listened to the discussion going on around her without comment, mulling over her own thoughts while still paying some attention to what was being said by the others. When she finally did want to speak, she pushed her empty plate away and waited while it and other empty ones were lifted off the wooden surface of the table and floated to the sink, where the scrubber had been poised for the last hour in avid anticipation of a good night's cleaning.

Donnie wiped her mouth one last time with her napkin, laid it down in front of her and folded her hands together, resting them on the soft cloth. She waited for a lull in the conversation to occur before announcing quietly, "We'll have to go the tower, you know."

When this elicited surprised gasps from a couple of the others, Donnie kept her gaze fixed on Sylvester, who was about to argue with her, and shook her head. "No, Sylvester, you'll have to give in on this one. I'm not sure why you don't want to go there, but I'm guessing it has something to do with one of those spells that has been cast upon you. I say that because it is very odd to me that you, of all the souls in this house, don't wish to visit the most extensive repository of magical information and history that Medregai has to offer."

Sylvester shot her a look of surprise. "One of the spells cast upon me? However did you come to that conclusion?"

"Because I remember reading in Catie's journals her warning about avoiding the Toren fi Førrens or Tower of the Førrens Sea Eagles at all costs, which is what the Forrieghness Tower is also called, isn't it?"

Donnie looked over at Falwaïn and he murmured, "Yes," to her query.

She redirected her attention back to Sylvester and explained, "Catie was weirdly adamant that she would never go back to that place and that none of those living with her were to go to it either. I suspect she was not welcomed there when she went, but I don't know if something more specific than that happened that caused her to vow to not step foot in the place ever again. But, since we know she had no issue with casting spells upon you, I don't think it's a stretch to figure one of them is likely about the tower."

"And because she wanted so much for it to be avoided, you think that means we must go there?" asked the cat, his voice rising in pitch.

"Well, sure," Donnie said brightly, grinning at his anxious response. "Don't you?"

"Not particularly, no!" the cat retorted. But he acceded that, "Well, if there is a spell upon me, as you suggest, then I *would* feel that way, wouldn't I? Oh, very well, Donemere, if you insist, we shall go, even if it compromises our safety, as I fear it may well do. But should we go before or after the Mîrlonds?"

"Before, most assuredly, just in case something there can shed light on what is attacking the Mîrlonds," Akanna suggested, and Falwaïn nodded his agreement.

Donnie shrugged, conceding, "Yeah, that might be best. And since the whole trip is going to take us longer now, we should get going as soon as possible, right?"

"Wait!" interjected Warren, his eyes alight with indignation. "You're not thinking of going without me, are you?" He looked around the table at his friends, read their expressions, and then sighed (it was really more of a groan) quite loudly. "You are. I can see it."

"Well, I'm not going at all," Diana said, her mouth set into a stubborn line. "As I've stated before, I won't go back there."

Ignoring her friend, Donnie turned an apologetic face to Warren and said, "I'm sorry," going on to explain, "We need to get going on this, yet you're not ready to travel. And it could be several more weeks before you can go anywhere. We have to leave long before then."

"Why do you say 'long before then'?" he demanded curiously. "Is there something you're not telling me—or is it something you're hiding from everyone and not just me?" This last he tacked on because of the startled looks that had appeared on most of the others' faces when he'd made the first conjecture.

And then Diego observed softly, "*Si*, according to this book she is most definitely hiding something; something very, very serious, *mis amigos*." He looked pointedly from the book in his hands to Donnie and then back at the book, which he had taken up again and resumed looking through.

Donnie brushed his remark aside with a small laugh, waving her arms carelessly, showing that she was totally prepared to argue the point. "Of course I'm not hiding anything," she chortled, "of course not! It's just that we need to get this all figured out and I think the Mîrlonds might be part of that and…"

Her voice tailed away as she realized that every single one of them was glaring at her except Falwaïn and he was shaking his head at her forlornly.

"It's no good, Donnie. You're going to have to tell them," he advised her. "Or better yet, you should show them."

When protests of, "Show us what?" sounded all around, with Donnie still looking unconvinced, Falwaïn held up his hands to shush the others and added, "Or they can read about it in the book, because, let me assure you, it's in there, right at the beginning, as Diego obviously just discovered for himself. I found it there earlier tonight. Like you, I had yet to read the new book in its entirety, so I was unaware of its contents and what they might reveal. I am very much afraid, my honey woman, now that Diego knows, you really cannot hide it from anyone else any longer. It is time to tell all. Besides, everyone who journeys with us will need to know what else to look for when we get to the tower."

Donnie, not liking the turn the situation had just taken, sat back hard in her chair and obstinately crossed her arms in front of her. She didn't want to unsettle the others and knew the news of her injury was going to rattle Rex, in particular. She had wanted to head off any kind of discovery like this, but she realized that this was her own fault because she hadn't taken the time to read the first few chapters of that darned book before giving it to Warren so he could reassure himself about Liz and Jesse's welfare. She frantically tried to come up with some avoidance mechanism that might turn the subject elsewhere for the moment, but her mind went perfectly blank and she found herself loosening her grip and slumping her shoulders in defeat.

"Very well," she carped mutinously. She stood and dragged her t-shirt over her head to expose the bandage on her left shoulder. Without saying another word, she pulled the bandage back and let the others see the wound underneath. Everyone except Warren stood up and gathered around her to get a better view.

The color drained from Diana's face when she got a good look at the black wound and she sent Donnie a disturbed grimace, while the others seemed mesmerized by the gaping dark hole in Donnie's shoulder.

Rex, the last to crowd around her, made her crouch down to show him. He took one look at the injury and cried out, "Oh, Mama, what happened? How'd you get that? You're not gonna die, are you? Please, don't leave me alone, Mama, please!"

Donnie cupped his snout with her hand, drew him close and kissed him in the mama spot right between the eyes, assuring him she was going to be around a very, very long time and was never going to leave him alone.

In the meanwhile, Falwaïn began to describe the wound's provenance, keeping his explanations succinct, while the others settled back down into their chairs. Donnie turned to allow Warren a good look at her shoulder since he had yet to see it. He scowled at it and then at her face.

While Falwaïn continued talking, Donnie sat down. She chewed her lip and studied the reactions of the others closely. Her injury was clearly not a surprise to everyone, as her friends' expressions told Donnie that both Diana and Sylvester, at the very least, had known of it beforehand.

"I am not versed with *vírat* lore," growled Warren quite vexedly once Falwaïn finished his expositions, "so I don't think I understand what this means, frankly."

"It means, that unless Donnie is able to find the *vírata* this Uncle of hers made her promise to lead to the sea and convinces them to follow her to that sea," replied Diana, her tone gravely ominous and her eyes glinting with blatant displeasure as she studied Donnie, "her wound will just grow bigger and bigger until it consumes her entirely and she no longer exists. I'm sorry to be the one to inform you of this, Rex, but there is nothing on this earth, or any other earth in existence, that can stop that process, other than her fulfilling her promise, no matter what she says to the contrary. And, as we all know, there are no more dragons on Írtha, so just where she's supposed to find Uncle's kith in this endless universe of ours is more than a mystery, it's damn near an impossibility!" She rounded on Donnie furiously and demanded, "Why did you have to make that silly do-gooder promise to that sneaky snake to begin with?"

Donnie refused to be goaded by her friend's outburst, instead focusing her attention on her bandage, flipping it over so that it once again covered her wound. When it was righted properly, she pulled her t-shirt back into place. These few moments of avoidance gave her time to think of a calm response to Diana's intense heat.

"I will make that same promise to anyone I think needs my help," she insisted blandly, looking not just at Diana but also at the others with a sweeping glance. Even though most were staring at her with exasperation, she maintained her cool attitude and added, "Because that is who I am and I will not change that part of me just because it has been taken so literally that it might one day kill me. I choose to believe in me and in my friends—those being you all, who I know with one hundred percent certainty will help me now that I need it, simply because that's who you are. So, tell me, am I wrong to believe in either you or in myself?" she challenged boldly, looking around at them all once again.

They each conceded, somewhat shamefacedly so, that, no, she was not wrong to believe that and they would of course help her.

Donnie beamed at them with a sunny smile. "And see, none of you are any different from me, are you?" she exclaimed with satisfaction. "I firmly believe that each and every one of you would have made the same promise to Uncle if you'd been there when he asked it of me. And I still maintain that he didn't get me to promise to help his people because he wanted me dead, but because he genuinely believed I could help." She lifted her chin and gave a short, emphatic nod. "And I will help the dragons—no, let me amend that: *we* will help them!"

After proclaiming this, she looked around expectantly, and, to a one, her friends nodded their agreement, however reluctantly.

"Fine," drawled Diana, "while you are off on this pointless trip west, Warren and I will research dragons and we'll see what's in your library about their current whereabouts. And," she added, with a determined grin on her face, "I may just take a little excursion of my own to see what's in Flat Finger's library."

"Are we agreed to leave tomorrow morning for the Mîrlonds?" asked Akanna.

While Warren looked as though he wanted to protest this decision, the others overruled him and began making their plans. Unsure of just how to get them all, including their horses, to travel over a thousand miles west in little more than one week—less if they could manage it—the discussion turned to logistics of fast-paced travel. It was agreed that the fastest route was to head south on the Annûar Path to where it intersected the Danduin

Road at Lænemeade, follow that to Hetwood Village, where the Eldaren Road could be picked up and travel that all the way to Anûmanétus. They would have to pack light, which was not a problem because Donnie could materialize whatever they needed whenever they needed it, just as she had on their last journey together when they had headed north.

"I believe it would be best to avoid towns because word of our presence will likely precede us and will certainly cause trouble," Akanna offered, looking around for agreement.

"And why would you say that?" inquired Donnie in mild protest.

The vincan regarded her a moment with steely gaze, then she explained in a strong, steady voice, "You are the most powerful witch Medregai has known for many centuries and news of your existence has reached even the ears of my people as far away as the Mîrlonds."

Donnie frowned at her, tipping her head to the side enquiringly.

Akanna cleared her throat, then admitted, "I have not been completely forthcoming with information that I possess and, for that, I apologize, but I had to make sure you were all trustworthy. Now that I am convinced of you, I will no longer hide what I know. I am able to communicate with my people in Canta'Lem telepathically and it was they who suggested that I approach you for aid in dealing with the beast attacking the Mîrlonds. I am afraid that it is, by now, widely known that you have agreed to help us fight this creature and will be journeying with me to the Mîrlonds. And yes, it is a creature that is attacking our home; that much we know for sure. And we very much fear that it is a Ghérôntog you will be facing."

"A Ghérôntog! What makes you think it's that?" demanded Falwaïn, looking apprehensive at the prospect, for Ghérôntogs were the most vile of creatures living in the entirety of Írtha.

"What else do you know that eats magic, poisons the earth around it, and sucks the lifeblood of the land into itself? For that is what's happening to my home. I know of nothing else that could do these things," Akanna maintained staunchly, trading her sardonic gaze from Falwaïn to Donnie.

Donnie made a face and murmured, "There are lots of things that can do that in my world, unfortunately, most of which are chemical in nature. But I agree that's unlikely to be what this is." She turned to Falwaïn and said, "Just what is a Ghérôntog? Mammal, reptile, fish, bird, worm, what? Or do I really not want to know that?" she jokingly tacked on, batting her eyes at him facetiously.

But Falwaïn turned a very serious face to her and replied grimly, "They are the most mighty and fiendish of all black magical beings here on Írtha. I only know legends about them, really; legends that originate from times long ago because it's been many ages since anyone encountered one of the beasts. They are said to bore deep into the land and then consume anything or anyone of substance within its reach, which grows larger with the more they subsume. What it actually looks like though, I have never heard."

He paused a moment, scratching his chin while he searched his memory for more information. "Their legends," he continued slowly, "were told to us when we young to keep all errant children in line, you see, and I must say that threat worked on a number of adults too. According to the stories, if you are unlucky enough to be caught by one, the Ghérôntog will steal everything that you are, beginning with your magic and your mind. When those are gone, it will then take your body and soul. It is said that, once touched by one, it is impossible to recover your wits ever again. It is also said that they care nothing for life, only power—or magic, if you will."

Donnie narrowed her eyes in thought and murmured, "Which is to say, basically, that they go after the spark of power we all have within us, the spark that underlies our triunes, including our sense of self. Is that about right?" she asked, trying to interpret properly Falwaïn's words and the glimmer of real fear that had flashed across his handsome countenance. When he nodded, she went on to add, "You know, that kind of reminds me of a disease called Alzheimer's from my world. If you have it, you slowly lose all sense of who you are and of those around you. It ends up taking absolutely everything of value from you."

"Essentially, then yes, that is exactly what a Ghérôntog does to its poor victims." Falwaïn grabbed his glass of beer and took a long swig from it. He put it down with a bang and added, "Déagmun said he faced one once. He fought it a hundred years, he told me, in a battle wild and furious, with both taking from the other and then turning the magic back upon their foe. He said he managed to defeat it only when two other Munus wizards joined him in the fray. The three of them together were finally more than a match for the thing and they eventually vanquished it."

"Oh, really?" Donnie grimaced before asking, "Um, did he happen to say how they did that? Vanquished it, I mean."

Falwaïn shook his head. "No, I was far too young and not yet versed in my novitiate's keldor to be trusted—er, my studies," he added as an aside and Donnie's knitted brow cleared. "As I say, I was too young to be privy to that kind of information. Déagmun was always afraid that we, his six apprentices, would take what little we knew and go out into the world, where we would likely be killed by a creature far more proficient than we. And he was undoubtedly right to think that, because we were all somewhat reckless in our ways."

He took another long pull of beer and sank back against his chair, his blue eyes focused on the years from his youth. "I had just made it to my third year of novit when I was recalled home by my father. I did not visit with Déagmun again for at least the next three long years, and by that time I had become both man and vaunted warrior, so the subject never arose during the several occasions I had the pleasure of his company thereafter." Coming back to the present, Falwaïn wiped his mouth with his napkin and sent Donnie a roguish grin. "But he was an inveterate scribe, so there is every likelihood he chronicled the battle. And, I just happen to know that all of his scrolls are catalogued and stored in Forrieghness Tower."

"Well, there is our reason to go then, if we were indeed searching for one," Diego pointed out, and the others nodded their agreement.

"We leave on the morrow," Akanna announced with satisfaction to Donnie, although her eyes bounced fleetingly toward Diana. "The sooner, the better, I believe."

Donnie leaned back in her chair and gave the vincan a short nod. "Yes, well," she began, "I'll need to speak to Bronadulach first, so don't expect to go anywhere until after that. Hold on a minute," she said, and she sent a telepathic message to Bronadulach. He responded that he would be at the cottage shortly after his rounds in the morning. Donnie relayed this to the others and then told them all to get a good night's sleep.

She and Falwaïn helped Warren to his bedroom, whereupon Donnie cast her healing chant once again, noticing that it helped to ease the tension and pain that had been building on their friend's features. They left him almost fallen asleep and went to their own bedroom, where the dog and cat were both snoring deeply on the bed.

Early the next morning, Akanna was already in the kitchen when Donnie shambled out sleepily in search of tea for herself and coffee for Falwaïn. The vincan sat at the table, looking down at it pensively, all the while tapping both her right foot and her left hand rapidly upon the nearest wooden surfaces.

Donnie mumbled, "Good morning," to her and Akanna swept her eyes upward to Donnie's face.

"I find I am having to enforce great patience upon myself rather than physically roust you all from your slumbers, so a good morning it is not," the vinca replied with a sharp edginess to her voice.

Donnie chuckled at this imagery. "No, I imagine it's not good for you," she conceded. "You've been waiting for this for a long time, haven't you? But I have every confidence that you will master your anxiety well enough so that we may experience a pleasant start to our journey, yes? Especially when we say goodbye to Diana," she said drolly, and Akanna had the grace to shoot her an apologetic look.

"Yes, of course. I will cause no trouble with her, I swear it."

Donnie nodded, holding her cup to her lips to take a small sip. Her other hand held Falwaïn's blacker brew. "Thank you," she breathed, beginning to make her way back to the bedroom with the same slow, shuffling steps as when she'd entered the kitchen, "because I'd hate to have to hurt you. But…if you deliberately piss off my best friend too many more times, I might just have to do something neither of us will enjoy."

Nearly two hours later, Donnie and Sylvester were still chatting with Bronadulach, having informed him of their departure and then moved on to discuss the needs of the Ganlonds while they would be gone. He nodded and otherwise kept silent until the end of their meeting, whereby he stated that he and his brethren would guard the borders of the Ganlonds and that nothing would be done with the refugees until Donnie's return. She made an unhappy face at him, but knew she had to agree to this stipulation.

"All right, if none of you feel confident in letting the refugees in while I'm gone, I will keep my blocking spell active. That way, no one can enter who has not already been accepted by the Ganlonds," Donnie relented with a heartfelt sigh, but then spread her hands in the air defensively when both Bronadulach and Sylvester looked like they wanted to argue with her. She hastily added, "It's just that I feel I should point out once again that the Ganlonds will decide who gets to stay, not me. But I understand there is apprehension about possible conflict before the Ganlonds can make its determination regarding each applicant, so I agree to keeping all refugees out until we get back and I can monitor the process."

It was another half hour before they were all ready and assembled in front of the stables. There they found Diana and Warren, who had hobbled out with Diana's help even though pain was etched in his every feature, sitting on the bench under Sisnos, the apple tree located nearest to the stables.

Warren looked decidedly put out, and Diana was giving him no quarter with that.

"Ha!" she crowed, letting out a rich, throaty laugh, "now you know how I felt the last time you all took off without me!"

"You were a cow then," he reminded her irritably, "so you could not very well have accompanied us on our journey to find Valledai."

"No, but that doesn't mean I liked it any more than you do right now," she rejoined, her chin set stubbornly.

They watched the others milling around and both felt a tug on their hearts, which each recognized as concern that they might not see their friends for some time, and possibly not at all if something disastrous were to occur. Neither of them liked the feeling and both contemplated calling their friends back but knew that would lead to nothing more than a short delay in the goodbyes.

Donnie and the others took off heading west, skirting Catie's salt works and then traveling southward. They passed Julia's practice ground, noting that several of its former inhabitants had moved back in and the little community of magical creatures there was beginning to thrive once more.

The group of travelers cantered farther south over the rolling moors of the Eotenmóras, turning west around noon so that they would eventually meet up with the Annûar Path on its southern course. It took the better part of the afternoon for them to reach the main road and once they did they settled into sets of two horses and their riders, with Rex, as usual, trotting alongside Donnie, Sylvester, and Wiwila. At times he would get bored and spring far ahead of everyone, only to return a little later to report on what they could expect to encounter in the next hour or so.

Donnie, apprehensive about the always explosive interactions between Diego and Akanna, had Wiwila fall back so that she could travel by Diego, which meant that Akanna and Falwaïn were in the vanguard position. They went on like this until they decided to stop for the night and Donnie set up camp for them about two hundred yards east of the Annûar Path.

***

As soon as the others had left the cottage, Diana helped Warren to the kitchen and together they consumed another pot of coffee and a round of cinnamon and sugar toast, slathered in creamy butter first. Her hunger satiated for the moment by the spiced and sweetened bread, Diana asked aloud for sandwiches to be made for lunch. Immediately, various utensils sprang to life, the refrigerator door opened by itself, and several fixings floated to the cutting board. In just a couple of minutes, three sandwiches and two apples were securely stored in a plastic container waiting on the counter. Diana rose to carry the dirty breakfast plates to the sink, then she reached up to a high cupboard to grab one of Donnie's travel canteens, which she filled with cold water from the tap.

"You're going to Flat Finger's library, aren't you?" guessed Warren.

Diana nodded vigorously. "Yes, I'm quite curious about it; aren't you? I can't help but wonder what giants find either entertaining or edifying to read, whichever is their particular bag, I guess." She picked up the plastic container and began to stride toward the front door. "I doubt I'll be home until late, so I'll probably see you at dinner but don't wait for me, okay?" She paused in the doorway and added, "Donnie said that Mickey T wants to come by today, so be expecting him soon. He likes to play *Murder*, you know, which should be in the games cupboard." She pointed to the left side of the big hutch and Warren nodded in acknowledgement.

She went out to the stables and found Otis already saddled.

"Diego got me ready earlier," he explained while Diana stuffed their lunch into one of the saddlebags hanging over the horse's back. "He said

Donnie asked him to because she knew you'd want to go to the cavern. He also told me to take good care of you. As if I would do anything else!" the horse scoffed proudly.

Diana chuckled. "He's a good friend, is Diego…as is Donnie," was all she murmured. She mounted Otis with a quick, graceful movement, then he trotted out of the stables and to the eastern path leading away from the cottage. It had been traveled so often of late, it was fairly well beaten down and easily traversable, so they made good time on it and arrived at the lake at some time shortly after noon, or so Diana judged by the position of the sun.

As they approached the lake, she was surprised to find a small crowd of magical animals gathered around its edges. The watery figure of the giantess Na'aven, displaying only her head and shoulders, had arisen from the deep lake and was engaged in telling stories to her enthralled audience.

Diana and Otis rode close quietly and waited without comment until Na'aven finished her tale about a young girl with two toes on each foot and how she had won a dancing contest. It was a lively, funny tale, and the smallest in the crowd were thoroughly entertained, while their parents and older siblings were also appreciative of Na'aven's message of acceptance. When she'd finished with it, Otis ambled over to the lake's edge and Diana called out to her.

Na'aven nodded at them in recognition. "You are Donnie's friends. I remember you from yesterday."

"Yes, I am Diana, and this is Otis." Diana introduced herself and her horse with a thumb pointed inward and then a couple of loving pats on the neck of the great white stallion she sat astride.

Na'aven smiled. "You are bond mates, I can tell. And have been for a very, very long time." She let out a small gasp of wonder. "You too are immortal, like Donnie and like me," the giantess said, and she smiled even wider. "And you are an Ér Ainíl, like Donnie, although not like Donnie, for your magic is very different from hers."

Diana rolled her shoulders uneasily as she sat back in her saddle and shot the water spirit a hesitant, curious look. "You are quite perspicacious, aren't you? Especially for a *yewiha meni*," she noted.

Na'aven laughed outright at this. Her laughter had a musical quality to it, as of water droplets falling down onto bells or striking strings on an instrument.

She replied, "I suppose I am that—for a water spirit, as you say. For I am made happy this day, because I am reaching out to touch everything around me and am receiving love and kindness in return," she explained enthusiastically. "I am reveling in my new life, I admit to that, certainly, and with much happiness. It is good to be in fresh air again and to be able to communicate with others freely. It is all making me very joyous," she reiterated simply, and Diana was reminded that she was actually still just a child emotionally.

Diana smiled back at the young giantess. "I'm glad you've been given this new life then."

Na'aven's eyes widened and she said with feeling, "Me too! And I have the Ganlonds and Donnie to thank for it. We giants are faithful to those who do us kindnesses, so Donnie has earned my eternal gratitude. And the Ganlonds and I will protect each other and those who live here. That is the pact I made with the magical lands when they helped me send my brother to his death, a pact I will never break or I will be sent on to Canavar just like Garin was."

It took Diana a moment to recall that Garin was Flat Finger. "Uh, yeah, well, I, er, I don't think he'll be missed all that much, to be honest," she muttered in embarrassment. "I, er, I'm sorry about that."

Na'aven shrugged, and many water droplets sprayed through the air around her. "He was never a nice boy and it was no surprise to me that he was not a nice adult either." She gave Diana a solemn look, and then her whole aspect changed and she asked brightly, "But you did not come here to discuss my brother, did you?"

Diana chuckled, shaking her head. "No, not really. Although I do want to know how to get to his library. Can you tell me that?"

The giantess blinked uncertainly at the question. "Well, my family's library is located at the top of the cavern, as I said yesterday. You just grab the handholds and pull yourself up to it."

"Oh, yes, well, that works okay if you're a giant, I suppose, but for those of us who are much smaller than you, that poses a bit of a problem. Is there no other entrance that might be easier for me to use?"

Na'aven's expression cleared by the time Diana was done speaking, but she now looked apologetic. "No, that is the only way I know of to get there. But can you not use your magic for this purpose?"

Diana considered the suggestion. "Well, it's just that my magic really is different from Donnie's and I can't do the sort of spell she finds so easy to cast. But, while it may take me some time, I will indeed find a way to that library, that much I know."

She said goodbye to Na'aven and those around who had been listening to their exchange and then she rode Otis into the cavern. Once there, she dismounted and stood with her horse in the grey light that stopped just beyond the cavern's entrance. "Hoo boy, Otis," she said quietly, unnerved by how her voice reverberated eerily back at her since they were alone. "I didn't think this through all that well, did I?" She laughed nervously and considered her next move. "Okay, first we need some light. Only thing is, I'm pretty sure I can't do light balls like Donnie can."

"You used to be pretty good at magical fire, as I recall," Otis suggested.

"Oh, yeah, I was good at that, wasn't I?" she said thoughtfully, glad to be reminded of the skill.

She went back outside into the bright sunshine and let her eyes re-adjust before she searched the surrounding area for nearby trees, soon finding a small branch that had fallen to the ground. Picking it up, she carried it into the cave proper and took it around the corner so that it was out of the drafty entryway. There, she stood for several seconds concentrating her power to the tips of her fingers. Blowing a slow breath, she touched the end of the branch in her hand with her index finger and now focused her magic into just that one fingertip, willing a small fire to spring to life from her magic.

It took her a few tries, but she was eventually successful and the tip of the branch was lit with a small, silver-colored conflagration. She held the branch aloft like a torch and moved carefully through the chamber over to the fireplace. Otis held the branch in his teeth while Diana dragged some of the smaller splits of wood into the fireplace pit. When she had enough wood piled there, she retrieved the small branch and lit the woodpile with it. In a couple of minutes, they had a blazing fire so that both Diana and Otis could see the contents and extent of the main cave, which made them feel much more comfortable about being there.

"Whew! That's a lot better, isn't it?" Diana commented with a chuckle and Otis snorted his agreement. They looked upward and simultaneously let out huge, deep, and long groans.

"Wow! Seriously, I have absolutely no idea how you're gonna get up there," said Otis, craning his neck high.

"Nor do I," Diana admitted, barely able to even see the ceiling high above them. But she refused to be daunted. "Let me see if I can find these handholds Na'aven said were here. Maybe I can jump from one to the other," she suggested, and they scrutinized the walls around them.

They found the handholds on the far wall, the one that blocked the cave entrance. The first one was about thirty feet from the cavern floor.

Otis whistled (or what passed for a whistle from him). "Guess they didn't want anyone but giants gettin' up there. I mean, you're good, but not that good," he observed, echoing Diana's own thoughts. "Even if you stand on my back, you won't be able to jump up there. Nope, there's got to be another way."

The two of them pondered the situation for some time. Diana paced the cavern, searching for anything that might help her. They discussed the possibility of moving the smallest of the chests, which stood about twice Otis's height, to the wall, thinking that they could perhaps build a ramp for

Otis to get on top of it, and then maybe Diana could jump to the first handhold that way. But even together, the two of them could barely move the chest more than six feet. Exhausted, they stopped and Diana sat on the ground, looking up again.

"You know, even if I made it to the first handhold, there's no way I can get to the second one. Look at how far it is from the first," she complained, pointing at the offending ledges in the rock face.

Otis grunted in response.

They contemplated the situation for another half hour until they were both hungry. Diana retrieved the cheese, tomato, and lettuce sandwiches, giving two to the horse after removing the cheese from them and popping the pieces into her mouth. She chewed happily on them before starting on her sandwich. In addition to the two apples the kitchen had supplied to her, she had grabbed a couple more from the bin in the stables. She munched on one while Otis ate a couple of the others. After this, they still could do nothing more than study the walls and furniture, hoping for inspiration. But, even several hours later, none had come.

Giving up, yet not defeated, they left the cavern and made their way back to the cottage, arriving just before sundown. Warren and Mickey T were surprised they'd made it back so early and invited Diana to join them in a game of *Murder*, but she declined, outlining her afternoon's efforts to them. They discussed possibilities throughout dinner, ending with the thought that perhaps a couple of ropes with hooks on them might suffice.

Deciding to move into Julia's old bedroom, Diana spent the next hour making the room just how she wanted it to be. First, she packed up her few belongings and carried them to the cottage, storing them in either her new room's wardrobe or its matching chest. Then, she changed out the artwork in the bedroom, swapping it for a couple of striking pieces that had been perched upon the knotty pine coffee table and end tables in the workroom, which were situated around Donnie's two wingback red Corinthian leather chairs. She also nabbed a couple of abstract paintings and hung them on the walls in her new abode, wanting to wake up to their vibrant colors and angled shapes. When she was done, she fell into her new and very comfy bed, happy with her efforts, and thereafter slept hard the entire night.

The next morning found her up early to work on two ropes in Catie's workshop at the back of the stables, where she set to fashioning some hooks out of garden implements. When she went into the cottage for breakfast an hour later, she complained to Warren that she was having trouble with the hooks because they would not bear her weight. He suggested she search the shelves in the rear of Donnie's workroom.

"You can find all manner of useful—and useless—things back there," he drawled with a yawn. "I've spent a few hours back there marveling at the assorted toys and tools she has on those shelves. One thing about our Donnie is she's certainly a procurer of very odd artifacts. Although, they could perhaps have good purpose in her world, I suppose."

Taking this advice to heart, Diana spent the morning searching through all kinds of weird stuff on the shelves, finally happening upon what was clearly some climbing gear. She took it out to the kitchen and she and Warren looked over the complicated apparatus dubiously. They carefully took it apart, piece by piece, with both of them ending up feeling like they'd bitten off more than they could chew.

"Maybe we're making this too hard," Warren posited.

Diana agreed with him heartily and said, "Okay, so I go back to my original plan and just find something here to use as a hook that I can attach to the ropes I knotted this morning." She glanced at her friend and added, "What d'ya think?"

"Oh, yeah, I definitely think that might be best," he chortled painfully, holding his ribs with a grimace.

So, Diana did just that, digging out a three-pronged claw and a single-pronged one, holding them both aloft triumphantly.

She had also found some other gear that would be helpful, like a couple of lanterns that she supposed must run on batteries, but which seemed to work just fine even though they could not have been charged in months. But, she surmised, they were likely charged with magic just like so many items of Donnie's seemed to be.

She waited impatiently for the day to end, and she and Warren looked several times for new text in the third book telling how either Donnie or Liz and those with them were faring, or even something regarding Julia and her exploits, but the pages remained blank except for those relating to their own activities. They finally agreed that might be good news, that at least none of the others were in danger…or so they hoped.

They went to bed a bit unsettled, though, and neither slept well, which meant that both were up before the sun and trudged to the kitchen around the same time in search of coffee.

Diana and Otis left almost straight after breakfast that day, this time making it to the cavern around mid-morning. She used a flashlight to get to the fireplace and relit her magical fire there. She added wood to the fire and spread it out over the firepit in back of the hearth, trying to create as big a light source as she could. She'd learned long ago that, with magical fire of the kind where you just need it for lighting purposes, providing it a widespread medium was usually best. Her efforts worked well enough today that she could now see upward a much farther distance than before.

The boombox decided to join them and, from its place on the woodpile, started playing lively music that set the mood for excitement.

Diana gave Otis a pat on the cheek when he wished her luck, and she readied herself for the first rope throw. After ten tries and as many failures, she was beginning to wonder if she could do this. After another ten tries and failures, she was nearly convinced that she could *not* do this. While she could get the hook to reach the handhold quite easily, with her aim improving fast with each throw, it invariably bounced off the rock ledge and crashed to the ground with loud thuds.

Somewhere around noon she finally had some success with the three-pronged grappling hook, so she climbed up the rope and clambered onto the first handhold. It took her only another ten tries or so to get to the second handhold. After an hour there, she looked downward, realizing she was about seventy feet off the ground with no safe way to get back to the floor, and here it was getting on in the afternoon and she'd had no more luck with the third handhold than she had with the first. She felt like crying out in frustration and did, in fact, release a fierce, low growl.

"Otis, I don't think I can do this," she said, keeping her tone evenly modulated.

"No," he replied in a subdued voice, "I don't think you can either. Come down now, okay? If you use one of the ropes, it should get you to at least about halfway down. I'll catch you after that. It's gonna hurt, but I don't think it'll kill either of us."

"Yeah, and then maybe I can read up on that other gear Donnie's got, learn how to use it correctly. It looked like it was for any kind of climbing," she mused aloud, setting the single-pronged hook into the lip of the handhold she was standing on. She carefully let herself down the length of the rope, then pulled her power inward, and let go of the rope.

She fell onto Otis's back and to her saddle, which caught her and gave her a much-needed soft landing.

"Oh!" she exclaimed gratefully to it. "I'd forgotten that Donnie cast the same spell on my saddle as she did on hers. Gosh, that wasn't bad at all for me. How about you, Otis?"

"I barely felt a thing," he assured her while she got down and strode all around him to check. She made him take a few steps so she could see if any of his legs were injured or if anything else might be wrong, but he appeared to be perfectly fine.

She walked over to the fireplace hearth and listened to the song the boombox had just started playing. It was one of Donnie's favorites, she knew, because it played quite often, so much so that even Diana knew most of its lyrics. Wishing it were a clue, like the ones Donnie would get from the musical augur, Diana chuckled to herself for her fancy. While she walked around the wood in the firepit and drew its flames toward the front log where she would then extinguish the fire, she and Otis both sang along with the song. It was not until the tune had ended, its final line having been blasted so loud that it went on to echo throughout the cavern for quite some time once the boombox fell silent, that Diana, suddenly slack-jawed, whirled around and stared at the musical box.

"A stairway to heaven?" she repeated in a whisper.

The boombox beeped at her and disappeared from its wooden perch.

Diana turned and studied the woodpile around where the boombox had been sitting and suddenly its hint blossomed into a full-fledged idea. "Oh, my good goddess!" she shouted, looking at Otis with unbridled glee. "This is a magical woodpile! Donnie even said so in that darned third book, that it had to be charmed so it was always supplied with plenty of wood. And that means, my friend," she crowed with anticipation, moving toward the great stacks of wood in front of her with her hands spread wide as if to reach out and touch their roughened surfaces, "that all I need to do is tell it to stack itself in such a way that…"

She did indeed lay both hands upon the wood, then closed her eyes and willed the wood to stack itself into a kind of stairway or ramp that would reach the ceiling of the cavern. The woodpile trembled and its top pieces began to float upward in long streams. Soon, whole trains of wood arose to curve and curl around in the air before finding their place in their new, zig-zagged configuration.

Diana stepped back and leaned against Otis's shoulder, and together they watched this show with utter enchantment, gaping with wonder as the woodpile rearranged itself into a perfectly passable ramp of split wood that climbed to the dark, inky blackness far, far above.

Otis insisted on trying the wooden staircase out first, running and jumping along it to see if it would in any way falter. When he was satisfied that it could hold them both, he allowed Diana to climb onto his back and he took them up the winding path. While he'd been testing the stairway, Diana had turned back to the fireplace and again spread her magical fire backward and outward to encompass the logs spread out over the big pit. She did such a good job with that they got quite high on their climb before she was forced to use a flashlight to light their way. She had no idea how high they went, but Otis was very tired and quite winded by the time they reached the top. He said he was mightily relieved to step off the stairs onto solid ground again and added that he needed another apple or two.

Diana slipped from his back, set out four apples for him to eat, and also pulled out the two lanterns she'd brought with them, setting both of these on the floor nearby with their lights turned on high.

The lanterns lent a ghostly glow to the large room they had entered, but nevertheless the bookshelves along the walls were fairly discernible, as were three dusty couches and several rugs and ottomans scattered across the floor.

Clearly, this had been a favorite place for the family of giants to congregate and spend their time. The room looked lived in and well loved.

Diana, and Otis too once he'd taken a break from eating apples, stared around the room in wonder for quite some time. For Diana, it was like being back in the *dirĭnĵ's* comfortable quarters with the other wives of her former husband and king, albeit with gargantuan furnishings instead of the normal-sized ones in the *dirĭnĵ*. But, whereas most of Hoeris's other wives had spent their days growing fat and lazy, Diana had Otis, so they spent all their time honing their riding and fighting skills.

Diana, shaking herself from her reverie of days from long ago, walked over to one of the thick rugs on the floor and knelt by it. Surprisingly, she found its threads were soft and plush, even still—although it was also quite dirty and great clouds of dust erupted from its surface when she ran her hand over it. Taking a couple hasty steps backward, she sneezed three times. She wiped her face and nose with her hands, then strode over to one of the ottomans to check it out. It was big enough to be a human-sized bed. She felt of its surface and was astonished that it was made of some very fine silk, with a padding beneath it that was firm, yet yielding enough to be pleasant to a giant's feet...or maybe an ovid's backside.

She turned back to Otis. "Do you believe this place?"

He shook his head, staring around at everything with big eyes. "I hardly can," he admitted wonderingly. "Geez um, I can't get over how much it's like your quarters back in Hoeris's old palace. I saw the inside of that a couple times when the light was just right so that it was visible from the outside," he explained when Diana shot him an amazed look. "Ya think it's possible giants come from Fal'Adîn originally and they lived like our people do? You know, with all these rugs and cushions, I mean."

Diana shook her head. "I don't think so, no. I mean, look at the room below. That's furnished in a pretty conventional, almost boring way, even though that one chair by the fireplace has some good rugs on it. But even those aren't like these ones here."

She turned around and pointed toward the nearest ones, saying as she did so, "These are some of the finest rugs I've ever seen in my life, but how could they possibly have been made in Írtha? I've never heard of looms large enough to create rugs of this size, let alone this quality. These have to be centuries old, if not older, and yet, other than being really dusty, they're still in near-perfect condition. I mean, okay, there are a couple spots looking a little threadbare here and there, but overall these are in great shape." She began to move around one of the larger rugs, following its contours. "I wish I could see them from higher up, because I think they have some wonderful scenes woven into them, almost like tapestries, you know?"

Otis too had been surveying the rugs situated around the room with a critical eye and he replied, "Now's a time you wish you had the same kind of powers that Donnie has, huh? Or that she was here." He stamped his feet a little and confessed, "I miss her. She always makes things like this more fun than it probably should be."

Diana chuckled absentmindedly. "She does do that, doesn't she? And yeah, I miss her too—and the guys as well. I really hope they haven't run into problems on the road yet."

Otis shrugged. "Well, even if they do, they'll be okay. Donnie is well able to handle anything magical and the others anything non-magical." He said this while he walked between a couple ottomans and approached the bookshelves towering over the whole room. Once he got to his destination, he let out a low, "Wow!", which drew Diana's eyes to the direction he was looking.

She too gazed upward, her eyes growing larger and larger. For the first time she realized that there were bookshelves everywhere, each crammed with books so big she wasn't sure she was going to be able to lift them. She took up both lanterns, depositing one in a spot for Otis to use and carrying the other with her while she explored the books on the next shelf over. They could only reach the books on the bottom two shelves for now, but by holding the lanterns aloft, they could read the titles of the books on the third, and in some cases even the fourth, shelves up.

They read off titles to each other, ruminating about just what some of them meant. A few were in languages neither of them recognized and they again lamented both Donnie's and Falwaïn's absences.

Diana pulled the smallest book she could find, which was still about three feet wide and four tall, and nearly half a foot thick, off the shelf and to the floor. She opened its heavy cover, then she and Otis stood back to peruse its first few pages. The book was apparently split into parts, with this one being about somewhere called Santarasa and its ancient peoples. It was not a place that Diana or Otis had ever heard about before and they were both fairly certain it could not be in either Medregai or Fal'Adîn.

They knew the other four continents of Írtha, of course, two of which were reportedly uninhabitable for more than a few days at a time because of either the extreme heat or extreme cold, as the case might be. They were called Haëtu and Glǿstlant, respectively, and were thought to have been dead for at least twenty millennia.

The other two continents, Neïlashagh Mançenan and Gubai, were both on the other side of Írtha from Medregai and Fal'Adîn, and their respective peoples never mixed. It was said that the inhabitants of the two continents were as friendly with each other as those living in Medregai and Fal'Adîn, which Diana presumed meant not at all.

She supposed this Santarasa place could be on one of those continents, but somehow doubted it. Maybe it was in Donnie's world or Donnie would at least recognize where it could be.

She and Otis settled down and began to read the book in earnest, as both felt drawn to the tome, as if it were destined just for them.

It was hours later that they realized the day had slipped away from them. Diana stood for one last time, leaving the book open to the last page read, leaving less than eighty to go, but she and Otis agreed they were both too tired to keep reading right now. Stiff from inactivity, she collected the lanterns and attached them to her saddle so that she and Otis could descend the wooden stairway.

When they reached the lower cavern, Diana slid off Otis and placed her hands on a couple splits of wood, willing it all to restack itself the way it had been originally. While the stairway was being dismantled, Diana again collected the magical fire she'd created earlier and snuffed it out, so that she and Otis had to exit the cavern using the flashlight.

They stepped outside to see a beautifully star-studded night sky. Diana gauged it to be about two in the morning and realized that she was more than a little weary and absolutely ravenous. If she hadn't been so hungry, she would have stayed in the cavern all night. Of course, if she hadn't been so tired, she would have hunted her dinner down.

Resolutely, they began the long trek home toward the promise of full bellies and soft, warm places to sleep. She couldn't wait to talk to Warren tomorrow, and to Donnie and Diego when they returned because the book she and Otis had been reading all night had detailed the beginnings of the Iquakawi peoples. They had left off reading at the beginning of a chapter that had started to explain why the Iquakawi lost their home in the fertile valley of Santarasa and were thereafter destined to roam the land.

They would come back tomorrow, she decided, no matter how late they awoke, so that they could finish reading the book. She and Otis began to discuss the plan for the next day, with each marking how excited they were going to be to continue their reading.

Secretly, they both felt something momentous was going to come out of their discovery today.

Chapter 12
Black Magic Woman

"So, you think Julia will be protected from her father as long as she has the Sôla?" Warren asked, gazing at Diana uncertainly the next morning at breakfast, after she'd explained her find of the previous day in the giants' library.

"Yes, I do believe that, because the Sôla, or the Balmaurii as the book we found said they were originally called in Elanéra, won't activate for someone who has no Iquakawi blood in them," Diana repeated, barely able to contain her elation at having found so key a piece of information. "As far as we know, Julia is the only one with him who is part Iquakawi and who could potentially work with the Sôla, so he's got to keep her alive and well."

Warren's jaw worked silently for several seconds before he nodded. "Good," he said tightly, with relief. "That means Donnie was right when she hoped they would make Julia more valuable to him and she was also right to let Julia take them with her." He breathed heavily through his nose, a great, long and expressive breath. "That really does make me feel better. Now, I only have to worry about Liz and Jesse, Donnie and the guys and Sylvester and Rex, and you and Otis while I'm stuck here in the cottage in bed most of the day. And I'll probably still worry about Julia, no matter what," he confessed with chagrin.

Diana smiled at him kindly. "I knew you were taking on that burden, my friend. I could see it in your eyes every time I looked at you. I know it's pure hell to not be able to help or protect us, but that doesn't mean you should worry so much about us either. And you need to stop carrying that damn thing around with you," she advised, making a face and pointing a finger at the third book of their adventures. As usual anymore, it lay within inches of Warren's hands so he could check it every five minutes or even more frequently whenever the mood struck him, which it seemed to do with increasing constancy.

He shook his head and stated flatly, "Oh, no, nobody takes this away from me, not yet anyways. I'd go nuts without it, because at least it makes me feel like I'm somewhat in the know, even if I can't do a wretched thing to help any of you if you do get into a bad situation."

Diana stilled her next protest about the book, noting that he really was getting more and more freaked out, seemingly by the hour, at not being able to assist in what his friends were all busy doing. "Okay," she relented with a sigh, "but I'm going to be monitoring your use of that book and, if I think it's getting too unhealthy, I will take it and hide it, like I'm pretty sure Donnie did with the other ones."

Warren's eyes snapped to Diana's face. "You think she hid them? But she said they were taken from her," he reminded her.

"Yeah, well, who would do that? And where could they put them where Donnie couldn't get to them? And haven't you noticed that she seems very unconcerned about them being missing or that she apparently cannot find them?" Diana shook her head slowly from side to side. "I'll bet you dollars to doughnuts that she has them stashed somewhere."

Warren frowned in confusion. "I hope you realize," he drawled, "that I have no more idea what that means when you say it as when Donnie says it. What in Gostock's dream is 'dollars to doughnuts' anyway?"

Highly amused, Diana chuckled happily with remembered pleasure, "Gostock's dream? Heavenly hags and horlocks, I haven't heard that mentioned since I was a kid and my friend's mother would tell us Gostock stories whenever she'd give us a treat."

Diana's eyes flashed with what were clearly precious memories to her and she breathed deeply before coming back to the present. When she did, she said, "Thanks for harkening me back to one of the happiest times of my life. Poor little Gostock, always doing the wrong thing, but for the right reason. As to Donnie's colloquialism about dollars and doughnuts, she told me it's kind of an unofficial betting term that simply means you're very sure of something. In this case, I'm very sure she has those books, no matter what she says to the contrary."

Diana downed the rest of her coffee in one swallow before setting the cup down on its saucer with a clatter. "Okay, that's it, I've got to get going to the cavern. And this time I'm taking plenty of food with me, so I may not be back for a few days. You'll be okay without me, right? I mean, if something happens, have somebody come get me fast." She stood, pausing on her way to the sink with her dirty dishes to inquire, "Mickey T's coming by again today, isn't he?"

"Yes, we're going to play more games, I guess," Warren said. "By the way, before Mickey T came yesterday morning, I checked the library here for information about dragons, but all it gave me were fictional novels. Although, to be honest, I was concerned I might ask for something from somewhere I shouldn't, so my request was composed in such a manner as to avoid taking anything from another repository. You know, from one that maybe we shouldn't access because it mattered where its documents would be stored. Anyway, I think today I'll question Mickey T about the history of Medregai. After all, like Sylvester said, he is the oldest animal on the Ganlonds so he might remember something helpful about dragons."

Diana, only half-listening to Warren, busied herself with packing a bag to carry enough food for herself for a minimum of three days. She nodded at him about his stated plans and then she strode to the door, going straight to the stables to feed Otis. Afterward, she grabbed a large feed bag, filling it with the special grain Donnie mixed for the horses so that Otis would have plenty of his own food while they were at the cavern.

She also poured a big mound of the special blend into the grain trough for Raleen, Warren's grey, and added extra hay to the grey's stall, patting the tall war horse on the flank as she walked by. Raleen tossed her head, stamping her feet impatiently, bucking a little and letting out some loud neighs.

Diana realized what the horse's problem was and said, "Hey, Otis, how about I take an hour and give Raleen a good run—would you mind?"

Otis told her with a full mouth of feed that he would not mind it at all, so Diana saddled the grey, rode her out the stable doors, and then let her have her head around the valley. They thundered in wide circles for nearly an hour until Diana felt the tension had eased off Raleen's taut demeanor.

Later, after having brushed the grey and saddled Otis, she stopped in at the house for a moment to see Warren and told him she was finally leaving, leaning over him to give him a tight hug. She laughed at Warren's surprise at the show of affection. She joked that she must be picking up some of Donnie's better habits along with her bad ones. They both laughed at this and said their goodbyes, with Warren warmly expressing his thanks to her for giving Raleen a good run.

Within another minute or two, she and Otis were leaving the farm and waving hello to Mickey T, who fluttered over her at low altitude and shouted, "Thee you later, Diana!"

Mickey T continued to the cottage, hoping the door would open for him instead of the window because it was too hard sometimes to get through the much smaller aperture of the window. It was as though the cottage door heard him because it opened wide and he dove for it, nearly breaking his neck when he ran into Warren's hardened belly.

"Oof!" he gasped, feeling Warren's hands grabbing for his small form so that he did not drop to the floor.

Warren managed to catch the bat, cupping him lightly between his palms and fingers. Ascertaining quickly that the old bat was unhurt, he turned back into the house and set Mickey T on his feet on the table.

"Sorry about that, Mickey T," said Warren warmly. "I was thinking I'd go out to walk around a little this morning, but clearly our timing was wrong."

"Yeth, Mynydd—er, Warren, I mean, our timing wath definitely off!" The old bat's body drooped a little and he admitted, "That juth about did me in, you know. I think I will take a retht, if you don't mind." And without another word, the bat collapsed onto the table's surface and began snoring.

Alarmed by the abruptness of these movements, Warren peered at Mickey T closely, glad that the old bat was breathing normally, even if he was also quite loud about it, especially considering how tiny his little bat body was. Reassured after a few more minutes of watching the bat and noting that his condition did not worsen, Warren went outside and walked around the cottage several times, even going out into the yard to do some wide arm stretches.

He gritted his teeth against the possibility of passing out and seemed to make it through the physical labor just fine. He continued taking exercise for another half hour or so before he made his way back to his room, where he too enjoyed a short nap. He felt safe in doing so because he could hear the loud rumbles from Mickey T resounding throughout the house.

When he awoke, he looked around him with alarm. He had intended to sleep only a little while, but when he walked to the kitchen, he noticed that Mickey T was gone and the clock on the wall showed that it was nearly two o'clock in the afternoon.

He spotted the book lying on the table and, unable to resist its call, read through scant new text that had appeared on its pages, disappointed that it was all about him and Mickey T.

His lunch was ready for him, so he closed the book and turned his attention to the thick sandwich that had been made for him. He was just popping the last delicious bite of it into his mouth when he heard the sound of horse's hooves coming toward the cottage on a dead run.

He made it to the front door in time to see Otis come to a stop in front of the porch. Diana slid from him in a quick, clean movement and bounded up the stairs, pulling up short when she realized Warren was standing right there.

"Crap, you startled me!" she exclaimed, not pausing a moment before adding in a breathless voice, "You'll never believe this, but somebody broke into the cavern last night and stole the book Otis and I were reading yesterday!"

***

Rex came into sight on the horizon, loping down the road. He called to his mama and the others and they stopped where they were to await his arrival and whatever his news might be.

"There's a big city just over the next ridge and they're sending out a whole bunch of guards this way," he relayed, once he'd drawn near enough to be heard. "I'm pretty sure they must be elves, 'cause they look all shiny and golden like the ones in the king's army, ya know?" the dog announced, snapping at a fly buzzing near his ear that was annoying him. "I made sure to get close enough to hear them talking, and one of 'em said something about the witch and her friends being near, so I think they're expecting us. But they sure don't look friendly, if you know what I mean." Falling silent, Rex waited, panting lightly.

"Cursed, black fortunes, it must be Lænemeade already," Akanna said with distaste. "I was hoping to simply skirt the town itself and bypass its elves entirely, like we've done with other settlements we've passed by in the last three days."

"How would they know we're here?" Donnie inquired confusedly, and both Akanna and Falwaïn shrugged at her.

"Well, they are magical," Falwaïn explained, "not like you, certainly, but they can nevertheless monitor the area around the city for anyone they might consider a threat."

"And I would be considered a threat, I suppose, right?" Donnie asked grimly, although she knew the answer already.

"Oh, yeah," Falwaïn replied with a dry laugh. "I think we can safely assume they would consider you a threat."

Donnie sighed. "You know, I want to like elves, I really do, but I keep havin' a lot of difficulty with that."

While Falwaïn and Diego chuckled at this, Akanna, Sylvester and Rex nodded their agreement with her.

"Most people do not like elves," Akanna informed her, "for they make it clear they care only for their own kind, while others are viewed as being beneath their contempt." The vincan shook her head and scoffed. "It is no wonder this attitude does not endear them to the other races of Medregai."

"Yes, well, we have but moments before they come over that rise, so if we are wanting to leave the path, should we not do so now?" asked Diego, pointing to the west side of the road, which broke off into forest within about twenty yards of the road. The other side was yet another rolling moor that would provide no cover to them at all.

"No, we should not do that," advised Sylvester. "For I feel their augur amongst those approaching and he or she would simply track us into the wood, rendering our attempts at avoidance quite pointless. We may as well meet them without subterfuge."

Donnie nodded. "Yeah, I feel this augur of theirs too. I think it's a she and she's quite impressive magically, I must say." She turned to her dog, who was sitting on the ground to her left, and said to him casually, "Honey, why don't you take a run to the cottage and check on Warren and Diana? I know you've been wanting to for a while, and now seems to be a good time for that. I mean, there's no sense in all of us getting delayed by the elves, and this way you can come back when we're done and let us know how things are going at home. Go on now, before they come near enough to see us. I'll let you know when and where to rejoin us, okay?"

The dog, looking a little troubled by this suggestion, finally nodded and replied, "Okay, I guess I can do that. Bye you guys. Love you, Mama!"

She said she loved him too and he disappeared instantly in a long blur of movement back the way they'd just come. She turned in her saddle to look forward again just in time to see the first line of elves and their horses appear over the edge of the hard-packed dirt road.

Donnie rode to the fore of their little assembly and muttered, "Well, here goes nothing," urging Wiwila into a canter that the others matched behind her.

The two groups came to within about fifteen feet of each other before stopping, with all four horses in Donnie's retinue standing in line to face the elves. The elves also stood four to a line, although there were about forty lines of them. Their leader, a big, strapping older man with bright white long hair and fading blue eyes that had a certain kind of meanness to them, raised his arm as a signal for his troops to halt. Those nearby did so immediately, with the back half of their procession circling around to surround Donnie and her friends.

Donnie surveyed the elves around her and noticed that every one of them had the same hard and mean look to them as had their commander. Except, he wasn't their true leader.

When he started to say something to Donnie, she held up a hand and said over him, "Where is she? Where is this Lady Bréagna you serve? I will speak only with her." Donnie ignored the indrawn breath she heard from her right, where Falwaïn sat upon Gallantry.

The elf commander leered in response to Donnie's protest, but he and the first three rows of guards behind him moved their horses aside so that a regal-looking elf noblewoman could ride forward.

Donnie thought this newcomer looked as though she had ice water in her veins, especially seeing as she was clad in a long white dress that clung to her like a second skin and an even longer white cloak that was clasped at her neck with a huge diamond encircled several times by slightly smaller diamonds. Her hair, intricately braided and piled high atop her head in a dizzying array of circles and lines, was ice blonde and literally glittered in the sunlight from all the small diamonds adorning it throughout its crazy gyrations.

She carried with her a cloud of sickly sweet-smelling perfume that was so thick and pungent that it made Donnie sway in the saddle, giving her a woozy feeling. The woman's eyes, as blue as sapphires, were haughty and cutting, and her lips, never destined to be generous, were currently pulled into a distinctly cruel smile. She was thin as a rail and her skin was almost translucent it was so pale, and it all added to the effect her hair, eyes, and very pointed ears created to make her look completely otherworldly.

There was no mistaking this woman for anything other than high elvish royalty and Donnie took an instant dislike to her.

"I am Lady Bréagna," the woman announced. Her voice sent shivers down Donnie's spine because there was such a queer tone to it that was accentuated by the deadened way she delivered her words. It was truly creepy and Donnie was properly creeped out by it.

Every movement the elf witch made, everything her gaze rested upon, even every breath she took seemed to be all too annoying to her, as if she were disgusted that she had to accomplish such mundane things in this mundane world she somehow found herself occupying against her will.

"You are not welcome in Lænemeade," she continued, and again her delivery screamed hatred for all that lived and breathed around her.

"That's fine," Donnie said brightly. "We have no desire to go there. As a matter of fact, we were just discussing a plan to turn into the forest so we could bypass your, er, fair city." She added the last line with her tongue lodged firmly in her cheek, but she made sure to keep her face impassive.

"You misunderstand us," Bréagna countered in her weird voice. "You are not welcome anywhere near Lænemeade. You will return from whence you came, and you will never step foot within fifty leagues of here again."

And then, with no warning, her elf soldiers attacked, starting by jumping onto Akanna, who was the last in line on the right side. Donnie, of course, used her magic to repel the attack, sending several of the elves careening backward into each other. But, feeling something had suddenly gone wrong, she whirled in her saddle and saw Ampago stamping and jumping behind her. He was rider-less.

She turned back to the elf noblewoman. "Where's Diego, where is our friend?" she ground out with clenched jaw. Falwaïn and Akanna turned in surprise, noticed Diego's absence and both grunted in anger, scorching the elves around them with murderous looks.

"If you are speaking of the Black Rider, he will be returned to you when you are the required distance from Balwedané Feûr and are again in your own province." Bréagna stated this flatly, then she showed the first sign of real emotion when she sneered, "We are not looking for war with you, witch, for we know you are not to be trusted to follow the Felaguine Rules, if you even know what those are."

Falwaïn answered hotly before Donnie could, "You'd be surprised just what she knows about our world, you filthy sorceress. And she's far more trustworthy than any of your lot will ever be!"

Bréagna focused her attention upon him, malice practically streaming from her gaze. "You," she said, making the word sound like an expletive. "I should kill you now, and would if you were not under the protection of this child of the Traitor of Avendin. You willingly keep the company of the cursed, and thereby will end your journey on her path when you betray her." The elf witch's eyes glittered when she added reprovingly, "You know this, for it was foretold to you long ago."

Donnie, stunned by this accusation, stole a glance at Falwaïn. She could tell he was fighting something internally. Donnie suddenly wondered, was she wrong to have ever trusted him?

"That was your prophecy, yes, but that doesn't make it true," he shot back, his voice tightly controlled, although his fury was evident. He did not look anywhere except at Bréagna. "I happen to believe in free will, something Donnie has taught me well. There will be no betrayal and none of us with her are cursed. But I know her well enough to know that, unless you give Diego back to us right now and let us pass through the forest here, she is going to make you pay sorely for your deeds."

"Ah, you have not shared our history with your witch." Bréagna stated this with flat certainty and Falwaïn turned red. "She does not know yet that there was a time when I was your whole world, when you saw *me* as your future and wanted to—"

"I was a child then, barely fifteen, and you took advantage of me just as you did my father and my brother!" he snarled, letting his control go as his own long-buried hatred of her welled up in his breast.

Donnie sat back in her saddle, said, "Huh!" and stared at first Bréagna, then at Falwaïn. "Oh, do tell," she murmured to Falwaïn, encouraging him with an inscrutable look and raised eyebrow to unload his burden now.

He caught her meaning, sighed, and slumped his shoulders with a kind of emotional weariness. "Okay, you know I was always attracted to magic, right? Well, so were my father and brother, but not in the same way I was. They didn't want to wield it, but they were perfectly content to have Lady Bréagna use it for their gain. As you know, the provinces of Balwedané Feûr and Faen Eárna border each other just west of here.

"Long story short, my father and brother got themselves enmeshed in Bréagna's plans to seize Sedarau, the province to the north that has long been controlled by the Sarn. That ended with my people being very sorry they had ever met Bréagna, for she made utter fools of them and turned all the blame for the failed overthrow upon them. The king saw through her calumny and did not order my family to be killed, as he otherwise might have done. Instead, he forgave us all, thereby solidifying the ties between us. That was also when he married his wife, who is the daughter of the elf queen and king of Balwedané Feûr."

Falwaïn swallowed hard and looked at Donnie with apology in his eyes for not having the courage to tell her this story from his past sooner. "With me, Lady Bréagna made me believe she would teach me what Déagmun would not, and I ran from my father to her and spent six months spellbound by her. That may even have been literally, now that we know I have those two spells on me that neither Déagmun nor Catie cast. To my great shame, I came to my senses only after she had accused my father and brother of what were her own evil works. As soon as I was told of this betrayal, I left her without looking back. I suppose *that*, more than anything else, must rankle with her, for she believes that no one can leave her unless she casts them away." He glared at Bréagna after snarling this at her.

For perhaps ten seconds there was silence, then from all around came the chant of "Lies. Lies. Lies."

Unnerved by the sudden synchronicity of the response, Donnie's gaze darted around her, wondering at the soldiers who all seemed oblivious to what they were chanting.

Lady Bréagna smiled at Donnie's bewilderment, then raised her hand and declared, "Lies! All of it, lies." She smiled with great wickedness at Donnie as the soldiers fell silent. "Falwaïn enjoyed my company and my touch upon his skin. And he reveled in our plans to overtake the kingdom. Oh, do not let him fool you, he was as much party to them as was I. He is filled with true evil, which you, dear girl, will find out far too late. But you will indeed feel the sting of his perfidy, and you will curse the day you let him into your heart." She moved her cold regard from Donnie to Falwaïn, smiling this time in triumph. "And you will come back to me then, foolish servant, and we will take up our plans and rule all of Medregai together! I have seen this in the stones, and they never lie to me."

A weird blackness overtook Donnie at this point and she felt like she was falling into infinity.

She awoke later with a start of dread, her head filled with wool. She groaned and moved her arms, comprehending that she was on the ground somewhere. The boombox was beside her and was playing "Black Magic Woman," although it took Donnie a minute or so to realize that part.

Daring to open an eye, she peered out at the world warily. There was waning sunshine glistening on the trees above her, which told her she must have been unconscious for hours. She opened the other eye and turned her head to the left, where there was open sky and no trees, and found she was on the side of the narrow road. A fast, scant look around told her that the others were scattered around the road nearby, as were the horses.

Donnie pushed herself up on her elbow and Wiwila's eyes flickered open briefly. Donnie, arresting all movement suddenly, blew an exhausted breath and complained bewilderedly to the boombox, "What the hell was that?

Black magic woman, my ass! She was more like hell's hags and what a friggin' nightmare!"

She raised herself to a sitting position, resting her weight on her hands behind her to give her head time to adjust and stop spinning. When that feat had been accomplished, she carefully got to her feet, swaying a little when she succeeded in reaching the extra altitude.

"Whoa," she chuckled, feeling almost drunk. "Seriously, what the hell happened to us?" she asked, but the others did not even move.

The boombox, though, beeped at her and disappeared into thin air, apparently contented that it had imparted whatever message it was trying to relay.

Donnie had to bend over to put her hands on her knees for a minute because the wooziness came back, but she managed to keep her feet and not toss her lunch. She knew her children were okay because they were, as usual, arguing over positions in her belly, so she tuned them out and concentrated on herself. She sniffed the back of her hand and smelled the same cloying scent the elf sorceress had brought with her. Donnie apprehended that the smell must have magical qualities associated with it when her head went spinning again. It was not a smell Donnie recognized, so she had no way of knowing how to combat it.

She heard a freshwater spring running nearby and thought it best to visit that, hoping that perhaps by dunking her head in it and washing away the elf-witch's magical perfume, her brain fog would dissipate. Groggily, she stumbled toward its cascading music and was relieved to find it was near where the others lay—although she didn't particularly like that it took her out of sight of them. But she knew she had to get herself awake, so she forced her legs to obey and take her to the stream.

Practically falling to her knees at the water's edge, she half-crawled into the stream. With shaking fingers, she cupped a handful of the cold, clear liquid into her mouth, drinking greedily of its freshness. She put her hands down onto some rocks in the stream's bed, steadied herself, then plunged her whole head into the swiftly running water.

As had happened before in similar circumstances with oddly placed streams, once her head was under water, she found herself transported to the same large clearing, deep within a forest somewhere, that was dappled by sunlight. And again, everything around her was still as death. Nothing moved and there was no sound other than her own impossible breathing.

Donnie was determined to stay as long as she could this time in what she knew to be the Escu'arík, or Waters of Chaos.

In the scene she was witnessing, her eyes roamed the illusory clearing and she suddenly caught the same strong whiff of blood as from before. It came from her right at first, but then she realized it was all around her. She looked down at her feet, which were shod in brown leather boots of some ancient design, and saw that the dirt there was soaked with a sticky, red substance.

For the first time, she noticed there was low plinth nearby and she followed its contours with her curious gaze, shuddering in horror when she found that it too was covered in dark red blood. Then, to Donnie's surprise, a bloodied hand shot up and grasped the edge of the plinth. The mangled hand was followed by the badly injured head and shoulders of a young, red-haired, blue-eyed maiden. She pushed herself upward, somehow seeming to know Donnie was there for she looked right into Donnie's eyes and, with gushes of blood spilling over her lips, gurgled, "Help us!"

Shocked into movement, Donnie whipped her head out of the stream and fell back onto her haunches in terror. She forced herself to take several deep breaths in order to refill her nearly too long-deprived lungs and to get her heart to slow its frantic beat. For several moments, she forced her body to just simply breathe.

She closed her eyes tight so she could concentrate on running through the event she'd just witnessed, trying to impress it upon her memory. It struck her that a memory was exactly what it had been—but just whose memory she had no clue. That had to be what it was, for that was the most logical explanation for the dying girl looking her straight in the eyes and begging her for help; plus, it also explained the strange boots she'd been wearing.

But why did the Escu'arík insist on repeatedly showing her that same event?

Confused, Donnie ran her hands over her face to wipe away the water and then combed her fingers through her wet hair, her mind still stuck in the midst of that disturbing memory as her breathing returned to normal.

Then she berated herself for staying so long in the Waters of Chaos that she'd nearly drowned—although, truthfully, she'd had a little while left before that would have happened, time that she could have used to look around longer if not for the startling unexpectedness of the red-headed girl's gruesomely delivered plea.

Still, she needed to remember that she couldn't breathe underwater the next time she dived head-first into the mysterious stream of time and creation.

She heard a noise from the road behind her and she got to her feet. At the same time, the stream next to her vanished and she was left alone with her thoughts. Pushing back her damp hair, she realized that she was indeed clear-headed and felt ready to help her friends.

Wiwila was standing, as were Akanna and Jora, with all three looking shaky. Falwaïn was sitting up, but hanging his head low. Sylvester was still out cold. The other two horses were struggling to get to their feet. Donnie waved her hand to help them up with her magic. They stamped their feet heavily, staggering a couple times, but they were both recovering quickly and stayed afoot.

Donnie looked beyond Gallantry and Ampago and gasped. "Diego!" She cried gratefully, "You're back with us!"

He nodded his head slowly, but both Akanna and Falwaïn gave him, and then Donnie puzzled looks.

"What do you mean, he is back with us?" asked Akanna wonderingly. "Where did he go and when did he leave?"

Falwaïn nodded with his eyes closed, pointing at the vincan to mutter, "Yes, what she said." He put a hand under his chin to prop his head up. He looked white and slightly harrowed under his tan.

Donnie explained what had happened to them during their encounter with the elf witch and her troops and then she turned to Diego to ask him where he had been taken.

But Akanna interrupted before Diego could answer. "No, that is not how it went at all," the vincan asserted. "What I recall is that we met the elves and they invited us to join them for a meal, so we went with them into Lænemeade, to this dark tent where they plied us with their best wine. We all got quite drunk." She smacked her lips and ran her tongue around the inside of her cheeks. "I can still taste its fruity elixir."

It was Falwaïn's turn to shake his head. "No," he interjected, "that's not what happened either. They took us prisoner and made us go into that dark tent, yes, but there was something evil in it, a creature of some sort. I thought. I remember listening to its breathing, which was ragged and heavy as though the beast was injured. Then it reached out its claw and ripped me on the arm—see, I have the wound still," he said, raising his arm to show them all the long rent in his sleeve. He twisted the arm around and stared at it in bewilderment. "But there's no blood, no wounds...I-I don't understand." He swept his hands over his face and pushed his long hair back away from his face with an unhappy grunt. "It attacked you too, Donnie, and I thought you and the children were—oh, that damnable elf whore!"

He swore several more times and motioned for Donnie to come over to him. With her assistance, he got to his feet. He met Donnie's eyes squarely with his and said, "I think your recollections might be the closest to the truth, Donnie, for I did know her in my youth. I had no idea she was back here though, as she had been banished from Medregai by the king when it was found out that she had engineered the failed coup attempt. But I do not believe I was ever anything more than her prisoner, for that is how she convinced my father and brother to help her, was by taking me and threatening to kill me if they refused her. I certainly did not go in search of her, that much I know. But I have never been clear on all the events that

happened during the half year she made me her captive or my part in them."
He shook his head despondently. "I can only hope that the rest of what she
said was utterly untrue, although to my extreme distress, I cannot swear to
any of it. The only truth I have is what my father and brother told me, and
much of that they learned from Déagmun, who rescued me from my
imprisonment with her."

Donnie's uttered a four-letter imprecation and posited, "I wonder if that's
why he put his protection spells on you. It would make sense for him to do
that after you were rescued from her, wouldn't it?"

Donnie considered this possibility carefully, along with the song the
boombox had been playing when she'd come back to consciousness. "Gosh,
if that's the case," she said, frowning in thought, "then we may not ever
want to mess with them. Just in case they keep you from changing into
someone awful...although, the wonderful, kind qualities you have now
should overrule any bad ones left over from yesteryear, so to speak." She
shifted her shoulders uncertainly and grimaced. "This will certainly give
more fuel to Sylvester's argument to leave the spells on everyone alone—
oh, that reminds me," she said whirling around to cry, "Sylvester!" She
darted to where he lay and watched him breathe for a few moments, grateful
beyond measure that he was alive.

She carefully picked him up, and with Falwaïn's help, she stuffed the cat
into her hoodie and zipped it up just far enough to keep him secure once she
was astride Wiwila again. The others pulled themselves up onto their
respective steeds, and by unspoken consent, they resumed a slow and
somewhat unsteady course down the road, all of them wanting to put as
much distance between their group and the elves as soon as possible.

Donnie, using her mind's eye to figure out where they were, told the
others, "Wow, we're nearly eighty miles down the Danduin Road, to the
east of Lænemeade!" She shook her head and said in amazement, "Jeez-um,
they really didn't want us to go there, did they?"

"That, my friends, is because they had a dragon egg and they were
attempting to incubate it!" Diego announced excitedly, his eyes gleaming
darkly. "It just came to me that that was what was actually in the tent! I
recall them forcing Donnie to blow an extremely hot breath at it to make it
hatch, and the thing that crawled out of the egg is what attacked Falwaïn and
Donnie both before the elves got control of it." He said all of this with an
assurance tinged with victory, but then afterward he faltered in both his
demeanor and his words as his mind obviously became muddled again. "At
least, I think that is what occurred, but I cannot swear to it, like any of the
rest of you. My recollections move in and out of my memory, but do not
stay. And then I see myself fighting with my captors, making my way into
the tent on my own, only to see...to see what, I do not know..." He sighed

with disappointment. "And now I cannot even be certain there was a dragon egg at all."

"Hmm," Donnie muttered, looking down at Sylvester, who was still unconscious, with his face just visible to her in the shadows made by her hoodie. She again remembered the last song the boombox had played. "I wonder what really happened with that black magic woman. And why is Sylvester still out? It must have something to do with whatever fragrance or potion, whatever it was, that that she-devil was wearing. I mean, he got the same amount as us, only it must still be overwhelming his system, presumably because his mass is so much less than any of ours."

"I do not think she was wearing it," Akanna mused thoughtfully, and Donnie leaned forward to glance at the vincan with curiosity. "It emanated from the ground, I am almost certain."

Donnie, her right eyebrow raised high, suddenly realized what this meant and shot Akanna an astounded look. "That means it's a protection spell, so if we were to get that close again, probably from any direction at all, we'd likely trigger the same spell again."

"I wonder, could it be something left over from years ago, say as many as sixty or seventy years, or would it have to be a recent spell?" asked Falwaïn.

Donnie shook her head. "I don't think age would matter so much, but it would depend more on who cast it," she replied to him. "I mean, they'd have to be super powerful for it to work for that many decades, or long years as you call them here, and they'd have to have really strong intent woven into the spell." She hesitated, still pondering the spell's provenance. At length, she said decisively, "It must have been Bréagna who cast this one. I mean, that's apparently what the boombox thinks, so I'm pretty sure that means it's her spell. And therefore, even if she cast it a long time ago, she was clearly strong enough for it still to be working today."

Donnie paused, looking down at Sylvester again and wishing he were awake because he would definitely know the answer to their questions. "Have you ever heard of anything weird like what we just went through happening to others?" she asked.

Akanna and Falwaïn shook their heads.

She thought a while longer, then mused aloud, "Maybe it works only on magical beings who wield sufficient power to give her real trouble. If so, it could have been here for who knows how long without any of the common folk tripping it, which would conserve some of its magical power. Just our luck, we're all more than likely strong enough magically to have tripped it, so there was no way to avoid it."

But Akanna shook her head again and said, "No, it is not us. It must be you, or perhaps your cat. I have passed this way several times and have never experienced anything like what we just went through."

"If it is an older spell, does that mean Lady Bréagna may not actually be in Medregai now? That part of the spell she cast was for the victim to hallucinate her as well?" inquired Diego.

Donnie shrugged uncertainly, making a face to match. "I dunno. But if it weren't for that tear in Falwaïn's sleeve, I'd be inclined to believe we imagined our respective experiences in Lænemeade; you know? Starting with seeing Lady Bréagna and her mean-spirited elves. If that's true, then the spell must have worked on Rex too because he saw the elves first and warned us they were coming and that they knew who we were. Hmm, I don't know what to think about that because so few magic tricks even work on him, so I'm a little inclined to believe that at least the elves were real. But that tear in Falwaïn's sleeve is certainly real and something very sharp made it. I'm just not sure it happened the way either of you remember it to have."

"Well, whatever did happen, we cannot let it delay us any longer," Akanna said authoritatively. "We must press on."

Donnie and the others nodded in agreement and they all sped up a little, although Donnie's expression showed that she was by no means done with either Lænemeade or Lady Bréagna and her black magic legacy.

She called out to Rex with her mind and told him where he could find them, warning him to stay far away from Lænemeade.

He said he would be back with them in just a few minutes and he was true to his word. They had traveled only another mile before he rejoined them. They'd heard his sonic boom behind them about a minute before, and thereby had been warned of his approach. Donnie decided not to say anything to him about their experiences and warned the others against it because she didn't want him worrying, as he was wont to do when it came to the safety of herself and the others.

Rex, for his part, knew something had occurred because Falwaïn, who he was beginning to like nearly as much as Warren, looked kind of shaken. But when his mama asked how Warren and Diana were doing, he forgot his concerns and launched into the tale of Diana's foray into the giant's library and the mysterious theft of the book she'd been reading about the Iquakawi.

Diego shot off a series of rapid-fire questions that had poor Rex looking stunned. The dog even stopped to sit in the middle of the roadway with his jaw hanging open since half of them were asked in Spanish.

Giggling, Donnie pulled on Wiwila's reins lightly so she would stop, then she turned to Diego and pointed out to him, with an amused smile on her face, "Um, that's maybe a bit too many questions to ask Rex, don't you think, especially since he can't possibly know the answer to most of them. How about we write your questions down sometime later and have him take the list back to Diana the next time he visits home?"

"He must go now, Donemere, he must go now!" whispered Sylvester in an urgent, but weak voice.

For the first time, Donnie felt the cat's body stir against her. She looked down at him and watched as he licked his lips several times, clearly trying to come awake more fully. Donnie unzipped her hoodie and carefully put him onto the saddle horn in front of her. Her saddle expanded, as it often did, into a small platform for the cat to settle upon.

She took out her canteen of water and poured some into the screw top, then set it down in front of Sylvester. He drank thirstily of it and sat back with a sigh, his head tilted to the side because he was waiting for the world around him to stop spinning.

The others gathered round and voiced both their greetings and their relief that he was going to be okay, to which he nodded gratefully once he could do that without collapsing.

Donnie put a finger under his chin and suggested in an affectionate tone, "Okay, my friend, tell us why Rex must go back to the cottage right now."

"Because," the cat explained patiently, "the giant's cave is not part of the Ganlonds, which means that whoever broke into it did so from within the mountain. That can only mean someone in league with either Valledai or the Iceni Meræ. And that means that whoever goes into that cave from the Ganlonds is in danger."

"But why do you say that? Someone from the Ganlonds could easily have entered the cave, climbed or flown up to the library and taken the book anytime during the night, surely," argued Akanna, but Sylvester shook his head.

"Impossible!" he retorted. "I know of no one who would have good reason to do such a thing. Furthermore, of those who might possibly be persuaded in a moment of extreme weakness to steal the tome and who would be able to reach the library itself, they would all be unable to carry such a gargantuan book out of it. At best, they would have had to push it over the edge, where it would have fallen a great distance to the cave below. It is unlikely there would have been no sign of this, which there was not, or Diana would not have had to access the library before realizing that the book was gone. Plus, Rex said she noticed that the draft at the front entryway to the cave seemed to howl particularly loudly, which must mean that—"

"There's another entrance into the cavern from the inner chambers!" Donnie finished for him with an incredulous shout. "*That* is what bugged me when Rex told us what she said about the draft, but I couldn't put my finger on why before you said something about it." She looked around at the others, who all gazed back at her steadily. She sat back in the saddle and crossed her arms in front of her, raising an eyebrow pensively. "I think Sylvester's right and someone must have blasted or dug their way into the back chamber—the one where Na'aven made her statues, I mean. Hmm, so maybe Diana shouldn't investigate the cavern by herself again, huh?"

"Ghira Ma'Hai is the Ér Ainíl of the Mîrlonds and the mightiest ovid ever to fight in any battle," Akanna reminded Donnie stiffly. "She is not one who should turn and run."

"No?" said Donnie, rounding on the vincan exasperatedly. "Well, I am Ér Ainíl of the Ganlonds and I'm a helluva lot more powerful magically than Diana, yet look at what that spell by Bréagna did to us all!" Donnie shook her head vehemently. "No, I don't want Diana investigating on her own again! Once Warren is well enough to help her, maybe, but even then, I think the council should send someone with her."

"Agreed," Sylvester interjected, looking down at Rex, who was taking it all in, but saying nothing. "Bronadulach must be informed of what has transpired in the cave and he must be allowed to accompany them once Warren recovers. But no one should step foot into that cave until they can all go together."

"Better yet," Donnie muttered, only half-jokingly, "they can wait until we get back, even if that's a year from now! I just don't want them putting themselves in danger like that."

Falwaïn leaned forward to catch her eye. "My honey woman," he said in a calm, reasoning kind of tone, "I agree with you that all precautions must be taken, certainly, but you cannot expect either Warren or Diana to do nothing until you return." He shook his head and gave her a knowing smile. "Your concern is admirable, my love, but misplaced with warriors of their fighting ilk."

She looked back at him unhappily and he chuckled with affection.

Rex, unsure of just what was wanted, asked, "Should I go back now or later? I mean, they probably know what you've said already because Warren's keepin' that new book about us really close by him and he checks it a lot. I mean, a lot!" the dog repeated, rolling his eyes. "He checked it like every three minutes while I was there. I was thinkin' about takin' the book somewhere's, you know like I did the—well, I just wanted to—"

"Ha-ha!" Donnie crowed, whipping her right arm in the air in front of her. "I knew you had them! I knew it!" She smiled at the others with glee and then sobered, looking down at her dog. "Where did you put them? I seriously cannot find them anywhere, which should be impossible."

Rex lifted his lips in a toothy grin. "I took 'em to the Exos. I can get there by myself, you know. They've been there this whole time. See, I just didn't want any of us obsessing over them like Valley Guy did, and I thought I'd help us all out by hiding them away."

Falwaïn interrupted this exchange to ask, "Are you talking about the first two books of our adventures, by chance?"

Rex and Donnie nodded together, while Diego and Falwaïn chimed in with, "Oh, that makes sense." They looked at each other and grinned in good humor.

"That is one mystery solved," noted Sylvester dryly before adding, "It is also interesting that you can access the Exos without Donemere's help. You really are quite the conundrum, my friend." he added, shaking his head in wonder. "But you should go back now, regardless of the third book and Warren's penchant for reading its new text. We must ensure that Diana knows to keep out of the cave unless she has others with her." He sighed, looking up at Donnie now. "It would be best if she and Warren had someone truly proficient, magically speaking of course, with them at all times, which means that Rex will to have to remain at the cottage. Do you not agree, Donemere?"

Appalled by the thought of being separated for an extended period, both Donnie and Rex began to argue back until Sylvester held up an imperious paw and intoned haughtily over them, "It would be for a matter of days to a few weeks, so do not lose your heads!" He hissed and they both stopped shouting at him. "Diana needs someone Ca'nam to be with her now, and Warren is not that someone because of his injuries, nor has he been trained to use his burgeoning Ca'nam magic. Remember, the majority of animals on the Ganlonds are Ísolé and would be of little use to Diana in a magical skirmish. Rex, on the other hand, is naturally skillful, capable of wielding magic like no other anigus I've ever seen or heard of, which means he will be able to give Diana a protection that no other can—of those left on the Ganlonds, I mean. No, I am telling you, Donemere, Rex will have to stay with Diana until we know who or what broke into the giant's library!"

Donnie didn't like it, but she had to admit she agreed with Sylvester. She looked at Rex to tell him so, but he was already offering up a gentle, "He's right, Mama, I'm gonna have to stay at home for a while. I'll meet you later, I promise. Don't go to the tower without me, though, 'cause I really want to see that place."

Donnie assured him they would not step foot in the tower without him and he smiled at her miserably. She got off Wiwila and knelt in front of her dog, hugging him tightly to her while raining kisses all over his face, ending by giving him a kiss right between the eyes. He reached up and licked her cheek, a hugely demonstrative move for him, then he nuzzled her neck for good measure.

"I'll miss you bad too, Mama," he whispered, and tears sprang to Donnie's eyes. They hugged each other for another minute, until Sylvester cleared his throat impatiently.

Breaking apart from Rex, Donnie laughed shakily and told him, "You be careful, honey, really careful, okay?"

"I will, Mama, I will," the German Shepherd dog reassured her. "And you too, 'cause I won't be here to help you, so you have to be really-really-really careful without me. But I'll take good care of Diana and Warren, I promise." Her pup blinked at her, said in a sad voice, "Bye, Mama," and disappeared from sight.

Feeling very glum herself, Donnie climbed onto Wiwila and urged the young horse to take off at a fast clip because she didn't want the others to see her crying.

They rode that day until the sun was nearly down and then made camp to the south of the narrow Danduin Road. Falwaïn stood and surveyed the area around them, turning to Donnie to tell her, "My love, tomorrow we will be closer to my home than I have been for some years, for in just another twenty miles or so, we will cross into the province of Faen Eárna."

She put her arms around him and together they watched the sun drop to the horizon. "Tell me, my lord and prince of Faen Eárna, if we were to meet up with any of your subjects, will they hate me, perhaps even try to kill or imprison me?" she asked in jest, thinking he would chuckle with his usual humor and assure her otherwise.

But he did not. Instead he sighed, admitting in a sorrowful voice, "Yes, darling, I'm very much afraid that is exactly what they'll try to do."

Chapter 13
Fortunate Son

A violent storm arose on the sea, tossing the *Drunken Knave* over its foaming waves like a toy until Catie and Liz got together and worked a little magic to keep the ship on a more even keel. After their spell was cast, the crew stopped looking scared and sickly green around the edges, instead applying themselves to their chores with renewed vigor, for once not minding that there were two witches aboard.

For Liz and Jesse, it meant that they were finally able to get some quiet time for her and a nap for him. For Catie, it meant that she was doing just fine as Liz's teacher, because she had made Liz take the primary role in casting the spell and it had turned out to be a good, strong one. For Neddy Cloys, it meant that he could keep a clearer eye on the dirigible overhead, watching it too get thrown this way and that in the rising winds of the storm. With relief, he noticed that it soon rose high and disappeared into the clouds. Later that night, just after midnight, he and Catie discussed this development over their usual flagon or two, or sometimes three, of rum in the sanctity of his cabin and agreed that their pursuers must have risen far above the storm to wait it out.

He wanted to make a run for it, maybe get to land or turn a direction they wouldn't be expected to go, but Catie was having none of that.

"Are ye daft, man?" she bawled at him impatiently. "They nowt be afollowin' us by sight, but by the dratted call of the watch-clock! They'd know afore long that we had changed course, so there be no sense ta tryin' that." She shook her head at her lover, sending him a reproving glare. "The best plan we got is still ta stay wi' these udder ships, 'iding in plain sight, like Liz says. She's a right smart one, that gal, and ye might wanna listen ta 'er some."

Neddy Cloys, not one to take criticism from anyone, always took it like a champ from Catie. This was not just because he was afeared of how she might retaliate if he did what he was wont to with someone who found fault with him or his actions—which was to plunge a knife deep into one or another part of their body until they either apologized or died. But he'd never do that with Catie, no sir. He found her fascinating and liked that she would seek him out occasionally to assist her in stealing yet another trinket from the toshes and yobs.

This was not his first time-travel with her neither, so he knew that, no matter how long they'd remain in this hellish future they were currently occupying, she would take him and his ship and crew back to their proper time and to safety, or what passed for it in his dangerous world of piracy and smuggling. He felt assured of this as much as he was of his own ability to navigate his beloved ship through the treacherous rocks off Cornwall or across the mysterious Devil's Triangle without mishap.

But upon hearing Catie extol the virtues of Miss Priss, he felt it was incumbent upon himself to argue the exact opposite.

"I canna see ware she be all that almighty right nor smart, meself!" he complained, looking Catie full in the eye as though daring her to refute his mulish claim. "She be clever a' times, I'll grant ye that, but I think they was mostly 'appenstance."

"Well, as I keep a tellin' ye, ye shouldn't think, my dear man. Nowt on this subject, ennyway," Catie maintained, jutting her chin at him just as stubbornly as he was projecting his at her.

The two could argue and carp at each other like this for hours and had done so many times while they'd fought a band of dragoons together, then gotten drunk, broken a little bread, and afterward made a lot of love, only falling silent once they'd both passed out. They were a matched pair who would likely kill each other if they ever attempted to spend more than half a year in each other's company in one long stretch. They both knew this well and neither had ever pushed for more than what was allotted to them by the Fates.

"I canna 'elp but think, woman, no matter wha' ye might want ta the contrary," he informed her haughtily, then mugged at her before adding, "I'm the capt'n of me ship and that is what capt'ns do!" He scratched his head, disarranging his hat while doing this, then righted it back onto his thick, dark hair, which was still pulled back into its tight queue, and added, "I mean it, Catie. I dunna like nowt takin' advantage o' this storm! I'm a tellin' ye, we owt to be doin' somethun and nowt jest lettin' this grand opportunity slip through ar fingers like ye're intent on 'avin' happen."

"I am not intent on that, ye old goat!" Catie shot back at him, huffing with indignation. "I too am uneasy 'bout lettin' the tempest pass wi'out gainin' some kind o' profit wherewith."

"Well, betwixt us, surely we can birth a plan ta deceive them high-flyin' yobs up there, eh?" Neddy said, pointing a bony finger heavenward. "Whaddya think, Catie luv?" he enjoined her persuasively. "Ye got any idees fer makin' 'em look elsewhere, somethun sech as that?" He added this last question absentmindedly because he was focused on lifting his full and rather large cup of rum to his lips so he could drain its contents.

Catie stared into her own cup of rum, considering the problem as put to her and marking the particular way her Neddy had phrased his question.

"Make 'em look elsewhere…" she mumbled, wondering if there was, in fact, a way of accomplishing that. And then it came to her.

"Decoys," she stated, her eyes glinting triumphantly.

Neddy, while bleary from drink, was also full of curiosity. "Wha'?" he asked, rum running down his chin and onto his breast, which he ignored.

"We set up some decoys," she explained, sending him a look that told him to sharpen his wits about him. "Liz and me, I mean," she added. "We figger out 'ow that watch-clock is bein' tracked and we cast the same spell on udder things. Then we puts those things on some o' the udder boats floatin' around us." She grinned at Neddy and cackled. "Them fly boys'll niver know which boat ta follow and we can go ware e'er we want!"

Neddy lifted his glass to her and smiled, his gold teeth gleaming in the soft candlelight. "My lovely girl, ye've dun it agin, 'avint ye?" He toasted her drunkenly with a lift of his nearly empty cup.

Catie downed the remaining portion of rum in her own cup, refilled it to the top from the nearest bottle to hand, and carried the sloshing cup along with her to Liz's cabin. She pounded on the cabin door for a full two minutes before Liz pulled it open and glared at her disapprovingly.

Catie ignored Liz's ire and simply brushed past the other woman as she busted her way into the cabin. Setting her sorely depleted cup of rum onto the table and smiling happily at a giggling Jesse in the hammock, Catie pulled out the clock-watch from her reticule and beamed at Liz. She put the thing down next to her rum, motioned Liz over, and pointed at the timepiece.

"We need ta figger out the tracker on this dratted thing," she said standing stoically while the boat swayed under her feet. She stumbled a step with the ship's movement, turned a bland face to Liz, and hiccupped.

Liz glanced down at the magical artifact and then crossed her arms in front of her, leaning back on her hips to inquire soberly of Catie, "And for what purpose would we do that?"

"Decoys," the little blonde witch announced, repeating herself from earlier. Only this time she didn't have to explain herself any further.

Liz, her eyes snapping down to the clock-watch and then to Catie's face, sucked in her breath and gasped excitedly, "That's brilliant!"

Catie bowed, clasping her hands behind her back while bending low at this surprising compliment. Unfortunately, she leaned too far forward and nearly crashed into the table.

She mumbled something about the storm making it difficult to stand, but Liz sent her a shrewd look from the corners of her eyes. While it was true the boat had again lurched a bit, Liz was certain Catie's stumbles had little to do with the storm because the stink of both stale and fresh rum was like a cloud hanging around the little witch.

Liz, just to try it out, waved a hand and murmured, "*Lavari.*" A dim turquoise light shot from her fingertips and encased Catie for a moment before disappearing. Little Jesse crowed with wondrous delight.

Catie did not see the spell, but felt its touch on her, and she turned to Liz, ready to berate the other witch for her audacity. But she realized that she felt and smelled so much better because of the spell that it would be quite rude to say anything other than a simple and firm, "Thankee."

Taken aback, Liz replied, "Um, sure. You want me to do the same spell on Neddy?" This she asked because she thought he was becoming quite ripe these days too. "And maybe the crew?"

Catie crossed her arms and put a finger to her chin to tap it while she considered the offer. Eventually, she advised Liz, "Mebbe Neddy Cloys, yes, but the udders not yet. We need ta conserve our magic for makin' the decoys and spreadin' 'em around."

Liz obliged and sent the spell to find Neddy Cloys, who had no idea what happened to him because he was passed out cold with his head on the table he and Catie shared during their dinnertimes. Even when he awoke later, he could not put his finger on just what was different about himself, other than his clothes suddenly seemed a lot cleaner than they'd ever been in the entire three years he'd been wearing them. And he was mighty glad his head had stopped itching.

Jesse gave another little squeal of pure delight when he saw the turquoise light shoot from his mother's fingertips and slip through the wall opposite her. Liz went over and picked him up, and together she and Catie swaddled him to Liz's chest, which had become his very favorite place to be. He especially loved it when he was turned outward so he could see the world approaching with every step his mother took.

Liz returned to the table and bent over the clock-watch, peering at it intently, and Jesse did the same, unknowingly mimicking his mother. "You know," Liz remarked, "Donnie did this spell on herself that allowed her to see all the spells cast on people—and on things too, I suppose. She called it, er, what was it now, the something…hand" She looked at Catie enquiringly and noticed the little blonde witch blanche.

"Egad, she did the Silver 'and spell on herself?" Catie shuddered. "Ye'd niver get me ta do a dance wi' the cosmoss. Many o' those who try it, die in the effort, I'm tellin' ye. And oh, poor Tanny's gonna want ta kill me when he finds out the spells 'e's had cast on 'im, even tho' only a few, reelly, are from me," she lamented, shaking her head slowly from side to side.

"Who's Tanny?" asked Liz.

Catie blinked at her. "Why, 'e's me cat, o' course! Er, well, I s'pose 'e's Donnie's cat now."

"Oh, him," Liz said, comprehension lighting her features. "Sylvester. Donnie calls him Sylvester," she explained when Catie gave her a look.

"Oh, yes!" Catie exclaimed, bobbing her head up and down vigorously. "I did know she'd dun that—renamed 'im, I mean, but I couldna recall what to." The little witch looked almost misty-eyed for a moment and then she repeated dryly, "Yessir, 'e's gonna want ta kill me dead, all right."

"Oddly enough, I can relate to that feeling most days anymore. But that's another matter entirely, isn't it?" Liz asked brightly, ignoring Catie's snort of disbelief at her response. "Right now, we need to somehow reveal the spell cast on this thing." With her right index finger, she pointed at the clock-watch.

She uttered a few, what she considered to be magical spells off the top of her head until Catie waved her hands wildly and spluttered, "Stop! Stop it right now, ye Yfel hag!" When Liz turned a bewildered look upon her, Catie demanded to know, "What in Fortin's name is that tongue ye be a speakin'? And why? Why are ye usin' it?"

Liz turned a couple different shades of red, replying, "Well, it's sort of Latin and it's from this wildly popular story about young kids learning magic. But it's not like it matters, right? Didn't you say it's more about your intent than anything else?"

"Well, o' course it is, but that dunna mean ye should jest say enny ol' thing in enny ol' language!" Catie roared at her. "Ye haf ta know what yer words mean tu a syllable, not jest what ye want the spell ta accomplish. Udderwise, enny one can come along and change it howe're they might. Which'll teach ye ta use words in a tongue ye dunna know!" Catie ended her reprimand by eyeing Liz severely, her one eye closed such that she was squinting ferociously at her embarrassed student.

Liz's cheeks stayed hot as she muttered, "Okay, okay, I'll use English from now on."

Catie sent her scorching gaze to the ceiling above and shouted an imprecation of, "Damn it, woman, ye dunna listen ta a word I say, do ye? It dunna matter what language ye use, as long as ye know what everee syllable means and ye fill it wi' yer intent! If that be in English, fine, or enny udder language, also fine, even if it ain't yer native tongue! Jest make sure ye know what ye are a sayin'!"

"Okay, okay, I get it! Okay?" Lis exclaimed, holding her palms up to Catie defensively. "What do you want to try next?" she asked, pointing down at the clock-watch again, wanting to move to a topic that didn't make her feel silly.

Catie chewed her cheek without replying, then went after her lip, and finally back to her cheek. Liz watched her, hope dwindling in her that they could indeed advance their chances of escape during the fortuitous storm raging around them still.

After several minutes of silence from them both, Liz decided to try a simple spell, leaning over the clock-watch and canting, "Let us hear or in some other way clearly show us the spell cast upon this clock-watch that allows it to be tracked by its matching orrery."

A small cloud of turquoise-colored magic hovered over the timepiece, and then settled down upon it.

Throughout this magical technicolor scene, Jesse cooed and giggled, for he loved it when his mama used her magic. He adored the pretty color of her power and how it moved into things and disappeared. As was his habit, he waved a hand toward the cloud, just missed it as it floated downward, then he strained forward to reach into it before it disappeared.

Liz's spell was caught in his right hand and he pulled it back to himself, thrusting his left hand into it so that both hands now held the spell firmly in their grasp.

So surprised were both Liz and Catie for the moment, neither thought to do anything but watch.

Jesse threw the spell back into the air with a happy giggle, and cried, "Ba ba ba ba!" and the spell started to settle downward once again, only this time it was mixed with his childish spell, which was colored glacial blue.

Catie, reacting decisively and thinking fast, reached for the mixed spell but could not hold it like Jesse had because her fingers slipped through it as if it wasn't there. Instead, she hastily added to it by canting, "Give us a way ta reproduce it on five more 'orloges, wi' each belonging ta someone on five diff'rent ships sailin' right around us naow!"

The gold of her spell twined itself around and through the colors of the two other spells, and then the combined spells, having settled all around the clock-watch by now, sank into it and disappeared.

The three of them gazed at the clock-watch expectantly, waiting for something to happen. It took a few seconds, but finally a long refrain was recited in an old German dialect that neither woman understood. They looked at each other with doubt, but then, from the clock-watch arose five balls of magical power, teeming with the brilliance of turquoise, glacier blue, and gold magic swirling around each other. These tiny balls of vibrantly colored magic split off and two went into Catie's hands, two into Liz's, and one into little Jesse's right hand.

This time, both women gulped at each other, pop-eyed.

Catie was the first to recover and she complained immediately that, "I was 'opin' the spell would bring the timepieces we want here, but I think we 'ave to go in search o' dem on the udder boats."

"Oh, crap, this means I have to take Jesse with me then, doesn't it?" Liz asked and Catie nodded, making a sorry face at the other woman. Liz noted further, "And it means we have to go to three boats, while you go to two; right?"

"Aye, I think it do mean that," Catie agreed, nodding her head still, and maintaining her sorrowful expression. "And we'd best get a goin', dunna ye think? This storm may blow o'er enny time and we want ta be done wi' it by the time it's quiet again or it gets light."

Liz hung her head a second and acknowledged to herself that Catie was right. She looked at her own watch and said, "It's now almost two a.m. We'd best be done by six, because that's when the sun begins to rise."

For the third time, both women looked at each other, only this time both looked scared.

"Don't get caught," Liz whispered and Catie inclined her head.

"Nor ye," she said, and Liz shuddered.

Together, they left Liz's cabin and made their way with difficulty to the side rail. Both were soaked within moments from the rain pouring down and the ocean spray booming over the rail as the tempest's raucous waves bounced all around the *Knave*. They looked toward the rough seas and could just barely discern the running lights of other ships in the distances around them. Deep inside themselves, they could each sense which boats they must visit and their directions, with Catie getting two shipping boats, while Liz and Jesse were assigned three passenger ships. They knew this simply because their hearts and their hands were pulled toward the ships in question.

Just as the women gave in to the haul and drag of their spell and were lifted off their feet into the air, they looked at each other one final time, both worried out of their wits, and mouthed, "Be careful!" to each other. Little Jesse, on the other hand, let out a high-pitched squeal of joy that was lost on the wind as he and his mother sailed into the black, stormy night.

***

Perhaps it was because of the afternoon's adventures with the elf witch and her army that, later that night, each of the traveler's found it impossible to remain awake. By midnight, all were asleep and snoring loud enough to wake the dead. At around two a.m., they were still sawing their proverbial logs when a group of ten strangers made their way into camp.

Wiwila and the other horses whinnied and stomped, being the first to awaken and being much surprised by the intrusion. Sylvester was the next and he darted out of sight before anyone could catch him. The alarm for him, naturally, woke up the other four, with Donnie being the last to rouse.

She woke to find herself bound from behind and being pulled to her feet unceremoniously.

She glanced over at Falwaïn in the dim light from the still burning fire and saw that he and the others were also trussed up like she was. He gave her a look that told her to wait before doing anything and so she merely made sure her bonds were not so tight that they chafed, and otherwise left them where they were when she was shoved to the ground with her friends.

A search was put on for Sylvester by the intruders, but after nearly a quarter hour, his location was still undiscovered.

Donnie let them search for another quarter hour before, taking pity on them, she said, "As I'm guessing you already know, he's kind of a special cat, which means you're never going to find him unless he wants to be found. Really, you might as well give up and tell us what it is you want from us." She smiled at the three men closest to her after she said this, each of whom were kneeling around the fire, which they had set ablaze with more wood so that it now illuminated the entire clearing of the campsite.

All three scowled back at her with utter hatred before returning to their quiet mutterings.

Rather flattened by the blatant intensity of the men's feelings, Donnie frowned, then puffed out her cheeks and let a long breath escape her pursed lips, her surprise showing in her eyes.

"Okay, so I hadn't expected to be welcomed outside the Ganlonds, necessarily," she remarked in a low voice to Falwaïn, who was to her left, "but I had no idea I'd be hated that much, especially since they know next to nothing about me."

He shrugged at her with sympathy, replying softly, "It does not matter what you are like, my love, because you are the most accomplished and skillful witch Medregai has seen for ages. It is unknown what you want with the world, or what you will do with your power, and there are many who would kill you to take that power from you, if they can. As we said before, the Sarn and the Valkérian are notorious for taking things, stealing what they will." When he said this, his face took on a sudden expression of enlightenment. "It occurs to me that, since the elves left us alone and did not take your magic, perhaps that means Bréagna really was not there, for I cannot imagine she would let such an opportunity pass by unheeded."

After almost half a minute spent considering this possibility, Donnie nodded. "Maybe," she allowed, speaking under her breath. "Although, Sylvester told me once that anyone who stole my magic but wasn't strong enough to handle it would simply and literally explode, and my power would come back to me. I suppose that could've happened back there while we were all unconscious, but I don't think it did because someone or something magical had to have transported us those eighty-plus miles.

Besides, while the Bréagna I met was quite strong, she wouldn't have been able to handle my power, I'm sure of it. Seriously, she wasn't anywhere near strong enough for that. Which argues for her being real, doesn't it? And, might I add, quite the friggin' psychopath!"

Their whispers had been noticed by one of the men guarding them. He came and stood over them menacingly. "If ye utter another word, I'll gut ye both," he threatened with a snarl.

Donnie sighed audibly while shaking her head slowly from side to side. "No, you silly fool, that you will *not* do!" she said with feeling, making sure to bestow upon him a stubborn and recalcitrant glare.

Before anything more could be said between them, the oldest man of the company, a great hulking warrior, returned from the hunt for Sylvester empty-handed and walked over to where the prisoners were sitting. He motioned for some of his guards to haul the captives to their feet, which was managed without too much pulling and jerking. He stood in front of Donnie and Falwaïn and informed them, "In the name of the Prince of Faen Eárna, I charge ye with treason and trespass, and tell ye now that we will take ye shackled and humbled to Hörthanc, where sentence shall be passed upon yer devious and ignoble souls. Be prepared to die, the lot of ye, for the brave Prince does not take kindly to a witch and her cohorts trespassing on his lands."

"But we are not on his lands," Falwaïn argued, eyeing the older man with a hardy stare. "And beyond that, the Prince of Faen Eárna stands before you, which you well know, Tather."

The old man looked back at him with as much hatred as the other man had stared at Donnie.

"Ye will not speak to me, treasoner!" spat Tather angrily. "Ye should have learnt yer lesson the last time ye meddled with a witch. We Eárnans will not forgive ye a second time and will never again call ye prince of anything but darkness and death."

Donnie, wide-eyed, looked from one man to the other. "Wow, there's more to that story about Bréagna that I have yet to hear, isn't there?" she said to Falwaïn.

He looked back at her and sighed. "Yes…well, it took several years after my rescue from her before my people trusted me at all. And even though I ruled as prince for more than three long years in total," he said sharply, obviously reminding the other man of this, "and improved the lives and status of my people substantially during that time, my past sins, whether real or perceived, were never erased, most especially from suspicious minds like Tather here, who was loyal to my brother, Mílwaïn."

Tather leaned forward and ground out maliciously, "He was a better man than ye'll ever be!"

"So you say," Falwaïn replied harshly, "but that's because you didn't know him as I did, nor have you the sensitivity of an okûn to understand the depths of my brother's depraved soul. He was neither a good nor kindly man; he was a brutal lout who, like my father, only wanted to kill or be killed by other warriors. Neither of them cared for me all that much, so their concessions to Bréagna really had nothing at all to do with me, although they argued differently to the king later. If it had not been for Déagmun, I would never have been rescued at all and would likely be dead or banished from Medregai along with her. And Tather here was their closest ally and sycophant, who believed the same as they did in every possible way."

Donnie's jaw had dropped. "Wow, there really *is* more to that story," she repeated, staring at her man with surprise. "When we get out of this situation, you're gonna have to tell me the whole dang thing from the beginning, okay?"

But Tather had had enough chatter. He literally spat on Donnie at this juncture, which landed on her shoulder when she moved fast enough to avoid it making it to her cheek, and barked at the man holding her to tighten her bonds and ready for her humbling.

From the pack on his horse, he got out an instrument that had a wickedly sharp, curved blade attached between the two ends of a wooden handle, and then he strode purposefully toward Donnie.

"I think we'll start with her," he said nastily, adding, "Tighten that rope even more. Cut off her hands if ye must to hold her firm." He approached Donnie and started to raise his hands, and the blade in them, to her head, apparently intending to cut her hair.

Donne concentrated on her power and froze everyone there except for herself, Falwaïn, and, of course, Sylvester, making sure to set the freeze charm on the others' minds, ears, and eyes so that they were completely unconscious of what she was about to do. "Sylvester!" she called out to her cat. "Where are you?"

His voice came from above and she and Falwaïn looked upward to see the cat's form appear out of thin air in the crook of the tree nearest to them. "I am here, Donemere. I was beginning to wonder just how long you were going to let this play on before stopping it," he commented, gazing down at her with a mild expression.

She looked over at Falwaïn and quipped, "Well, at least now I get why you don't want your hair cut if that's what constitutes humbling! Geez Louise, you all have some weird-ass customs here, don't you? I mean, that one's kind of Samson and Delilah-ish, huh? And why do it? Is your power supposed to be in your hair?"

"Yes, they are indeed quite similar happenings," shot back Falwaïn, grinning at her surprise. "And yes, I have read that story from the Bible. But a humbling merely begins with cutting the hair—and, by the way, hair is cut from all over the body, not just the top of the head. For instance, your eyebrows and eyelashes are also cut, as is the hair around your genitalia, and then whatever body hair you also have is removed, and not in a gentle sort of shave, if you understand my meaning."

Donnie gaped at him. "Oh! My! God! Are you serious? That would take forever to do to all four of us! What was that fool thinking—that we'd just let him do that to us?"

Falwaïn chuckled at her. "My honey woman, you are rather naïve at times, aren't you? He does not expect us to let him, he expects us to fight back so that he can then justify killing us."

She suddenly caught on and rolled her eyes. "That's right, slow little deducting dowager that I am. You just said not two minutes ago that he was just like your father and brother, who either wanted to kill or be killed by another warrior. So, of course, he's looking for any excuse to make this lethal." She fell silent a moment and stared at Falwaïn with apology. "I promise I won't hurt them, but I can't let this go any farther, you know."

Falwaïn nodded complacently. "I know."

She looked up at her cat and said, "Stay there for now. I'll let you know when I want you to be seen by these idiots, okay?"

Sylvester nodded and settled back down upon the thick branch of the tree, becoming invisible again almost immediately.

Donnie dematerialized the ropes binding her and her friends, transferring them to the guards' wrists that were standing behind each of them. While it was not a perfect fit, it was enough to encumber the guards' hands, which gave her friends time to turn and dispatch them with relish once Donnie unfroze them all, meting out some effectively powerful blows to Tather's men. Each of their captors fell to the ground unconscious just as the boombox appeared on a small boulder to Donnie's right and began playing "Fortunate Son."

Falwaïn was quite pleased to take care of his and Donnie's guards, while Donnie kept sidestepping to avoid Tather's advances.

Tather, for his part, spluttered at her, bug-eyed, "Wh-wha-how?" He grunted angrily at her as he missed yet again, then recovered himself and asked, when he suddenly found Falwaïn's knife at his throat, "Why, if ye could have done that before, did ye not?"

"Oh, I was just being courteous," Donnie replied, looking at him with pity. "I mean, I didn't want to turn you into a toad without getting to know you a little better first to see if you actually deserve that."

Her friends all snickered at this, even though the rest of Tather's men were closing in on them threateningly.

Donnie waved a hand and the other guards, all five of them, were pushed into a circle and bound by a rope she had fly over from one of the saddles so that it could wind around their middles a couple times before a knot was tied at its ends. She took the precaution of having their knives and swords and anything else metallic disappear from their hands and scabbards, to reappear ten feet away on the ground in a pile. She spared a pensive look at the boombox before turning her attention back to Tather.

"So, who's this prince you're serving?" she asked curiously, although she thought she might already know the answer, especially when Tather moved his head as though he wanted to see Falwaïn's reaction to his reply.

"Prince Malwé has returned and is twice the sovereign his father ever thought to be," Tather told her arrogantly, an ugly sneer on his somewhat wizened features.

Donnie noted the shock on Falwaïn's face, which was to the left of Tather's. She said, "We thought he was back in that Año Nuevo place—er, yeah, yeah, I mean Anûmanétus, and he's supposed to be learning to be a page or knight or something like that." She nodded her thanks to Akanna for the assist, which normally would have come from Falwaïn, but he had yet to process the new info bomb just dropped upon him. "Are you saying that's no longer true?"

Tather looked like he didn't want to respond at first, but when Donnie shot him a reproachful glare and looked meaningfully at the knife still held to his throat, he reluctantly explained, "The king sent him back to us four months ago."

Donnie gaped at him, and then she noticed that Falwaïn's hand slipped, leaving a long nick in Tather's neck that immediately started spurting blood. Donnie hastily waved her hands and the cut healed. She touched her forefinger to Tather's forehead and he dropped to the ground where he stood, knocked out cold.

The boombox was wailing on the song by now and Donnie grunted loudly at it in exasperation. "Show a little respect for his feelings, will you?" she exhorted, gesturing toward the still-stunned Falwaïn. The music box turned down its volume with a series of flashes and beeps.

The five guards who were tied together were looking at the box like it was a demon come to feast upon their flesh. Each of them appeared about to have a heart attack, with several gasping for breath and all with their eyes as big as saucers and filled with abject terror. As a group they were scrambling away from the box as fast as they could, which made for a very comical sight as they tripped and fell, were pulled to their feet by sheer force of will by one or two of their number, only to fall again almost immediately. Thereby, they made practically no progress in their retreat.

Donnie noticed their antics and had another rope fly from one of their saddles and tether the frantic five to a tree, just to make sure they did not somehow wander off. Then she pointed at the boombox and reassured the men airily, "No, really, it's not possessed—well, I'm pretty sure it's not possessed. It's got lots of attitude, though, I'll give ya that. And you're not necessarily wrong to want to get away from it."

She focused back on Falwaïn and heaved a concerned breath, as did Diego and Akanna. Sylvester climbed down a ways from his high perch, then jumped to Donnie's shoulder. They all crowded around and stared at Falwaïn, who did not look at all well, and then they turned to each other helplessly.

Donnie, after a few moments, asked Akanna, "You had no idea the king had ordered Malwé back to Faen Eárna?"

The vincan shook her head, speechless. She licked her dry lips, swallowed hard, and finally managed to say, "No, I thought he was still in Anûmanétus, still training." She glanced at Falwaïn guiltily though before adding, "But I did know that he was not exactly the favorite that Belnesem and Galæron convinced you he was. You see, he was a bit small at first, when he came to the main garrison, I mean, and he…he suffered at the hands of older and larger boys." She now looked distinctly uncomfortable and confessed, "I believe there were several incidents, some of them quite vicious, until he suddenly sprang up tall and earned a bit more girth. The other boys stopped playing their tricks on him then, but it was widely known that the master did not. He had the boy beaten regularly because he said the king wanted to make sure the young prince…" she hesitated here before completing the sentence, "the young prince was not weak like his father."

Donnie looked at Falwaïn, noting that, while he was taking in most of what Akanna was saying, he was also still reeling from the fact that his friend and king had lied openly to him about his son's whereabouts and his life at Anûmanétus.

Unsure of what to say right now, Donnie turned away to go saddle Wiwila so they could get back on the road as soon as possible, but was stopped when Falwaïn suddenly spoke, advising her bitterly, "There you go, Donnie, that's the truth of us all. Every Sarn and their cursed kin, every Valkérian and their pointy-eared fold, maybe even every vincan, noakie, okûn, troll, ogre—every Mountain Man and Woman, and everyone in-between except for your magical creature friends—and Diego and Warren, I guess—every one of the rest of us in western Medregai is nothing more than a cheat and a liar, a thief and a murderer. Trust none of us, my darling, because none of us are even a hair's breadth as pure or noble as you and your animal friends. We none of us have finer qualities to recommend ourselves to anyone and we all should be shunned and left to rot in our iniquities and abominations, waging wars with each other over power and greed and imaginary injustices that are as fallacious and specious as we are. In short, leave us to die by our own hands and get yourself and your magical charges to safety, far, far away from us and the baseness of our paltry existence." He stopped, took a shuddering breath, and wiped his face where his own spittle had flown to while he had so passionately cursed himself and the peoples of Medregai. He raised his eyes but could not hold Donnie's gaze. "I mean it, Donnie," he entreated her, misery pouring from him, "leave me here, go save the Mîrlonds, then get the hell out of this world and find the dragons so you can save yourself. And never look back to this god-forsaken hole. Promise me you'll do that. And that you'll never let our children think that their father was in any way worthy of their mother or of being their father."

Diego and Akanna had stayed to listen to Falwaïn's diatribe, but they now walked away. As they left, Sylvester jumped down from Donnie's shoulder to follow them.

Donnie raised her chin and squared her shoulders before walking right up to Falwaïn. She placed her hands on his shoulders and made him look at her by putting her face an inch below his. "You know full well that I will do none of that, not without you by my side. In case you hadn't realized it yet, nobody is born all that noble or all that terrible. Life makes us what we are, but we also have the ability to make ourselves into who we want to be. That's certainly what's happened with me. When I first came here, I was a silly, spacey, crazy idiot, but I'm not any of that now because that's not who I want to be anymore.

"And if there is any purity or nobleness to me," she continued dryly, employing a sardonic tone and mocking expression, "it has more to do with my purpose than with my personality, believe me. You see, I fully comprehend that there are thousands of magical creatures relying upon me to protect them, to give them a better life if I can. And I have taken those responsibilities and their related tasks on willingly and knowingly, just as I took you on. While at first I thought you were the pure and noble one, I've since learned that you are merely a man, a man who has made good choices and bad ones in his life. But you too have good purpose now and that has changed you, molded you ever more firmly into the man you really want to be in your heart."

She stepped back and added crisply, "So, no, I will not leave you here to die, nor will I leave your son here without trying to reach him. He can make his own choice when it comes right down to it, sure, but we can give him a new choice and maybe, just maybe, he might decide to join us and find a good purpose for his own life. And now, dear heart, go get our horses saddled so we can begin the journey to rescue your son. In the meantime, I think I'm going to do something silly, spacey, and crazy with your old friend Tather."

***

Liz put her hands over Jesse's face to shield him from the worst of the wild storm raging around them, but he kept trying to brush her hands away, still squealing with unbridled joy at the wind and water streaming over him and his mother while they flew through the roiling air just above the turbulent sea. Liz resolutely concentrated her power on coming up with some kind of protection for them and felt a modicum of relief once a heavy, black wool coat appeared on her small form, its folds falling to the tops of her shoes, its generous proportions big enough to hide Jesse completely, even though he was strapped to her chest. She chuckled a little when she realized that it reminded her of a coat her mother had kept in a trunk where she stored all of Liz's dress-up clothes from when she was a child. Liz pulled the large hood on the coat over her face and held it so that there was just enough of an opening to see with one eye that the first boat they were to visit was approaching.

In another minute, they were standing on the ship's deck, having landed in the deep shadows near the bulkhead. Liz's stomach lurched in time with the heaving boat and she had to fight to keep down the remnants of dinner.

She noticed there were lights on in the salon down the way from where she and Jesse stood, so she edged forward cautiously to where she could make out that the room was occupied by some men who were playing cards and drinking whiskey. One of the men, who looked to be the oldest judging by the snowy white hair covering his head, detached himself from the others and stood unsteadily, downing the last half of his whiskey into his gullet in one go. He then wiped his white beard with his handkerchief and apparently emitted a long belch that Liz heard but took a moment to identify. There was laughter and muffled voices among those present, and then the man stumbled out onto the deck and dove for the stairs that would take him to his cabin.

Liz felt a pull on her heart and hands again, and so she followed him, making sure to cross in front of the salon only when everyone inside was focused upon their cards. She too made her way down the stairs to the enclosed deck below and watched as the highly inebriated man wove a drunken path to his cabin. When he tripped over the threshold into it, Liz walked up to its closed door and conjured a small light ball so she could see the lock. It would be a simple thing to pick it, she could tell. Her gaze rose for a second to the cabin's number, number one, and held there as she saw a card underneath it that had printed upon it, "Professor Horace Gottleib-Lange."

Something stirred in her breast and in her memory, and she knew there was something written in history about this man, but she could not yet recall what. But the pull on her heart was unmistakable and so she extinguished her light ball, concentrated on the lock and its workings, and soon heard the click as it shot open.

Keeping her hands, and more importantly her fingerprints, covered by the wool of the coat, she gently turned the door's handle and made her way inside the cabin, where she heard its occupant already snoring loudly. She debated whether to dare another light ball and decided she had to risk it or face possibly tripping over something and waking the man. She conjured the smallest light she could imagine and let it glide over the bed, where it dimly illuminated the man's prone body, face down, upon the bed.

Breathing silently, Liz tiptoed over to him and saw that his watch was still on his left wrist, which was, thanks be to the keepers of divine fate, outstretched right in front of her. She opened the big coat and slipped out of it so that her hands were free and clear of its folds. It fell to the floor around her feet. Once freed from its confines, Jesse cooed up at the light ball in a small, sleepy voice, enchanted as always by the sight of his mother's magic at work.

Liz reached for the man's watch, her cold fingers stiff from their freezing journey over the ocean waves, and she wondered what she was supposed to do next. But she had no real reason to worry, for before her fingertips even touched the watch's surface, one of the brilliant balls of magic that had come from the clock-watch earlier cruised smoothly from her left hand and into the man's watch, where it glowed brightly before settling into the timepiece's innards. Peering more closely at the watch, Liz saw that it was also a stop watch and had been manufactured by the Swiss great, Girard-Perregaux.

Jesse started to giggle in earnest, so Liz scrambled into the coat once again and hopped over the man's drunkenly discarded shoes toward the door, pulling it open just as she felt another strong tug on her heart and her hands. She extinguished her light ball and looked back, realizing that the man was staring at her bleary-eyed, too drunk to tell if she was a threat or not. She slipped out the door and pulled it closed behind her, then started to hurry toward the stairs.

With her heart lodged in her throat, she heard two voices approaching her position. She looked around frantically, seeing nowhere to hide, and felt her terror rise when the spell began to pull her again, dragging her toward the advancing men. Not knowing what else to do, she gave into its pull and was lifted off her feet once again, the heavy wool coat flapping around her and making her look like one of the great, winged Furies as she flew toward the two men, who yelped and dodged out of her way at the last moment to the wooden floorboards of the top deck, a sort of sixth sense warning them of her presence and her direction in the darkness. They both screamed something at her in German, but Liz's brain was too scattered to realize then what it was.

And then she was soaring over the waves again to the next ship, which had to be the largest of the lot sailing within the nearest ten-mile radius. This time, she met no one, and it all went much more smoothly. She was drawn to the cabin of Ester Babette Chagall, breaking into the woman's suite easily. Madame Chagall was, from what Liz could recall of her from memory, a society maven and so-called philanthropist from Paris. She was apparently on her way to the Panama Pacific International Exposition in San Francisco with her three daughters and one son, or so Liz gleaned from papers lying on a table in the enormous stateroom.

She'd perused the cut-out articles regarding the Expo with enthusiasm but admittedly only glanced at the photographs of Mrs. Chagall's children that stood proudly upon the chest of drawers in the suite's main bedroom. This bureau was positioned at the foot of the bed in which the *grande dame* reposed in total oblivion, snoring loud enough to wake the dead.

Liz quietly chuckled at the snorts and chorts coming from the woman's open mouth, then she turned back to the chest and her eager fingers dove into its top drawer. There she found the timepiece the spell was searching for, and she suddenly felt the little ball of magic leave her right palm. When its colorful brilliance died out, she noticed it had settled into what was a Cartier gold watch, exquisitely rimmed with gleaming diamonds on the outside of its round face, its faultless design sleek and gorgeous.

With fleet steps, Liz left the woman's room and hurried through the suite's darkly silent stateroom. Jesse was asleep under the heavy material of the woolen coat now, reassured and made warm by his mother's body heat, and Liz could feel his rhythmical breathing against her chest. She opened the outer door to the suite and swiftly traversed the hall, climbed to the open deck, and was again pulled into the air and sent hurtling over the still foaming waves of the waning storm, its fury seeming to be nearly spent.

Was it her imagination or was the sky to the east getting suspiciously lighter? Liz groaned softly, hoping the last of the timepieces was residing somewhere easily accessed.

The third boat was smaller than the second, but larger than the first. Liz felt the draw of the last timepiece and followed its pull down to what was generally called steerage. Here, she could no longer avoid anyone, so she pulled the coat's hood over her bright red hair and wound her way through the many groups of nervous people disturbed by the tossing of their boat upon the whimsical waves of the storm. Most of these folks were standing around smoking cigarettes or pipes, or filling spittoons with their redolent chew, while others were gripping either each other or the poles supporting the two levels of sleeping berths provided for this deck and its particular class of passengers in order to keep their feet. What little heat there was in the place came from some large, bare pipes that groaned and thumped overhead as steam was pushed through them. What little light there was came from lanterns attached to the posts demarcating the various rows of beds.

The spell drew Liz toward the very back of the large hold, far away from the two entry doors and quick escape, if escape was needed. Near the last row of beds, a little blonde girl of about seven or maybe even eight sat looking down at a sleeping woman in the bed beside her. Liz and Jesse were pulled to the little girl, so Liz looked around and saw that the berth across from where the girl sat and the woman slumbered was not currently occupied. Liz gave a friendly smile to the little girl as she passed close and got a whiff of stale, sick air from the mother's bed clothes. Liz sat on the edge of the bed and opened her coat, looking down to check on Jesse, who was still fast asleep. Grateful that the lighting was so terrible in here, she pushed the hood back from her head and gave the little girl another smile, admiring the girl's tight ringlets, even though it looked like her thin hair had not been washed for some time.

The little girl did not return her smile, but she did say in a bold voice, "My mommy doesn't want me talking to darkies. And you shouldn't be here anyway, you know. It's whites only back in this area." She had a distinct New York accent, although her diction was excellent and far beyond her apparent years. She gazed back at Liz without fear or any sign of trepidation at all.

"I am not a darkie," Liz said, adopting a strong Spanish accent. "I come from Spain, both *mi hijo* and *yo*." She pointed to herself and Jesse. She strongly suspected the girl was fibbing anyway, because there were several people of color nearby, while most of the whites had been berthed at the front of the hold, near the entries. She figured that likely meant the woman and child had no one to protect them nor money to procure a better berth.

Still intent on making friends with the little girl, Liz added in a kindly voice, "And we can go anywhere we need to in this class, just like any of the other really poor folk."

She shrugged out of her coat, intending to use it for a pillow. In the meanwhile, she introduced herself and Jesse and then laid back on the bed, her hands wrapping around Jesse's so his didn't get cold.

"Your mama smells sick," Liz stated and the little girl nodded.

"She said she wants to die, she's so sick," the little girl told Liz. "But I don't think she really wants that. My daddy died this past winter and Mommy was quite sad about it and told me it's not a good thing to die and leave a little girl on her own, like Daddy did to me and her." The child blinked her solemn, blue eyes at Liz.

Liz shook her head and replied, "No, that is not a good thing, I agree. But it's not usually our choice of how and when we die, you know?"

"Where'd your accent go?" the little girl interjected and gave Liz a reproving look.

Liz, taken aback by her error, chuckled a little ruefully and conceded, "Well, okay, we're not from Spain. But you wouldn't believe me if I told you the truth about where we're really from."

"My daddy always said the truth will out, and it's best to just own up to it right away. That way, you don't get punished so bad for telling lies." The little girl stared at Liz meaningfully and she reached up to rub the side of her nose. When she did that, Liz caught a glimpse of a pocket watch hanging around the girl's neck on a thick, silver chain.

Liz sat up and Jesse stirred. She kissed the top of his head and looked over at the little girl, who was watching her wistfully.

"I ain't never seen anybody wrap a baby like that. Does he like it?" the little girl asked, forgetting just for a moment to be a grown-up, but Liz could see the girl catch herself and knew from the child's frown that she was silently berating her regression.

Liz nodded, giving the little girl a sweet grin. "Jesse loves it, actually. Like I said, that's his name, Jessop Campos, or Jesse for short. And I'm Liz, his mom. Er, what's your name?" she asked breezily, not wanting to scare the girl off.

The little girl considered the question for a moment, then supplied, "I'm Maeve Rae Danaher, but Mommy says I'm going to be called just Maeve Rae when we get to Hollywood." The little girl blinked her solemn eyes at Liz again. "I'm going to be in moving pictures, see. I've already made a couple of one-reelers back in New Jersey, but Mommy thinks Hollywood is where I should be, so we're going there to make our fortune."

"Wow," Liz said, looking at the girl with widened eyes. Feeling flushed with excitement she could hardly contain, Liz realized that this was indeed little Maeve Rae, child star of the silent screen who would go on to become internationally famous for her singing and dancing in numerous movies and just as infamous for believing in the occult and magic. She would get railroaded out of Hollywood by the time she turned nineteen and tragically end her life in a drug-induced suicide two years later.

"Do you want to become a movie star?" Liz asked her, a question she'd always wondered about this very talented young child.

"Is that what you'd want for him?" Maeve countered, pointing at Jesse with her cornflower blue eyes widened in disbelief.

"No, of course not."

"My daddy didn't want it for me either, but my mommy snuck me back and forth to Hoboken so I could act in some films her special friend was making. His name is Herbert Flint and we're supposed to be meeting him in Los Angeles, although first we have to go to San Francisco for a big fair."

Liz, digging through her memory and recollecting that Herbert Flint would go on to direct the little girl in her first four movies until he and Maeve's mother had a falling out and broke off their torrential affair, finally realized it was her turn to say something.

"Er, why are you going to the San Francisco fair?" she asked curiously.

Maeve shrugged. "Because Mommy booked me for a film there that's going to be about fairies and magic."

"Do you believe in fairies and magic?" Liz enquired, not able to keep herself from wanting to know if the girl was already on that path.

Little Maeve frowned at her. "That's silly," she said, and clearly meant it. "Fairies aren't real, they're just stories. Everybody knows that."

"Well, sure," Liz gushed, turning different shades of a dull red, "that was indeed very silly of me, wasn't it?"

Maeve agreed that it was and the two of them fell into silence.

Liz had no idea how she was going to get Maeve's watch close enough to Jesse so he could release his part of the spell, she only knew she couldn't go back to the *Drunken Knave* until she had somehow accomplished that very thing.

It was perhaps an hour later that Maeve's mother began to mutter gibberish and, for the first time, Liz realized that Florrie Danaher wasn't seasick, but was ill in a very different manner. Little Maeve glanced over at Liz worriedly, put up a small hand to cover her mother's mouth and said to her, "Mommy, stop that. There's a lady here and she's going to think bad of you if you don't behave."

Liz's heart twisted. That was such a grown-up reprimand for such a little girl to give, and she somehow knew that young Maeve was merely repeating it because it had likely been said to her on occasion.

Jesse was awake now and had been watching Maeve intently for some time. Maeve had mostly ignored his coos and giggles, making it clear she did not want to get caught up in conversation again. Nevertheless, Liz felt great concern for the little girl's mother, so she got up from her bed and lurched over to the other one. While the seas had calmed a good deal by then, it was still a rough ride here in steerage.

Liz put the back of her cool fingers to Florence Danaher's forehead and sucked in her breath with surprise. Mrs. Danaher was burning up, she was so feverish. Looking around, Liz could see no one who could help.

"Do you know if there is a doctor around?" Liz asked Maeve, but the little girl just lifted her shoulders and stared back at her in doubt.

"No, I don't suppose doctors come down here much, do they?" Liz mumbled to herself, pulling the sick woman toward the side of the bed so she could get a proper look at her. She was a beautiful woman, a little worn around the edges and far too thin, but that was to be expected for the times and her lot in life thus far. Liz noticed that her hands were pressed to her abdomen and so Liz asked Maeve, "Has she been having problems with her belly, Maeve?"

Wide-eyed and solemn as ever, Maeve nodded.

Liz wracked her memory, knowing there was something she should be remembering about Florrie Danaher, and was glad when it came to her. Mrs. Danaher suffered as a young woman from a serious infestation of helminths, or intestinal worms, and it was suspected that she had gotten them long before she brought Maeve to Los Angeles. Liz knew she had to do something, but she had no idea what that would be for several minutes as she debated her options.

She finally decided to send Maeve to the front of the hold to ask if there was, in fact, a doctor available to help. It took her some time though to convince Maeve to leave her mother, but Liz finally prevailed by telling the girl quite honestly that she feared Mrs. Danahur was going to die.

The girl slid off the bed and strode off purposefully, and Liz turned back to the sick woman. She concentrated hard on visualizing what she imagined Mrs. Danaher's parasites looked like and then she willed them to dematerialize from the woman's intestines and onto the floor at Liz's feet. Liz figured that was best, so then she'd know what she'd actually removed from the woman.

A wave of turquoise light flew from her hands and settled over Florrie Danaher's abdomen, sinking into her a moment later.

Liz heard a gasp directly behind her and turned in time to see Maeve start to scream. She grabbed the little girl and put a hand over her mouth, willing Maeve to be calm. Again, a soft wave of turquoise magic came from Liz's hands and this time sank into the girl.

Maeve stopped struggling and stared up at Liz deliriously, obviously more greatly affected by Liz's calming spell on her than intended. Pushing Maeve onto the bed beside her sick mother, Liz looked down at her feet. She shuddered at the sight of the tangle of long worms roiling around on the wooden floor and sent the nasty parasites to the sea outside. This time, the small wave of turquoise magic she used seemed to hold Maeve still with fascination.

The child's serious gaze traveled to Liz's face and she said gravely, "You're a fairy."

Liz gave her a somewhat miserable smile and answered, "No, no, of course not. Fairies aren't real, remember?"

"I remember." The girl said the words but she looked unconvinced.

"Look, I need to do something, something I should have just done an hour ago and then left." Without asking permission, Liz took hold of the pocket watch on its chain and raised it to Jesse's hand.

The last bit of the spell that she, Jesse, and Catie had cast enveloped the watch and then disappeared into its innards.

Maeve gasped again.

"Don't worry, it won't do anything to the watch. But you might one day meet up with some very strange Austrians or Germans who want to buy it from you." Liz made a face. "At least, I hope they'll try to buy it instead of stealing it from you. Is it your father's watch?" she asked, and was not surprised when the girl nodded.

"I'm going to leave you now, Maeve, and you'll never see me or Jesse ever again, okay?" Liz told the girl, tucking her small body in beside her mother, who looked much better and was breathing easier. Liz touched the woman's forehead and swore it felt cooler already. She looked back again at little Maeve Rae and said seriously, "But I need you to promise me that you will never tell anyone what happened here today or that you met me. Nobody will believe you anyway, so it's best to just not say anything at all, you see?" she pointed out, and the girl gave her a slow nod.

"Are you going to do something to me so that I don't remember you?" Maeve whispered, staring at Liz with a touching glint of fear in her pretty blue eyes.

Recalling what the famous young actress would claim later in her life, Liz knew she could not do anything to alter that outcome, even though it broke her heart not to help the girl. "No, sweetheart, I'm going to depend on you to keep your word and not say anything about us." She answered Maeve in a voice just as subdued as the one the little girl had used for her question. "You're young enough you may well forget us completely in just a few days and will probably soon be convinced we weren't even real. But your mother will be able to get the help she needs when the worms come back, because they're going to come back, Maeve. I only got the ones that are grown, but there are others in the larval stage that will bother her again throughout the next few years. But she'll be okay, trust me," Liz reassured the girl, knowing full well that Florence Danaher would eventually die of the parasites ten years from now. And it would be her mother's death that would trigger Maeve Rae's recollections of "fairies" and send her on her long and fatal dive into madness.

Liz left them quickly, already feeling the pull of the spell wanting to send her flying across the sea. She hurried through the groups of people, many of whom were now preparing to march into the dining room for the first breakfast sitting at six o'clock. She let herself be herded out the door with them and down the hall until she was able to slip up the stairs and make her way to the main deck. She could feel, more than hear, that other people were congregating on her position, people who were also making their way to break their fasts of the night, but this in the higher classes of the ship's hierarchy. She ran to the railing and slipped over the edge, hearing a shout that someone had gone overboard, and felt the spell drag her close along the side of the boat, then pull her behind it and back toward the *Drunken Knave*.

The sky was beginning to lighten significantly by the minute. She passed the second ship, trying to keep low to the water so that early risers on that ship would not see her as anything other than perhaps a large bird. She concentrated on skimming the water until she felt she was sufficiently far enough away and then let the spell take over again.

She saw the first boat, the one with the German professor on it, approaching to her right. She thought about what the two men had shouted at her, trying to translate it but realizing forlornly that her German was a bit rusty. She was almost past the boat when she finally understood what they'd said to her and also just who Professor Gottleib-Lange was.

She immediately changed directions.

Fighting the spell's intentions, Liz flew toward what she could now see in the waxing light of day was a converted fishing trawler and found a place where she could go over the railing and be hidden by a buttress that was anchored right in front of the bulwark there. For several minutes, she waited and listened, trying to get a good read on where everyone was. Her senses told her that nobody was immediately around her on this deck, so she crept from her hiding place and snuck over to the other side of the ship. Here, she heard voices, loud and distinct ones, coming from the salon.

Holding her breath, she edged toward one of the open portholes used to air out the heavy fumes of the passengers' cigars and pipes.

The first man speaking had a thick, German accent, although he was speaking English.

"I tell you, der vas a voman in mein cabin."

A lazy, humorous, and richly American voice noted, "Lucky you, my good fellow."

"No!" the German protested. "Eez not like zat! She had a *kinde*—er, a child, a child mit her!"

A cynical chuckle dismissed this remark and the American voice drawled, "Oh, well, if she's claiming it's yours, tell her to go to the devil! Otherwise, make her prove it."

"No-no-no, eez no ting like zat!" the German man spluttered, wonderfully indignant and horrified by the American's responses. Liz knew that he had to be Professor Gottleib-Lange, the man who had been responsible for designing most of Germany's zeppelins used in World War One. "*Sie war eine Hexe, sage ich dir!*" he howled in outrage. "She vas a vitch, I tell you! And she vas seen not just by me, but also by my comrades! She flew at zem and nearly threw zem overboard!"

Liz could hear the restrained laughter in the American's voice when he said, "And you think she's still aboard the ship? Well, by all means, gentlemen, we can search for her high and low. But I hardly think a little woman like what you've described would be able to throw two grown men overboard. Really, that's most improbable!"

"Zat is because you do not understand!" the German rebutted angrily. "Ve believe she iz de one who has zee *uhr-uhr*, Herr Kepler's clock-vatch! Und she did zometing to meine uhr, but I don't know vat! Derefore, ve must let our people in de zeppelin above know dis, so zey know to vatch for her on ze decks of ze ships around us!"

Liz had heard enough. Also, the spell was becoming more and more insistent that she give in to its pull. She tiptoed back to her hiding place and readied herself for flight, but stopped herself just in time, for around the corner strode three men, each of whom Liz recognized from earlier that morning. She concentrated on blending into the shadows, feeling elated when she realized that her form had become transparent and she was impossible to discern in the dim light of morning. The men passed by her without noticing her presence, although Professor Gottleib-Lange paused at one point in his footsteps, sniffing the air. But he moved on with the others almost immediately.

Still concentrating on keeping herself and Jesse transparent, or at least able to blend into their backgrounds like chameleons, Liz again slipped over the bulwark of the ship and felt herself falling through the air. This time, she nearly hit the water before the spell took hold of her and shot her low over the water and toward her temporary home on the *Drunken Knave*.

Catie was waiting for them in Liz's cabin. She appeared unconcerned at first by Liz and Jesse's long absence, although Liz soon smelled that Catie's breath was clear, which meant she had not had her usual two or three early morning cups of rum yet.

The two witches traded stories while Liz gave Jesse a bath and fed him. Liz learned that Catie had had a much simpler time of it than she had. Catie, of course, had immediately thought to make herself invisible to the eye and had managed to conclude her part of the spell within the first three hours, with most of the time having been taken up in travel to and from the ships she'd been sent to because they were nearly twice the distance from the *Knave* as those Liz had visited.

Catie, after hearing Liz's tale for each of her three boats, especially her second visit on the first boat, sat down and snapped her fingers. A tin cup and a bottle of rum materialized in front of her. "Damnation!" she opined thoughtfully and immediately poured a more than generous helping of rum for herself.

"Yes," agreed Liz. "But, to stay positive, I'm going to be glad that we have four other decoys out there that may yet fool our pursuers. And there is always the possibility that the professor, his German comrades and their American friends will not realize we are using them as a decoy."

"Yes," Catie nodded. "Ye would look at it that way, all right. But not I," she stated dryly. "If we 'ave any good luck left wi' us, I can only 'ope we'll reach a major port b'fore they realize that we're the ones with the real watch-clock. Then mebbe, jest mebbe, we can lose ourselves in the crowds along wi' at least one o' our decoys. Udderwise, we'll 'ave ta think about time-jumpin' agin and who knows what we'll run inta then. It may well be somethin' even worse than 'ere."

Liz looked at her and sighed. She reached over to grab the bottle of rum, glancing at Jesse, who was sleeping again. She poured herself an inch worth's, downed it in one go, then climbed into bed beside her son and said goodnight.

Catie, amused, saluted her with another full cup of rum and watched the mother and child slide into a deep sleep. Finally able to breathe with relief that they had made it back to the ship safely, she decided sleep was a capital idea. Not wanting to be seen on deck, she used a finger to draw a doorway in the wall, sent a wave of golden magic at it, then stepped through it when it opened into the captain's chambers next door.

Chapter 14
John Barleycorn Must Die

Despite her friends' arguments to the contrary, Donnie allowed Tather and his men to go free. Although, before untying and leaving them behind at the campsite, she first placed a sleeping spell on them for the next twelve hours. She reckoned that would give her and her traveling companions a healthy head start to Hörthanc. She'd debated making the spell longer, but was concerned that someone else might come along and harm them while they lay sleeping. They were ruffians, yes, but she didn't want them hurt, only to get away from them.

Besides, since she and the others left camp right after the incident with Tather and his men, that gave them full use of the twelve-hour window, so she was feeling pretty good about their odds of being the first to make it to the Keep of Hallishead. Hallishead, as Falwaïn explained to them while they were riding through the dark night with only a couple light balls from Donnie to illuminate them their path, is where the Princes of Faen Eárna traditionally make their demesne. It was also where Falwaïn spent much of his youth, and Donnie could tell that it held many bittersweet memories for him. He nearly quivered with anticipation the closer they came to his family home.

They veered off the Danduin Road at a certain point and Falwaïn had them catch a scarcely trafficked trail he said was called the Harlowe Cut-off. This shortcut had them plunging southwestward on a more direct line to Hörthanc, the capital city long protected by the province's Sarn leaders with their keeps and their castles. Often, this so-called cut-off was little more than open field, but because of how well Falwaïn recalled the route they were able to maintain a fairly fast pace.

When they stopped later in the morning for the horses to rest and for everyone to eat breakfast, Falwaïn began to describe his home province to his friends. He informed them that there was nothing at all special to the North Castle of Hörthanc; whereas the Keep of Hallishead was a true engineering marvel, soaring to a height of nearly one hundred and fifty feet at its apex. He added as an aside that the more distant and long-abandoned Sørenur Castle to the south was little more than ruins and had fallen into disrepair before even his father's time.

He began to wax poetic about the green farmlands far and wide within the province, discussing proudly how he had improved their yield during his tenure as prince and had built an irrigation system that was the best in the land—although, he added with a wink to Donnie, there was still plenty that could be done in that regard, seeing as he now knew, because of the books and magazines he'd found in Donnie's library, so much more about the subject. From reading them, he had learned new and clever methods of building upon what he'd already installed and he was sure he could easily make the province the richest in the land, richer even than Sedarau with its endless orchards and green fields around Cairnost, or than Nœthlangan with its widespread gold and silver deposits situated throughout the White Tower Mountains' northern peaks.

Falwaïn then moved on to tell them of the verdant chalk hills northeast of Hörthanc, called the Cordis Downs, where he and his clansmen had, for centuries, maintained six carefully drawn signes, or signs, in the limestone. He brushed smooth the ground in front of where he was sitting and drew several shapes in it with a stick, which were basically as follows:

"These signes are known far and wide," he said, staring at his artwork critically, "and are greatly feared by anyone who sees them in the distance, for they represent the six sons of Eárnas Ba. She was the legendary leader of the Gossalyn Forces that held the Red Warlock's armies at Canta'Lem. Eárnas Ba and all but one of her sons sacrificed themselves in that battle, and their signes are sacred to the people of Faen Eárna."

Grinning, he added, "My bloodline came from the one surviving son, Thûlemt, who was my great-great grandfather."

"Is that perhaps why you were able to repel the evil effects of the *Book of the Var*?" Diego asked from his perch on a branch of the large oak tree they'd stopped under. "Because of your bloodline?"

Falwaïn got up and walked over to lean against a low branch just across from Diego. Once settled, he gave a small shrug. "I have never understood why the book had no effect upon me, but it did not. I doubt, though, that it had anything to do with my bloodline, because my brother and my father were sorely tempted by the book and they were hundreds of miles away from it when each answered its call."

He shook his head in thoughtful remembrance. "I'll tell you something little known about its destruction." He paused here to take a drink from the coffee cup in his hand before continuing. "So," he said, beginning his new tale, "when Dreena and I stood before the fires of Adergoth, deep in the heart of the Perminden Mountains, Dreena flung the book away into the flames just as we were tasked with doing. But it stopped in mid-air and stayed still, suspended there. It reached out to him in what appeared to be some sort of mystical entreaty, with its very form stretching toward him, as though begging him to save it. Before he could retrieve it, I pulled him back behind me and the cursed thing recoiled immediately. The next instant, it had dropped to the flames and was soon destroyed."

Sighing heavily, Falwaïn frowned as he looked down the long road of his past. "Three days later, when we approached the Velga'arík, Dreena and I discussed the book's strange behavior for the one and only time. That's because he is still so frightened by what the book did to him at the last moment, and I don't wish to remind him of it unnecessarily. I told him I thought the book may have called to him because of the great burden he had endured after bearing it for so long, and he and I both wondered if it had finally broken through his natural defenses."

Falwaïn bit his lip contemplatively before continuing, then said, "By then, of course, it no longer mattered because the book had been consumed by the magical fires of the old dragon lair and its affects reversed so that all peoples and creatures previously caught by it came to their senses—which, from what we were told later, occurred the very moment the book was taken from this world. And, I assure you, it did not go quietly!" he told them, letting out a wondrous, but rough chuckle. "That book's wail of fury was deafening when it went. As a matter of fact, it was a full day before either myself or Dreena could hear anything said to us."

"What was in the book—do either of you know?" Donnie asked curiously, looking at first Falwaïn and then Akanna.

"Dark spells, fiendish curses, black histories. Or so it was reputed," replied Akanna, and Falwaïn nodded in agreement.

"Black histories?" Donnie echoed, struck by the term. "What does that mean?"

They both questioned her with raised eyebrows.

"Well, I mean, were they alternative versions of history, that sort of thing?" she clarified. "You know, maybe as told by the bad guys, giving their viewpoints or explaining their backgrounds or detailing their actions during seminal moments in Medregai's history, for instance? Something like that."

Appearing thunderstruck by Donnie's question, Akanna squared her shoulders uncomfortably before observing, "If it indeed meant what you suggest, that would make the book an interesting read, certainly. If only to compare how it tallied with what we have in our recorded history."

Donnie looked at Sylvester to gain his opinion and found him shaking his head vigorously.

"One would be unlikely to obtain real truth from a book of that ilk," he said dryly, further pointing out, "None of the authors of that rubbish were at all trustworthy, you know."

"Sylvester's right," Falwaïn interjected, "it would be unwise to trust anything you might find in that sort of book, but…I must say, Akanna has a good point too." He was silent while he grouped his thoughts, and then explained, "When I held the *Book of the Var* in my hands, I had no desire to use the book to vanquish anyone or to rule over others, but I *was* curious about its contents; I admit it. I asked Dreena if he'd ever opened it and he reluctantly admitted that he had, and on more than one occasion, he said."

"Did you ever open it and read it?" asked Diego.

Falwaïn shook his head. "No, any curiosity I had for it disappeared after asking my question of Dreena and then seeing how deeply affected he was when he described its contents. He told me that within it he'd read some of the saddest admissions of evil, puerile confessions of abused power and sadistic dreams unfulfilled, and he said that it tore his heart asunder to be subjected to that much pain and hatred." Falwaïn shivered with dread at the memory of Dreena's twisted face on that day long ago.

"No," Falwaïn averred, his great sympathy for the heroic little noakie showing plainly, "I wished to never be tainted by its contents, so I let it alone and chucked it back into the bag in which Dreena carried it."

"Hmm," Donnie murmured, staring off into space and lost in her own thoughts. "I can't help feeling that the truths behind several events here in Medregai have been hidden from everyone…like, it's all been left out of the history books deliberately or the stories changed, that sort of thing. And I think that might have happened with some rather important events." She grimaced, adding, "I don't know, maybe we'll find there's more reliable information in the Forrieghness Tower." She pushed her hand through her hair, then came back to herself suddenly and slapped her hands upon her knees. She stood tall and stretched with a yawn, noting afterward, "Gosh, we've been here for an hour already. Shall we move along?"

The others agreed it was time to go and they resumed their travels, again making good time because of the easy terrain and the horses' ability to maintain a steady canter throughout much of the day. By the time they decided to stop for the night, they were more than a hundred miles from their campsite of the night before. They took turns standing watch in increments of two hours, managing eight hours of rest for the horses.

Donnie took the last stint and Sylvester joined her for the final hour. The two of them sat in silence until Donnie, with half an hour left in her watch, decided to materialize the kitchen table, which was now laden with coffee and tea pots and cups, scrambled eggs and hash browns, and heaps of toast, along with jams and jellies and butters to suit everyone's tastes. The delicious smells awoke the others slowly and each soon joined her at the table to assuage their aroused appetites. Within another half-hour, they were all moving with light steps, feeling satiated by both food and sleep. The horses too were wonderfully refreshed and impatient to regain the trail once more.

That day passed just as the one before had, with the same nighttime schedule repeated, as was Donnie's method of awakening her friends the next morning. And again, everyone seemed almost uncommonly well-rested. The horses took to the path eagerly and, in fact, had to be restrained from their apparent inclination to gallop the rest of the way to Hörthanc.

It was in the afternoon that Donnie suddenly understood that all was not completely natural in this collective sense of well-being that had settled amongst them. They were approaching a series of rounded hills that in the distance appeared to glow brightly in the sunlight. The boombox, which had decided to join them about half an hour earlier, was playing minstral music, which somehow befitted the day.

Donnie blinked several times, sure that the great glow being reflected by the looming hills was an illusion. She rubbed her eyes and waited for them to adjust to the landscape's brilliance so she could see beyond it to what actually lay ahead for them. Finally growing irritated by the enduring ethereal brightness of the oncoming hills, she shifted her squinting gaze to her friends and realized that they were all fine and had noticed nothing amiss at all. She looked down at Sylvester and knew that he could see what she did, because his eyes, when she leaned forward so she could get a good look at his face, were locked onto the hills as though he was caught in a spell that was centered around them.

Donnie gasped, then gently put her hands around Sylvester's ribcage and picked him up, turning him around and placing his limp body upon her shoulder while she waited for him to disentangle himself from the effects of the magic shining so vividly before her now.

Falwaïn, positioned behind Donnie and Wiwila, astride Gallantry, at first just stared at the cat's blank face, which was hovering directly in front of him. "Is there something wrong with Sylvester, Donnie?" he inquired, breaking the others from their reveries.

Donnie nodded and called back to him, "Yes, there's something highly magical ahead, and it's put Sylvester into a trance. It almost did me too," she admitted, "but I found the brilliance of it too much to take and had to close my eyes."

The others came up to flank the two in the lead and they all gazed into the distance, with Donnie shielding her eyes with her hand.

"You really can't see that, none of you?" she asked in amazement and the others shook their heads.

"No, my darling, we see only the Cordis Downs covered by their green grasses," Falwaïn informed her matter of factly.

Ten minutes later they began to round the first of the chalk hills, and thereupon they saw what Falwaïn told them was the first of the signes his forefathers.

The boombox cut to the old classic, "John Barleycorn Must Die," and Donnie glanced down at it with curiosity. But she said nothing until the song ended, and then, still avoiding looking at anything directly by holding her hand up to her eyes, she exclaimed, "You know, I think it's the signes that are glowing!" She looked at Sylvester, who had roused himself a couple minutes before and was again curled up inside her hoodie, his face peering at her from the shadows. He'd been concerned with how easily the glow had entranced him and had therefore decided to hide himself from its influence.

"They must be on consecrated ground," he replied, which she repeated when the others said they couldn't hear him.

She decided to see if her sunglasses would be enough to protect her eyes and materialized them onto her palm, then put them on. Relieved, she found that she no longer even had to squint. She duplicated a small pair of glasses for Sylvester that were the same as hers, but shrunk down to match his size, then fashioned a loop for the back to make the glasses stay on his head. At first he refused to try them, but when the others encouraged him, the cat reluctantly put them on, then turned toward the first signe, which was finally coming into full view. With the aid of the darkened lenses, he too was able to view the landscape without being mesmerized by its highly powerful charm.

Everyone peered up at where the first signe resided on the hillside and saw what appeared to be a length of chain cut into the chalky ground. Truth be told, if they had not known what to look for, it would have been impossible to tell what form the signe took because of how overgrown the grasses were around it.

Falwaïn exclaimed at the sight, looking both bewildered and angered. He turned to Donnie and spluttered, "How could they? This is our heritage! Not just my family's, but all of those who call Faen Eárna home. These signes protect the lands, making them fertile and viable, or so their legend goes. And if the signes are neglected, then so too will be the land and the people. Even my father, who was never the most benevolent of leaders, understood this and ensured the signes were always well kept." He stared up at the ragged edges of the chain links, their outline barely visible, and then brought his unhappy regard back to Donnie's sympathetic face.

"Can you help?" he asked, and she nodded, murmuring, "Sure."

But Sylvester checked her with a loud, "No, Donemere, not like this! We must first ascertain the root of the problem and fix that, otherwise anything you do now will not work."

Donnie shot Falwaïn an apologetic smile, which he acknowledged with a begrudging and distinctly grim nod.

For the next two hours, they rode past unkempt signe after unkempt signe, each one seeming to infuriate Falwaïn ever more as they passed by. In addition, the fields they trotted through, once green and lush according to Falwaïn, were now mostly brown and yellow, with deadened crops from the previous year visible with no apparent tending to the soil for this year. And this fact seemed to stun Falwaïn even more than the signes not being maintained.

By the time they came within sight of the province's capital city, they were all riding silently. Each was fully aware of the dark anger rolling off Falwaïn's hunched shoulders while he led the way through the neglected lands of his beloved Faen Eárna, where even the once-tidy cottages, farm buildings and fences were looking seedy and uncared for everywhere they went.

It was nearing twilight when the citadel of Hörthanc appeared on the top of the next hill. The Keep of Hallishead rose above the rest of the city, its towers darkened and deserted.

Donnie asked Wiwila to halt, which meant the others had to stop with her. She slipped to her feet and beckoned for Falwaïn to follow her out of earshot.

"You're really angry," she noted flatly.

He scoffed. "You think?"

"Yes, I do think. I also think it's not a good idea for you to go in there determined to throw your weight around!" she retorted, pointing a finger at the city standing about a half mile away. She, like the others, had noticed that, while the keep looked black and forbidding, the castle at the back of the city was ablaze with light. "It seems a number of things have changed here—some drastically—since you left."

"So?" he shot back truculently.

"So," she returned with a forced smile, maintaining her patience with difficulty, "I am simply reminding you, as gently as possible, that you are the one who decided to leave here. You gave up your position as prince, whether that was for good or for just a short while, it doesn't matter, because you willingly gave it up. And that means you have forfeited any right to be angry about what's happened here since."

"No, it doesn't!" he countered, his eyes fierce as he looked at her and then beyond her at the city. "I gave up nothing when I—" he began, but Donnie cut him off.

"Yes, you did! You're a fool if you can't see that, and you'll deserve it when your son tosses you out on your ear!" she huffed at him, getting in the way of his angry glaring at the city's outline. "And understand this, my love, I will not interfere in that! If he so desires to toss you and the rest of us out, we will go without argument!"

"What?" Falwaïn exploded at her, moving his glare to her face.

"That's right," she said, crossing her arms in front of her defiantly. "I will not help you overthrow your son. He has been put in charge and he will remain in charge unless and until he abdicates, which is what you did two and a half years ago!"

"I am his father!" Falwaïn ground out between clenched teeth. "He will do as I command!"

Donnie sighed and grimaced before saying, "I rather suspect he's going to feel you gave up the right to be his father when you sent him away to Anûmanétus. By the way, just how old was he when you sent him there? And how old is he now?"

Falwaïn, rendered speechless at first, recollected himself, swallowed hard, and replied, "He was seven when he went. He is nearly sixteen now."

Donnie gaped at him in outrage and snapped, "Do not ever expect our children to be raised by anyone other than us! And they sure as hell aren't going anywhere until they're ready for college—and that'll be when they're eighteen!" She huffed and puffed again, anger and distaste growing in her breast. "You sent your child away when he was only seven years old? You sent him to that life, knowing he was so young and small that he would get the crap beaten out of him for years and years?"

Falwaïn shook his head, moving his shoulders agitatedly, and then shot back, "I had no way of knowing anything bad would happen to him!"

"That's bullshit!" Donnie cried furiously, stepping right up close to Falwaïn. "You knew only too damn well, didn't you? I can see it in your face! Why did you really send him there?" she demanded.

"If you must know, it was not my decision to send him away," Falwaïn informed her coldly and then it seemed like all the air went out of him and he shrunk several inches inwardly. He let out a long and heart-broken sigh before he said in a voice just above a whisper, "I had no choice in the matter, Donnie. As part of my family's reparations for our…unfortunate involvement in the plot to overthrow the kingdom all those years ago, it was decreed that I must send my first-born child to live in service to the king when he or she turned seven."

Falwaïn's eyes glistened in the waning light as they filled with the tears of a repentant and devastated father. "By the time Sémere and I held our handfasting ceremony, I had risked my life on numerous occasions for the king, fighting with full heart and all my strength beside Belnesem in battle upon battle. And I single-handedly saved the kingdom during the War of Unity, which literally no one else could have done, by destroying the *Book of the Var* when Dreena could not."

He turned his head away and wet his lips with his tongue, swallowing with difficulty again. "I then, not unnaturally, assumed our family debt to be paid in full and therefore joyously fathered a child. But the king did not agree with my simple hopes of fairness and compassion. Instead, he insisted the conditions of my family's pardon be met by us in full. I was commanded to send Malwé off to Anûmanétus, and all I could do was hope for the best for him, even though Sémere and I knew his life would be made an awful hell at that place!"

He swung from Donnie and stalked away several feet before stopping with his back to her.

She followed silently and stood right behind him, her forehead resting upon his shoulder in love and sympathy.

"Why are you still friends with Belnesem?" she asked, unable to stop herself.

Falwaïn shook his head, started to turn toward her, but he then whirled away again, his face wet with forlorn tears. "No one refuses the friendship of the king of Medregai, Donnie," he choked out, his voice thick with sorrow. "Not if you want you and yours to live." He wiped his face with the backs of his sleeves and sniffed at himself in contempt. Then he twisted around to grin ruefully at her when he added, "Except for you, of course. You didn't seem to like him almost from the beginning, did you?"

She shook her head. "Not really, no. He's far too dismissive of others for my taste," she complained, as if that was the only way to explain her complicated feelings toward the king. Realizing that she should add more, she said, "He's handsome and all that, sure, and a girl can be swayed by someone with his good looks as I was the first time I met him, but pretty soon after that I noticed that he wanted to kill everything in sight that wasn't part of his army." She shrugged. "That told me a lot about him right there and then, and none of it was good. And I can't say as I've ever trusted him."

Falwaïn snorted in agreement. "Nor he you! But you got the better feel for him than he of you, I must say. I believe he thinks you want to ally with the Mountain People, which is why he's marching his army there to teach them a lesson, I think."

Donnie stared at Falwaïn aghast at this news. "Are you serious? He's going after them because he's afraid of me?"

Falwaïn looked at her with a touch of helplessness in his torn gaze. "Very likely, yes," he admitted. "And there's nothing you can do about it, by the way. Belnesem would never believe you wouldn't want to take over the kingdom from him." Falwaïn drew her close and put his arms around her, hugging her tightly while burying his face in her long, loose hair. "It's what he would do, you see, so he can't imagine you not wanting the same." He lifted his head to look at her, his eyes hooded now. "I'm not sure you need to worry about the Mountain People, Donnie. There's a very good reason why they are not really part of the kingdom, you know, and that's because they've never wanted to be, not for thousands of years. During that time, they have solidly and forcefully resisted every attempt to crush them. I imagine the same will occur this time and, yes, some will indeed be sent to Canavar far before their time. But the king will feel as though he has impressed upon his enemies the message they need, which is that he is watching them and will not let them spread beyond their agreed upon borders. And he will not tolerate them treating with you."

"But, in the meantime, how many will die in this stupid and needless lesson of his?" Donnie asked, her thoughts reeling.

Falwaïn turned them both around so they could begin walking back to the others and then he set off with slow strides, his arm holding Donnie close to his side. "Typically, a few score all around," he said. Like Donnie, he contemplated the thought sadly and gave a small shake of his head. "This will be the fifth such skirmish in the past fifteen years. Which means it is time for the two sides to meet again, irrespective of your involvement. And that was why the king agreed to let me leave my province and travel to the Brumal Mountains two and a half years ago. He hoped I would learn the whereabouts of their strongholds and discover their weaknesses, such as their supply routes and storage locations."

Donnie's eyes grew big as she asked, "And did you?"

"Naturally." Falwaïn grinned at her. "But I only told him of one such depository, and that one I knew was going to be abandoned and did not figure in the Mountain Peoples' plans for survival. They will lose it and its guards, sadly, but that will not cripple them the way it might have if I had told him of the three others I know exist and that are planned to be in use for several years to come." He shot her a look of satisfaction. "The Mountain People will be all right and the stalemate we've been at for many long years will remain intact."

Donnie sighed and stopped just a few feet away from their friends, who were regarding them both with interest.

"Do you even like him?" Donnie asked disbelievingly, "Belnesem, I mean?"

The other three laughed at the question, as did Falwaïn.

"There is no liking a king, Donemere," Sylvester chided her, and the others nodded in agreement. "By definition, his position makes that utterly impossible. The same is true with a ruling queen. They must both make decisions that others will neither countenance nor comprehend, but they must not explain themselves or they will be seen as being weak."

"Which means death for themselves and chaos for their kingdom," Akanna explained. "It might interest you to hear that Belnesem is by no means the worst king to rule Medregai. He is strong and has maintained a lasting peace for more than seven long years now. Which is, in itself, no small accomplishment. If he can continue that record, he may well rule until his death. Since he is a Sarn and has yet to reach middle age, he could conceivably rule effectively for another two or three centuries."

"If he can maintain a relative peace like what we have now throughout the remainder of his reign," Falwaïn added, "that will be a monumental accomplishment and he might well be considered the greatest king ever."

"And for a king, that is the only reward that matters. To be thought great," Diego chimed in helpfully, "to be celebrated as such, and to be honored by his people in manners such as with the great pyramids in the land of the pharaohs—this is what motivates a king, *mi amiga*. And the same is true with queens, as Sylvester reminds us." He grinned at Donnie. "At least, this has been my experience with the kings and queens of my world."

"Humph!" Donnie grunted unhappily. "Well, if you all think that way, then I suppose I need to readjust my viewpoint of Belnesem."

Akanna scoffed the loudest at this and declared, "None of us said that, Donnie. It is clear to all concerned that you have his measure and will be properly wary of him should your paths ever cross again."

"And that is a good thing, my darling," added Falwaïn, giving her a light kiss on the tip of her nose. "Now that you have successfully diffused my anger from the day, I believe we can enter the city without me making a scene."

Donnie giggled at the very idea and shot back facetiously, "I do so hate it when you make a scene!"

Falwaïn was true to his word and did not make a scene when they entered the city. No, that was left for Donnie to do.

Posted to the one side of Hörthanc's main gate was a list of items considered to be illegal and which could not be brought into the city. Every person or similar, every horse, goat, cow or other farm animal, every wagon, barrow, and handcart—every one of them—was to be searched thoroughly according to the list. This list was quite long, and some might say excessively so. Donnie certainly said so and quite loudly once she got into full swing a little while later.

When the guards came over to search Donnie and her friends, it was clear that they recognized Falwaïn and were determined to snub him. All but one that is, and he inadvertently began to bow to his former prince until his captain slapped him on the side of the head and the man was sent flying onto his bottom.

For his part, Falwaïn seemed to have almost expected this treatment and he ignored it, striding nonchalantly over to the gate to closely review the list of contraband items. He was finished with that in seconds and came back to Donnie with a grave expression on his face.

"Donnie, I don't really know how to tell you this, but, er, well, Sylvester is not allowed entry," he informed her quietly in her ear.

"What!" she squawked indignantly, not at all happy with the way their belongings were being tossed onto the ground by the guards, who were just finishing up checking Wiwila's saddle bags and were about to start searching the biological entities in their group, starting with the horses.

The guards ignored Donnie's outburst and began running their hands carefully over Wiwila, going so far as to check the horse's teeth and ears in the bright light of the four bonfires built at the gate. The guards were taking their time with the search, obviously looking for any excuse to refuse entry to these visitors.

They were also obviously buying time for themselves, because the moment their former prince was recognized, a messenger was sent to the castle with the news of his arrival.

Donnie, for her part, noticed the messenger and correctly suspected his mission. On the other hand, she was not ready for her cat to be denied entry and she fumed while she waited, watching as the moment for confrontation regarding Sylvester approached. And when it did, she gave it her all.

"You will not take my cat from me, nor will you tell us that Lord Falwaïn is not allowed anywhere near the castle! And, no," she added, shouting at the top of her voice so that people began to crowd around on both sides of the gate, "we will not stay outside on the moors or with the pigs in their pens, no matter how good their roofs are!"

The guard who had made this last suggestion turned several shades of red as many of those congregating around them recognized Falwaïn and started calling out to him in warm greeting and encouragement. Falwaïn graciously acknowledged each of these remarks and thanked their owners for their support.

Several of these fine citizens then began to berate the captain and his guards, complaining how bad it was that they were already burdened with such onerous restrictions, could they not even welcome an old friend without persecution? And as to the cat, well, that was just plain ridiculous and nobody had ever enforced that silly rule before, one woman shouted, pointing a bony finger at three cats who crossed right in front of the crowd, chasing a fat rat. Just because the Lord Chancellor did not like them, the woman maintained, seconded by several of her friends, that was no reason to be banning them entirely, as everyone with half a brain well knew.

Donnie got the impression that many of those voicing these perfectly reasonable complaints were relieved at finally having an opportunity to do so with what they felt was relative assurance there would be no reprisals upon themselves, for here was the prince who had abdicated and left them in this mess in the first place. While he might be sorely missed, as one complainer expressed caustically, it was also his fault the Lord Chancellor was even needed and now that Falwaïn was back, surely he could stop the "Lordy Lord" from being such a pain in their collective asses and they could get back to living a decent life.

Donnie egged this lovely man on with a few of her own outraged comments about the contents of the list and how its length must surely be overcompensation for some quality lacking in this Lordy Lord, whoever he was. Or maybe it was something lacking in the captain of the guard, she posited dryly and with a knowing wink, which was met by sufficiently lewd rejoinders and much laughter from the rabble.

The throng continued to grow and soon even Donnie quieted down to let others shout their insults at the guards. This continued on unabated until an older man, who was dressed in better-made clothing than most of his fellow citizens, pushed his way to the front and stood staring at Falwaïn. A ripple of excitement went through the crowd and they hushed as one.

The man turned to the captain and ordered gruffly, "Let 'em pass," then he turned around and waved at the crowd to disperse, which it did with alacrity and in veritable silence.

Donnie and her friends picked up their belongings and repacked them swiftly. At a sign from the man, they led their horses through the streets, while the man walked about twenty feet in front of them. Nobody said a word to them as they passed by the homes and businesses of the townsfolk, but it seemed like everyone came out to stare as they went by. Over the ten minutes, they climbed to the highest part of the city, turned a deserted corner, and were suddenly confronted with the Keep of Hallishead.

The man, having grabbed a torch at some point in their trek, lit what appeared to be heaps of wood and dry debris in the each of the ten braziers that stood sentinel to the keep's entrance and along the keep's outer wall.

Beyond this wall, the keep itself soared high into the night sky, blocking out the stars behind it, its darkened windows cold and forbidding in the dim light from the fires that threw shadows up and down the keep's length. Donnie brought her gaze downward and noticed that the keep's outer doors were barred and the whole building looked abandoned.

The man motioned for Falwaïn and he stepped forward, with Diego and Akanna two steps behind him. The four of them took hold of the boards that were nailed to the keep's large oaken doors and ripped these off the old doors with a couple of crowbars that somehow found their way into Falwaïn and Akanna's hands after Falwaïn glanced at the doors and then at Donnie meaningfully. Within just a few minutes, they were all inside the cold keep.

In response to Akanna's softly spoken question, Falwaïn pointed to the stables and the vincan took hold of Jora and Wiwila's reins to lead the horses to their abode for the night. Wordlessly, Diego grabbed Ampago and Gallantry's reins and followed Akanna.

The older man led the way through the entry courtyard and into the main building, still carrying his torch. Inside, he lit several candles around the ground floor's receiving area, then handed a set of candelabras around, one each to Donnie and Falwaïn, and they all climbed to the third floor, where the living quarters were located.

There was a general air of decrepitude to the place, and dust was settled thick and fine over everything, including the floors, the furniture, and the wall sconces and chandeliers. In addition, the whole place smelled musty and unused.

Falwaïn turned to Donnie and asked her, "Can you clean it up some?"

Donnie glanced at the man, who avoided looking at her by turning his back on her. She bit her lip at his rudeness, but nevertheless waved her hand to lay her cleaning spell. In a pique of displeasure, she concentrated on dematerializing all the loose dust within the keep and its fixtures to the fire pits outside the city's gates. She hoped it was enough to snuff the fires right out and make it impossible to light them again until tomorrow. As she was to find out the next day, it was indeed more than enough to suffocate the big bonfires, all four of them, because the keep, its stables, its armory, and its underground cells and tunnels were quite extensive and their entirety had been covered in nearly an even inch of dust.

When the spell had finished and the dust was cleared, the man who'd led them to the keep carefully placed kindling and smaller logs in the fireplace, using his torch to light them. He stood with his back to the room, giving Falwaïn the opportunity to ask Donnie to provide food and drink for them all and for Donnie to do the providing. By the time Diego and Akanna found them, they were just sitting down at a large table to enjoy a light feast of ale, wine, bread and cheese.

The older man hesitated before reaching for any provender, but then he seemed to come to a decision and took up his tankard of ale in one hand and a big chunk of cheese in the other. He raised his ale to Donnie, looked at Falwaïn, and observed amicably, "She is nothing like the other."

Falwaïn eyed him for two or three heartbeats before replying in a calm voice, "No, she's better tempered most of the time—although she has her moments, as illustrated tonight at the main gate."

The man let loose a snicker of laughter. "That is true," he admitted humorously. "Beasing will not forget her soon."

While Donnie wanted to ask which of the guards had been this Beasing, she refrained from interjecting herself between the men, as she had ever since they'd entered the keep. There was a comfortableness between the men that spoke of long affection and she instinctively knew it would be best to just let it all play out without interruption from her.

The man studied Falwaïn intently while he sat back in his chair and chewed some cheese. When he'd swallowed, he said, with a nod toward Donnie, " 'Tis being said that she has the better of ye."

Falwaïn nodded, answering, "That she does…that she does. As a matter of fact, all good left in me is hers to do with as she will." He smiled and winked at Donnie, then added with a dry chuckle, "I count myself lucky that she has decided to hold me dear, even after learning the very worst of me."

"Then she really is nothing like the other!" the man rejoined and Falwaïn laughed outright.

"You would know, being as you were her father!" he pointed out, and then smiled at Donnie's raised eyebrows. "My love, this is Dantheus, Sémere's father."

Donnie and the others murmured their surprise, but otherwise kept quiet, each of them watching the two men with interest.

"The last time I saw him," Falwaïn told his friends, turning his bright gaze back to the man, "he had just been named steward of the province and was hoping I'd be successful at finding myself a warrior's death, and the sooner that could be achieved, the more preferable."

"Aye, that I was. I was a hopeful man then," Dantheus observed, taking up a thick slice of bread and tearing off a bite with his strong teeth. He looked at it, seemed impressed when he swallowed it, and said, "Now, I am simply called Grandad and there is no hope at all rising in this tired old breast." He returned Falwaïn's warm regard blandly, adding, "And I count myself lucky to be called anything at all these days."

Falwaïn sighed and gave him a hangdog look. "What happened here, old friend?"

Dantheus shook his head, his face taking on a bewildered expression. "I cannot tell ye, for I do not know myself. In truth, it seemed the moment yer feet left the province, everything went wrong."

"Everything like what?" asked Falwaïn, leaning forward to place his elbows on the table and cross his arms.

"The crops, the animals, the river and its tributaries, the weather—name it and it went bad," Dantheus explained with wonder, still shaking his head. "Everything, as though we were cursed as one. There was fear of that, ye know. Fear that Bréagna had returned and found a way to destroy all that we have with one of her wicked witchly curses." He glanced at Donnie guiltily, then took a long pull from his tankard and set it down with a smack onto the wood of the table. "When it came time to pay our tribute that fall, we could not meet our quota and the king's emissary wanted to know why. That fool soon went away and, in his place, came the Lord Chancellor, who has ruled here ever since. I finally got word to the king that the region was dying even with the Lord Chancellor's meticulous guidance and that perhaps we needed more help than a Lord Chancellor with no experience at either farming or raising sheep. A week later, Malwé arrived home. Not unnaturally, I suppose, the Lord Chancellor decided to stay and advise the young lad, and our problems remain as ever they were."

He picked up his tankard again and realized it was full once more, which stopped him in astonishment. Then he considered the liquid inside and downed it one long gulp, watching in fascination as it refilled itself. When he went to lift it to his lips again, Donnie felt it was time she should say something.

"You know, that comes from my private stock, of which there is a limited supply," she noted coolly. "Seeing as I don't know how to make it and have nothing with which to barter for more from my neighbors, it's going to be a while before I can replenish it." When Dantheus just looked at her with an impassive expression, she chuckled, waved a hand, and said, "Drink to your heart's content."

And so he did, lifting the tankard high.

"Who is this Lord Chancellor?" Falwaïn asked.

Dantheus put the tankard down again and his eyes hardened. He spit out, "Gullrick."

Falwaïn hissed and blew a hot breath. "That bastard?"

"Yes, except that he is now a very influential bastard, as ye'll soon see for thyself." Dantheus indicated the keep around them and explained, "He ordered this place closed the day he arrived and told us that no one was to set foot in it again." Dantheus grimaced. "He will not approve of me letting ye come to stay in it."

"Hmm," grunted Falwaïn. "What will Malwé think, that's what I want to know."

"Thy son," Dantheus said, pointing a finger at Falwaïn, "is nothing like ye or his mother. I think ye will find him a changed soul, but not in the same direction as thine."

"What do you mean, in the same direction as mine?" asked Falwaïn in surprise.

Dantheus scoffed at him. "Well, 'tis clear to see thy heart has changed. Firstly, ye no longer wish to die, do ye? Secondly, ye seem to have other things in life that might consume ye rather than the problem of increasing our crops' yields," the older man noted and Falwaïn nodded his agreement.

"Yes, well, we, er, I mean, Donnie, that is, er, well, she's with child," admitted Falwaïn, looking at Donnie with apology. "A-and it's mine," he said stuttering a little at her expression, which had just turned decidedly wooden. He cast his attention back to Dantheus and added, "We figure the birth will be before the end of the year."

Dantheus glanced around at them all and then at Falwaïn scurrilously. "Be it a witch as well?" he demanded to know.

Donnie sat forward and replied stiffly, "The babies, of which there are two, as Falwaïn well knows, are indeed magical, but I have no idea of their exact standing within the magical community. Not yet, anyway, because they are far too young for such needless classification." She looked the old man in the eye and stated unequivocally, "If anyone seeks to harm them, they will fail, and they will then have me as their enemy."

Dantheus let this soak in, before he shrugged and said with surprising approval, "Ye cannot say fairer than that, can ye?" He lifted his tankard again to Donnie and added, "The Lord Chancellor is going to have a fine time with ye, I can tell. I can only hope thy reputation for separating chaff from grain is warranted, because there is plenty of chaff around here that needs to be cleared away." He turned to Falwaïn to note, "And I do not mean by her, although I can see where she is going to be a might helpful to ye when ye fix our woes, as is thy duty."

Falwaïn sat back in his chair, glanced at Donnie, who was really giving him the stink eye now, and at his other two friends, who were also looking less than pleased at this potentially lengthy delay in their journey, and he sighed—a great, long and loud one. "It's good to be home," he quipped, and drained his own tankard of ale.

Chapter 15
Start Me Up

Diana was being driven nuts, plain and simple.

She returned to the cottage for lunch, sat down at the table, moved her plate to the side, and began slowly hitting her head on the wooden surface in front of her.

Warren watched her amusedly for several seconds before asking, "Kids a bit of a handful this morning, were they?"

Diana stopped banging her head, sat up, and stared at her friend. "They are a handful all the time, not just this morning," she deadpanned. "I don't know how Donnie does it, how does she get them all to stay quiet for the lessons? How?"

She made a frantic face at Warren and he laughed a wheezy laugh.

"Ouch!" he exclaimed, sobering because of sudden, intense pain. He instinctively grabbed his chest, then put out a hand when Diana made as though to rise. "No, I'm okay, I just have to be careful not to laugh too hard," he explained. The spasm passed and he was able to sit back with relief, commenting, "And I don't think she does."

Confused for a second, Diana said, "Huh? Oh, I see. You don't think she gets them to stay quiet?"

"Well, I don't know, really. I just meant that I don't think she's ever had to teach as many students as you are, so she's never even had to try to keep that many in line," he replied, then grinned at her slyly. "You are Diana the Savior, after all. I believe that just might explain why so many students keep vying for your attention in the classes," he posited, keeping his face straight.

She threw half of her sandwich at him, which he dexterously caught and shoved into his mouth. The two of them laughed at each other until Warren again had to hold his chest and Diana was waving her hands and repeating, "Sorry! Sorry!" at him until he sat up and said he was all right.

They resumed eating, with Diana pilfering half of the sandwich on Warren's plate instead of taking one from the platter and munching on it happily as he chuckled at her.

Rex came into the house and a couple of sandwiches floated over from the platter on the table to his ceramic food bowl. Noting this, he trotted to his feed station and wolfed the unexpected feast down in seconds, then came back to sit near the corner of the table, gazing up at the other two.

"How's your day going?" he asked, looking from one to the other.

Warren stifled another chuckle and said, "Mine's fine, boring as ever, but Diana's has been frustrating."

When Rex raised his eyebrows in surprise, Warren went on to explain confidentially, "I think she's acquired a number of students who are maybe a bit too ardent in their admiration for her and she just doesn't know how to deal with them."

Rex turned to Diana and said blandly, "Oh, is that all?"

To which response she started to repeat her earlier complaints until she heard what came out of his mouth next.

The German Shepherd traded his gaze again between the other two and suggested artlessly, "Why don't you have the classes here at the cottage so that Warren can help you?"

Warren fell totally apoplectic, spluttered pure nonsense for twenty seconds or thereabouts, finally got hold of himself, with Diana laughing like crazy throughout his antics, and retorted, "And why doesn't Rex help with that too?"

Rex grinned widely, winked at Diana first, then shrugged at Warren. "Yeah, I guess I can do that," he assented, and the matter was settled.

That afternoon and the next morning, the three of them held reign over classes for reading and writing and basic math, all of which Donnie had felt would help the Ganlonds' magical community as a whole to improve relations and communication amongst the differing species and their varying ways of life. It was yet to be seen how successful these endeavors would be, but the young animal students were certainly avid learners, if nothing else. And many of them were quite devoted to Diana, who was trying very hard to remain courteous, but was having more and more difficulty as the impassioned classes traipsed through the house.

The following afternoon though, once the second class was taught and its students sent on their way home, Diana began pacing the kitchen floor, obviously absorbed in something cogitating in her brain.

When she came to a standstill, she announced to the other two crisply, "I can't do this all day anymore, not without having something physical to do as well."

Rex was lying on one of his thick dog beds in a tight circle, his head resting on his big paws, while Warren, as usual, was sitting at the end of the oak dining table. When she spoke, they gazed at Diana's tense figure for a moment before grunting to acknowledge her statement.

"What do you suggest?" asked Warren, raising a curious eyebrow.

She turned to him and then Rex, biting her lip nervously. "Oh, nothing, really," she said, her voice a little too airy. "I just mean that I'm done for the day, even though we still have another class coming. I, er, I would like to take Otis for a run, I think, get us both some exercise, breathe in fresh air, that sort of thing." She paused, moving her shoulders up and down in a semi-nonchalant shrug. "Maybe you guys can handle it by yourselves the rest of the day. What do you think?" she asked, smiling elatedly when they nodded and agreed they would be fine with that for one afternoon.

Wasting no time, she hot-footed it to the stables where she saddled Otis quickly and efficiently, telling him she wanted to head east. That was all she said to him about their destination.

With her urging the horse to a sustained canter, they found themselves at the Giant's Lake in just a couple hours. Na'aven was not visible and the horse and rider did not veer toward the lake where the giantess's water spirit resided. Rather, Diana kept Otis on a straight track to the cave and dismounted him in a smooth leap as soon as he opened his mouth to protest their journey's end. Thereafter, he had no choice but to follow her through the darkened doorway to the cave beyond.

"We're not supposed to be here alone," he reminded her sternly as she lit the stick she usually used for her magical fire.

The fire burned brightly, its silver flames dancing and leaping high to dispel the pitch black of the cave.

"What are the chances that whoever took that book are still here right now?" Diana scoffed. She made her way deeper into the cave, but did not head for the woodpile. Instead, she directed her footsteps toward the strong breeze she felt coming from the other chambers.

Feeling mighty apprehensive, Otis followed her in, his hooves clicking on the hard floor and echoing over the low humming sound of the draft flowing between the chambers.

They passed through the chamber with the childish drawings on its walls and moved into the larger cavern where Na'aven had spent her time creating statues.

They threaded their way through the statues, heading toward the back of the cavern and in the direction of the draft, which was increasing with each step they took. Here, the howling of wind grew, and Diana felt herself even more intrigued by its source.

They came upon the hole in the cavern's far wall and paused in front of it. This large rift was near some of the earliest statues of an adult Flat Finger that Na'aven had created. Judging from what they could view of the wall's remains, it seemed the more than twenty-foot thick block of hard rock had been blasted outwardly, and by something magical, for there were no signs of any kind of incendiary device having been used to create the high and wide entrance.

Diana picked her way carefully over the layer of rubble from the blast, studying it closely, searching for anything that might tell her who had been through here recently. After noting that the largest chunks of blasted rock were piled up outside the cavern, she spent some time looking down at the floor. There she found distinct footprints in the thick dust and small rocks that covered the ground from the blast. She decided these might have been made by either human or okûn shoes and she followed them through the debris, into what was apparently one of the tunnels the giants had built long ago that ran the length and breadth of the Brumal Mountains.

Ignoring Otis's repeated warnings, Diana tracked the footprints to where another smaller tunnel T'd into the main one, a distance of over a half to even three-quarters of a mile from the giant's cave. Otis stayed with her all the way, but he was getting more and more nervous he said, because he felt like maybe they weren't alone anymore.

Diana held her torch high and peered through the darkness all around them, finding nothing to reflect light back at them. "You're crazy!" she exclaimed to him, turning toward the smaller tunnel, where the footprints disappeared into the darkness. "The tracks lead here and then they head to the east. I'll bet they go to Mount Gjendeben and the filthy okûn lair there."

She looked back at Otis, adding, "Well, we knew that Donnie and the other goddesses hadn't gotten them all, just the ones actually involved in the battle." She shook her head, confounded somewhat, and mused, "What would the okûn want with that book about the Iquakawi, I wonder? Unless they were just doing the bidding of someone else, like maybe Ixifír and his freaky monsters. But what do the okûn have that could blast a wall apart like that?"

She started to say something more, still lost in her own thoughts, but then Otis hissed at her in an urgent voice, "I'm telling you, Diana, there's something else here and it's not far away from us. Look, you've always trusted me before, so trust me now! Get on me and let's get the hell out of here!" he implored emphatically.

Diana, her eyes widened in reaction to his vehemence, gave him a quick nod of acquiescence. She stepped over to his side and reached for the reins, which were wrapped around her saddle horn, but suddenly found herself pulled off her feet by what felt like bands of steel wrapping themselves around her torso.

A voice, rough and dangerous, snarled, "Not so fast, little 'un. We want to have a conversation."

Diana was caught firmly within the giant's fist. He held her high in the air with her feet kicking wildly, but there was nothing to gain purchase anywhere nearby. She shuddered and closed her eyes, cursing her stupidity and her bad luck. Licking her lips, she looked down and saw by the light of her torch, which she'd dropped when grabbed, that Otis was standing where she'd left him, staring up her attacker.

He was furiously angry and whinnied shrilly, stomping his feet before shouting, "Let her go, you great beast, and I won't hurt you!"

The giant chuckled, finding this threat enormously funny. "Ye be quite the firebrand, eh?" he observed in his thick, northern accent, and Diana felt his breath draw nearer to her neck as he strained to see Otis. Once satisfied as to what it was that was defying him, he called out, "Ye hear this, Ma?" turning his head back around so that Diana's left ear caught the brunt of his call to his parent. Mercifully, her eardrum did not break, although she did almost pass out from the high number of decibels the giant employed with his shout. "This itty bitty little horse is going to hurt me!" he cackled, sending Diana into another swoon.

And then a new voice joined them to say, "Okay, maybe he can't really hurt you, but I sure can."

Diana opened her eyes to see Rex standing beside Otis and, to her utter amazement, the dog took one step forward and began to grow, enlarging himself until he stood eye to eye with the giant.

That massive person still held Diana in his fist, but she felt his hold slacken as he drew his breath at the appearance of the gargantuan dog.

"Put her down gently," Rex ordered, and he bared his very large, very sharp teeth in a growl that filled the tunnel with its roar.

The giant hastily complied and, when Diana was back on the ground, he backed off a heavy step or two from the dog, protesting and apologizing profusely. "Forgive me, forgive me! I would never hurt her; I swears it! We just wanted to talk to her, that's all, and then her horse there said that he was gonna hurt me and that tickled me sideways, ye see," he assured Rex, his arms stretched out in front of him with palms showing. He sat down where he stood and gestured toward Diana. "Ask her!" he prodded. "I didna hurt ye any, did I?"

Diana, at first astounded by this claim, ran her hands up and down all over herself, then she realized she was just fine and replied, "Well, no. He actually didn't hurt me, Rex."

"O' course he didna," an exhausted female voice sounded out from the black behind the male giant, a touch of the north in her voice too, although it was not so overt as her son's accent. "Neither of us has a reason to hurt anyone these days." There was a dragging sound from behind the giant as this new entity brought herself forward.

Rex concentrated on his magic and, like he'd watched his mama do on countless occasions, he conjured up a brilliant blue light ball, split it into fours, and sent these flying around so they could all see better. One of the balls went to the male giant's face and lit up his swollen, battered features, while one stayed with Diana and Otis. A third flew to the face of the new personage, and the fourth zoomed on down the tunnel for a while in search of any other beings, finally returning when it found no one else nearby.

The third light ball lit up the face of an elderly female giant. She looked dirty and drained as she crept up behind her son and sank down next to him with a great sigh, leaning her back against the stone wall of the tunnel with a heavy thud. When she was situated, she turned toward the others, ran a shaky hand over her grey hair and its untidy bun, and added, "We just want to go home. It has been such a long journey and I want to see my children. With any luck, they still live in our home."

Diana, thinking she probably knew the answer already, asked, "What are your children's names? And what's yours, by the way?"

The giantess looked down at Diana where she stood beside Otis and Rex, and replied, "I am Ma'oma, and this is Feirth, my son. My youngest son Garin lives at the end of this tunnel with my beloved daughter, and—well...I do not know how to explain my daughter Na'aven, but I wish for nothing more than to see her one more time before I die. And while my youngest son be a fool and a traitor to his people, he is still my child and I wish to lay one last blessing on him before I make the journey to Canavar."

Rex shrank back down to his normal size, trotted over to his friends and cleared his throat. He said to Diana encouragingly, "Maybe you should tell 'em what happened now."

Diana mulled this over for a second before nodding. "Yeah, I guess I might as well do it now." She turned to face the two giants and explained in a quiet voice, "Garin himself has made the journey to Canavar, while Na'aven is the spirit of the big lake outside your old cave."

Both giants exhibited great surprise at this news, but neither responded in any other way. Rather, they merely looked at Diana expectantly.

Diana obliged their somewhat dull curiosity and told them what she knew about what had occurred between the two children when they were young and what their lives had been like all the years they'd been locked away with each other in the cave.

When Diana finished, Ma'oma explained that she and her husband had strongly suspected Garin of pushing Na'aven over the falls when she was a young girl, but they'd had no proof and had therefore accepted his claim that he was nowhere near his sister when she went over the water's edge to her doom.

Ma'oma began to cry and Feirth put his arm around her, shoving a filthy square of cloth into his mother's hands for her to wipe her tears. Out of respect for her grief, the others turned away and waited until the giantess said to her son, "It seems I am to be defeated here the same as we were in the north, dear boy. But perhaps we can go home for a bit, at least until the king's men come and rout us out into the open again and this time end our days forever."

Diana whirled back around then to enquire sharply, "What was that you said—you met up with the king's men? Where?"

Feirth nodded, pulling his mother's head onto his shoulder as her tears continued to fall. "Aye. Ye see, for many a long year we have lived at the Bulgassarhar Pass, where the Brumal Mountains meet the Moênas Flírgin. Well, 'twas less than two weeks ago, I believe, that the Mountain People of Marn Dím warned us the king and his company would surely be comin' to attack them and so they asked for our help."

He paused here to sigh and pass his free hand over his begrimed face before continuing. "In the past," he explained, "our communities regularly give each other mutual assistance, if ye ken me."

"For a week we worked and worked and by the end of then we were convinced we were well enough prepared to thwart any assault on the city that might possibly come. But then they arrived. Ah, it were terrible. We were attacked from all directions, or so it seemed," he cried, shaking his head. "They cut us down like we were fish in a northlander's barrel, using an evil instrument we learned later was called a 'gun and its bullets.' Those cursed metal missiles from that gun thing tore into everyone as if we were made of naught but air. We scattered ourselves to the four corners to avoid extinction. And then it turned out it was just one wee dragon doing all that damage—can ye imagine?" He shook his head again, this time in painful wondering. "No *vírat* has been seen in Medregai for ages and ages and the first one found ends up trying to kill us all!"

Feirth gazed at the wall opposite throughout his recounting of these events, his eyes unfocused with remembrance and filled with sadness, their sorrow somehow emphasized by the glare of Rex's light balls.

Unknown to himself, his restless fingers picked at the worn cloth of his trousers as he again took a moment to collect his thoughts.

"Ennyway," he recommenced his story, still lost deeply in those days of terror, "most of our people headed north, but we got separated from 'em and nearly got shot by that little dragon tyke. 'Twas lucky for us that Ma here remembered how to get to this tunnel from the old rookery by the Withering Hills. And then, just when we made it to the entrance of the old nursery, we heard a trumpet sound to the west and figured we best strike off the path to investigate it, in case it were something we needed to account for to keep ourselves safe. That was when we saw the king's men and realized that the ones who'd attacked us could not have been his. So, we slunk back to the rookery and fled into the tunnel. Who the fiends were at Marn Dím, I cannot say. But the king was on his way there and it was evident he was wanting to conquer all who opposed him."

Here, the giant roused himself, and brought his gaze over to Diana, Otis and Rex. "Ever since then," he continued tiredly, "Ma and me have been traveling south as quick as we could, which ain't been all that fast, as I'm sure ye've seen fer yerselves. We've been on our feet most of the last eight days, counting all that came before. And we've only had a bit of water to drink since we left the city, and that was just what we could find draining into the tunnel, ye ken me on that? But we've brought no food or anything else with us and now," he announced glumly, "we've come to the end of our tethers. We truly have, for we are both done in all the way and cannot take another step."

He squeezed his mother's shaking shoulders and grimaced forlornly at his listeners, who were watching him in silence. "Ye might as well leave us here to die, I suppose," he finished weakly, letting his big head loll on his thick neck to rest on the wall behind him. He managed a deep, ragged breath before adding, "But it would be a kindness if ye could bring us some water or food, and maybe tell us where we are. Are we near Mâlendian yet?"

Diana, taking pity on them, said honestly, "Look, if you *can* somehow make yourselves go just another half mile or so, you'll be at your old home. It's really not that far from here."

Both giants raised their heads and stared at her with disbelieving eyes.

"Are ye certain about that?" Feirth asked, wanting to be convinced but not daring to let that happen.

"She's quite sure," Rex assured him. He moved forward and let himself grow large again, but not as big as the previous time. Then he walked over to the giantess and directed her to climb on top of his back and hold on tight so he could carry her. He indicated her son with a toss of his canine head, adding, "You'll have to walk because I can't carry you both."

As much as he could, Feirth helped his mother onto Rex's back and then began shuffling down the tunnel himself. From the way he basically inched along, using the wall for support, it was clear to them all that every muscle in his body screamed for rest and he was operating on auto pilot. Everybody did their best to inspire him to keep going with kindly verbal encouragements as they waited again and again for him to catch up.

It was almost an hour later when they reached the blasted entrance to the cavern where Na'aven's statues resided. Rex could no longer maintain his enlarged size through the obstacles they were about to encounter, so Ma'oma had to go back to walking. It took a few minutes to wake her because she'd fallen so deeply asleep, and she cried with abandon when she came to, her grief and exhaustion getting the better of her again. She finally rose to her feet, wobbly and unsure, then stumbled and nearly fell, but she managed to wend her way with the others amongst all the statues without any real mishap.

Neither giant noticed what it was they were weaving through because both kept their eyes on the ground, following the feet of whoever was in front of them. Their way was lit by Rex's light balls and Diana's torch. Diana, sitting upon Otis so she could see the most direct path through the statues, led the group, with Rex right behind. Ma'oma came next, while Feirth brought up the rear.

Ma'oma ended up having to crawl through the tunnel between the statue and pictogram chambers because she was too weak to crouch within the low structure, which delayed their final steps. By the time they reached the main chamber, both giants were close to passing out and, after helping Ma'oma onto the bed, Feirth tumbled into the chair by the fireplace and immediately fell comatose.

Diana, Otis, and Rex left them and went outside to discuss the situation.

"Once they wake again, they'll need both food and water," Otis noted, and the other two nodded in agreement with him. "D'ya think they're allowed to come onto the Ganlonds?" he asked curiously.

Diana's eyes widened and her lips formed an 'O' in surprise. "Golly, I have no idea! They must've been able to before though, don't ya think?" she reflected. "I mean, the cave entrance opens onto the magical lands, so the family must have been on the Ganlonds before."

Rex shook his head hesitantly. "I dunno about that," he argued. "Didn't they have an entry somewhere inside the cave that led to the big tunnel? That could be what they used to get in and out of their cave when they lived here before. Who knows, maybe this entrance was made by Valley Guy when he let Flat Finger out," the dog posited, glancing at the darkened doorway to the cave.

This struck Diana as odd and she said so. "Are we even certain it was Valledai who let Flat Finger out? I mean, I think it might've been the Iceni Meræ because I can't see Valledai wanting to potentially face Catie under those circumstances."

"True," Otis agreed. "Flat Finger couldn't have been freed while Catie was here. She must have been off time traveling when that happened, right? Otherwise, she would've known that her spell on the cave was being broken and she would have tried to stop whoever it was, wouldn't she?"

Diana crossed her arms in front of her and leaned back on her hips, nodding her head while she idly watched Rex shake his whole body, his fur twisting this way and that. "Yeah, she would have," Diana answered. "And if she was off time traveling, then Valledai would have been with her, like Donnie said he usually was. Which means it had to have been the Iceni Meræ who let Flat Finger out."

After his much-needed shake, Rex crouched in a long and deep stretch because his back was sore from all the weight he'd had to carry so friggin' slowly down the tunnel. When he stood tall from that, he sighed with relief and looked at his friends, suggesting, "Unless it was someone else entirely. I mean, why would the Iceni Meræ care about Flat Finger? What could he do for them?"

Mystified, both Diana and Otis made faces and shook their heads.

"Maybe Valledai asked them to do it?" Diana pondered with a shrug. "Who else would have wanted him freed?"

"Impossible for us to know," Otis said, grunting. "At least for now."

"Yeah, agreed," said Rex and the three of them fell silent.

This lasted until Diana exclaimed, "Oh," with her features assuming an inquisitive expression. She looked at Rex, raised in eyebrow, and inquired, "Were you and Warren reading the book? I mean, how the heck did you know where Otis and I were?"

Rex sat down of a sudden and he huffed, shooting her a reproving glare. "Of course we were reading the book! We both knew something was up with you when you left, so we had to keep an eye on you somehow. If the book hadn't started telling us what you were doing, I was gonna come find you anyway. But then it said you were in trouble, so I ran here as fast as I could, which, as you know, is pretty darn fast. I just thank the heavens and their stars that you weren't in any real danger! Well, that is, unless giants include humans and horses in their diet," he added, now giving her a dark *and* reproving glare. "Do you know if they do?"

Diana and Otis exchanged contrite glances and shook their heads.

"Um, not real sure on that, to be honest," conceded Otis, heh-hehing nervously.

"And what if they do?" Rex demanded exasperatedly of him, before turning to Diana and giving her the same stink eye he was showing Otis. "What if they consider you a delicacy and they lied to us about not wanting to hurt you just so I wouldn't hurt them? Did you even think about that before you went off exploring in the one place my mama didn't want you to go to alone?" the dog berated them, this time bestowing even more dark and reproving glares upon them both.

They each groaned and assumed suitably shamefaced expressions and then began to apologize to the dog.

He listened for about a split-second before he raised an imperious paw to interrupt them. "I'm just glad you're okay," he said, his former worry evident in the tight look he gave them now. "You two acted recklessly and could've really been hurt. If anything bad had happened to you, I would be feeling really, really terrible right now, you know that? And you can thank me later for having saved your lives. Right now, I'm gonna go ask Mickey T if the giants are allowed on the Ganlonds, 'cause if anyone knows the answer to that question, it'll be him. In the meantime, do you two think you can stay out of trouble?"

Diana and Otis nodded vigorously, and both offered effusive praise about how smart he was to have thought of Micky T regarding the question on the giants' access to the Ganlonds.

Rex, clearly not buying their fluff yet again, added that he would also find some of the council members so they could deal with the giants' food and water needs, which meant that Diana and Otis could go home where it was safe.

"I'm serious, I want you to just go home—and nowhere else for today!" he ordered, his gaze uncharacteristically flinty.

After the dog disappeared without uttering another word, Diana began to stride away in the direction of the lake, but Otis, wise horse that he was, quickly blocked her path.

"No, Di, Rex is right—we've done enough for now," the horse advised, turning so he could look her in the eye. "It's almost dinnertime and I'm starving. Nothing more can be done today and it's no good telling Na'aven anything yet. Plus, we need to let Warren know what happened and that we're okay, just in case he hasn't read it in the book already."

It turned out that Warren did indeed know what had happened in the cave and was waiting for them by the well when they arrived home. He followed them into the stables and watched while Diana unsaddled Otis and fed him, then started to brush the horse, before he too started to lecture them both on their foolhardiness.

Granted, he did this last bit half-heartedly, if truth be told. After only a couple remarks, he stopped himself in mid-sentence, changing gears by telling them frankly, "Oh, well, I can't say as I blame you, really, since I would have done the same thing myself, if I could."

Diana turned to him with a raised, critical eyebrow and he smiled back at her in anticipation.

"As a matter of fact, there's something I want to try, but I'll need your help," he explained in a rush. "See, I think it's time for me to visit the Gahal Glæd and find out if its magic can heal me. Whaddya think?"

Diana shook her head at his excited face and resumed running a brush over Otis's back. "You can't even ride a horse yet to get you there," she reminded him.

"True," he conceded, "but we've got Plug and I'll bet the ride in her is a whole lot smoother than on any horse."

Diana's movements were arrested in mid-stroke.

"I hadn't thought about Plug," she murmured, turning toward him now with a faraway expression in her eyes. "Huh. I guess she's worth a try, at that."

After breakfast the next morning, they both, along with Rex, went out to where Plug was parked. When Diana lifted the canvas cover off the SUV,

Plug responded by revving her engine and taking off almost before she was clear of the cover to complete several self-indulgent doughnuts in the yard before she rumbled to a stop in front of Diana, straining to be on the road once more. Her windows were open and she was blaring the rock classic, "Start Me Up."

Clamping his jaw shut tightly and looking like he might pass out from pain, Warren walked over to Plug and climbed into the vehicle's passenger side. Diana joined him, claiming the driver's seat for herself, while Rex jumped into the back seat, his youthful voice singing along happily with the radio's choice of tune. Only when they were all in did the SUV take off with a screech and a lurch.

Warren braced himself for the hard turn up the hill they'd have to make, but no such sensation reached him and he remained sitting upright in his seat as though on a straight and level road. He breathed loudly with relief and thought he might begin to relax a little.

The trees situated along the footpath to the Gahal Glæd were very accommodating and most of them moved as quick as they could out of the way when they heard Plug approaching. And Plug could be heard for at least a two-hundred-foot radius as she drove along because the SUV had continued to blare out a whole repertoire of anthem-style rock songs with her elite sound system during the entire ride to the glade because she was that glad to again be doing something with purpose.

Those few trees too stubborn or slow to move from the footpath were merrily sideswiped by Plug as she squeezed by them. Which meant that, by the time they arrived at the Gahal Glæd, all three of her passengers were more than a little traumatized by Plug's antics and all three spilled out of her gratefully; albeit, in Warren's case, most agonizingly. The SUV revved her engines again, spun in a tight circle, and parked herself just outside the entrance of the glade to wait, unrepentant of her joyful actions. Truthfully, the trees she had hit had merely felt bumped and received no injury from her, but her passengers were unaware of this fact and all three glared at the vehicle as if it were possessed—which it was not.

Diana strode immediately to Warren, who was bent over with his hands on his knees and wincing in pain, and put a warm hand on his back, trying to concentrate her magic to help him feel better. While she had never been very good at that sort of thing, she managed to conjure a small spell that went straight to his chest and relieved some of the tautness there.

He straightened, nodding to her as acknowledgement of the relief she'd just afforded him. Glancing at Plug again, he observed under his breath, "I suppose that was a better ride than with a horse, but only just."

Diana chuckled her agreement and gently took him by his arm, helping him shuffle into the glade, while Rex led the way.

Once inside, they found the young bat queen, Sephala waiting for them. With her was a sleek, grey-colored feline who watched their every move with her marbled blue eyes, and a small sparrow who twittered nervously and flounced her feathers with practically every step the newcomers took.

These creatures were gathered together on a couple of pedestals that had arisen out of the ground in the center of the glade. Upon one of the pedestals were two wooden perches, one for the bird and the other for the bat.

Sephala, who was Mickey T's eldest daughter, bade them welcome and motioned for them to approach. "Come in, the glade awaits you," she said, and they all walked over to the center of the clearing.

"How are the giants this morning, Sephala?" asked Diana, posing the question to the inverted bat while she continued to help Warren make his way.

"They are well, Diana; both much recovered from their journey south to their home of old," the beautiful brown bat told her, gently swaying in the air as she spoke. "They were reunited with dear Na'aven this morning and are a happy family once more."

"Are they going to stay in the cavern for long?" Rex inquired curiously.

All eyes were turned to the bat queen.

"Yes," she replied, nodding in her gracious way, "they will remain until Donemere returns and helps us to decide their future on the Ganlonds. I believe the magical lands have no issue with the giants, but the rest of us might, for you see, they eat rather a lot, which means our ecosystems must be able to provide food for them and everyone else. They are vegetarians, by the way, in case anyone is concerned. My father says he can remember them making some of the finest vegetable stews he's ever had in his life." She chuckled with affection, adding, "Not that he's eaten all that many stews, truth be told, be they vegetable or otherwise."

She stretched her wings as though wanting to take off in flight, then folded them again with a small sigh. Turning, she looked at the cat beside her and said, "This is Galansa of the forest felines."

The compact cat looked at the three newcomers and bowed her regal head to them ever so slightly.

"She will invoke the magic of the glade," Sephala continued, "while Hilati here will release the magic when the spell is done."

The little sparrow tittered to them in a high, happy voice, "It is my great pleasure to meet you all."

Warren's grateful gaze encompassed everyone there when he said with warmth, "Thank you for helping me with this."

Each acknowledged this with nods or smiles, then Sephala indicated that Warren should come closer using the long, spidery toes of her left foot to gesture to him. When he was but a step away, she said in a low, serious voice, "As you will recall from your former days as wolf king, you must stand in the heart of the glade. You will know when you are there, but you must find it by yourself."

He nodded because he did know this and had on previous occasions watched others struggle to find it. For, when asking something special of the glade, the petitioner must listen to their heart and somehow tune it to the rhythm of the earth and its magic below the ground. Only then would they be able to call to the heart of the glade so that it came to the surface where they could successfully connect to it.

Closing his eyes, Warren put his hands to his chest and listened to his own heart, its beat finally stirring his feet to move him three steps to the right. He felt something like a wall there, but then he was pulled forward two paces by a force that was almost magnetic. He continued to be led through a complicated series of steps that eventually led him to a place he knew instinctively was right above the glade's heart.

Opening his eyes, he saw that he was only about ten direct strides from where he had started. He looked down and saw that his feet were rooted to the ground where he stood, already steeped in the magic that would soon course through his body.

At the moment Warren's eyes opened, he heard the cat hiss something, and the glade's blazing white magic began to creep up his legs, its fire and life rejuvenating every cell as it passed through them. In what was probably seconds, but felt like a lifetime, it engulfed him, and that was when he felt only pain. It was so much pain that he could not breathe when the white magic moved into his chest and found every crack and crevice made in his bones by Julia's dark intent. Certain he would faint, he clung to consciousness for dear life, envisioning Liz's face and imagining little Jesse's through the blinding white brilliance of magic that he was now fully immersed in, determined to hang on no matter what for their sakes. They would need him, he told himself, and one day soon. He must be well for them, he must be ready to defend them from whatever Ixifír Bíun wanted from them all. He must hang on for them, he chanted to himself, gritting his teeth against the unrelenting torment wracking his body.

And then it was done and he was falling, falling through the sky and to the earth. He fell for ages and ages, perhaps hours even, but then he knew that it was only seconds and he found himself crouching upon his knees. He listened with shuddering breaths to the sparrow's chant as the magic of the glade receded from his body and fell back into the sacred ground of the glade.

Diana ran to him to place her hand under his arm, pulling him upward until he was standing. "Are you all right?" she asked anxiously, her face a study in alarm and worry. "You screamed so awfully," she whispered, her brows knitted together as she turned him toward her.

Warren looked at her, noting that, as tall as he was, she was even taller. He said, grinning, "I've only just now realized that you are as tall as an oak tree, my friend, and just as strong."

Stunned by this nonsensical statement from him, she barked in sudden laughter and let her hand drop away from him. "I ask you again," she said through her chuckles, "are you all right?"

He chortled along with her and slowly began testing his movements. He patted his chest and his legs with his hands, beaming happily when he found that he was indeed healed to perfection. "Yes," he finally replied, "I am more than all right. I am better than ever, I believe." He looked over at Rex, adding, "And I think we can now set off to join your mama and the others!"

Rex stood up and wagged his tail furiously. "Well, it's about time!" he cried with feeling.

They heard chuffing noises and, as one, they turned as the Kaerdír of the Ganlonds walked through the entrance of the glade. Bronadulach, the greatest of the Cave Bears, advanced toward them, remarking, "Good, you are all still here."

When he came to a stop, he sat back a little on his haunches, looking from one to the other before explaining earnestly, "I was on my way here to see whether the ceremony was successful when the Ganlonds sent me a message. It seems the magical lands are aware of the giants' battles with a small *vírat* only days ago, and they want you all, now that Warren is well, to take the giants back there to retrieve the dragon."

Diana whistled softly, her dark eyebrows raised high, and she leaned toward Warren before quipping under her breath, "The news of your good health certainly traveled fast, didn't it?"

Their gazes met and he nodded humorously.

In the meanwhile, Rex was goggling at the giant Cave Bear. He closed his mouth, opened it again, closed it again, and then squeaked, "Really, we can't just go get my mama? And why do we need the giants with us?"

Bronadulach turned his piercing regard upon the dog, replying, "Your mother is on a very important mission of her own. Believe me, my friend, she is missed by us all. And you will need the giants with you because they are the only ones who can tame *vírata*, and it seems this one is quite wild."

Sephala's breath caught, and she too looked agog at the bear. "Then the stories my father tells of the old times are true?" she said with wonder and the bear nodded.

"Yes," he told her, "my grandmother had tales much like your father's, only hers were not first-hand accounts like Mecholætera's are. She told me the giants tended the dragons in their rookery at the Withering Hills, although the area was not called that at the time. The giants were there to raise and train the young hatchlings so that they could go out to the many worlds to help maintain peace, or so it was believed. But then it was found that many were not spreading peace of any kind, and the war with them began. This, of course, meant that many giants left Írtha to fight *vírata* on other worlds. And then the peoples of Írtha were left with the final five dragons, whose history lives on only in legend."

"But why do the Ganlonds want us to capture this dragon, and why can't that wait for Donnie to get back? And, not to belittle the finer points of this insane mission, but just what are we going to do with the dragon if we somehow manage to get it away from whoever its master is?" Diana inquired skeptically. "It's a dragon, after all, which means it's gonna want to burn everyone it encounters."

The bear stared at her impassively, having learned by now not to react to this kind of sarcastic expression of frustration. "The Ganlonds know of Donemere's injury and that it is only the magic of the cosmos that she acquired for the Silver Hand spell that is keeping the *badûr* she made with Ungôl from killing her," he explained. "But that magic will not hold off the *badûr* forever. You see, Donemere is very much needed and must not die, for she is the last in her line right now."

"She has a sister," Diana reminded him, "back in her time, I mean."

Bronadulach nodded, his eyes glazing as something seemed to take him over. His voice, when he spoke this time, sounded oddly echoing. "You are correct, Ghira Ma'Hai, but the sister by name is not a witch and never will be. Donemere's children may, in time, and only together, be able to wield the magic of the Codlebærn line. Therefore, Donemere remains our only hope for survival for the foreseeable future. The dragon must be retrieved and brought to Donemere, for with its assistance, she can find the *vírata* home world and fulfill her promise to the dragon king, thereby settling the *badûr* and healing her wound."

The bear's eyes cleared, and he shook himself, his thick fur raised and spiky in appearance. "Is it my imagination or did the Ganlonds just speak through me?" he asked, clearly stunned.

The others were just as confounded as he and most nodded slowly.

The little sparrow, Hilati, twittered, "Yes, it seems so!" and she rose up on her tiny feet, her feathers fluffed with fear or excitement, it was hard to tell which, to where she looked nearly twice her size before she settled back down on her perch.

Galansa hissed something to Sephala, and Sephala nodded. "Galansa says there are three instances known where the Ganlonds have spoken this way before, with each occurring only in very grave times."

Diana frowned at the cat questioningly and Bronadulach explained, "Galansa lost her tongue many years ago and cannot speak in words."

"That is true," Sephala added, smiling gently, "and I am one of the few who understands her when she hisses, so I often translate for her. Galansa," Sephala explained, looking at Diana, "is the historian of the Ganlonds. That is how she knows that the spirit of the Ganlonds has spoken through a Kaerdír three times before. Or as she reminds me now, strictly speaking, there were three previous times that are known," the bat added when the cat again hissed to her. "The Ganlonds may have done it hundreds of times, but, if so, it was not marked by anyone."

Rex cleared his throat, and when everyone looked at him, he said, "Uh, okay, that part's weird and all, sure, but I'm more interested in just how we're supposed to find this dragon and bring it back here. I mean, can a giant tame one all that quickly? 'Cause we won't have a lot of time, I'm guessing. And so, what, do we fight the king's men for it, along with the other guys the giants' mentioned, the ones who seem to be its masters?" The dog shook his head and frowned at the others grimly. "I'm sorry, but I don't see how we're gonna do any of that without Mama."

"All species of the Ganlonds will provide however many animal soldiers are needed to complete the task," Bronadulach replied stiffly, his ire finally roused a little. "Surely, we can mount a party of sufficient size."

Warren shook his head. "I don't think it's a matter of numbers, my old friend, but rather one of cunning and stealth. Rex is right, we'd never get through all those forces successfully with a large contingent. We must be a small team—small, but mighty and clever." He looked at Diana, saying to her, "I think we need a few wolves, perhaps, plus you, me, Rex, and Feirth. What do you think?"

Diana considered it, her eyes narrowed while she thought. "Yes," she agreed, "although I suggest we also take some birds to act as scouts."

"And some bats," interjected Sephala, "for nighttime scouting."

"Agreed," said Warren, looking from Diana to Rex, both of whom nodded.

Diana still had a studied air about her when she mused aloud, "What if we all travel in Plug and have her drive us as far as she can? That would save us a tremendous amount of time."

Warren shot her a look of surprise. "But you'll want Otis to go too, won't you? How would we get him and Feirth into Plug?"

Diana turned to Rex. "What if they touch you while you make yourself smaller so they can fit through Plug's doors?" she suggested. "Then, once they're inside, Donnie's spell should allow Plug's interior to adjust to their size, wouldn't you think?" She raised a questioning eyebrow at the dog.

Rex shrugged diffidently. "I dunno about that. Maybe. We can try it right now with Bronadulach and then we'll know if it'll work or not."

The great Cave Bear did not look happy at the prospective experiment, but he agreed in the end to help them test the theory. So, Diana called Plug into the glade, told her to refrain from doing doughnuts and wheelies and such while on the hallowed ground of the glade, then gave a rough outline to the vehicle of what they wanted to try.

Since there was no way the huge bear could ride on Rex, the dog instead scrambled atop Bronadulach with some magical assistance from Diana. Once he was in a steady position, he concentrated on his magic and making himself smaller, and, when ready, urged the bear to move forward toward Plug's open rear door. The two of them grew smaller and smaller until the bear was of a size to fit through the SUV's door opening.

Inside, Rex leapt off the bear to land upon the seat of the middle row. Bronadulach began to return to his normal bulk and fill the back of the vehicle. But when he got to a certain size, the SUV seemed to waver for a moment, then the inside got much larger and the bear sat down on the back seat to look at the others through the window. He looked like he was a long way away from the outside because of how small he appeared, but when Diana and Warren got into the front seats, they looked back and saw him as normal sized.

"Damn," grunted Warren, marveling at his witch friend's prowess, "Donnie's so good at magic!"

The four of them traveled back to the house in Plug. The trees along the route had, quite smartly, realized there would have to be a return trip and so had not moved back into their usual places yet. Which meant the track back to the house was unencumbered with obstacles.

When they arrived at the cottage, Rex once again climbed onto Bronadulach's shoulders and, when the bear moved toward the open rear door, he and the dog were reduced to a size to make their exit possible without harm to either.

Knowing now that they could indeed take Plug at least part of the way, they began to lay plans for their mission.

In the meanwhile, the kitchen's pans, pots, bowls, utensils, and appliances were already working overtime to make enough salads, sandwiches, and snacks for the soon to be adventurers to take with them. While all of that went on merrily around them, Diana, Rex, and Warren met with most of their traveling companions.

The wolves had sent four of their best fighters. Janah and Binurg were both male and Kueray and Maga were females. Janah and Maga were of the ruling Bau tribe, while Binurg was from the Cabadis tribe and Kueray from the Tamlal tribe. Two falcons, Leaco and Salu, and two bats, Jiliriaf and Dornam, would accompany them on the journey.

All told, there would be fourteen biological members of their group, that is, counting both horses and assuming that Feirth agreed to go with them. They decided their journey did not depend upon time of day, so they set forth as soon as their food was packed and they had all climbed or flown into the SUV. Raleen took some convincing to allow Rex to hop onto her back and for them both to jump into the back of the vehicle, but with Warren, Diana, and Rex all concentrating their magic on soothing the horse while urging her on, she eventually leapt aboard. To everyone's surprise, Plug's interior adjusted to provide both horses with narrow stalls that would assist in keeping them on their feet as the SUV traversed the sometimes-winding trail to the Branmar Plain.

They arrived at the giants' cave in little more than half an hour. At the lakeside sat both giants, looking much better than either had the previous day. They were enjoying some time with Na'aven and looked at the vehicle's approach with curiosity, but nothing more.

Diana, Warren, and Rex all climbed out of the SUV and went over to where the giants sat on the grassy embankment of the lake. From the nearby forest strode Bronadulach and Mórbaen, the Giant Deer stag. With them flew Mickey T and his daughter. When Sephala and her father neared the giants, there arose from the ground a tall stone pedestal with two perches for each of the bats to descend upon.

The giants now eyed the converging groups expectantly and even Na'aven surged forward so that she was closer to the shore.

The Animal Council members presented the idea of the mission to the giants, with Bronadulach taking the lead.

Diana, Warren, and Rex stood off to the side, listening to the great bear explaining the desire to capture the dragon and bring it to the Ganlonds, each noting that nothing was said about Donemere or her *badûr* with Uncle in the telling. They turned slightly to each other, a clear understanding in their shared glances that, while the giants were to be allowed to stay, they obviously were not to be taken completely into confidences.

When Bronadulach finished speaking, Feirth studied his mother, then turned back to the Cave Bear. "No, I am sorry, but I cannot leave Ma here without me and she certainly cannot travel back north with us, even if we go in that contraption there," he said, pointing at Plug. "There be a great gaping hole in the back of our home, which means anyone could walk right in through that tunnel and hurt her if I were not here," he added by way of apologetic explanation.

Sephala fluttered her wings and sighed. She looked at her father, who was staring at the giantess, Ma'oma, with great fondness.

Sephala turned to Feirth and replied, "Because of the many kindnesses your mother and father committed so long ago, the Ganlonds have provided a small cave that can serve as a suitable abode for you and your mother until Donemere, the Ér Ainíl of the Ganlonds, returns. Ma'oma is welcome to stay in this safe haven while you are gone on the proposed journey." She moved her gaze to Ma'oma and asked, "If you could add this kindness to your list, the Ganlonds will be greatly appreciative. My father tells me you know what it means for a *virat* to be here, for it to help with guarding the magical lands and the creatures who dwell here. This is the only dragon in all of Írtha, it seems, and it can have no better life than living its days here with other magical creatures who will tend its needs and give it a home while it keeps us safe."

Ma'oma smiled at Mickey T and then at Sephala. "Your father knows the way to my heart, he does. I always loved *virata*, even more than most giants did I, and Mecholætera knows this well." She chuckled and sighed, turning her attention to her son. "Ye will have to go with them, my darling, for the wee dragon cannot be let to stay with the awful folks who have it now. Ye must rescue it, and I shall tell ye just what to say to it when ye do."

She began to speak in the strangest tongue any of them had ever heard before and not one of them understood even a syllable. Ma'oma and Feirth got to their feet and started to walk back toward their cave, with Ma'oma continuing to speak in the unknown language the whole time.

Rex stared at Na'aven, asking disbelievingly, "What the heck language is that?"

Na'aven laughed, a light, watery sound with a slight gurgle to it. "It has no name, little wolf. And no matter how many times you hear it, you will never understand its sounds, cadence, or anything else about it. Just when you think you might have gleaned a word or two here or there, it will all change and nothing will mean what you think it does. It is that way for everyone but giants and *virata*."

"But why?" the dog inquired. "Why can't anyone else understand it or speak it? And why do you even need it?"

Again, the water spirit laughed. "Because it is meant just for giants and dragons. And it is the only language that will calm a dragon, any dragon, and that is why we must have it."

With that, the water giantess rolled back into the lake and disappeared with a gentle whoosh of water.

The others looked at each other and most just shrugged. Diana, Warren, and Rex got back into Plug and Rex sat on Warren's lap so that Diana could hold his collar while everyone else made sure to touch the animal in front or beside themselves, creating a daisy chain so that, when Rex concentrated on making himself small, the vehicle and all her occupants were also made small enough to fit through the cave's opening. Staying small, they made their way through the inner caves until they were at the entrance to the long tunnel running north, which Plug could traverse at normal size.

Half an hour later, Feirth found them where they'd parked. Diana explained to him how he was to get into the vehicle and, although he looked doubtful, he said he would try. When he was finally buckled into his own, very large bucket seat at the back of the vehicle, Plug took off with a slight squeal of her tires and everyone settled down for the long journey back to the Withering Hills and its abandoned dragon rookery.

Chapter 16
Zombie

Their first meeting with Malwé did not go well. Dantheus brought the teenage prince to the freshly opened Keep of Hallishead the morning after the arrival of Falwaïn and Donnie and their friends. From the start, it was daggers all around as far as Malwé was concerned. The regal youth was tall and gangly, with raven-colored hair grown down to his shoulders, which was combed back off his forehead by careless fingers. He exhibited a thoroughly contentious mood and attempted to fight with just about everyone except the one person with whom he was truly angry.

He showed some sense at first because, having met Akanna before at Anûmanétus and knowing full well what vincans were like in arguments, Malwé merely shot her a nod of acknowledgement, which she returned, and he then stayed away from her.

He also avoided Donnie initially, instead focusing his ire upon Diego, who, to his credit, kept his temper and his tongue, and merely stared back at the boy without expression as the slightly pimple-faced juvenile tyrant continued to bait the darkly handsome foreigner.

So Malwé started in on his grandfather, who, from his recent practice with the capricious emotions of this particular blossoming adult, adroitly tried to turn the subject to the state of the province's farming and grazing lands. Alas, the old man's efforts were in vain.

Falwaïn, the real object of Malwé's diverted derisions, hunched in a chair at the large table in the center of the room and stared at his son, his guilt clearly eating away at him until he seemed to have been diminished by it. But because of the many overtly encouraging looks and prompts he received from Donnie, he attempted several offerings of peace, or at least courtesy, to his son, all of which were steadfastly ignored or summarily repelled by the bellicose boy.

Malwé, whenever he deigned to look at his father, did so with loathing and reproach, and Donnie could tell that Falwaïn felt every day of his son's long absence and probable hardships anew and with a lash across his heart for each cutting glance, rude gesture, or dismissive response the young man was showing him now. Inside, she began to get a little angry at the young prince's constant digs at his father and his friends and at his father's complete lack of defense, and had to bite her tongue on more than one retort, knowing it would do no good at all. But when Malwé, looking sly and obviously wanting a more direct and combative response to his aggressive tactics, called her a witch-whore and her unborn children filthy bastards, Donnie had had enough.

Just to let him know that she was holding back deliberately, she shot to her feet and moved to stand in front of him before any of the others were even able to see her flex a muscle.

Malwé's blue-grey eyes went wide with shock when he suddenly found himself nose-to-nose with her. Stumbling backward, he stayed upright, spluttering gibberish at her as he fought to keep his footing.

She heard Falwaïn's muttered plea of, "Donnie, please, no; don't do anything," and she sighed loudly, sending Malwé an irritated glare.

"Call me whatever you will, dear prince," she said lightly, forcing a smile onto her lips that turned out to be a lot snarkier than she intended. "But you might want to be nicer to your half-sister and brother because they are definitely magical and will likely be able to kick your ass quite thoroughly by the time they're maybe half the age you are now."

When Malwé showed her a stunned look of comprehension at this well-aimed jibe, she spread her hands wide, giving him a mockingly deferential bow as she backed away, adding, "I say that in all good faith, my lord, looking only to protect his princeship's future."

She then stalked over to Falwaïn and said in a pseudo-whisper that everyone in the room heard quite plainly, "My love, while I'm all about peace, love, and understanding most of the time, this kid is taking it a bit far even for me. Tell you what, you know how I have that penchant for locking people in rooms to make them get along with each other..." she paused, letting her voice trail away meaningfully.

At this point, Falwaïn straightened and looked at her apprehensively. Diego also was brought to attention, but with perhaps a decided touch of amusement rather than trepidation. Both men recalled being locked in the library at the cottage and forced to read about each other to establish peace between themselves. While the gambit had worked then, it had not been without its complaints, and who knew what the result might be if Donnie tried it today with Falwaïn and his son.

"I know I promised I would never do that again without first trying to talk to the people involved," she continued, turning now to glance at the young prince before telling Falwaïn, "therefore, I heartily suggest you two begin to have a productive argument. I'm serious, say all the nasty things you need to say, get it all out, or at least start to, and the rest of us will just leave you alone while you're at it. Okay?" She said this and motioned to Akanna and Diego, who each nodded and moved toward the door with alacrity. She looked expectantly at Dantheus, who came to himself from deep thought and hastily followed them out.

Sylvester, as she'd suspected he would be, was in the stables with the horses. He felt distinctly uncomfortable around Dantheus and had done his best to avoid the man because of Dantheus's apparent aversion to magical creatures. Donnie scooped the cat up and put him on the railing in front of her, then turned to the others.

She looked directly at Dantheus and said, "I don't suppose you'd like to give us a tour of the area? Maybe show us some of the trouble spots—by that I mean, the fields and such that are in the worst shape, just so we can see what we're dealing with, that sort of thing?"

With obvious reluctance to leave his grandson in the keep alone with his estranged father and to travel anywhere in the region with this bold and rather baffling witch without Falwaïn, Dantheus grudgingly agreed to her suggestion. While the old man went to get his horse, Donnie, Akanna, and Diego saddled theirs. They met Dantheus at the city's gate, where he eyed Donnie's linen saddle with dubious curiosity. He remarked nothing about it though and, with a sharp word from him to the captain of the guard, they were allowed to exit the gates without being searched even once.

They headed west, which was where, according to their guide, the very worst of the land's problems had arisen during the past two years. They soon understood exactly what Dantheus meant because the grasses turned from lush, vibrant green to a dull, yellowish brown not three miles from the city. It looked as though nothing would grow here anymore and that couldn't be from lack of water, for there was plenty around—too much, in fact.

Donnie dismounted from Wiwila to the soft, squelchy ground, as did the others from their own steeds.

For the first time, Dantheus got to see Donnie's saddle in action as it retreated from around her legs and tush so she could get down. Shocked, he sat still upon his horse in awe, his mouth hanging open unattractively until Akanna muttered to him impatiently, "It does that. She is a witch. Get down and let's move on."

Sylvester alone remained aloft, sitting with his tail wrapped around his front paws at the front of Donnie's magical saddle. Donnie had warned Brindle, the house tree her stirrups were made from, to be quiet when around strangers, so if he was there instead of at the cottage, he made no indication now.

Donnie and the others began to explore the general area, remarking on their findings as they discovered more and more signs of definite degradation of the soils in the vicinity, such as worms and beetles dying in great numbers, and the presence of too much water everywhere, as if it would not penetrate any farther into the soil than a few inches. Even the muddy and deeply grooved, water-eroded road they were on appeared to be more of a mired pit than an actual man-made surface.

"Is this the same sort of thing that's happening with the Mîrlonds?" Donnie called out to Akanna, who looked up and shook her head.

"No, there everything is withered and dry and black, not wet and sickly and brown, like here," the vincan replied, eyeing the ground with distaste. She was standing perhaps fifty feet across from where Donnie was, with Dantheus and Diego farther away and moving in opposite directions away from the horses.

Donnie nodded to the vincan's response absentmindedly and continued to explore the area around her until she realized that her unborn children were beginning to rebel. She stood quite still and placed her hands upon her baby bulge, concentrating on communicating with her little magical embryos. They immediately relayed to her lucidly and quite emphatically that something was indeed very wrong and they could feel it, and soon it would begin to affect them and not in a good way.

In response, Donnie opened her eyes, turned on her heel, and strode back to Wiwila. She urged the others to join her, saying, "C'mon, we have to get out of here now. Something is definitely wrong here and we need to go before it starts messing with us."

No one gave her any argument and they all climbed back onto their horses and left the area at a fast canter, following Donnie's lead.

They rode for a mile or so before Donnie asked Wiwila to slow down, and when Wiwila did, she stopped the horse entirely and turned her toward the others, so that they all came to face each other in a circle.

"Okay, Sir Dantheus, what else is happening around here?" Donnie inquired, sitting back in her saddle.

He looked surprised by the question, but gave it some consideration before replying, "Several things, if I am to be honest. But I presume ye mean anything that is out of the ordinary, is that correct?" When Donnie murmured in the affirmative, he took a deep breath before answering.

"Well," he began, looking melancholic as he spoke, "we have had far too many children dying of late, and in the most terrible manners one could realize. Some had great growths protruding from them in all areas of their bodies, while others simply wasted away and nothing our healers have tried has managed to alter their condition. That is happening not just to children, of course, but mainly to them," he noted sadly. "Besides all of that, many adults are losing their hair, and even their teeth, and they too are developing tumors of the grossest sorts. An alarming number of them are also leaving this life far too soon and we have no way of understanding why." He stopped speaking there and spread his hands wide in a helpless gesture.

While everyone else looked as lost as he, Donnie was sitting with her mouth open, staring behind the others at whence they came.

"Shit!" she swore softly. "How the hell did that happen?" she asked, and they all turned around to look back too, but none of them saw anything amiss and so they each looked forward again.

In the meanwhile, Donnie was musing aloud. "Okay," she muttered to herself, "it's something magical, which I already suspected. But it's gone everywhere, all over the friggin' place. And that makes no sense to me, unless…" Her voice tailed off as she continued to stare into the distance.

When Diego asked her, "*Querida*, do you know what is wrong here? And perhaps how it can be fixed?", Donnie's face twisted into a grimace of something like anguish.

"I have no clue how to fix it, to be honest," she admitted. Diego emitted a stunned gasp and she nodded in acknowledgement of his surprise. "That may seem odd, but, while I think I know what the problem is, fixing it is going to involve knowing exactly how the spell was originally worded and just where it was set. I mean, I'd probably have to be in the same spot as whoever cast it, or as close as I can get to that."

"Ye believe it to be a curse set by a witch?" Sir Dantheus challenged, directing the question at her with an accusing glare.

"I don't know if it was a curse or something else, and whatever it was, it wasn't necessarily set by a witch or even a wizard," she shot back at him defensively. "It could have been a sorcerer or a god who set it." She shook her head, blowing a fractious breath. "But how I'm going to figure that out is beyond me, especially since it could have been set anywhere within a thousand square miles of here."

Sylvester, who had until now refrained from saying anything in the presence of anyone not of their usual group, posited, "What if you were to simply replace the affected soil?"

Donnie turned that option over a couple times in her mind before nodding. "That might help, yeah. But where the heck am I gonna find that much topsoil? And what do I do with the contaminated soil afterward?" She considered that question for a moment and then immediately answered it with, "Well, okay, all I'd have to do is send it to outer space where it couldn't do anymore harm, so that's pretty easy." She shrugged, gazing down into her cat's upturned face. "But there's still the issue of finding sufficient soil to use as replacement. If I could figure out a way to create topsoil, then that might be a viable option. Otherwise, we'll just have to come up with something else."

Dantheus, not having understood a word the cat said, but cottoning to the fact that he had said something intelligible to the others, brought his horse closer to Wiwila and stared at Sylvester. He looked up at Donnie and snapped, "It too is magical?"

Donnie, ready to argue for Sylvester's right to be anything at all in this life, sat up tall and answered disdainfully, "*It* is a he and he can understand you perfectly. May I point out that you are the only one who is lacking here since you are apparently unable to understand *him*."

Dantheus was taken aback by her affronted air and he himself looked offended for a moment, until he finally growled, "Well, ye do have a way of looking at things that is a bit different for these days, do ye not?"

"*¡Si!* Of course she does, because she is not from this backward place!" Diego interjected. "You could learn from her perspective, *viejo hombre*." He said this as haughtily as Donnie had spoken a moment before, his dark eyes flashing sparks. "My friend Donnie honors all life equally, holding everyone as sacred. And she expects those around her to do that as well, so if you want her help, you would be wise to accept each of us traveling with her just the way we are and without judgment. That includes the cat, the horses, myself and Akanna, and most especially, Donnie and her little magical babies! Oh, and her saddle as well!"

He huffed a little when he said the last part, and Sir Dantheus raised a confounded eyebrow at him before turning to Akanna, as if prodding her to have her say too.

But Akanna merely shrugged at Dantheus in return. Obviously not wanting to get drawn into any discussion of the kind being pushed on her, she ignored the tension between everyone and instead turned to Donnie. "Please, if you will tell us: what exactly do you see out there that we do not?" She tossed her head in the direction of the farmland behind them as she asked the question.

"Well," Donnie began, frowning at the dismal vista showing over the shoulders of her companions, "firstly, let me point out that I didn't see anything wrong until the kids noticed there was something amiss and told me about it. And now they're helping me so that I can see what's really there. Because I needed them to show it to me for me to see it, I have a feeling that the spell or curse or whatever it is, is something that's targeted toward children and the land itself, and that adults are being affected by it only because the land is affected by it and they're coming into contact with the land. So, they are collateral damage, if you will." She paused to frown again. "Why whatever is doing this to the land is focused on kids, I don't know, but it sure is crappy of whoever set it in motion."

She made a grim face and tightened her lips together with displeasure. "Granted, I can't swear to any of that yet, but I have a feeling that's the main thrust of whatever the spell is supposed to do, is to harm children. As for how it's manifesting and what I can see of it," she continued, staring out again at the depressing sight of the hills and fields in her view, "it's like there's this ugly brown mist hugging close to the ground everywhere. It looks muddy and dirty, you know? And when I say it's everywhere, I mean it's all over the fields for as far as I can see." She shuddered with disgust, breaking her gaze away from the brown mist-covered landscape to face the others.

Dantheus had been staring at her intently throughout her explanation and now ventured thoughtfully, "Several children have said much the same as ye just did. They describe a low-lying, muddy mist all around that they cannot escape. It frightens them because they feel it has a presence or soul to it; although that would be impossible, would it not?" he asked Donnie, his brow furrowed.

Remembering Na'aven and her melding with the Mist of Avendin, Donnie shrugged uncertainly at him. "Normally, I would say yes, of course that's impossible, but we recently encountered such an entity in a benign mist, so I can't say it's either impossible or possible in this case. But I will say that this mist, to me, feels more like a...like it's a strong and willful intent and simply that," she answered in reply, her gaze returning to the distant landscape. "By that, I mean that I don't feel it's an entity with any kind of intelligence behind it, but it certainly has a will. For instance, when we were out there in it, it left us adults alone, but not my kids. They could feel it trying to attack them and they got quite scared by it, which is why I had us leave so abruptly."

"Could the children say in what manner this mist was attacking them?" asked Sylvester anxiously.

Donnie shook her head. "No, they just knew it meant to harm them, but they didn't know what it would do to them if they stayed in it any longer."

"That does not bode well for you to fix it, then," Akanna pointed out, "because you will need to be in it or near it to deal with it."

"Well, I have ways of protecting myself and the kids, if it comes to that," Donnie said confidently, "so I think we'll be okay. But if not, then I'll just have to be quick about whatever I do and limit our exposure to the mist and its effects." She silently prayed her declaration would prove true when it actually came down to dealing with the curse or whatever it was that was causing all the damage.

They decided to return to Hörthanc and to the keep. The captain of the guard forced them to halt at the city's gate while he insisted upon having them searched, and quite thoroughly at that. Donnie decided to be nice and said nothing, submitting herself and Wiwila to a general pat down without protest. But when the captain opened his mouth, after eyeing the cat, she lifted a finger to him and said, "I think not, dear sir. I may very well cause another riot, and will do so happily, if provoked."

The man looked at her and shrugged wearily, finally motioning for her to move on.

When they were inside the city's walls and were beginning their traipse back up to the keep, Donnie noted to Sir Dantheus, "I see that not even you are exempt from the security measures," and the old man nodded.

"There are only two who are," he replied, and before he could go on, Donnie interrupted him.

"Ooh, ooh, let me guess," she crowed excitedly, waving her arms to underscore her facetiousness, "that would be...um, lemme see...the pugnacious prince and the lordy lord! Am I right?" She grinned widely at him when he gave her an exasperated snort.

They were passing by some street singers who were draped languidly over a small, raised dais on the side of the main street leading into the city. The troubled troubadours were intent upon warbling to all and sundry the bittersweet tale of the sons of Eárnas Ba and the blessings laid upon them by none other than the great Morrían. Donnie, having caught that much of the tale as they were walking by, thought back to last night when she'd heard this same lay about halfway through their trek through the city on their way to the Keep of Hallishead. She supposed it must have been these same singers practicing then, just as they were now.

"My grandson has good reason for his behavior, I assure you," Sir Dantheus replied to her, a sharp snap to his voice, which brought Donnie's attention back to him. "And he will soon make peace with his father, there can be no doubt, for it will behoove us all to listen to the wise counsel of Lord Falwaïn."

"Oh, no doubt," Donnie repeated, making her voice change to a serious tone and sending the old man a gentle smile. "I am sure Malwé is, at this moment, seeking his father's advice on how to handle the farmers' issues."

That, of course, was not the case at all. When they returned to the keep, they found Falwaïn in the second floor greeting chamber with an oily-looking man who turned out to be Gullrick, the Lord Chancellor, and about ten armed guards, two of whom were standing outside the keep and did not want to let them pass until Sir Dantheus ordered them to stand down. Two more guards stood sentinel on either side of the thick, oak doors of the reception room. The others stood in two lines just inside the room. Of Malwé, there was no sign.

But their old friend Tather was inside, as well, and seemed to be in high dudgeon, if one takes into consideration that his face was suffused with blood and his features were screwed up into an expression of outrage.

Falwaïn seemed to have recovered himself fully for he sat in the large, intricately carved oak throne that dominated the room looking quite comfortable and somewhat smugly pleased with himself.

The Lord Chancellor was trying to persuade Falwaïn of something, using the threat of arrest as encouragement. Falwaïn was sticking to his guns, though, and was refusing to go anywhere with the "Lordy Lord" or his guards.

When Donnie and the others appeared at the doorway, Tather did not hesitate to order his guards to take them all into custody immediately. Akanna and Diego both stepped forward with readied swords and lustful gleams in their eyes, for it had been a while since either had encountered a good fight.

Falwaïn jumped to his feet and called out to them to stand down, briefly explaining his opinion that the prince's guards were good men and woman, and did not deserve to die today because of two ambitious men's whims.

In response, Akanna and Diego slowly sheathed their swords, neither looking all that happy to forego a fight for freedom. But Falwaïn had not said anything to Donnie, who took her wand out of her coat and, with a quick wave, froze every soldier where they stood. Not one could move, except for their eyes, which grew big as they all panicked.

Keeping her eyes trained on the Lord Chancellor, who was staring at her with undisguised hatred, Donnie waved her wand once more and said softly, "Guards, you may relax, for I will not hurt you in any way." The alarm in the guards' eyes faded and they all calmed to the point where they merely kept watch on the proceedings that followed.

Donnie went on to explain to them in the same soft and soothing voice, "You will be able to move when it is time for you to leave, but not until then. That keeps us all safe, doesn't it?" She seemed to ask this question of Gullrick, but he did not respond to her.

Instead, Gullrick looked at Sir Dantheus and informed him with a snarl, "You have been treating with the witch and her friends. That is treason and you shall pay for it, as you well know. As if that were not bad enough, you also brought our beloved prince here this morning without my consent." His dark eyes were small beads in his face and his oily hair gleamed wetly in the sunlight filtering in through the open shutters. He had an aquiline nose that came to a thin, sharp point at its end, and his eyebrows were so light-colored they were hardly there. He was unsightly to behold and even more unseemly to listen to, for his speaking voice was commonly that of a vicious sneer.

"The prince," Sir Dantheus replied to the man carefully, his expression one of carved stone, "ordered me to bring him to the keep. As I am sure ye are aware, the boy does what he wants and seldom asks for counsel."

Gullrick flashed a hateful glare at the older man. "He will do as I tell him or he too will learn there is a price to pay for disobeying the king."

"And do you really believe you know what the king would want in this situation?" asked Falwaïn, his voice quiet, but firm.

Gullrick turned his sneer onto Falwaïn and shot back at him, "I am the king's emissary, his mouthpiece. I speak only his truth, ever his orders."

Somewhere above them and within the tower, Donnie heard music being played. It was the boombox and its sound produced a tinny kind of echo throughout the big tower's main stairwell. It was playing "Zombie" and was in full swing on the chorus.

Donnie's eyes darted around, searching for the supposed zombie here with them. Her gaze lit first on Tather, but she dismissed him as being too inconsequential for it to matter if he were doing someone else's bidding and could not therefore warrant the boombox's warning. It then moved to Gullrick and she instinctively strode forward to stand very close to the odious man, who took an involuntary step backward when she approached him. Donnie studied his face, noting the bravado in his eyes, along with something much darker behind that. She also noticed that, above the floor-length, brown, richly braided tunic he wore, there was a strange-looking collar made of what appeared to be gold that was inlaid with three colorful gems of sapphire blue.

This torque, of sorts, bore upon it beautiful intaglio engravings. Donnie closed her eyes and looked at it with her mind's eye and saw a faint, weird haze emanating from it. This haze hovered over the entire piece, but was densest at the embedded jewels.

She was certain she had found the zombie. Her eyes flicked open and she noted quietly, "That is some collar you have there, Lord Chancellor. How do you take it off, if I may be so bold as to ask?"

Gullrick turned away and ignored her question, but his movements gave Donnie the chance to see the back of the thing that lay around his neck so tightly. For the life of her, she could not see how the piece could possibly be taken off without cutting it off. Or without magicking it off, she supposed to herself silently. Which likely meant it had been put on the same way it was intended to be removed.

Who did this distinctly unmagical man know who had the ability to do that kind of magic, Donnie wondered, and what did the collar do, exactly? And why did it have similar engravings to those she'd seen up close on the young dragons she'd been forced to kill that terrible night during the battle on the Branmar Plain?

While she'd been musing over his collar, Gullrick had apparently said something that had made everyone else very angry.

Donnie stepped in front of him, waved her hands frantically, and said, "Whoa, everybody! Seriously, we have a big problem here." She pointed to the man behind her, who was looking furiously at the back of her head. "That collar he's got on is really something, magically speaking, but I can tell he has no magic of his own, so he sure didn't put it there. Which means someone else did and, whoever they are, they'd have to be highly, *highly* magically to control that collar."

"Ye are lyin', ye daft witch!" accused Tather

Donnie forced herself to ignore him and turned back to Gullrick, who had pure hate pouring from his body toward her. She put a hand on his shoulder and he flinched as though struck. His hands came up to throttle her and she, of course, froze him in place. She motioned for the others to come over to see what she was pointing at. "See this," she said, pointing to one of the sapphires. "If I'm right, then when I touch it, it should react in some way."

She was indeed correct, for when she touched the jewel, she was sent flying backward at an unnaturally fast rate of speed, a circumstance for which she was prepared enough that she managed to keep herself from hitting the far wall, although just barely, stopping only inches from it.

There was a malevolent light in Gullrick's eyes now, and it burned a bright green as he fixated on her face. They could all see the moment when the collar sent a green flash outward and Gullrick was freed from Donnie's freezing charm. He grabbed Diego's stiletto from its sheath and threw it at Donnie, his aim unerring. She moved in time to avoid the sharp blade penetrating her throat, but then found the thing came after her again, and then again. Each time she avoided it, it continued its attack until she finally put it in stasis in a thick ball of her own magic, letting it float high above them all as it strained to break through the protective shield of Donnie's magic.

By then, Akanna and Diego had the Lord Chancellor pinned with his back to the wall and were tussling with him as he writhed angrily in their strong grips. Sir Dantheus was also there and had his palms on Gullrick's chest, pressing him flat to the wall. Tather became perfectly still where he stood, staring at Gullrick with increasing horror.

Falwaïn had a stool in his hands that he had been using to block the knife from getting at Donnie, and it bore at least five holes in it from where the sharp tip had penetrated the soft wood by more than an inch.

Sylvester was standing on his hind legs on the table and was shooting a stream of his own magical power from his two front paws at the brilliant blue prison surrounding the knife to lend an extra layer of protection in case it somehow got through Donnie's shield. While he seldom made such an overt display of his Ca'nam powers, the cat had practiced alongside Donnie on many an occasion when she was learning to wield the incredible power she'd been gifted.

It was upon this scene that Malwé strode in, looking as though he was ready to start yet another argument, but with whom this time was unclear because he must have known that his father certainly was no longer alone.

He made it to the center of the room and stopped, looking around him with shock. After uttering a surprised shout of, "What is happening here?", he commanded that his Lord Chancellor be set free immediately, an order to which only Sir Dantheus paid any heed.

Gullrick surged forward again and broke away from Diego's grip, and in another second had torn his arm out of Akanna's as well. He turned toward Sir Dantheus and from his hate-filled eyes shot two beams of green magic that hit the old man squarely in the chest. Sir Dantheus fell to the floor senseless and nearly dead. The Lord Chancellor whirled to face the two warriors trying to restrain him, attempting to do the same damage to them, but they dove away, landing in rolling motions that carried them to other sides of the room.

Falwaïn stepped in front of Donnie, who gave a snort of annoyance at his inherent chivalry at a time when he was clearly not matched for the foe standing before them.

With a snap of her fingers, she transported herself and Gullrick to the courtyard outside, where the two of them began to circle each other warily. The chancellor's guards at the entrance to the keep were still frozen in place, but made enough noise in trying to call to each other that Donnie's friends were alerted and they ran to the ground floor and out of the keep to witness the battle that was about to begin. Sylvester alone stayed behind to watch over Sir Dantheus.

Donnie waved a hand and shouted, with a glance at Falwaïn, "I've let the guards go now so they can attend to Dantheus. He's alive, but barely. Tell them to put him in our room, my love. If I can beat this, this—" she motioned toward Gullrick, "magical zombie, then Dantheus just may live another day."

"You may not kill my Lord Chancellor, witch!" shouted the young prince, his face red with fury.

"She is not allowed to kill anyone," interposed Diego quietly, his voice barely above a whisper when it came to the boy's ear, "except under specific circumstances. A condition imposed upon her by someone with much more power than you, *principito*, will ever have. And she is much contented to have that restraint placed upon herself. Could you say the same, if you were her?"

Malwé, who turned to find the dark foreigner standing directly behind him, flushed bright red all over in embarrassment and he stared out at the world with growing confusion. Falwaïn turned away from the scene sadly and strode inside so he could direct the guards where to move Dantheus.

Donnie blocked the first two bolts of murderous magic from Gullrick's eyes with a small shield she conjured with her wand, not happy when they bounced away and exploded holes in the keep's ancient walls. But then she decided to use that to her advantage and, on the sixth shot that she deflected, was able to direct it to an already weakened spot above Gullrick. With this shot, the third in that same area, enough stones fell to knock him unconscious and cover him in their dusty rubble, as she'd hoped.

Several seconds ticked by, with no movement from the small pile of stones and human flesh, and Donnie breathed normally again. Falwaïn returned from inside with two guards and the three of them cleared away the rubble over the Lord Chancellor, with Diego and Akanna joining in to help haul the unconscious man into the keep's tower. The young prince stood by watching, obviously not sure where he should be because he kept looking back at the keep's tower throughout all this movement. Tather too seemed unsure of what he should do or where he should stand and, after several moments of indecision, he went off after Falwaïn and the guards carrying Gullrick.

Once Donnie was sure the Lord Chancellor was truly knocked out, she ran back into the tower and to the bedroom she shared with Falwaïn. There on the soft counterpane covering the bed lay Sir Dantheus, his breathing shallow. Sylvester sat on the table beside him, staring at the old man's deathly pale face.

Donnie barely noticed that Malwé had followed her in. She went over to Sir Dantheus and held her hands over him, closing her eyes while she looked with her mind's eye into his chest. There was a ball of green magic compressing his heart. She dared not touch it with her magic in case it reacted to her the same way the collar had and thereby killed the old man.

She opened her eyes and said to the prince, "He needs a healer, a strong one, one who is perhaps versed in lifting enchantments—if one exists here, that is," she amended hastily, unsure of just what this world's healers could do against magic. "He has a layer of magic, the collar's magic, encasing his heart. I won't even attempt to touch it because I fear that may only worsen his condition. But a healer might be able to do what I feel I should not even attempt."

Malwé stared at her for a very long time, then turned a stony gaze upon one of the guards and ordered, "Fetch Quillirana the Elder."

The guard left immediately, and so Donnie sank onto a chair that stood in the corner. She sighed as she sat back and let her tautened muscles relax. The fight had made her jittery and tense, with so many sensations flitting through her, from worry for the others' safety, to concern for the poor man being used as someone's pawn, to curiosity about the maker of the collar, to wondering if she'd done the right thing in leaving Sir Dantheus to the ministrations of a healer instead of trying to help him herself.

She considered the last part and realized that she did not wish to be the instrument of his likely death, and that was really why she had called for a healer. To begin with, she didn't want Dantheus to die because she liked him and she could tell that he and Falwaïn had been close for a long time, so his death would be a heavy blow to take. But, further to that, she did not want to give Malwé yet another reason to hate her and his father.

Biting her lip, she looked at the young prince, who was brooding over his grandfather with his back mostly turned to Donnie. Strangely, he in no way reminded her of Falwaïn, and she wondered what Sémere had looked like. But Malwé did have his grandfather's hawk nose, that was clear, for Donnie could see them both now in silhouette against the bright light shining in from the windows and noticed how strikingly alike they were. While Malwé was tall like Falwaïn, that was about all they seemed to have in common, at least physically.

During the few minutes Donnie spent ruminating, the others put the Lord Chancellor in wrist and ankle shackles that were recalled from the dungeon. These were made of maurichalcum, that precious metal believed impervious to magic—although it had been many a long year since the shackles had been tested thusly.

After being impeded by the shackles, as quaintly called in Medregai, Gullrick was carried inside the reception room and his shackles attached to four maurichalcum rings set deep into the flagstone floor over in the far corner of the room from the door. His unconscious body was then sat up in one of the many high-backed chairs placed in all the rooms of the keep's tower.

A guard was dispatched to the bedroom chamber to inform the prince and Donnie where the "prisoner" was being held. Malwé, with one last look at his grandfather, strode out of the room without saying a word.

Donnie asked the guard still in the room how long it might be before the healer would come and, though he looked at her with a hint of fear in his eyes, he responded in a firm voice that Quillirana the Elder lived only five minutes away. Nodding her thanks, Donnie settled back into her chair to wait and not long thereafter heard an old woman's voice chatting with someone about how nice it was to be back in the Keep of Hallishead, that it was a fine building that had served the city well for centuries and should be given its freedom to breathe, just like any building should.

This made Donnie smile and she stood in anticipation of meeting the wise woman about to enter the room. The weathered face that appeared around the door a moment later was curious and kindly, with a sense of calm about it that was belied by the lively and intense blue of her eyes. She seemed to recognize a kindred soul in Donnie and approached her with a smile and a light step. She was in her twilight years definitely, but given how long everyone lived in Írtha, her age was indeterminable. She wore a dark, hooded cloak of thin wool and carried a large, carpeted bag with her, which she set down just inside the door.

"I am Quillirana the Elder and ye must be the witch the entire city is nattering on about endlessly since thy arrival," she croaked, an amused twinkle beaming from her eyes. "Ye might think none of them have ever met a witch before, but a fair number have indeed, so I am at a loss to understand what makes ye such a topic for their gossip. Well, other than ye brought our good Lord Falwaïn back to us, looking healthy and happy, which are two traits long missing from his handsome self."

Donnie chuckled and greeted the woman with a slight bow. "It is very much a pleasure to meet you, Quillirana the Elder. I am Donemere of the Codlebærn, Ér Ainíl of the Ganlonds. And, while I thank you for your courtesy, I take only small credit for Lord Falwaïn's state of being, for he is very much his own master in every way, as I suspect you know."

Quillirana's smile widened. "Ah, the stories I could tell ye of him in his youth!" she exclaimed, and would have begun regaling Donnie with some such anecdotes, but her gaze fell upon Sir Dantheus and she gasped in shock, letting out a soft, "Oh!"

Donnie stepped backward and motioned for Quillirana to move to the bed. "He was felled by an enchantment that emanated from the collar the Lord Chancellor wears around his neck. I presume you've seen the collar," she stated, not really expecting a reply.

She paused and frowned, extraneously recalling Rex's message from Gwydion the night of the Battle of the Branmar Plain regarding the secret lies about Sylvester. She wondered now if there was a secret lying about *his* neck. Her eyes darted to the cat sitting on the bedside table, who was watching the two women with interest, and she noted that he, naturally, wore his locket and chain, its silvery metal suddenly blazing with reflected light from the windows opposite him. His calm gaze met her meditative one and, when she did not immediately continue, his eyebrows raised expectantly and he murmured her name low.

This prompting was sufficient for Donnie to shake her head and recall herself to her purpose. She turned to Quillirana, who was also staring at the locket because of how brightly it had glinted a moment before, and cleared her throat before speaking.

"I discovered that the collar is itself enchanted and it reacted violently to my touch, therefore I dare not go near Dantheus myself," she explained and Quillirana digested this news carefully.

The wise healer pushed back her hood to reveal wildly curly, dark grey hair pulled back into a loose bun at her nape, and rolled up her sleeves a little. She then did the same actions Donnie had made previously over the man's prone body, which were to hold her hands over him with palms down and concentrate on "seeing" inside his body. When she opened her unusually blue eyes a minute later, she said, "His heart is imprisoned by the magic of the collar."

Donnie grimaced and gave a diffident shrug.

"Ah, ye knew that already, did ye not?" Quillirana noted thoughtfully. "That means ye have the gift of inner sight, along with thy Ca'nam powers. And probably more than that runs through ye, or so I suppose."

When Donnie nodded in hesitant confirmation of this supposition, the healer then turned to Sylvester and said, "And what about ye, little one? How be yer own magic these days?"

Both he and Donnie stared at the old woman wide-eyed. She cackled and told the guard who had come with her and the one who had been in the room all along to leave the chamber and close the door tight behind them. When they were alone, she crossed her skinny arms in front of her and beamed at Sylvester.

"Ye do not remember me, do ye? Ye never do," she said mock-sourly, looking a little put out at the realization.

"We have met before, madam?" Sylvester asked, his surprise manifest in his tone.

"Aye, several times, we have," Quillirana replied cheerfully, chuckling as she turned away. She walked to the door to get her bag and came back to the bedside with it, talking the whole way. "But, as I say, ye never remember it even oncet, just like ye never know why ye still wear that ever-bright trinket 'round yer neck. She always sets a spell on ye, Catie does, so ye forget it all, and ye have to get to know me over and over again, each time we meet." The humorous old healer had arrived back at the bed by now and she opened the carpet bag held in her grip, pausing to laugh lightly again before telling Donnie slyly, "Catie is a great one for bartering for my metheglin, she is. And that is how I come to know yon cat and Catie herself."

It took Donnie a moment to understand this, but she finally recalled the many casks in the buttery that were marked with that word, which she kept forgetting to look up in a dictionary. Greatly curious, she asked, "What exactly is metheglin? Some type of drink, I gather; right?"

Quillirana started taking from her bag a supply of candles, stones, and packs of herbs tied with string which she would place along the outline of her patient and around the edges of the bed. She paused in her work upon Donnie's inquiry to smack her lips lasciviously and rub her tummy with big, calloused hands. They were the hands of someone who had performed much hard work all their life and continued to do so, for the digits were strong and nimble and showed no sign of arthritis or weakness.

" 'Tis spiced honey meade, it is," she explained, adding proudly, "and I concoct the best brew to be found anywhere, and that is not just me sayin' so. See, I brew it for near everybody in these parts and for those traveling by who stop in town 'cause they're feeling a touch parched by their long journeys. Most people in Medregai know they can always find refreshment at my home."

She beamed at Donnie and busied herself with her primary task again, that of attending to Sir Dantheus, her amused smile becoming warm and carefree. "M'dear father brewed it the best afore me, and now my lovely, sweet granddaughter is learning the craft. She'll be taking over the trade after I go to Canavar," said the old woman, looking like it might well be several long years before any such thing as that were to occur. "Catie is one of my best customers, as she was my father's before me, as she was his father's before him, and so on and so on for ever such a long, long time. I tell ye, when she did not turn up at the start of spring, I feared something bad had happened. I say that because for her to miss her appointment with me and mine is uncommon to the extreme. Then we learned about ye and that Catie had left Írtha, so 'twas all made clear and my worry abated."

Quillirana grinned again, coming around the bed to place her candles on the floor on the other side, which meant Donnie had to move backward so as not to be in the way. After placing one candle near the foot of the bed, Quillirana chuckled throatily before assuring the world at large, her arms spread wide in the air and her hands full of her medicines and tools, "There'll be plenty meade waiting for my old friend when she comes back, I guarantee!"

"And she'll be happy for that, I'm sure," remarked Donnie, privately thinking she was glad she hadn't had any of the stuff in the buttery at home. She'd tried meade once and had found it a bit too hard for her palate. She wondered if Falwaïn had drank any of Catie's stash, because he'd certainly been down there enough times to know the casks had to have come from Quillirana.

As if reading her mind, Quillirana stood up from bending over to place another candle, leaned closer to Donnie, and shook her greyed head before saying, "Lord Falwaïn cannot tolerate anything from the bee, so he has never tasted my tempting brew."

Sylvester cleared his throat importantly at this juncture. "Catie comes here to visit you, does she?" he inquired, unsure what to make of this oddly talkative woman.

"No, not her," Quillirana replied, glancing over at the cat. It was clear from that one look that she was quite fond of him. "I would meet her at an arranged place, and with me would be her renewed stock of brew. This, she would send to her cottage with the blink of her eye, along with me and herself, and thereafter I would enjoy a long spell of sittin' and chattin' with her. And Tanny, ye would ask me the same serious questions every year and I would provide ye with the same silly answers every year, and it..." here the wise woman's eyes gleamed with happy remembrance, "it were the best start to my spring imaginable!"

She exhaled a long, slow, heartfelt sigh and this time smiled an almost beatific smile, all the while gazing serenely down at her patient's pale face.

Donnie found Quillirana endearingly enchanting and took a steadfast and immediate liking to the older woman, feeling quite glad she was here to help with Sir Dantheus.

"I will sit here with my old friend Tanny," Quillirana announced to Donnie, holding a taper to one of the lit candles by the bedside and using it to light her own small candles, "and we will chant over Sir Dantheus a while with my bits and bobs, and hope for the best."

Donnie looked at Sylvester questioningly.

He nodded back, encompassing the other women briefly in his gaze when he replied to Donnie, "Yes, I will stay with Quillirana, for I am most curious to learn something of our previous encounters together. Perhaps I will glean a clue from her memories of us regarding my locket. As you know yourself, Donemere, Quillirana is quite correct when she supposes I have no idea why I wear it, only that I must never remove it."

Donnie did know this, for the subject had arisen more than once in their conversations since she'd been brought to Medregai. The locket, or rather, the chain, had resisted all effort on both their parts to be removed from his neck until they'd finally given up on it, agreeing that its provenance would likely be revealed only when they finally caught up to Catie.

Quillirana had listened to their exchange with curiosity, but she now prompted Donnie gently with, "Well, my dear, we best get to our task for Sir Dantheus. And I expect ye wish to return to the Lord Chancellor."

Donnie agreed with obvious reluctance but, nevertheless, she moved toward the door after telling the other two, "It's not so much that I wish to be anywhere near him, because I'd rather be anywhere *other* than near him, truth be told, but I do think I should join those guarding him, if only to see for myself what he says or does next. With any luck, maybe he'll be in his right mind by now."

Chapter 17
Morrian's Blessing

When she descended to the reception room, Donnie entered it quietly, not saying a word to anyone. She stood to the right of the big double doors, peeking between two guards at what was happening at the other end of the chamber. Malwé was standing in front of his shackled chancellor and had just demanded to know how long Gullrick had been wearing the collar. Donnie assumed this was not the first time the question had been asked because Gullrick merely gave him a nasty smirk and stayed silent.

"It will do you no good to ignore my questions," the prince berated him angrily, "for I will simply have my guards beat it out of you."

Gullrick bowed his head to reply with a scornful sneer, "As you wish, my liege. As I have told you many times before, my life is nothing without your trust and...*your love.*" His dark eyes gleamed with sheer impudence and the young prince's face turned a dull red.

At a hissed command from Malwé, Tather stepped forward. In his big hand, he gripped a thick cudgel that had small, sharpened bolts of metal embedded into its fatter end. Tather hefted this menacingly at the prisoner a couple times before swinging it back over his shoulder.

Donnie was about to freeze everyone in the room to take control of the situation when Falwaïn strode over and wrenched the lethal weapon out of Tather's hand.

He turned on his son reprovingly. "This is not how we do things in Faen Eárna!" he reminded Malwé through clenched teeth. "Have you forgotten all of my lessons such that now you know only what you were taught at court?" He threw the weapon to the floor in disgust and Akanna kicked it away and out of sight, the expression on her face showing just how much she agreed with Falwaïn.

Diego seemed to somehow become aware of Donnie's presence, for he turned around and searched those assembled until his eyes met hers. He glided back with almost no sound to join her and whispered in her ear, "*Hola, mi amiga.* The fiend in this Gullrick person comes and goes at will. It seems the man has no control over it, although it has not attacked any of us again."

Donnie acknowledged this with a nod and turned her attention back to father and son, who were now arguing over Falwaïn's right to interfere in the province's affairs. Even the prisoner sided with the prince and said so with relish, an unnatural glitter of green showing in his eyes.

Diego again leaned in to whisper in Donnie's ear. "The *demonio* is intent on having the prince kill the man it possesses, and the *principito* is so angry at everyone and everything, he wishes only to strike as he himself has been struck far too often."

Donnie turned to Diego and gave him a concerned look. "That sounds like the voice of experience," she noted in a low whisper.

Diego grimaced, conceding, "My father was a violent and angry man, as were his friends from his days in the army. When he took us with him to Mexico City, we did not have a pleasant life with him, for he did not like losing the war with the French. And so, he beat us daily to release his fury. His friends did even worse things to us for an entire year…" Diego's eyes narrowed and his face filled with hatred as he recalled those terrible days of his young life, and he could not look at Donnie for a moment. But then his expression cleared, he raised his gaze and squared his jaw, adding with satisfaction, "Until it happened that they could not, and from then on, they never did anything ever again."

Taken aback by his response, Donnie's eyes widened and she stared at him questioningly.

"One day, perhaps I will burden you with that sickening story," he told her quietly, "but for now, I cannot."

She squeezed his forearm sympathetically and they returned their attention to the other end of the room, watching as Malwé, looking sullen, flung himself onto the seat of the throne with a shout of, "You sound like Dantheus! Well, go on then, *Father*, confound us with your interrogation methods!"

Falwaïn sighed, straightened his back until he stood to his full height, and replied gently to his son, "I think you were on the right track earlier, Malwé, when you reminded Gullrick of better times back in Anûmanétus. He seemed to come more to himself then."

Malwé snorted derisively, glaring at his father. "Better times? And just when were those?"

Falwaïn moved his shoulders restlessly and conceded, "Well, you are correct if you're thinking that Gullrick and I have no such better times to recall, for we certainly do not. But I am hoping that perhaps his hatred of me will be even stronger than his regard for you and that this may bring him to himself, even if just for a short while, so that we can finally advance to some real answers."

The prince scoffed again and shot his father a piteous smile.

Falwaïn turned from him in resignation and glanced toward Donnie and Diego. Once he noticed her presence, his gaze lengthened upon her.

This prompted her and Diego both to move deeper into the room, with Donnie keeping her eyes locked on the prisoner in case he tried to attack anyone again because of her. She came to stand beside Falwaïn, her green eyes flitting briefly to the knife still suspended in the air where she and Sylvester had left it, with her blue shield encased by the cat's orange one.

Gullrick sat forward suddenly and snarled at her, his eyes glowing with the weird green light of the collar's magic again. "Let it fly, witch, and by the will of my power over magic it shall drive itself into your wicked, wicked heart!"

"It's not my heart that's wicked though, is it?" she retorted blithely and stepped behind Falwaïn so that she was now hidden from Gullrick's view. As she suspected would happen, he settled into his chair with an impassive expression and his eyes, from the quick glance she stole seconds later, had returned to their normal color and expression.

When Falwaïn moved forward to approach their prisoner, Donnie smoothly hid behind a nearby guard. For the first time, she noticed that there were several more of these in the room than previously. Someone must have sent for reinforcements.

Falwaïn was talking in a low voice to Gullrick, reminding him of a few of their more contentious interactions and rubbing it in that Gullrick had failed so miserably on more than one occasion to best Falwaïn. There was a growing whine in the imprisoned man's rebuttals, and he was slowly getting angrier and angrier, but Falwaïn kept reminiscing his victories over the other man and how, several times, he and the king had laughed over poor, useless Gullrick.

Donnie kept moving around the room and finally figured out a path that would bring her close to the prisoner from behind without him seeing her. She utilized several guards to hide her progress toward him and his collar because she wanted to know if the collar could sense her proximity without Gullrick watching her approach.

But first, she wanted to see if Falwaïn might be successful in his tactics.

She peered over the shoulder of a guard, watching with fascination as Gullrick became so angry he was literally spitting at Falwaïn. His vile words were about his own assumed superiority and he went on to revel in the fact that Falwaïn was deeply hated by everyone at Anûmanétus, but he had always been too ignorant and stupid to recognize that. She noted that Falwaïn flinched at this taunt, but he grimly pushed the prisoner even further, telling him that here in Hörthanc it was much the same and the townspeople laughed at Gullrick behind his back, calling him names like "Lordy Lord" and "Weaselcock." It was perhaps the last insult that did the trick.

Gullrick lunged at Falwaïn, who caught him in a taut embrace. And then Gullrick was crying and spouting gibberish about being trapped for the last two years, and that someone, he apparently had not seen who, had come upon the cortege escorting him to the province. He stammered that they had all lost at least an hour of the day, although no one could recall why except for himself, but he could say nothing because the demon in the gold collar had kept him at bay ever since. After the attack, he had been brought to Hörthanc as planned, where he was left to rule. Only it was not himself in charge, he said, weeping, but the true owner of the collar.

Falwaïn was looking down at the man with distaste, unsure whether to trust anything he said.

Malwé approached them and positioned himself so that he faced the prisoner square on, his whole body oozing contempt for the man. "If you are telling the truth, then you will know what you said to me when I was nine and came to you for help against those who were beating me every day and every night."

Crying desperately, Gullrick shouted, "Nothing! I said nothing! To my shame, I said nothing!"

The young prince slapped him and Falwaïn shoved the man back into the chair behind him, looking from Gullrick to his son in bewilderment.

Malwé, his face twisted into rage, snarled, "Nice try, demon, but you are wrong, for Thyton Gullrick had much to say to me that night, and all of it was about my father and how he had always secretly loved him!" He turned on Falwaïn and added, "Your tactics have gotten us nowhere near the truth, so perhaps now we employ mine! Tather, have your guards take the prisoner out of his shackles so I can beat him!"

Donnie, taking in Malwé's words now and from before, together with Akanna's confession of his treatment in Anûmanétus, finally understood several things all at once, and every bit of it was heartbreaking. She moved to stand behind the prisoner and put her hands on either side of his head and concentrated hard with her magic, listening to the chaos within the man's mind. She knew no one would attempt to stop her from doing this because Falwaïn wouldn't let them. Faint at first, but then roaring into her ears, she heard the cry of the man deep inside and the name he was bawling out in agony.

"Bréagna!" she repeated it to Falwaïn, who looked back at her, startled. "She was the one who did this to him. He speaks her name in his mind, calling out to her to rescue him from us."

Falwaïn's arms, which he had spread to block the guards from getting to Gullrick before Donnie was done with him, fell to his sides and he stared at her in defeat. "No," he whispered, anguished, "she can't be back!"

"Well, she was at the time Gullrick came here to rule," Donnie pointed out. "Who knows where she is now, though."

"That could be anywhere," Falwaïn acknowledged with a sigh. "Does any of this help us with Dantheus?"

"Hold on a minute," Donnie replied, and she again placed her hands on the sides of the prisoner's head, just over his ears. She infused his mind with calming thoughts because he was beginning to resist her, doing so both physically and psychically.

Delving in deeper and deeper, Donnie found a memory of the supposed kidnapping, which did indeed occur somewhat as Gullrick had described. He left out, of course, that he had readily agreed to be the witch's servant and do her bidding if she helped him secure and hold on to the position of Lord Chancellor of Faen Eárna, a temporary post he was seeking to make permanent. A bargain was struck between them and, to his great surprise, the collar was emplaced around his neck and no amount of protesting, begging or praying had helped him in removing it.

Beyond this information gleaned from Donnie's quick foray into Gullrick's mind, there was one thing said that might help them now with Dantheus. To save them more confrontation, Donnie set a sleeping spell on the man and he immediately passed out.

"We need to give blood to the collar," Donnie informed the others, opening her eyes and looking straight at Malwé. "Bréagna said that only family blood would release its power, so I think it must be the blood of the afflicted one's family. For Dantheus, that would have to mean you, Prince Malwé."

"No, Donemere, that is not what it meant!" cried Sylvester as he wove his way through the feet of the many guards in the room and finally came into view. To those who could not understand him, his speech sounded like long, angry hissing and many of the guards stepped aside warily.

Donnie waited for him to get closer and, when he sat down a few feet away from her, asked, "Well, then, what is meant by family blood?"

He gazed up at her uncomfortably, started to say something, but then stopped. He tried again, failed again, but finally managed to explain breathlessly, "Quillirana just informed me that Bréagna is Catie's aunt."

Donnie was staggered by this news. She stared from the cat to Falwaïn, who was looking as stunned as she was, and then back again to Sylvester with dismay. "I-I'm related to Bréagna?" she croaked, her throat suddenly dry. "Holy hags of horror, if she's Catie's aunt, that means she's my aunt too or something close to that, doesn't it?" Involuntarily and without even realizing it, Donnie began stepping backward until she found herself in the corner of the room.

"Of course!" Falwaïn gasped, looking excited now. He reached his arm toward Donnie and cried, "The book! The new one being written of our adventures! It has a prologue that talks of some sisters, all of whom were Ér Ainíls of Írtha's magical lands long, long ago, if I remember my history correctly. It doesn't mention Bréagna, but it does Margawse. Apparently, she and the others listed were set to visit their sister Gwillagan on Fellowes Island, where the old Ferlonds were. And now I begin to understand!" He paced back and forth, lost deep in thought while everyone else watched him in silence. Abruptly, he turned to point at the collar. "And those jewels there, the ones in his collar, I think they're connected with the Five Jewels of Light."

"Weren't those just used to control dragons?" Donnie interjected, and several heads shook "no" at her.

"They can control anyone, *even* dragons, would be a more accurate description of their power and their purpose," Akanna explained, her voice matter of fact as usual. The vincan watched Donnie step forward and come to a halt directly behind Gullrick, her sharp eyes following Donnie's slow, dazed movements closely. "The only other ones who can control dragons," Akanna added, "are the giants and they need no magic to do so. It has long been believed that Abé, the god of creation whom all peoples in Medregai know and pray to, gave the giants to the *vírata* as a way to appease the dragons' need for belonging, for the giants offer a friendship that the dragons would otherwise never know."

"Oh, how nice," Donnie murmured, favorably struck by the vincan's sentimental phrasing. She turned to Sylvester and asked him, "And you think if I give this collar and its jewels my blood, I will be able to control its power?"

"Of that, I have no knowledge," the cat admitted cautiously, "nor am I counseling you to try."

"But you *must* attempt it," Malwé demanded, trading a steely gaze from her to the cat and then to his father. "After all, Dantheus was hurt because of you."

Falwaïn grunted at him unhappily, "Must you lay blame for that, most especially when there is none at all to assign?"

Before Malwé could respond, Donnie replied to the prince's directive. "Give me your knife, my lord," she said, "and I will comply with your request. My family's blood with your family's weapon—it's only fair, because I happen to agree with you that it's my fault Sir Dantheus was injured. And now it seems it was my kin who gave Gullrick the power to hurt anyone at all."

Malwé moved closer to place his knife in her outstretched hand and murmured under his breath, "He did not need that collar to hurt others, for he is quite capable of doing that without magical assistance."

Donnie put her other hand over his when he dropped the knife onto her palm, which made him look into her eyes. She held him with her gaze, stepping them both outside time so she could tell him that he might find a friend in Diego, someone in whom to confide because she suspected they had had similar upbringings. She brought them back before anyone could possibly have noticed anything amiss.

Malwé, his face white, turned on his heel and resumed his former place, although he stole a glance at the dark foreigner. Diego raised an enquiring eyebrow, then nodded and returned the boy's glance with a friendly, placid smile.

In the meanwhile, Falwaïn stepped up to Donnie and took the knife off her hand, urging her, "No, Donnie, not like this. I think we should discuss it first."

"Discuss what?" she replied in surprise.

He looked at her apprehensively, but continued in earnest, his brow furrowed with worry. "I mean it," he said. "Normally, I would never dream of telling you what to do magically speaking, but this one—no, I can't let you do anything like this without knowing the consequences. If those really are some part or even the whole of any of the Jewels of Light that feature so predominantly in the ancient lore of Irtha, then they could have almost any effect on you and that—that, my love, could spell disaster for us all."

Sylvester cleared his throat and seconded Falwaïn's passionate plea, "I agree with Lord Falwaïn on this matter, Donemere. We must take our time and think before doing, especially when it is something so rash as blood magic."

"But what if Dantheus doesn't have that kind of time before he dies?" she asked, and the others looked back at her miserably. She contemplated them silently for a moment, then queried in a firm voice, "What can you tell me about these Jewels of Light? What do they do?"

Akanna was again the one who answered her, telling Donnie, "They control the minds of others using any one of five emotional…lures, shall we say? One of the jewels is said to target a person's successes and failures and their ability to have them. That includes those in the victim's past, present, and future, naturally. Another uses love and sex, in all their forms, to entice a person under its control. Still another targets wealth and power; with a fourth aiming its control directly at the safety and health of the victim's loved ones and of themselves. The final one…" she hesitated here, sending Donnie a bleak look that in itself spoke volumes, "that one taps into your deepest fears, which are all the things that keep you from sleep at night or make you old before your time because they are always perched on your shoulder, waiting for an opportunity to torment you yet again."

No one spoke for a moment, in a kind of collective acknowledgement that they all knew those kinds of fears too well.

"All right," Donnie said, running her hands over her face and then her hair tiredly. "So, that's how they get someone under their control, using those emotional lures. But how is that actually accomplished? Must the jewels be touching the victim, like this one here appears to be, or is it done some other way?" she asked, pointing at the collar around Gullrick's neck. "And then what? They must be able to provide the victims some magical power, given the damage Gullrick managed to do earlier. Is that typical of the jewel itself, or is that only because, in this case, it's being wielded by Bréagna and it's really her power that was used to attack Dantheus? Has anyone seen Gullrick show any sign of magical possession before now?" she asked, turning to the prince first, and then looking at Tather and his nearest guards.

Everyone shook their heads, some murmuring that they had never seen anything like what Gullrick had done today.

Malwé took his knife back from his father, turning away to sit on the edge of the throne, from where he watched Donnie without speaking.

"Do any of you know how to fight the jewels or their effects?" she asked, but no one could answer that question. "Well, then," she tried again, "besides controlling others, what else are the jewels known to be capable of doing? For instance, can they create or destroy, or track or display the whereabouts of their victims or their foes, that kind of thing? I mean, it seems to me that nothing much is known about them, but if we have one of them here, shouldn't we do all we can to learn more about it? Especially since it seems Bréagna is back and is determined to use them against us?"

Falwaïn allowed the truth of this, agreeing to it with a combined nod and shrug, and then he commented, "I think this just gives us even more reason to visit the Forrieghness Tower, where maybe we can find answers to your questions about the jewels. But doing anything here and now seems unwise to me," he added.

Donnie, giving this due consideration, mimicked his nod and shrug of a few moments before to show she agreed with him, however reluctantly. She left her position behind Gullrick and moved to stand beside her love, gazing up at him with admiration, for, if she were honest with herself, he was right to keep her from acting so recklessly.

The tension in the room seemed to have dissipated almost totally at this apparent détente and no one paid much attention when the prince rose from the throne and went to stand in front of Gullrick. Nor did they notice that, with a quick, sure movement of his hand, his knife slashed the entirety of Gullrick's throat, from side to side.

The sleeping man died without ever regaining consciousness.

Gullrick's murder might have gone undetected for another minute or two if not for the wave of green magic that shot outwardly from the dead man, causing everyone to look at him, and the clatter of Diego's knife as it fell to the floor when the force fields created by Donnie and Sylvester, being no longer necessary, dissipated to free the stiletto.

Someone exclaimed in surprise and then several people crowded closer to see what was happening. But by then the collar had disappeared. Only Malwé had seen it go and he said it happened the instant the main jewel was covered by Gullrick's blood. He told them this later, when he finally said anything at all, adding that the jewel absorbed the lord chancellor's blood and then the entire magical apparatus vanished from around the man's neck.

While Donnie hurriedly tried to heal Gullrick's wounds, even though she could see that he was already dead, Falwaïn hustled Malwé out of the room, shoving him against the wall and shaking the boy's shoulders once they were outside the reception chamber. He badgered his son to tell him why he had just committed murder, but the boy would not utter a word to him. Tather followed them out and began to threaten Falwaïn loudly if he didn't release the prince at once.

Donnie gave up on Gullrick pretty much immediately because the murdered man's wounds refused to do anything except gape at her, no matter what she tried with them. She accepted his death and backed away from him, then she asked Diego and Akanna to deal with the situation in the hall, which they managed without further bloodshed.

Then Diego, his stiletto returned to its sheath, took Malwé for a walk within the grounds of the keep. Malwé showed him the tunnels leading into the mountain on which the keep was built, and described to him its two egresses—one directly to the north and the other to the east, to the Cordis Downs and the first of the hills bearing the brotherly signes.

Later on, when he was alone with his fellow travelers, Diego quietly informed them that Gullrick had been one of Malwé's main abusers and, being emboldened by the witch's presence (meaning Donnie, of course), Malwé decided to finally rid himself of an enemy who had indeed used the collar's magic against the prince on numerous occasions. The boy had been too afraid to admit this earlier when Donnie had asked about it.

This news hit Falwaïn hard and he shrank within himself once more, refusing to converse with anyone for some time.

In the meanwhile, Donnie ran upstairs to see how Quillirana was faring with Sir Dantheus. The elderly nobleman lay pale and unmoving upon the bed, his breathing perhaps a little less ragged than it was before, but it was nothing near normal yet.

Donnie called Akanna and Falwaïn into the room and, along with Sylvester and Quillirana, the five of them continued Quillirana's chanting. Donnie stood at the foot of the bed, while Sylvester and Quillirana were at the head on either side, with Akanna and Falwaïn posted near Dantheus's knees. They chanted for an hour or so until Dantheus's condition showed marked improvement.

They stayed to chant for another half hour, at which point Quillirana chased the two warriors away and bade Sylvester and Donnie to join her for the final half hour. By then, Dantheus was breathing effortlessly and all three agreed that there was not even a wisp of the collar's magic left around his heart, so their work was done. But that did not mean their vigil was over, of course, and so they sat down and watched over the old man, with Quillirana soon breaking into humming and then outright singing a familiar melody. Donnie recognized the tune as the same one the minstrels of the previous night and earlier this day had sung.

It was again the reverent tale of Morrían's blessing for the six sons of Eárnas Ba, with specific verses, or blessings, for Ignis, Carûn, Migdenon, Freágorn, Bëdelbas, and Thûlemt, the youngest of the six. Her final blessing was for them all, though, and went:

> For love of mother and faith of son,
> There is no fitter work to be done,
>   For crowning king and gabled throne
> Shall forever be thy noble bone
>   Until sad tidings may upon ye break
> When all glad hearts surely wilt ache
>   And dark day brings a new house to rule
> For this the final and awful blow so cruel
>   But when the line is broken thus
> With all good sons in lying dust
>   The land shall fallow and turn to brown
> As children wither and fall to ground
>   Leaving mothers of few to cry
> And fathers of many to die
>   So shall the land mourn the passing
> Of the sons of Eárnas blood.

Quillirana, by this time, was waving her hands in a very specific and repetitive manner, her fingers working out their pattern in the air in front of her. To Donnie's great surprise, she realized that she could see a faint, but quite beautiful web of reddish gold being woven by the wise woman, which Quillirana set free upon completion of the verse. It faded away and Donnie watched it go with fascination. And then Quillirana began the lay again, and Donnie could see a new web being woven in the air.

"What is that song?" she interrupted Quillirana to ask, and the new web dissipated into nothing.

"Why, 'tis the blessing of the great Morrían for the sons of Eárnas Ba, of course," Quillirana replied, beaming an angelic smile upon Donnie and Sylvester. "It has served this province for centuries, protecting our lives and enriching the land. All people of Faen Eárna sing it whenever we become a bit bored or sad, because it reminds us of the greatness from which we all come." Quillirana again glowed at Donnie and Sylvester. "It makes all good people joyful to hear it and to sing it," she added, her eyes twinkling merrily. "Plus, it teaches us the names of the six sons!" She cackled at her joke and Sylvester chuckled along with her.

Donnie, a little anxious about where her thoughts were leading her, bit her lip before asking carefully of Quillirana, "How…accurate is this lay? I mean, how close is it to what Morrían actually said? Do you know?"

Quillirana, although taken aback by the odd query, answered it readily enough. "Well, 'tis reported to repeat every word from Morrían's blessing, or so that has always been my own idea, which I believe, is the same as most others'." She smiled confidently at Donnie and resumed her singing.

Donnie sighed, which was more of a low groan, and looked at her cat. She motioned for him to follow her out of the room, where they went to one of the other bedrooms. Donnie closed the door behind them and turned to the cat, who was sitting upon a small table beside the bed. "Did you listen to the words of the lay? The last verse, I mean," she inquired, and the cat at first nodded carelessly, then he gasped and nodded vigorously.

"It describes what is happening here in Faen Eárna!" he whispered, as distressed as Donnie by where this clue might possibly lead them.

"That's why the signes are becoming overgrown," Donnie said, her voice matching her expression of misery because she was way ahead of the cat. When Sylvester regarded her questioningly, she explained with obvious reluctance, "Because, according to the terms of the blessing, for the province's lands to fallow as they are now, the Eárnas Ba line has been broken, which means that Malwé can't be Falwaïn's son. At least, not by blood."

Donnie hung her head low. It was one thing to say those words to her familiar, but it was going to prove impossible to say them to Falwaïn.

It turned out that she was right about that; Falwaïn did not believe her when she told him her theory that evening after supper. He ranted and raved at her angrily for at least an hour, informing her coldly that she was insane to believe anything so idiotic.

She nodded.

In fact, she nodded to everything he shouted at her, every accusation he hurled, every hurt-filled protest he raised to contest her theory, her entire aspect slumped and saddened by concern throughout his tirade. She told him she didn't like where her deductions had taken her either, but there it was, what could she do? It was not she who had put the blessing on the land or on Falwaïn's family.

Eventually, he started talking to her more normally, even going so far as to concede that her hypothesis had some good points. The lay, which he of course knew as well as anyone from Faen Eárna, did indeed describe exactly the conditions Donnie described as occurring where Dantheus had led her that morning.

But for Malwé not to be his biological son? No, that was impossible. Sémere would never have lain with another willingly and she certainly would have informed him if it had been an unwilling coupling. They were so close, such good friends, and he had loved her mightily, thought her beautiful and proud and brave, and he could never believe anything else of her, he said, his voice rising in pitch once again.

This remark was heard by Sir Dantheus, who had awoken perhaps half an hour before Donnie made her unfortunate announcement to Falwaïn. The old man shuffled into the room Falwaïn had always used for his office, where Falwaïn and Donnie were now having their loud and quite angry (at least on Falwaïn's side) discussion. Dantheus came in without knocking or any such preamble as that, wanting to know why they were discussing his daughter thusly.

Falwaïn, as though wanting to throw Donnie's words back at her, said in an outraged tone, "Donnie believes that Malwé is another man's son!"

Donnie turned to Dantheus wearing much the same expression she'd been using on Falwaïn. And so, with yet another apologetic grimace, she explained, "It's because of that darned lay I keep hearing, the one with the blessing Morrían gave for the sons of Eárnas Ba. The last verse is just so close to what I saw today in the fields…" she said, her voice tailing away with regret.

Poor Dantheus looked even older than he had a few moments before, when he'd already looked like someone recovering from a long illness. He made his way to the nearest chair and sat in it heavily, heaving a great, long sigh before facing his former son-in-law. "Ye know," he murmured, his voice catching, "that she loved ye, yes, after a fashion. She respected ye and liked ye best, I can swear to that. But her heart belonged to the Sarn king, or at least a part of it always did after they spent that week together. Remember that? When she nursed him well again when he was injured, I mean. She tried, but she could ne'er get over him; he haunted her to her dying day, he did," the old man added softly, his worried eyes searching Falwaïn's recalcitrant ones.

"I have often wondered, because the boy looks so different from ye," Dantheus confessed sorrowfully, "tho' I can see a likeness to the king in most lights." He moved his shoulders in a helpless shrug. "I cannot say with assurance that he is yours or that he is the king's, but I will not pretend it is impossible that he be not yours. I know there was a day before the wedding when she and the king went off to discuss whether marrying ye was what she truly wanted. He always showed his concern for her, as ye know, because of the debt he felt he owed her for saving his life. But I never thought, nor did she, that he loved anyone other than his own wife, for he still speaks of that lady with a reverence fair and true. Always!"

The old man wiped his leaking eyes with a handkerchief that Donnie materialized and stuffed into his hand. He looked back up at Falwaïn and gulped, "If what we're fearing happened, then it had to have happened that day. And that was three days afore the wedding, if I recall rightly."

Falwaïn was still having none of it and he shouted this to all and sundry. Malwé was his and that's all there was to it. End of argument.

Which, of course, it wasn't.

After seething for a whole two minutes without saying a word to either Dantheus or Donnie, Falwaïn finally barked at her, "So, what if he isn't my son by blood? How would you fix things?"

Donnie wetted her lips with the tip of her tongue and replied soberly, "I would have to either lift the blessing entirely, or modify it, if possible. It helps that the lay purportedly provides the exact wording of Morrían's spell—er, blessing, I mean," she amended when Dantheus looked at her in alarm. "It's a blessing, not a spell, really," she reassured the old man and he looked sufficiently mollified with that because, apparently, a blessing was a thing of love and beauty, whereas a spell was clearly not to be countenanced for even a second.

Donnie frowned in thought, finally musing, "There's a bit in the verse regarding Thûlemt that describes the sons of his line. I can modify that, maybe, to include the sons of the heart, not just the blood." She nodded slowly, satisfied with this potential fix. "Yes, I think that should be good enough," she declared to Falwaïn, "because of how much you love Malwé. But the lay itself will have to be changed too because I have a feeling that every time someone recites it as it's known currently, that just reinforces the old blessing. Therefore, we need to make sure the corrected blessing gets reinforced instead, see? You can maybe tell everyone something like, um, that I happen to know the blessing from Morrían's papers back in the Ganlonds and was therefore able to tell you that there is a slight error in the one you are all reciting. You know, something along those lines. That might convince people to use the amended blessing after that."

The two men nodded at her, Falwaïn stiffly so.

"Or…you could have someone write a different lay to, er, well, I suppose it's to represent the peoples' feelings about their land, right? So, maybe something not used as a blessing might be better for everyone to sing all the time?" she suggested to Sir Dantheus, and he murmured that he would give the idea some thought.

Later that night, under the cover of darkness, Donnie and Sylvester used the hidden tunnel beneath the keep, which was right where Diego had described it to be, to get to the first of the signes. They were grateful that it was the only one whose blessing needed to be amended.

It took them five minutes to complete what they needed to do to the blessing, then another twenty-five to reinforce the change by repeating the new blessing numerous times, letting as much magic go with their spell as they could put into it.

By the end of the next day there was a noticeable difference in the land and in those made sick by it, so much so that reports started pouring in from all around about how the earth was finally soaking up water that had laid on top of it for so long, of how the brush around the signes had begun to fall back some, and of how the many afflicted children were looking brighter and better by the hour.

It was hard to say exactly what the people of Faen Eárna believed had occurred, whether it was Falwaïn's return, the presence of the new witch, or the death of the Lord Chancellor that effected the changes in the land. To be honest though, no one really wanted to look that deeply into it, with everyone being much relieved that the blight upon them seemed, at long last, to be lifting. There was much joy and laughter in the streets after that, and Falwaïn hugged Donnie to him, not caring himself what had caused the turnaround in the lands and peoples of his beloved province; he was just happy to see it all begin to prosper once more.

They remained in Hörthanc for another five days to make sure that all fortunes really had been turned, with Donnie and Falwaïn visiting several of Falwaïn's favorite old haunts. Sylvester even accompanied them a few times of his own free will on these excursions. Donnie grew to love the beautiful vistas from the top of the keep almost as much as Falwaïn did. It afforded stunning views of the farmlands to the west and the south, and because the skies in the area were so remarkable in color and form, Donnie became absolutely enchanted with them. Fluffy clouds scudded across the skyscape and continually inspired all three of them with pareidolia, where faces and figures of all sorts of creatures abounded to amuse and amaze them as the white and grey canvases floated eastward.

While visiting the North Castle, Donnie also marveled at the fabulous views framed by its windows, most of which opened onto the rolling chalk hills of Cordis Downs. Here, the green grasses covered the white limestone beneath, but with recognizable patterns woven here and there that Falwaïn said had long ago been cut by the children of the province as paths on which to run and play. From the farthest east tower of the North Castle, one could clearly see the five-pointed star that was the signe of Thûlemt.

Diego and Malwé spent these same days together talking. The boy found in the Black Rider the trusted confidante he had been wanting for years. While it was a bitter pill for Falwaïn to swallow, knowing that his son did not wish to spend time with himself, he came to be glad in his heart that the boy felt a connection with Diego. And he declared openly that the boy could have no better mentor than the dark foreigner who had become a close friend to both father and son.

Akanna alone sat hunched in a chair in the keep's reception chamber, her feet and fingers tapping a constant and impatient tattoo. She was saved from herself by Sir Dantheus, who soon came to her and asked if she would train some of their younger recruits in the use of standard weaponry. She entered into this endeavor with decided gusto and was long remembered thereafter for her fighting prowess and willingness to teach the youngsters to defend themselves.

The evenings they all spent together as a family, at Donnie's insistence. She stressed how important it was for them to know each other and for Malwé to learn to like and trust her and Falwaïn. She also worked to make sure that Sir Dantheus, who spent most of his time with affairs of state so that Malwé could cement his friendship with Diego without fear of reprisal or consequence to the province and its peoples, came to understand that not all magical creatures were bent on harming anyone not magical. She felt that the dinners succeeded where nothing else could have and, when the day arrived for her and her friends to continue their journey, this news was met with real sadness. Malwé even asked not if, but when they would return so that he could make sure to have a feast set for them.

Diego announced that he would stay a day or two extra just to make sure that the good turn that had occurred to the province was not, for whatever reason, reversed once Donnie and Falwaïn were absent from it.

And so it was that Donnie, Falwaïn, and Akanna set out together to the northwest to catch the Eldaren Road, with Sylvester sitting comfortably on the saddle in front of Donnie, as usual. Once they were traveling on the ancient road, they took their time so they could enjoy the beautiful sights and sounds of the Beldawuda, which lay on the north side of the Eldaren Road. Many of the forest's trees had grown as tall as two hundred feet and had trunks more than twenty feet in diameter, reminding Donnie of the giant redwoods of California and making her a little homesick.

Even Akanna did not chafe at this new delay, for she too enjoyed the presence of the large trees around them and felt connected to the sense that much wisdom was contained within the forest and its woodland denizens.

Four days later, when they had nearly reached Anûmanétus, Diego rejoined them and told them that all was well, or had been the day before, in Hörthanc, and that he'd left quite early the morning before this one and had ridden hard all the way so he could catch up with his friends.

They decided to stop a while to give Ampago a chance to rest his legs and lungs, and they therefore camped to the west, where the Lengaheld

River met the confluence of the two tributaries to the Donbragh'arík. They found a secluded spot downriver to stay until the following dawn, when they resumed their sojourn to Anûmanétus.

Later that morning, they began the descent of the Eldaren Road as it approached the kingdom's capital city from the south. The White Tower Mountains stood to the west of the city and, living up to their name, towered above everything. They dominated the landscape and had been visible from the road for most of the last two days of the travelers' journey.

It took a little while, but Donnie finally came to realize that they were dropping down into a very large basin that lay below the White Tower Mountains. The roadside was heavily wooded, blocking the view of the city until the road curved to the east a little and dropped down even farther. Here, the forest stopped, and the ancient city of the gods and royalty of Medregai was revealed.

Donnie, Sylvester and Diego and their horses were leading the way and for those of the party who had never seen the city before, it was an amazing and wondrous sight to behold…as for the others, meaning Akanna and Falwaïn and their horses, it was much less so, and they all had to steel themselves to make the trek down to the capital's gates.

When the others let out loud gasps of admiration, Falwaïn called, "The city is made up of sinter spires, as you can see. It is the only city thusly composed in all of Írtha, or so its legend goes."

"We call them tufa, where I come from," Donnie replied, turning her head to make sure she was heard by everyone, "but these are of a size and arrangement I've never seen before." She turned in her saddle to Falwaïn to explain further, "There is this lake in California where the tufa towers are exposed like the ones here, but those are miniscule compared to these!"

She breathed in and out excitedly, her eyes sparkling when she looked at the distant city. "This whole basin," she said, gesturing widely at the landscape set before them, "must have once contained a humongous and really hot lake for those spires to have formed like that! What happened then, after it dried up, I wonder? I mean, when these tufa towers were discovered, were they carved out," she asked, looking back at Falwaïn and Akanna, "and turned into habitable towers and homes? If so, that is just incredible! What a tremendous feat to accomplish!" she added, breathing in wonderment again.

The city was utterly remarkable in every way, with thousands of tufa towers, or rather, sinter spires grouped in a sprawling arrangement that spread the city for miles to the north and east, with the mountains forming the western border of the great metropolis. Some of the tufa towers reached close to easily two hundred feet high, with most topping off at about half that. All around these giants were several smaller formations, which had also been turned into public venues and private homes and tunnels and streets and bridges and plazas and everything that constitutes a grand city.

Donnie, Diego, Sylvester, and even young Wiwila were enthralled by Anûmanétus, and each had their mouths open and their eyes glued to the magnificent city they were approaching. They were completely ignorant of how their traveling companions behind them felt.

Falwaïn and Akanna turned to each other at the first sight of the city and shared a grimace.

"I hate this place," Falwaïn shared in a low voice.

"As do I," agreed Akanna wholeheartedly. She motioned at the ones in front and added, "as will they by the time we leave. I give her a week," she added, nodding her head at Donnie's back before turning her gaze to Diego. "And him a day. The cat will not like it immediately."

Falwaïn chuckled to himself. "I think you might be right about Diego and Sylvester, but not Donnie. No, she'll hate it before two days, or three at most, have passed." He grinned widely at Donnie's back, sending her a grin filled with adoration and fond good humor, explaining to Akanna, "She loves her comforts, my honey woman does."

Akanna nodded in comprehension. "Of course she does. I did know that, given the state of her cottage." She too chuckled to herself, but not with anything like good humor. She darted her eyes back to Falwaïn and prognosticated in a grave voice, "Well then, she is *really* going to hate Anûmanétus, isn't she?"

Chapter 18
Diamonds Are a Girl's Best Friend

The three warring factions at Marn Dím were at a standstill, with each positioned in a location they felt was most advantageous to their cause. The Mountain Peoples and their surprising allies, the okûn of the Brumal Mountains, were holed up deep within the farthest north and the uppermost reaches of the city, nestled back into the mountain itself into various keeps and caves. The army from Lænemeade, made up mostly of elves and their young *vírat*, were entrenched in the lower reaches of Marn Dím, just inside the main wall, but outside the second inner one, which had held them back thus far, even though they had that dragon in their command. The king's forces, all those who had left the Ganlonds after the Battle of the Branmar Plain, were encamped outside the walls of the city, with almost all of them taking refuge in the nearby mountain caves and forests in order to hide from the dragon, which was regularly out on patrol throughout the day and night.

Diana, Warren, Rex, and the others were staying in a large cave Feirth knew about that was situated above the city and where there were some ready provisions stored—more than enough for their purposes anyway.

All parties had been in these same places for several days, with the fighting that occurred before today being heavy and vicious, with many casualties on all sides, as witnessed by Diana and her friends. Even the dragon had been wounded. It turned out that the Mountain Peoples, or more likely the okûn, had been to the dragon rookery in the Withering Hills and were the actual thieves of the missing pallets of weaponry that Donnie had feared Valledai had taken, but not used. There were guns of various sorts and sizes being employed now, and it was these that finally downed the dragon, clipping it multiple times in both wings until the beast could no longer take flight.

It was two days before the dragon rose into the air again, and when it did, it made as though to attack any and all it could see, although Feirth noticed that it did not actually kill anyone. He told the others that meant the dragon wasn't really under the elves' control and it wasn't yet killing on its own, so he felt confident that, if he could get within earshot of the thing, he could convince it to abandon the elves and come back to the Ganlonds with him.

The question was, though, how was he ever to get within earshot of the young dragon?

Whenever he saw it rise into the air, Feirth would stand at the mouth of the cave shouting at it and waving his big arms, hoping to arouse the beast's attention. Thus far, he had no luck with that approach at all.

The cave they were in overlooked the entire city, so they could see down into the Mountain Peoples' outer battlements. Of the elves, they could see much more, although there was always the possibility that what they were seeing was just glimmer. As Diana knew well, the elves of Lænemeade were notorious for their glimmering abilities, pooling their magic to produce an image, or front, that was deliberately deceptive.

They could see the king's forces only when scouts were reporting in or were being sent outward to collect more information on, what was likely, just what the elvish forces were truly comprised.

Rex and the wolves had descended the mountain toward the city that morning, hoping to get some kind of contact with the dragon or at least locate where it was staying whenever it was not in the air. The two falcons had accompanied them. The bats were still hanging from the ceiling and were currently asleep.

Their group had really begun to chafe at their confinement earlier this morning, so Diana had sent out the most restless of their number on the reconnaissance mission.

Now, for what seemed the hundredth time, Feirth growled, "I tell ye, that little 'un is not being controlled by one of the Jewels, even though, if yer friends are right, Bréagna has returned and she has at least one of those cursed gems in her possession!"

He said this to Warren, who, as usual, had his attention focused on the current book of their adventures. He had read them aloud to the others, so they were all aware of the events that had occurred in Faen Eárna and of their friends' progress to Anûmanétus.

"Furthermore," the giant added to Warren's bent head, "if the filthy scoundrels in Lænemeade had this 'un's brother, that may be how they convinced this 'un to join in the attack on Marn Dím."

"You keep saying that," protested Diana with exasperation, "but you never tell us why the elves are here in the first place!" She began to pace around the large cave, a habit of hers these days.

She stopped and glared balefully at the giant. "And besides that," she huffed, continuing her ill-tempered snit, "we don't know for certain if this dragon here is who we think it may be, so you're just conjecturing about its motivation. Maybe it's with the elves because it wants to be—have you thought of that yet?"

Feirth ignored Diana's complaint and began to wax poetic about *virata*, lecturing them all on the instructions his mother had given him regarding how to soothe and calm a dragon. Since he had done this many times over the duration of their trip thus far, Warren and Diana both rolled their eyes at him and went to stand out at the mouth of the cave. They settled down onto some boulders and studied the vistas set before them.

The boombox joined them, turned itself on, and began playing an iconic version of "Diamonds are a Girl's Best Friend." They listened to it for a couple minutes before both essentially tuned it out because it was definitely not their kind of song.

"Feirth is hiding something," Warren remarked absentmindedly, stretching his long legs out in front of him and leaning back against the stone wall behind him. "I don't know what it is, exactly, but I think he may know why the elves are here."

"Of course he knows why they're here," replied Diana with a shrug. She considered possibilities and finally said, "They must have something the elves want."

"Yeah, like maybe another Jewel," Warren half-joked, nodding toward the boombox facetiously, which was still happily telling them all about the precious stones. But then Warren saw Diana's stunned face and hurriedly added, "No, that can't be it, can it?"

She turned to him and demanded incredulously, "Why not? It has to be something big, and there's not much else that's bigger in Medregai than finding one of the Jewels of Light!"

Feirth finally realized they had left him and he had just come around the big bush that hid the cave from direct view when he heard what they were discussing. He gulped and started to go back to the cave, but Warren and Diana both sprang to their feet and stopped him by standing in his way so that he had to turn back around or run them over. Protesting their high-handedness loudly, he finally sat upon an outcropping of rock and looked down at them glumly.

The boombox, apparently feeling it had fulfilled its duty, disappeared with a small beep.

"Are we right?" Diana asked crossly, looming in front of Feirth with her hands on her hips.

He gulped again and looked guilty.

"Hell's hags, how?" Diana asked, inching closer to the giant, a frown marring her chiseled features. "How did you know it was one of the Jewels of Light? And where was it found?"

Feirth sighed. He moved his shoulders in a helpless gesture, and then sighed again—a great, heavy one that he expelled with much force over several seconds.

"There was this mage, see, a wizard he is, though not a much talented one," he explained reluctantly, "name of Hadronica Perlusgo, and he went to the Forrieghness Tower, didn't he? Well, to be honest, he stole into it or so he swears to all and sundry. Says it weren't like he was invited there or anything such as that. And that's where he found a parchment that said the White Jewel could be found amongst the pearls of the *vírata*." The giant sent his two listeners a sorrowful grimace and said, "Well, for anyone from these parts, it don't take much to know what that meant. So, he came back and told the leaders of the Mountain Peoples that all they had to do was search the dragon rookery. They sent out a whole party of us, myself included, and me Ma, and we looked through every one of them eggshells until we found the Jewel."

"When was this?" asked Diana, her eyes widened in amazement.

"Not more'n six months ago now, I expect," Feirth replied. "Prob'ly a little less. We found it in one of the shells set back in the tunnel from the great hall, down in the warren. We picked it up in a cloth and carried it back to Marn Dím. We all hoped it would get us freed from the kingdom, but nobody knew how to use it, and..." here the giant hesitated a moment before admitting, "we were all afraid to try it out."

"I should hope so!" Diana snapped in a pointless reprimand. "Those things are very dangerous!"

"We know that!" allowed the giant, his head nodding vigorously.

Warren looked from one to the other and said, "That means Bréagna knows that it's here; but who would have told her?"

"Oh, she has her ways of finding things out, as I suspect you and I both know quite well!" Diana retorted pointedly, shuddering with remembrance of some of her own run-ins with that Madra witch from long ago.

Warren indicated his agreement with a nod and a shrug and turned to Feirth to ask, "Where is the Jewel now; do you know?"

Feirth nodded. "I doubt anyone's touched it, so it's likely still hidden in the cloth we used to carry it to the city in, and that's stored in a chest in the treasury." Anticipating Warren's next question, he added, "And the treasury is at the very back of the farthest chamber dug into the mountain. There's only one way in or out, and that's guarded by two of my friends, giants the both of them. It's as secure as it could be, so we don't have to worry about Bréagna getting to it."

Diana scoffed loudly at this and reeled away in disbelief. "If she's here and she thinks that Jewel is nearby, she will stop at nothing to get it." She slumped her shoulders and let out a wail of discontent. "Gadam's babbit! Not only do we need to rescue this damn dragon of yours, now we have to get our hands on that Jewel and take it back to Donnie too, because if Bréagna gets hold of two of the Jewels, she is going to be nearly as strong as Donnie. And that means we're all doomed then!" She whirled on her heel and stalked back into the cave, where she resumed her pacing.

Hours later, Rex and the wolves returned, preceded by the falcons, who had alighted on a niche in the wall and huddled together without saying a word to anyone as usual. With Rex came a party of a dozen soldiers, their rough clothing marking them as Mountain People. Leading their number was the mage, this Hadronica Perlusgo that Feirth had told them about. His face looked distinctly like a weasel's and, to complete the picture of a rotund rodent, he was even small and round in the body.

The soldiers with him had their weapons out and gave the impression they might start a fight at first, until they got a good look at Feirth, and then they greeted him as they would any long-lost friend, which he was, in fact, to a couple of them.

Before Feirth could give explanation of their presence, Diana jumped in and exclaimed, "It's good that you found us! We were just about to come in search of you, for we are come to your aid. We too want our freedom from the king's yoke and are prepared to stand with you and die if need be!" She said this while adopting her most fearsome warrior's stance, her tall frame dwarfing everyone except for Warren and Feirth.

The Mountain People could not believe their luck at this news, and together they gathered as much of the food and other provisions stored in the cave as they could carry and carted it down the mountain. They took a winding path to descend hundreds of feet, and then they came upon an entrance to another cave, which had a tunnel at the back that ran all the way down to the city level of the mountain fortress.

Leaving the provisions with the rest of his group, Hadronica Perlusgo led Diana and her traveling companions to the chamber where the City Council was in session. Hadronica had a high-pitched, whiny voice that grated on Diana's nerves and she was relieved when he handed them over to the self-proclaimed leader of the council, the handsomely rugged and very blond Calgar Bane. Calgar, as Diana soon realized, was a bit of a loose cannon who wanted to kill everyone in sight; most especially, Diana and her friends.

But Ulma Marg, the real de facto leader of the council, knew how to handle him, obviously, and had him calmed with just a few, quiet words spoken in a private aside.

She approached the newcomers, her faded blue eyes wary and grave, and asked Diana, "Why are ye here, ovid? What do ye want from us?"

Surprised, Diana blurted, "How did you know I'm an ovid?"

Ulma shook her shaggy grey head. "I have met a few of ye before. Ye all carry yerselves the same way." She gave Diana a tired smile. "I have answered yer question, now will ye answer mine?"

Instinctively, Diana knew she could not give the same glib response to Ulma as she had to Hadronica Perlusgo and his compatriots in the cave earlier. She squared her shoulders and replied, "We are here to steal that dragon away from the elves. It belongs on the Ganlonds, and that's where we aim to take it."

Ulma digested this silently, her head moving up and down in a slow nod. "Ye're not that new witch we been hearing about, though, are ye?" she observed, and Diana shook her head no.

"So, ye say ye want the *virat*. Is that all ye be after?" she inquired, peering up at Diana with distrust.

Diana spread her hands wide and asked innocently, "What else is here that we might want?"

Ulma's eyes snapped to a sharpness not apparent before. She looked over at Feirth, who wore a decidedly hangdog expression. "Ye told 'em, did ye not?" she barked at him and he winced.

"If you're talking about the Jewel, we guessed that, to be honest," interjected Warren, drawing Ulma's gaze to him. "Although, Feirth is not exactly good at hiding truths, as you seem to know."

A momentary smile flitted across Ulma's weathered face. "He never has been, no," she admitted. She turned back to Diana and asked with impatience, "Are ye wanting to take the Jewel with ye, as well as that *virat*?"

Deciding once again to be candid, Diana nodded slowly. "My friend, the new witch you were referring to, could maybe use it to do some good. She likes to do good. So much so, that's she's convinced all of us to do good ourselves from now on. You should meet her one day."

"Where is she now? Why ent she here wi' ye?" asked another of the council members, an old man who went by the name of Parkle Conrad.

"She's off saving the Mîrlonds. They're dying, you see," replied Warren. "But she'll figure out what's wrong with them and fix it. She does that, fixes things, I mean. And people too! Or rather, she does just enough to give you real choices on how to live your life a new and better way."

"And if ye disagree wi' her and her ways?" asked another council member, Derlen Kreg. He squinted at Warren disapprovingly.

"She lets you go your own way, no matter what," Warren answered without hesitation.

"Ye're Mynydd Uchaf, aren't ye?" asked Calgar Bane. "Ye're that wolf king that became a man."

Warren said nothing to this, but he held Calgar's gaze until the other man looked away nervously.

Ulma stared down at Rex throughout all this and finally said to him, "I dunna know who *ye* be, but I can feel the magic rollin' off ye. And the rest of ye, as well, though none of ye is quite like him," she added, looking around at the other animals in their group. "I always had a sensitivity to it, and that's why I know that we have no business having that vile gem in our midst."

Diana and her friends all started with surprise at this remark. Behind Ulma, most of the ten council members nodded their heads sagely. Besides Calgar Bane and Derlen Kreg, all seemed to agree with Ulma's bald statement.

"We dunna know how to use it, let alone how to stop using it if we was to start," Ulma explained ponderously, her jowls heavy with doubt. "And we dunna have anyone with anywhere near enough magical prowess to wield the thing. Hadronica Perlusgo would like to pretend he do have it, but he don't, and we all know that without question. Then too, the okûn feel like it should be handed over to them, but nobody trusts them any more than we do the elves, to be truthful and all. That is why we have sent what's left of 'em in our ranks to patrol our outer defenses, along with our own most experienced soldiers. But the cursed creatures fight amongst themselves as much or more than they do with the enemy and, since their king refuses to leave his stronghold in order to lead them, they ent doin' much good here. Most of 'em have gone back to either Moên Grím to be with their king or to Gjendeben to be with who knows who is runnin' the grand show there and they've left us to deal with the elves by ourselves." She sighed, and for the first time seemed to be letting her guard down. She even motioned toward a table and chairs and then ambled over to sit at the head of that table. She waited silently until all were seated with her. What she had to say then completely stunned Diana and her friends.

Ulma sighed again, her gaze sweeping the newcomers. "I swear, yer bein' here is a godsend, if it be anything at all," she assured them, adding, "and the sooner ye can take that evil thing away from here, the better off we'll all be. And I ent talkin' about that dragon, although it'll be a blessin' to have that dratted thing gone too!"

***

Liz had no idea they were so close to San Francisco until the *Drunken Knave* was already in the middle of the bay. She was alerted to this by, more than anything else, noises of other boats suddenly coming close, their whistles and horns blowing as they sailed nearer to the island of Alcatraz, and then Yerba Buena—sans Treasure Island, of course, which would not be built for nearly another twenty years. Liz marveled at this as the lone island passed by her window. Jesse had just gone down for a nap a few minutes before and, taking a quick look at him, she felt confident he would be fast asleep for at least an hour, so she thought she might be able to enjoy a little time outside if she was careful.

Fascinated by the youthful nakedness of the Bay Area she'd called home for decades of her life, Liz turned this way and that, staring around her with wonder. She made sure she stood in the shadows of the masts on the main deck as she drank in the amazing sights so that the crew of the dirigible above, if they were looking down at the ship at that time, would not easily make out her form.

Liz felt a thrill rush over her as she looked toward the sparsely populated Oakland hills and knew her mouth hung open, but she couldn't have cared less what anyone thought of her right now. There was no one from this time period alive in her world anymore, not in 2026, which meant that she was the only one of her contemporaries who had seen the Bay Area look like it did here. And that made her head swoon. She had to squint at several of the views because she kept expecting to see structures that weren't there yet— the most notable being the two bridges connecting San Francisco to Marin and to Oakland.

It was a bright, sunny day, a little warm for the end of June, but the water served to generate a cool breeze that ruffled Liz's hair. She turned as Catie came over to stand beside her.

"It seems that all five o' the boats we visited have followed us to here," Catie observed. She was again dressed in men's breeches, boots, and shirt and had stuffed a wide brimmed hat upon her blond hair. She and Liz had materialized the proper sort of clothing for themselves and Neddy Cloys and his crew, and everyone but Catie and Liz were already dressed to meet the officials they'd have to deal with once they made it to the Alameda shipyard.

Upon Liz's advice, they had decided to dock there, just in case there was not a slip available in San Francisco. This was because the PPIE or Pan-Pacific International Exposition was in full swing in the City, and everything there was priced at a premium, if it could even be had.

By the time the *Knave* was berthed two hours later, they had found out that it was going to cost them forty dollars a day for the slip. Liz, unsure whether that was a good price, nevertheless urged Neddy Cloys to accept the harbor master's terms and Catie seconded her. Neddy had no choice but to hand over the first forty. He swallowed hard and passed the money to the grinning master, then scowled with displeasure at Liz as if she were somehow at fault.

Nearly half the crew, with Smitty the talented boatswain among them, stated unequivocally that they had no desire to leave the ship, for they were not at all curious about seeing what the future would behold for their great-grandchildren, five or six generations on, some of whom they reckoned were sure to be alive in 1915. The rest crowded off the boat behind Liz and Catie and Neddy. Jesse was, as usual, swaddled to Liz's chest in the big shawl.

Mindful of the times they were living in presently, Liz made sure to walk behind Catie and Neddy, keeping her head down, for she had already received several severe stares directed at her from some of the dock workers when she'd inadvertently ordered a couple of the crew to move aside. One worker, an older man with skin just a little darker than her own, stared down his nose at her and muttered, "Come the day when one o' us be givin' orders to white folk! Why, I never!"

Catie had changed into a tan-colored skirt that came to just above her ankles and its matching jacket, with a pale-yellow hat perched jauntily upon her head and stylish ladies' boots upon her dainty feet. She looked cool and quite natty, and could easily pass for a woman of means, which was the plan. Beside her, Neddy was dapper in a blue-striped seer-sucker suit with straw boater. He had washed and shaved, and almost looked handsome.

Liz, passing as their faithful servant, was dressed in a plain brown skirt that went to the floor and a matching fitted jacket, complemented with a high-necked white shirt, along with a simple dark brown cloche on her head to cover her vibrantly red hair.

The crew behind them were all dressed in light woolen suits that each obviously found uncomfortable as the dickens to wear and every one of them kept running their fingers around their collars or scratching their legs or their arms, unaccustomed to the feel of wool against their skins. This would, of course, stop as soon as they left the dock area and were taken by skiff to the Alameda Mole, where railroads and ferries awaited thousands of passengers. No one questioned their destination. It was nearly eleven o'clock in the morning and the exposition had been open for hours. While the fair would not close for the day until midnight, there was still a sense of urgency in the crowds of passengers awaiting the next ferry to San Francisco.

The crew of the *Knave* were in awe of the trains, having never seen anything mechanical like this ever on land. It had been a revelation to them when Liz and Catie had converted the sailship to a steamship, and now the crew talked excitedly amongst themselves about the belching monsters rolling loudly along their tracks.

At first, Liz thought to rebuke their loud discussions of the rolling stock of the East Bay's Key System. But then she realized that they were by no means the only ones there who had never seen a train before and she had to remind herself that, in 1915, modern technology such as railroads, while being old hat to the many people living in the cities, had yet to reach the hinterlands of the country. And that was one of the purposes of a world's fair like the PPIE, to introduce new ideas and technology to the masses.

Almost an hour later, they disembarked at the Ferry Building at the foot of Market Street in a buzzing San Francisco. No longer worried about the crew looking like a bunch of rubes to anyone, Liz suggested to Neddy that they all go their separate ways and meet back at the Ferry Building to take the next-to-the-last ferry boat to Alameda, which would leave around one a.m. Anyone who didn't make it by then should meet up with the group again the next day at noon at the main entrance to the fair, which was at Scott Street.

With these arrangements made and understood by the ship's crew, they moved as a group to where the streetcars that would transport them to the fair were loading. In all, it took almost three hours just to get to the fair, which meant it was past two o'clock before they made it to the entrance.

They had decided to spend a few days going back and forth to the fair just to see what kind of response this would kindle in their pursuers. This turned out to be necessary because of the important piece of information that Catie had not given to Liz until two days ago. It came out when Catie slyly suggested they spend a week in San Francisco before using the clock-watch to send Liz home, just to maybe see some of the sights.

Liz, her internal radar aroused, had turned on Catie and asked flatly, "And why would we need to do that?"

Catie moued at her, wrinkling her nose and bugging her eyes humorously at Liz, before saying, "Well, I wouldna go so far as ta say we 'zactly need ta do that, but it mebbe would be helpful."

Liz, practically glaring red-hot daggers at the other witch, demanded again to know why.

After much hemming and hawing, Catie confessed that the dimension they were currently occupying was not the one in which Liz and Donnie had been raised nor was it the dimension that contained Medregai, and therefore...well, therefore, they needed the orrery to get to the correct dimension.

Liz, listening to this news without uttering a word back, felt the ire rising in her belly and had to turn away before she totally lost it and began yelling her head off at Catie. She had paced the cabin for probably five minutes until she felt the anger ebbing away and thought she could safely face the other witch again. When she did so, she said, "So, all this time we've been running away from the bad guys, now we want them to find us, is that what you're saying? Once we get to San Francisco, of course."

Catie beamed at her. "I knew ye'd understand it quick like that! Ye be such a smart girl, ent ye?"

"What happens when they find us?" Liz asked, wondering if Catie had thought that far ahead yet.

Apparently, she had, for she responded with a jaunty, "Well, they're likely ta have their own witch or wizard or mebbe a sorcery fool wi' 'em, aren't they?"

"But that means we'll have to fight them for the orrery! With magic, I mean!" Liz spluttered.

Catie nodded, and a serene, knowing smile played on her lips. "See, ye really are quick, ent ye?"

Liz growled out loud and shot Catie a cutting look. "Don't push me too far, Catie! You know darned well that you should have told me this a lot sooner than now, instead of springing it on me at the last minute!" she'd complained with angry heat flushing her cheeks.

The little witch had backed away contritely at this point, spread her hands and bowed in wordless apology, and the two of them had gotten down to discussing logistics of what might happen if such a fight were to occur and how they could best pool their powers together. Liz was not looking forward to anything like what Catie posited, but she also knew that Donnie had been in a magic fight with Valley Guy and had bested him easily with her ingenuity. She reminded herself that she could do that too and nobody would have to be hurt, no matter what Catie might warn to the contrary.

And so now they were intent only on enjoying themselves at the fair, although Liz was on her guard regardless. She found herself looking at the faces of the people around her, searching for any sign of recognition either in herself or in them. Thus far, there had been no such happening, and she began to relax, allowing herself to look around her with barely suppressed excitement. She was about to attend the PPIE and that fact made her smile a little wider than it had perhaps ever been before. This was history in the making, and she could hardly wait to see how similar or different it all was to the events in her own dimension.

They got off the streetcar and suddenly found themselves queuing up to get through the turnstiles. Each of the crew had plenty of money with them in both coin and paper, so they were able to enter without making it obvious they were all together in a group. To make their performance of employer and servant work, Neddy Cloys paid for the tickets for Catie, Liz, and even little Jesse, who got in at a price of a penny. Liz had swaddled him to her so that he could see out instead of the usual position of turned toward his mother. He laughed and giggled at the sights, staring at people moving by him like they were players in a movie that was being filmed just for his enjoyment alone.

Liz was disconcerted when she realized that most people would look at Jesse's light-colored face, then at her darker face, then Neddy's pale one, and then pointedly back to Jesse as if to say wordlessly, "He doesn't look much like his father, does he?" She found herself offended by this obvious assumption of an employer taking liberties with his servant, but had to let it go because there was certainly nothing she was going to say that would change these people's minds.

And for the first time in a long, long time, Liz found herself feeling frustrated by the fact that she was considered inferior, as though she were somehow lacking because of the color of her skin. And she hated that Jesse was being treated that same way. Her back became straighter and her chin set more squarely, and she found herself not able to enjoy the fair. Even the glistening, soaring Tower of Jewels and the majestic Fountain of Energy held absolutely no delight for her, and the Court of the Universe was little more than a tired battleground of jostling idiots for her to navigate.

Surprisingly, it was Neddy Cloys who first noticed Liz's discontent. He nudged Catie and pointed at Liz, shooting Catie a questioning look. Catie watched Liz out of the corner of her eyes for a few minutes, realized what was happening, and then sidled up next to Liz and Jesse to say, "Shall we flatten the lot of 'em? I know a good spell that'll do jest that, if ye'd like."

Liz, taken by surprise, almost cried in her laughter. "No," she replied shakily, still halfway between laughing and crying, "no, I don't suppose that'd be very nice of us; would it?"

Catie shrugged in a lazy kind of way and said, "Nice ent got nuthin' ta do wi' what's in these people's minds, do it? They dunna know no better mebbe, but still, it's an ugly side o' humanity that I sorely do not miss whenever I can get away from it and spend some time with Tanny at the cottage or Neddy on the open water—both o' which make me 'appier than a witch oughter be, if ye catch me drift!" She cackled a little and smiled kindly at Liz and then gave Jesse a dazzling grin, which he returned ecstatically.

After that, Liz felt much better and she again reminded herself that she was witnessing history in the making. So, instead of paying attention only to what people were doing immediately around her or how they were reacting to herself and Jesse, she looked beyond them to the larger population at the fair, watching those people's enjoyment and excitement, studying how they reacted to all the different stimuli available.

And, good heavens, was there ever a *lot* of stimuli available for the ears, eyes, hands, and tongue! For instance, the Zone, or Joy Zone as it was alternately called, was filled with a huge variety of concessions and amusements, and was, in and of itself, a wonder to behold. There, one could taste all sorts of exotic fruits and vegetables and other foods from faraway lands and from the U.S. itself, delicious palate teasers like coffee and grape juice and chocolates. The Zone also hosted live exhibits with people and animals from countries all over the world. There was alligator wrestling, bull riding, and even a Wild West shootout for the public's entertainment.

Liz and the others made their way to the Joy Zone around six o'clock because their stomachs were beginning to protest the lack of food and they thought that might be the easiest place to find it. At the Zone, they found all manner of new-fangled foods available, ranging from peanut butter to hot dogs to popcorn and way beyond, with ethnic foods abounding because of all the different countries participating in the fair. Liz ate an enchilada that tasted different from any she'd ever had before, although she could not pinpoint why until she found out they'd used ostrich meat in it, and she had a peanut butter concoction on a stick that one vendor touted as being better than ice cream. He was right, it was better than ice cream, and was so sweet and smooth, like nothing she'd ever tasted in her own time. She even put a fingertip of the creamy confection into Jesse's mouth and he just about swooned with delight.

They stayed at the fair throughout the evening and enjoyed walking around a couple of the halls, with Liz nearly choking when she saw the exhibit with luminous radium crystals on display. She hustled them all away and carefully explained to them why they should never go anywhere near that exhibit again because of the radium and the very bad things it would do to them if they touched it, as everyone was being encouraged to do at the exhibit. She would have told even more people this, but Catie forbade her to, admonishing her severely about interfering in life's natural course of events. But, since their trip here was not by any means a natural event, it was okay for her to stop them from irradiating themselves, she said and then turned away to walk on, effectively ending the argument before it could even really get going.

They wandered around some more and got to see a Ford automobile being assembled by hand in the Palace of Transportation, with Henry Ford himself hawking its virtues. And, of course, Liz made Catie and Neddy try out the hugely oversized 14-ton Underwood typewriter, all of them laughing uproariously at its great bulk as they sat down upon its keys. They even convinced Neddy to get into the Aeroscope, a double-decked cabin that lifted its passengers two hundred and fifty feet above the ground with a huge steel arm, swinging the cabin around in a great circle over the Zone. He decided at the first lift-off of the cabin that the sea was where he truly belonged and the birds could have the air to themselves forevermore as far as he was concerned.

Eventually, they made their way to the Marina Green so they could watch Art Smith take off in his hand-built biplane. They, like everyone around them, marveled as the flying machine rose to the heavens and let off a long series of fireworks that rivaled any Liz had ever watched back in her own world. By the time they decided to leave the fair, it was nearly midnight, and they made it to the Ferry Building just in time to catch the boat that would return them to the *Drunken Knave*. All but two of the crew managed to make it back that night, but they rejoined the group the next day, this time making sure they were around when the others decamped back to Alameda at midnight. Each successive day, more of the crew went with them, until there was finally only Smitty left on board all day, and he only stayed there so he could be near the rum.

It was on their fifth day at the fair that they saw the Germans. For the first time, Liz was thankful for her guise as a negro servant to Catie and Neddy Cloys, for Professor Gottleib-Lange was searching the faces of everyone present who passed through his range of view, but he did not think to look at anyone of color. Surreptitiously, Liz pointed him out to Catie and Neddy, along with his two German comrades and a group of seven others, most of whom seemed to be American, judging by their accents. Liz made sure to stay near them for a while, hoping to glean some information that might help in discovering where the orrery was located, but all she actually overheard was that they were staying at the historic Palace Hotel on Market Street.

They hotfooted it to the hotel immediately, wondering if it would be possible for their luck to be so good that the orrery could be hidden somewhere in the hotel rooms right now. Catie had to do a small spell of remembrance and then another of forgetfulness on one of the bellhops, who went to the front desk and found out the names of the Americans, all seven of them, and the names of the Professor's countrymen. This bellhop, chosen because he could read and write, produced a list of names and room numbers, was given his two bits' tip, and then was made to promptly forget everything other than that he had helped a nice lady with a dog and that's how he'd earned the tip.

Neddy Cloys stayed in the hallway while Catie and Liz searched each of the rooms. Catie was faster than Liz and got through four rooms to Liz's two, although, in her defense, Liz took the larger suites, while Catie had two small suites and two single rooms, one of which was occupied by the professor, with the other being booked by one of the Americans. In addition, Liz took the opportunity to feed little Jesse from her breast.

Neither woman found anything of interest in the rooms, other than some plans the professor had for modifications to the dirigible design, but Catie had not understood them so she had not taken the time to study them. Liz, deciding the plans might come in handy, went into his room, found the papers and scrutinized them carefully. From them, she determined that the professor seemed to be having second thoughts about using hydrogen gas and was starting to investigate other possible fuels.

Liz figured that he must end up rejecting this new research considering that, by the time the famous Hindenburg disaster were to occur in about twenty years, hydrogen was still being used as the fuel source for German dirigibles.

While none of that particularly interested Liz, she did find something that Catie had missed. It was a telegram stating that the *Reisender* had landed in a clearing at the Presidio and would be there for only two more days before they would be forced to leave by the U.S. government. It was signed by a Cpt. K. Haufenstahl, whom Liz took to be the captain of the dirigible. Made curious, she decided she wanted to see how well-guarded the airship might be, because that was certainly where the orrery must be.

She was just pulling the door to the professor's room closed when she heard voices approaching. Turning, she noticed that Catie and Neddy were down the hall a bit, so she hurried to catch up with them, making sure to slide into her place behind them smoothly before the people owning the voices appeared.

Liz was stunned as they rounded the corner, for here was the son and youngest daughter of Ester Chagall, whom she recognized from the photos she'd seen on Ester's highboy dresser the night she, Catie, and Jesse had set up the decoys. With them were two of the Americans, both tall young men in their early to mid-thirties. One was exceedingly handsome, while the other was buff and quite rugged, and both looked like they spent a fair amount of time outdoors. Judging from their finely made, bespoke suits, whatever they did for work certainly paid well—if they even worked, that is. She had to remind herself that they were in the Palace, after all, where young sons of the day's tycoons would be more than likely to stay while in San Francisco.

As they passed this group, who were discussing their dinner plans for that evening, Liz realized that she recognized one of the voices as being the main one the Germans had been complaining to on the ship. His laugh was unmistakable because of its roguish qualities, and she saw now that it belonged to the handsome one of the two. Liz turned to stare after him once they'd passed by her and the others. There was something about him that piqued her interest, although she could not say what it was other than perhaps how good-looking he was, with his curly blond hair falling off to the side and onto his high forehead. The young Mademoiselle Chagall apparently thought so too because she was fawning over him, as was the young monsieur, but he in an eager, star-struck kind of way, and not in the same coquettish manner of his sister. Liz wondered just who the handsome man was exactly.

Then, to her consternation, the rugged-looking one suddenly turned to look back at her, his penetrating gaze meeting her surprised one with cool reserve. She gasped, blushed profusely and hurriedly turned around, stumbling a little in her haste to catch back up with Catie and Neddy, who were several feet in front of her by now. She decided she needed to study that list of names from the bellhop, see if any of them might jog something in her memory.

They turned the corner at the end of the hall and found themselves at the top of the main staircase. No one was looking at them so Catie twisted around and said to Liz in a worried voice, "Thems two are who we have ta be mighty careful o' crossin'."

Liz's eyes widened. "Why?" she asked.

Catie looked back at her with asperity and exasperation. "Did ye not feel the power jest about pourin' offen those two? The Americans, I mean, not the silly chit of a girl and her useless brother. Those two could be twins," she noted dryly.

"Are you sure?" Liz asked, adding, "About the Americans I mean."

"O' course, I'm sure," Catie responded huffily. "I'm a Madra witch and when I tell ye we've jest walked by a couple o' powerful sorcerers, ye can rely on me being right! One day," she added, poking Liz on the shoulder, "ye might even know what it means ta be Madra yerself, and when that day comes, ye'll not ask a silly question like that one ever agin!"

"Okay, I'm sorry, I'm sorry!" said Liz, spreading her hands up high to protest. "I believe you!" She turned around and looked behind her, then down the stairs again, still seeing no one in their vicinity. She brought her attention back to Catie and asked worriedly, "Do you think they were able to feel our magic? Oh, hell's hags of perdition," she suddenly swore, hitting herself on the forehead with the palm of her hand, "of course they did! That's why the one looked back at us!"

"And how would ye know he did that?" Catie asked, an imposing scowl forming upon her face.

"Well," Liz admitted sheepishly, "I was looking back at them because I felt there was something odd about the handsome one, when the other one turned and stared back at me, cool as a cucumber, as if to tell me to go to the devil for all he cared!"

Catie was shaking her head and grousing under her breath. She shot Liz a look to kill and observed with a snap in her voice, "Ye really are no good at this stuff, are ye?" She turned away to float down the stairs in disgust, Neddy Cloys following close behind her.

They decided to take afternoon tea in the hotel's Garden Court restaurant so they could discuss their plans for the rest of the day. They were seated as requested, although the maître d' looked unhappy about Liz and Jesse joining them. He seemed relieved when they asked to be given one of the tables at the very edge of the room, back where it was somewhat secluded and anyone standing in the entryway would be hard-pressed to see them.

They placed their order as soon as they were seated and, when they were alone again, Liz asked to see the list the bellhop had made for them. Catie handed it over and Liz, for the first time, perused its contents. She got through most of the names before she recognized one of them and then she gasped aloud, "Oh, heavens, I should've known it! The handsome one upstairs is Herbert Flint. No wonder the poor Chagall boy and girl were falling all over themselves to get his attention!"

She explained who she meant by that and how she knew who the youngsters were, then added, "Bertie Flint is one of the pioneers in movie producing and directing right now, and..." she paused for effect, "he knows the owner of our third decoy, the one that Jesse set. It belongs to the little girl, Maeve Rae Danaher, soon to be known around the world as just Little Maeve Rae. She's already worked on a couple of short movies for Flint and she's supposed to do four feature length films with him before they part ways for good. He and Maeve's mother were having a fling for a while, but it must have cooled by now because he sure didn't pay much for them to get here, only giving them the cheapest berth you can get." Liz shook her head in amazement, murmuring, "What are the odds of all that being so tied together, I wonder?"

Catie snorted at this and announced, "Magic is full o' coincidences like that, only they aren't coincidental, if ye gets what I mean. No, the force behind magic, and no one knows who or what that is, did this on purpose," the little blonde witch informed her sagely, nodding her head. "And ye need ta be mindful that this is not yer dimension, Miss Priss, so ennything can change here and ye wouldna know if it were meant ta be or if ye somehow changed events when ye shouldna. And that means we all need ta be on our best behaviors while we're here! Don't be tryin' ta make things better fer someone or enny such silliness as that." She shot Liz a dirty look again and Liz, blinking back at her guiltily, wondered if she could read minds like Donnie could because she had, in fact, been wondering if she could somehow help Little Maeve Rae avert the sad destiny that fate had in store for her.

Wanting to avoid more confrontation on that or any score, Liz picked up the copy of the afternoon paper that had been left at their table and began to flip through its pages. She ignored the other two adults and made sure that little Jesse, who was asleep again, was not being disturbed when she turned a new page, leaning back so that the paper's corners stayed clear of his sweet little nose.

She had read the first half of the paper, most of which was about either the fair here in San Francisco or the war raging over in Europe, the Great War that would end all wars, when her attention was caught by a couple of articles that were positioned together. She re-read them twice and then folded up the paper into a small square with these articles displayed, sliding that over toward Catie.

"Aren't those the names of the ships you visited when we set the decoys?" she inquired, pointing to the two articles.

Catie, taking a moment to finish her latest *petit fours*, brushed the crumbs from her fingers and picked up the newspaper to read. Her face turned pale as she went on, until she was pasty white by the time she lowered the paper and said to Liz in deadened voice, "Yes, that be them. And the murdered men be the two I visited. I know, because that Petey McNair and I had a nice, wee chat. He thought I was his mother's ghost, ye see, and I let him believe I was." She shook her head and looked sad. "Ta die like that, wi' his insides all blown up. And the other one, this Callum Bligh fella, suddenly bein' decapitated by a runaway streetcar, of all things! And then their ships, both of 'em sunk and their crews lost for good in the deepest part of the bay, with no one able ta help them, it seems? Well, it dunna take much ta see the work o' a sorcerer in all that. And I'll bet ye it was one or both o' them two upstairs!"

Liz's nerves were jumpy and she picked at her napkin with restless fingers. Her shoulders even began rocking back and forth with worry. "Y'see what this means, don't you?" she hissed. "They've found the two decoys you set, Catie. There's no way they didn't find the one I set with the professor. And I'll bet they've already found the one I set with Madame Chagall, and that's how and why they know the Chagall kids. Thank heavens, they didn't kill them like they did your two, or sink their ships. But..." she paused, shining big, luminous eyes at the other two, "this means the only one they may not have found yet is little Maeve's. I somehow doubt they'll be as nice to her and her mother, or their ship, as they were to the very wealthy and well-known Chagalls."

Catie nodded in agreement and gulped audibly. Both women looked like they were ready to cry.

It was up to Neddy Cloys, or so he decided, to make them feel better, so it was he who declared to them both simply and stoutly, "Well, then, that jest means we 'ave ta find the wee child and her ma b'fore them bad men do and git that darned decoy away from 'em!" He looked pleased with himself a moment, then chewed his lip and added, "Er...anyone got enny idees 'ow ta do that?"

Liz and Catie agreed that the first thing that had to be done was to get the *Drunken Knave* and its crew to safety, which meant sending them back to their time this very night. The newspaper accounts they'd read had put quite a scare into the two witches and neither wanted to see their friends meet the same fate as the poor, hapless sailors from the sunken ships.

But that would mean the two women and little Jesse would need a place to stay from tonight on. They left the Garden Court and went to the hotel's front desk where, after paying a hefty premium, they were able to procure a suite of rooms that had just miraculously opened up. They had conjured suitable luggage on the spot and then visited the suite so they could see the rooms' layouts. This was so they would know just where to materialize themselves when the night's events were over.

They walked around the rooms importantly and Liz directed the bellhops where to put their luggage, while Catie pronounced the rooms as being more than suitable for their needs. The head bellhop who'd shown them up to the suite handed them the door key with a devil-may-care tip of his hat, especially after Liz pressed a two-bit tip into his eager hand.

Neddy Cloys spent the rest of that day getting the word to his crew that all were to make this night their final visit to the fair and everyone who intended to return home had best be back on the boat by two a.m., which was when the *Knave* would sail for open water.

He also collected the clock-watch from the crew member carrying it presently. Early on, they had worked out a system whereby every man was to have it with them for at least half an hour before passing it off to another crew member. This way it kept moving in a varied manner that would be more difficult to follow. These exchanges were managed surreptitiously each time since every sailor knows perfectly well how to palm any item given to them by another. But this was the first time Neddy had carried the artifact and he was nervous to have it in his charge until he got back to the ship and surrendered it to Catie.

While he was off doing all that, Catie, Liz, and Jesse returned to the *Knave*, and the two ladies spent the rest of the afternoon going over the stores of the boat with Smitty the boatswain, with Liz summoning to the ship's hold everything the crew would need to get them back to the Caribbean without the shortcut of the Panama Canal. This, of course, would mean the *Knave* must pass Cape Horn, which could only be possible during the summertime in the Southern Hemisphere, several months from now. And that meant there was need for more food and drink stores than usual. By the time Liz had finished with that and had helped Smitty to store it all and stack it to his specifications, it was nearly midnight, and most of the crew had returned.

Catie, in the meanwhile, had been busy devising a plan on how to best convert the sailship back into just that. She and Liz were both worried if whether, by removing the steel plates and machinery installed to turn the ship into a steamship, that would compromise the integrity of the ship's original hull. Since Catie was much more familiar with this structure than Liz was, they had divided their workload to reflect each witch's strengths. By midnight, Catie had not just created a plan for de-installing the steamship materials, she had also come up with a spell to repair the underlying wood of the hull once it was unencumbered with the steel plating. She was, if nothing else, very good at mechanical spells of this sort, she said, and she was confident that they could convert the ship in less than five minutes, working together to do so, of course, and that the *Drunken Knave* would be as seaworthy as ever she was by the time the witches were finished with her.

Time was of the essence, something they both knew instinctively. Surely, their enemies in the dirigible would be aware that one of the two possible clock-watches was on the move the moment the *Knave* sailed away from Alameda. And that meant that the sorcerers could soon know it as well via another telegram from the airship. While the Germans did not frighten the women really, the sorcerers certainly did.

Their plan was simplicity itself: they would sail to the middle of the San Francisco Bay in the deep of night, where Catie and Liz would climb aboard one of the *Knave's* small rowboats. From it, they would set the spell for converting the *Knave* back into a sailship, and then they would use the clock-watch to send them back to the year 1722. The women would row as far away from the sailship as needed while the conversion spell was doing its work to the ship, then they would use the clock-watch to return themselves to 1915. They would then wait a while, if they could, to restore some strength before materializing themselves into the suite at the Palace.

The first obstacle they faced came from Neddy Cloys. He was not about to leave the three of them stranded without himself to help them, he said, digging in his heels mulishly. He showed them the revolver he'd bought earlier that day and said he'd practiced with it while waiting for some of his crew to get done with their time at the fair, so he was a crack shot now. He stubbornly clung to the notion that they would need him and refused to budge on the matter. He and Catie argued about this until the very moment they set sail, with nothing resolved on either side.

The next bump in their plan involved four missing members of the crew. While everyone agreed that all had wanted to go home, these four had been some of the keenest to wring as much from their time at the fair as possible. It was debated whether to wait for them another hour, in case they'd made it to a later ferry, but it was Smitty who pointed out that all four were grown men and knew well the consequences of their actions. He recommended they get their plan in motion by uttering a pithy, "We should vamoose," before turning away to bark at the rest of the crew to ready for departure.

They had unloosed the mooring lines and were pulling away fairly quickly from the pier when a plaintive cry was sounded nearby. From behind a tall stack of crates came one of the four missing crewmen. He was badly bloodied and beaten and could barely walk, limping his way to the edge of the pier. He waved to the ship, looked behind himself with a quick glance, then, apparently surprising his attackers who were hiding behind the crates, he dove into the water and tried to swim to the *Drunken Knave*, even though he had a broken and useless right arm.

It was Smitty who threw a kisbee ring at the man and hauled him to the ship. With the help of a couple others, he was pulled aboard and laid on the deck. Straining upward, he gasped to Neddy, his eyes filling with tears, "They knows, Cap'n! They knows it all! They kilt Slew and Cobb and Parker and nearly did me, but they reckoned ye'd come back for one, so they kept me alive ta call out ta ye. They said they 'eard one o' us talkin' 'bout goin' back ta our own time tonight, and now they be a' waitin' for us in the bay!" He got all this out and then slumped to the deck, lifeless.

Catie stared up at Liz from where she'd been holding the dead man's head before he left this world on his own, and told her defiantly, "We ent changin' the plan now, so ye be on yer best guard from here on out, ye savvy me?" Her gaze fell to Jesse, who as usual was swaddled to Liz's front side. She leaned toward him and reached out a hand, pointing a finger. "Ye too, little 'un!" she declared. "We will, like as not, need yer special bits t'night as well, so be prepared, son!"

While Liz was sure Jesse could never possibly understand what had just been said to him, she did note that he cooed as though in agreement and squirmed excitely in his wraps, managing to get one arm free and wave it. She looked around at the scared but resolved faces of the crew and shivered with fear herself. For they would be facing two very crafty and ruthless sorcerers who had already murdered more than eighty sailors just to get their hands on two decoy clock-watches. They would be unlikely to show the *Knave* or its crew any kindnesses, and no one could rightly expect anything like mercy tonight.

It was up to providence to help them, it seemed to Liz, for they had no idea what it meant to have their enemies waiting for them in the bay. But, right now, none could believe it meant anything other than death for them all.

Chapter 19
Hole in My Heart

Warren sat back against the hard rock wall behind him. His gaze, as ever these days, lifted to the moon, its crescent shape lending sufficient light to the landscape below him so that he could, if he were to go to the nearest ledge, see down into the heart of Marn Dím. As it was, from here, where he sat on his favorite boulder out in front of the cave, he had a clear view of the rolling hills that covered the eastern expanse away from the city. There were trolls out there, he knew, trolls who would just as soon see your throat cut by their own hand as hanging by the neck from a tree by someone else's.

The trolls had attacked the king's men earlier this morning and the king's army looked to have lost at least a hundred soldiers in return for killing nearly twenty trolls. Not necessarily a good trade, he thought to himself, but the king's army refused to yield its position. That meant the elves remained in their camps just inside the walls of the city, while the Mountain People kept to their fortresses in the mountain, and the trolls maintained a hungry watch of everyone from the western hills.

Other than the deaths today, nothing had changed since he and his friends had arrived in the area. Well, he conceded to himself in his internal monologue, they had one Jewel of Light in their possession now. Diana kept it in a pack that she slung across her back. She never took it off and never gave anyone a glimpse of the Jewel except when she turned the pack to the front and looked in it each morning to assure herself the Jewel was still there. She said she felt nothing coming from it, so it appeared to want nothing from her.

Warren understood what she meant by that because he too had been around powerful crystals like the Jewels before and his experiences had taught him that, if they were going to affect you in any way at all, you could feel their pull on you almost from the moment you were in their range. If you felt no influence from them, then they would more than likely leave you alone.

He too felt nothing from this particular Jewel, nor had any of the others in their group, or so they said, but there were clearly some among the Mountain People who did harken to the Jewel's call. That was why Diana had secreted it out of its former hiding place, with Ulma Marg's blessing. The only one who suspected that Diana had it was Hadronica Perlusgo, which they had guessed because he kept visiting them in the cave, where they had insisted they would stay rather than down in the city. They had all, as a group, decided to leave the city and return to the cave three days ago, figuring that their retreat with the dragon, once they had managed to capture it, would be much easier from here than from the city.

But since that removal of themselves, the weaselly mage had visited in the mornings and evenings, and today had come three times. On each of these jaunts up the mountain and to their camp, he had sidled up next to Diana, his thin hands and beady eyes working busily at nothing. She had confronted him tonight and told him that if he came near her again, she'd take his head from his shoulders and throw it into the elves' camp. From that, everyone took her to mean that she thought the rat-like wizard was in their employ—which he might very well be, Warren supposed to himself thoughtfully. That would certainly account for the elves having known the Jewel's whereabouts in the first place.

He focused on the moon again, his thoughts turning to Liz and to the child he had yet to meet. Rex had taken the third book of their collective adventures from him when they'd returned to the cave and told him he would give it back only when it was finished or when he knew for sure that everyone was safe. Warren had wanted to argue, but there was a quality about Rex that was so like Donnie, he found himself acceding to the dog's demands without quibbling.

Since then, Rex had been helping him and Diana explore their magic. Diana, of course, didn't really need much help, just prompts to air out her powers, which the dog kept supplying at a regular pace. With Warren he was encouraging and informative, but with Diana he was wily and sly, throwing a stream of power at her at the most innocent of moments or having the elements swirl around her to match her moods. Which meant that whenever she was angry, dark thunder clouds appeared around her head, with miniature bolts of lightning striking the ground and whatever else haphazardly in her vicinity. If she were feeling bored or depressed, grey clouds heavy with rain would materialize over her head and proceed to soak her good and proper until she dissolved into giggles. And then the clouds would dissipate and around her would form a halo of light, which would make her laugh even harder.

Warren, a slight smile of warm remembrance of this kinship with his magical friends playing on his lips, concentrated on the latent Ca'nam powers he was finally getting to know through his lessons with Rex, and flicked up a small ball of light from his palm, its glacial blue color shining bright in the night. Into his mind came the memory of someone talking about these kinds of magical spheres, and how one could perhaps use them to see into the future, or into other worlds, at least, if one concentrated hard enough.

Not knowing why he felt the need to do just that right now, he gave into the idea and sent the small sphere into the air in front of him. He gazed at it steadily, eventually working himself into a meditative state where his only focus was Liz and Jesse.

**

As so often occurs in the San Francisco Bay area, a thick marine fog descended upon the entire region. Whenever that would happen, the Alameda harbor master would commission tugboats to lead ships on a continuous basis slowly through the bay's waters to a place well past Alcatraz. Once there, the captain of each pilot tug would shout, "Go on from 'ere by yerselves, laddies, due west!" and then they would turn their noses around, get into their return shipping lane, and head back toward Alameda, careful to call out to the tugs from the bay's other harbors as added identification, in addition to keeping their ships' radios tuned to the correct frequency for all ships moving about the bay. Without these tugs, nothing big would get either out onto the open ocean or into the bay's waters safely.

The entire crew of the *Drunken Knave* was tensed for action as they slid through the somewhat choppy waters of the bay behind their pilot tug, for a storm looked to be headed this way in just a few more hours. Liz and Catie were holding hands and standing near the small rowboat they would be using to separate themselves from the ship once they had made the return trip to 1722. They would have to get at least forty feet from the big ship so that they needed just one turn of the clock-watch to send them back here to 1915. The only change to their original plan was that, instead of having the women drop into the water here in 1915, they would now do that once they had gotten the *Knave* safely back to her time two centuries earlier.

They had to wait for the tugboat leading them to sail far enough away for the little boat to be well outside the distance affected by the six turns needed from the clock-watch to make sure all of the *Drunken Knave* was safely transported back to the past. Six turns were necessary because the *Knave* was a long ship—sleek, but long. They all knew this meant a wait of at least five minutes once they could no longer hear the tug, just to make sure there was sufficient separation between them and the smaller boat so that they did not inadvertently take the tug back with them to the past.

The sail past Alcatraz felt like it took a lifetime, although it was actually less than two hours before the tugboat's captain shouted his directive to them, and the little tug began to pull away, its lights obscured by dense fog almost immediately.

Everyone aboard the *Knave* waited silently. At about the time the two witches thought it might be safe to make the time jump, there came the noise of two high-pitched engines approaching fast, and before anyone understood what was happening, the *Drunken Knave* was rocked by something that resounded off her steel plating and bounced the great ship to the side.

The decks lurched starboard, and several of the crew lost their footing and would have been tossed into the sea if not for both Liz and Catie catching them with magic and pulling them back onto the ship. And then the *Knave* was struck again, this time from starboard, and she listed to her port side. And still the keening of the oncoming boats' engines rose above the sound of the waves.

Neddy, who was at the helm, made the choice to spin the wheel of the *Knave* to starboard, and she came about sharply to begin racing to the north, toward one of the attacking launches. Another hurled bolt of quite distinctive magic, a swirl of red, plum, and purple light edged and threaded with bright yellow, all colors somehow looking deep and angry and frightfully deadly, skittered off the side of the turned boat and hit something farther beyond. Considering that the second engine seemed to die out right then, Liz figured that meant providence was indeed on their side tonight and had just disabled one of the groups pursuing them.

She and Catie were doing all they could to keep their feet, for this last shearing shot from the one sorcerer still coming toward them was soon followed by two more. These shots hit the *Knave* more squarely and got her listing to port again.

Catie, with a wave of her magic, sent all the crew she could see around her flying through the door of Neddy's cabin to comparative safety. Liz realized what she was doing and began to help so that, within seconds, every member of the crew that had been on deck was huddled in that room except for Neddy and Smitty. A couple of the crew were not happy about this turn of events and tried to leave the cabin, but Smitty saw what was happening, understood what the witches were attempting to do, and made his way across the heaving ship to the cabin's door. Once there, instead of entering it himself, he closed it, took something from his pocket, and fastened what turned out to be a padlock to the door's handle. While it would not keep the crew in there forever, it would keep them safe for now.

While he was doing that, Liz and Catie turned to each other and decided they had to risk using the clock-watch now. Catie's fumbling and frozen fingers—for she and Liz were both soaked from head to toe by now and it was a chilly night—drew the artifact from her reticule and pushed it into Liz's hands. Catie lit a small light ball that hovered over the timepiece and Liz carefully placed her fingers on the numbers 1 and 2, while Catie was struggling to get the key out of the bottom enclosure to wind the clock.

Before Catie could do that, a brilliant red light hit the other side of the deck and with it came the sorcerer. Because of the bright flames burning around him, they could see that it was the rough looking man who'd been with Herbert Flint and the Chagall youngsters earlier in the afternoon. The two women gasped aloud and took a step backward together. Liz almost dropped the clock-watch, barely managing to hold onto it, her throat and chest filled with sudden and immense fear. Without really thinking about it, she stuffed the timepiece into Jesse's swaddling cloth until she was sure they were someplace they could use it without losing it into the sea.

Behind them, they heard the rowboat being pulled up and over the side of the *Drunken Knave* by a pulley, and they both turned when Smitty shouted at them, "Get in the boat naow! I'll drop ye down, then ye gals git away from 'ere and get ta safety. Only then should ye use that blasted thing ta get us all back ta our time! Ye 'ear me well, wimmen, do not use that thing until ye three are far enuff away from the *Knave*! And ye take good care o' that bairn this night, or ye'll 'ave me ta contend wi'!"

He barked this at them as he shoved the women into the boat and began to lower them to the water. While they descended, they got just a quick glimpse of a small figure running and tackling the sorcerer, sending both men careening to the deck.

Catie leapt to the near side of the rowboat and screamed, "No, Neddy, no! Don't ye dare get yerself killed, ye 'ear me?" but Smitty had already dropped them so far down the side of the boat that there was no way anyone but him could have heard her plea.

Their rowboat fell the last quarter of the way to water and landed hard, sending both women to their knees. They scrambled hurriedly to a sitting position and each took up oars after releasing the pulley lines to the ship. With a few deft strokes of Liz's oars, she turned their little dinghy so that it was moving at a right angle away from the foundering *Knave* and they began the hard haul to gain separation.

But Catie had her back to the *Knave* and was turning around so often that Liz finally yelled at her to pay attention because they were heading north themselves now, with Catie having altered their path without meaning to. They could hear the sorcerer's launch, the one still with a working engine, whining toward them from the other side of the *Drunken Knave*, getting closer and closer, and both women felt fear fill their hearts again. They pulled harder on the oars.

Moments later, Liz looked back at the *Knave* in time to see Smitty's form outlined at the near rail within a blaze of red light and she screamed in grief and terror when he crumpled to the deck like a puppet cut from its strings. The sorcerer hurled a bolt of magic toward her and Catie and their rowboat, but providence again got in the way, and he ended up hitting his own boat this time. The launch exploded into flames and the night was rent by long, pain-filled shrieks of agony as two men could be seen stumbling around the burning deck for perhaps twenty seconds before their screams were silenced.

Liz fell forward to her knees again, sobbing, and her fingers dug the clock-watch out from beside Jesse, pulling his right arm free as well as the timepiece. She begged Catie to help her. Catie, who was also sobbing and crying, fell forward too, and she again created a little light ball for them to see by.

The deed was done in seconds and the skies above them cleared miraculously, because on this date in 1722, there was no fog to shroud the night and the moonlight dazzled the eye. The displaced water around them surged and rocked the little boat crazily, but the women held on and the rowboat stayed afloat.

But they were not out of danger, for the sorcerer had taken another of the rowboats, employing magic to get it to the water. With a wave of his hand and red sparks shooting from his furious fingers, the boat began to cleave the waves between him and his prey at a fast pace.

Both women stood in the rowboat and held hands as was getting to be their habit of late. They watched the sorcerer's approach with something like acceptance or maybe even resignation as he got closer and closer.

Catie said to Liz, "Listen, Miss Priss, we have ta hit him hard and quick, because if we use a long stream o' magic, he'll jest absorb it and get stronger, and then he'll turn it back on us."

Liz turned to the other witch and cried, "What?" in astonishment.

Without looking at her, Catie nodded grimly. "Yes, my love, 'e will. And if 'e gets close ta us, he'll take the rest o' our magic and with it our lives. So, we're both gonna make sure 'e dunna catch ye and the babe, ye 'ear me? Ye can take yerselves back to 1915 wi'out me, if need be."

Suddenly, Liz understood that Catie would sacrifice herself before letting this monster touch either herself or Jesse. She felt the shock of this but was unsure of what to do. With only seconds left, Liz put her faith in Catie and in magic itself and waited with her friend for the lethal attack that was sure to come.

But then four shots rang out, in fast succession, and the sorcerer, whose boat had gotten to just about twenty feet away from the women, stalled in the water and came to a stop. At first, the man's face showed disbelief in the bright moonlight and he started to put a hand to his back, a look of determination now overtaking his features as magic crackled from his fingertips and jumped to the nearest of his wounds.

Liz let her power build up, formed it into a blazing ball, and then gave that over to Catie to direct, and the little blonde witch combined it with her own blazing ball of magic, soon sending the whole thing shooting at the sorcerer.

The man's hand not engaged in healing himself came up, palm toward the women, and he bounced their magic back at them so quickly they would have no time to avoid it. Both would have gone flying through the air and into the water to who knows what end if it were not for little Jesse's reaction.

About the time the two witches let their combined magic ball fly free, from the babe's tiny hand came a pack of phantom wolves that encircled the sorcerer almost instantly, he was so near to them, and they caught the reflected magic, refracted it, and bounced it back at the sorcerer in ten different directions. He had no time to defend himself from this surround attack and he dropped to his knees, he eyes bulging wide. And then the wolves were upon him and both witches turned away in horror, clamping their hands over their ears so they did not have to listen to the carnage the wolves brought with them.

Magical power of all ilk and sources, that which the greedy man had stolen by artifice and by murder throughout the many years he'd been practicing his most cruel of the magical arts, burst into the air and fell like rain around his rowboat, the beautiful colors sinking slowly into the bay's waters made black by the night. And then the wolfpack vanished and the man's lifeless body fell backward onto one of the rowboat's seats with a thud.

Liz looked down at Jesse and saw that he was staring at the dead man, whom they could all see pretty well in the bright moonlight. Her child's baby face was set in a serious and solemn expression that seemed years, not weeks old. She noted with wonder that, when the wolves disappeared, Jesse's features again took on their youthfulness and he turned his face up toward his mother, smiling at her trustingly. She caught her breath and said to Catie, "You know, I don't know what it is that comes over him, but it's not Jesse who's calling the wolves here."

Catie had also noted the transformation of the baby's face and nodded now. "I agree. My guess is that it's one o' yer Indian gods, them An'ugadi of the Iquakawi. He's got that blood runnin' strong in 'im, ye know." She eyed Liz circumspectly and added, "And so do ye, which is why ye're so advanced already."

Liz, taking this in, nodded. She had heard of the Iquakawi, of course, and known that her adopted mother had had several good friends among them when she was a child and living on the reservation. But Selma had not shared much of the ways of the Iquakawi she'd known or of her own heritage of the Lakȟóta Sioux. Liz now suspected that had something to do with the magic she now felt running through her body, the magic that Selma had bound and worked so hard to conceal, even from Liz herself.

A shout came from the *Knave* and it was Neddy's voice who called to them. Catie replied that they were all three fine and that their enemy was well and truly dead. Neddy, his voice breaking once, said the same was true of Smitty. Both women wrapped their arms around the other and Liz called to him that they would return to the ship, but Neddy bawled back that under no circumstances were they to do that. They had a plan and they all had to follow it, no matter what.

He let out a forlorn cry of, "Goodbye, me love, go on and do what ye must. We will be fine 'ere a spell, until we can sail back ta warmer shores." He seemed to be choking back tears as he added, "Except for Smitty, who will 'ave ta be buried 'ere in these cold, foreign waters."

A certain look passed between Catie and Liz, and with a wave of their joined hands, they sent Smitty's body back to his beloved Caribbean Sea.

Neddy, his voice a faint and hollow echo, said, "Thankee, ladies. That meant the world ta me. Goodbye, Catie luv, and goodbye, Miss Priss."

Catie then began to chant her spell to turn the *Drunken Knave* back into a sailship only, with Liz joining her on the second round of chanting. As they rowed away, they could see and hear the steel plates, their rivets and trusses, and the steamship machinery with all its bits being materialized off to the side of the ship and then dropped into the water to sink to the bottom of the bay.

When the spell had run its course and the beautiful ship's sails were unfurled and looking majestic in the moonlight, the two witches again drew deeply from their innate magical power and, holding the clock-watch between them, put their fingers on the 1, 9, and 5. With all their might, they concentrated on the year 1915. At first, they went nowhere because of their extreme exhaustion. But they both took a deep breath and glanced at the graceful ship far in the distance. Then they looked into each other's eyes and refocused their power, combining it like they had with the magic ball they'd shot at the sorcerer, and instantly they were back in that same foggy night nearly two hundred years in the future.

They heard a couple of tugboats in the area rescuing the men from the first launch that the sorcerer had inadvertently disabled with the magical blow meant for the *Drunken Knave*. The women, both of whom felt they could no longer stand or fight or do much of anything at all, slid to their seats in the rowboat and whispered their worries to each other. What if someone found them now? They could not defend themselves against another assault and they did not want the rescued crew to know for sure who it was they had attacked tonight. There was always the possibility that, while the *Drunken Knave* might have been known to the enemy, they themselves might not, for they both felt instinctively that there were other witches in San Francisco, some of whom were as strong as either Catie or Liz. They hoped dearly that Herbert Flint could not know for sure it was they two who possessed the timepiece, even if he were to meet them face to face in the street tomorrow. Which meant they could not let themselves be rescued now, or he would indeed have the certainty of just who had the clock-watch with them. But how they were going to make it back to San Francisco without help, let alone all the way to the Palace Hotel, they had no idea.

Wet and frozen and suffering from shock, Catie forced her stiff body to move so that she was sitting beside Liz. The women huddled together for warmth, too tired and too low on magical power even to conjure a couple of blankets to wrap around themselves.

Liz put her arm around Catie and pulled Catie's head to her shoulder, grateful beyond measure for all that the little blonde witch was doing for her. She said Catie's name quietly and the other woman nodded

In a voice just loud enough to be heard through the sounds of the waves and the watery rescue happening not far from them, Catie replied, "I know. Ye dunna 'ave ta say a word. I wouldna let ye or baby Jesse be 'urt fer all the magic in the world." She took her index finger and used it to caress Jesse's cheek. He was staring up at her with utter adoration, a look she returned whole-heartedly to him, even though neither could see it in the dark and gloomy fog surrounding them.

Jesse grabbed Catie's finger, curling his little ones around it tightly, and then the three of them were suddenly on the floor of their suite at the Palace. Without the rowboat's seats behind them, they rolled onto their backs with soft cries of surprise, and then with joy and much relief at finding only soft carpet surrounding them.

***

Donnie had gotten lost again. The streets of Anûmanétus were mean to her, always seeming to rearrange themselves so that she was unsure which would take her back to the inn where she and her friends were staying.

Sighing ruefully, she supposed that none of the cobbled passageways had actually moved or any such thing as that, but rather it was that she kept getting turned around in this area of town. With Falwaïn's advice to use the rooftops whenever she was lost echoing in her ears, she climbed onto the nearest roof that was high enough to provide her with a good view and from there she plotted the correct route to her destination.

While it was easier to navigate up here, it was also a lot more dangerous than down below because far fewer people used the connected rooftops of the city's slums. She knew she'd have to keep a wary eye out for thieves and cutthroats, who, according to Falwaïn, ran rampant all over the city's poorer neighborhoods.

She began to follow her chosen course, ducking around chimneys and scaling up and down the walls of taller and shorter buildings as she went, turning at times to look back at the general spot she knew to be the location of their inn to make sure she was heading due east away from it.

As she hopped down onto another low roof, she idly hoped that Falwaïn and Akanna would come back with good news tonight. They had spent the previous two days with Belnesem's wife and Medregai's queen, the lovely Miramdahl of the Woodland Álvar, trying to persuade her to grant them access to the Forrieghness Tower. But they had had no luck in convincing her royal highness to give her approval to them thus far. While she had not told them no outright, neither had she told them yes, and instead changed the subject every time they importuned her with their repeated request.

Queen Miramdahl was the stunningly perfect and seemingly ageless elf princess who had married King Belnesem at the end of the War of Unity. She ruled the capital city in his absence with a graceful, but nevertheless tightly clenched, iron-hard hand—figuratively speaking, of course. She was revered almost to the point of idolatry in Anûmanétus and no criticism of her was allowed to pass unchallenged. Falwaïn had warned Donnie about this and Akanna had added her cautions to his, with both regaling her with stories of the terrible fates of those who had been careless enough to voice an untoward opinion of the fair queen.

The royal marriage had been entered into all those years ago with the intent of solidifying ties between the anointed Sarn families who ruled the many cities, fiefdoms, and provinces across Medregai and the unrivalled and magically powerful elves of the Province of Balwedané Feûr—leaving out those who dwelled in Lænemeade, naturally, who no one anywhere in Medregai trusted.

The union had served its purpose, that of stabilizing Medregai overall, and had proved to be a relatively successful instance of matrimony for both the king and queen. The king could go off and do his warring and lording bit whenever he wished, taking to his bed whatever wenches caught his fancy, and then he could return to his home city, ever the hero, to find his wife complacently holding reign over the several factions presently invited to maintain a representative at court.

Which was not to say the fair queen didn't enjoy lovers of her own, of which there seemed to be a plentiful number hanging around the royal court. This was something Donnie had cottoned to instantly upon meeting the elf queen during her one brief audience with that regal lady on their first afternoon here.

Another aspect to the queen that Donnie spotted immediately was the rather weird magical power smoldering inside her slim, elfin breast. While she possessed nothing like Donnie's power, she was by no means plagued with a paucity, so to speak. Nor did it resonate like normal elf magic, which was decidedly odd to Donnie. All the other elves she'd met to date had a similar magic that was not quite like that of vincans, nor of witches, sorcerers or gods, which were really about all Donnie had thus far encountered of the higher magical creatures, other than those resident on the Ganlonds. Something about Miramdahl's magic felt unfamiliar and misplaced in the elf queen's body to Donnie.

After only a few minutes' in the queen's presence, it was clear to all there that she desired Falwaïn to be yet another royal lover and she would go to whatever lengths to maneuver him into that position, something she was still working on several days later.

In the meanwhile, Donnie was just as committed to keeping him out of Miramdahl's clutches, but without using magic, which was officially banned inside the walls of the capital city. At least, any overt sign of magic was banned. But that didn't mean it wasn't there, beneath the obvious.

Nor did it mean that Donnie couldn't set a home spell with herbs, a simple spell that would remind Falwaïn lovingly at all times of his growing family. Not that she distrusted him, no; but she definitely did Miramdahl. And Donnie did not, for one second, believe the ban on magic included the queen. Therefore, Donnie saw her current quest as merely a method of protecting her family and friends.

And that was what she was in search of today, was some rosemary for Falwaïn and an aloe plant for Diego. They were difficult herbs to find in Anûmanétus, but her chambermaid had whispered to her this morning that there was a certain woman, arrived to the city only last night, who was reputed to carry all sorts of plants that were not strictly illegal, but were heavily regulated. The chambermaid offered the opinion that it was likely rosemary and aloe would be two such herbs the woman would carry with her.

Donnie had set out that morning as soon as Falwaïn and Akanna had left for the palace. Sylvester was off on his own as usual. He was trying to find a path to the Tower but having no luck with his quest because the way was either hidden or blocked, something no one they'd talked to yet were sure about because they'd never traveled it before either. Although, it had to be said (and had been said by everyone they'd asked), everybody in the city had certainly seen the Tower in the distance and knew that the queen's mages tended it daily, so there must be a well-traveled route somewhere.

Diego was back at the inn in his room. He'd learned within a day and a half of their arrival that it was best for him to limit his time in the streets, seeing as he was attacked by bigots and thugs four times his first afternoon here, and seven times his second day. His attempted excursions outside ended after the seventh bout of violent bullying was perpetrated by some of the most destitute but also the most belligerent citizens of the poorest parts of the city, where their inn was situated. These slums were referred to locally as the Drass, and they were the closest the queen would allow any witch to get to the palace, or so she deemed after her one meeting with Donnie.

With the seventh attack upon Diego's person, prompted of course by his similarity in looks and coloring to Medregai's current and most reviled enemy, the Mehen'Adríum, he had agreed to remain at the inn until they were either allowed access to the Tower or told to leave the city. And Donnie was now seeking aloe to help his more prominent abrasions heal because some were more severe than she felt could properly heal on their own.

She hopped from roof to roof to her clandestine destination, careful to land on only reinforcing boards nailed to the rooftops of the Drass. Once she felt in her heart the tug of magic that signified a healer was nearby, she climbed down to the street level in search of her quarry.

Twenty minutes later, she was back up top, with the sky as her ceiling, and feeling excited because her mission had been a success. She'd found the mother of two small children and had handed over a sizable (really, it was nothing short of extortionate) payment for the herbs, tucking them into her waist belt for safekeeping, and had beat it out of there as quick as she could make it, not liking the way any of the locals were eyeing her and her money belt. She stood tall on the roof of a blacksmithy and observed the clear day around her with satisfaction, noting the Tower in the distance, and the palace's numerous man-made cupolas and intricately and naturally formed tufa turrets in the foreground. Nearer to where Donnie stood were the city's other public buildings and most of those were crumbling around themselves, for none were so well kept as the palace. It occurred to Donnie that it really was disgraceful how nobody seemed to care at all for anything in this city other than the Tower or the palace.

She began to move in the direction of the inn, watching more where her feet were landing than anything else, and was therefore surprised when her cat ran across her path and dropped to a sitting stance in front of her. Donnie halted her progress, stopping somewhat precariously upon her tippy toes, as she was wont to do when leaping from one board to the next. She settled back down on her heels and gave her cat a grin.

"Hi, Sylvester!" she welcomed him, adding with a chuckle, "Man, you came outta nowhere, didn't you?"

He shook his head and sighed. "No, I did not come out of nowhere, because that would be impossible for most beings and most improbable even for me. I came from the north and did so without subterfuge." He shook his head, got to his feet and began to approach her, jumping high onto her shoulder, where he once again sat down and said to her in a low voice, "I am being followed, as are you, you know."

Donnie nodded and resumed picking her way across the rooftops to a street she knew. "They are Queen's Guards, I believe, although the ones following me are in disguise as bandits and cutthroats. Kind of thrilling, ain't it?" she informed him chattily. "And there was one who stayed back at the inn when I left. I'm guessing he's there to keep an eye on Diego."

"You do not seem perturbed by them," noted Sylvester, and again Donnie grinned at him, her eyes sparkling with mischief.

"Naw, but I'm thinkin' they might be about ready to pick me up for acquiring contraband," she said, and he let out another sigh, this one even more telling of his frustration than the previous one had been.

Donnie said to him in mild protest, "Well, Diego needs something for his abrasions, doesn't he?"

"And you are, no doubt, still intent upon setting a home spell on Lord Falwaïn. Which is nothing more than a waste of good rosemary," the cat commented acidly. "Any fool can see he is completely besotted with you and no elf queen is going to lure him away, not even for a dalliance of no consequence."

Donnie screwed up her face in displeasure. "No consequence? I don't agree with you there, my friend. And besides, it's not him I'm worried about."

By this time, they were almost to the main thoroughfare, where Donnie felt she could safely vault down to street level and still find her way to the inn. But before she could accomplish that acrobatic move, she and her cat found themselves surrounded on the roof by eight brawny men and women, all looking mighty rough and each carrying a bludgeoning weapon of one sort or another.

Donnie gave them a feeble grin and greeted them brightly with, "Hello there, fellas! Sure is a lovely day for a stroll up here on the roofs, innit?"

"Gimme yer money belt," the one standing in front growled at her, and they all took another step closer, so that now all she could see was them.

She reached down and opened her belt, showing that it was empty, which it was because she'd already sent everything, including her money, back to her room at the inn. Its emptiness seemed to arouse the ire of all of the ruffians surrounding her and a couple of them even took another step toward her, but Donnie suddenly threw up her hands and shouted at the top of her lungs, "Okay, okay! You got me, you incredible and oh-so forceful Queen's Guards! I surrender, I surrender!"

Taken aback by just how loudly she was yelling, her attackers retreated a step. One or two of them realized they were suddenly being watched by several pairs of curious eyes in the crowds below and they muttered this to their cohorts. Since they were all standing near the roof's edge, their little scenario could be viewed quite clearly by the crowd traveling the street, a crowd that was quickly gathering to a standstill. It was a crowd that grew and grew while Donnie continued to cry, "I give up, I give up! Really, I give up!" Her final cry was one of triumph, when she held out her hands, wrists together, and shouted dramatically, "All right, all right, I'll go with you! You can take me to your queen, if you insist!"

Disgusted by this unexpected turn of events, especially since not one of them had said a word to Donnie about going anywhere, the captain of the Queen's Guard, the one who had growled at her, signaled for the others to stand down, and then for two of the guards to take Donnie in their grasp so they could roughly and unceremoniously escort her to the palace. Sylvester hung with her throughout these shenanigans, to his credit, although he was ready to bolt at any second should the need arise.

When they reached the palace, they were shown into the great hall's anteroom, which was decorated with nothing except for some tapestries hanging on the smoothly sanded tufa walls. Donnie supposed there was no furniture here so that petitioners or visitors to the court who were required to wait in the room would not get comfortable before the queen agreed to receive them in the great hall.

Donnie decided to kill time studying the tapestries, all of which were exceptionally good, with excellent likenesses of the places depicted upon them. She recognized the cities of Marn Dím, Lænemeade and Hörthanc in three of the tapestries. The only other place she recognized beyond them was the Forrieghness Tower, which stood off to the north-west of the capital city.

This tapestry she studied more closely than the others, noting that a path was shown that led straight from the west side of the palace's outer walls, where the mages made their homes, all the way to the Tower. Donnie pointed this out to Sylvester, who shook his head and said, "There is no cleared path there now, that is all I can say. When was this tapestry made, I wonder?" he asked, and they both began to search for a legend of some sort. They found it to the lower right corner of the tapestry, where several sentences were stitched there.

They both studied the first few passages sewn into the tapestry, and then Sylvester turned to Donnie, his manner hesitant. "My facility with the language of the gods is improving as my own magic increases, which you know. But I am unsure in this case…er, I mean to ask, does that relay what I think it does?" he inquired, cocking his head curiously at her.

Donnie could see him looking at her out of the corners of her eyes and so she gave him a sly and humorous grin, quipping back, "Well, if you're thinkin' it's our ticket into the Tower, then yep, it relays exactly what you think it does!"

She chuckled happily to herself and, after further study of the long lines of text stitched around the tapestry's edges for several minutes, she leant with her back against the stone wall and her arms crossed in front of her, content to wait now for as long as the queen thought necessary.

It was, in fact, after three o'clock in the afternoon, by Donnie's watch, before Queen Miramdahl deigned to see her. Donnie was led into the great hall by a couple of the guards who had arrested her, although they were dressed in their normal gear once again, the blue and white crosses of the king's banners emblazoned on the guards' chests. Inside the sunny hall, with its high and wide windows, there were easily a hundred or so ladies and gentlemen in waiting who were either standing or sitting around, depending on their rank within the court, while the queen was acting the regent over all from her bejeweled throne. The king's simple, yet imposing throne, as always whenever he was away, stood empty with only a fur cape of brown and black to adorn it, and this was slung carelessly across its wooden seat and right arm.

Standing to the left of the queen, upon the king's side of court, stood Falwaïn and Akanna, both of whom watched Donnie's approach with a combination of wariness and dismay that made Donnie wonder just what the heck had been said about her before she was shown in.

She moved her money belt a little higher up and tightened it so that her pregnant belly was accentuated because she instinctually felt this would bother the lovely Miramdahl to no end. It seemed she was correct in that assumption, because she saw the queen's lips tighten disapprovingly as her ice blue eyes roved down Donnie's tall figure and lingered on her curvy midsection. Donnie made sure to turn to the side to nod to both Falwaïn and Akanna, her hands pressing her long skirt against the slight roundness of her swollen belly to give the queen an eyeful. She then turned back to Miramdahl and did a modest curtsy.

"Your eminence," she murmured, keeping her head bent. "I thank you for seeing me today."

The queen's eyebrows both shot upward and she repeated nastily, her voice also raised an octave or two, "You thank me for seeing you today? That statement is nothing short of idiotic." And then she asked, "Do tell me, just what kind of idiot are you exactly?" Her velvet voice dripped with ridicule and condescension now, and the crowd in the hall giggled their appreciation of their queen's wit.

Donnie laughed along with those behind her and, before the queen could add another remark to it, patted her belly to again accentuate it and shot the queen an obviously conspiratorial wink. "Oh, I'm sure you know how crazy your hormones get with pregnancy! Ha-ha, you must remember what's that like, right? Or don't you have any children at all?" she asked innocently, knowing full well the queen had not been able to provide the king with an heir. Donnie figured that might have something to do with all the many lovers the king and queen both kept.

The court gasped and tittered at her remarks, and Donnie heard Falwaïn groan over to her left. Sylvester finally jumped to the ground and sat down beside her, bowing his head and shuddering with disbelief.

The queen, her face set in a mask of barely restrained anger, snapped at Donnie with cold impatience and overt dislike, "You have been accused of procuring banned substances by the captain of my Queen's Guard. What say you to that charge?" After her question, she looked at Donnie with narrowed eyes, her long fingers tightening on the arms of her throne.

Donnie, who'd begun rocking back and forth on her heels and toes as though she had not a care in the world, stopped, opened her money belt to show that it was empty, and replied blithely to the queen, "Prove it."

"Wh-what?" stammered Miramdahl, her glittering eyes suddenly large and hard with outrage. "You dare?" she spluttered, beginning to rise from her seat in her fury. "You dare—"

Donnie faced her boldly, seemingly unfazed by the queen's growing ire, and recited in a strong and firm voice, "*An bala, eav fi Ca'nam raegune aduer'kätal leâna'sen ahn lu Toren fi Førrens.*" She then turned to look at Falwaïn and Akanna, and explained, pointing for a moment behind her, "Those words are stitched on one of the tapestries out in the hall's antechamber and they mean, loosely translated, that anyone with Ca'nam power is welcome in the Forrieghness Tower anytime. And it goes on to decree that anyone who recites the proper request and wields Ca'nam power within themselves *must* be allowed access to the Tower. There is a long bit included on the tapestry that states it's considered treasonous for anyone to prevent any Ca'nam being, creature, or entity from going to the Tower and reading its scrolls. If any such interference is raised, retribution for the offense shall be swift and automatic, and there is no avoiding that because, if any such subterfuge is discussed or worked on in any way at all to prevent access, then all beings involved with the planned obstruction attempt will be struck dead by the powers of magic, with no recourse open to them or their loved ones."

She paused and added dryly, "Now, I am reasonably certain that both the king and queen are fully aware of this condition of the Tower's use, but I doubt they've ever discussed it since they're both still alive. Anyway, it's just a guess, but I'm pretty sure neither of them has made any of that public knowledge before now."

About halfway through Donnie's explanations, the court had erupted into gasps of disbelief, followed by wild chatter.

Triumphant in her victory, Donnie turned to the queen and reminded her rival loudly so she could be heard over the rabble, "And now that I've recited the proper request for access, you can either grant me leave or stand for treason in a court of magic yourself. Which will it be?" she asked, leaning back on her hips with her arms folded in front of her while she stared crossly at Miramdahl.

With an abrupt and furious gesture from the queen, the guards made sure the room was cleared of everyone but those standing near the throne. When their restive audience was gone, Miramdahl eyed Donnie with the intent of open war.

"Lord Falwaïn was under a spell to make you with child, you know," the queen hissed, rising to her feet and approaching Donnie. "Even he knows this. He knows he used *ofett víratula*—dragon fruit—in that hen egg concoction he made for you that night. Otherwise, he would never have bedded you." She came to a stop about a foot from Donnie and raised a finger to her own temple. "I see it with my mind. I know it to be true, as does he—as do you!" she sneered.

Donnie turned to Falwaïn and looked at him inquiringly. "Is this what you believe, my love? That you were under a spell to bed me as soon as possible so you could impregnate me?"

He looked at her somewhat sheepishly, then nodded with uncertainty. "If I am honest, yes, it is what I *fear* happened. But I swear I've never told that to anyone, so the queen must have magicked it from my mind, because I did not share it with her willingly," he added, glaring at Miramdahl with open defiance.

Donnie let out a mirthless laugh before turning back to the queen. "You are some piece of work, aren't you? Digging into him like that without caring about the truth behind what you saw," she chided the other woman. "Well, let me tell you something, sister: he didn't have to use anything magical to make me with child because magic itself had already decided I would get pregnant! I knew that the moment I realized I was going to have Falwaïn's babies. Previously, I had wondered if Ixifír Bíun, whom I am certain you know well, had a hand in our romance in any way, but then I realized that he wants many things, but none of them involve me furthering my magical line. And these babies will do just that," she said, her eyes filling with joy when she caressed her tummy gently. "I know old Ixy dude told Julia his suspicion that someone else wanted me to get pregnant, but he was dead wrong there, unless you count that someone as being me. But then, getting pregnant was not on my mind that night at all, believe me, not until I felt the quickening. No, my dear, magic itself made it possible for me to create that everlasting bond with the man I love."

She turned back to Falwaïn and smiled at him tenderly. "Our kids will carry on long after you and I are gone, luv, and they'll fight if and when they need to! They are our legacy, our gift to this world, and they are our gift *from* magic," she explained earnestly, tears forming in her eyes, "for all the bad things we're going to endure. Like this horrible woman." She grimaced and pointed a thumb at the queen. Forcing a quasi-smile onto her lips upon returning her attention to the queen, she added, "If you don't believe me, ask Sylvester about how much magic likes to keep things in balance."

The cat nodded vigorously to this, although no one in the room was watching him. When he realized this, he intoned hastily, "Magic is very curious in that respect—oh, yes, it is indeed quite determined. It goes to the extreme, always, to find the proper balance between objects, or events, or anything it might touch or harm or enhance in any way at all. Those in Donnie's world might call it the Yin and the Yang, if you will, or the Great Duality of All. Many civilizations are based upon this belief, which seems to stem from the—ah, yes, of course," the cat interrupted himself when the queen turned to shoot daggers at him with unmasked hatred in her ice-blue eyes. Swallowing hard, he cleared his throat and said carefully, "*An bala, eav fi Ca'nam raegune aduer'kätal leâna'sen ahn lu Toren fi Førrens.*"

Then Akanna joined her voice to the mix and recited, "*An bala, eav fi Ca'nam raegune aduer'kätal leâna'sen ahn lu Toren fi Førrens.*"

Everyone turned to Falwaïn, who started to say it, stumbled, started over, and then looked at Donnie with a plea on his face, but it was Sylvester who ordered him, "Repeat after me, Lord Falwaïn." And a few moments later, all four of them had stated their desire to visit the Tower.

"Oh, and our friend Diego says it too," Donnie interjected. "So, you'll have to let all of us go to the Tower." She lifted her chin at the queen, whose hardened and furious expression made it obvious that she did not like the position she was in, nor did she appreciate losing out on any man to another woman, even one he considered his wife.

"There is still the matter of the contraband you were seen procuring this morning," she reminded Donnie acerbically. "The sentence for that is within my discretion entirely, and I believe I shall give you—"

But Donnie had her right hand raised and, on it, her index finger was wiggling from side to side. "Oh, no, you don't!" she crowed with glee. "Y'see, all I did was give that woman a large donation so that she could feed her two sweet children, Gabby and Dugal, and in return she slipped me a thank you gift. What it could be, I do not know because it got lost between there and here, probably when I was so roughly accosted by your guards. Go on and ask the kind lady—I know she'll tell you the same thing. And there is nothing illegal about any of that on her part or mine!" Donnie declared saucily, her hands on her hips. "So, see? You've got nothing at all to charge me with!"

The queen looked like she wanted to rain hellfire upon them all, but she somehow held her temper and ground out, "Very well. You will be granted access to the sanctuary in the morning. You will stay at your rooms in the inn at nighttime for only as long as you need to remain in the city to obtain whatever information you require from the Tower, and then you will leave Anûmanétus together! And none of you should ever venture anywhere near here again, witch!" she spat at Donnie, leaning toward her menacingly. She turned to Falwaïn and Akanna and came even closer to losing it as she added, "None of you at all!" After saying this, she turned on her heel and swept majestically out of the reception room.

Donnie and the others turned to stare at each other, their eyes bugging wide, and—unable to stop themselves—they burst into stifled peals of laughter, barely able to believe their sudden good fortune. Finally, they were going to Forrieghness Tower!

Later that night, Donnie, as usual, called out to Rex with her mind while she was in her bath and her pup responded with love, but without much enthusiasm. When Donnie inquired as to what was wrong with him, he sighed heavily before responding.

"We haven't been able to get near that dragon, which means we're still stuck here in Marn Dím. I'm beginning to think we'll never get out of here, and we certainly won't be able to take the dragon with us when we do finally go. The closest we've come to it was yesterday, when Kueray and Maga actually got its attention at one point and it followed them for nearly a minute. But then the dratted thing turned away once a bugle or something similar sounded from the elves' camp."

The dog sighed again, and Donnie wished she could give him a hug.

He added forlornly, "I don't know exactly what the bugle signal meant, but the dragon listened to it and was gone in a second back to the camp."

Donnie grunted sympathetically and then informed him gently, "Um, yeah, well, we've had a bit more success than you."

"Whaddya mean?" the dog asked with fake interest.

Biting her lip, Donnie admitted, "I found a way to force Miramdahl to give us leave to visit the Tower. We are going in the morn—"

"But you said you wouldn't go without me!" Rex's voice rose as he uttered this objection, his tone relaying hurt and an accusation of betrayal.

"I know, I know!" Donnie conceded, wanting to placate him. "Tell me how I can fix this. I mean, we have to get to the Tower as soon as we can, we all know that. Do you want to leave Marn Dím now and come here so you can go with us tomorrow?" she suggested.

Rex was silent for several seconds before grumbling, "No, I don't see how I can leave everybody here. I mean, Warren's just learning how to use his powers some, while Diana's are pretty good now and she's remembering a lot about them, but that's it besides me. None of the others are super strong magically and we might need my powers to fight off the elves or the king's men or who knows who whenever the final showdown does come around to us; ya know what I mean?"

"Well, then, maybe you need to make sure it comes when you want it to and by whom, not when one of the other groups decides all that," Donnie observed.

Again, her dog was silent for a bit. Finally, he said, "Yeah, I get that. But I'm not sure how to force it."

The boombox appeared on the floor of the bathroom and, with its volume set low, began playing the metalcore song, "Hole in My Heart."

Donnie blew a raspberry at the music box and thought hard for a while, listening to the song without consciously noting anything about it. She played absentmindedly with the hot water and suds in the inn's copper tub, which, as usual, she had scrubbed magically and filled with clean water, soap and bath oils from home. She figured nobody would know she was using magic here in the bath, so she could at least have a few comforts. Otherwise, this place would have been just too unbearable for her to countenance for longer than a day.

The silence between Donnie and Rex stretched to minutes before a hard truth edged its way into her thoughts, helped along greatly by the boombox's song, and she finally gave it voice.

"You know, honey, if it's one of the dragons that I thought I killed the night of the battle, as I strongly suspect it is, all you'll have to do is tell it that you're my boy, my heart and my soul, and I'll bet nothing will recall it to the elves. No bugle call in the world will penetrate its fury then." She gulped before admitting, "And I don't blame it one bit."

The dog, aware of just how his mama felt about that night and what the gods had decreed she do to the dragons, felt the deep morass of her guilt and self-loathing open up in her and suddenly he was the one wishing he was there to comfort her. Instead, all he could do was remind her sweetly, "Mama, you would never have killed them, or even hurt them, if the gods hadn't told you to."

Donnie shook her head, the burgeoning tears in her eyes spilling over onto her cheeks like they always did whenever she relived that nightmarish part of the Battle of the Branmar Plain. "That doesn't matter," she said stiffly, "I did it and I have to live with it. Now you can use it as you have to, my love, but be very careful because that dragon's going to want to kill you and it's gonna be hard to stop. Whatever you do, beware of its eyes and the lasers in them. You'll have to figure out a way to calm it down once you get it away from the elves. Distract it, maybe give it something else to do so it changes its focus from you to this other thing. But what you can use for that, I don't know. There must be something to hand that'll work; you just need to get creative."

The dog agreed with her and they began to chat of more mundane things until they both felt a little bit better. When Falwaïn knocked on the bathroom's door a while later, Donnie and Rex told each other they were sending nothing but love between them and made their goodbyes, then Donnie let her man enter the steamy bathroom.

He joined her in the bath and, in about another half an hour, her mood had improved exponentially so that she went to bed that night thoroughly contented to be with her man on this day and every day.

The next morning found them bright and early at the gates to the mages' sanctuary, which was officially called the Chapter House for High Wizards and Witches, although the last two words were seldom recognized or even used anymore, ostensibly because of the betrayal by many witches to the causes of the righteous victories and policies of the Sarn.

Donnie could hardly contain her excitement, for she felt intuitively that here she would find answers to her own predicament, not just that of the Mîrlonds. She started to rap loudly on the big, heavy oaken doors of the sanctuary, but Falwaïn pulled her back and pointed to a bell pull to the entry's side. Her face a little pink, she grabbed the rope and pulled on it with enthusiasm. It must have triggered a bell far away from the door because there was no sound of it nearby that any in their group could hear. They waited a full two minutes before Donnie was allowed to pull it again, and she did so vigorously thereafter every two to three minutes for the next hour or so.

Finally convinced the intruders were not going away anytime soon, old Brother Asaph shuffled slowly to the front door of the sanctuary, pulled it open a crack, stuck a distrusting eye to that slim opening and called out in a peevish voice, "Who's there? Stop that racket, will ye? Stop it, I say!"

Before Donnie could respond, Falwaïn stepped forward, explained who they were and reminded the venerable mage that surely the queen must have sent word to their order that he and his friends would be visiting the Charter House today so they could be shown the way to the Tower, yes?

Brother Asaph pulled the door open a little more before turning to walk away, mumbling to himself that it was scandalous how just anyone at all was to be given access to the sacred Toren fi Førrens these days. He made several rude comments about witches and their consorts, which they all prudently ignored while he led them through the byzantine sanctuary halls to the presiding bishop's quarters, where he left them at the closed door. He tottered off, his thin shoulders hunched and his long head drooped so that his pointy chin and scraggly beard lay on his chest. He was still grumbling about the unwelcome disturbance to his day as he disappeared around a corner far down the hall.

Akanna knocked on the bishop's door and a cold voice bade them enter. Donnie went in first and the others followed behind her.

Donnie studied the bishop sitting before her with undisguised interest. Last night, Falwaïn had explained to Donnie, Diego, and Sylvester that the office of presiding bishop within the Førrens Order of Manûs Mages was an elected one and the same man had held it for more than nine long years presently. To be even more precise, Aldalis Munkinum had worn the starry crimson robes of the order's presiding bishopric for ninety-four regular years. And prior to that he had lived as a journeying bishop who'd traveled the central provinces of Medregai for forty-five regular years, performing whatever small miracles he could, where he could, in order to provide aid and comfort to the common folk. Donnie thought he looked to be, at most, a middle-aged man, but she remembered that Akanna had informed them last night that he refused to tell anyone just how long he had indeed been alive, so there was no knowing how old he actually was.

The bishop rose to his feet at their entrance and, if there had come a cunning sneer over his face at first sight of his visitors, it passed fleetingly and was replaced by a composed, though nearly infinitesimal smile of acknowledgement. There was no welcome in his expression or his words, but he at least hid his distaste for them a little better than Brother Asaph had.

He, of course, knew both Falwaïn and Akanna and greeted them first. Diego, he ignored completely, while his faint sneer returned (again, fleetingly) when he was introduced to Donnie. Akanna had made sure to add her title of Ér Ainíl of the Ganlonds to the introduction and this did not pass unnoticed by the bishop.

"Ah, you remain intent upon bringing a high witch to the Mîrlonds to assist with your little problem, I see," he drawled to the vincan, and she nodded once curtly. "W-e-l-l…" he added, letting the drawn-out word fill the air with a plethora of meanings as he stared from Akanna to the others, eyeing each of them, one by one, with disapprobation. "I suppose you have that right as Kaerdír of those magical lands. Although, as I have mentioned to you innumerable times now, it really would be best to let us, the mages, those who truly know what we are doing, investigate and devise a plan to improve the Mîrlonds' chances of surviving its lessening to at least some small degree. As a matter of fact, my brothers and I have discussed this extensively and we all agree that we could no doubt save the core of the magical lands."

He inclined his head and assumed an air of sadness which he clearly did not feel when he added, "Many magical creatures will die, naturally, in the process, but that cannot be helped. What is most important is that some small measure of the original lands is retained. The rest will simply have to be sacrificed."

Akanna's back had stiffened and the vincan, normally quite tall and menacing in stature, somehow seemed to expand another four inches in all directions, a common physical reaction in vincans about to enter battle.

It was one that Falwaïn recognized instantly and he stepped forward with haste, almost fumbling in his hurry to diffuse the situation, to say, "Ah, yes, well, forgive us, Bishop Munkinum, we are all quite eager to get to the Tower. Therefore, if you would be so kind as to have someone show us the path to it, we will bother you no longer this fine and glorious day."

While the bishop was clearly affronted by Falwaïn taking control of the situation, he could not refuse the suggestion without being openly churlish, something he was apparently reluctant to be at this point. He picked up a small bell on his desk and rang it, then sat down to ignore his visitors until the call was answered by a beautiful young man with a haughty, upturned nose.

This thin and unpleasant novitiate was named Billy of Mayweather and he was sure he was destined for great things. He was just as sure that the witch he was charged with leading to the Tower gate this morning would never have bested his master in a duel of wits, as had been the case with Queen Miramdahl. By now, everyone in the city had heard of how the witch had manipulated the queen only yesterday into letting her and her friends come here to the Tower.

The general consensus at the dinner table last night, when the brothers had discussed this audacious Donemere of the Codlebærns and how she had resorted to trickery to get her way, was that she was no better than a charlatan and would, no doubt, betray the kingdom just like the rest of her kind always did.

Therefore, it was with a decided sense of superiority that he led them the long way to the door that served as the gateway to the Tower path, and it was not until the second time they passed through the corridor to the dining hall that Akanna took hold of his arm tightly and told him in a snarl, "You will lead us straight to the Tower gate now. If you take longer than the time it takes me to count to one hundred, you will die by my sword. Do you understand me, boy?"

Brother Billy sniffed and clasped his hands upon his wrists within the sleeves of his robe so that he looked rigid and unmoving, but he led them to the door before Akanna made it to eighty, and she had been counting rather quickly. Once there, he slid back each of the twelve thick and heavy iron bolts locking the door down its length, then let the door stand open and flourished a hand to usher them through before him.

Akanna and Falwaïn went first, with Donnie and Diego taking up the rear. Sylvester was atop Donnie's right shoulder.

They got no more than six feet outside the sanctuary before they heard the door slam shut behind them, and then each of the twelve bolts was shot home with a loud clang that split the morning.

Turning back just for a moment to glance at the closed door, Sylvester looked forward again. "Now I understand why I could not find the path to the Tower before this. There isn't one," he observed dryly, noting the overgrowth all around them with displeasure. "The Order must have other means of access to the Tower, and of course they would not share that with us," he said, making it a statement.

Nobody felt they could refute this in any way, so they nodded as a group and moved on through the scrub surrounding them, three swords held at the ready. The Tower stood distant, perhaps half a mile away, but it seemed less than that, for they were all made aware the moment several giant eagles took off from their great eyrie at the top of the Tower. These eagles soared gracefully downward in their direction and begin circling above the intruders, moving lower and lower with each spiral they made. When they got close enough, the birds' great wings thrashed the air and sounded like death hunting its prey, which, naturally, was exactly what was going through the minds of these mighty predators of the skies.

Donnie watched with fascination as the birds drew closer. She heard the others muttering beside her something about running. She stopped where she was and waited, still looking up at the birds, until her friends realized what she was doing and returned to stand around her, with obvious resignation showing from both Falwaïn and Diego. Within seconds, they were effectively hemmed in by at least ten of the huge birds, who all began to strut around them in a circle, their movements quick and disturbing, as if they were barely being restrained from attacking. The three warriors with Donnie tensed and took up combative stances, raising their weapons.

Shaking her head with amusement, Donnie stepped out from behind them and said in a loud, clear voice, *"Gralad'a'bine, Ér Ainíl et Anigus Magur."*

Every Førrens Sea Eagle there stilled instantly and turned their heads slowly to stare at Donnie, obviously thunderstruck by her greeting. The eldest of their number, a crusty old bird with sharp, intelligent eyes, took a couple steps closer and peered at Donnie for about ten seconds before he replied, much more slowly than she had and in a rough, cracking voice that had a whip-like quality to it that was more than a little unnerving to listen to, *"Gralad'a'bine, Anigus Magur et Ér Ainíl."*

He then turned his penetrating gaze toward Sylvester, who was sitting upon Donnie's shoulder as usual, and to him added, "*Aht, gralad'a'bine, Anigus Magur et Anigus Magur.*"

Chapter 20
Why Can't We Be Friends?

With little else to do, Rex ran over the plan for luring the dragon away from the elves in his head once more, hoping that nothing would go wrong. To begin, while he and the falcons in their group, Leaco and Salu, were stationed here above Marn Dím, the others were waiting at the dragon rookery near the Withering Hills. Last night after he'd talked with his mama, they'd all gone back to the dragon breeding/birthing ground to set a trap, hoping to capture the young dragon—whose wingspan was over a hundred feet wide, Rex reminded himself wryly, wondering for the umpteenth time whether the trap was of sufficient size and interest to lure the dragon in and restrain it for long enough.

He and the others had fashioned a very large net using vines of dragon flowers from the large hall outside the rookery's warren last night. The net was decorated with enticing dragon fruit which, according to Feirth, was considered an irresistible delectable by all dragons. While Rex was fairly confident the vine net was large enough, he secretly doubted it was strong enough to hold a wildly flailing dragon, as this one was sure to be once it realized it had been caught in a trap. But, he told himself firmly, if it would give them the time they needed to talk to the dragon, with Feirth using whatever "words" his mother had taught him to use in that weird language that apparently only giants and dragons could understand, they might be able to convince the young monster to leave its elf masters for good and go to the Ganlonds with them instead.

Earlier this morning he and the falcons had returned to Marn Dím, biding their time until it got near to an hour when the dragon would be in the air and, more importantly, away from the elf camp. The falcons were then to have a conversation about Rex somewhere within earshot of the dragon, however they could manage that. They were to name Donnie specifically several times, stressing that she was the new witch who was thought to have murdered three dragons at the Battle of the Branmar Plain. They were to then mention that Rex, her little love as she called him, was resting in a cave high above the city and then they were to take off in the direction of the cave, ostensibly so the one falcon could show Rex off to the other.

As if all of that wasn't unlikely enough to occur without a major hitch, it was further hoped that the dragon would then follow the falcons to the cave and give chase to the waiting Rex. Rex, after "escaping" from the cave, would maintain a pace fast enough to elude the dragon as he raced over the top of the mountain and down its eastern slope. But he had to be mindful not to go so fast as to lose the dragon, or else it wouldn't follow him to the rookery. It should take them a little over two hours to get to their destination, judging from the fastest speed he'd seen the dragon fly.

And that right there was a hugest problem of all and constituted the most pressing of his concerns, because who was going to chase him over mountain, field and moor for two whole hours? Even his best games of keep away with the skunks lasted maybe an hour at most. There was no way the dragon would stay interested in chasing him that long, was there?

So he had set his mind to determining what could be the key to keeping the dragon's focus upon himself all that time, even if that meant letting the thing get close enough to actually harm him a little. He supposed he could always taunt the dragon with more comments about his mama, which might really drive it wild...well, as long that didn't make it so frantic that they couldn't calm the beast once they'd captured it. He knew the dragon had no more ammunition in its gun barrels, nor, it seemed, was any of its other weaponry loaded, but he figured the lasers in the dragon's eyes were probably working just fine. And those, as everybody knew, were lethal.

Hmm, maybe he could let the lasers do a little damage to himself on the way to the Withering Hills...but that would work only if he could successfully minimize the damage they did to him. And then what? How could they make sure the lasers weren't used once they had the dragon in the trap? None of the others in their group had any real defense against it, or so he feared.

Rex paced the cave worriedly.

He stopped, reminding himself that he had to think positively and trust that Feirth would have better luck than Rex suspected he might at making friends with the dragon...after all, that could happen, right?...

His thoughts tailed away and he looked back down the hillside, noting with disappointment that nothing seemed to be happening, even though the dragon had been on patrol for the past fifteen minutes. Granted, he did not actually see the dragon at the moment, but it must be down in the trees or something like that. He decided to lay down for a little while and then he'd check again. He turned around seven times where he was, as was often his habit, before dropping his length carefully to the ground. He huffed impatiently, his breath raising a small cloud of dry dust around his nose, enough so that he sneezed, and then sneezed again until something caught his ear. It was the keening of the falcons and they were getting very close.

He jumped to his feet and looked out over the ledge just in time to see Leaco and Salu veer off to his left. The dragon, right behind them, pulled up and hovered in front of him, its darkly orange, yellow-rimmed eyes glaring at him with hatred, while small puffs of thick, black smoke billowed from its nostrils angrily. It was out for blood—Rex's blood.

Acting out of instinct, Rex dove to his right and leapt toward the path up the mountain. He felt the dragon's rage in the form of red-hot flames burning up his footsteps behind him. He let himself grow bigger so he could use his enlarged muscles to propel himself up the mountainside faster. The dragon's fire spurred him on more than once when it reached his tail and he knew his fur there was singed short almost immediately.

He dug even deeper into his reserves and leapt up the mountain a little faster. The thing was, he wasn't *letting* the dragon get close—no, it turned out the dragon could fly a heck of a lot faster than Rex had thought it could, and it was having no trouble keeping up with him right now. But Rex couldn't go to Mach speed or he'd lose the dragon for sure, which meant he had to maintain his fastest regular speed without going into overdrive. He hoped it would be enough to keep him from getting too badly injured.

He raced off the path and under some trees, thinking they might provide cover, but realized his mistake too late, for the forest around him erupted into hot flames that he could feel licking at his fur with their demonic tongues. Usually, he never got touched by things like this, but this dragon's fire was different and he reckoned his mama hadn't known it would be or she would never have suggested he use himself as bait.

Rex concentrated hard on his magic, glowing a brilliant blue just like his mama did whenever her magic was running high. He encased himself in a magical shield to protect against the burning flames shooting all around him, which sort of worked and sort of didn't, because he could feel his fur everywhere growing hot and even more slightly singed. Plus, the dragon fire was making the air thick and heavy so that it was difficult to breathe and hard to move through.

He felt concerned for the people in the city below, for the fire would surely reach them too, and they might have no defense against it. It would be several hours later that he would find out from Feirth that dragon's fire only went where the dragon wanted, which, in this case, would be in the direction the dog had been running—that is, away from the city.

By now, Rex had lost his sense of direction within the conflagration and a new terror from that situation lasted for several utterly miserable minutes because the firestorm around him was so intense it negated all his other senses. But he kept moving upward, kept focusing on increasing his speed, and luckily kept climbing toward the mountain top. He reached its peak, saw some landmarks he recognized that were just now being engulfed in flames, and then he shot down the mountain, rejoining the path they'd used the night before. This time, he made sure he stayed ahead of the dragon's fire and did not get lost again. He no longer wondered how he'd get the dragon to follow him for two hours. This dragon would keep after him indefinitely, for he could feel that its hatred was that great for himself and Donnie.

***

The young *vírat*, recognizing upon the dog a smell that reminded her of her greatest enemy, grew incensed that she could not obliterate the beast as easily as she desired. But fire was all she had at her disposal right now because she had to marshal all her thoughts to use and control the lasers in her eyes, something that seemed impossible to her at the moment. But she kept chasing him in the off-chance an opportunity would arise and she could then incinerate this silly little creature so dearly loved by the murdering witch. And then that horrible woman might—just might—get a small taste of the pain and grief she had caused the dragon's family.

***

After spreading out the new texts and scrolls she'd collected from the shelves of the Forrieghness Tower Library, Donnie sat back down at the table she'd been working at all morning and breathed in the musty smell of the great library with extreme pleasure. She had always loved libraries and books and maps and any collection of tangible knowledge that could be physically amassed. She glanced at Falwaïn at the next table over and saw the same rapture on his face that she was certain was displayed upon hers.

Sylvester too was deeply ensconced in checking and cross-checking several magical treatises, stuffing his fertile brain with new knowledge that he hoped would be of help to them one day. His primary search was for any information on his locket, but to his disappointment, nothing could be found regarding any locket with a similar shape or constitution as his. He had then moved on to researching other things.

Akanna and Diego, while also buried under mounds of texts, looked as though they could use a break, and a long one at that. They were studying Ghérôntogs and their known characteristics and potential weaknesses, and were also learning what they could regarding other creatures of similar terrifying ilk.

Turning her attention back to her own finds, Donnie smiled to herself as she carefully set about opening the Scroll of Talbula Halladd D'Orsti, the scroll that Na'aven had recommended she read. She was thrilled to have it because she'd been sure she'd have to wait a very long time for it since it was in use by two of the mages tending the Tower, or so they had informed her yesterday, going on to say that it was not available to her and they could not possibly predict when it might be. But, only a few minutes ago, the library itself had presented it to her as one of the scrolls on a shelf she'd been searching about dragon *badûrs*, and she'd scooped it up without saying a word to anyone.

Intriguingly, it was written in five languages, the first of which was Elanéra, the language of magic, as Gaia had informed her after the Battle of the Branmar Plain. Some called it the language of the gods because the more magic you could wield—in essence becoming more godlike—the better you could understand Elanéra. Since Donnie was now an actual goddess, minor though she be, her skill with the language was pretty good. She skimmed the text of the scroll, noting happily that she was able to understand somewhere around two-thirds of it straight away.

The next two languages the scroll was written in she did not recognize, but the fourth was in Sarn—or rather, English. She did not know the fifth either, but figured she could probably get a complete translation between the two languages she did comprehend. She set about reading the first version in Elanéra, and then the fourth in Sarn, noticing immediately that there were subtle differences between portions of the two versions that could potentially have far-reaching consequences.

She was just rechecking the beginning paragraphs of her work when the main library doors opened once, closed firmly, and then they opened again with a loud bang of their wood against the walls of the Tower. Next came sounds of a heated kerfuffle that echoed throughout the small and large chambers of the enormous old library. The fracas made its way deeper into the magical repository and, to Donnie's great astonishment, she saw that it was being made by the Bishop of the Førrens Order of Manûs Mages himself, Aldalis Munkinum. He was sternly commanding someone, as yet unseen by those in the library's main chamber, that they were not allowed inside the library and must leave at once. He reiterated this several more times, but whoever he was talking to must have gone on ignoring him, for his tone rose with increasing stress upon each iteration.

It took another ten seconds or so before the objects of the bishop's ire shuffled into view. These turned out to be five of the mammoth Førrens Sea Eagles who, for whatever reason, had seen fit to invade the library. Three of the hulking raptors trailed the two in the front, and these three kept their eyes sweeping the hall around them for any sign of advance from the order's brothers.

But it was to the two in front that the bishop addressed his increasingly vigorous remonstrations. One of these was the male bird who had spoken to Donnie and the others when Donnie had recited to them the traditional greeting between magical beings of the higher orders. She had read of the greeting in one of Catie's diaries and had dearly wanted an opportunity to use it, so she was completely delighted by its reception with the Sea Eagles the day before.

Their leader of yesterday, who was called Gak, looked over at Donnie and murmured something to the one by his side. That eagle looked ancient, blind, and frail, and it moved quite slowly.

As a group, the Sea Eagles approached directly toward Donnie, their movements not exactly clumsy, *per se*, but certainly rhythmic as they swayed from one side to the other depending upon which clawed foot they were stepping with.

The bishop had apparently given up his objections for the present and watched silently while the imposing birds marched farther into the library until they came to a stop about ten feet from where Donnie stood. But he again interjected himself between Donnie and the majestic raptors at this point, grinding out between his clenched teeth, "Ye are not allowed here, and ye must leave or we brothers will force ye out."

Donnie, about to protest this threat, was cut short by the sharp cackles of laughter this inspired in the eagles. They laughed and laughed, their loud screeches making the bishop and his order brothers ever more uncomfortable. Donnie, on the other hand, materialized some cotton balls which she shared with her friends. They gathered around her so they could stuff their ears too and thereafter looked on serenely at the interaction of the birds and the mage.

Donnie, after filling her own ears with cotton fluff, crossed her arms in front of her and leaned back casually on her hips, making a clear, wordless statement that she had decided to let the scene play out before her without her interference.

Eventually, the ear-splitting, shrieking laughter stopped. Donnie and her friends removed the cotton from their ears and all stood at attention now, looking politely from Gak to the blind eagle beside him.

The bishop huffed and stared down his nose superiorly at the eagles.

Gak ignored him yet again and locked gazes with Donnie instead. He croaked, "*Gralad'a'bine, Anigus Magur et Ér Ainíl.*"

Donnie recited her reply in a grave voice, at the same time briefly glancing with satisfaction at the dumbstruck bishop, who had whirled toward her. "*Gralad'a'bine, Ér Ainíl et Anigus Magur.*"

The ancient-most eagle cackled again, but mercifully kept her laughter brief and not so ear-piercing as before. "Ah, 'tis good to hear the old words spoken again, Ér Ainíl," she said with obvious satisfaction. "My name is Nagba, and I am the High Convoke of the Førrens Sea Eagles," she declared proudly, going on to explain, "We are the guardians and keepers of the Toren fi Førrens, although this foolish wizard appears to believe he and his kind own that honor." The bird turned her unseeing eyes unerringly to the bishop and, her voice cracking like a whip, she snapped at him, "By what divine order do ye claim keepership of this tower? Show me, as I will show ye ours!" she demanded, and she threw her head upward to the high ceiling above.

No less than five tapestries, hung for many long years upon the Tower's walls, zoomed down toward the group that was gathered around the great eagles. In succession, these tapestries showed the greatest of the magical races bestowing upon the Førrens Sea Eagles the cross that still adorned the Tower's highest pinnacle.

"Bring us a record of any kind that names ye as the keepers of the Tower!" she challenged the mage again, waving a wing at the tapestries, which moved around so that they hung in the air above the birds now, their scenes clear and utterly convincing. "Unless it be something from that elf queen ye serve, for magic does not recognize her as its own and ye know this well, for she has turned her back upon magic, except for the black arts she practices in secret and which ye assist her in learning."

When the bishop gasped and straightened his back in affected outrage, Nagba cackled again before inquiring, "Did ye think we didna know what ye were doing with her? Ye are as big a fool as ye seem then, ye are. Mark my words, false mage that ye are becoming, magic will take back its own and ye will rue the day ye decided to take up with that sly elf queen o' yourn."

When the bishop started to protest this, Gak stepped forward and let out a blast of sound at him that was a cross between a screech and a grunt and which said in that one note that the birds were letting him live only through sufferance. The message was so plain that no one could mistake it for anything other than the threatening reprimand it was, and Aldalis Munkinum, feeling its inherent warning, shut his mouth on his rebuttals.

Nagba returned her attention to Donnie and noted with satisfaction, "Ye have read the scroll ye were seeking, ye have. And did it provide ye with the answers ye sought?"

Donnie grinned, awestruck that this magnificent being, blind as she was, was apparently so in tune with her library that Donnie suspected she knew exactly who was reading what at all times.

Shaking her head slightly with bemusement, Donnie replied, "Well, to be honest, I think it has raised more questions in me than provided answers." She twisted around to carefully pick up the Talbula scroll and heard several of the brothers snort indignantly when they recognized what she held. She looked 'round, her innocent gaze finally settling upon the bishop. "The Tower Library provided the Scroll of the Immortals to me this morning and I have been studying it ever since," she explained crisply. "As to its answers, all I can say to that is I cross-checked the Sarn text with the Elanéran text and have found some discrepancies that could have quite an impact on what is considered to be fact around here, most especially since the Sarn text seems to be taken as the truth. And yet," she mused almost to herself, "the original text is clearly the Elanéran one, so to my mind, that should certainly hold precedence over any of the translations. And that means the Sarn version, if not the others as well, appears to be incorrect."

Several order brothers scoffed pompously at this bold statement and tittered amongst themselves with scathing denunciation. The bishop even stared down his nose at Donnie this time before jeering, "Ye lie, for ye could not possibly know the tongue of the gods sufficient to make a reliable comparison between the texts of the Talbula Halladd D'Orsti."

Falwaïn stepped forward, puffed out his chest, and retorted fiercely, "She does not lie! And she knew enough of that same language to get us here, remember? Or did you forget about the tapestry that dictated the terms for any Ca'nam being looking to visit the Tower? Can you yourself read that? How many of you can, I wonder?" he demanded, huffing with the heat of his convictions and then glaring around at the fifteen or so brothers that had congregated to watch their leader's confrontation with the Sea Eagles and the unwanted witch. To a one, their expressions showed that Falwaïn's shot had hit its mark.

That is, except for the bishop, whose face was as impassive as stone when he extended his hand toward Donnie for the scroll, commanding her peremptorily to, "Give it to me, for ye should not have that venerated scroll in thy vulgar clutches."

Donnie took a half-step backward. "In my vulgar clutches?" she echoed in disbelief. "And you're not even joking when you say that, are you?" she remarked, chuckling with forced amusement. "Well, I'll tell ya, brother, if the library is okay with me reading it, then I guess you'll have to be too," she added dryly. Then she turned back to Nagba and said seriously, "The Sarn text says that there are four immortal races in all of Írtha, which I gather has been taken to mean there are four and only four immortal races. But the Elanéran text says there are four immortal races known to be on Írtha. As I say, the distinction is subtle, but I think it must mean there are more immortal races, and maybe they're on other worlds if they're not here—or would that be other dimensions? Well, anyway, because of that, I question if what's known as the Symbol of the Immortals represents something else—unless it's a symbol only known on Írtha, then I suppose someone from here might have created it for the Immortals. Do you know?" she asked the old she-eagle curiously, setting the scroll carefully back down onto the table.

Nagba cackled again and threw back her head, her beak held wide as though in a smile. "Ah, ye look like thy mother and argue like thy sisters!" she crowed with approval, her unseeing eyes glistening in the daylight illuminating the great library chamber.

This statement was met with confused silence.

No one moved for at least ten seconds, until Donnie shook herself and spluttered, "Wha-what? How do you know my mother? A-and I have only one sister," she assured the still-beaming eagle confidently.

"Nay," demurred the High Convoke. "Ye have twelve sisters and I have met them all, even the eldest, Briganna, who is dead now, alas. After her demise, the sisters congregated here no longer. But before then, I came to know them all well and I can tell ye that none wielded more power than Briganna, none was wiser than Margawse, or more knowledgeable than Melchira, more beautiful than Philînan, nor more passionate than young Vessica. Even Gwillagan had her staunch beliefs and would not be swayed from them easily."

Donnie stared at the old eagle with consternation, her thoughts reeling. "But...but that means you think I'm a daughter of Morri—no, you can't possibly think that!" she admonished, her disbelieving voice just above a whisper. Her startled gaze drifted toward Falwaïn, who was wide-eyed with astonishment too.

"But ye are a daughter of Morrían!" Nagba exclaimed, making it sound unequivocal. "This I have been assured of from the moment ye stepped foot near the Tower, although I suspected as much when ye first accepted thy birthright erst-year and magic informed the entire planet of that with its flood wave. And then it happened again, during the conflict with the mad sorcerer, Valledai who was in truth Orgos, at the Battle of the Branmar Plain. I knew the Nine had arisen in full once more and that only a powerful witch, a daughter herself, could warrant the swell that engulfed us all in that moment. I recall well the magic of the mother and every one of her daughters has had it alike, it is that distinctive. It resonates the same and cheers the heart and soul to be near it—well, except for the one who turned from the light and the other who followed her." The eagle frowned a little when she said this, but then her expression cleared and she observed brightly, "And ye have a goodly round of companions with ye, I see. They be companions who help ye on thy path, and whom ye are supporting in turn."

Nagba tilted her head toward Donnie's friends in her bird-like way, blinked her eyes as if she could indeed see each of them and were studying them singly, and then she cried out happily, "But there are more, are there not?"

"Yes," admitted Donnie, made completely awash and confounded by the eagle's claims.

What the bird had posited was crazy...wasn't it? Nagba had to be wrong...but she seemed so positive she was correct.

It took Donnie a few seconds to realize that more had been said. She shook her head to clear it, glanced over at Falwaïn again and noticed the look of concern he was giving her, which made her turn back to the Sea Eagle to ask cordially, "I'm sorry, what was that last bit you said?"

"Ye must believe me, Donemere," the eagle urged, "although it may be hard, for ye have been hidden well for such a long time, being as ye were the youngest, and therefore the most powerful of all the sisters, for thy mother died to give ye life." Nagba paused in remembrance and bowed her head, her harsh voice softening somehow while she had relayed all this. She lifted her head after a moment's gravity and informed Donnie, "In doing so, she gave ye her all, including her powers and her will, so ye can be the one to lead thy sisters home."

Donnie stared at the old eagle dazedly and was suddenly engulfed in a wild mix of emotions that took her breath away and made the world spin around her wildly. She felt herself falter backward and Falwaïn was there instantly, helping her sink down onto her chair safely.

Nagba moved closer to her, so that she now stood almost directly over Donnie. Donnie, too stunned to speak, focused her eyes forward until the spinning stopped and she saw that the eagle's feathers looked silky and shiny in the bright light angling through the natural windows of the tufa-built library. She suddenly realized that each of the birds made a small rustling noise every few seconds and had been doing so all along, but she had been too distracted to notice it before now. The sound was created when they ruffled their dark feathers, which they were all doing as though it were a nervous tic. Its strangeness somehow seemed to underscore the impossible revelations of Nagba's declarations.

"Ye have been told many lies to protect ye all these years," the High Convoke continued, "but the veil is being lifted now, for ye must rise to thy destiny, as ye already know from dear Catie, I am sure."

"Oh, Catie...well, she's told everyone almost nothing *but* lies, it seems," muttered Donnie, her voice sounding faint and far away to her ears.

Nagba tossed her head upward and cackled yet again. "Catie truly tries to be a goodly girl, she does! And she *is* one at heart, or magic would treat her very differently from what it do. While I have not seen her for many a long year now, I always enjoyed her visits here to the Tower."

This, of all things, was finally too much for the bishop. He had barely restrained his cutting tongue for the last five minutes and it had been painful for him to do so. But upon this latest pronouncement by Nagba, he stepped forward to protest biliously, "Ye have had no visitors the entire time I have lived here, which means ye are lying to this witch and therefore she is no daughter of Morrían! Wicked, wicked bird!" he remonstrated, shaking an angry finger at Nagba.

But Nagba found him only amusing and again threw her head back and cackled with abandon. When she was finished, she said, "Have ye never heard of a *fír'mäela*? 'Tis is a portal between places protected by magic. Almost any Fægre Witch can create them, but not so many Munus Wizards can. And Caterin of the Codlebærn visited me and this library through hers for centuries, starting long before ye came here to darken the Tower's halls!"

Donnie sat up straight and gasped with sudden recognition. "Oh, my goodness!" she cried. "You're who Catie calls Ornithorn in her diaries!"

The High Convoke looked much pleased by this. "Yes, indeed, that is her name for me because she thinks me prickly about her doings and not-doings, while mine for her is Gilded Lily. I call her that because of the innumerable trinkets with which she so loves to adorn her body and which make her gleam in candlelight like a gilded flower." Here, the bird paused, adding with a touch of sadness, "Or so I thought before I went blind and my sight became that which I borrow from others."

Donnie shook her head, marveling to herself. She again missed the next thing said and had to ask for it to be repeated.

"I merely noted that thy little ones are powerful already, even in thy womb," the old bird repeated, although she was beginning to sound impatient with Donnie and, to be quite honest, Donnie couldn't blame her.

Sitting up straight, Donnie took a deep breath, shook out her shoulders and her hands, then she stood up so that she and the eagle were nearly eye to eye. "If what you are telling me about my parentage is true, will the library be able to give me information on my family, such as what they're like or what they've done? Perhaps even where they are?"

The bird blinked and considered this, her head tilting in jerks while she unconsciously listened to every sound being made in the great chamber around her. After several moments, she replied, "There are texts in the library that may indeed help ye to know them, but there is little here about thy sisters other than the five eldest and young Vessica and, of course, Bréagna and Duínagh. Of thy mother, Morrían, there is much told of her deeds, most especially in the early days of Medregai's civilization, although of her deeds in other places, very little is known. There may be hints of where they all went, but nothing in the library tells what their fates be, except for poor Briganna, whose body was buried by her most beloved sisters, but only they know where. Together, it is all much more than thy mate could read in many months or perhaps even a year, so ye must establish thine own *fír'mäela* and, if the library accepts it, ye will always have a conduit to its material, no matter where ye travel, as long as ye are on sacred ground when ye call it forth."

"Can I do that now, here?" Donnie asked curiously, and Nagba nodded.

"Either here or home will suffice," the High Convoke assured her.

Once again, this proved too much for Aldalis Munkinum, and he surged forward in protest. "I will not have this witch being given unfettered access to the library's holy texts! No, she may not create any such portal to it, either now or later!" he commanded explosively, greatly irritated by his loss of control over the situation, and perhaps also by the fear he could feel invading his heart that this witch's magic would grow far beyond what his own abilities could ever match. Even now she had clearly surpassed him, and yet he was the second-most powerful wizard in all of Medregai. And that would not do, he told himself; no, it simply would not do.

Nagba turned to him, her blind eyes filmy and eerie. From the sneering expression on the mage's countenance, he obviously felt only revulsion for the bird.

She croaked to him, "Where is that proof ye were going to show us that gives ye the right to call thy order the keepers of the Tower?" The tapestries still floating above her began to flap loudly in the air and she tossed her head at them. "Here is mine, but where is thine?" she inquired almost musically. "While thy elf queen may believe she possesses some rule here, she has none in the Tower, nor do ye. If the Tower wishes to open itself to the last daughter of Morrían, there is not a thing ye or any other daft wizard can do about it, for the Tower *is* magic. And, as we all know, magic has a special bond with the daughters of Morrían."

So saying this, she waved her left wing a little and a new scroll came flitting toward Donnie.

Donnie caught it in her fingers and unrolled it. It was instructions, if you could call them that, on how to create a *fir'mäela*. She herself would call it mostly just advice. It was written in the Elanéran language, which made Donnie wonder if perhaps that was the main reason that few Munus Wizards could create one, seeing as most could not read Elanéra. A bit of a catch 22 there, she supposed with amusement.

Muttering this to herself, she turned to walk to the middle of the room, where she stood and let her magic reach down toward the center of the earth, connecting almost instantly with the vast sea of magic beneath her feet. She let her magic mix with that of the Tower, feeling its warmth and vibrancy fill her soul with gladness. This sense of well-being she used to wrap herself in a thick blanket of blue magic, the Tower's magic creating streaks of different colors within Donnie's bright cobalt. She closed her eyes and visualized an open doorway connected to her cottage, feeling it most apropos to link directly to her own library. When she saw this image in her mind, she pushed it outward and opened her eyes.

And there, in front of her, stood an open portal to her library, looking very much like a real, open doorway. Donnie chortled with amusement because it seemed the chickens had made their way into the cottage and were, as they had so loved to do during the winter months, now engaged in roosting upon the bookshelves, bawking and squawking companionably to each other. But they sensed the moment the portal opened and this aroused their attention. Once a few of them saw Donnie at the other end, they raced to her and began crowding around her feet, happily greeting her with loud squeaks and squawks of affection. Soon, nearly twenty chickens were milling around her on the library floor demanding her attention.

Donnie could just hear the house trees calling out to her over the din of the chickens and so she too called back warm salutations to both Mournful Jack and Sophie, who were the only ones awake, they said.

The order brothers were going pretty much ballistic by this time, what with all the feathery confusion going on, and some were threatening to use violence to clear away the chickens. Donnie sent several of these wizards dirty looks in return, then she reached down and started shooing the birds back through the portal.

When they were all back home, she bade them goodbye, shouting super loudly because of the noise going on behind her now that she would try to visit again soon and they needn't be so worried about her. She visualized the portal closing and it did, with just the slightest "pop" of compressed air.

She turned around to near-bedlam. Even the boombox apparently thought so, for it had appeared and was currently occupied in blaring out that wonderful old classic, "Why Can't We Be Friends?"

While she'd known that what she was doing was sure to upset the brotherhood, Donnie had gotten a certain satisfaction from it regardless, and she now looked upon the angry protestors with no small twinkle in her eyes. It was a twinkle that she was sure would also have been in Nagba's eyes if the High Convoke had been able to see.

As it was, the four younger Sea Eagles had taken it upon themselves to stand in front of Donnie's friends with their wings spread protectively wide, defiant expressions on their feathered faces as their large, sharply curved beaks sliced the air here and there, brief, muted squawks of menace emanating from each of them. The five tapestries that Nagba had called down earlier were herding the wildly running and jumping wizard brothers together into a circle, beating at them until they complied.

Whatever spells the mages shot at the tapestries were bounced back upon themselves, which made for an unexpected circumstance that most caught on to fast enough that no real or lasting harm was done to anyone. And then more tapestries joined in the fun and had the wizards scuffling ever closer toward each other. The birds advanced on the wizards from the other side of the room as the brothers' grouping got tighter and tighter, and the tapestries stiffened and folded as necessary to beat the wizards about their heads and shoulders to show them that the birds (by means of the tapestries) meant business.

Donnie couldn't help but chuckle, especially since none of the wizards were being hurt by any of this, but she still thought it had gone about as far as it should go, and so she clamped down on the laughter escaping her lips and moved forward to call out in cheery voice, "Okay, everyone can stop now! Really, there's no reason at all to fight. Now there, that's much better, isn't it?" she said in what she hoped was a soothing voice, meeting the darkly furious gaze of Aldalis Munkinum boldly.

The boombox was having a great time, repeating the chorus over and over again, making it sound like a DJ was working their turntables, with, "*Wikki, wikki, wikki! Why can't we—why can't we—why can't we be friends, why can't we be friends?*" echoing loudly throughout the Tower's chambers. It had materialized on top of the table where Donnie had been sitting, so it was just a couple feet from Nagba, who was grinning in its direction with absolute delight on her wizened features.

Donnie went to stand by the ancient bird and said over the music, "Um, that's my boombox—it's a music box, obviously. And, er, it has a mind of its own," she explained, glancing at the bishop as she shouted this, "which means I can't control it. Nobody can," she added, "but it sometimes listens if you're nice to it." She smiled at nobody in particular, bent down a little to look straight at the boombox and asked it respectfully, "Uh, boombox? That's pretty funny, as you know. It really is, but the moment's kinda over, so would you mind going elsewhere?"

As if to show how little it cared for Donnie's futile requests, no matter how politely put, the music box cranked up its volume and ran through the whole song at just below a deafening roar. Donnie grimaced apologetically at the others and passed around more cotton. The tapestries that had come loose to chase the brothers danced in the air with the music, twirling and twisting around the wizards they had corralled, generally keeping pretty good time to the beat.

At the end of the song, the boombox disappeared and Donnie turned to the others to say, "I think perhaps we should listen to its message, don't you? We have no real reason to fight here, so let's just go about our business, accept each other as we are, and we'll all be good." At least, that is what she'd intended to say, but she was interrupted halfway through it by the sound of the outer doors opening for an extended period, and then several voices in general conversation could be heard approaching.

Through the open archway of the main chamber came about thirty creatures of all sorts and sizes, all of whom were looking to visit the library for their first time. Their eyes were filled with wonder as they took in the thousands of tapestries hung all around the inside of the massive main chamber and the shelves behind these that were filled to capacity with texts of all kinds. To a one, their gazes roamed the walls first, their mouths wide in wonder, and then dropped to the group huddled near the center of the room, where about ten tapestries were now floating freely and seemingly aimlessly above the heads of those gathered there.

Nagba sent the tapestries zooming to their original places with a small flap of her wing, then she stepped toward the newcomers, her voice raised when she said, "Hail, curious visitors, to the Forrieghness Tower Library! It has been too long since any other than wizards came to study our texts, and we, the Førrens Sea Eagles, keepers and guardians of the Toren fi Førrens, bid you greetings of hearty welcome!"

Aldalis Munkinum was shaking his head from side to side, moaning, "No, no! This cannot be happening. How is this happening?" His brothers were staring at him, then the witch, then the old Sea Eagle, then the new visitors, and back to their leader with hooded gazes, each calculating for themselves just how best to react.

The brotherhood, which looked from the outside to be a conclave of like minds, was in fact anything but. Each of its members secretly hoped the bishop would meet his downfall in a public, if not necessarily lethal manner, however that could be effected, so that his title and position were open to others to claim. Excitement began to build in their breasts at the possibility that today might bring such an unexpected gift as the ousting of Aldalis Munkinum, and their already sharp gazes honed ever further into focusing on their greatest mutual desire.

It can be said that Aldalis Munkinum was not unaware of this reaction by his brethren, and he therefore schooled himself to return to his normal stature and demeanor. He leaned forward to take a step, his right hand gripping his wand and holding it forth, opened his mouth, and then the strangest thing happened. He felt his feet drag as though in heavy sand, and his bones crackled and popped, so he stopped moving for a moment, then pulled himself back to a resting position, looking bewildered.

Nagba, who had been facing away from him, now turned and advised him, "It seems the library has heard enough from ye today, Aldalis. Unless ye wish to be no more than a statue, I suggest ye bend to the will of the Tower and bid these good souls a greeting of welcome." She turned a little further and encompassed the rest of the brotherhood in a small wave. "And that goes for the rest of ye, as well. A daughter of Morrían is back amongst us and that can only mean that magic is not yet ready to fade from this land. We must encourage its resurgence, do ye not agree?" she asked, although she didn't wait for a reply before facing the new visitors and urging them to, "Come one, come all! Tell thy fellow compatriots and companions that all be welcomed here in the Tower, no matter how little Ca'nam magic they wield. They will not be turned away and their path shall not be barred by anyone or anything, for if it be, then we, the Førrens Sea Eagles, will make it clear, and we will have the might of the library and of magic itself with us! Magic shall always prevail!" she cried, and her rallying call was appreciated by several who clapped and cheered loudly, with Donnie and her friends being perhaps the loudest and most enthusiastic clappers going.

Sitting back down at their tables and resuming their work was nearly impossible, but after another hour, everyone had slowly become immersed once again in the texts open before them. The order's brothers had left the building immediately after Nagba welcomed the new visitors, ostensibly to regroup and decide their future moves. Donnie could not anticipate what those might be but she kind of hoped that she and her friends would be long gone before the bishop and his followers were able to mount any sort of real offense toward the Sea Eagles. She supposed that magic would not allow anything to happen that it truly did not countenance, so her worry quotient was really rather low about it all.

As to the question of her own parentage, Donnie refused to think about it. She needed to be alone when she finally confronted it, because she was pretty sure it was going to be an emotional session and she was not about to have that here in front of a bunch of strangers or even her friends. Besides, it wasn't like she could ask a million questions about her mother and sisters today, could she? After all, the library was busier than it probably had been in many a long year, so Nagba would have no time for her. She kept glancing over to see where the High Convoke was, but Nagba remained busy with the Tower's newest visitors for some time.

There was something Nagba had said that echoed in Donnie's ears and it kept on bothering her. When the old bird was finally freed from showing the newbies how to use the library, Donnie ran over and stood by the bird, grinning at Gak first, whom Donnie had surmised was mostly who Nagba "saw" through, and then at Nagba.

Nagba returned the smile and said, "Donemere, what can I do for ye?"

Donnie replied, "Oh, please, do call me Donnie; all my friends do." When the bird inclined her head, Donnie smiled wider and explained in a low voice, "You said something earlier that made me quite curious, which was that magic did not recognize Queen Miramdahl because she'd turned her back on it. What did you mean by that?"

In response, the High Convoke was silent.

Donnie searched her mind for a persuasive argument, then she realized that simple truth would work best, so she added earnestly, "I'm not asking for gossipy reasons or anything such as that. You see, it strikes me that, if I really am the thirteenth and final daughter of Morrían, then she made me for a purpose. As you said yourself, I am rising to meet my destiny, but I don't yet know what that is, although I am guessing that Morrían did, otherwise why would she give me so much of herself? As for Miramdahl, I don't know how deeply she's involved in what's happening, I just know that she has her part in it, no matter how small that might be. And what I'm asking now is whether the answer to my question is something that perhaps has influenced my situation or had a part in defining my destiny, or rather, my purpose. If you believe it does, then I could use all the information I can get, because I'm having to play catchup to some very powerful beings who all seem to know a lot more than I do about who I am and *why* I am."

She waited a few moments for a reply, got none, and began to draw away, telling herself that she was not going to pester Nagba. She calmly reminded herself that if the High Convoke didn't want to tell her Miramdahl's story, then she would just have to accept that.

Donnie had not even completed a full step away before Nagba said, "Child, do not run from me. I am merely composing in my mind the proper way to describe the incident." She lifted her head upward toward the top of the Tower, then she lowered it to ask Donnie, "Can ye fly?"

Donnie shrugged. "I can levitate myself, yes, if it's to up there," she replied, pointing straight up. "To go somewhere else, I'll need my broom and saddle."

"Levitation will work just fine then," the bird said, and she spread her wings, lifting herself into flight effortlessly. Gak went too, only a second behind his convoke.

The rush from their beating wings made Donnie's heart flutter a little. Shaking off that disturbing feeling, she crossed her arms in front of her and laid her hands upon her shoulders, concentrating hard on centering her magic within herself. And then she too was lifted into the air toward the very top of the Tower. She ignored the many gasps and exclamations that sounded all around the main chamber the moment her feet left the floor.

She rose to a dark hole in the wooden ceiling, high up within the Tower, and glided through it. She was now in an unlit passageway that had several more holes cut into its ceiling. Gak was waiting for her and told her which hole to take and how many floors of the eyrie to rise through to follow Nagba. In another minute or so, Donnie found herself in a warm, friendly room lit brightly by filtered sunshine. This room was fortuitously situated at the very top of the Tower, so the view from it was stunning and Donnie was appropriately astounded. Made speechless as she gazed through the room's many arched openings toward the mountains and over the city of Anûmanétus, Donnie turned where she stood and admired the beautiful vistas surrounding the Tower.

Nagba let her have her fill of this delicious feast for the eyes and then cleared her throat, inviting Donnie to sit. Donnie looked around, spied what looked like a chair in the corner, and lifted off the several rugs that were laid over it. She was right, it was a chair and, after placing the rugs very carefully upon the sand-colored tufa floor, she sat down, noting how comfortable the chair was as she sank into its cushions. She was facing the High Convoke now, who was settled upon a very large and plush perch, which Donnie assumed is where the ancient bird spent much of her days and nights.

Nagba's beak fell to her breast and she looked to be almost asleep. But before too long went by, she began to speak.

"I can tell from the texts ye and some of thy friends are reading that ye know of the *Hèset fi Bâslen*, or what is commonly called the Jewels of Light," she said heavily, keeping her eyes closed and her head down. "There are no texts in the library that address the beginnings of the Jewels, but they have been in Írtha since history has been recorded, that much is known of their origins. Each of the Jewels has its own way of working and are known to control any and all creatures, including *vírata*. In ancient times, they were rescued by seven of Morrían's daughters and hidden for more than two millennia by the second eldest of the girls, Gwillagan. Her younger sister, Philînan, met a comely young sorcerer from the Iceni Meræ and he convinced her to steal the *Hèset fi Bâslen* from their hiding place. To her downfall, Philînan succeeded. When she gave the Jewels to the young man, he disappeared with 'em. All of this is exhibited in the tapestry called Philînan's Betrayal, which resides here in the library. Ye should study it a while, I think. In fact, I believe it might be meant for ye."

Donnie, intrigued by such a possibility, murmured, "Really? Meant for me?"

Smiling briefly, Nagba said, "See it for thyself."

A brightly colored tapestry appeared over the archway directly across from Donnie.

Donnie pushed herself to her feet and approached the wall hanging. It showed a man with ice-blond hair holding a staff, almost pointing it at the woman depicted on the other tapestry in front of him. Behind him was an open doorway to a city that looked different from any Donnie had ever been in, but that seemed to be oddly modern. Moving closer to the tapestry, she saw that the woman, a beautiful young girl with dark, curly hair, held in her hand some jewels, a couple of which were falling from her extended fingers. In the midst of the woman's breast protruded a knife, while blood had only just begun to seep from the wound. It was a knife that Donnie recognized only too well, seeing as it had attacked her on several occasions and was currently encased in a cage of her own magic at the cottage on the Ganlonds.

"What the hell?" she whispered disbelievingly. Without thinking about it overmuch, she reached her hand toward the tapestry, gripping its nearest edge to pull it closer for her to study, only barely registering Nagba's low and sudden mutter of protest.

To her complete astonishment, her mind was taken over by a vision of what she soon came to realize was an encounter between two of her sisters that she had read of before when she'd started to look through the third book of their adventures, just after retrieving the tome from Julia.

***

After tending to the fire, Gwillagan stood tall as her critical gaze swept the main room of her cottage, for she knew her sisters would be searching for signs that she was either too old or too crazy to still be guarding the hiding place of the *Hèset fî Bâslen*, or Jewels of Light as they were commonly called. This was a task that had been hers for a millennium or two, she could no longer remember which—it might even be three or four by now, for all she could recall. The hundreds of thousands of days that had passed since she'd been given the guardianship duty had meant nothing to her and yet she had enjoyed every single one as "Keeper" of the mystical jewels, for it was Gwillagan's way to be eager and interested in both her gifts and in her life here in the frigid north of Medregai, far from what she thought of as the devious civilizations of the elves, the men, the vinca, and all other mortal races dwelling upon this fair continent.

In the summertime, the normally frozen temperatures of the Icebay of Nœthlinga retreated just far enough south that, for a few weeks, the world Gwillagan knew so intimately bloomed into riotous jumbles of flora that proudly exhibited nature's entire spectrum of colors. While she loved these bountiful days and rejoiced in them with an abandon she otherwise would never exhibit, the stark whites and blacks of the rest of the year drew her in and made her triune sing with its purpose and its joy. To her, there was nothing more splendiferous than freshly fallen snow, a pristine delight of incomparable beauty grown several inches thick and coating everything around her in its icy blanket, and nothing more dazzling or shiny than the crystallized wonderland in which she resided for ten months of every year.

Gwillagan was not the first daughter of Morrían, but she was the first to be truly fulfilled, for here on Fellowes Island she was home and had no need of traveling elsewhere, nor did she wish for the adventures of her youth. She no longer desired anyone else's company or comfort, for she had her tapestries to weave and those kept her both contented and occupied night after night, day after day, their rich colors and vivid scenes lending a sense of acute history to them as if they were occurring right before her as she wove, with only herself and her loom to witness and record their allegorical messages.

These skillfully *wefan* hangings she gave to her sisters as payment for the supplies they sent to her throughout the year, including the food and fuel for her sustenance and the fine materials for her weavings. What her siblings did with these tapestries, she did not often know. She suspected that some were traded to the mortal races through third parties and others went directly to the giants and their friends and the more powerful witches and wizards of lands both north and south; and she knew that the gods had been gifted more than one by her mother long ago, while still others may have found homes in lands not even located upon Írtha.

Gwillagan viewed each of her tapestries like precious children while in the midst of witnessing and weaving them, a process that was as innate to her as breathing air. Her need to weave had come upon her long ago and she had succumbed to it with her whole heart when she'd agreed to take on the duties of Keeper. While weaving, she operated her magical loom slowly, working its many pieces carefully in order to precisely illustrate her tapestries' abstruse, but inevitably reliable auguries. Once a tapestry was complete and she had severed its final thread from her machine, she wished only for it to find its way, however long and twisted that path might prove to be, to those who had need of its message, and so she seldom complained as to where any of them later landed.

To ward off an odd apprehension that had been plaguing her all that morning and that was threatening to overtake her once more, Gwillagan allowed her thoughts to turn to the new panel she was weaving. It showed a man standing before an open doorway and through that door was the view of a citadel made of stone and steel, with gleaming appointments lining the darkened outlines of the citadel's soaring towers. It was a place she did not know, but it stirred within her a vague sense of familiarity. She once again wondered, as she did whenever contemplating this particular tapestry and its uncluttered vignette, just who the man, dressed strikingly in brilliant red robes and obviously only just come through the open door, could be.

The first points to notice about him were that his ice-white hair flowed in luscious waves down his back and that his staff of elder wood, held firmly in his powerful grip, stood nearly as tall as he and had a blood-red stone attached to its crown. This staff he held before him, its tip slightly leaning forward in a menacing stance. The sorcerer himself was divinely handsome, almost too beautiful to believe even, and utterly unforgettable. But his blue eyes, seen so clearly in Gwillagan's visions, were not the eyes of a trustworthy or virtuous man and he made her shiver when she dreamt of him.

Striding over to her loom, Gwillagan took up the completed end of the tapestry and held it toward the light. No, those were not the eyes of a good man, she told herself, and the hair on her arms arose from her skin. He frightened her, yes, but he also fascinated her for he was the most exquisite creature she had ever known. In her visions and dreams she heard his voice call to her, its timbre strong and deep, and she knew from it that he wanted her to reveal to him how he could retrieve the *Hèset fî Bâslen* from their hiding place, those lovely bright dragon jewels she guarded so well.

But she would not tell him and this he had come to know, for his calls were diminishing from her dreams. He had not been the first to demand from her this knowledge, nor would he be the last. But through all of these exhortations shouted at her by so many in their own dreams, she remained steadfast in her appointed purpose, for she remembered only too well what life had been like before the cursed jewels were recovered by her family.

Feeling strangely jumpy, Gwillagan sat at her loom to calm herself, deciding to work on the new *wefan* for a spell before her sisters came to her door, for today was to be their centurial visit and soon they would begin arriving to test her ability to remain as Keeper of the Jewels. In the meantime, though, she thought she could perhaps begin weaving the face of the woman who was to join the mysterious warlock in the tapestry. Disturbingly, Gwillagan had not been able to see the woman's features in her visions and she wondered how she was to weave them if she could not see them. But she had faith in her loom and soon she had it clacking away busily, its parts moving faster and faster as she went, belying her normally cautious manipulations of its treadles and shuttles as her unusually fretful mind turned to her sisters.

Not all would come today, for some were not in Írtha at this time. But Margawse and Philînan certainly would, and likely Rianilmas. She hoped that Vessica would join them because her next-to-youngest sister was invariably cheery and sweet and so refreshing to be around. Melchira and Mehitable were, as usual, off with their fathers, while Affray and Fridilin could be traveling anywhere through time and space because neither could be counted upon for any purpose other than ones of their own choosing. Their two dark sisters, whom she could not even think of by name, never joined their siblings and were not welcome to do so, for they had betrayed their mother and her teachings and had joined with the álvarat long ago in believing that the Jewels should be shared with the mortal races.

And then, a mix of images, some lived long enough ago to be ancient, arose unbidden from deep within Gwillagan's memories, and filled her mind with melancholy. They were of Morrían's first and eldest daughter, Briganna.

Brave, bold Briganna had died by her own hand, for she had willingly walked into a conflagration set with the Flame of Ívers'Fa some thirty long years ago when she'd returned home to find that the magic had somehow faded from the Ugelonds of Oganæ, the magical lands bound under her care.

Briganna believed this loss of magic to be her own disgraceful fault and that her beautiful lands had withered to such a miserable state due to her neglect of them. To her infinite shame, she had fallen in love with a mighty warrior and had left Írtha to be with her lover in his world. She had informed none of her sisters that she was leaving for this extended period, which was most unlike her, and so none had even thought to check upon the Ugelonds in her absence. In the end, her lover had spurned her and she had come back to Írtha broken-hearted and desolated to find her wondrous magical lands changed to nothing more than ugly withering hills, their former radiance having died an awful death.

Gwillagan's most beloved sister had then branded herself a complete failure, a witch of the lowest magnitude, as Briganna had written in a letter for Gwillagan and the others to find, and she had thence decreed that she was unworthy of living a minute longer. The missive detailed her sad tale, ending with her intention to call upon the almighty Flame for her deadly intent. The letter said that she dared not talk to any of the sisters in the worry that they might somehow alter her decision.

Still decimated by that tragic event all these years later, Gwillagan felt the old anger flare in her breast, for Briganna's letter had not sufficiently explained her sister's extreme measures to her satisfaction. But it was all that Briganna had left for those who loved her best.

Briganna's death had been felt keenly by each of her sisters. It was only afterward that they had discovered, from one of Gwillagan's subsequent tapestries, that a sorcerer, his hooded form too far in the distance within the tapestry for identification, had emplaced a Ghérôntog secretly beneath the heart of the Ugelonds and the horrid beast had eaten away at the magic there, consuming its wondrous properties until its power was no more. The small satisfaction the sisters felt after destroying the hypogean monster had done nothing to assuage their grief over the demise of their eldest.

Gwillagan's flashing hands stilled and the loom was abruptly silenced. She stared unseeingly at the floor beyond her shoulder, her throat closing upon her rising pain as she pushed it inward once more, clamping down on it before it overwhelmed her. She disliked thinking of Briganna, for her heart felt wounded afresh each time her dead sister came to mind. Briganna had been the strongest and most powerful of Morrían's daughters, with a depth of will, skill and talent that only Margawse could rival. Briganna, daring and courageous, had seemed indestructible to Gwillagan.

Oh, how she missed her dear sister and always would, for they two had grown up close together, being born within three regular years' age of each other, while all the other daughters had come along much later. In fact, by the time little Rianilmas was born, both of her elder sisters had earned their

Fægre calling and were traveling the many worlds with their celestial fathers through the *giât y teithiwr*.

Gwillagan rose from her sitting position at her loom and began pacing back and forth from the fire to the door, impatiently wanting her sisters to arrive immediately so that their visit would be over and she could safely return to her solitary life and her prophesying tapestries. Which would also mean that bittersweet memories such as those she'd just experienced of Briganna would not intrude into her thoughts or her visions. These things made her desperately unhappy and she hated being unhappy.

It was perhaps twenty minutes later that a light tap sounded upon the cottage door. Gwillagan strode over to it eagerly and flung it open, glad to see Philînan, her darkest haired sister, standing there. Drawing her witch sibling inside, they began to chatter about their lives. Although they were so unalike in appearance—what with Gwillagan being tall and wearing her thick blonde hair pulled back in an abundant plait that hung straight down her back nearly to her knees, whereas Philînan's short dark curls somehow seemed to accentuate her small, slight frame—Philînan was Gwillagan's closest and most trusted friend. That is, if one could say that Gwillagan had any friends at all seeing as she had no visitors other than her sisters.

The two of them nattered on comfortably for quite some time, knowing full well that the others would not arrive for hours yet, for their journeys were longer even than Philînan's had been. They sat at the table eating and drinking while Philînan shared stories of a new lover, whom she'd met in Morlant. She confessed to Gwillagan that he had stayed with her several times upon her beloved Mîrlonds, which were under Philînan's magical care just like the Ferlonds were under Gwillagan's care, and the Noäglonds were under Rianilmas's care, the Ganlonds were under Margawse's care, or the Callalonds were under Vessica's care, and just as the Ugelonds had been under Briganna's care many long years ago.

After imparting titillating tales of romance for nearly an hour, Philînan noticed the loom and crossed to it, her blue eyes lively and sparkling with mischief. "Ye hath begun a new augury! I know ye do not like anyone to behold an unfinished one, but these colors thou art using are most striking and I simply cannot resist my urges!" She sent her sister an arch smile over her shoulder. "Ye will not mind if I take a small peek, will ye?" she asked.

Gwillagan sat back with a chuckle, waving her favorite sister on.

Not more than a couple seconds later, Philînan gasped, choking out in a thin, strangled voice, "No! No, it cannot be!" She stared at the front end of the loom and its newly woven threads, then turned her head back to the completed end of the tapestry, staring mutely at the figure of the handsome man.

Instantly, Gwillagan was at her Philînan's side, exclaiming, "Tell me what it is that distresses ye so, dear sister!"

Shaking her head helplessly, Philînan turned to Gwillagan and pointed at the unfinished wall hanging, inquiring, "Was that born from one of thy visions?"

"Surely it was; they all are. Ye know this!" her sister replied tartly.

Philînan shuddered and squeezed her eyes shut, shoving herself away from the loom as though burned by it.

Gwillagan bent over the loom's frame to study the image, noting the new weave from that morning. She had added what looked like the *Hèset fi Bâslen* falling from the hands of the woman on the unfinished end of the tapestry. The woman's face was also there now and showed clearly in the strong light of the many candles lit around the room. The young woman's familiar features displayed faltering disbelief, most obviously because of the knife handle protruding from her bleeding breast.

Like her sister moments before, Gwillagan gasped in horror and stood away from the loom as though it had scorched her fingers, whirling upon her white-faced sibling in a worried frenzy. "B-but, that woman is ye!" And she demanded of her cringing sister, "Who is this man? Do ye know him?"

Philînan admitted that she did as she drew a thick rug from the stool before her, buried her face in its soft wool and began to weep.

Gwillagan straightened her shoulders and clasped her hands in front of her, looking sorry for her sister. "Ye can never meet him again, Philly!" she reproached the younger woman sharply. "For he means us all harm, as anyone can see from the tapestry's prediction. He means to have the *Hèset fi Bâslen*, the Jewels of Light we seven fought so hard to regain and protect, and ye know I cannot give them to him, nor will I let ye do so, as ye are offering in that, that *wicked* weaving." She pointed an indignant finger at the offending tapestry, heaving a string of heavy sighs fraught with fear and frustration. "Philly, ye must stay away from him!" she urged almost righteously when she finally got her breathing under control again.

Philînan, her shoulders bent, let out a wail and a sob before lifting her tear-stained face to the towering Gwillagan. "I know it, sister, I know it," she agreed woefully, her voice cracking with sorrow. "I only hope I can do it, for I love him with all my heart, ye see."

Gwillagan let her sister cry herself out, handing the distressed woman clean handkerchiefs as needed, saying nothing until the torrent was finally over. "We shall not tell the others, not yet ennyways," she said in a quietly composed voice. "And I shall put the thing away for a time. All right?" she asked and Philînan nodded, her eyes desperate still.

Gwillagan waved her hand and the unfinished tapestry was tied off in seconds. She cut its threads and let the terrible piece fall to the floor in a heap. With another wave of her hand, she set the tapestry to folding itself, so that soon it was rolled up into a bolt such that no one could possibly see the images upon it. She sent the thing to the darkened cellar of the cottage, far at the back and underneath all the other old tapestries that she had not had the heart to give to anyone or had been too wary of their content to let them go freely into the world. There were more than fifty of these stored down there, she knew, and swore to herself that one day she would ask Philînan to bring the Flame of Ívers'Fa with her so that Gwillagan could burn them all in the magical flame, in the hopes that the mystical fire would cleanse the tapestries of their malignant intentions and ensure that the terrifying scenes in them never came to fruition.

Chapter 21
The Gunslinger's Ballad

Donnie came back to herself with a start, realizing her fingers were still clutching the edge of the tapestry.

Noticing that her new friend was aware of her surroundings once again, Nagba sighed deeply. "Poor Philly," she intoned sadly, pausing. "She lost everything because of that sorcerer of hers; everything except her sister Margawse." The bird shook her head slowly and sighed again. "Tell me, what did ye see in the tapestry?" she inquired curiously.

Donnie described the scene she'd just witnessed to the old Sea Eagle and Nagba quirked her head to the side thoughtfully.

"Perhaps ye saw that instead of what occurred between Philly and that vile sorcerer who tricked her because ye touched only the edge of the weave instead of connecting directly with any part of the event depicted in the tapestry itself," she posited.

It was Donnie's turn to think. She swiveled back toward the tapestry in front of her and lifted a hesitant finger to the knife in Philînan's breast. Somewhat mercifully, nothing more happened and Donnie let her hand fall before she went back to her chair to sit down.

"Well, if there is to be no more gained for ye from that wicked rug, ye can certainly learn more about darling Philly from other texts in the library whenever ye feel ready," Nagba assured her knowingly. "Her sorry tale is told in several ways here and I urge ye to read them all before passing judgment upon her. She was a silly girl, yes, but still just a girl who was taken in by a handsome lad, even with Gwillagan's warning to her. And all but Margawse forsook her. Philly hid with Margawse afterward and they two stayed on the Ganlonds for a time before they left Írtha together. That was when Catie was sent back to replace them, although she wanted no part of being a goddess of any kind and she refused to wield the magic that was needed to become an Ér Ainíl."

There was a long pause here and to fill it, Donnie observed, "Yes, Catie writes about that in her diaries, more than once. She's an adventurous witch, that Catie, but she's not particularly power hungry."

"No, that she is not," seconded Nagba, this time lifting her head to smile in agreement.

Donnie, still sifting through what Nagba had told her so far, prompted the bird to go on, asking, "What happened to the Jewels then? Did they also leave Írtha?"

Nagba shrugged restlessly. "It is believed they did, yes. But they were returned somehow. Some say that is because objects like them will always come back to where they feel at home, for that is where they work the best. As for myself and my own opinions, I canna say, for I have none on the matter. And as to where the dangerous trinkets are now, that is anyone's guess. But that elf queen had one of them for a while and what she did with it was unspeakable!"

The bird grunted disgustedly and looked like she was going to spit out something that tasted very, very bad in her mouth. "Ye see, the daughters of Morrían were the Ér Ainíls of several magical lands throughout Írtha, one of which was the Callalonds. Those were on the border between the Balwedané Feûr and Trenethera provinces, just outside the Avenwuda, and had been overseen by young Vessica for quite some time. But Vessica, perhaps the most impetuous child of Morrían, was needed at the Ganlonds while Margawse was birthing her second child and she left the Callalonds alone for three moon cycles. When she returned, her lovely magical lands had been destroyed. Those who witnessed it and survived the carnage swore that the Blue Jewel, that evil stone which heightens both the successes and failures of its prey, was used to unleash a wave of pestilence, fire, and dark magic such as this world had never seen before. The survivors all agreed that it was wielded by the elf princess, Miramdahl. Ye see, she hated Vessica deeply, for the High Commander of the Woodland Elves had fallen in love with the fierce Ér Ainíl, 'though she offered him no encouragement. Ever since that day, magic has forsworn Miramdahl. What magic she commands with her fingertips she has learned to steal by the counsel of Aldalis Munkinum and his foolish ilk, just like a common sorceress."

Donnie let this sink in for a few moments before she inquired, "What did she do with the Blue Jewel, I wonder. Do you know?"

"Aye, for her father and brother were both more than furious with her, for the Callalonds protected the elf realm from the southern countries and without them Balwedané Feûr was open to attack. They forced her to tell them what she had done with the Jewel. She said she gave it back to the same sorcerer that Philly had fallen in love with, Ixifír Bíun be his name."

Donnie grunted in frustration. "Him!" she snarled. "I've still not met him, but I already don't like him!" She shuddered with revulsion and asked Nagba, "Did he ever become involved with any of the other sisters besides Philînan?"

Nagba nodded. "Oh yes, he did at that. It was, of course, one of your sisters who had turned away from the light: Bréagna be her name."

"I thought as much," Donnie said. Her lips were set grimly. "And I'm pretty sure we've already had a run-in with the Blue Jewel in Faen Eárna. If I'm right, it had been set into a collar and used by Bréagna to control

Gullrick, the Lord Chancellor sent by the king to guide Malwé, the young prince of the province. It disappeared the moment he was killed by the prince. Do you know if the Blue Jewel was of a size to be used like that?" she asked curiously, her gaze turning to the tapestry to look at the Jewels falling from Philînan's hands.

Nagba nodded and assured her, "Aye, it was certainly that, as ye can see for yourself. None of the Jewels of Light was larger than a hen's egg."

Donnie, lost within her own turbulent thoughts, murmured, "Then what we encountered in Hörthanc must have been the Blue Jewel. Once it was discovered, you know, Gullrick attempted to kill me, along with anyone else who got in his way. He very nearly did kill the prince's grandfather, Sir Dantheus." Donnie looked pensive for a moment and then she said, "That must mean that Bréagna got the Jewel from Ixifîr Bíun."

The old Sea Eagle nodded, and both fell silent, each caught deeply in their own ruminations. They stayed like this for some while and, for the first time, Donnie began to consider in depth what Nagba had revealed to her today.

If she was indeed the last of Morrían's daughters, what was to be her purpose, she wondered. And what did Nagba mean by saying she would be the one to lead the sisters home? Home to where; here? Or somewhere else? And why was it her task to lead them anywhere?

She pulled herself up short in her chair with a start of surprise. Someone was calling her name. And yet, they weren't here at the Tower.

Before she could do or say anything, she felt her essence being drawn elsewhere and suddenly she was looking through the eyes of Maga, who was chanting her name in prayer. The wolf was running beside Diana and Otis as they left the concealed entrance to the dragon rookery and bounded toward the Withering Hills beyond.

To her everlasting shock and future nightmares, Donnie saw her beloved Rex was pinned to the ground by the young female dragon Donnie had been charged with killing the night of the Battle of the Branmar Plain. The dragon was rearing back, focusing her lasers on the dog's face, getting ready to incinerate him with its intense heat.

"Run, Rex, run! Shrink yourself first!" screamed Donnie, amplifying her words with magic to make sure Rex heard them. Her voice, when it came out, was a mix of hers and Maga's timbres and tones and it sounded frantic.

"Donnie?" Diana yelled uncertainly, staring down at the wolf running beside Otis.

"Yes," Donnie replied, as Maga panted with exertion. "Maga prayed for me to come and help you all and, well, she somehow pulled me here. I am just as bewildered by that as you, believe me," Donnie added fervently.

"Oh, I'm not bewildered by that at all," Diana countered in amusement.

They were still racing toward where the dragon, after Rex obediently disappeared per his mama's command, had not had time to shut down the lasers in its eyes, resulting in the earth and rock in front of her exploding into smithereens. The young dragon had been hurled back by the force of the blast and was still tumbling away.

With a small, slightly humorous grimace on her face, Diana explained, "I always kind of hated it when that would happen to me. Only those with Ca'nam magic can actually summon their Ér Ainíl to them in situations of extreme duress, like this one!" the warrioress added dryly, gesturing with her free hand toward the dragon. She looked back down at Donnie/Maga and said, "If you focus really hard, you can leave Maga's body and become a sort of phantom that floats around, although you can't do that for long. As a matter of fact, you'll only be here a few minutes before you get sent back to your body."

"Um, okay, if you say so," Donnie replied dubiously. "So, what's the plan here?" she asked, and it was Maga, weirdly enough, who answered.

"Well, *this* is not part of the plan," the wolf panted anxiously, only it was just her voice doing the talking this time. "The plan seems to have gone badly awry. We had hoped to lure the dragon into the rookery, where we have a trap of sorts laid. From there, we thought to harness the beast to the top of Plug and let it drive the thing thusly all the way to the Ganlonds through the tunnels."

"Plug's here?" Donnie asked incredulously, starting to turn the wolf's head to look back the way they'd come, but the wolf stopped her and said impatiently, "Your metal friend is almost out of power and is awaiting us in the meeting hall beyond the warren that leads to the rookery."

Donnie concentrated hard and Maga's body began to glow blue. In just a few more moments, a long bolt of cobalt-colored magic separated from the wolf and shot back toward the rookery. "That should give Plug plenty of power to come and help us," she explained to the others. "But we have to find a way to get the dragon to follow us back to the rookery."

Diana shouted to the others behind them, "Go back inside and get set! We'll bring the dragon with us!"

Donnie, through Maga's eyes, looked up at her friend and asked dryly, "How? I'm not gonna hurt another dragon, so don't ask me to do anything at all like that."

Diana grinned down at her wide eyed and chortled, "Oh, we won't have to, trust me. It's time for you to either become that phantom or at least project an image of yourself, say somewhere close to the dragon first, then again over by the entrance to the rookery?"

Donnie immediately grasped what her friend was proposing and she replied, "Yeah, I can do that. But let's get closer, right, Maga?"

When the wolf answered in the affirmative, Donnie again concentrated on her magic and visualized a "ghost Donnie" that she willed to appear near the dragon, who had come to a stop in its tumbling and was now searching angrily for Rex over what appeared to be the remnant of some sort of ancient geological vortex that had ravaged the area eons ago. Even from where Donnie was viewing the scene, all the rocks, shrubs, and small scrub of the general vicinity swirled toward the same point in the center of the vortex.

The dragon spotted Maga and Diana moving toward her and she began to lift herself onto her back feet just as the apparition of Donnie's form appeared nearby. Enraged by this sight, the dragon screamed her fury and shot a long, powerful stream of fire at the ghost Donnie. The ghost Donnie disappeared, while the real Donnie, still entwined with Maga, went along for the ride as Maga turned them around to head back toward the rookery on an all-out sprint. Otis and Diana were retreating alongside the wolf, for the dragon had finally gotten fully righted and was readying itself for a low, sweeping run of either fire or lasers at the racing wolf and horse.

Donnie let her magic extend over her two animal friends' forms, and soon both the wolf and horse were running twice as fast as they normally could, which was a good thing because the dragon was very fast. Donnie could feel it coming up from behind, and so she prompted the wolf and horse to split off into different directions, while she projected an image of the ghost Donnie standing at the darkened entrance to the dragon rookery. She felt the dragon's wings as it passed overhead and she sent Maga rolling off into the dead grass outside the abandoned dragon breeding ground.

Maga, with Donnie still entwined with her, scrambled to her feet and dashed into the rookery seconds behind the dragon. Otis and Diana were not far behind Maga. When they entered the main chamber, where not so long ago the great *Badûran Vírat*, Ungôl, had died from drinking a poison given to him by his so-called master, Valledai, Donnie felt a sense of grief overwhelm her and she could only hope that poor Maga did not feel it too.

Donnie's thoughts went back to that day, recalling, with a deep sadness in her heart, Ungôl's impressive stature, his intelligent countenance and demeanor, and his absolute and burning conviction that he must lead his people back to their home in the sea. It was a task which he then passed to Donnie when he died in front of her, the poison having eaten at his organs until he felt only pain and begged her to kill him. For mercy's sake, she had found morphine amongst the supplies that were stockpiled in the main rookery chamber by someone as yet unknown to Donnie and her friends, and had administered it to the great *vírat* to ease his transition into death. He had been genuinely grateful for that, but only Donnie had witnessed his change of heart toward her.

Now, all that was left of the great *Badûran Vîrat*, who had been wingless and whom Donnie had long mistaken for a Great Serpent, was a long, thick pile of ashes where he'd died. Donnie assumed this was because his family had incinerated his body. She knew it was their custom to gather around and, as a group, burn the bodies of their dead, which she'd learned from the research she'd done on methods she could potentially employ to kill them the night of the Battle of the Branmar Plain.

While Donnie had called him Uncle just to cause mischief, she had always understood that, no matter what, she had a soft spot for him and for his mate, Murlaín, who would forever haunt Donnie's dreams. She had been convinced that their two children, Téman and Smault, were dead by her own hand, like Murlaín, but now she'd learned she had another chance to connect with at least one of them, and she was determined to make the most of it.

A magical net crafted by her friends was released from above onto the dragon when the beast entered the main chamber. The dragon twisted and turned and flailed helplessly at first against the binding vines, her rage making her ever more reckless, and Donnie grew concerned that she would do some very real damage to herself, even though the vines seemed to break apart easily enough.

Concentrating on her magic hard again, Donnie separated herself from Maga with great difficulty, and then made sure the dragon could see her form. She was aware that she was not exactly solid, but there was nothing she could do about that because her body was, after all, far away in the Forrieghness Tower.

Rex came to stand by her and tried to lean up against her, but he merely stepped into her, got a little freaked out by that, then sat down and sighed, staring up at Donnie with such love that she was very sorry she could not scoop him into her arms.

Instead, she smiled at him and then stood tall, calling out to the young dragon, "Stop, please, before you hurt yourself!"

This just incensed the dragon further and she fought harder to escape the magical netting, getting more and more of her wings and their empty weaponry tangled up in the great heaps of vines. Dismaying her captors even more, she completely ignored the dragon fruit pelting her writhing frame that was being tossed by Feirth the giant toward her. Clearly, she did not find that particular bounty at all irresistible.

But then Plug careened through the far tunnel and raced across the main chamber's floor, laying rubber down when she slammed on her brakes. Everyone turned to the vehicle at the sound of its breaks and tires squealing and, at the last moment, several of them realized the SUV was going to slide through the trail of Uncle's ashes. And they instinctively knew this would make matters worse with the dragon.

There were shouts and screams for Plug to stop before it got to the ashes, but it was Donnie who shot a blast of magical power that sent the vehicle flipping backward as though it had encountered an impenetrable wall. The SUV landed a good twenty-five feet back the way it had come and turned itself off, unsure of what had just happened and why.

But the dragon had understood and this, more than anything else, got her to stop fighting the net. Utterly exhausted and out of breath, she glared at Donnie silently…watchfully…ignoring the soothing sounds that Feirth was making to her. He was edging closer and closer to the dragon, while Rex, Warren, Diana and the four wolves were encircling the dragon from about ten feet back. The falcons flew in and joined the bats circling above.

Donnie moved to stand in front of the dragon and said to her gently, "Please, Téman—it is Téman, isn't it? Please, let us help you."

The dragon drew back and looked at Donnie in astonishment, her face covered by the netting of dragon flower vines. "Help me?" she screeched, and everyone took a cringing step backward. "You want to kill me, so am I now to simply let you do that, execrable witch?"

Donnie shook her head vehemently. "No-no, I don't want to kill you," she cried, "and I won't try to ever again! That I swear to you and to those here and to those who are guiding my path, whoever they may be. I mean it, not now, not ever will I contemplate killing another knowing soul. I will give up magic willingly before I will murder again, even for the gods!"

Diana stepped forward to add, "None of us want to kill you, dragon. But you should know that we have been asked by the Ganlonds to retrieve you and take you there, although we don't know why you are wanted by the magical lands. Do you know the answer to that question? Why would the Ganlonds want you to seek refuge with it?" she asked, and the query had the furthering effect she had hoped for.

The dragon sat down and stared around at them in disbelief, making it clear she was wondering if this was just another trick being played upon her. But after a minute had gone by with no one making any menacing moves toward her, she slowly replied, "I do not know why these magical lands you speak of would want me there. I only know that, when we were very young, my mother would tell my brother and me stories about the magical lands of Írtha and of a witch named Morrían. Many of her tales back then centered around the Ganlonds and their connection to my world. But she threw away her stories when we were brought here, so it has been a long time since I heard them and cannot remember them well. My brother might know them better than I."

Diana turned to Donnie and whispered to her urgently. "Donnie, we need this dragon if we're ever going to get your shoulder healed."

Donnie nodded, mouthed, "I know," and then she turned back to the dragon. "Look, you have no reason to trust me, we all know that, but these folks are here to help you, so will you let them? I'm not really here anyway and I can already feel myself being pulled back to my real body, so I must be quick about this next part. Let me just ask you this—is your brother in Lænemeade?"

Téman jerked backward. "How do you know this?" she demanded as though all her prior suspicions were being re-confirmed.

"I had a run-in with some elves and a powerful sorceress there, who, it turns out, is my sister Bréagna." Donnie looked at Diana when she said this last bit so she could see her friend's reaction. She was not let down by it. "You knew, Diana, didn't you, all along? You knew I'm a daughter of Morrían!" she accused her friend, her mixed feelings plain on her face.

Diana put her hands up defensively and ignored the loud gasps from the others, focusing solely on Donnie's transparent figure, which was visibly fading now. "I didn't really know it, no, but I strongly suspected it, yes." She sighed heavily. "Nagba told you, I suppose. Well, it must be time for you to know it then too, or the gods would have stopped her from saying anything to you."

Donnie brushed this aside with a snort and faced the dragon again. "I will make you the following deal, Téman," she said. "If you will trust in my friends and let them help you, I promise that, not only will I take you back to your home world, I'll rescue your brother with you when I get back from the Mîrlonds. That's going to take a few weeks, though, which is okay because you're going to need that time to heal." Donnie pointed to the dragon's wings, which were tattered and torn in several places now. "You'll get help with that on the Ganlonds."

She looked around at the others to say firmly, "When you take the net off her, if Téman wants to leave, you are to just let her go, you hear me? No one is to stop her. But she is welcome on the Ganlonds, however she gets there. And if she so desires to take her father's ashes with her, then would you please come up with a way to get them into a box of some sort that you can transport home? Check over there," she said, waving toward the corner where she'd found a hodgepodge of modern equipment and several crates of weapons stockpiled the day she'd encountered Ungôl here in the dragon rookery. "I sent all the weaponry and equipment away when I was here before, and most but not all the crates and cupboards, so some might be serviceable, if they're still there."

Donnie turned to Rex and suggested, "Honey, why don't you come to the Tower now? That way you can spend a day or two with us in the library here. But then we'll have to leave for the Mîrlonds."

With the last fading word, she was gone from the dragon rookery and almost instantly found herself back in her own body in Nagba's quarters at the very top of the Toren fi Førrens. Feeling slightly woozy, Donnie looked around. Nagba was on her perch asleep and snoring lightly, so Donnie very carefully got up, replaced the rugs onto the chair, and made her exit. She flew back down to the floor of the main chamber, making sure to do so very quietly and off to the one side so that she was not really even noticed by the new users of the library. Once she was back on the ground, she hurried over to where she'd been sitting earlier and motioned her friends to come to her, explaining in terse whispers what had just happened at the dragon breeding ground.

"But, just what does the Ganlonds want with a dragon?" asked Falwaïn, giving Donnie a puzzled look.

She shrugged, then hooked an eyebrow at Sylvester. "Do you know?"

The cat scoffed at this and replied with feeling, "I wish I did, but no, of course I do not. If I ever did, it has been wiped from my memory like so many other pieces of vital information that could assist us now. I will say this though, I long for the day you manage to refrain from making illogical and dangerous promises to every dragon you encounter!" He shot her a glare and then turned his back on her to stalk away, resuming his studies without another word.

Donnie grinned sheepishly at his retreating backside and turned the grin upon the others, who looked about as happy with her as Sylvester had. She quickly altered the grin to a grimace when they all turned their backs on her too and sat back down at their stations.

They were right, of course, and Donnie knew it was her guilt that had made her promise to rescue Smault and take both dragons to their home world. But, after all, she *had* tried to kill them and had been convinced for months now that she'd succeeded all too well at that. Yet here she was, being given a small, but very real chance to perhaps redeem herself with them and she was going to make the most of it.

Nevertheless, she also comprehended that she needed to rein in the need to assuage her guilt or else she might get thrown off course entirely, and then who knows what would happen?

She bit her lip and looked at each of her friends, acknowledging how much they were all investing in her and in their journey together, and she felt bad about potentially jeopardizing any of that for them. She could feel their disappointment with her and her shoulders bowed a little as she bent down and re-applied herself to the Talbula scroll.

It was getting to be dinnertime when the outer doors opened again and light, quick steps could be heard on the stone flooring. Seconds later, Rex came trotting into the room and bounded straight to Donnie. By that time, all of the new visitors had gone home, so it was just Donnie and her friends inside the library. Of the order brothers, nothing had been seen since that morning.

Donnie greeted Rex's arrival with a shout of glee, met him with a big welcoming hug, and then rained a hundred kisses down upon his head while she squeezed him tight with love. He wriggled in pure ecstasy in the comfort of her grasp and wrapped his neck around hers, which was his way of returning a hug. They were both sitting on the floor and hugging tightly when the outer doors could be heard opening again.

Their friends had gotten up and gathered around Donnie and Rex, all of them greeting the dog with genuine gladness on their faces and in their voices. Sylvester in particular looked much relieved by the dog's presence, although he would likely deny that if asked about it.

At the sound of the door, they all turned toward the entryway and waited to see who had just come into the library. It was Gak and Nagba, and they were alone this time.

Falwaïn pulled Donnie to her feet and they waited for the Sea Eagles to reach them before smiling at the giant birds and murmuring hellos.

The birds nodded and both looked down at Rex, who was grinning widely, he was so happy. "Hi, again," he crowed, sitting down and staring at them pertly.

Surprised, Donnie asked, "You know each other already?"

Gak answered, "Yes, we have met. The guards at the city's gates were not going to let young Rex in, but Nagba felt his presence and sent me and a few others to fetch him."

Rex nodded, turned to Donnie and gushed, "Yeah, you should've seen it. The guards didn't wanna let me in at all, Mama, but Gak came and told them they had to so I could get to the Tower. And when they still refused, Gak got, er, real convincing, ya know? I mean, he gets really-really-really loud when he wants to, and kinda scary too. They thought about it a split-second and decided to let me in right away. Then I raced here! I had fun jumping over all the guards that were after me and that big wall that separates the city from the Tower. It was great, Mama, 'cause you know how much I love to be chased!"

Donnie frowned at him while asking in a puzzled voice, "Um, if the city guards let you in the gate, why were they then chasing after you?"

"Well, thinkin' about it, maybe they weren't so happy at my comin' in, were they, Gak?" said the dog and the Sea Eagle shook his head.

"Gak tells me that what the city guards are not happy about mainly is the sudden influx of magical creatures demanding to be let into the city and subsequently the Tower," interposed Nagba, and her face transformed into what Donnie took to be a radiant smile. "We are having to maintain a presence at the gate, which is perhaps not helping the situation. The guards are trying to hunt down those we let in, but are finding it a most difficult task," she added with satisfaction, and even Gak looked pleased.

"The Tower has not seen such potential use in many long years, if not centuries even," Gak noted, his harsh voice cracking a little with emotion. "We have also blocked the underground entry the mages made in order to avoid us, which, really, we should have destroyed long ago." Gak stole a look at Nagba, who cackled merrily.

"That is Gak's way of reprimanding me, for it was my decision to let the mages have their own passage into the library. I allowed it because I was as weary of their fear of us as were they, but Gak argued with me that we should not condone such separation of the higher magical races and that only together will we survive and thrive." Nagba smiled again and she said fondly, "He was quite right, of course, and I was wrong. But I am working to rectify that mistake now."

She turned to Rex, her blind eyes seeming to see him, and asked, "As for ye, my boy, did ye get the *vírat* back to the Ganlonds safely?"

Donnie gasped, "How did you know about that?", with others around her seconding the question.

Nagba chortled again and admitted, "I could hear what ye were saying to thy friends when ye were called for a divine visitation. I recognized it as such when ye screamed for young Rex to shrink himself and run." She chuckled low once more before continuing. "When ye gave instructions for letting the dragon go to the Ganlonds on its own, I lost interest and fell asleep." She shrugged and noted a little wistfully, "That seems to happen more and more these days."

The great old Sea Eagle turned to Rex and prompted him with, "Well?"

Rex, utterly fascinated by the massive bird, took a moment to realize that he was supposed to answer her previous question. So he flashed her a smile and replied, "She rode on top of Plug, our SUV, which is a metal vehicle that can go really fast and really far. It took us the whole afternoon to get back home, but when we did, Ma'oma, the giantess mother, took charge of Téman—the dragon, I mean—and I said goodbye to the others and hurried here, although I let Warren have the book back before I left—you know, the one being written now?"

Donnie nodded, knelt to him and gave him another hug. "That was very thoughtful of you, honey. I am sure he appreciated it."

Rex nodded and murmured, "Yeah," but he was clearly distracted by something on his mind. Donnie released him and looked questioningly at him, but he was staring at Nagba.

The Sea Eagle somehow noted this and urged him, "Go on, my boy, ask me what ye want."

"You seem to know so much about everything and, well, it's just that I've been wondering about me, you know? I mean, I'm not like the other dogs on the Ganlonds or the wolves there, or really any of the other beings we've met, so I'm kind of curious as to what I am," he confessed, glancing up at his mama uncertainly. "Do you know?"

Donnie was surprised by his question, yes, but since she herself had ruminated over this same issue more than once, she too turned to Nagba with an air of expectancy. After all, the High Convoke had been able to tell her about herself, so surely she could tell Rex about himself, right?

"Ye are like no one I have ever known here in Írtha, my friend," Nagba conceded, causing Rex to groan a little in disappointment. "That is not to say I cannot help ye," Nagba assured him with a smile. "Morrían had many a tale to share whenever she came here, and some of her favorites were of what she called her dearest friend ever. His name was Lućac and he died saving her from the evilest sorcerer ever born."

"Ixifír Bíun?" murmured more than one of her listeners, but she shook her head.

"No, his name was Keurelis Jakahn and he had hated her, Morrían said of him, since time itself had begun, although she never knew why he did so," explained Nagba, and she seemed to be airing her feathers more often than usual, as though the talk distressed her some, which it did, for she had been great friends with Morrían for a long, long time and still missed the elder witch sorely. "She told me that Keurelis threw a deadly spell at her and Lućac hurled himself into its path before her to take its blunt. Because of Lućac's sacrifice, the spell was rebounded onto its caster. The result of that attack was that Lućac and Keurelis both died, and so for quite some time Morrían was left without friend or foe, she lamented. Eventually, she fell in love with a man, a hound she called him, but he died in battle and so she gave up on love for a time. That was when she came to Írtha. She told me that Lućac had also been a hound, but of the more literal sort. Him, she called *cúrem ga'ra*, or hound of love." Nagba smiled again and bowed as though looking straight at Rex. "And that, I believe, is what ye are—*cúrem ga'ra*. There are many texts in the library that mention Lućac, and they are at your disposal to peruse," she added, and an armload of scrolls, hand-sewn books and folded texts floated over to the table where Falwaïn had been working by himself earlier, and piled themselves carefully atop each other.

Rex hopped up onto a chair across from Falwaïn's and the first of his scrolls opened before him. In seconds, he was lost to those around him.

Donnie looked around at her friends and at Nagba and Gak and smiled. "I think that describes him perfectly, a hound of love..." she said, her voice tailing away with affection as she turned to gaze at her dog.

"This Keurelis Jakahn," interjected Falwaïn curiously, "did Morrían tell you more about him?"

"Some, yes," the great Sea Eagle replied, "ye were not far wrong by asking about the other sorcerer, his son. No, Ixifír Bíun was not he, but he hates as hard as his father and nearly as long, it seems."

Donnie sighed and grumbled, "Oh great, I suppose that means he thinks we're in some sort of blood feud, doesn't he? Because of my mother and his father. Well, maybe he knows why that should be, but I sure don't." She looked upward at the library shelves and said, "If there are any texts explaining that feud, I'd be grateful to read them."

Nothing stirred anywhere and Nagba chided her gently, "Perhaps if ye look for something a little less specific from that long ago, ye might have more success." She lifted her head and said, "Bring her texts that mention Keurelis Jakahn."

This time, more than twenty items came flying off the shelves and piled themselves on top of those that Donnie already had.

Donnie surveyed the new mound of material for her to go through, pursing her lips in thought and feeling like she'd just learned an important lesson about using the library.

She turned back to Nagba and Gak, opened her mouth to apologize for being an idiot, then shut it when Gak said over her, "Ye will all stay here in the library until ye are ready to leave the city itself. It appears the queen would like to see ye in the dungeons, given half a chance. I suggest we not provide her with that opportunity."

The big bird flipped his beak toward a doorway at the rear of the Tower. "There are plenty of rooms there for ye to use," he added. "I have sent for thy horses and belongings in thy rooms at the Blackthorn Inn, and both should arrive here soon. Ye will be as comfortable as we can make ye, but it will be nothing to what ye are accustomed to enjoy at home."

While the cat and two men snickered at this statement, it was Akanna who leaned forward to demur dryly, "Nobody in all of Írtha has the kind of comforts Donemere is accustomed to enjoying at home. It is most fortuitous she does not expect them elsewhere, is it not?" the vincan asked, hooking an eyebrow at Donnie.

Donnie gave her a shrug and a smile in return, then chuckled good-humoredly along with the others.

The accommodations were sufficient but by no means comfortable, as predicted by Gak. And it turned out that the birds would offer the use of the Tower's thirty-something spare rooms on the floors below the library to other guests as well over the next few days. Meals were served in a large common room under the main chamber of the library and were provided by a couple of inn keepers who were siding with the Sea Eagles in the dispute between the birds and the mages, which had escalated somewhat.

In what they viewed as their right to improve access to the Tower, the Sea Eagles had torn down the mages' sanctuary gates, both front and back, and cleared a straight path in between them to the Tower. This really only disrupted a couple of hallways, one or two classrooms, and the main courtyard, which Aldalis Munkinum had had enclosed when he was first voted bishop.

Aldalis, particularly, had never been a friend of the Sea Eagles and had wanted to marginalize them as much as possible, so he had been proud to have ostensibly succeeded at that throughout his long tenure as bishop and he took this assault on his sanctuary as a personal affront. He told his brethren that these walls had been erected solely to protect the Tower, its prized library, and the many artifacts contained therein and he encouraged his fellow mages to disrupt, although never outrightly thwart access to the Tower whenever possible, for the library was certain to experience all sorts of discomforts and injuries with all these foreign, dirty creatures accessing it so freely and thoughtlessly now.

Previously, he'd left it to the king and queen to decide who was to come through the gates of the sanctuary. Once they were inside the sanctuary, then and only then was it discussed whether they would be granted access to the Tower. It was a slight deviousness on his and the sovereigns' parts, but it had been enough to circumvent the requirement to not willfully keep visitors from the Tower.

Unfortunately, because Nagba had allowed this physical separation to go on for so long, many denizens of the city believed it to be the natural state of affairs and the city found itself divided immediately. Some took the side of the mages, who they said had always kept to themselves and, it was claimed, had tended the Tower and its prohibited library to perfection for years and years, hadn't they? Others, those who had had dealings with the brotherhood, argued that the mages were pretentious saps who were finally getting their paid comeuppance and good riddance to the lot of them.

Who the royals blamed for the upheaval in their city was unknown, but the consensus was that it may well have been the mages, as was debated on more than one occasion in pubs and taverns all over the city.

To soothe some of this unrest, the Sea Eagles were explaining to all and sundry at regular intervals during the day that it had been a mistake to allow the segregation and it was high time to fix that most egregious error, hence the need for restructuring the sanctuary's entrance, it walls, and, further to that, the Tower gates so that easy access was granted to any and all Ca'nam individuals.

The mages, quite naturally, did not accept these aggressive actions by the Sea Eagles without retaliation. Walls were rebuilt on a daily basis, as were gates, and visitors were redirected back to the city streets whenever possible. This all seemed to be just fun and games until beautiful Brother Billy, still convinced he was destined for greater things, used his meager magic to seal the gates against some lemkins (this group being minor fairies of the Beldawuda who had never set foot in Anûmanétus or had even thought of visiting the Forrieghness Tower before now), and was turned into a pile of billowing ash by a wave of magic that arose from the ground, accompanied by what the lemkins described as thunder rolling the word, "Treasoner!" at Brother Billy, before the wave then smote the young mage to dust from toe to head.

If it were not for the fact that no Sea Eagle had been in the vicinity at the time, this act might have started a war of the magical races. But when it happened again a little while later with Brother Derrigult (who was smote just as violently and suddenly as Brother Billy) when he stood in the path of a pair of imps and screamed at them they were not allowed access to the Tower because they were just low-bred imps, for Haggats' sake, it became apparent to pretty much everyone that magic was on the side of the Sea Eagles and even the mages accepted the changes to their revered sanctuary with no further repercussions to anyone.

Oddly enough, the queen had, from all appearances, decided to sit this entire argument out, and after that first terrifying night for all newcomers seeking access to the Tower, the city's guards were no longer hunting anyone down and the influx of magical beings continued to grow, with the capital city's inns and stores all swelling with heavy, brisk trade. More gloriously, the library was in daily use by growing multitudes and the Sea Eagles were ever the gracious hosts.

Which is not to say they did not keep a close eye on the users of the magical repository or its invaluable materials. Several texts, ostensibly on their way out the door with different personages, fluttered from hiding places as soon as their bearers left the rarified air of the library and they all flitted back to their shelves with alacrity. Their would-be thieves were sharply reprimanded and informed that it did no good to even attempt to steal from the library as all of the magical texts within the library wanted to be there and would therefore go to extreme lengths to remain in the building.

This was a new one for Donnie and her friends, so when they first heard it, they stared at each other with marked surprise. Donnie, of course, then wondered if the texts in her own library wanted to be there or not, but when she was unwise enough to give voice to this thought, Sylvester sent her a stony glare before demanding in a condescending tone, "And which of yours are magical texts?"

Properly rebuked, Donnie sat silent for a moment and thought about this before protesting mildly, "Well, I do have some awfully good stuff, you know. But, no, none of them are exactly magical, are they? Not even those that are about magic or magical spells or its history. What makes these magical, I wonder, versus just regular texts like what I have in my library? Do you know, Sylvester?"

The cat had to admit that he did not know the answer to this query, but they were all saved from wondering further by Gak, who had overheard their conversation and interrupted it to enlighten them. He said, "The High Convoke recites a dwelling spell on any and all texts and such when they are submitted to the library. If the article in question accepts the spell, which is shown by if the item then finds its own place upon the shelves, it will remain in the library thereafter and never leave. All other texts are stored in the ancillary rooms near the entrance and can come and go as our guests please."

"Oh," said Sylvester, sounding impressed, "I was unaware that type of text is here. I would rather like to appraise what you have before we leave for the Mîrlonds," he added as he jumped off the table and scampered away toward the front of the library and these ancillary rooms.

During these last days spent at the Tower, Donnie, Rex, and Diego got to see, for the first time ever, several types of magical creatures they knew of only from stories. In addition to the aforementioned lemkins and imps, there were popkins (the major fairies of the Beldawuda), pura-puras (hairy pixie-like creatures that spoke in purred voices that were impossible to understand), tiny pixies (most of these had been hiding in attics and cellars all over the city and now felt free to show themselves), drapers and kelsies (who, for reasons known only to themselves, insisted upon always living together although they were nothing alike in any way), wood sprites and their conjoined spirits (all of whom were quite friendly but nevertheless astonishingly ethereal and therefore a little disturbing to see and hear), hobgoblins (vegetarian to a one and thoroughly disgusted by their goblin cousins' omnivorous ways), and to Donnie's everlasting delight, a couple families of noakies even drifted into the Tower the afternoon before she and the others left to continue their journey to the Mîrlonds. The noakies were just as depicted in the movie version of *Songs of the Earth* from her world and withstood Donnie's gushing over them reasonably well before shooting her a bright smile that displayed their wooden teeth to their best advantage and then marching off to look up some lore that had been argued about in their village for years.

On the morning when Donnie and her friends were to leave the Tower and head south, six solemn Sea Eagles gathered to lead them through the city to the outer gate, with several others descending from their eyrie to follow behind them. Their route was lined with magical creatures of all manner and ilk, some of whom Donnie had yet to meet and so she could only stare and smile at them, wondering who or what they might be.

As they set out, the boombox attached itself to her saddle and, to her amusement, played at low volume the haunting and mournful movie score called "The Gunslinger's Ballad," where the harmonica, flute, and piccolo almost speak their parts. Humming, "Wah, wah, wah," under her breath in time with the instruments, Donnie thought back to last night and her time with Nagba.

She had met the High Convoke in her chamber at the top of the Tower, and her attention, as always when there, was drawn to the heavens. Last night the moon had been new and darkened, while billions of brilliant stars carpeted the sky in a dazzling array of pinpoints that Donnie admired for some long while before she turned around, sat in the chair across from Nagba's perch, and thanked her new friend for all the help and information she'd given to Donnie and her friends.

Nagba, as usual, cackled with glee and told Donnie that, while she liked Donnie and her traveling companions, it was her purpose in life to impart information to other magical beings so there was no sense in thanking someone for fulfilling their purpose. Donnie had laughed with the ancient Sea Eagle and they had sat companionably for some time without speaking at all, both content to delay having to say words of farewell to the other.

After that, there had been no further revelations or surprises, just simple regret at parting, with them both bonded deeply in their mutual respect and appreciation for each other. Donnie would visit again, this they both knew, although when that might be could not be known or guessed, and the two new friends merely held their hearts open and let their mutual love flow between them. It had been a beautiful experience that Donnie suspected had been enjoyed by other members of her family on many occasions with the wise old bird.

Donnie still had not given herself the time to think about her blood family or anything of what she had learned about them since coming to the Forrieghness Tower. They were shadows to her and she could see none of them clearly in her mind except for the two from the tapestry. Because of this, the others seemed unreal to her and she felt ridiculous for thinking of herself as a daughter of Morrían, no matter what Nagba or any of the others might argue in rebuttal to that.

They said goodbye to Gak at the gate to the city and let the horses carry them off at a brisk trot toward the upper part of the Eldaren Road. It was a dreary sort of day, with heavy grey skies that seemed to mirror the sadness they all felt at leaving their Sea Eagle friends. Rex summed it up perfectly by looking back for a moment and then telling the others earnestly, "I'm really gonna miss them, especially Nagba and Gak."

To which, his friends all nodded.

Nearly an hour later, Donnie was riding alongside Falwaïn and noticed that he was casually scanning the horizon, both in front and behind them, along with the forests on either side as they traveled, as if he were trying to hide his deliberate gaze. She questioned him about his furtive looks, turning to stare him in the eye when she spoke.

He shook his head, letting out a small chuckle before replying ruefully, "I should have known you'd notice that." Bringing Gallantry a little closer to Wiwila, he said quietly, "Gak told me there was a rumor that the queen planned to send soldiers after us and that the mages would be with them. It seems none of them wants us to make it to the Mîrlonds, for whatever reason of their own. Whether that's because of you or what is happening on the Mîrlonds is anybody's guess, at this point."

Akanna, behind them, leaned forward and added confidentially, "As I am sure you recall from our first meeting with him, the bishop has been wanting to get himself and his mages onto the Mîrlonds for some time now. I do not trust his intentions, and I have never liked his methods. I believe he will try to set something in motion that he and his brothers cannot control, something that many of the magical creatures living on the Mîrlonds will pay for with their magic or their lives. Seeing as he does not hold those in high regard, I cannot sanction his stated desire to help us with our problem."

Donnie nodded, looking back briefly at the vincan. "I do remember the first time we met him. I came away from that interview with the distinct impression you didn't want his help in any way."

"Well, he and his brother mages have been known to use their magic for furtherance of their own needs rather than those of the people they are reported to be assisting," Falwaïn interjected dryly. "It's been a problem for many years and is why most mages are in Anûmanétus—because they are not welcome in other places unless the king decrees they must be given agency to practice their craft upon the locals."

"Jeez, I thought you said it was witches who weren't welcome here in Medregai," noted Donnie sardonically, rolling her eyes.

"Oh, the gentry have no use for witches," Akanna assured her, adding, "but the plain folk feel differently, for the most part. Witches have usually helped the poor, while wizards help the rich. Therefore, officially, wizards are welcome, while witches are not. But unofficially, it's a very different story."

Donnie hooked an eyebrow at Falwaïn who was looking unhappy with this characterization, but then he nodded, conceding, "If I am to be honest, I must confess that she is quite correct. Witches are not popular with the Sarn; no, not at all. But with the peoples the Sarn rule, witches and wise women are often one and the same and are a mainstay of local life."

"Quillirana," Donnie murmured, and Falwaïn grinned at her.

"Yes, she is indeed the local witch of Hörthanc, although we, like other communities in Medregai, employ the euphemism of wise woman or healer to her and those of her ilk so that any laws prohibiting witches cannot apply. As I intimated, this is a common practice throughout the land," he admitted. "That being said, anyone who calls themselves a witch or who is branded one publicly is ostracized from their community and is forced to seek shelter and livelihood elsewhere."

Donnie snorted derisively at this and noted, "Oh, I see, as long as they don't call themselves a witch, they're okay. But once they're branded as a witch, they become pariahs. Nice."

"No, it is not nice!" snapped Sylvester, staring up at Donnie from where he sat on the saddle in front of her. "It has never been nice. I wish I could say that it only occurs in human populations, but it does not. I have been told that witches are excluded in elf, dwarf, vincan, troll, goblin, fairy, woodland, and of course the fluvial communities as well."

"Is there good reason why this is so?" asked Diego, who had been listening intently to all that was being said.

"No," Sylvester answered flatly, still looking up at Donnie. "No good reason that I have ever heard, but rather for the worst reasons. Witches are notorious for flouting authority and working magic their own way instead of following the same rules that the rest of us generally do. I myself have prejudice against them, a prejudice I have learned to swallow mostly because of you, Donemere. While I still find you capricious and willful at the worst of times, I trust you more than anyone else I have ever known."

Donnie blinked at him, worked her mouth a little and screwed her face into a few different expressions, then said, "Well, thanks for that. I think."

He shrugged and turned around to look toward the front again. He then tossed out carelessly, "I feel the mages around us, so I believe they will attack soon."

Falwaïn jolted with surprise, spluttering disbelievingly, "What?"

Donnie turned a remorseful face upon him. "Sylvester's right. There are eight of the darned fellows—three on each side and another one in front and behind us." She made another face at her man, an expectant one this time, suggesting to him brightly, "Ya know, if you've already devised a plan to avoid them, it might be best to implement that now."

Chapter 22
Auf Wiedersehen

Catie and Liz, with little Jesse bundled tightly to his mother's chest in her shawl as usual, had been following Maeve and Florrie Danahur around for days, making sure they came to no harm as they moved between their cheap hotel on Van Ness Avenue, the fair, and the Palace of Fine Arts within the fair, where most of Maeve's fairy movie was being filmed. So far, there had been no sign of Herbert Flint or his cronies, the Germans. Nor was the dirigible still docked at the Presidio, although the two witches had spied it just below the clouds more than once since that fateful night when they'd sent the *Drunken Knave* back to its proper century.

Catie said she could still feel Herbert Flint's magic in the Palace Hotel each morning and evening when they left and returned to their suite. They figured that meant he must be holed up in his room, perhaps recovering from whatever injuries he had sustained when his fellow sorcerer's bolt of dark magic missed the *Knave* but hit the small boat carrying Flint and some of his lackeys. The incident had not made the papers, curiously, even though a major rescue had been mounted that night by the port authorities.

What did appear in the papers though was a small blurb detailing how an abandoned rowboat had been found floating in the middle of the San Francisco Bay in the early hours that morning. The article said it was supposed that whoever had been using it had either fallen or jumped overboard and was presumed dead. It went on to inform the paper's readers that the investigation was hereby closed until the day a dead body should wash up on one of the many shores within the bay.

Catie, closing her copy of the morning's *San Francisco Times* in disgust a couple days after the incident, commented that it was a ridiculous statement for both the police and the newspaper to make since dead bodies turned up quite regularly all around the bay upon its many shores. Liz had to agree with her, seeing as the paper reported daily on a body or two washing up on this or that beach, or having been found floating at this or that harbor, so finding the one body that might belong to an abandoned rowboat did seem a somewhat farcical impossibility. She mumbled her agreement, folded her own paper, drained her coffee cup, then stood so she could follow Catie out the door of the Garden Court. At six-thirty exactly they caught the streetcar that would take them to the Danahurs' hotel.

It turned out that the movie filming process of 1915 was absolutely fascinating to Liz and she watched it unfold with avid and undisguised interest. This new movie, really a series of shorts that related a naïve and saccharine sweet tale, was based off an earlier promotional film that had been shot about a fairy who sprinkled the city with inspiration after the devastating earthquake of 1906 and, from that magical act, the Pan-Pacific International Exposition was born.

On the other hand, Catie was bored by the whole thing, so she spent her time playing with little Jesse or staring at the crowds gathered for the filming. While the movie people had wanted what they called a closed set, that was impossible given the sheer numbers of the fair's attendees. The most deserted sets were those where the filming began in the early morning, which did not occur often because the entire crew was usually enjoying the fair until its closure at midnight and then liberally partaking of the pleasures provided in other parts of San Francisco until the wee hours of the day. At that point, those still standing might call together the young actresses and their mothers and shoot some of the scenes that were meant to be of just the fairies. This would last until ten o'clock at best, and then, one by one, the remaining crew would disappear until no one was left and none would reappear until later that evening when the fun would start all over again.

This naturally meant that the young girls, five in all, who were playing Queen Aurelia and her four handmaids, were then free until the next day, when they would be called upon to cavort at the beloved Palace of Fine Arts amongst its magnificent colonnade and rotunda for a few hours more. The girls, none of whom were older than eight, were having a grand time and looked adorable in their fairy costumes.

Afterward, the young starlets, who all seemed to accept each other without quibble or quiz, at least for the time they spent together, would convince their mothers to let them explore the "Jewel City" for a few hours and off everyone would head to other regions of the fair. This way, they got to see most of the fair's exhibits, as did Liz, Catie, and Jesse.

Liz admired the Tower of Jewels so much each time they passed it that Catie set a spell on five of the glass jewels adorning the building, one each of the original five colors manufactured for the tower, such that they would one day find their way to Liz. At the last moment, she told the jewels that the sooner that could happen, the better it would be for she prophesied they would be leaving this particular year and dimension in less than a week. Liz protested this frivolity sternly and maintained that she could never accept the "Novagems" as they were called. But Catie noted the sparkle in Liz's eyes and knew she would have been hard-pressed to come up with a better gift for the novice witch, who was, by now, certainly Déadl qualified and might soon make it to Madra if she continued to progress as quickly in her daily lessons with Catie as she had thus far done.

For those lessons, each afternoon at one p.m., the two witches would make their way to the field where the *Reisender*, the Germans' dirigible, had been docked for a few days. This field and its two big barns were used as a sort of airstrip and hangar for the airships associated with the fair, and it was always deserted at lunchtime except for one guard. Here, the witches felt safe practicing different defensive moves on the dirt airstrip that ran down the middle of the field. These practice sessions lasted no more than an hour and were curtailed by the airfield employees returning from lunch.

The one guard who remained at the field would be charmed to sleep by either Catie or Liz, and he would wake up moments before his colleagues returned feeling refreshed and not one bit guilty about having taken a nap when he should not have. Since nothing untoward ever happened during these practice periods, both witches thought it a fine way for Liz to learn more about the exciting power she could feel coursing through her body that was wanting to be let loose by her fingertips. To her credit, she worked hard and quickly became adept at turning harmful spells away, almost bending them to make them glancing blows at worst, while her own aim was nearly unerring and her release was soon faster than Catie's.

Even Jesse was fascinated by his mother's attempts and sometimes extended his little hands to assist his mother with whatever spell she was working at that moment. His power during these instances was strong, but nothing like what would have been needed to call forth a whole pack of wolves and control them, leading both Liz and Catie to be even more convinced that Jesse was not the one calling them forth whenever they had erstwhile appeared.

When the ladies returned to the fair after these magical lessons, one of them would set a spell to find Maeve, and they would spend the rest of the day tailing the bright and curious little girl and her faded mother around the exhibits and concessions. Maeve Rae seemed to love the airshows the most, which consisted of not just Mr. Art Smith and his daredevil flights in his bi-plane in both the day and night skies, but of brave jumpers with parachutes or hand-made wings or gliders from varying heights, hot-air balloon tricksters. A couple of these aero-dynamic kite balloons and their audacious, or as some might say, foolhardy daredevils ended up in the drink when the wind caught them just right. They then had to be rescued by the admiralty, which was typically positioned at the mouth of the San Francisco Bay during daylight hours. There were other types of flying, floating, and gliding machines as well, of course. Many of these were still in prototype form, and most failed dismally and sometimes hilariously, with no one getting too seriously injured. There were hot-air balloons for public rides, of course, that were tethered by rope and went no higher than a couple hundred feet. Oddly enough, these did not appeal to the young actress because she never once asked to be allowed to ride them, but the airplanes certainly held her attention and she would protest strenuously if her mother or anyone else tried to move her before she was done watching their acrobatic antics for the currently running show.

During this week, no one had approached either Maeve Ray or her mother except for those few people associated with the film, and there had therefore been no cause for alarm. So, it was with apprehension that the two witches noticed that the youngest Chagall girl suddenly appeared one morning, accompanied by a couple of rather tough-looking men, and the three of them stood silently watching the filming taking place. When the director called it a day at just a few minutes past noon and the hungover crew packed up their equipment and trudged away to their beds, leaving the young actresses to play tag through the colonnade around the Palace for a while, Mademoiselle Chagall waited by herself for the girls to pass near her. She looked awful and had dark circles haunting her eyes, while her shoulders were hunched and seemed to shake with either fear or grief—Liz and Catie could not agree which. They themselves melted back into the shadows and watched as the young miss, having been unable to raise the attention of Maeve, spoke to Florrie Danahur, who ignored the younger woman, marched over to her daughter and drew her by the hand away from the Palace's beautiful gardens, off to the thicker crowds of the fair's main thoroughfares.

Having frequented the PPIE for so long and so often, Catie and Liz had gotten to the point of recognizing some of that week's fair visitors since they'd seen them several times over the past few days. It occurred to them both that neither had seen the Chagalls since the previous weekend, which would probably have alarmed them if they'd noted it before now. As it was, the two witches agreed in quiet voices that nothing felt right about the way the young Chagall girl had approached Florrie and Maeve today, nor about the men who even now were roughly prodding the thin young lady to follow the Danahurs.

The next attempted contact by Mademoiselle Chagall occurred at the Joy Zone. The two men pushed her toward the older woman and her young daughter and shouted something after her.

Catie, thinking quick, espied some ear trumpets on sale at a stand to their right, so she ran over and picked up the nearest two, one long one of brass and wood and a shorter one of ox horn. She tossed some money at the vendor, not even looking at how much she gave him, and raced back to Liz and Jesse, handing Liz the metal and wood trumpet after she canted:

"These we put to our ears
So that we may hear
　That which we want
And not what we dunna!"

Liz took hold of the ear trumpet, raised it to her ear uncertainly, and then was utterly amazed when she heard the youngest Miss Chagall say, clear as a bell, to an obviously angry Florrie, "You've got to come with me, really you must! You don't understand, they have my brother and they've threatened to kill him if I don't bring you and your daughter to them."

The outraged Florrie grabbed hold of Maeve's arm and pulled her away, scalding the other woman with a sharp look, and the two of them marched toward the Joy Zone's exit.

The meaner looking of the men with Mademoiselle Chagall clasped her elbow in his big paw and pulled her close, hissing into her ear, "Mebbe ye should've told 'er it were yer life 'angin' in the balance; mebbe she'd'a listened to ye then, eh? Now, it'll be up ta that bruther o' yourn ta save ye, which is ta say, farewell, me lovely, for 'e ain't 'alf as in love with ye as 'e is wi' 'imself!" And the young miss, if possible, turned even paler than she already was.

Following this group when they set off briskly after Florrie and Maeve, Catie grasped Liz's hand and pulled her through the crowd only a few feet behind the Danahurs' pursuers. They headed up the Avenue of Progress and turned left onto the Esplanade. At Hudson, they went right between the New York City and Pennsylvania buildings, then jogged left again onto the Avenue of the States. At the North Dakota building, they turned right again and soon found themselves in the midst of the aeronautic-loving crowd thronging the Marina Green, who were waiting for their favorite flyer to hold his noon show. Little Maeve had found a place for herself and her mother near the front of the grandstand, which afforded the best views of her favorite fearless pilot and his agile bi-plane.

The thugs after the Danahurs were smart enough to wait until Art Smith had finished his show. It was a little after three o'clock now, and the skies were clear of flying machines for the moment, although the public balloon rides were still open. The crowds began to thin and Liz and Catie lost sight of Florrie and Maeve, but not of the Chagall girl and her companions.

Another man had joined them about halfway through the airshow and was now making his way purposefully toward the grandstand. He pushed his way to the top of the steps and waited. When Florrie and Maeve came upon him, Florrie cried out and gave him a horrified look.

Liz and Catie again lifted the ear trumpets to their ears.

"It can't be you—you're dead!" gasped Florrie as she fumbled to shove little Maeve behind her.

The man, who had his back to the two witches so they had yet to see his face, replied in a low voice that was edged with steel, "And yet here I am, in the flesh." He pulled Florrie to the side and looked down, adding in a much more pleased tone, "And there she is, there's my little girl! I'm your father, Maeve Rae."

By now, enough of the crowd had gone that the trio on the stairs were by themselves and Maeve's reaction could be seen. She looked up at the man, her eyes widened and she gulped, then she looked at her mom for direction but found none because Florrie wouldn't take her eyes from the man's face.

Maeve shrank away from him and replied precociously, "I don't have a pa anymore, so I ain't your little girl! I don't know who you are, but you are not my daddy!"

The man had both Florrie and Maeve by the wrists and was twisting them hard so that both stilled their protests and stared at him with growing fear. "I didn't say I was your daddy or your pa," he growled at the little girl. "I said I was your father, and your mother here knows it to be true. Why else do you think she's shivering right now? She knows me well, perhaps even remembers just how much I like to touch her…all over, I like to touch her." He had pulled Florrie close to him and pushed his face into her neck, smelling her and groaning with pleasure while he said this.

Poor Florrie looked like she wanted to die right there and then.

Liz started to take a step towards them, but Catie held her back by thrusting her arm through Liz's left one and turning them both around. "Not yet, Miss Priss. We got ta let this develop some and keep ourselves 'idden and out o' it fer naow. But we'll get there, that I promise ye, we'll get there. Come on, come over 'ere wi' me," she said in an urgent whisper and herded Liz toward a group of palm trees that had been installed for the fair. She had noticed that they had been starting to attract the attention of onlookers since they were both holding ear trumpets to their ears. Catie had lowered hers but instructed Liz, just as they found the sheltering shadows of the palms, "Ye keep on listening and be sure ta tell me if anything important 'appens, all right?"

Liz nodded and went back to listening, telling Catie, "He's still just threatening Florrie. He seems really sick and mean, Catie. I don't trust him with either of them."

Catie sighed and shook her head, her eyes scanning the crowd, spotting the original two thugs and Mademoiselle Chagall who were walking west, the young lady between the two ruffians with her. "Ye find that kind o' man all over, it seems. I wisht they'd all turn good, but I guess they jest canna do that."

"Oh, he's taken Maeve up in his arms, I think, because she's started screaming," Liz said, wanting to come back around the palm trees to take a look, but Catie beat her to it and then she drew back again and said, "Ye dunna need a trumpet ta 'ear that little girl, do ye?"

She was correct, for Maeve Rae's cries were quite loud and insistent, but then so was the man's laugh when he scolded her, making sure to inject a note of amusement into his voice, "We have to go, darlin', because the airshow is over for now. I promise you, we'll come back and catch his next show, so pipe down, will you?"

But Maeve Rae did not pipe down, and the man would have to repeat his reprimand several times as he strode though the fair with the little girl hoisted over his shoulder kicking and screaming for all she was worth. Poor Florrie was by his side, walking numbly and keeping silent while he continued to threaten her and his daughter with all manner of harm. Liz wanted dearly to knock him unconscious and save the woman and little girl, but Catie reminded her that they needed to find out where Herbert Flint was, and by association, the Germans and their orrery. Liz didn't like doing nothing, but she kept the disgusting man and his captives in earshot, if not eyesight, and nearly an hour later, they found themselves at the field being used to store the fair's airships.

The *Reisender* was back and both women turned to each other in shock when they realized this. If they'd had their practice session as usual that day, they'd have found the dirigible hours ago, but then, they might not have known the fate that seemed to be in store for the Danahurs either.

As the two groups in front of them disappeared inside the airship, the witches used the trees that ringed the field to remain hidden from view while they made their way to a point where they were directly opposite the ship. Both women put their ear trumpets to their ears and focused on any conversations going on within the enclosed gondola, which was held fast to the ground by several strong ropes. These tethers creaked and moaned as the huge metallic balloon floating just overhead swayed slightly in the light breeze that had arisen. The listeners ignored the sounds made by the ropes and concentrated on voices. It took Catie a little longer than it did Liz to find the main lounge, where it appeared the two groups they'd followed to the ship had assembled with Professor Gottleib-Lange and his two German comrades.

It sounded as though a few others were also present. A young man's indolent voice, having somewhat peevish notes to it, was complaining about being hauled from bed with a terrific hangover. He said he needed a drink to right himself, and there came the sound of a few snorts from some of the others present.

The man who'd identified himself as Maeve's father snarled at him, "Have whatever you want, if it will shut you up!" He paused and then added, "I mean it, drink the damn thing in silence."

"Kapitän Haufenstahl, ve are nearly ready to take off, *ja?*" asked the Professor, and a smooth male voice responded that they were still waiting for Herr Flint, who had said he would return before midnight.

"But I vant to be gone by 'zen," the professor demanded indignantly.

"You hear that Klaus, our esteemed Professor Gottleib-Lange wishes to be gone by then," sneered a cold voice that once again unmistakably belonged to Maeve's father. "Why don't you send one of your crew after Herr Flint and tell him what the good professor wants? I'm sure Bertie'll race right back here to do as the professor pleases."

Someone snickered with amusement at this remark, but mostly it was met by a pained silence that lasted for nearly a minute.

Then there was a period of perhaps a quarter of an hour where multiple conversations were being carried on at the same time. The Chagall sister and brother, who were apparently named Adrien and Lela, spoke together in hushed tones that Liz listened to because she felt responsible for them being there in the first place. After all, if she hadn't set their mother's watch as a decoy, Herbert Flint and his cohorts would have had no reason to go after any of the Chagalls.

It seemed that Lela wanted Adrien to give up his association with these people, but he was having none of that and told his *petite sœur* to remain calm, assuring her blithely that no one was going to harm either of them and he had everything under control. It was clear that Lela did not believe him, but she nevertheless remained where she was and did not attempt to leave either the room or the ship. Their exchange, carried on in French, at least reassured Liz that neither of them was in dire danger, although she suspected that no one on that airship was in any way truly safe.

The afternoon wore on, with the two witches still hiding outside about two hundred feet from the small gangway to the gondola's door. They both sat down on the grass after the first hour and leaned against the big oak tree they were behind. One of them generally kept their ear trumpet in and they changed off listening every so often, although Catie did most of the listening while Liz attended to Jesse's needs.

There had been ground crew working at the airfield throughout the day, but none of them noticed the women or little Jesse and so they went about their business unhurriedly, which consisted mostly of ensuring that the fair's aircraft were all in tip-top shape and that Art Smith's plane was reloaded with fuel and fireworks after each show. His biggest show of the day wouldn't run until ten o'clock that night, but all other shows he put on daily still had quite a few fireworks in them. That evening, the seven o'clock show went off without a hitch and the plane landed in the hangar field, as usual, at about eight-thirty. Mr. Smith parked the plane just down from the *Reisender* and hopped off it to help the crew attach the tie-down ropes. He had a talk with some of the men and they began to replace one the plane's tension wires that Art thought was coming loose. It seemed he was correct, and the wire was replaced and tightened in no time at all. The two women watched with fascination as Mr. Smith, his gamin face wearing its characteristic smile, as shown in the light of the portable lamps the crew set up so they could work at night, not only did most of the work himself, but managed to maintain a cheery atmosphere that seemed to buoy the spirits of the entire airfield crew, for they began to laugh and joke more than they had done all day long.

Interested enough to listen in on them, Liz put the ear trumpet down after just a couple minutes, her face flaming red with embarrassment and a little shock. Catie, on the other hand, giggled and cackled lasciviously until Liz hit her on the shoulder, knocking Catie's ear trumpet onto her lap, and hissed that the other woman was making far too much noise and they were sure to be caught if she didn't shut up.

Which was when a tall figure separated itself from a nearby tree and drawled, "Too late, little eavesdroppers! Get inside the *Reisender* now or I'll have to hurt you."

Closing their eyes for a moment in regret, the two women scrambled to their feet, turned around to face their captor, and could just make out the handsome form of Herbert Flint standing in front of them. He studied Catie's face, barely looking at Liz or Jesse, and said, "You're a witch, both of you. Well, no funny stuff, or the babe will be the first to die." He made this threat so matter of factly while gesturing for them to turn around and march to the dirigible that it was unimaginably creepy to Liz and she felt her skin crawl.

When they entered the gondola, it was ablaze with light. At first sight of the women, an alarm went up, but then Herbert Flint stepped in behind them and the hue and cry died down immediately. He pushed the women to a set of stairs to the right and they climbed obediently. At the top, they were in a hallway and Flint indicated they should head toward the one open doorway about halfway down the hall.

This was the lounge, where most of the others were either languishing on couches or playing poker at the big table at the back. Little Maeve Rae and her mother were tied together to some chairs that stood back-to-back and both looked over their shoulders at the newcomers in wild desperation. When Maeve recognized Liz and Jesse, her eyes popped wide in surprise. Liz moved her head to the right negatively, staring at the little girl intently and willing her to say nothing about their previous meeting. She needn't have worried because the child wouldn't have been given the chance to speak anyway.

Florrie's face was bloodied and battered, and very difficult to look at. The beating that had caused her injuries, which Catie heard and warned Liz at the time was happening, had been perpetrated by Maeve's father shortly after they had arrived at the dirigible. She said it sounded as though his ire with Florrie was centered around her escape from him when Maeve was not yet half a year old. Catie had refused to allow Liz to listen with her ear trumpet during the beating, for they really could do nothing to stop it, she pointed out sadly, and it would just make Liz feel bad, so there was no sense in her listening in right then. Liz, convinced this made her weak of spirit, was nevertheless grateful that Catie took on the horrible burden of listening to it by herself.

The moment Florrie realized someone new had entered the room, she began to cry, begging tearfully, "Please, help my little girl out of here and take her away with you!"

Maeve's father, recognizable by the cornflower blue eyes and long dark lashes which his daughter had inherited from him, surged to his feet from the poker table nearby, took three long strides to Florrie, reared back his arm and smacked her hard across the face with the flat of his big palm. Mother and daughter were thrown instantly to the floor, their bound chairs flipping as one onto their sides. Maeve emitted a small scream as they went over before bravely clamping down on the cry, whereas Florrie neither moved nor said anything.

Liz would have stepped forward to protest this renewed assault if Catie had not slid in front of her right then, effectively stopping Liz from doing anything. Herbert Flint pushed the two women farther into the room, then passed by Liz, studying her intently, a stern warning in his eyes for her. She bit her lip and pushed back the tears of frustration and grief that were forming in her eyes because she was pretty sure that Florrie was dead. Adding to that, Maeve had moved her head backward so that she could see Liz from where she was lying on the floor, and the little girl was watching her with barely dared-for hope.

Herbert Flint went over to the drinks cart on the left wall, poured two fingers of whiskey, and tossed half of it down his throat. He sighed with pleasure and turned around to survey the room. Whatever injuries he had received that night on the bay had not scarred his features, that was for sure. His curly blond hair, cut short on the sides but allowed to grow long on the top, fell onto his high, smooth forehead and made him look even more handsome than he truly was. He was as easy on the eyes as ever and carried himself with an assurance that was wickedly alluring.

The three Germans were seated at the table and had been playing poker with Maeve's father and the two ruffians seen earlier that day with Lela Chagall, while the Chagall brother and sister were sitting together on the larger of the two couches. Lela had her arms around Adrien's shoulders and her face burrowed in his neck. She had been frightened by the renewed assault on Florrie and had turned to her brother for protection.

Liz thought that was probably not the wisest move on the girl's part, because Adrien Chagall looked half-drunk and wholly arrogant. He was trying to push his sister away, but she was clinging to him determinedly and he finally gave up and merely pulled himself into the far corner of the couch so that his sister was nearly laying on top of him.

Liz noticed that the professor was staring at her and at Jesse with his mouth hanging open, so she turned away from him slightly, but was not surprised when he gasped, "*Das ist sie!* Zat is her, ze vitch who wisited my cabin ze night on ze boat. And zat is her *kind*! I remember now, she was a negro!"

Adrien roused himself enough from his languishing to scoff at the professor and sneer flippantly, "You Germans are such fools. You really think you know everything, yet you can't even see that she's a redskin, not a darkie!"

Liz pushed back her shoulders and looked around the room with anger. These people had touched an old hurt she could feel burning deep within her, adding fuel to the blazing fire of her soul.

Catie took her hand and squeezed it, holding on tightly.

Herbert Flint chuckled to himself, emptied his glass and set it on a small table to his right. He walked over to stand in front of Liz and Catie, and stared at Catie for a long, menacing time before demanding, "Where is it? It's certainly not the watch that silly child's stepfather gave to her when he died, which means you must have it because yours is the last possible one."

Catie met his gaze without blinking and said nothing.

A small, vicious smile played around Flint's mouth. "That was a clever move, I'll admit. It took us some time to hunt down all your decoys, yes, but we're done with that now. I know you have it," he stated dramatically, adding, "and I want it!"

"Ye canna 'ave it," Catie argued bravely, her spine straight and hard. "But I will take the orrery from ye, with pleasure." She looked around the room and asked with only slightly feigned curiosity, "Where be it? Or are ye afraid ta show it ta me?"

Flint threw his head back and laughed, his eye glinting with arrogance. "Oh, I like you. Which one are you, by the way—or are you *not* one of the daughters?"

"I am not," Catie assured him, still holding his gaze steadily.

The smile on Flint's face faded and he said, "No, but you're related to them, I can feel it. You all resonate the same." He spit at her in disgust.

The spittle never made it to Catie's face. Instead it hit her protective shield, which she had raised over herself, Liz, and Jesse when she grabbed Liz's hand. The spit hung for a second a couple inches from Catie's cheek, then it disappeared into nothing.

"Give me the watch-clock and I might let you live," Flint suggested lazily, crossing his arms in front of his chest.

It was Catie's turn to scoff. "No, ye won't do that." She lifted her chin and made her own offer. "If ye let the children go free, along wi' my friend here, I might consider givin' ye the watch-clock wi'out fightin' ye. 'Cause if I fight ye, I guarantee this big ol' balloon will go up in flames. I'll make sure it do, and none o' ye will git out alive." She had tightened her grip on Liz's hand for a second when Liz had tried to protest this scheme, which made Liz fall silent again, knowing that here was a situation where she had to simply trust in Catie and in magic once again.

"The children can go, but not her," Herbert Flint stipulated after a few moments' consideration, flicking his eyes toward Liz and then returning his attention to Catie. "And you will show me how to work the clock-watch without argument, yes?"

Catie nodded, both knowing the other was lying through their teeth. But before anyone could say anything else, Catie shot a small bolt of power at Maeve and the ropes around the child disappeared. When her father moved to stop her from rising up, Herbert Flint raised a hand and a stream of his magic held the other man back.

"We'll release her and the other child as agreed," he told his comrade firmly, and Liz knew that in his head he'd added the words, "for now," to the reprimand.

Maeve Rae got to her feet, glanced once at her mother's still form, and then ran to Liz, her eyes wide with fright but also with determination. "Give Jesse to me," she whispered solemnly, which Herbert Flint noted with interest. "I'll keep him safe, I promise. I'll always keep him safe."

Liz looked over at Catie, who nodded to her. Just how the hell they were going to get out of this dilemma, she had no idea, but she did realize that the kids needed to be away from the crossfire of whatever was about to happen here. She unwrapped the shawl that bound Jesse to her chest and handed him over to Maeve, carefully re-wrapping him in the shawl so that he was now positioned tight to the little girl the same way he'd been to his mother, leaving Maeve's hands free to do whatever she needed to.

Maeve Rae stood tall and took hold of Jesse's fingers with her own. Liz had left Jesse's arms unbound so that he could help himself and Maeve get away with his magic, if at all possible. When Liz was done tucking the ends of the shawl into its folds and she straightened to stand, sweet little Jesse stared up at her and gave her a trusting smile, cooing at her with delight and love.

Liz smiled back tremulously and made a silent promise to both Jesse and Maeve that she and Catie would not die tonight and leave the children with no one to protect them. She blew her son a kiss and lifted her gaze to Maeve, sending the little girl a reassuring smile and nod. She murmured, "Go now, Maeve," and pushed the girl behind her and toward the door.

Flint motioned for one of the two ruffians at the table to go with them and ordered, "See that no one stops them from leaving the ship. I would hate to renege so soon on my bargain with our guests." He chuckled low and flashed his eyes meaningfully at the women.

Liz clenched her jaw and returned his look with an angry glare.

When he started to say something else, Catie held up a finger and snarled, "Not until the children are safely gone! I can feel 'em, ye know, and once they are outside and away, we can resume our negotiations. But not until!" she repeated, and she sent him a glare that matched Liz's.

He wheeled away toward the drink cart again and poured himself another two fingers of whiskey, turning to stare at Catie until the ruffian returned to the lounge and muttered that the children were gone.

Catie nodded with satisfaction and said to Herbert Flint, "Proceed."

Flint took a sip of his drink, regarded it for a few moments, and then remarked, "Emery Gold is one of the most powerful sorcerers I know and he would never just let you get away from him. Therefore, you must have taken him to another time and left him there that night on the bay. I want to know what year you took him to."

Catie shrugged, returning his stare brazenly. "It dunna matter ennyway, 'cause 'e ent livin' no more."

"You killed him?" Flint asked, shaking his head slowly, disbelievingly. "No, you didn't do that. You *couldn't* do that!"

"I saw 'is body, and it were as dead as poor Florrie's over there," Catie assured him, and Lela, who had not realized the battered woman's fate, let out a delicate gasp of horror.

Herbert Flint stood looking at Catie and Liz with a mixture of rage and hatred. He turned to his right and stood with his fists clenching and unclenching, and the others in the room all sat up or stood to attention.

Adrien shoved his sister away and got to his feet, lurching over so that he could stand on the other side of the room with the three Germans, behind the poker table. Once there, he leaned as nonchalantly as he could manage against the wall, took out his cigarette case and, with shaking hands, lit one, taking a deep drag from it as he watched Flint battle his fury.

His sister, who had cried softly when her brother had thrown her across the couch, sat up for a moment, then she seemed to melt into the corner of it, trying to make herself as small as she could.

Flint strode over to the phonograph, caught in his hand a record that came flying toward him from a pile on a nearby table, then placed it on the turntable and set the needle upon it. It was a rendition of the old classic "Auf Wiedersehen" and was sung by two of the current titans of the operatic world. It was his favorite song to play or sing to himself whenever he killed someone.

Maeve's father stepped forward and began cracking his knuckles, a nasty grin on his face. The two ruffians moved up next to him and did the same, all three staring at Liz and Catie with something akin to lust on their faces, although it was not clear whether that was blood lust or sexual lust.

It was Herbert Flint who took hold of Lela Chagall's shoulders from behind the couch, lifting her up to her feet and pushing her in the direction of her brother, snapping at her, "Get out of the way, you little fool."

A calmness overtook Liz, even though she doubted that she'd ever been this scared before in her life. She and Catie glanced at each other, neither saying a word aloud, and both lifted their hands. The two that were as yet unclasped, they now joined together just as each woman turned to face the other.

Their clasped hands began to glow brightly with their respective gold and turquoise magic, and Adrien Chagall slurred drunkenly, "You see that, sis? That's what I want—I want to be able to take that and use it for myself. And Flint's going to show me how to steal it away from untalented, filthy bitches like these two who should not be allowed to ever possess anything so pure and wonderful as real magic!"

Catie ignored him and concentrated only on Liz, gazing at her with confidence and reassurance. She began to chant,

> "Together we are one,
> not to be undone.
> We are safe and whole,
> no matter the toll."

Liz repeated it with her and when they'd recited it for the third time, a solid wall of turquoise and gold power had been built up around them.

Herbert Flint stood only a few feet away from them and had mustered all his own magical power into his fists and was sending blow after blow of black magic reigning upon the witches' shield. It shook and cracked, but the women kept up their spell and the cracks disappeared almost as soon as they formed.

Maeve's father and his two friends leapt at the women and began punching the shield, using some sort of brass knuckles that were able to penetrate the magical wall a few inches, gouging out great chunks of it with each punch.

Again, the witches renewed their efforts and the wall was reinforced.

The Germans were yelling in their language and suddenly the professor ran across the room, opened a cupboard in the wall that contained a small lockbox, opened that, and took out what had to be the orrery. It was folded flat, but both Liz and Catie saw its gold metal frame glint in the professor's hands and knew they'd have to let their shield collapse if they were ever going to take possession of the magical artifact.

Just then, the doorway to the lounge was filled with the shapes of two men fighting in the corridor outside. One man hit the other and he came flying into the room where he landed onto his back. It was the captain of the airship and his attacker was none other than Art Smith himself. He stared with shock at the women standing behind their magical shield and at Herbert Flint shooting bolts of magical power at them. Smith shook his head once before shouting with resolve, "All right then!" After that, he resumed his fight with Captain Haufenstahl, who had climbed back to his feet.

Behind Art Smith came five members of the airfield crew who leapt onto the shoulders of Maeve's father and his two thuggish friends. And when the Germans tried to leave the room, a couple of these heroes separated from the others to corral the foreigners back to the far side of the room.

Catie said to Liz in a low voice, "We let the shield go, I block Flint, and ye go for the orrery; agreed?"

Liz shook her head and replied firmly, "No, I'm faster than you at both defense and offense, so you get the orrery and I'll handle Flint."

"No, ye must 'ave the orrery, girlie, since ye've got the clock-watch. They should stay together, and ye should 'ave them, not me! Trust me, Miss Priss, I'll be fast enough for this," the little blonde witch asserted confidently. "And then ye go, ye find them kids, and ye git them away from 'ere. Go back ta yer time, and make sure ye get ta Donnie's ma as quick as ye can, 'cause she can protect ye well."

"Lorraine's a witch too?" Liz gulped at this news in surprise, and their shield cracked in several places.

Both witches refocused on their shield and it soon stood firm against Flint's blows, which were becoming stronger, more precise, and harder to deflect. They both knew this without either saying it. They also knew their shield could last for only another couple of minutes before they ran out of power, so it was definitely time to try something different.

Catie looked over her shoulder, then at the Germans, and then back at Liz. She nodded toward the Germans and said, "Ye go that way, and I'll turn to deal with Flint, like we agreed. On the count o' three, all right?"

"No!" Liz exploded. "You can see the Germans, so you deal with them. I'm going after Flint—now!" And she did just that. She let her magic fall back into her hands, dove behind Catie and shot a magical netting of pure power that landed on Flint's head and shoulders, binding his arms.

Catie had no choice but to race over and tear the orrery out of Professor Gottleib-Lange's hands. When the three Germans tried to grab her, she twisted to the side and slid away from them. She shouted to Liz that she had the orrery and dove for the door, hardly able to believe that they were going to make it out of there.

But then Flint fought free and he shot a bolt of angry red magic at her. Catie felt it hit her squarely in the chest and suddenly she couldn't breathe. She staggered forward a few steps, knowing that her life was flowing out of her like a river. She faltered, came to a stop, and fell to her knees. One of the Germans grabbed the orrery from her and disappeared out the door with it, his two compatriots and the Chagall siblings escaping behind him. No sooner had they left did several men from the ship's crew race into the room to attack Smith and his friends. The ship's crew had knives and guns with them, she noticed, and Smith and several of the others fell where they stood.

Catie tried to tell Liz this, tried to call out her name, but the words wouldn't form properly in her mouth and she realized that something was filling her mouth and running down her chin. She put up a hand to wipe whatever it was away and her hand came back covered red with her own blood. She looked at it strangely, felt her body begin to droop, and knew that she was seconds from dying, leaving Liz to fight alone. She shot a weak bolt of golden-colored magic at Flint, which he deflected easily with a crow of laughter. He deflected a much stronger bolt from Liz and then he aimed a second shot of angry red magic at Catie and she toppled backward in death.

Liz, watching all this unfold, screamed her fury at the gods, the ancient beings who she was sure had started this mess in the first place however many eons ago, shouting at them, faceless and nameless though they were to her, "Help me, damn you! Save her and send me help!"

She screamed this over and over in rage until her voice grew hoarse.

And this time, through her own breast, she could feel the wolves arise. They shot from her in a pack and filled the room. If the dirigible's crew hadn't gotten in their paths first, Herbert Flint would not have had time to blast a hole in the wall behind him and flee, his coattails disappearing into the night with a soft pop of noise.

The wolves killed the dirigible's remaining crew in seconds, including Maeve's brutal father and his two thuggish comrades.

Liz ran to Catie's body and chanted a healing charm that the other witch had taught her only yesterday, but Liz's frantic voice shook so much with fear and grief that the charm could do no good at all. She reprimanded herself, choking back her tears, and forced her magic to flow into Catie's chest, willing it to fix her, ordering it to do just that, shouting at it over and over again that it must fix Catie.

But Catie just lay there, her features set in an expression of surprise at the suddenness of her death, not breathing.

Liz raised her face to the heavens and wailed with sorrow.

The wolves, their carnage complete, came to circle the witches. They raised their heads to howl mournfully along with Liz and then three of them disappeared into streams of silvery magic that poured into Catie's open mouth.

Blessedly, her chest began to rise and fall again with life.

***

Warren turned the page and waited impatiently for more text, but none came after several minutes. He got up and paced the bedroom, the room he should be sharing with Liz and Jesse. He ran his hands over his dark hair and worried. What was going to happen to them next, he wondered? Where were Jesse and Maeve by now, and how were Liz and Catie going to catch up to them in time, because this Herbert Flint, who Warren badly wanted to meet in an open field one dark and deserted night, was going to go after the kids, he just knew it. He hadn't managed to get the clock-watch from Liz and Catie, and the only leverage that would work with the two witches would be the children.

Warren went back to the bed and picked up the book, reviewing its last few pages more carefully. He got to thinking about the wolf pack that, for the third time, had rescued his family. But this time, instead of coming from Jesse, they'd come from Liz—no, that was wrong, because the book said Liz had felt them arise *through* her own breast, not *in* her own breast. Did that mean they came from elsewhere and had only been channeled through Liz?

Well, it had to mean that, didn't it?

He sat down and positioned himself so that he was leaning back against the headboard. Running through his memory, he realized that the previous two times the wolf pack had appeared, he'd been meditating on his magic and had lost himself in it, thereafter having no memory of anything after he'd begun his meditation.

What if the wolf pack came from him and he somehow channeled it through Jesse and now Liz?

But no, that couldn't be right because he hadn't been meditating this last time, so the wolves couldn't be his conjuring, could they?

Idly calling up a small ball of glacial blue magic from his fingertips, he let it float above his palm, staring at it intently like he was trying to see beyond the visual into the very essence of it. He fancied that he could see "threads" of magic in it, each interwoven and entwined with other threads that moved constantly throughout the ball, making it an almost solid, teeming mass of living power.

He chuckled a little then because that was exactly what it was. As he'd found out for himself, magic was very much a living thing, always moving and vibrating through him even when he slept. He assumed it was that same way for others, as well, remembering what Donnie's power had felt like as it surrounded him when she'd cast the spell on him a few days after he'd met her. That spell had changed his life, not just his appearance, and it had been the first time he'd felt a magical power that frightened him not because of its intent, but simply because of its greatness. He recalled so clearly being grateful that her power was not in his own bones, for he knew he could never handle it. Whereas Donnie had accepted it as second nature and had even deliberately welcomed other types of magic to run through her body.

Suddenly distracted, Warren's eye caught something different in his magical sphere and he shook his head, peering closer at it. The next thing he knew, he felt like he was being sucked out of his body and, when he realized he'd arrived at his destination, he looked around.

He found he was in a dark cave. He could not see much at first, then the walls became almost transparent or misty with a weird haze that would occlude almost all light before it would clear to show what was happening somewhere else.

To his great surprise, he began to watch, through the cave's walls, the scene he'd read only minutes ago in the book get played out in real life. He witnessed Catie dying, saw Liz lose it and scream at the gods, and then saw the wolf pack erupt from her.

His senses kicked in and he whirled where he stood in the cave. Behind him were two men, both of whom were tall and strong, with dark hair and swarthy complexions.

"Who are you?" he demanded from them and they both raised their right hands, palms turned to him. It was a friendly, placating gesture, and by it he knew they meant him no harm.

Warren relaxed and the one standing directly behind him replied, "I am your father."

Then the other one stated, equally as solemnly as the first, "And I am her father."

The first one explained, "We are Iquakawi and we watch over all the people of our tribe."

The second added quietly, "We protect them when they cannot protect themselves."

Warren looked from man to man, then turned to gesture to the scene still being played out on the wall behind him. "You did that? You conjured the wolf pack to save them?" he asked.

They both shook their heads.

"No," his father corrected him gently. "We *are* the wolf pack."

And from the shadows appeared perhaps another thirty people, men and women of all ages.

Liz's father took two steps closer to Warren so that he was now right next to him and put his hand on top of Warren's shoulder. He said, "We are the An'ugadi. We are the middle gods of the Iquakawi and we do the bidding of the Sasdá Añon." He nodded slowly and smiled. "They are watching over you and my daughter. But mostly, they are watching over our grandson, who is the one we have all waited for so long to be born."

His father put his hand on Warren's other shoulder and patted him with affection. Warm tears sprang to his black eyes and he smiled through them at his son. "Like you, your son will be thrice blessed, and he will bring our peoples together from far and wide. But he has much to learn before he can accomplish this. You will teach him as he grows, his mother will teach him, and there will be many others who will also contribute to his wisdom and his reason. His path is long, but he will bear the best and worst for us, and it will make him into the leader he must become."

Liz's father squeezed Warren's shoulder and, when Warren turned to look at him again, he said, "But for now, we must make sure he survives the next attack. Forgive us, but we must return to watching over him."

Warren blinked and found that he was back in bed in the cottage. He grabbed for the book beside him and opened it hurriedly. If not for the new text describing what he'd just experienced, he would have thought it all an impossible dream.

Chapter 23
Stories of Old

After a short discussion of options, Donnie and the others bolted away from the trap the Førrens Order of Manûs Mages and the Queen's Guards had waiting for them, sprinting into the forest, careening around trees and crashing through thick undergrowth as they went. They were about thirty miles southwest of Anûmanétus and were headed in the general direction of Muneer, where the Lengaheld River crossed the Donbragh'arík. There, Falwaïn had assured Donnie with a hurried shout, a ferry boat was set to take them down the mighty Donbragh, which was the most imposing waterway in all of Medregai. This giant river sourced from deep within the White Tower Mountains in the north and flowed to the Sôlom Ocean in the south.

With a snap of her fingers, Donnie had sent the two closest mages and their squads of soldiers, who stood directly between her and the two rivers' conflux, to a specific spot she'd recalled with clarity on the road about a mile outside the capital city. She might have done the same to more of their pursuers, but she told herself she should play fair, so she assiduously followed Falwaïn's instructions to remove the mages and soldiers in that direction. With the way free and clear, she bid Wiwila to head for the forest as quick as she could.

When Donnie shot her transport spell into the thicket of trees lining the road, its path was viewed with anger by the remaining six mages and also by the troops with them, all of whom had been assembled in their places for several hours. Within moments of the spell's release and the perceived disappearance of their comrades' magic, the mages ordered the Queen's Guards to converge upon the hated witch and her traitorous confederates.

Aldalis Munkinum had been the one mage stationed at the front of the planned ambush and he had sat upon his horse silently and without moving throughout the entire wait for the enemy to appear. While he seemed at his ease, he was, in fact, as impatient as any of the guards might have been, for he had been wanting to stage a confrontation with this witch for some time. As the powerful wave of blue magic left Donemere's fingertips and shot straight into the forest, undoubtedly to kill two of his most learned fellows, he felt the thrill of combat come over him and he urged his horse with his whip so that it leapt into the trees on a direct line to intercept the woman he secretly feared just might be his nemesis.

There was a large wharf at Muneer, near where the tiny settlement of river folk who tended it was established just off to the southwest of where the two great rivers converged and crossed. This wharf was what the riders were intent on reaching, each group before the other.

The mouth of the Lengaheld River was situated far up the western slope of Tumbenhaigh Mountain, the southernmost peak of the White Tower Mountains. It was the steepest mountain in the White Tower Mountains' range and because of its proximity to the summer branch of the Baldean Current, which brought warm winds and high precipitation, the forests covering the mountain were thriving, growing green and lush all year long. The Lengaheld, as it descended down the sometimes-sheer mountainside, ran faster and faster until it reached the bottom of the mountain, which was within a couple hundred feet of its narrow confluence with the Donbragh. The Lengaheld ran so swiftly and shallowly that it rammed a path across the Donbragh and continued east, surging toward Hörthanc.

Conversely, the Donbragh ran slow but deep along its length, with its bed widening the farther south it flowed as it gained water from several tributaries originating in the west from the Tegere Mountains that marked the northern boundary of the lands controlled by the vincan tribes. At the conflux with the Lengaheld, though, it filled a narrow gorge that plunged the depth of the river to hundreds of feet. This provided the Lengaheld, being the faster and shallower river, the opportunity to cross the larger waterbody instead of joining it. It was quite a phenomenon to see, for the Lengaheld was so murky and muddy with the sediments carried in its flow as it crashed down the side of Tumbenhaigh, it streaked across the deep blue of the Donbragh as if it sought to cleave the mightier river in two.

The folk living in the settlement of Muneer were plain watermen and lightermen, and they did their best to stay away from the politics of the Sarn or any group wishing to make trouble with the Sarn. Not that they agreed with the Sarn or their politics, which was why they had built their settlement west of the confluence of the two rivers upon land where the vincans of Gainál and the northmen of Nœthlangan ruled in peace with each other. But it was better for business if the Sarns were allowed to believe they were calling the shots whenever any of them were around, as they had been two days ago.

Poblench, who was the leader of the river folk and a family man of devout and pious nature, had listened without question in his small office on the eastern side of the Donbragh'arík to the instructions given to him by the Sarn captain who'd come to make sure that the new witch everyone was talking about, and who would reportedly soon be coming to Muneer, would not find escape on the ferry.

He had listened just as quietly to the vincan ambassador who paid him a goodly sum to make sure the ferry delayed its departure a day to wait for a few particular riders who would be traveling fast because they would undoubtedly be chased to the east wharf by Sarn guards.

The ambassador, a fierce vincan male by name of Juree of the Marcons, had been the vincan army commander in Morlant for many a long year before his ambassadorship. Taller than most other vincans, he confidently assured Poblench that the vincan government would assume responsibility for the ferry and he himself would inform the Sarn guards that the witch and her friends were under the aegis of the vincan realm the moment they neared the wharf. If the Sarn thereafter had any issue to raise, they must do so with the vincan high council in Morlant at its next convening in two moon cycles' time.

At that point, the vincan ambassador had stood from his chair, sent Poblench a meaningful stare, and had left the wharf's main offices—which were located on the western side of the Donbragh and was where the river folk usually met with the vincans—without saying another word.

Poblench had considered his dilemma but momentarily and thereafter had had a very large and simply framed barge constructed that stood ready and docked at the farthest end of the eastern wharf. It was not quite half the size of the shipping ferry the lightermen used to transport goods south and was made of long, thick logs lashed and bound together. A couple of long lean-to shelters covered with animal skins were installed on two of its corners.

He felt righteously certain that this solution would free him from all fault with both the Sarn and the vincans because the shipping ferry and the passenger ferry would both leave on time and would not be used by anyone to escape from anyone else, although escape could still be providentially made with the new barge. He had not mentioned this plan to anyone but his fellow dock workers, as was considered right and proper for those of his ilk, and some of his most trusted folk were currently posted as lookouts for the potential refugees.

It was the northern-most of these lookouts who spotted Donnie and her friends first. This was the youngest and smartest daughter of Poblench—he had two other not quite so smart daughters and three even less smart sons, if one is being truthful—and she whistled the alarm not because of seeing a woman, two men, and a vincan riding their horses hard toward the wharf, but more because the woman let loose what looked like blue light from her fingertips as she cleverly moved about ten large trees across the path behind them—where the trees still stood tall with roots and dirt and everything intact, mind you—so that they completely blocked the path to the wharf for the small company of loudly whooping and hollering Sarn guards following a ways behind the witch's little band of fugitives.

The witch and her friends passed below the hemlock tree where the lookout, whose nickname was Midge because she was quite a tiny young thing, had made herself comfortable in a large joint of the tree for the afternoon. Midge's heart pounded in time with the horses' hooves, which were thundering down the path and throwing up mud below her, and the young girl, willing someone to notice her, pointed toward the wharf and shouted. The darker of the men and the vincan caught this and called out something to the others and the horses renewed their purposeful galloping, notching it up by a couple more miles per hour.

When she heard some trees behind her explode, Midge whirled around in her seat to look back up the well-worn path. Being such a smart girl, she realized almost immediately that this meant mages from Anûmanétus were with the Sarn and it was they who had just blown up the trees the witch had moved into their path. And, of course, they had not taken the same care as the witch had to safeguard the trees' well-being when moving them. Midge scrambled down her tree in seconds and raced toward the Donbragh, where she wanted nothing more than to be well out of the path of the dreaded mages of Anûmanétus, who were known throughout Medregai for letting fly whatever spell they decided might be required, uncaring who or what got in its way, irrespective of the damage it might do or to whom it might do it.

Another lookout farther down the road and almost to the wharf itself, an oldish man named Thomb, waved the first group of riders by, pointing at the end of the pier, although it was impossible for anyone but himself, really, to know it was the end of the pier he was pointing at. The riders passed him, with the witch smiling and saluting him with a wave that made him grin in return, and then he looked back at the path behind them.

Thomb barely had time to dive to the forest floor when a spell from one of the mages coming around the bend two hundred feet away hit the tree he had climbed earlier, exploding its thick base into smithereens that shot everywhere. Thankful at first that he had somehow managed to land in a heaped bed of drying grasses several yards from his tree, he shook himself hard and rolled to his feet, having realized by now that it had been magic that had moved him to the grass pile when he fell. He stared up the road toward the witch, saw her salute him again with a wide grin before turning away in her saddle, and old Thom felt what he thought just might be love blossom in his bosom.

Falwaïn had also turned in his saddle to watch behind them and he now looked at Donnie, grinning as he shouted, "I think you made a conquering there, my love!"

She let out a full, throaty kind of laugh and retorted, "Then you'd better not take me for granted, my darling, or I might just come back here and see what it's like to be admired by a river man!"

Her man nodded and said he would take note of that, all the while his eyes scanned for more direction from someone or something. It came in the form of a white and red flag being raised in the distance, one that not many would know was meant to mark a target. Akanna, of course, was one who did know this and she shouted it a split-second before Falwaïn did.

"There!" the vincan called, pointing at the flag so that Diego saw it too, with Falwaïn unknowingly making the same gesture for Donnie's benefit.

"At the end of the wharf, Rex!" added Falwaïn, leaning forward in his saddle and looking down.

The German Shepherd dog racing along just in front of Wiwila and Gallantry yelled back, "Got it!" and sped off out of view.

The wharf itself was quite deserted and had been so from the moment the first explosion of trees by the mages had been heard. The contingency of vincans and their ambassador, all watching from the woods nearby, were waiting for the right moment to come up behind the Sarn so they could stake their claim for the safety of the witch and her friends. They were destined to have to wait for some time because the train of Sarn guards was quite long, with most of the mages having fallen back as one by one had witnessed the witch let off a spell that was completely beyond any of them without her tiring even a little. After having chased her for the last forty minutes, they knew full well they were outgunned, so to speak, and most had decided to save their own skins by moving toward the rear of the company.

Aldalis Munkinum was not among them and was, in fact, right up front along with his second in command for the skirmish, Brother Hectern Mire. Brother Mire, as he liked to be called by his constituents, was known more for fighting and stealing than for comforting or healing. He had spent a mere month in the field before realizing that the city was where he belonged. That was when he found his rightful place with the order of mages at Anûmanétus, which was home to many a thief and soldier, his two favorite kinds of people to assist. It was he who had shot the tree out from under old Thomb, while Aldalis had been recovering from blasting apart the trees the witch had moved to stall the Sarn and the mages on the path.

Both wizards could normally last some long time while battling like this, but the witch had sent all manner of detritus flying at the mages in a swarm, targeting each man with these whirlwinds of tiny sylvan objects at least twice or thrice, forcing each mage to nearly exhaust his supply of innate magic while protecting themselves from the mini-cyclones' bites, stings, and cuts. They were each having now to call upon what magic they could muster from the earth, but this was stingily drawn and not so easily wielded on the run. Since Aldalis and Hectern had shot most of the spells, they were the most hunted by these ruthless objects, which even now were chasing them down once again.

Both mages whipped their horses harder and harder and the steeds had no choice but to speed up and race at far too fast a pace onto the wooden boards of the wharf. Their sharp hooves slipped and slid and both horses stumbled more than once, which meant their riders had to waste even more magic on keeping them upright during these near disasters. The Queen's Guards, on the other hand, who all knew and appreciated the roles their horses played in their lives and in their battles, had slowed down to let the two mages go on ahead alone.

By the time the mages got within clear sight of the barge, its passengers were already loaded upon it and the tie ropes had been cast off.

The mages shot bolts of dark green and blue magic at the barge which bounced off the shield Donnie had raised around the watercraft and ricocheted back at the wizards, knocking them both off their horses and onto their asses. She made sure they landed softly enough that neither had any lasting injury, but she was deeply distressed by how much damage they had created on their wild ride through the forest and she was, by now, quite angry with these men whom she felt should be her compatriots and counterparts in magic, not her enemies.

She held up her hands and, with a small wave of them, stepped outside time with both Aldalis and Hectern to hold a private discussion with them. All movement everywhere stopped and the two men looked at each other and then around them in fear.

"What's this ye fashion naow ta cower our hearts, ye dark witch o' hell!" cried Brother Hectern Mire.

Donnie snorted and shook her head in disbelief, looking mainly at Aldalis Munkinum when she said, "Have you never stepped outside time before?"

He stared at her as though he thought her a lunatic and so she sighed long and loud.

"Wow, our experiences with magic are really very different, aren't they?" she noted sardonically. "Like, why are you so determined to destroy trees? Trees are our friends, and they help to circulate magic everywhere, so when you blow them apart like you did back there, all willy-nilly and such, it's no wonder they came after you the way they did!" She noticed both mages' surprised looks and she chortled, "What—did you think I'd sent them to attack you? Oh, no, I had nothing to do with them at all—well, except of course that, because of who I am, magic swelled up to the surface just below us like it seems to do wherever I go these days, and that must have triggered something in the trees' memories. Maybe it simply awakened them and they didn't like being woken up from a really long sleep only to get blown into a million pieces by you guys."

"What do ye want with us here?" snarled Aldalis, and he gestured in the air, apparently meaning the Exos.

"Well, the Exos is meant to be used for things that you don't necessarily need to have others partake in or listen to, like this conversation we're having now. If you'd prefer to go back to real time, we can do that, but understand that your guards will hear it, as will the vincans who are about to come out of hiding." Donnie had, by now, crossed her arms in front of her and leaned back on her hips. She raised an eyebrow expectantly at the other two and prompted them with a, "Well?"

"We have nothing to discuss with ye, witch. I say, release us so we can go on with our battle and we'll see who is victorious in the end," Brother Aldalis snapped, his eyes flashing with anger.

Donnie made no reply, but everything around them sprang to life again. The two angry mages, with zero innate power reserves left, called up what they could from the well of magic flowing below them and proceeded to fling many more bolts at the barge, which Donnie's shield easily deflected and shot back to the mage who had originated it. She also made the barge stay where it was—close enough to talk to those on the wharf, but too far to be reached physically. After five minutes, the crowd at the end of the wharf's pier had become quite large and the two mages, who were still insistent upon fighting, were looking more and more foolish to all. At a certain point, Donnie had had enough, and so she shot a bolt of her own magic that encased the two mages, freezing them in mid-action for more than a minute before letting them go.

"Be still!" she entreated them wearily, and several people in the crowd nodded their heads and called out in agreement, the most important of these being the captain leading the Queen's Guards, an enterprising soldier from the little town of Kendel in the western region of the Sedarau province, who informed the mages in a voice that brooked no argument that they had lost and the battle was over.

Juree of the Marcons stepped forward, made his ambassadorial speech about the witch and her friends being protected by the realm of the vincans, and then put his hands on his hips to add in a bold, threatening voice to the Queen's Captain, "Leave this place now and there shall be no war between the Sarn and the vinca. Remain here and you will know the high council's decision on this situation within the week."

The Queen's Captain scoffed in outrage and sent the ambassador his most scathing stare. "This witch's lands, these Ganlonds we keep hearing about, are within the realm of the Sarn, and I will thankee to remember that. My king has been thy friend and lord for many a long year, and our peace agreements mean more than this vile witch does, certainly!"

Juree shook his head, intoning flatly, "Not if she is able to save the Mîrlonds. If she does that, then no peace treaty is worth more!"

"And if she isn't able to save them, what then?" interjected Falwaïn, frowning at the vincan ambassador in suspicion.

Juree turned to gaze at him steadily and without expression. "Then we will hand her over to the Sarn to do with as they please," he rejoined.

Donnie and the others turned to Akanna, who had strode to their front in protest and was glaring at her fellow countryman with deep anger etched upon her face.

"That was not our agreement!" she spat at Juree through clenched teeth, but the ambassador merely shrugged at her in response.

Donnie cleared her throat quite loudly before pointing out, once all eyes had turned to her, "Firstly, why don't we see what happens when we get there? I may not be able to save the Mîrlonds, as I've already explained to Akanna. Nevertheless, and at the very least, anyone on the Mîrlonds can seek refuge on the Ganlonds, so there is that to consider. As for handing me over to anyone, none of you seem to appreciate who I am. I mean it, think about what's happened. Magic is once again on the rise, as evidenced by my ascension to Ér Ainíl of the Ganlonds and by so many other magical beings regaining magical strength ever since I came to Írtha—or hadn't you noticed that yet? I certainly have," she noted dryly, looking around the crowd assembled on the end of the wharf. "It's happening everywhere I go. And this is after magic had been dying out for many, many long years, right? But I arrive and suddenly magic is on the rise again. I imagine that has more than a little to do with my being a daughter of Morrían, and especially with my being the last and supposedly most powerful of those. Therefore, you can tell yourselves whatever you want, but I seriously doubt my fate is up to any of you here or to your kings and queens to decide.

"Just sayin'..." she quipped tartly, giving an exaggerated and careless shrug. "I have a long road ahead of me, longer than anything the likes of you can even think of, so it behooves no one to believe that you or your kin and kind are going to determine anything for me other than whether you help or hinder me in my tasks."

She let this sink in for a few moments, all the while gazing expectantly at each of the Førrens Order's brothers in turn before she added, "And that means you mages need to stop attacking me, at least until after we get to the Mîrlonds and see what we can do together toward saving them."

Falwaïn was the first to comprehend what she had just said. He put a hand on her arm to turn her slightly toward him and spluttered, "You can't mean that! You're going to let them come with us to the Mîrlonds?"

She looked at him wide-eyed and conceded with some aplomb in her manner and in her small smile to him, "I'd have to be crazy to turn down the help of six wizards and, as you know, my darling, I'm a lot of things, but crazy isn't one of them."

For the next twenty minutes this option was discussed in detail, the result of which was that the mages were indeed disposed to come along with them to the Mîrlonds, although the Queen's Guards were not. Not that anyone in Donnie's group wanted the guards along anyway. But several of the mages felt they would be much safer with them than without them, a point to which more than one person chuckled. Donnie shut these naysayers and lovers of irony down with a firm frown and offered to host one squadron, which would be ten soldiers, to go along with them on the journey. The Queen's Captain shook his head, but nevertheless agreed that he and a squad of his best soldiers would accompany them to the Mîrlonds. Of course, the vincan ambassador, Juree of the Marcons, insisted that he too must be allowed to travel with them.

And so it turned out that thirty people, plus their horses, and one dog and one cat were crammed upon the makeshift barge, leaving not much room to do anything other than sit or lay upon the rough logs covered by the thick rugs provided by the river people of Muneer.

Any boat trip down the mighty Donbragh typically took a week from the port of Muneer to the Ka'lametan Wharf, but everyone realized that would not do for this journey, given the close quarters and their present circumstances. Donnie, after some hesitation, fashioned a large rotor fan out of flattened tin the river folk had stored, strengthened that with magic, then attached it to the barge, also with magic, and set the thing spinning fast in the water. Their speed increased substantially and in only four hours they passed the regular shipping ferry, which had left on time the day before and was jammed full with wagons and horses and a few cramped passengers. It seemed to be standing nearly still when the new barge zoomed by. Not two hours after that, the regular passenger ferry was surpassed in similar fashion. The new barge was in goggling range for only a few minutes though, so many of the ferry's passengers missed the sight of Medregai's first motorized watercraft.

But, with the aid of this mechanical assistance, the vincan-owned wharf of Ka'lametan was reached around eleven o'clock the very next morning. Everyone gratefully disembarked from the barge and soon found that their land legs had not completely deserted them.

The Ka'lametan Wharf was overcrowded, busy and loud, so staying together as a group would have been impossible if it were not for the determination of the two factions traveling with Donnie and her friends. For both the mages and the vincans were intent upon being there when the Mîrlonds were saved or to see the witch in her first real defeat. It could not be said that either group truly felt strongly either way, although the vincans would have denied this vigorously. The Mîrlonds, while certainly an area of distinction and source of pride within their home lands, were not revenue producing, nor were they filled with voting constituents, so their importance to the vincan government was perhaps more symbolic and ceremonial than anything else, and to the ambassador and his soldiers, ceremony was not high on their list of priorities, although symbolism was. Hence their desire to see the magical lands thrive once again, if possible.

For the duration of the trip south, the Tegere Mountains had shadowed them on the west, their outline distant and imposing. Akanna now headed their group toward the high peaks of the infamous mountain chain, the sun high in the sky by the time they left the Ka'lametan Wharf and its outlying settlements. Akanna set a vigorous pace and she did not relent it until very late in the afternoon. The road to that point had been functionally smooth and well preserved, so making good time had been no hardship on either the horses or their riders.

It took some time to realize it, but eventually everyone became aware that they were heading into a large canyon, one whose walls grew ever higher each quarter mile in and whose shape was that of a wedge. The long faces of the wedge directed the travelers to the wedge's point, which they reached with only about two hours of light left in the day.

At its apex, the wedge point gave way to a towering but slim corridor that, once entered, appeared to be endless and curved slightly to the right a long distance from its entrance. Akanna, who had said nothing to anyone the entire ride from the wharf, plunged into this corridor, which was no more than twenty feet at its widest and stood easily a hundred feet high on either side, without any sign of acknowledgement for the others with her. Diego entered next, keeping almost abreast with Akanna, while Donnie, with Sylvester on the saddle in front of her, and Falwaïn and Rex beside her, hurried after. The mages and the Queen's Guards hesitated for several moments, but having come this far, felt committed to going the rest of the way, and so they too directed their horses into the corridor. The vincans showed no apprehensions about the approach to Canta'Lem, and therefore nearly herded the Queen's Guards before them.

Every sound in that corridor seemed amplified and startling because it was impossible to tell if it came from in front, behind, above or below. Donnie reached out with her mind's eye and her magic to explore the area around them and its many cracks and offshooting alleyways. It seemed there were a few places where well-hidden steps, carved in spirals, climbed to the stark plains above. The stairways were in convoluted corridors of their own that penetrated the main passageway's walls sometimes as deep as a hundred feet. These offshoots were formed by nature apparently and were filled with debris from the ages through which they'd stood. While she noted three of these stairways in the first half-mile of the main corridor, she suspected she'd missed a few.

At times she used her natural vision to survey the main passage as they went through it, marveling at how its dark walls soared straight upward, leaving only a slim crack of light and sky showing above. Every so often, stone bridges arose from one side to the other, each looking as naturally made as the corridor itself. The corridor, which Falwaïn had warned them about, having described it in much detail as they neared it, was named Bu'kelle's Challenge, and had been known to defeat many an enemy simply because of its great length and haunting eeriness. It was, in fact, the most perfectly defensible approach to a fortress or city known anywhere in Írtha, not just to Medregai. It had never been breached and was unlikely to ever be so considering that even the Malacham An, the evil Red Warlock's fiendish monster army, had failed to penetrate past more than the city's outermost gates during the War of Sorrow.

They came upon the first gate about the time the sun fell completely over the horizon and darkness raced to fill the corridor. By then though, they had gotten close enough to the city that the guards stationed in the corridor knew who they were and had lit the system of torchlights that lent just enough light for the horses to see their way around the boulders and such that were strewn along the path. They traveled another slow hour before coming upon a large portcullis that currently stood open, its heavily timbered and reinforced door suspended nearly fifteen feet in the air. This gate, worked by chain and winch, closed heavily behind them, making the mages and Queen's Guards even more nervous than they already were, which was mighty nervous and no doubt about it. Each of them stared around them with either fear or apprehension and had their hands ready on their weapons of choice, be it wand or sword.

Over the next two hours, they crossed through another six gates, each more heavily and greatly reinforced than the last. Donnie mentioned that she thought this was overkill, but Falwaïn assured her that the riches to be found within the mountains and beyond were well worth such precautions. Canta'Lem, he explained, was the only passable opening in the Tegere Mountains from their start near Muneer to their end in the south at the sea, a distance of somewhere around five hundred miles. While many attempts had been made to find alternate routes through the mountains, all had failed and usually left no one in the exploratory party alive unless they retreated in time to miss the long winter's kiss, which raced around the soaring peaks for all except four cycles of the moon per year.

It was well past midnight when the travelers passed through the final gate and journeyed into the city proper. In the dark there was not much to see, but they did note that each street they traveled was lined with silent and watchful vincans who came out of their dwellings to eye the newcomers.

Akanna took them to the vincan army command center to explain their purpose in the region, her explanations supplemented and supported by the vincan ambassador. They were subsequently given leave to stay in the city overnight. The ambassador took charge of the mages and the Queen's Guards and had his captain show them to an empty barrack, informing them it was theirs for the night. They trudged away unhappily, obviously convinced that the witch and her friends would be gone in the morning, but since they had no standing to argue for any other conditions, they swallowed their protests and strove to make the best of the situation, such as it was.

Donnie and the others watched all of this without uttering a word, and merely shrugged to each other when the mages and guards were led off. Akanna left the high commander's side and drew his lieutenant away, and they spoke to each other in low voices. Akanna was clearly not made happy by whatever that lieutenant's reply had been to her queries.

She left him, stalked over to Juree of the Marcons, and stood in front of him with her hands on her hips, her chin jutted out truculently. "You will issue the order to release him immediately," she demanded stonily, her expression as cold as her tone.

Juree raised his hands, palms to her, and replied defensively, "It was not my decision to incarcerate him again...for the *third* time, might I add?"

"But you knew he'd been arrested soon after I left here last." Akanna stood completely still when she said this, staring at the other vincan with hooded gaze.

Wearily, the ambassador lowered his hands and clasped them in front of him, his shoulders drooping with disappointment at having to resume an old argument. "Daughter, he is no longer my responsibility, nor yours. He is an adult and must claim his actions for himself. And that means he must pay the price the same as any other criminal for his misdeeds."

Akanna snorted at this accusation and shot back, "He was drunk and started a fight with a superior officer. That makes him a dunce but not a criminal! And certainly not one who should be in gaol for nine moon cycles because of it!"

Again, the ambassador raised his hand, this time exhaling a long and quite audible sigh. He turned to the high commander to say, "I request that you release the prisoner Durreen to his half-sister's custody. If she wishes to take charge of him, she may. As you are aware, I no longer will." And with that, Juree of the Marcons got on his horse and rode away, his guards following behind him.

Donnie stared over at Falwaïn and whispered, "He's her father? And she has a half-brother too? Did you know any of that before now?"

He shook his head, whispering back, "No. But vincans are not known for opening up about their private lives to outsiders; most especially ones like Akanna."

It was another ten minutes of standing around watching and waiting before a young vincan male emerged around the corner of the command offices. He was flanked by two armed guards. His bright and lively yellow eyes darted from person to person and settled for a moment upon his sister and his ready smile widened.

"I knew they'd have to let me out the moment you arrived back," he crowed smugly, leering at his captors. "You sure took your time about it, sister mine," he added in a low and humorous voice.

Akanna ignored him and demanded to have his horse as well, which the commander assured her was being brought. And indeed, moments later it was led straight to him. With no more words said between them, the young vincan and his sister climbed onto their steeds and whirled them away from the army command.

Donnie and the others had no choice but to follow.

The house Akanna had them enter a quarter of an hour later was ablaze with light. She knocked on the door and a small vincan woman opened it, standing back to let the light fall upon the visitors' faces.

The woman instantly recognized Akanna and started to bow, but then her gaze drifted behind Akanna and she stopped and stared, a slow smile overtaking her darkened, but chiseled features. "Durreen's home!" she called to someone in the rooms behind her, and several footfalls could be heard rushing through the house. She ushered Akanna inside and curtsied to her, then nearly fell into the young man's arms with a cry of relief. "Nephew, thank the gods you are free!" she cried, her voice cracking.

There was a flurry of greetings from three more people who welcomed the two newly arrived vincans, all staunchly ignoring Donnie and the others. This situation might have gone on for some time if Akanna had not cleared her throat and issued several orders, telling a matronly woman currently clasping Durreen in her arms that they were hungry and therefore needed food, drink, and beds, in that order. She turned to a male and ordered him to ready the horses for the night, and then she pointed toward the inner rooms and said to the other vincans, "Go on." Without turning around, she followed them into the house, leaving her fellow travelers to trail after her.

Once inside a large, raftered room that had its low fire stoked down for the night, Akanna gestured toward a table and chairs and the visitors sat down, gratefully accepting the ale or water that was offered by the matron, who Akanna introduced as Kairalee.

A cauldron of thick stew had been hanging over the fire and several bowls were filled with it and passed around. A loaf of bread was chopped into pieces for the weary newcomers to enjoy, with Kairalee encouraging them to partake and regain some of their strength and good cheer.

The young man, Durreen, had disappeared through a door across the hallway when Akanna led her fellow travelers into the main dining hall, and the other vincans went with him. Kairalee followed them the moment the food and drink were served to the visitors.

The boombox appeared at the end of the table and began playing softly, reaching back for several New Wave classics with mellow grooves that somehow captured the mood between them all. When the song "Stories of Old" came on, which was a favorite of Donnie's, she knew that the time must have come for Akanna to explain what was going on, something none of them had felt comfortable questioning her about up to that point.

With the music playing quietly in the background, Akanna waited until everyone had finished eating before announcing, "I know you are curious about what has happened here in Canta'Lem and you have the right to some answers. I admit that, so I will give you those I feel I can share. To begin, you are in the house of the Zal'Dorek. It is the largest house in Canta'Lem and extends over much of the city. My mother's people have owned this part of it for generations and my Aunt Bellett and my Uncle Gellen still live here with me, as does my half-brother and his mother, as well as the husband and children of my aunt. Each of the main house's smaller ones, like this that I and my immediate family occupy, are connected in ways that only the family knows and will never divulge to anyone outside the family.

"Nearly one long year ago, or more specifically nine natural years ago, I welcomed to it my half-brother Durreen and his mother Kairalee, both of whom hail from the house of the Marcons in Morlant. They came to me when our father Juree disclaimed the boy and demanded he quit the house of the Marcons and take his mother with him, whom Juree had tired of long before then and had replaced with another mate. Durreen and Kairalee had nowhere to go but to me, and I took them in. Durreen is young and unruly, and in trouble more often than not. He is the shame of the family and is its heart, for he is a simple, joyful boy who is unlike most vincans. I cannot fault him for his ways because he seeks adventure and entertainment of a sort that does not include killing, a goal that is difficult for a warrior's son and half-brother to achieve in this often-violent world."

For much of the time Akanna had been talking, she had looked at no one, choosing instead to turn and gaze into the moving flames of the fire. She paused now and took a drink of her ale before she continued speaking. After licking the ale's froth from her lips, she went on to explain, "Kairalee has since mated with Gellen and has officially sought kinship to the house of the Zal'Dorek. I believe she will be given that status soon and will henceforth be taken care of by the house for the rest of her life, however long that may be. My half-brother, her only child, refuses to seek such an alliance and is barely tolerated here in Canta'Lem, most especially because my—*our* father is the ambassador to the Sarn and no one wishes to offend or provoke him by welcoming his estranged son to their midst. They are also careful not to offend or provoke me whenever I am here, and I have made it plain I expect the boy to be accepted without question. I fully comprehend how difficult that makes their decisions on how to handle Durreen's antics and bear them no grudge for their punishments of him. Any enmity for that is between myself and my father, whom I know to be a scoundrel and a cheat. I have known this of him since he betrayed my mother when I was but a child.

"As you know, she was Kaerdír before me, and had known the Ér Ainíl of the Mîrlonds intimately since their association was several centuries long. My father accused my mother of interbreeding and swore before the vincan council that she and the Ér Ainíl of the Mîrlonds had exchanged letters that would prove this miscegenation of the races. It was lucky for him that he could never produce these letters, or I might have had to kill him at some point in my life. As it was, my mother was forced to foreswear whatever feelings she had for the Ér Ainíl, denounce her, and swear to the council that no children had been borne as the fruit of this liaison, which of course was ridiculous because I was the only child my mother had ever birthed and we all knew this. From that point forward, my mother refused to live in another vincan village or city. When she became ill from the sting of a malina bae frog, she told no one and died within days of the wound's inception. I felt her death and immediately set out to return home, only to arrive little more than a week later to be told that her body had already been burned and her spirit released. When I questioned why she was not placed in the icehouse until my return, I was told it was my father's decree that the burial be performed while he was still present. It seems he left a few days before I arrived."

"Um, the Ér Ainíl your mother was involved with was Diana, right?" Donnie interjected. "It wasn't the one before her, was it? Which would've been my sister Philînan."

"I do not know because it happened when I was quite young, although I have always assumed it was Ghira Ma'Hai, or as you know her, Diana."

"And this was all a problem because you vincans do not mix with other species, *si*?" asked Diego. "I recall our previous discussion regarding this same subject."

"That is true," replied Akanna, but Donnie was shaking her head.

"Well, that's true *now* with the Sarn and the elves and any other of the races in Medregai," Donnie corrected them both, "but as you admitted before, Akanna, a long time ago the vincans were allied to the southern peoples and the texts I read about those days implied heavily that vincans mixed with more than one of those races, or species, if you will."

Akanna shrugged.

"Why would they have thought a child might have been born from this *amorio*, seeing as both parties were female?" inquired Diego curiously.

Falwaïn and Sylvester held their tongues, although both looked like they wanted to answer the question themselves. Instead they let Donnie do so.

"Vincans carry both sets of reproductive organs," she murmured in a low voice, and Akanna regarded her for a long time without speaking.

"You seem to have completed much research on my people and our ways," she observed, her yellow eyes narrowing in the firelight.

Donnie nodded unconcernedly and chirped, "Sure, of course I did. Did you expect me not to?"

Akanna shook her head once and chuckled, glancing in the direction of the boombox when it shut off and then vanished. "No," she said to Donnie, "I researched you as much as I could in your library, although I understood very little of what was there."

She returned to staring at the fire and expelled a long sigh before she continued talking. "And now my father is here in Canta'Lem once again and he is sure to make trouble," she noted in a tired voice, "which means the best I can do for my brother is to seek for him a different life. I therefore formally request, Ér Ainíl, that you consider taking him with you back to the Ganlonds when you go."

Her appeal was so unforeseen and surprising that Donnie, Falwaïn, Sylvester and Diego all stared from one to the other without speaking for more than a minute. Rex was sleeping peacefully by the fireplace and his light snores were the only sounds throughout that awkward silence besides the crackle of the fire.

Akanna eventually turned from the flames and back to the table, her eyes now seeking Donnie's.

Donnie's mobile face had gone through a series of expressions until it ended in a kind of stunned, but watchful look. Her eyes moved from one friend to the next, finally landing back upon the vincan's face. "I have to admit that I did not see that one coming, Akanna. Nope, I did not anticipate that one at all. Er, that being said, I am not exactly averse to what you are proposing," she said in a careful voice, "but you realize that I cannot make a determination like that without even speaking with the young man or spending time with him. Nor is it my decision alone—there are others to consider and their opinions *will* matter." When she said this, she gestured toward her friends, even the sleeping dog.

Akanna nodded and turned back to the fire. "He will be journeying with us to the Mîrlonds for just that purpose. You can tell me your decision after the Mîrlonds are freed from whatever is killing them."

So saying this, she swept to her feet and called to Bellett, her aunt, to ask her to show the guests to their sleeping quarters. She then walked out of the room without uttering another word, leaving those behind at the table to process for themselves her stunning behavior of the day.

By the next morning, they were all ready to leave. The vincan people, while being hospitable, did not lead lives of any kind of comfort. The beds were hard and cold, breakfast consisted of more stew and bread and ale or water, and all other functions of the household were primitive and stark. Donnie, of course, was not well-pleased at having ice-cold water in which to freshen up her face, so she zapped it a couple times to warm it and then did the same for Falwaïn.

Their horses were already saddled and waiting for them when they went outside the house to find the stables. Akanna was there and was also waiting for them, along with her brother Durreen, who was chatting low with his mother Kairalee. When Donnie and the others walked outside, the two vincans climbed onto their own horses, saluted their family, and led the way through town back to the military station.

This was the first good look at the town Donnie had had and she was not surprised that there was not all that much to see. The walls were built of either rock or a cement-like composite, and were plain, unpainted, and unadorned in any way. The rooftops were of a dark grey or black tile, and there seemed to be no trees or shrubs anywhere.

It made Donnie shiver and feel sad for the vincans as a people until Falwaïn noticed her face, brought Gallantry up next to Wiwila, leaned over and whispered to his honey woman, "Anything of beauty is contained within the houses and is for the family only to view. The houses are very strong and their secrets, including their wealth, are kept from any outsiders such as us." He gazed up at the current walls towering over them and mused, "I'll bet you there are trees and flowers and all manner of artful and amazing objects on display only a few feet from us at this very minute. Vincans," he added before moving away, "are very secretive people."

At the high commander's offices, they found the rest of their party, including all the ambassador's people and the mages and Queen's Guards. Once again, Akanna took lead and kept up a brisk pace, although this time Durreen was riding close beside her, while Diego and Rex and then Donnie and Falwaïn came after, with Sylvester, as usual, on the saddle in front of Donnie. Behind them rode the other two groups.

It turned out that Canta'Lem was situated near the western edges of the Tegere Mountains, something that had not been apparent the night before and so it took them less than an hour to leave the mountains and travel onto more level ground. The landscapes around them were breathtakingly gorgeous, with rich, vibrant greens of grasses and trees, with some of the deep greens morphing into deep blues almost. The sky was clear and vivid in coloring, nearly cobalt blue to the west, fading to pale blue above. What clouds existed were small and fluffy and drifted lazily over rolling hills that seemed to extend forever. It was barely seven o'clock in the morning and the air was still quite chilled.

By late morning they came in sight of a ridge that rose several hundred feet in the distance. Akanna made for this ridge and urged her horse to a fast canter, and the others followed suit. Less than an hour later they stood atop the ridge and looked down upon the verdant valley below.

Akanna stopped, dismounted her horse, and walked to a place where two large boulders stood side-by-side. She climbed onto one and placed a foot on the other, straddling the space between them. She crossed her arms in front of her and placed her hands upon her shoulders, closing her eyes as she concentrated on communicating with the magical lands before her.

The Mîrlonds' response was weak, but she felt it course through her body as it usually did, she said to those nearest her. It had replied yes to her question, telling her that whatever help the newcomers could give would be appreciated, and they were thereby granted access to the magical lands.

With a clap of her hands, the view changed to that of more rolling hills and trees, while the valley scene disappeared. Akanna swung herself back into her saddle and they were again cantering across the land toward a place that only Akanna knew. They rode fast for a few hours to where the grasses were no longer green, but were yellow.

Their destination, when it was apparent, was a glade much like that of the Glimmering Glade on the Ganlonds, although this one was called the Eireni Glæd or Peaceful Glade and was even larger than the Gahal Glæd.

This was the heart of the Mîrlonds and Donnie could feel its magic pulsating rhythmically around and below them. But there was a strain to it, and she felt keenly the pain it was experiencing. She directed Wiwila to a place a hundred feet or so past the glade that looked particularly parched, a pull on her heartstrings drawing her there. Rex felt it too and he walked in concordance with the horse almost as though in a trance. The others stopped at the glade except for Falwaïn, who urged Gallantry after his family and the horse hurried to catch up with them. He had no sooner done that when they all disappeared from sight.

Those watching behind them gasped in surprise, a surprise that became even more pronounced when Sylvester suddenly appeared in mid-air and landed several feet back from where the two horses, their riders, and the dog had vanished.

The cat, twisting in the air so that he would fall upon his feet, let out an angry yowl and shouted in outrage, "She threw me back, damn her! We were falling into nothingness and she threw me back over her shoulder! And now none of us can follow to wherever it is they've been taken!" He landed in a crouch and hissed his ire at Donnie's recalcitrant actions, even though they may well have saved his life.

While they searched desperately for a clue of any kind to the fate or the whereabouts of those missing, with several of their number venturing to the exact spot where the disappearance had occurred, the cat was right and no one else was taken. Sylvester could sense Donnie's magic somewhere below, but it was muffled, as though blocked by something much stronger than his own magic could penetrate.

Akanna, as Kaerdír, was able to communicate with the Mîrlonds and was told that the Ér Ainíl was in grave peril, but there came no more than that from all of Akanna's repeated inquiries.

The mages also tried to do something helpful, but they could not even sense Donnie, and they soon gave up trying. Instead, they settled into a circle, their arms over the shoulders of the two standing beside them, and began to hum their spell, hoping to call up enough magic to get a location on any of the missing souls. When this was unsuccessful, they motioned for the cat and Akanna to join their circle, and even Diego went along to lend whatever magic he could. Before too much longer had passed, most of the vincans shuffled over and joined the group, forming another circle behind the mages.

Three hours later, the circle broke apart. Sylvester climbed upon a large boulder near the glade's entrance, sat down, and stated wearily, "It is no use. They will have to somehow free themselves because I do not believe we will ever find them to free them, not as we are now." He shared a worried look with Diego and Akanna and let out a heartfelt sigh. "Now is when we truly need Diana," he pointed out fervently, adding, "Let us pray that she and Warren are still reading the book and can divine a way to assist us. Otherwise, we are defeated before we have even begun."

Chapter 24
Keep on Keeping On

Liz was feeling distraught and nervy, which was nothing new anymore because it had been five days since the fight in the *Reisender* had occurred and every one of them had filled her with terror. She relived that terrible hour when she'd dragged Catie from the burning wreckage of the dirigible and carried her on her back out of the Presidio every time she closed her eyes. After the fight, she had somehow hobbled painfully, still bearing the full weight of her critically injured friend, for two more blocks until she'd found a cabbie willing to convey them to the Palace Hotel.

The horse-drawn, enclosed cabriolet had taken what felt like forever to cross the city to the hotel and panic had arisen within Liz's chest with each second that took them farther from the airfield and the last known place for the children. But she forced herself, no matter how unwilling she was, to return to the hotel with Catie since she had no way of knowing where Maeve and Jesse could possibly be, which meant there was no sense in staying near the flame-filled dirigible. Besides, before she'd barely gotten herself and Catie into the shadowy trees surrounding the airfield, the area was already teeming with firemen and fair officials.

She tried not to worry about the kids, figuring that at nearly eight years old Maeve was smart enough and resourceful enough to have gotten them both as far away from the airfield as she could manage. As though to assuage Liz's fears, Catie had come to just long enough to reassure her that they were not within a good mile of the children and then she had passed out again, and Liz had looked up and spotted the cab approaching from some ways down the street, whistling sharply for it to come to her.

In their suite later, Liz had undressed Catie, bathed her, and redressed her in a long nightgown that covered her small form in a pretty pink silk. The wound over Catie's heart from the sorcerer's deadly spell looked black and spidery still, but it was obviously receding with each passing quarter hour, so Liz had finally stopped worrying that Catie was going to die on her again that night. Having noted the mark that Diego, as Galto, had made some time ago upon Catie's chest, that scar very light but still visible, she said a prayer over the unconscious woman's form and asked that Catie and the children all be watched over by the most benign of gods and goddesses that might be inclined to care about them. She then climbed into bed with the other woman, who was shaking with cold and reaction to the great trauma her body had suffered, and the two of them eventually fell into a deep and dreamless sleep in the early hours of the morning.

Liz awoke late the next morning with her breasts heavy and bloated, so she rose and stumbled to her room where she had some bottles for Jesse that she'd used only a couple of times before, and manually expressed milk into one until she felt empty. Not knowing what else to do, she willed the milk and its bottle to find the children and could only hope that when it disappeared it had gone to the desired destination. Over the next few days she continued to do this, each time willing the full bottles to find the children and the empty bottles to be returned to her. While the bottles were returned less than an hour later of being sent away, Liz fretted that the kids were not getting sustenance, let alone safety and sleep, and she herself looked more and more haunted and wan as each day passed.

Catie did not come to again for three days, and then she managed only a few minutes before slipping back into oblivion. By then, Liz was a wreck, jumping at every sound from outside, whether it was in the hotel or out in the street. She had all her meals delivered to their suite and only pecked at the food, staying faithfully at Catie's bedside in a chair she pulled up to the bed. Liz found herself just watching Catie breathe while she slept because she was so dreadfully scared to be on her own and, as long as Catie's breast rose and fell, she wasn't alone.

Several times Liz lost it completely and cried up a storm, missing Jesse so badly, worrying over him and Maeve and Julia, wondering what Warren was doing and if he ever thought of her, and doing her best not to look too closely at her dire situation, especially when her mind started wondering what she would do if something horrible happened to Catie permanently.

But this morning just after sunup, Catie had opened her eyes for good, blinking rapidly before rising groggily up onto one elbow, licking her lips and indicating she wanted something to drink. Liz had handed her a glass of water and helped her drink as much of it as she could get down. From that point on, Catie seemed to grow stronger by the hour and, not long after rising and moving to the sitting room that stood in the middle of their suite, she demanded to be given the newspapers from the past week. These were stacked on the reading table by Liz's armchair. She and Liz perused these carefully, discussing with each other any stories either of them found that referenced the events at the *Reisender* and the fallout from them as they ate the breakfast that had been delivered by room service.

The police were continuing to scour the city for Herbert Flint and the three Germans but had found none of them thus far. They were being charged with the murders of Florrie Danahur, Art Smith and the airfield crew. Also charged with these crimes were two surviving crew members of the *Reisender* who had apparently slipped out before all hell had broken loose inside the dirigible's lounge and had later provided the police with Flint's name and those of the Germans.

The Chagall siblings had also been named by the two crewmen, but Ester Chagall had refused to let anyone see them and it was clear from the newspaper reports that she intended to convey her children as far from San Francisco as she could get them before anyone had the slightest chance of interrogating them. One report said as much in plain language, but the police, it seemed, were helpless to stop Madame Chagall because of her connections to the mayor and the governor, not to mention her many friends within the federal government back in Washington, D.C. Their exodus from the Bay Area was confirmed in today's morning's paper, with the article citing the entire family having boarded a train traveling east from Sacramento the previous day. How they'd gotten to Sacramento was unknown, but it seemed the Chagalls were by now no longer in California.

Catie and Liz agreed that the siblings were well and truly out of the story and so they concentrated on looking for the trail of either Jesse and Maeve or the Germans and their sorcerer in other stories in the papers, but to no avail. As far as they could tell, there was no hint or sign of them in any of the happenings being reported around the City.

That evening, the two witches emerged from their suite and stepped out onto Market Street for the first time in nearly a week, the sun only a couple hours from setting. They had decided to check Chinatown because they both recalled having followed Florrie there to a particular shop a couple of times and hoped that Maeve had perhaps visited it over the last week. Catie even went so far as to predict that that is exactly where they would find the children, saying she felt it in her bones and her bones were never, ever wrong.

All afternoon, Catie had tried to teach Liz how to reach out to feel Jesse with her magic, but Liz had not succeeded. She had been unable even to sense Catie's magic and yet she was standing right next to Liz during the entire lesson! All of which made Liz droop her shoulders and call herself a complete loser. After Catie finished chiding her for her gloomy outlook, she informed Liz dryly that Jesse was being shielded by something or someone anyway, so it was unlikely that Liz would have been able to penetrate that protection even if she could feel Jesse's magic.

Therefore, they struck out together for Grant Street, Catie's left arm entwined with Liz's right one, with a clear mission ahead of them. They would find the children tonight, they had vowed to each other and to themselves. And neither was going to get too far away from the other because both women were still deeply shocked by what had happened in the dirigible and only felt safe when touching each other because they were convinced, and rightly so, that together they were much, much stronger than ever apart. It was perhaps this thought in Liz's mind that made her suggest that they try to find Jesse's magic together now.

It was a good suggestion and it worked, to a degree. It certainly made Liz finally understand what it was she was supposed to be looking for and feeling and thereafter found she could do it by herself. With mixed emotions, they found that whatever was shielding Jesse and Maeve was still doing so, but when they approached the store on Sacramento Street and tried one more time to find Jesse's magic, they became greatly excited because they both felt him and knew that he was very, very close indeed.

Catie opened the door to the curio shop, which, like many others in old Chinatown, was overcrowded with myriad imported goods from China. The smells were especially overpowering for the unprepared person and both women had to take a moment to adjust to the heavy perfume of the incense haze that hung over the narrow aisles of the store. All around the front counter, herbs and spices from all over the world were displayed for buyers to browse, their fainter scents mingling with the pungent fragrance of the incense.

The shop was named Fong's Emporium and looked like its better days were long since lived. It was dark and dusty and the floorboards creaked with each step the two witches took. They were so intent upon speaking to the woman behind the counter that neither noticed the large figure moving behind them to lock the shop's door.

The woman at the counter gave them a nod, said something to them in Chinese, which neither witch understood a word of, and when they got close enough, she surreptitiously passed a note, which she slid under Liz's hands when Liz placed them upon the counter and readied herself to speak to the woman. The note surprised Liz and she took it without saying a word at all, instead backing away to look meaningfully at Catie.

Catie had no inkling of the note, but she realized something had passed between Liz and the shopkeeper and so she stepped forward to inquire of the woman if she had the herb known as Astragalus, but which she thought was perhaps called Huang Qi in the shopkeeper's native language. In the meanwhile, Liz looked down and read the note, which was written in English and told her that the children were in the cellar below being held by a sorcerer, and that everyone in the house of Fong Chu Fu had pledged to give their lives for them both, so the visitors were to escape with the children without thought for anyone else. Liz, wide-eyed, looked at the woman in shock, carefully passing the note to Catie. Catie, under the pretense of opening her purse to pay for the small bag of herbs the woman was pushing to her, also read the note, swallowed hard, and with shaking fingers retrieved the coins owed to the shopkeeper. She folded the note back to its small square and placed it in her mouth to swallow it.

She had no more than done that when she and Liz felt strong hands clamp onto their shoulders and then a rough voice growled in their ears, "To the back room, nice and easy does it."

The man pushed them toward a curtain and they both moved to it, the small bag of herbs forgotten on the counter. The woman swept that up with her slim fingers and hurried to shove it into Catie's hand before preceding her down a long, dark hallway. At the end of that passage, she turned right through a door and led them down some rickety wooden steps until they reached the cellar, where the earthen floor was covered in thick straw. The woman led them through two rooms until they reached a larger one whose purpose was obviously for worshipping and praying. Several alters were built around the room, some with gold or stone statues of the Buddha sitting atop them or others bearing the carved forms of bodhisattvas. Hundreds of lit candles gave the room a shadowy, but warm glow, while thin trails of smoke wafted from several incense burners.

From behind one of these alters came Herbert Flint, his eyes dark and glittering in the candlelight. He motioned to someone off to his right and a woman stepped out from behind another alter, her hands on Maeve's shoulders, pushing the girl before her. Little Jesse was wrapped in Liz's shawl against Maeve's body and he cooed and gurgled happily at the sight of his mother and his other favorite person, Catie. He reached for Liz with his tiny fingers while the woman shoved Maeve toward the newcomers.

Liz bent down and clasped them both in her arms, checking each to make sure they were unharmed. When she was satisfied they were fine, she stood up and said to the two Chinese women, who were now standing side-by-side, "Thank you for taking such good care of them."

The women nodded, their dark eyes mysterious. Both of these women had their jet-black hair piled out in puffy buns atop their heads and wore blouses and long skirts of different shades of blue and white. The elder one, who looked no older than either Catie or Liz, murmured, "The milk you sent to your son each day was much welcomed, because we have no other suckling children in the house right now. You seem surprised to find these two in good condition. Perhaps you do not know that to us, children are sacred and are never to be harmed. This is our way of life and no one may sway us from it. We will die before harming any child who comes into our custody. Maeve Rae knew this and that is why she sought us out five nights ago."

Liz and Catie both looked down at Maeve, who was nodding her head. She met Liz's questioning gaze and told her, "It's true. My mother brought me here a couple of times and told me to come and wait here if anything should happen to her while we were in San Francisco. She said she knew a lady in New York City who was a member of the Fong family there and they had told her that any child would be safe with the family anywhere in the world. So, Jesse and I have been here since the night that my—since the other night." She amended herself subconsciously, the expression in her eyes sad but determined. "The night I became an orphan, I mean," she added, raising her chin bravely as she half-turned toward Flint.

Liz gave Maeve's shoulder a squeeze and hugged the little girl to her side, then she pushed the child behind her and faced the sorcerer, her hand clasping Catie's. She assumed a calm demeanor that Catie matched and the two stood together in their defiance.

Herbert Flint motioned to someone else and the Germans walked into the light. Professor Gottleib-Lange held the orrery by its top and bottom and the whole thing moved in his hands as though possessed. It was fully extended outwardly and had somewhere around eight to ten planets on fine wires or filaments, each of which were circling the main stem at different rates of speed.

The professor looked pleased and announced, "Zey have it vith zem, for ze orrery can feel it, as you can see for yourself! Come," he snapped his fingers impatiently, "let me have it! Let me have ze clock-watch!"

The hair on the back of Liz's neck bristled at his tone and she turned to look at Catie, who challenged Flint boldly with, "Why should we just give it over to ye?"

Flint smiled at her evilly and replied, "I've given you back the children with no fuss or fight, haven't I? And too, I want you to be assured that I have no intention of harming them myself. They are free to go, as are you two once you have surrendered the clock-watch to us. I think a fair trade for my consideration on your behalves would be the clock-watch, and the professor agrees with me. So, you see, it's quite simple; you give us what we want and no one else gets hurt."

Catie studied him before observing astutely, "What ye're not sayin' is that ye dunna want that wolf-pack o' little Jesse's a'comin' back ta git ye, do ye?" She shook her head and sighed. "I canna say I blame ye there. But I have ta wonder how ye knew ta get outta its way the other night. Could it be ye'd seen it b'fore?" She continued to study him thoughtfully, his smile becoming even oilier than it had already gotten. "Ah yes, I can see just a flash o' yer memories. Ye were on Tortuga, along wi' them soldiers. Ye had yer hair mighty blond back then, but a little berry juice fixes that, eh? And ye saw then what little Jesse could do. Well, at least ye've had a long time ta prepare fer us, ent ye? A couple o' centuries seemed ta be jest what ye needed," she noted, and he smiled even more widely.

"The boy won't call the wolf pack now though, because I'm not going to hurt either you or him," Herbert Flint said persuasively, his eyes never leaving Catie's face as he took the steps necessary to bring him right in front of her, where he stopped. He raised his hands in the air and, as Catie and Liz flinched, he laughed richly, waving his palms benignly before them. "You see, I will do nothing. No tricks, no spells, no nothing. I will harm you no more."

Catie eyed him suspiciously, prompting him with, "Ye know we would never jest give ye the clock-watch, so what is ye're reelly after, I wonder?"

And then as if it were the easiest thing in the world to do, Herbert Flint turned to the younger woman of the two standing behind him, raised his hands again, and the most god-awful scream was wrenched from the woman. Liz and Catie both grabbed Maeve's hands and pressed close to each other, staring in horror as the young woman's body writhed where she stood. Only when a field of deep yellow was slowly ripped from the young woman's form and soared over to disappear into Herbert Flint, did she fall to the floor, now silent and lifeless. Flint gasped and shivered as though he'd just orgasmed, his eyes closing in ecstasy and then opening to show their fire and delight at the new magic being absorbed by his body.

Catie spat at him in revulsion, but he waved her spittle away carelessly and it disappeared in mid-air. He breathed hard, groaning with pleasure as the dead woman's magic settled through his skin, into his bones, melding with the magical power already there. Behind him, the older woman was joined by another young one and the two of them collapsed upon each other for just a moment in shared grief. But they pushed their emotions down inside themselves and stood tall, staring at the sorcerer with cold eyes as dead as those of their sister.

Flint, still visibly high from his kill, turned back to Catie and Liz and crowed at them, "*That* is what I will do! And I'll do that to all their kith and kin in this filthy establishment before I'm done. Will you live with that, knowing that more than fifteen souls died so foully because you were too stubborn to see that I had already won?"

An old man suddenly came from the left, his almond-shaped eyes mere slits in his unhappy face, and he clapped his hands. Two older women appeared from the right, each carrying a silk pillow with various glittering and glowing objects on them. He said something in Chinese, which was obviously a plea for a bargain.

Herbert Flint turned to him with impatience, but then he saw the wares being offered for barter and he stopped. He studied these objects with naked greed, turning back to the old man to begin negotiations. Professor Gottleib-Lange was also interested in these objects, so much so that he put the orrery down on an alter beside him and stepped up to the women with the pillows, his two companions crowding around the objects with him. Without asking, he picked up first one object and then the next, while he and his countrymen discussed their possibilities in German.

It was as though Catie and Liz were forgotten, and they both looked at each other in bewilderment. Should they just leave with the children? But then Liz noticed something that made her blood run cold in her veins— Maeve was standing behind the alter with the orrery and was reaching around the front now to grab it. Liz heard Jesse coo and she looked down to see him lying on the ground. A moment later, Maeve was back and she'd stuffed the orrery at Catie, who flattened it and shoved it into one of her skirt's two voluminous pockets. In seconds, Maeve had Jesse bound to her and stood smiling up at Liz and Catie.

And then the odd spell upon the Germans and Herbert Flint broke, with the Fong family uniting in a wall surrounding them. Someone screamed at Liz and Catie to leave. Scared and unsure, they nevertheless pushed Maeve up the stairs ahead of them, through the store and out the door, which Catie blasted open when she saw the key had been taken from it. Behind them were screams and sounds of blows and explosions, and then a thundering of footsteps started up the stairs, only to be stilled almost immediately. But by then the two witches and the little girl and her baby passenger were racing up the hill, with a thick crowd suddenly seeming to form behind them, filling the street with a throng of people.

The three ran and ran until they thought their lungs would burst. They stopped to catch their breath and saw that they were at Hyde Street. No word was said between them, but all three ran to catch the oncoming cable car toward Broadway.

Panting, Liz huddled with the others on the steps of the cable car and said breathlessly to Catie, "You still have it, right? And do you know how to use it?" She gave her friend a hopeful look and was relieved when Catie gave her a small smile and a nod.

"Yes, 'tis easier ta use than the clock-watch, ta be sure," she claimed. "We need ta go toward Pacific Heights, so we'll have ta get off here at Broadway." She pointed at the upcoming stop and a minute later the three of them climbed down from the cable car and looked around for a cab or something. But none seemed to be available and both witches knew they had at most a two-minute head start on the sorcerer.

Looking around for something, anything to aid their escape, Liz spotted one of the day's popular tandem bicycles, a two-seater, standing along a restaurant wall on the corner. She pointed to it and said, "Let's take that and Maeve can ride on the handlebars between us!"

Catie looked at it doubtfully, but Liz hopped onto the front seat and told Catie to just balance herself at first in the back seat, then help pedal once she got the hang of it. They nearly fell twice and poor Maeve soared into the air both times, only to land safely upon her feet like a cat, but by the time they reached Van Ness Avenue they were operating the bicycle with grace and synchronicity. Maeve was seated on the wide bars Catie was using, holding on for dear life and dangling her legs over the center bar as they raced toward the west, where the sun's rays were now fading to a warm orange glow. Jesse, still strapped to Maeve's wiry little body, was cooing and laughing and enjoying the wind against his cheeks.

But the two witches knew they were losing ground to the sorcerer. They could feel him approaching behind them, significantly advancing on them with each block.

As her breathing allowed, Catie was shouting instructions for how and when they would use the clock-watch and orrery together, admonishing them severely that they were all to concentrate on taking only people with them and what was on their bodies because otherwise they might bring a tree with them, for Fortin's sake, and that just wouldn't do.

Maeve flipped her head backward to look up at Catie and said, "What?" and so Catie took a couple minutes to explain that they were about to travel through time and dimension and they meant to end up at the house of a witch more powerful than either herself or Liz. That witch would take care of her and Liz and Jesse, and everything would be all right if they could only reach her before that bastard—er, evil sorcerer, Catie corrected when Liz shouted a reprimand back at her. She started again and said they wanted to be at Lorraine's house before Herbert Flint could get to them and if they didn't manage that now, they never would, so they should all concentrate and pedal hard, she urged, and then she got quiet because she knew he was only a block behind them.

Liz felt him back there too and she doubled down on her pedaling, turning the bike sharply from Broadway onto Divisidero, doing all she could to move them ever closer to the Ellinwood mansion and safety. Here the street was more level, running almost downhill so it was much easier going for them on the bike and they could only hope it would help them regain enough distance between themselves and Flint.

The difference between how it looked now and how it would look in another minute or two, if they were successful in their time and dimension jump, would be enormous, Liz knew. Right now, in 1915, there were only a few houses built along Divisidero and each of them had such extensive grounds that the street itself was deserted.

And then, even though they were half a block away, at Catie's urgent behest, Liz took out the clock-watch, wound it less than half a turn, removed her shaking hands from the handlebars and placed her fingers on the numbers for the year 2026. She concentrated with all her might on sending just the four of them through time and space to their desperately needed destination. She closed her eyes and shouted back to Maeve to do the same and then she felt herself floating, opening her eyes after a few seconds just far enough to know that everything was still whirling in dizzying circles around her. She heard Jesse giggle and Maeve yelp, then they were flying through the air and there was no bike to stop them from scraping the pavement or hitting the parked cars lining the street. Liz reached back with her hand and got hold of Maeve's arm, using her magic to give them a cushioned landing down the center of the street, upon which they tumbled and rolled until they came to a stop.

Suddenly, an ear-splitting, bloodcurdling scream rent the night and Liz felt her heart begin to bang even more wildly in her ribcage. The scream had come from Catie, who was somewhere behind them.

***

Falwaïn awoke, knowing instantly that something was very wrong. He was lying on his back and Gallantry was standing over him, nudging him in the side. Falwaïn opened his eyes and saw nothing because there was no light to see by. He remembered being on Gallantry and following Donnie on Wiwila, and that was it. He thought harder and after a minute recalled seeing Rex fall first through the earth, like it just went down in a swirl and took him with it, then Donnie and Wiwila fell the same way, only she must have thrown Sylvester back up because he went flying by Falwaïn's face as he and Gallantry fell.

But where was Donnie now? Falwaïn paused and took a deep breath, knowing she must be close to him because he could smell her scent, that of the flower gardenia, the one he considered as her special fragrance.

He rolled onto his left side and reached out with his arms, finding Rex's body there. The dog was breathing, but just barely it seemed. Falwaïn ran his hands quickly over the canine and found no wound to account for the slow, long breaths Rex was taking. He tried to wake the dog but could not, and so he climbed over Rex and tried to find Donnie.

She was there, just a few inches beyond Rex. Beside her and the dog lay Wiwila, her back to the others. Like Rex, both Donnie and Wiwila were breathing very slowly and were also unconscious.

Falwaïn pulled up a knee and sank back onto the floor, shaken to his core. He didn't know what to do, how to awaken them, how to battle whatever it was that was holding them unconscious.

This was strong magic and was something he could not fight. He was a warrior, time-tested and battle-hardened, and he could match any other warrior blow for blow in the physical world. But this was nothing to do with the physical world. Here he had an unseen foe, and how do you fight an enemy that traps someone you love behind earthen walls, hiding their purpose for, according to Akanna, for decades, slowly infiltrating the dirt beneath your feet while eating away at the magical force that keeps the land and those upon it alive? This was Donnie's realm, but she was down and out right now, and his greatest fear was that she would maybe never rise again. His body jerked at that thought and he shook himself hard and then tried again to rouse his sleeping family, shaking them gently and calling their names.

But he still could get no response from Donnie or the animals. Placing both of his hands upon Donnie's rounded belly, the belly that was usually so lively these days, Falwaïn reached out with his mind to the children.

He received no reply from them either, which he hoped meant only that they too were unconscious and nothing worse than that.

Feeling defeated, Falwaïn lay on the ground beside Donnie, leaning his back against Wiwila's and arranging Donnie next to him so they were both curled against the horse. He found Rex in the dark and pulled the dog up between his legs and then he gathered Donnie into his arms. Only then did he give in to the grief, his body shaking with silent sobs.

He was frightened they were all going to die and he would be the only one left alive because his magic was nothing like theirs and their unseen enemy had no use for it. It was just a paltry little thing inside his triune, and the only one it could ever do any good for was himself. It had helped him survive, it had opened his mind, had given him a new life even, but it was now taking all of that away because it did not make him formidable enough to warrant being killed along with his powerful family.

He drifted in and out of consciousness for he knew not how long. When he was awake, he felt the bodies around him getting colder and colder, and he would let the deep black of despair overtake him once more so he did not have to witness his entire world dying around him. And then he went so deep he thought he too might never rise again.

It was the dream, the same dream that had haunted him for years now. Falwaïn struggled against its message, not wanting its painful visions to float up from his unconscious mind to the dream world, knowing how the nightmare would end and dreading it.

But he could do nothing to stop it.

He saw Sémere and Malwé and then his unborn child whom he had not had the heart to name after its murderous death had taken Sémere away from him, its one act in the living world to send its mother along with it to the distant shores of Canavar. Their beloved faces smiled at him at first, then their expressions turned to fear, and finally to anger, and he felt their hatred for him in his heart as if it were three knives piercing his breast. He had not protected them, they were all dead because of those people, those terrible, horrid people who murdered everyone light-skinned, people who wanted the world to be dark, only dark, to fill it with dark people and dark thoughts, to rain tyranny over anyone with light eyes and light skin, deeming them as slaves as a form of retribution for the centuries of their own unremitting, forced slavery to the white people and their white gods, and whose only purpose now was to make white ghosts bow down and grovel to the dark gods worshipped by these unforgiving, dark people. As always, Falwaïn felt the dream draining away his hope and he was lost to its blackest depths. He would never rid himself of it, it was part of him, just as was his growing hatred for the dark people.

But now in his mind came images of Diana and Diego, and his conflict returned, for they were his friends, not his enemies, and he would not hate them. No, he would not, for they were Donnie's friends too. And he called out to Donnie, hoping she would somehow help him out of this monstrous dream.

"Malwé is not dead," her strong, warm voice reminded him, "and your wife and child were not killed by anyone other than Fate, and Fate knows no color and would not have taken them simply because they were white. They were taken for another reason or perhaps even no reason other than their time here was over."

"But I did not protect them!" he shouted to Donnie, only it wasn't Donnie, it was the black goddess from the Nine. Sonndimar was her name, and she was looking at him with disgust.

"You really should have protected your family," she agreed, contempt morphing her fine, chiseled features and making them run, her cheeks bleeding in rivulets down her neck, her eyes melting downward to her lips, and Falwaïn knew only fear again, because she was reaching for him and he tried to back away, but he could not, and she was going to touch him and when she did he would hate her and want to kill her and anyone who looked like her, and his heart would turn to darkness and be lost to him forevermore...

And then a light began to burn through the deep shadows threatening to overtake him. He felt it warring with the black magic of the dream and he watched in fascination as the light and the dark were hurled at each other, and, in their great clashing, brilliantly colored sparks flew outward, this sudden mêlée created by two supreme forces that threw bolts of lightning from their centers, uncaring what they hit, this spiraling skirmish for his soul taking place inside him while he was powerless to do anything at all, and he wanted to give in to the dark, to admit his defeat, for surely the light could not win and he did not deserve its loyalty. And his greatest fear then was that, when it lost, it too would lose itself to the dark.

It was at this, his lowest point, that from the light came a call, a call echoed by two voices—two childish voices—who named him 'Daddy.' And it was their love, and the love of their mother that reached him, that pulled him up and made him fight the dark and push it out of his heart, pushing it so far away that none of its long tendrils could reach him any longer.

And this was what did it for him, what ended his torments, for the light, which this time really was Donnie, enveloped the dark, absorbing it and transforming it, remaking it into his resolve to decide his own choices and to choose his own paths. When she was done, he accepted this part of himself back into his triune in the same manner as a long-absent friend might be welcomed, and he knew with certainty that the dark dream would never return to him again.

He looked down and felt Donnie snuggle deeper into his embrace, her breath warming his chest above his heart.

She murmured quietly, "It was a spell set by Bréagna. We defeated it as a family, you know."

"I know," he said back. "And I am more grateful to you and the twins than I can ever express," he added gruffly.

He felt her smile against his skin. Then she kissed his bare chest, told him he was a silly man, and sank back down to a deep, deep sleep.

Falwaïn let his love for Donnie fill him with its light and when it had lightened every corner of his soul he came awake again in the darkness of the cave, knowing that what had just passed was a dream and had occurred only on that plain, but that made it no less real or potent. His eyes opened in the dark and though he could see nothing he could feel Donnie, Rex, and Wiwila's bodies all around him in their magical comas, and he knew that everything had changed because of that dream.

Falwaïn released his hold on Donnie and Rex and got to his feet, calling Gallantry to him. He searched in his saddlebag for the canteen Donnie had given him and allowed himself three normal swallows of water. Then he poured some for Gallantry and trickled a few drops into the mouths of the three unconscious forms huddled together on the ground, hoping to keep them somewhat hydrated.

He checked through everything in his saddlebags and then searched those on Wiwila. He found two flashlights and lighters and several candles he could use for light if he chose to do so, two more canteens of water, some cheese and crackers, two chocolate bars, and some assorted clothing and other sundries. At the bottom of Wiwila's first bag was the best item. He had seen Donnie use it before on their trip and then fold it back together before replacing it in her bag—it was a small, sturdy shovel.

He used the flashlights to see what the cave they were in really looked like and found that there was no egress from it. He had known their entry had been magical and this merely confirmed it. The cave was about twenty feet wide and long, and nearly ten tall. He led Gallantry over to a wall, climbed onto the horse's back and knelt on his knees, then used the shovel to begin breaking away at the ceiling. It was rich, soft dirt there and came away easily.

Music started playing behind him and Falwaïn whirled, spotting the lights of the boombox flashing and winking at him from the cave's floor. He turned back to his task.

It didn't take long before he was covered in dirt and roots and bugs and worms, but he also had a large hole developing. In another ten minutes or so, he broke through the ceiling, made the hole large enough to pull himself through, then pulled the flashlights from his waist belt and shone them around this new cavern. It was the same size as the one below it and contained the dead bodies of three owls and a bear. He assumed they must have been powerful magically and that whatever was attacking the land had wanted their magic and had therefore entrapped the animals the same as it had done to Donnie, himself, and the others.

He again returned to his task. This time, he carved out a platform in the wall, which took him a good hour, and he climbed upon that and started digging a hole in the ceiling.

The boombox had followed him to this new cavern and lent its encouragement, now blaring the classic soul tune, "Keep on Keepin' On."

After listening to it a minute or two, Falwaïn grunted his agreement with the boombox's sentiment and worked even harder. No matter how long it took, he was going to dig them out of this trap.

***

Warren finished with his last students and watched them race out of the house to join their friends in play. While he understood that Donnie's goal in teaching the youngsters all these varied subjects was to build a working society upon the Ganlonds that would soon be thriving and progressing, he was not sure he was the best teacher for subjects such as mathematics. Thank the gods he only had to teach them simple addition, subtraction, multiplication and division, all of which he could handle with ease. But he had looked into some of the more advanced maths and knew they were nothing he should ever even attempt to teach anyone, not even himself.

He stood tall and yawned, saw by the clock that it was nearly four in the afternoon and allowed himself to feel glad that classes were over for the day. After putting away his own textbook and moving the chalkboard to the far wall, he surveyed the room and decided it was just fine as it was and anything else could wait a while. He needed some sunshine.

Stepping out onto the front porch, he was surprised to find Diana sitting by herself on the steps. He figured she would be out riding Otis or working in the workshop at the back of the stables.

As he descended the steps, got to the bottom, and turned to look back at his friend, his attention was brought up to the roof, where the Ganlonds' entire flock of Sûlrím, or Wind Wings, were perched. The crowded birds chirped and cooed, and their feathers rustled impatiently. Most of them stood in one place, but a couple were moving, which made those around them wave their wings and chirp or almost bawk with either annoyance or friendly concern, Warren couldn't tell which.

His mouth, which had opened to say hello to Diana, stayed opened while his eyes widened in wonder. Collecting himself, he tore his amazed gaze from the birds and sent it to Diana, asking her, "What are they doing here?"

Diana snorted, eyeing him guardedly. "They are following me," she announced, obviously not happy about it. "As a matter of fact, everywhere I go, they follow me."

Warren's eyebrows were drawn high up his forehead.

"They started doing it late this morning," Diana went on to explain to him in a matter of fact tone, "but I didn't really mark it until I came out after my last class. Whereupon they followed me to the barn, then to the workshop, then to the well, and then to here, where I figured I'd wait for you to help me. And, as usual, they've been changing colors about every minute or two, which is always just weird—the way they do it, I mean." She sighed. "Maybe you can find Bronadulach and see if he knows what they want. I mean, if I didn't know you were checking that damned book every hour, I'd be wondering if something had happened to the others that we should know about."

Warren gave a start of surprise. "Actually," he said, "I haven't checked it since first thing this morning because I've been too busy. Last I knew, events still aren't going particularly well for Catie and Liz, but they're both alive and, as I told you, the An'ugadi are watching over Jesse and his friend Maeve. As for Donnie and them, I know they reached Canta'Lem, and the last I read of their travels, Akanna had just asked Donnie to let her half-brother come back to the Ganlonds to live. But I already told you about all that last night and at breakfast this morning."

Diana nodded. "Yeah. Well, maybe you should take another look now, just to see if anything else has happened."

Warren indicated his agreement with a nod of his own and called for the book to come to him. It zoomed out of the house a few seconds later and landed upon his open palms.

He turned to the last page he'd read several hours before and saw that there was indeed more text. After reading a few minutes, he looked up in alarm and told Diana, "Something's taken Donnie, Falwaïn, Rex and their horses and made them disappear. While it was taking them, Donnie threw Sylvester back to safety and he and the others have been trying for a while to find them, but without success. He even says something about hoping we're reading the book because they need you. See?" he asked, showing the page to Diana, who looked at it with something akin to dread in her expression.

Warren flipped the page and added, "Oh, wait, there's another chapter started here…give me a minute."

He took the book up again and read for a while, his face going paler as he went on until Diana finally snatched the book out of his hands, went back to the page he'd shown her and read on from there herself. Warren sunk onto the step beside her and watched her read the text about Liz and Catie going to Chinatown and finding the children in the cellar below. When she got to the part telling of the sorcerer killing the young Chinese witch, the blood drained from Diana's face like it had from Warren's.

After that, she and Warren shared the book while they both read avidly of the witches' escape on the cable car and the bicycle, and just when it seemed they might have made it to safety, the subsequent scream of Catie. At that point, they turned to each other with apprehension on their faces.

Then Diana flipped the page and they read the text regarding Falwaïn and the horrors he had gone through and, by the time they were done with that, she and Warren were both dumbfounded and speechless. Diana let the forgotten book slip out her hands and onto her lap as she directed her unseeing gaze toward the other side of the valley, all the way up to the ridge and the line of trees where several of their younger animal students were playing games.

The silence between them lasted for a long while before Diana broke it, breathing a sigh that sounded as though it came all the way from the bottom of her lungs. "I must admit," she said to Warren ponderously, "I think I've known that I'd have to go back to the Mîrlonds from the moment Donnie left here for them."

Warren turned to look at her and lifted an eyebrow. When she met his gaze, he noted dryly, "Oh, I think we've *all* known that, my friend."

Diana deadpanned it for a good twenty seconds, then chuckled, finally breaking into a full-on laugh. "You are such a smart ass anymore, a habit you seem to have picked up from Donnie."

He threw his head back and guffawed. "I'd call it a quality myself. But nevertheless, thanks for the compliment!"

And then their expressions changed to identical ones of worry.

Warren spoke first, saying, "I know there's nothing we can do to help Liz, Catie and the children other than pray the An'ugadi are still watching over them or that they've made it to exactly where they wanted to go and Donnie's mother can save them. But we have to do something for Donnie and the others. Do you have any ideas about how we can get there before whatever that thing is that's holding them takes all their magic and they die?" he asked, running his hands over his upper arms, then lifting them to push his long, thick hair off his forehead, afterward placing his elbows on his knees and letting his hands hang loose.

Diana shrugged and looked up at the sky, then at him. "Well, I was thinking that's the easy part," she said, "or at least I hope it is. I think I can establish a *fîr'mäela* from here to the Mîrlonds, glade to glade, if you know what I mean. I formed one a long time ago that goes between the Eireni Glæd and the Forrieghness Tower, so I know how to do it. I just have to call up enough power and control it such that it does what I need it to, which sounds simpler than it is."

"No doubt," agreed Warren, nodding his head vigorously. "But how do we free Donnie and the others?"

Several of the Sûlrím stretched their wings right then, flapping and extending them, chirping loudly, and of course they changed color again, this time from a dark red to a brilliant blue, all of them, all at once.

Diana and Warren stared around at them in surprise and Diana replied to Warren's question in a thoughtful voice, "I somehow think that might become apparent once we get there, don't you?"

Chapter 25
Every Breath You Take

Liz whipped around on her knees, ignoring the pain this action caused while instead furtively scanning behind them through the darkness for any sign of Catie, but she could make out nothing except cars and streetlights. She shoved Maeve ahead of her so they could crawl behind a large-sized sedan that looked pale blue in the light from the lamp overhead. She put a finger to her lips and waited until Maeve nodded her understanding, and then she inched back around the car's bumper to look down the street.

And there was Catie. She was moving toward them slowly and right behind her was Herbert Flint. He had one arm held loosely around Catie's waist and the other, his right hand, was pressing the tip of his wand to her neck.

"Very well," he called out, and he seemed to be looking in Liz's direction even though she didn't think he could actually see her. "You have made it to the time and place you desired and now it is my turn to use Kepler's *Sonnenzeit und Ortungsgeräte*. Witch, you will give them to me now." He gave this order as though it was incomprehensible that anyone would thwart him in his desires.

Still walking toward Liz and the children, he raised his wand and Catie screamed differently this time. While the last had been a wail mixed with fear and warning, this was a cry of crippling pain.

Liz gasped in horror as Catie stumbled and stopped, almost crumpling to the ground in a heap when the sorcerer's wand pulled a golden cloud of magic from her chest. When Liz saw this, she sprang to her feet, holding the clock-watch high above her head to display it to Flint, all the while babbling in distress that, "Yes, yes, of course it's yours and you should take it! Really! So, take it—here!" she urged him, her dark eyes wide with terror, her breath shaky as she reached out to him with it.

Flint looked at the clock-watch in her hands, then up at her face when he growled, "Where is the orrery?"

Liz shook her head from side to side frantically, her agitated fingers shooting turquoise-colored sparks into the air as she waved her arms in front of her and declared, her voice rising anxiously, "I-I-I don't have it, I swear! I-I don't have it! All I have is this, the clock-watch and, seriously, it's yours. Take it! Please, please, just don't hurt my friend anymore!" she begged, her voice breaking with her emotions.

Flint released his wand's hold on Catie's magic and it settled back into her body. Catie groaned with relief and sank back against him, then Liz heard him ask her where the orrery was.

"I told ye, I gave it ta the other witch!" Catie ground out between her clenched teeth.

"She swears she doesn't have it, so where is it?" shouted the enraged sorcerer. He pointed his wand at Catie's throat and again started to pull her magic from her body.

But another voice sounded nearby, a strongly melodic one that Liz recognized and that stilled Herbert Flint immediately. "Catherine sent it to me," the firm voice said, "not to Liz."

Liz swung around, but she was not certain where Lorraine could be. In another few seconds though, the tall, graceful form of Donnie's mother slowly walked into the circle of light from the nearest streetlamp. She came up to Liz wearing a welcoming smile and a long, colorful caftan of silk, then she looked beyond Liz to the children, at whom she smiled even more warmly. With a cheeky wink, she took the clock-watch from Liz's restless fingers, then she opened the orrery up fully and placed the clock-watch onto the top of it, where it clicked into place. Liz looked from Lorraine to the device and back again with surprise.

Lorraine repeated her cheeky wink, her curly ginger bob hiding it from the sorcerer. Balancing Kepler's solar time and locus devices on the palm of her hand, she seemed to be proffering them to Flint, who was now only about twenty feet away.

"Here they are," she told him with a cheerful insouciance to her voice, "and all is well with them. I'm glad they're reunited again, aren't you? Dear Nicolaus was so proud when he made them and had confirmed what they could achieve together. I must tell you though," she breathed in excitement, as though imparting a confidence to the sorcerer who was still approaching her with Catie held captive, "their use this time certainly has brought four of the most precious people to me and for that I am most grateful to Herr Kepler and—well, to anyone who had anything to do with getting them here safely. But, as for you, you depraved murderer, I'm sure you realize that I cannot let you take the devices away from here." Her tone when she said this was again bright and cheerful.

Liz looked apprehensively from Herbert Flint to Lorraine and then back at Flint.

Flint made as though to threaten Catie again with his wand, but Lorraine put up her other hand to stop him and this time stated in a wholly serious voice, "You are working at a disadvantage, villain, and you don't even know it." She handed Kepler's device over to Liz, then took a couple steps toward Flint and Catie, who had finally come to a standstill. "But I think it is time for you to be made aware," she announced with importance, "the reason you cannot feel me or my magic is not because I'm so damned good at creating protective shields, although I am quite proficient at that. But no, it is because I am what is known in our circles as a Fundamental."

Liz had no idea what a Fundamental was, but it was clear that Flint did, and so did Catie because a flash of exultation passed over her small face, whereas Flint's features froze into a watchful mask that had fear behind it.

"Now," Lorraine went on, as though she were speaking with one of the interns or nurses at the hospital where she practiced obstetrics, "we can do this slowly, which of course means you will survive, although there will be plenty of times you will wish you had not. The problem with that choice is that the process takes several years before I am finished. That is a *lot* of pain for you to experience over a very long time," she assured him with a dry, but sympathetic nod and chuckle. "Or I can do it all at once, which, as I'm sure you know, will kill you most excruciatingly. On the plus side though, it also means that your death will last but a second or two. You choose!" she added cheerily, and Liz could almost hear her add, "Tick, tock!" to the command.

With a wave of Lorraine's hand, Flint was encased in a field of grey light, which forced him to let Catie go. When she was free, Catie shook herself, inhaled and then exhaled a deep breath of relief, and turned upon Flint a hateful glare before she ran to Liz, threading her arm through Liz's while turning her friend away from Lorraine and Flint. Maeve ventured out from behind the car and squeezed in between them.

"We dunna want ta watch this, fascinatin' though it might be," Catie whispered quietly as she pulled both Liz and Maeve back toward the house with her.

"What's she going do?" asked Liz with a concerned frown marring her brow. "And what's a Fundamental? What does that mean?"

Catie sighed heavily, but she wasn't actually irritated even though she exclaimed severely, "Always so many questions wi' ye!" Nevertheless, she continued shepherding her charges toward the house as she explained the answer. "Well, there are among us a few witches who ent like us others, and my sister is one such. They can do things the rest of us canna, nor would we want ta do them, for they carry a heavy burden that goes along wi' 'em. Lorraine tries ta make light o' what she does when others are around, but that's jest so's they can feel okay about it, because she never do. Nope, she does what she must, but she never feels good 'bout it and never crows ta anyone because o' it."

They were nearly to the front steps now and Catie stopped them but didn't let anyone look backward. "Ye see, she strips sorcerers and their like o' their magical powers," Catie said, both her voice and expression uncharacteristically solemn. "As ye know, sorcerers' powers come from other magical creatures' triunes. That means their victims all die 'cause nobody can live wi'out a soul and therefore the more powerful the sorcerer is, the more creatures were done away by 'em—ye understand me?" she asked, and Liz nodded. "And 'tis jest as painful to strip each o' those triunes from the sorcerer as it was from their original owners."

Liz took this in for a second and then gasped, "Oh! Oh, my goodness! You mean like what Flint did to that woman back in the Fong Emporium, don't you?" She gulped, looking askance. "And that's what Lorraine's going to do to him now?"

"Aye, that she is. Either slow or quick, dependin' on which 'e chooses." It was to Catie's credit that she kept all hint of satisfaction from her voice when she pronounced these words, but the gods knew how much she hated sorcerers and that to her, the only good sorcerer was a dead one.

"Oh, my god!" Liz squeaked.

She looked utterly terrified for a few moments until she recollected herself and hustled Maeve up the steps and through the open front door of the house. She took the child's hand once inside and pulled her all the way to the formal receiving room, which was the nearest room where a light was turned on and which faced the street. There she found Ben Saunders, Donnie's father—or rather, the man she'd always known as Donnie's father. He was a tall man, well-built and handsome, with medium-length reddish-blond hair combed back off his high forehead and somewhat oddly blue eyes that had always made Liz wonder if he wore contacts to colorize them to their uniformly brilliant blue. Liz had no idea what to think of him as now, or of Lorraine for that matter, since she had learned that they were not actually Donnie's parents, so she just simply called him Ben.

"Ben, we're here," she told him unnecessarily and he came forward to enfold her in a bear hug.

He released her after a few moments and looked down at the children questioningly.

Liz explained Maeve and Jesse as succinctly and quickly as she could because she was nervous of the way Catie and Ben were staring at each other. She could tell they were both uncomfortable in the other's presence, but she had no idea why that would be. When Liz finished her explanations and introductions, Ben roused himself and shook Maeve's outstretched hand politely, then he brushed a gentle finger across Jesse's cheek.

When Ben straightened, his gaze went directly to Catie as he said, after clearing his throat first, "Catherine. Always good to see you."

Catie gave a short nod and murmured, "Ayep." Then she moved over to the window and looked out upon the street as if drawn by a magnet.

Liz could see what was happening from where she stood, and her breath caught in her throat. Lorraine was outlined in a glowing field of her power and it crackled and boomed all around her. When she threw a bolt of it at him, Herbert Flint died just like his evil friend in the rowboat beside the *Drunken Knave* had died, with magic of all sorts and colors bursting from his body and raining through the air, falling and floating to the ground where it was absorbed all the way into the planet's core.

Even though it was muffled, Liz heard his sharp cry and then she felt all the power he'd stolen over the many years of his very long life passing down into the earth close by. Somehow, she knew that over three hundred souls had died to give Herbert Flint his magic, and all those captive triunes had just been released into the ether. She shivered, revolted by it all, most especially by the knowledge that anyone could have murdered so many people in such a vicious and intimate manner...to rip out someone's soul, ending their life and all their hopes for any chance of happiness, to bend their magic to your own will and use it as though you had every right to do so...well, she began to see why Catie hated the Iceni Meræ so much.

And then she noticed that Maeve and Jesse were watching out the window beside her. Actually, everyone seemed almost hypnotized into witnessing the sorcerer's death, because even Ben had moved so that he had a clear view too.

Liz reached down to take firm hold of Maeve's shoulders and turned her around just as another figure strode through the doorway, her hands stuck nonchalantly into her back pockets and her luxuriant auburn hair—so like her mother's in color and texture—bouncing in long curls over her shoulders and down her back.

"Hey, Dad, is something happening outside? Oh, my gosh, Liz is here! Where's Julia? Is she here too? And Donnie?" cried Emily, hurrying over to crush Liz in an anxious hug, holding her close for a long time while shuddering with emotion. Then she held Liz at arm's length to study her appearance, declaring with forced brightness, "Oh, my goodness, you look absolutely exhausted and far, *far* too thin! Come on, you need something to eat, and this sweet little girl with you looks like she could do with some cookies and hot chocolate!"

Liz smiled back and nodded in tired agreement.

Emily took charge, herding Liz and Maeve out of the receiving room and across the main hall into the brightly lit kitchen. She had them sit at the small, round oak table in the corner and then went about making them the promised food and drink.

After confirming for Emily's curiosity the name of the short blonde woman with her, Liz took the opportunity to finally unwind her shawl from Maeve's small body and then she gratefully swept Jesse into her arms as she sat in a chair. Her eyes teared up when she realized that he'd grown a little bit while they'd been separated. But by then, Emily was asking more questions and they were having a lively conversation, with Liz explaining what had happened to them that day. At first, she gave only general answers to Emily's queries because she wasn't sure how much Donnie's sister knew about how things were, but it seemed Emily had been filled in rather fully by her parents.

"Yes, they told me everything after Aunt Catherine came to get Donnie because they insisted I move back in here—something about us all being potential targets now. I didn't believe them at first, of course, but then Mom showed me what she could do and proved to me that magic is real." She shook her head in wonder, grimacing somewhat comically when she brought over a plate stacked with ham and cheese sandwiches and another with chocolate chip cookies that she placed in front of Liz and Maeve.

Nodding to their muttered thanks, Emily returned to the kitchen area to continue getting drinks around, chatting all the while. She went on to say, "And then, with you and Julia being taken at the same time as Donnie—was that because you were sleeping on Donnie's furniture?" she threw back over her shoulder as she got out mugs for the hot chocolate, which she had warming on the gas stovetop in a small pot. "Mom figured it had to be something like that, that my aunt would not have made her spell look for that kind of thing when it was set and that she probably had you all in storage for who knows how long before Donnie unpacked you!" She giggled with amusement over this thought but stopped when she saw Liz's face. She hurried over to the table, plunked the two mugs in her hands down onto the wooden surface and cried with both regret and concern, "Oh, I'm so sorry! Judging by your pained expression, I gather that's not at all what happened, is it? I really am sorry. It's just that we didn't know how you two got taken, only how Donnie did, but we had hoped for the simplest explanation. If you don't want to talk about it, I'll understand."

Liz reassured Emily that she was okay talking about it and that she honestly hadn't thought about it all that much in the last couple of months because of everything that had happened since that awful experience. She gave Emily a brief explanation of her and Julia's time with Valledai and the cruel and grotesque okûns working for him. And then she went on to tell of the big battle on the Branmar Plain and how she came to be with Catie after Donnie sent her through the time portal created by the amulet. Going on, she gave a brief outline of her and Catie's adventures together, all the way from Tortuga to San Francisco, unconsciously gushing a bit about the Pan-Pacific International Exposition of 1915.

When Liz realized that her reticule had been bothering her since their arrival because it was heavier than she'd remembered it being earlier that day, she untied it from her undergarments and, upon opening it to inspect its contents, received the somewhat ridiculous but happy surprise that Catie's spell had been fulfilled and five jewels from the Tower of Jewels had been placed in the bag. Liz extracted them with care from the reticule and showed them off to an enthralled Emily.

Meanwhile, Emily, having served the steaming hot chocolate, stood behind a chair until Liz pulled out the jewels, and then she sat down in the chair to listen to Liz's adventurous tale with alternating expressions of interest, horror, and utter amazement upon her face. When Liz was finally finished with her recitation, Emily sat quietly ruminating for a little while before asking Liz, "What kind of a place is this Medregai?"

Liz shrugged uncertainly. "Donnie seems to do okay there, but I don't know as it'd ever be for me," she admitted.

Emily sighed wistfully. "I miss Donnie so much," she said in a forlorn voice and Liz nodded her agreement.

"Yeah," she replied. But wanting to reassure Emily, she added, "She's taken to magic like a duck to water, you know. I mean it, she's really quite clever with it and it just seems to flow from her and around her and to all those who care about her. Seriously, it's her natural state of being, you can see that immediately now. Oh, and she's found love!"

Nearly choking with mock shock, Emily spluttered, "No! My sister is in love with someone? Oh, do tell!"

And so, Liz told Emily all she could about Falwaïn, going on to describe how easy his relationship with Donnie seemed to be and how they both were so obviously in love with the other, even though they'd known each other only a few weeks. "Well, I don't know how they're doing now," she amended, "seeing as it's been a few months since I saw them last, but they fit together so well then, I can't imagine they've parted yet."

Sitting quietly and chewing her bottom lip for several seconds, Emily's sapphire blue eyes teared up. "She's always going to be my sister, even though Mom says she's her aunt and my great aunt." Emily shook her head as though to clear it of unwelcome thoughts and sighed again. "Sometimes this is all just too much to take in, you know?"

"Oh, yeah, I know exactly what you mean by that!" Liz exclaimed with feeling, thinking back over the events of the past year. "I would never have thought anyone would kidnap me, or that magic was real or something that I could tap into myself one day, or that Julia's father was so dangerous."

"Her father?" inquired Emily, bewildered. "What does he have to do with all this? Didn't he die in Arizona a few years ago?"

Liz shook her head. "No, that man was no blood relation to either of us. No, Julia is my child and I had her when I was only fifteen. The story of how I got together with her father is so weird, I never thought I'd ever understand him or why he got me pregnant. But then I was kidnapped to Medregai, and a lot of that history began to be explained." She passed a hand over her eyes wearily and noted, "It's funny, I thought he was a dream for so long and I struggled to remember him for years, but now I know he's a nightmare and I can hardly get him and his kind, the Iceni Meræ, out of my head. I've been so scared of them ever since Catie told me stories about them and of him, Ixifir Bíun. That's Julia's father. Catie says they'll stop at nothing and will use whomever to get what they want, which is always more power, more magic, and more magical articles like the ones we used to get here."

They discussed Kepler's magical clock-watch and orrery until Emily understood what they were, which occurred at about the time both turned their attention to the voices they could hear approaching. The others walked through the open doorway a moment later, with Catie entering first and Lorraine and Ben following right behind her.

Catie darted immediately to the counter where Emily had another plate of sandwiches waiting. She grabbed one in each hand, taking turns biting from each, rapidly chewing mouthfuls as though she thought she might never be allowed to eat again. Emily got up and reheated the chocolate drink, smiling tentatively at Catie when she turned the gas burner on again.

"I'm Emily," she introduced herself a little shyly to her aunt and Catie cackled with amusement.

"And I'm yer Aunt Catie," she said, smiling widely at Emily. Then she realized that she had a mouthful of food and she glanced at Liz a moment before turning a shade pink and muttering under her breath, "Er, 'scuse my manners, if ye please. I could eat a pig all by meself, if given the chance, I be that hungry, but that don't mean I ought ta act like one!" That being said, she popped the last two bites into her mouth, wiped her hands on her skirt, then held them out to Emily, who took them in hers and beamed at her aunt with amused delight.

Emily looked over at her mother and demanded mock severely, "Mom, why didn't you tell me you had a sister, and one that's so very nice?" She turned back to Catie with a smile and asked, "Why did you never visit us before now? Is it because we were hiding Donnie?"

Catie turned to Lorraine, who eyed her critically, and then she replied to Emily discreetly, "That and other reasons. P'haps one day, I might even tell ye my story. I gather Miss Priss—er, Liz, here, has been filling ye in on what's happened wi' us together, eh?"

Emily nodded and said enthusiastically, "Yes, she certainly has, but I have yet to ask her any real questions about Warren. And I want to know all about him!" she declared teasingly, smiling over at an embarrassed Liz and a happily cooing Jesse. "After all, he is the father of the sweetest little boy ever!"

"Oh, he's just been fed," Liz demurred quickly, smiling with love and humor at her son nevertheless. "You'll think differently of him when he's on the other side of feeding or is in need of a nap."

"Warren is the baby's father?" Lorraine echoed slowly as she regarded Catie with shocked disbelief.

Catie nodded and took a big gulp of the warm chocolate drink that was now in her cup. "Aye," she said after swallowing the rich, creamy elixir and smacking her lips appreciatively, "he's back ta bein' 'imself, or so I gather from Liz. Although, I dunna think he knows hisself yet."

Liz, having noted the exchange of odd looks between the sisters, threw in her own question. "Are you saying he wasn't born a wolf or a werewolf, but as a human?"

To this Catie shrugged noncommittally, while Lorraine kept a steadfast gaze upon Catie and showed no sign of answering Liz's inquiry.

"And I gather he has just happened to be called Warren again, even without knowing himself, as you say he doesn't?" Liz persisted with a soft breath, staring at Catie with incredulity.

Again, Catie shrugged. She started to say something, then stopped, then started again, finally quipping, "Quite a coincidence, ent it?"

Lorraine shook her head in wonder and turned to Liz to tell her kindly, "Another time, we'll explain it, I promise. It's just good to know he's back to being human again. I presume it was something Donnie did, yes?"

It was Liz's turn to shrug. "If so, she doesn't take credit for it, but says that she merely opened to him the choice of who he wants to be. After that, it's all him."

Lorraine's smile was like sunshine upon receiving this news. She glanced at Ben and nodded once to him, then she drifted over to the table and stood for a moment, radiating her happy smile down upon Jesse. "I see both Warren and you in your son," she remarked.

Liz gazed down at the contented and sleepy little boy in her arms. "Yes, I see us both in him too. Which, I guess must mean that Warren, without realizing it, has chosen to look like himself again or at least how he looked when you knew him." She tried to see if either Catie, Ben or Lorraine would confirm this assumption in any way, but their faces did not change expression, so she let it go. Looking back down at her son, she mused, "I think Jesse's eyes are changing color though. They've been dark like mine since he was born, but now I think they're turning blue like Warren's."

Emily cleared her throat and said in a low, facetious tone, "Um, just who is this Warren anyway? And what do you mean he's human again? And what, exactly, do you mean by *werewolf*?"

Lorraine laughed musically, striding over to where her daughter stood by the stove to place a long, slim arm along Emily's shoulders. "As I said before, honey, that can all wait. We need to get everyone sorted, into beds and settled for the night. Maybe a bath or two before though, yes?" She made this suggestion with a twinkle in her eye.

Liz pushed loose tendrils of her hair back from her face and nodded, but she remained sitting, studying the others pensively. Finally, she asked Lorraine in a husky voice, "What did you do with Flint's body after you, er, stripped him of his power?"

She was sorry to see that Emily, after taking this in and realizing what it meant, became so badly shocked by the question. The young woman looked pale and lost as she struggled with the knowledge that her mother had just killed someone, even if her mother's "victim" been a very evil sorcerer. Liz knew she had to fix her blunder somehow, so she said Emily's name and, when the other woman held her gaze, Liz told her, "He'd killed more than three hundred people to accumulate his power, and in whatever manners were most painful and awful for each of his victims. He was no good at all, and he enjoyed killing others as meanly as possible. I know, because I've seen that side of him. What your mom did to him released all those souls from his capture, so they can now be at peace. Remember that, okay?"

Lorraine's smile had died away and her face had gone blank after Liz had asked her question about Flint's body. She stared at the floor silently when Liz continued to speak and then also for some time after while composing her thoughts. When she was ready, she regarded Liz with an impassive expression and replied, "The only safe thing you can do with a dead sorcerer the likes of him is to burn his remains. This man, this Herbert Flint, who chased you here is scattered to the wind as ash and dust, and there's not much that could possibly bring him back." She gestured toward herself and the other two who had come in with her, adding, "We've made sure of it."

"Does that mean there is something that could bring him back, even now?" gulped Liz.

Lorraine bit her lip in response to the question and gave Liz a somewhat wistful shrug. She was avoiding looking at Emily, who had shrunk away from her mother and was huddled in the nearest corner.

"Or would that be a someone, as in Ixifír Bíun maybe?" Liz clarified, sudden perception flashing into her eyes. She traded her gaze from Ben to Lorraine and inquired, "I presume you know that he's Julia's father?"

They both nodded slowly, although it was Lorraine who said, "Yes, we've known it since we met you and your sister," she admitted. "Or is it all right now to say who Julia is truthfully?"

It was Liz's turn to nod and she did so vehemently. "Oh, yes, it's past time I claimed her as my daughter with everyone we know instead of hiding behind lies. I had Julia when I was very young. I now know that it was Ixifír

Bíun who tricked or magicked me into having sex with him and Julia is the result of that coupling. And that makes her half Iceni Meræ and therefore, I presume, half a sorceress, right?" Liz's breathing had gotten noticeably shaky by the time she had finished speaking, but she was determined to know the worst and so she looked at Lorraine expectantly.

Lorraine rubbed her hands together almost nervously before replying. "Well, no one is ever half of one or the other, but rather, it depends on which side is stronger in a person, in their DNA, I mean," she replied carefully. "If Julia has shown signs of becoming a witch, then she's a witch. If, on the other hand, she's shown signs of being a sorceress, then she's that. Even though magical bloodlines have been crossed several times throughout history, it's never been recorded that a true mix has ever been achieved. One is either a witch or wizard, or a sorceress or sorcerer."

Liz had already sighed in relief and, when Lorraine stopped talking, she stated firmly, "I'm fairly certain she's a witch. I don't know why I feel that, but I do."

Catie nodded and murmured absently, "As do I, so I b'lieve it ta be true. Both yer dotter and yer son are of the witch and wizard variety."

Liz glanced at her in gratitude, then she turned to Emily. "What about you? Have you accepted your powers yet? Isn't that what all Codlebærn have to do first?"

For no reason that was apparent to Liz, both Lorraine and Ben were clearly alarmed by this question and each started to speak at the same time, one over the other. Ben stopped first and motioned that he was deferring to Lorraine, who took a moment to regroup her thoughts before addressing Liz's questions.

"While that is true, yes, we've all decided that Emily shouldn't claim her powers at this time," she explained, glancing at Emily and beaming at her with pride and love, "so she's still not practicing magic."

Catie snorted cynically and glared at her sister. "Reelly?" she said with another loud and disbelieving snort. "That's the line ye be takin' wi' 'er, is it?" the little blonde witch demanded skeptically and her ginger-haired sister held her regal head high while she warned Catie to stay out of it, that they had discussed the subject as a family and the three of them together had come to the logical conclusion that now was not the time for Emily to claim any kind of magical birthright. Lorraine stared at Catie meaningfully when she said this, but it was obvious that Catie was impressed by none of what her sister had just said.

Before Catie could make a rejoinder though, Emily murmured quietly, "Well, Mother, I've been thinking tonight that maybe we should discuss it again, now that they're here." She waved a hand toward Liz and the kids, and then at Catie.

But Lorraine shook her head quickly, giving her daughter an imploring look. "Oh, no, my dear, now's not the time for that, trust me," she said, extending a hand to Emily. "Look, your Aunt Catherine should not have said what she did," she reproached her sister, shooting Catie an icy glare and huffing at her in exasperation, "and I pray she apologizes and goes no further. No, believe me, darling, we don't need you to accept your powers or anything like that right now. You'll just make yourself more of a target." Lorraine reached over and gathered her daughter to her, putting her arm around her again to give Emily's stiff shoulders a gentle squeeze. She grimaced at her daughter questioningly. "Okay?" she whispered, pressing her forehead to Emily's, and Emily nodded her agreement reluctantly.

But Catie simply wasn't having it.

"We've had this argument b'fore and it tore us asunder!" she reminded her sister hotly. "When I told ye—when me own gifts told me what yer daughter would be, and ye didna want ta know! Ye didna want ta b'lieve! But naow, if ye be claimin' the truth fer yerselves, dear sister, then ye ought ta *be* truthful! Lies should have purpose and that one does no one no good service!" She looked sharply at Ben and, pointing a thumb toward the front door, which lay behind her, with a jerking motion, challenged him with, "What was that sorcerer's real name? It surely weren't Herbert Flint. I reckon ye must have known him back in yer days with them awful people o' yourn, them Iceni Meræ!" She almost spat the last two words when she said them.

Liz and Emily gasped aloud and they each looked several times from Ben to Lorraine with widened eyes and dropped jaws. Even Maeve had followed the adult talk enough to understand that Catie had just accused Ben of being one of the enemy, and she put her almost empty cup of hot chocolate down and sat back in her seat, her eyes as wide as either Liz's or Emily's.

When no response came from Ben or Lorraine, Catie turned to Emily and informed her regretfully but with firm resolve in her eyes and voice, "What yer parents ent tellin' ye is that ye are a sorceress and fer ye ta have magic, ye'll have ta kill someone and steal their triune! Ye ent no witch and it dunna matter how much ye may want ta be one! Ye are a sorceress, born and bred, and that is why yer parents dunna want ye ta know yer true birthright!"

***

The boombox, which had joined them earlier while they'd been sat on the cottage's front stoop after classes and then followed them here, for at least the fifth time in the last hour started to play the creepy stalker song, "Every Breath You Take."

Diana eyed the music box with extreme disapprobation, heaving a thoroughly disgusted sigh in its direction before turning to face Warren with a raised and questioning eyebrow.

He, more than a little amused by the music box's antics, was chuckling to himself until he caught Diana's look. He then straightened his grin and nodded back that he was indeed ready for whatever she was going to do next.

They were both mounted on their horses and standing in the middle of the Glimmering Glade, with the great Cave Bear, Bronadulach, watching from the entrance. He'd insisted on going with them at first, but they'd both turned him down flat, arguing that his absence would leave the Ganlonds with too little protection, even with the giants and the dragon around. He'd given in to them eventually, but he was not at all happy about it and he stood now watching them with a hard glint in his eyes.

The Sûlrím were all perched in tree limbs above the glade, the flock's color changing every couple of minutes as they too waited with impatience for something to happen. Diana glanced upward at them as they went from bright blue to dark goldenrod in one grand wave, making the trees glow in what little of the evening's sun still penetrated the glade.

She and Warren had discussed how to dissuade them from following her but neither had come up with a method they thought might achieve this purpose. And each time she'd even thought about somehow dodging them and leaving them behind, the boombox had started in on its annoying song again. In the end, she'd decided to give it up and let the birds do as they pleased and so the flock had followed her and Warren from the cottage to the glade, alighting in trees ahead on the path and waiting for Diana to pass below before flying ahead again, never letting her get too far away.

All that was left to do now was for Diana to establish a *fir'mäela*, or portal, from glade to glade, Ganlonds to Mîrlonds.

Ha-ha, that was all she had to do, she thought to herself, just that one simple, highly magical act.

Nervously wiping her clammy hands on her leather-clad thighs, Diana let her mind drop into the magic within her soul, connecting it to the magic welling in the ground beneath Otis's feet. Through him, she drew up as much of it as she could, letting the power flow from him to her and focusing her mind on increasing it and letting it fill them both. From times of old, she knew that she was strongest when funneling magic through her bond-mate into herself, so she fell back into that familiar habit and let its comfort fill her heart. She allowed the magic to fulminate within her until both she and Otis acquired identical looks of sublime contentment.

Warren watched them from atop Raleen, wondering what was making them look so peaceful and figuring astutely that it probably had something to do with their connection to each other. They were glowing bright silver and emanated an ethereal kind of air about them. The Sûlrím in the tree branches above them changed colors twice restlessly as though urging Diana and Otis to hurry, a sentiment he was beginning to feel himself.

And then there came a bright flare from Diana's breast, which formed a moment later into an archway, and in a moment more, this archway outlined another glade far away. The Sûlrím darted through it and were gone from sight in but an instant. Diana slowly opened her eyes, as did Otis, and they both viewed the archway with satisfaction. Noting the absence of the birds over her head, she looked at Warren and again asked if he was ready by hooking an eyebrow at him.

He responded by urging Raleen through the portal, and Diana and Otis trotted close behind them. When they reached the other side, Diana let the portal close and they all looked around the new glade, only with Diana and Otis their expressions were nostalgic, whereas Warren's and Raleen's were curious.

The Eireni Glæd was empty of all creatures except for the groves of magical trees encircling the glade and some non-magical insects flitting through the air and giving off a low buzzing sound. The moment she and Otis arrived, Diana felt the trees' recognition of her and their resulting resentment toward her and her horse. She knew instinctively that they would tell her nothing of value, so she urged Otis toward the glade's entrance and they left the silent, angry circle without saying a word. While Warren did not know what had just passed, he too had felt the sudden menace of the trees, so he and Raleen followed the others out of the glade at a fast clip. Of the Sûlrím there was no sign.

Immediately in front of the glade there was a field of tall grasses. They rode through this for a couple of minutes, all the while scanning the hills around them sharply. Being as they were so far west now, there was still plenty of light to be had and sunset was at least three hours away. At about the same moment, they each noticed what looked like some sort of gathering on the nearest hilltop, a good half mile away, and so they headed toward that at a canter. They were soon greeted by the sight of Akanna and Diego riding down the hill upon their horses to meet them, with Sylvester clinging tenaciously to Diego's saddle. Their welcome when it came was warm but brief because of the other groups now also riding or running to meet them.

Akanna started to explain the various comers hurriedly but Warren interrupted her to say that they knew of those who had journeyed south with them from Anûmanétus because of the book.

"We hoped you would be reading that," the vincan observed fervently, and both Sylvester and Diego nodded with her, looking relieved. Akanna continued, telling the new arrivals, "The mages are insisting that we blow up the glade as violently as possible because that's where the heart of the Mîrlonds is and Donnie and the others went missing near there. They believe only a hard, sudden attack on the glade will work to free our friends. We've been arguing about it for hours amongst ourselves because there are many of us who believe that just because that's where they were taken from, it does not mean that's where they are being held—below the glade, I mean."

Diana and Warren both nodded that they understood.

"You're right; they're not being held under the glade," Diana assured them grimly, having caught sight of the Sûlrím from the corner of her right eye. She turned and pointed at the flock of birds, all of which were soaring in an agitated but concerted manner around a ragged point off to the east on a high bluff. "They're being held below there."

Warren looked at the birds and let out a small gasp, saying excitedly, "You're right, and that proves why the Sûlrím were following you all day! They must have known you'd get us here so they could show us where to look for Donnie and the others." He turned back and explained, "The entire flock followed her from the morning on, never letting her out of their sight, they were *that* determined to come here with us."

At about this time, they were joined by several peoples on horseback and some animals who were all members of the Mîrlonds' animal council. While many stared at Diana with curiosity, most of the animals did so with something more like animosity. Apparently, they knew who and what she was.

This was even more evident when two horses, both towering black stallions, stamped the ground and snorted at her angrily.

She eyed them for a while without speaking, folding her arms in front of her as she sat back in her saddle and met their angry, flashing gazes. Clenching her jaw in defiance, she acknowledged them in a clipped voice, saying, "Radocan. Ludrid."

Both horses tossed their heads at her and the one on the right sneered, "This is the result of what you did, you traitorous coward! Our lands are dying because of you. You must be quite happy about that, yes?"

She scoffed at him and retorted, "Of course I'm not happy about that, but the Mîrlonds could have called out for another Ér Ainíl, you know! And you could have voted for that to happen, and maybe if you had—"

"Oh, believe me, we did vote for that many long years ago!" interjected the other horse acidly. "But the Mîrlonds ignored us."

Akanna leaned forward in her saddle and reminded the two magical horses, "There are many here who still believe in her and clearly so did the Mîrlonds, so let's not argue old issues that are not ours to resolve." She shook her head and sighed. "Besides, she is here now, and there is one who believes in her beyond us all, and that is the other Ér Ainíl, Donemere of the Codlebærn. While you and the other denizens of the Mîrlonds don't know Donnie yet, I assure you that, if she believes in Ghira Ma'Hai, or as she is known now, Diana, then so must we. For we know what doubt will do to our efforts. We *must* work together as one or we are doomed."

Of course, this did not stanch the flow of arguments, but Diana told Otis to go and he began walking toward where the birds were circling. Warren and Diego urged their horses to follow her. Durreen and his steed hurried so that they were only a few steps behind this vanguard. Akanna did the same as her brother, and soon the entire group of combatants was moving in that direction. Those in the front and rear stayed out of the quarrels that sprang up amongst those in the middle, and nothing more got settled the entire five-minute trip to the bottom of the bluff. There, Diana searched for a path up and Durreen jumped ahead to show her. He and his horse led the way until they'd reached the top of the bluff and their groups slowly congregated around the area the birds were still flying over, each coming to a halt and all silenced by the spectacle of the birds.

The Sûlríms' percussive murmuration was felt in everyone's hearts whenever the birds passed nearby, and the hairs on the backs of many necks were raised when the birds' flight suddenly become faster and even more mesmerizing. So intent on watching the birds were they all, nothing more was noticed by almost anyone until the birds flew together in a thick stream and divebombed the earth.

Diana, looking downward by mere happenstance at the right moment, was the only one to notice that a hand had reached out of a small hole that was centered in the middle of a vortex that stirred a memory in her brain. It was exactly the same spiral pattern that was at the Withering Hills, near the dragon rookery.

The birds flew into the hole, somehow managing to not eviscerate the hand sticking out of it. Diana jumped off Otis and ran toward the hole. She leaped backward when the phalanx of birds erupted a few seconds later from the same hole and back into the fresh air. They circled around and dove back into the hole, slicing through its edges and enlarging it. They did this four more times, each cycle widening the hole until it was quite large enough for a horse to pass through, the birds' razor sharp and diamond hard beaks cutting through the thick layer of earth with the ease of a knife through warm butter.

When they appeared in the sky no more but could distinctly be heard moving around below, Diana approached the edge of the opening they had created and stared down into it. She saw Falwaïn crouched on a ledge right below her that he'd apparently dug out for himself. His arms were raised up to cover his head and great globs of earth had rained down upon his form. Many of these had been cemented to him by sweat so that he was barely discernible from his surroundings. Diana called his name and his head jerked up, his piercingly blue eyes bleary and blank and his whole body exhausted.

"Help them!" he cried, and then he collapsed into unconsciousness.

Chapter 26
In the Dark

"Get out!" Lorraine snarled, pointing a manicured finger toward the front door, her face contorted with rage. "Get out of my house!"

Catie turned bright red, gave a short, stiff nod in acknowledgement of the command and started to stalk out of the kitchen.

Liz jumped up, shouting, "If she goes, we go!" She grabbed Maeve by the arm and pulled her to her feet, pushing her around the table.

Emily, her face stricken and her motions jerky, brushed by her mother and she also strode after Catie, throwing over her shoulder, "I'm going with them!"

Lorraine stared after them all in disbelief and turned to Ben helplessly.

Ben hurried to the front door, somehow reaching it before Catie did. He stood in front of it and shook his head, his expression anguished and his shoulders drooping with sadness.

"No, please, don't go, not like this," he entreated the three very angry women standing in front of him now. "She's not used to telling everything she knows. We've all been hiding for so long, none of us is good at that anymore." He zeroed in on Catie and reminded her, "You know this; you've always known this, all your life! And you're no better about being forthcoming than she is." He turned to his daughter and pleaded with her, "Your mother only wanted to protect you, and to protect me, because she's worried you'll hate me for what I used to be. Is she right about that? Do you hate me like your aunt does?" he asked, staring his daughter bravely in the eye. "Because you can't hate me any more than I did for many, many years. After your mother stripped me of my powers, I went away and spent a long time hating myself. But then she sought me out and taught me that every person has value, if only they themselves will let that value count for something."

He sagged back against the door, passing a hand over his forlorn face. "It took me years to overcome that feeling of dread every time I looked at myself in a mirror," he confessed grimly, "or when I met up with someone who knew me from before. As for making friends with strangers, I found that impossible as well because I had no right to feel anything as clean as real friendship. I was completely convinced of that. But Lorraine made me see that I could become a force for good if I so wanted, that it would take even more strength than I had already shown, but that it was possible and was the most noble goal I could ever attain."

He sighed and moved away from the door, opening it a few inches before standing clear of it. "And so I have spent the last sixty years doing everything I could to pay retribution to my fellow humans and to injured magical beings. I help them find themselves. I help them discover their true strengths so they can broaden their lives into something so much more meaningful than they had ever thought possible. And I'm proud of my work, I'm proud that I'm helping others to achieve their best. I can't ever forget what I was and the terrible, terrible things I did, but that doesn't mean I can't do all I can to stop others from making similar bad decisions in their own lives."

He focused again on Catie and said to her, "Go on, continue hating me all you want, but don't let that stop you from reconnecting with your sister. Lorraine needs you. She has always needed you, Catie, more than you ever needed her." He turned to his daughter now and begged her, "Please don't walk out on her, Emily, but rather, show her how to be open, how to be honest, and how to earn your trust back." And to Liz, he said, "Dear, brave Liz, give her a chance to teach you how to get the most out of your talents. She's such a talented witch, and she has much to give you all. Please, don't any of you abandon her now or yourselves and the growth you may all experience together. No," he said abruptly and with finality, and then he sighed, shaking his head sadly. "If anyone is going to leave here, it will be me." Coming to this decision, he reached over to shut the door and then headed up the stairway, intending to pack a bag.

Emily caught his arm and stopped him as he passed by her. She looked deeply into his eyes, urging him passionately, "No, Dad, stay! I'm gonna need you beside me to make sure I don't make the same mistakes you did. I'll be honest with you, all I can think about anymore is using magic like Mom does," she confessed, "but I don't ever want to kill anyone just so I can have the privilege of being magical." She let out a small, anguished groan. "You've got to help me, Daddy, help me be strong."

He drew one arm around her and the other he lifted so that his hand cradled the back of her head, holding her close to him. He buried his face in her hair and began to silently weep.

Catie hung her head and blew a dark, shuddering breath. When she looked up, her face was set. She pushed her shoulders back, stood tall, and motioned for Liz to accompany her back to the kitchen. "Let's give 'em some privacy, eh, Miss Priss?"

Liz nodded, taking Maeve's hand to lead them all back to Lorraine. When they entered, Lorraine was standing with her back to them at the sink, for all intents and purposes cleaning the dishes. She must have heard them return for her back stiffened and she hesitated for just a moment before continuing washing up. It wasn't until Catie went up to her and leant her forehead on her sister's back that Lorraine stopped. Her shoulders slowly began to shake, and a sob escaped her lips.

Catie reached around to turn off the water, then she put her arms around her sister, who turned in her embrace and, just as Ben had done to Emily, she buried her tears in Catie's hair and had herself a good cry.

Liz heard them murmuring to each other about how each had missed the other and how glad they were to be together again, for however long they might be granted that pleasure this time. They said something about the gods, but Liz couldn't catch it all, and so she let Maeve finish her hot chocolate and eat one more cookie, waiting for some decision to be made as to where they were going to be spending the night.

***

Diana cleared her throat, pointed at Bishop Munkinum and Brother Mire, and then motioned toward Falwaïn, commanding sternly, "Get him out of there already, will you? Then arrange the dirt so we can ride down it. We've got to get to Donnie and the others!"

The mages stared at her with unfriendly gazes. Yet still, they complied with her peremptory demands because they could feel the power she was emanating. They both recognized her as an ovid and knew better than to ever thwart one of those, if it could at all be helped.

The bishop focused his own power and raised his hands until Falwaïn was lifted clear of the dirt ledge where he had lain slumped and moved him onto the grass. Both Warren and Diego jumped off their steeds at once and went to check on their friend.

In the meanwhile, Brother Mire had started the process of getting the loosened dirt from the enlarged hole into the form of a rough ramp. He had barely gotten the first ramp finished before Otis stepped onto it, sank down a few inches, and then carefully made his way along it to the cave below.

The two senior mages went next and the others followed so that soon only some of the Queen's Guards were left above, with all others following Diana and Otis.

Warren brushed the dirt from Falwaïn's clothing, while Diego went back to his horse and got a canteen full of water. Taking out a square of cloth he usually employed as a handkerchief, he used that and the water to clean Falwaïn's face. He put the canteen to Falwaïn's lips and was gratified to see him drink a few mouthfuls.

Falwaïn's eyelids fluttered and he groaned heavily before muttering, "Are they okay? Did you find them?"

Warren put a reassuring hand on his friend's shoulder and said, "Diana is on her way to them, along with the others. They're going to be fine, so don't worry about them."

Falwaïn frowned up at his friends, shaking his head in frustration. "You don't understand! That thing that captured us, whatever it is, has them in some kind of magical coma. Diana won't be able to get them out of that!"

In response to this statement, Warren sat back on his heels and drawled, "I wouldn't be so sure Diana can't do that. She's come a long way with her magical powers in a short time, as have I. As, I'm sure, have several others. Together, there must be something we can do to free them. Plus, Donnie herself must be fighting that thing on some metaphysical plain that none of us could probably ever achieve."

Diego nodded, interjecting confidently, "I believe in Donnie. She will get free of the creature, which I strongly believe to be a Ghérôntog and not just any Ghérôntog. Whether she accomplishes that herself or someone else does, it will not matter, because when she is free she will no doubt make that thing wish it had never gone after her."

"Oh, yes, she will certainly do that!" Warren chortled in agreement. "Donnie is going to make that thing very, very sorry it messed with her."

They each took one of Falwaïn's arms and hauled him to his feet. He stood for perhaps a second and then he dropped to his knees, exhaustion overtaking him once more.

A look of non-verbal communication passed between Warren and Diego and they nodded to each other. For the first time, they recognized the kinship of their people between them, their Iquakawi blood singing in their ears. The two stood together, one arm over the other's shoulders, with their free hands gripping Falwaïn's shoulders. They concentrated on their magic, intent upon doing what they'd seen Donnie and Diana do, which was to draw magic from the earth below them and let it flow between them and into Falwaïn, focusing on their urgent purpose of rejuvenating their friend after his near-fatal ordeal. It took them a while, but when they got it right, they both felt magic coursing through their bodies and then, with great joy at their success, they sent it into Falwaïn.

Its effects were immediately evident, and it was not long before he himself was standing before them, flexing his muscles and nodding to his friends with gratitude. And then the three of them leapt down the first ramp and the second and then the third, each level growing darker and darker. Warren snapped his fingers and a small light ball appeared. While its wan light was not enough to light the entire chamber, it was sufficient for them to find the next ramp down and so on until they came into the crowded chamber just above where Donnie, Rex, and Wiwila still lay.

Diana had led Gallantry up from below and he was now standing near the last ramp. She turned to see the others coming down from the upper level and reached over to grasp Falwaïn's arm in greeting.

"We can't go down there yet," she informed them crisply. "The Sûlrím are still doing their thing, and believe me, none of us wants to get caught up in that." She shuddered and grimaced expressively before explaining, "They're shredding the walls, especially the ones in what must be the central part of this damned prison. Apparently, that's where the creature is, or at least part of it's there. I went down to that level for a minute or two and saw all these weird little monster things with slimy black tentacles that are about thirty feet long being released from the holes the Sûlrím are cutting into the central shaft while they're flying their circles around the room. Not that any of those *things* lived for much longer than about two seconds after the Sûlrím noticed them." She shuddered again. "There is nothing like seeing a living creature sliced and diced into little bits to make you gain a whole lot of respect for those birds. And to have a desire to stay far, far out of their way!"

Then she threw back her head, snorted and said, "And you know what? Not a damn one of 'em is changing their color to anything but blazing pure white! Every time I look down there, all I see are hundreds of white streaks flying in big circles, rippin' everything to shreds. Well, everything except the A'Rontauk, because, as Otis reminded me, the Sûlrím have been known as the Salvation of A'Rontauk for centuries and I guess now we know why! Akanna says it's another prophecy from that good ol' mage in the mountain. He was quite an accomplished guy, it seems," she quipped, her worry and nervousness showing plainly to her friends by the chattiness that had overtaken her normal reserve. Even those who didn't know her noticed the agitated edge to her voice. "In case you're wondering, an A'Rontauk is a magical triad. In this instance, it's those three still out cold on the floor below us."

Diego stepped forward and put his arms around her to draw her close, just for a moment. He whispered something calming into her ear and then moved back after releasing her.

Diana gave him a tremulous smile and heaved a heartfelt sigh as she shook out her arms and shoulders. "Yeah, I know she will," she murmured, "I do really. It's just that I kind of hoped she'd be awake by now."

Diego let out a small chuckle. Then his face sobered and he said in a low voice, informing them all, "I believe those things with the tentacles are called Aspheira. They are known to be found wherever there is a Ghérôntog, but whether they are part of the Ghérôntog or created by it, or are something completely separate from it, no one seems to know. But it is certain they communicate with the larger beast; whether that is by actual sound or telepathy or by some other means, is also unclear."

Akanna nodded and said gravely, "Yes, and they are deadly if they get those tentacles around you. They will strangle or squeeze the breath out of you in seconds. If you encounter one, you must attack the tentacles first and cut them from the main body or you will not escape with your life."

"And that is why, I for one, am most content to let the Sûlrím take care of as many of them as possible," added Diego, and just about everyone nodded or grimaced in agreement.

And so they waited for the birds to finish their gruesome task. The sounds coming from below were often sickening, for when a new Aspheira creature appeared out of one of the holes created by the Sûlrím, it would screech momentarily and then a noise like many knives cutting through a slab of meat would sound, with a corresponding patter of small thuds as the pieces hit the ground.

It was several minutes before there came a total silence from the lower chamber. Diana was the first to bound down the earthen ramp. She threw several balls of silver flame outward and the chamber walls were covered with dancing shadows. When the mages followed her, a couple were able to create light balls and these were added to the light of the fires zooming overhead. These lights revealed a large, gaping hole in the far wall, open from floor to ceiling, where the central shaft connected the chambers, or cells, of the prison to each other.

Diana strode over to look down into this wide shaft but had to step back almost immediately because the Sûlrím were flying straight for her face. She jerked backward and held her breath as they streamed upward in front of her, shining brilliant white as they passed. A few moments later, she detected some faint rays of natural light filtering down to where she was, then those were eclipsed as the birds dove downward into the central shaft again.

She turned and looked at the three figures lying still on the ground. She realized that a protective shield of someone's making had kept Donnie and the others from being plastered with viscera from the Aspheira that the birds had shredded.

Suddenly, there seemed to be way too many people in the chamber and Diana's heart started pounding because the damn A'Rontauk had yet to awaken and were not responding to anyone's ministrations. She felt panic rise in her breast just like it used to do before she'd given up on magic and had decided she couldn't be much of anything to anyone anymore, even her bond-mate Otis, and she had left everyone and everything behind. She tried to clamp down on this feeling, but it was getting the better of her and she knew she had to release it somehow or it would release itself badly. Already she was pacing rapidly back and forth behind everyone while they tried to get Donnie and the others to awaken and respond.

She made another full pass and then she could stand it no longer. She drew in her power, crossed her arms and pressed her palms to her shoulders, crying out in her loud, overpowering goddess voice, "Wake up, Donnie! For Fortin's sake, wake up!"

Even though her cry shouldn't have worked, it did, for Donnie's head lifted, her eyes opened, and she retorted sleepily, "All right, already, I'm awake! Sheesh, there's no need to shout like that. Hells hags, Diana!"

Falwaïn, who was kneeling at her side, swept her up into his arms and he buried his face in her neck, sobbing tears of joy.

Rex and Wiwila were roused too by Diana's bellowing and they lifted their heads, stared around them with cautious, blinking eyes, and slowly got to their feet as Diana, Diego, Warren, and even Akanna ran frantic hands over their bodies and legs, just to make sure the animals were okay. Sylvester stood under Rex's head, rubbing his head and neck against the dog's chest and purring affectionately, he was so pleased to have them all back.

Donnie extricated herself from her lover's grasp only after kissing him soundly and fully upon the lips, and then she strode up to Diana and threw her arms around her, giving the other woman a long embrace.

"It's about time you got here," she drawled, finally putting Diana from her and studying her friend's face. "I can't do this without you, you know. We're both going to be needed, believe me. While I was under that darned enchantment, I took the liberty of doing a little investigating of my own and I've learned a bit about the thing entrenched below us." She turned and looked around at the others, telling them, "By the way, I could hear you all talking, I just couldn't respond. But I certainly heard and marked what Diego said about this being not just any Ghérôntog." Her gaze settled on him and she gave him an encouraging nod.

He grinned in acknowledgement and said, "I believe there has always just been one Ghérôntog. The same Ghérôntog." He turned to the others, many of whom had gasped or were staring at him skeptically, to explain, "While it is believed that two separate Ghérôntogs have been killed throughout history, once by the daughters of Morrían and once by Déagmun and his fellow wizards, I think it was the same Ghérôntog both times and it was not killed, just driven farther into the bowels of the earth. And then something would make it come back near the surface, which I think is when it found or was led to another magical land." He looked back at Donnie, who was nodding thoughtfully, and said, "As a matter of fact, I believe that this one Ghérôntog has destroyed the Ugelonds of Oganæ, the Ferlonds on Fellowes Island in Nœthlangan, the Callalonds of Trenethera, and now the

Mîrlonds of Gainál. And that means that if we don't kill it now, it will attack the Ganlonds next."

Looking impressed, Donnie smiled at him and quipped, "Well, then, we'll have to make sure we destroy it for real this time, won't we? I won't have it attacking the Ganlonds. They are the last true magical lands here in Medregai other than the Tower, which is magical because of the way it was blessed, or so Nagba explained to me in one of our talks. So, I don't think it would ever be attacked by the Ghérôntog."

She turned to Akanna with regret and told her, "I'm sorry, Akanna, but I don't think we can save the Mîrlonds because they have been too far gone for many long years now. I think Diego is correct and this one Ghérôntog was already attacking the Mîrlonds even before Diana—or Ghira Ma'Hai as some of you know her—I think the Ghérôntog was already emplaced here and feeding before she left, and that was why she was tricked or driven away, so that it could feed freely without anyone strong enough being around to stymie its reach. But even if Diana had remained here, she would not have been able to stop the Ghérôntog, only slow it down, and would probably have died doing that." She looked at each of the other vincans and the mages singly, and finally landed her gaze upon Diana.

"All of which means," she said to her friend softly, "the Mîrlonds were doomed with or without you. Catie was not strong enough to have been able to help you stop the Ghérôntog, none of the mages here are strong enough for that either, but I think together you and I and all those with us can. As a group, I believe we can vanquish this demon." She waved a hand that encompassed everyone assembled. She smiled solemnly at her friend and asked, "What do you think?"

Diana swallowed hard, then set her lips to a firm line. Nodding once, she replied, "I think you're right, especially with those damn birds helping us. No matter what, we have to give it our best. And if there's anything, any weapons or such that we can use to help us, we should figure those into our plan."

Diego again spoke up to say, "The lore states that blades tempered in magical flame are reported to be more effective against the tough outer hide and the many branches, if you will, of the Ghérôntog. You see, the main body of the beast is covered by layers of thick skin, and each layer is purportedly tougher than the next. But we must somehow cut through these layers and slay the branches that are attached to it and whatever Aspheira are protecting them. Be aware that the whole thing may move underground, as it did with Déagmun and the wizards, and, if or when it does, it can take whole mountains with it, so we must all be prepared for anything to occur around us. Expect sneak attacks and cave-ins, and anything else you have ever encountered in any fight in which you have participated." He was silent a moment, chewing his lip and considering, then he looked at Akanna and asked her, "Can you think of anything else we learned at the Tower that they should know?"

She shrugged diffidently, her strong features set with disappointment ever since Donnie had voiced her assessment of the Mîrlonds' fate. "Not really, no," she replied quietly, "other than it is best if we work in pairs so we can watch each other's backs. Between the beast's unpredictability and the tentacles of the Aspheira, it is likely to be a battle many of us will not survive."

Donnie shot Akanna a sympathetic look. Nevertheless, she cleared her throat and said to the vincan a little reprovingly, "None of us can afford to go into this with a defeatist attitude, my friend." She paused meaningfully. "I want us all to survive and to enjoy many long years of friendship and comradery upon the Ganlonds, where all magical creatures of good and kind intent can thrive and will always be welcome." She touched the vincan's grey-skinned, muscular arm and sent a blessing for love and calm soul through her touch. She understood that Akanna's heart was breaking, for Akanna had convinced herself that the Mîrlonds could survive the beast that was consuming its life blood, so to find out now that those hopes had been in vain was a crushing defeat for the vincan, who was unused to losing any fight. But Donnie was not going to let anyone go into this new battle feeling so low.

Akanna felt the blessing, heard its message for her, resisted it for a few moments, but then she gave in and nodded in acceptance. With the help of the blessing, she steeled her heart for battle, and also hardened her resolve to make the Ghérôntog and whoever had helped it pay for their misdeeds.

Diana, who had been thinking hard about what Diego and Akanna had described of the Ghérôntog's traits, suggested tentatively, "If that thing can move a mountain, then what will it do to the land above us? And can it move, say as far as either Canta Lem or Morlant?" She looked at Donnie, who had moved over to one of the balls of flames that Diana had created and was studying it thoughtfully.

She caught the question in Diana's voice and turned to her friend with raised eyebrow. "Are you thinking that we should send out messengers to warn of possible calamity?" When Diana nodded, Donnie said to Akanna, "She's right. The magical community needs to be warned, as do the two cities and their outer settlements."

Akanna glanced over at her father, then at her brother, and ordered, "Durreen, you go to Canta Lem. Father can go to Morlant."

Both men protested this vehemently. Durreen refused to go anywhere at all and Akanna finally had to give in to him as he got wilder and wilder in his refusals to leave. When the ambassador also refused to countenance such a move, his guards argued with him that he must indeed be the one to go. They even implied that they would force him, if necessary, and he eventually agreed, though it was clear he was quite angry about it. In the end, the two stallions, Radocan and Ludrid, were sent on a swift gallop to warn what was left of the magical community living in the Mîrlonds, while the vincan ambassador headed toward Morlant and safety with one of his guards. Additionally, two Queen's Guards were sent to Canta Lem to warn that vincan community, along with the youngest and most inexperienced mage, leaving eight Sarn guards, eight vincan guards, five mages, and ten magical creatures from the Mîrlonds, including two eagles, a crow and an owl, two deer stags, two wolves, and two bears.

During this discussion, Donnie continued to eye Diana's balls of silver flames with great interest. When the messengers had gone, she extended her right hand, palm up, and a ball of blue flames sprang to life just above her skin. She sent this fire toward one of Diana's. The two flames whirled around each other, going faster and faster until there was just one flame, which was still silver, but with blue tips.

With a satisfied smile, she looked around at Aldalis Munkinum and, with a gesture, invited him to add to the fire if he could. His fire, small but bright, was hot yellow in color and it too was soon mingled with the others. Brother Mire lent his green fire, and Warren his glacial blue. Diego and Falwaïn were unable to produce a flame by themselves, but only just. Both were so close that Diana and Donnie lent a touch of their magic to those of the man beside her and two more flames were added to the mix. By the time the entire assembly was finished adding to it, thirty flames had been mixed to create one big ball of flames that still burned mostly silver at its base, with tips of varying colors dancing about in all directions.

Donnie crossed her arms in front of her and pressed her palms to her shoulders, sending a request down into what was left of the magical lands to ask for any other help it could lend to the flames. For a long time, nothing happened, so Donnie sent her request down farther, deep into the earth, and this time the Flame of Ívers'Fa appeared upon her shoulder. It was there for but a moment, just long enough for a small splinter to become enjoined with the group's main flame, and then the ancient magical flame, as was its wont, disappeared back to its hiding place upon the Ganlonds.

A crystal sphere had also appeared and it hovered in front of Diana. It was about three inches in diameter and had hundreds of small facets that glittered and refracted the light from the flames floating a foot away.

Diana gasped and reached for it, her voice full of happy wonder as she cried, "I thought these were all gone!" Her fingers wrapped around it and it began to hum instantly. Its color changed, ranging randomly from white to gold to orange to red to purple to blue, then green and back to white, then the color shifts started all over again.

Diana glanced over at Donnie excitedly, her gaze falling back to the crystal as she explained, "It's an ovid weapon called a *vandonen*, or tracer. Each color it exhibits does something different, like if I choose it to be green it will cover any object it hits in a sort of strait-jacket, making it so the object or person or whatever it hits can't move for at least five minutes. The blue shift encases its targets in ice, and red engulfs them in flames."

Others had crowded around to get a closer look and so she showed it to them on her raised palm.

"It only works for ovids, which I guess is why only one came—if there are any more than that still in existence, I mean." She shook her head and again looked at Donnie, a bemused smile upon her face. "There were never that many around, but most of those were stolen and never recovered."

"Stolen by whom?" Donnie asked curiously, peering more closely at the stunningly beautiful ball displayed on Diana's open hand.

"Mine was stolen by another ovid who'd lost hers in a rigged game of chance she was foolish enough to play with a sorcerer named Gilo Barren. That was centuries ago," Diana replied, her eyes filled with remembrance. "I'm not sure about all the others, but I do recall that the three or four sister ovids I met over the years had theirs stolen as well." She shrugged. "I don't know much more than that. But these tracers, in the hands of an ovid who knows how to use them, are impossible to defeat." She bounced the crystal *vandonen* up in the air a few inches and caught it deftly in her hand, her fingers tight around its circumference. After catching it, she nodded to Donnie with satisfaction. "This makes me feel much more confident about how much I can help you," she said quietly.

Donnie smiled widely at the other woman. "Oh, my dear sister goddess, trust me when I say that you and I will do all kinds of good deeds together. We've barely begun to scratch the surface of our combined talents. We two shall stand together for a long time to come. Don't ask me how I know that, but I definitely do know it."

She felt the restlessness of the others around them and so she turned to the flame and announced in a strong, commanding voice, "Those with weapons to be tempered in our flame should join around it now in a circle." She herself stepped back to allow others to come closer and gather around the ball of flames hovering in the air.

All of the remaining Queen's Guards and the vincans stepped closer to the ball of fire, as did Diana, Falwaïn, Warren and Diego. Upon Donnie's directive, they all lifted their blades to the flames. The flames brightened so that they were blazing, and then the fire traveled the length of each blade at the same time, making for a kind of spoked star effect. Donnie told them to hold their swords high and they all did so. The flames blazed and roared for a few seconds more and then, as one, they fell into their respective blade and disappeared, leaving the metal shining with silvery gilded edges.

One of the mages asked if they could do the same with their wands and Donnie nodded approvingly. This time, it was only she and the five mages who stood around the ball of flames. Their wands were lit with the magical flames for a few seconds until they too absorbed the fantastical fires.

Before anyone could say or do anything else, the ball of flames itself split into several smaller balls which then zoomed to the claws, hooves, beaks, horns and such of the animals in the group and lit them brightly for a moment before they too disappeared.

Donnie chuckled and said to the surprised onlookers, "And now we all have either a weapon or a tool that has been reinforced with the magic, intent, and will of us as a whole." She turned to make sure she was facing everyone and said, "We must all choose a partner. Diana and I will be the lead team. There are amongst us some who will not be comfortable attacking another fellow creature." She paused and looked at first Rex and then at Durreen, smiling at them both. "I respect that choice, especially since I am one myself, but we can certainly protect our partners and we can do other things to ensure our success today."

She paused, smiled ruefully at the ground, and allowed, "I understand that I will likely be forced to harm the creature entrenched below us, and I will accept any and all consequences for that. But I am not a warrior like so many of you are, so if you feel I am endangering anyone by my actions, step in and do what I cannot. I will not resent that. I fully comprehend that we are here to destroy the thing, not save it, as is my chosen way of living."

She felt a hand squeeze her shoulder and turned to see Warren smiling at her reassuringly. Grasping his fingers in hers for a moment, she smiled back at him gratefully.

Before mounting Wiwila, she strode over to Falwaïn and they shared a long and lingering kiss while the others readied themselves. Parting from her man reluctantly, she climbed aboard her horse, then looked around for Sylvester. He was murmuring something to himself and when he was done, he transformed into his black panther form, his claws and teeth both shining with silver light. Apparently, he and Rex were pairing up, and so Rex came to stand beside him, staring up at Donnie and waiting for her to get things rolling.

She turned Wiwila to face the others and said to them, "We have to go deep, which is why the Sûlrím cleared out the central shaft, enlarging it where they could. Some of them will try to force oxygen down to us when they can, while others will join us in the fight. Just be prepared, because it's going to be very hot and airless down there."

She wheeled Wiwila back around and lifted her wand, but before she could say her spell the boombox appeared and bound itself to the saddle. It belted out the first scream of the classic "Immigrant Song" and she screamed along with it, if only to release some of the tension inside her tight chest, for she was as worried as any of the others of what would occur in the next few hours, although all were facing the coming battle bravely. Her voice rang out above the song as she canted,

"Our path must be cleared,
and to danger we will ride.
    Our hearts may be filled with fear,
but we have purpose on our side.
    Together we shall fight,
two by two and all in stride.
    Unyielding in our might,
for magic's homeland to survive."

The ground in front of her moved and its soil was rearranged into yet another ramp like those leading to the surface. Donnie snapped her fingers and four very bright light balls flew into the chamber below, with Wiwila following them immediately and Otis fast on her heels.

Down, down, down they went, and it did indeed become hotter and hotter. Several among their group threw off cloaks and capes, leaving them where they fell onto the rich, black soil of the deep earth of the caves below. Donnie calculated that they were nearly half a mile down when they reached the final level of cells. Underneath this level was a huge cavern that dropped to inky black. Donnie's spell built a ramp for them to descend that was several hundred feet long and, when they reached the cavern's floor, only darkness greeted them.

The boombox was still with them and had played hard-driving rock songs during their entire sojourn to the bottom. It bucked that trend a little by playing the haunting rock ballad "In the Dark."

Donnie, not telling anyone what she was going to do other than to shout out, "Everyone get ready!", had the four light balls split hundreds of times in an instant so that suddenly there was enough light to make it look like daylight had just broken through from above.

And the moment she did this, several objects near and far began to move until it was clear that all of them were part of the same creature. The branches that Diego had spoken about moved like ribbons that could cut through both earth and rock with ease. Several of these snaked around the feet of the horses, who had to jump and wheel around so that they were not caught up by the branches or any of the spidery smaller branches that shot from the thicker ones like thousands of sharp fingers clutching at its enemies.

Donnie and Diana urged their horses to the center column, jumping and hopping as necessary to get there. This central trunk of the monstrous beast was blackened and looked like hardened tar. Diana threw the tracer and it sliced through this outer layer, revealing pink flesh within the cut, and another dark layer beyond. Donnie used her magic as a wedge to widen this cut, pointing her wand at it and streaming a wide swathe of her power into it which pushed on the edges, forcing them apart. A cloud of Sûlrím dove into this wound and shredded it until it ripped all the way around the central column and the layer snapped apart.

In the meantime, Diana was hacking at flying branches, making sure that none of them reached Donnie or Wiwila. She glanced around and saw that all of the others were engaged in similar battles as she, with everyone fighting desperately for their lives. The mages were each paired with a Queen's Guard, while Falwaïn and Warren were battling at each other's side and Diego and Akanna were fighting back-to-back, both having let their horses go free.

Their group had managed to wade deeper through the many branches of the Ghérôntog and all were hacking or slicing away at arms and fingers with every blow or spell that found their targets. And when some Aspheira showed up, the mages worked up a spell to set their long tentacles on fire and the spherical demon creatures smashed to the floor with satisfying thuds. They were then set upon by blade, teeth and claws and were soon nothing but mounds of pulpy flesh.

Donnie and Diana, with the aid of the Sûlrím, made it through another three layers of the Ghérôntog's tough hide and were starting on the fifth one when a terrifying scream rent the air.

Diana called to Donnie that she would take care of whatever was happening behind them as she recalled the crystal tracer to her hand. She whirled atop Otis and cringed as she saw one of the mages impaled on the tip of an infiltrating branch of the Ghérôntog. The branch had penetrated through his chest and his lifeless body swung awkwardly upon it as it shot toward the Queen's guard who had been fighting beside the dead mage. Durreen sprang from his horse, his sword arcing toward the branch. He severed the branch, but too late for the guard, whose scream it was that had cause Diana to whirl.

Donnie called to her, "What's happened?" She was focusing her power on the cut Diana's *vandonen* had made in the Ghérôntog's hide.

"Two of ours are down for good," Diana panted back to her, throwing the tracer again to help widen the cut Donnie was working on. "Several others are hurt, some badly, but only those two are dead."

"I think we're almost through," Donnie said, twisting her stream of magic so that it ripped at the edges of the tracer's cut. And a moment later, that layer also snapped open all the way around. Beyond it was nothing and so, with apprehensive looks at each other, they moved with their horses to the edge of the central column and leaned over to look down. Shooting up at them was a whole phalanx of Aspheira. The horses jumped back just barely in time. Donnie threw up a protective shield in front of them all, which the Aspheira bounced over into the cavern behind them.

The Sûlrím swarmed overhead, soaring in concert toward the main flow of Aspheira coming from below. The hundreds of birds poured into the cavern and swarmed the spidery invaders.

Donnie jumped from her horse to the ground, as did Diana, and the two stood together, facing each other calmly with clasped hands. Donnie shouted over the din everyone was making, "Let's concentrate on tying their tentacles together, really tightly. So tight, in fact, that they break off! Ready?" she asked breathlessly, and Diana gave a short nod.

The two goddesses reached down into the ground and drew up a huge stream of pure magical power, passing it back and forth between them for about ten seconds. Their faces were set in determination and they had their eyes closed. Each heard, but did not heed, the bellowing coming from below while they retrieved the stolen magic from the Ghérôntog.

In moments, they both glowed brightly, Donnie with her blue-colored magic and Diana with her silver. At the same instant, both let loose like a bomb, and their magical power, which was infused with their intent from their combined spell, shot outward from their chests in all directions to fill the cavern.

The Aspheira were crushed, tighter and tighter, until tentacles dropped to the floor, torn off by the women's spell. The dark creatures screamed and screamed, and then it was as though the entire world tilted and fell.

Donnie and Diana were still standing together, their eyes closed, and their expressions set grimly. Both felt themselves falling. Diana opened her eyes, saw what was happening and leapt for the open central shaft, dragging Donnie with her. Donnie, knowing that Diana would keep her safe, concentrated on sending all the others to the Eireni Glæd.

The two Ér Ainíls fell toward the open maws of the Ghérôntog. Its giant head was lifted up toward the main chamber, the floor of which was falling right alongside the goddesses to the even larger cavern below. The black beast was bleeding profusely from the cuts made by the goddesses and it was holding an injured appendage to the side as it screamed in its fury and its agony.

The two women fell and fell and neither said a word, knowing that being in the belly of the beast was exactly where they needed to be. Around them dove the Sûlrím.

Far above, the rest of their group, who were weary, sore and bleeding from the battle, tumbled to the ground or staggered to keep their feet within the glade, which was already filled with the denizens of the Mîrlonds. Falwaïn and Warren both sprang up furious to be transported away from the fight at this point, as were Sylvester, Brother Mire and several of the others, but both Diego and Akanna were the ones who understood that they had succeeded in getting the goddesses to the best point possible and they shouted this over the remonstrations the others were making.

"I am telling you, we have done all we can do!" Akanna cried, standing tall before those who were clamoring to go back, her hands placed firmly on her hips and a reproving expression set upon her face. "We always knew someone was going to have to go into the chamber where the beast was nested and dig it out. To get there was nearly impossible, we feared. But we just did exactly that, don't you see? And now they two alone are able to fight the beast effectively. We, the rest of us, have to stay here where it is safe, especially if they fail. We will be safe here because it is the safest place on Írtha, just like the Glimmering Glade on the Ganlonds, because here we are protected by Írtha herself." She looked up and around at the glade and added, "Trust me, if they fail, we'll have to regroup once the ground stops shaking. And we will have to decide if we try again to kill the beast or if let it kill all magic here in Medregai and eventually in Írtha."

She shivered and hung her head, so tired she thought she might not be able to stand even another minute of this life. All during the fight there had been so many fingers and branches snaking and sneaking everywhere, in all directions, catching them each by the ankles or the wrist or somewhere even more tender before they were saved by some brave member of their group. All had risked their lives several times over and all were white and drained with shock from the sudden pandemonium that had occurred the moment Donnie's light balls had awakened the beast. All, deep in their heart of hearts were grateful for their abrupt rescue to the Peaceful Glade.

The sights and sounds of the battle that had just been fought would haunt everyone there for years to come, that was certain. And now all any of them could rightly do was to sink to the ground and breathe with relief that they did not have to hear another screech of an Aspheira; or get strangled by their rubbery tentacles as one bear and three Queen's Guards had been at the last; or feel the tough, roughened skin of the Ghérôntog's thousands of fingers clamping down onto their own flesh; or watch anyone else get impaled by a deadly, sharply pointed branch of that evil beast that seemed to be far too large to be bested by anyone.

Two of the mages were crying, whispering near gibberish to each other and staring at their leader, Aldalis Munkinum, with blank and watery eyes. He and Brother Mire were on their knees facing each other, and both had their eyes closed and their hands clasped and laying upon their laps. They, like many others all around the glade, were running through every prayer they knew to recite, all hoping against hope that the goddesses would somehow be victorious.

Chapter 27
The Promise

Donnie stopped their descent with a wave of her hand and around them the wings of the Sûlrím seemed to beat in rhythm with her heart. She and Diana floated about a hundred feet above the screaming Ghérôntog and both were covering their ears to abate the sound. The Ghérôntog's face and ears were covered in old scars and wounds that had not healed well, from the looks of them. The closer they got to the beast, the more scars they could see on its numerous appendages, many of which were flapping and reaching upward. Donnie scanned the ground below, her eyes darting here and there with increasing dread, but she was afraid to land anywhere because she had no idea what was rock and what was monster.

"We have to go in, Donnie," Diana shouted, pointing downward at the monster's mouth.

Reluctantly, Donnie acknowledged this, and they resumed their fall, only this time she controlled it with her magic. The Sûlrím dove in before them and shredded the beast's throat, with the tongue and teeth all ripped to pieces before they were done and had moved on.

Diana shoved Donnie behind her as they flew through the air, and then she threw the tracer straight down the throat of the profusely bleeding and mortally wounded Ghérôntog. The weapon's color was orange when it was thrown and, when it hit its target, they were blasted backward. Donnie kept them righted so that when they fell again, they were still on track to fall straight down the thing's throat.

The *vandonen* returned to Diana's hand and she threw it again, only this time it took a while to return. Diana caught it and said, "The real beast is not this. I'm not even sure if the next one is."

This statement was explained when Donnie sent out some light balls once they were through the throat and the balls showed that they were in another cavern, but its sides were heaving with pain, so it must have been part of the beast. Another battered and scarred head lay still on the floor of this new cavern, with fresh, gaping holes cut into it by the Sûlrím, who were now not only out of sight, but out of hearing range. Diana and Donnie fell into the torn throat of this next beast and found themselves inside an ice cavern, with yet another badly scarred and deformed monster down below.

And here were the birds. This ice beast they were struggling greatly with because they could not penetrate its skin quite so easily. Diana threw the tracer down its maw and the crystal weapon exploded again. The ice beast broke into a million pieces, and then it reformed and broke again. It went through this four times until Diana again threw the tracer and flames shot out of the beast's throat while it screamed its death agonies.

The Sûlrím dove past the flames and into the beast's throat. Donnie put up a protective shield for her and Diana and they too fell through the fire.

And now they were in a cavern so vast, Donnie's light balls had almost no effect at all; they were just lights falling downward in an endless sea of velvety blackness. Donnie sent more light balls shooting in all directions, but it was a long time before any of them lit up anything solid.

And still they fell downward.

By the time they got even remotely close to the beast awaiting them below, they knew that this one was it, this was the final aspect of the monster that had to be destroyed. They both felt this with such surety in their hearts. Donnie again sent out several light balls, having them zoom at twice their normal speed so that she had a good idea of what was there before they got too close to change course. They landed on top of a bluff that the creature had a portion of its tail wrapped around. Even though this bluff was a couple hundred feet tall, the beast's massive head hung high above them. It snorted suddenly, and the magnified sound reverberated for what felt like half an hour.

Donnie studied it with her mind's eye and was soon marveling over its size and weight. It was larger than anything she'd ever encountered or thought to encounter—in fact, it was hundreds of times larger than both Uncle and Murlaín put together, and they had both dwarfed Donnie. When the Ghérôntog snorted again, it was more of a growl, and they could sense its very long tail slipping into a tighter curl around the bluff they were standing upon.

"Er, hi!" Donnie called out to it, and Diana turned to her in disbelief. Donnie shrugged and muttered, "It's worth a try, isn't it?"

The beast batted at one of her light balls, sending it arcing far away. It did the same to several more and, when Donnie called them back to her, a massive head was lowered and one word was hissed at her. "Stop!" it said, and Donnie did.

She looked at Diana, who was looking back at her with raised brows. "I guess it doesn't like light," she whispered, and Diana whispered back, "I think you're right." Nevertheless, Donnie kept a light ball on either side of them so they could see if the beast was about to come too near.

Donnie had no idea where the Sûlrím were at the moment. She could not hear them, nor see any sign of them. She'd noticed that when they flew they were white in color, but when they were motionless, they went dark. What this meant now, she had no idea, but she knew they had to be somewhere here in this cavern.

"Who are you?" she said conversationally, looking up at the monster, which she could just see outlined by the light balls far behind it and which was more of a shadow in the wan light of the one light ball floating by her side. She went on, introducing herself and Diana. "Er, you might even sort of know Diana," she said musingly. "I mean, she was Ér Ainíl by the time you came here and started feeding on the magic of the Mîrlonds."

The thing moved its head closer and both women could see large, dull and milky circles shining back at them.

"It's blind," Diana said in a low voice to Donnie. Her voice dropped to a mere whisper when she noted, "It must be its skin that's photo sensitive."

"I can feel you well enough, ovid. I do not need eyes for that," it hissed back, its voice gravelly and edged with a what felt like a long-sustained fury. Its words echoed around the cavern for a very long time.

When silence finally came, Donnie noted to her friend, "I think he does know you. Well, I say he, but he could be a she. Correct me if you want," she suggested, looking up at the beast with a forced, bright smile.

The beast lifted its head and they could no longer see its dully shining eyes. "There is another of you here. Show yourself, witch, or I will kill these silly novices standing before me."

Donnie and Diana looked at each other and then into the darkness around them in surprise. Neither had felt anyone else's presence.

And yet, there came the sound of the Sûlríms' wings from behind them. Both women crouched low, readying themselves for battle, in case the birds attacked the beast. But all that happened was that the Sûlrím began to alight in the darkness behind them on the bluff.

The Ghérôntog sniffed the air, then its head again was thrust forward so that it could peer at those upon the bluff. It hissed angrily, and raised its head back up, snarling, "You! I know you from the Ugelonds."

A voice, low and melodic, sounded from behind Donnie and Diana, startling them. It said simply, "Yes, it is I, Briganna."

And then a woman, tall and fit, with long dark hair and blue, blue eyes, dressed in a blue robe that fell to the floor in glorious, white-edged folds strode into the circle of light from Donnie's light balls. She herself seemed outlined in a faint, white aura that made her glow ethereally.

Donnie took a staggering step backward in shock. "Briganna? It can't be you!" she gasped, and Diana looked between the other two women, her own shock registered plainly on her face.

Briganna came to a stop beside her youngest sister and smiled at her, murmuring with delight, "Little sister, it is a pleasure to finally meet you in my old form. I cannot sustain this body forever, but I will hold it for long enough today." She smiled again, this time quite sadly. Her gaze traveled over Donnie and she said, "You are more like Mother than all the rest of us, except perhaps Margawse. I can feel Mother in you, you know. She really did pass on to you all she could of her power and her talents. And you are doing well with them. She would be proud of you, as am I. You and your friends were the only ones, besides myself, who figured out that the same beast had destroyed all the magical lands here in Medregai." She beamed at Donnie again and said, "You have surrounded yourself with far more trustworthy friends than the rest of us ever managed. That says something about you, you know. I suppose that, like Mother, you instinctively read a triune and know its true nature. That is a trait none but you share with her. I have been glad to be able to know you these past months, even though it has been from afar."

"B-but how can this be? I mean, didn't you die long ago?" exclaimed Donnie, her voice filled with awe.

Briganna chuckled bitterly. "For all worldly intents and purposes, yes, I did. But once I returned to Írtha from my travels, I knew exactly what had been done to the magical lands under my care—my dear, wonderful Ugelonds. You see, I too was tricked into leaving them abandoned for a long period of time and this beast was then entrenched below them to eat away and destroy all the magic it could ingest. When I came back and found them dead and withered, I knew all of this with absolute certainty. And so I vowed to trick the trickster."

She took a few steps closer and stared up at the monster, who was still peering down at them from not all that far away.

"Your master, Ixifír Bíun, underestimated me," she told it, her voice gruff. She looked back at Donnie and explained, "I separated my mind and my soul from my body when I found my magical lands dying and knew there was nothing I could do to help them then. So..." she said softly, pausing, "it was just my body that died in the Flame of Ívers'Fa. The rest of me went into the creation of these most righteous birds. And ever since that dismal day, living freely as the Sûlrím, I have fought any and all dark magic wherever and whenever I encountered it, ripping it to shreds the way my love and my heart were destroyed by Ixifír when he betrayed me."

Briganna's eyes glittered with tears, but she sighed heavily and closed them. When she reopened them a few moments later, they were clear and bright with renewed determination. She turned to regard Diana critically for several seconds, then she nodded toward the beast and asked, "Can you get us inside?"

Diana looked from her to Donnie and to the beast, and then back again. She squared her shoulders and replied, "Yes, I can."

While the Ghérôntog may have anticipated the suddenness and method of the attack, it could not stop it. Diana threw the *vandonen* and it struck the beast squarely. The crystal buried itself in the beast's flesh, burrowing in deeper and deeper. Donnie conjured a thick shield around them to protect them from the Ghérôntog's grasping arms and tails, which wrapped themselves around the shield, trying to crush it. Donnie felt it weakening but knew it would hold long enough. And it did.

The tracer, set to white in color, worked much like the Sûlrím would. It shredded flesh and bone and soon the many arms and tails of the beast left Donnie's shield and clawed at its throat, trying desperately to stop the crystal weapon's destruction. But it was too late, and flailing appendages fell limp to the ground, and the great head toppled to the side and slumped down with a great shattering and shaking of the cavern.

The tracer returned to Diana's hand and Briganna looked at her with admiration. "I have known only one other ovid who could do that. She must have been your mother, you know. At least, you look just like her."

Diana's eyes widened and her jaw dropped. "What?" she spluttered.

Briganna nodded. "Yes. When you go in search of her, look for an ovid named Averie Bagam Am'Bal." She turned to Donnie and held out her hand. "And now, Sister, we must destroy the final beast. There is only one way for us to do that, so be sure to shield your eyes," she warned Diana, twining her fingers with Donnie's. "You'll know when."

"Here, Di, here's some welding goggles. They will help," Donnie said, materializing a pair, which she handed to Diana.

Diana, still stunned, could only nod and take the goggles, trying hard to keep her wits about her. She had always thought her mother had been a whore of the Mehen'Adríum and that she herself was a bastard child, but now...Briganna's conjecture filled her heart with excitement. Could she have been that wrong about her beginnings?

She watched bemusedly as Donnie floated herself and Briganna over to where an opening in the Ghérôntog's flesh revealed what looked like perhaps yet another cavern, this one much smaller than any of the others. Diana watched them settle to the floor and squinted so she could see the odd blob that was situated right in the center of this smaller cavern. She thought that it looked much more vulnerable than any of the other layers had.

Donnie had this same thought as she landed on the floor of the small cavern and looked at what it held. She and her sister had drifted slowly to the center and found there what looked like a sack of blood or some other dark liquid, which moved and pulsated almost like a heart would.

There was no form to it, just a great membrane over what could have been muscles, bones, or some type of internal organ. It nauseated Donnie to watch it, because it was wrong, just wrong in so many, many ways. That should not be a beast, it should not be anything, she thought to herself.

She looked at Briganna uncertainly and her sister squeezed her hand. "Ugly, isn't it?" she said, staring at it intently.

"Yes."

"I believe it was created from the beating heart of a sorcerer, one that lived as a man many millennia ago." She glanced at Donnie, who was as tall as she, but slimmer. "I found that out on Gallena, which is the world I followed Ixifír to all those years ago. Of course, he didn't call himself that when I knew him. To me, he was Lee." She sighed, then shook her head slowly. "Anyway, they took that sorcerer's heart, some evil man named Halis or something like that, they took it right out of his chest, did some dark magic on it, and created the Ghérôntog. It can duplicate itself under the right circumstances, or so I was told on Gallena, but I do not know how much to believe of anything from there."

It was Donnie's turn to squeeze Briganna's hand reassuringly.

Both women looked at each other and then they readied themselves for their task. Briganna, setting herself in a strong stance, said to Donnie, "You will have to be quick about getting yourself and your friend out of here when we're done. I will soon return to being the Sûlrím and we shall again be parted."

Donnie interjected, "You can't...you know, you can't stay like this?"

Briganna said, "No, I am okay for the moment, but only because this is what my purpose is, and I have saved my energy for it. After this, I may occasionally be able to visit with you thusly, but only rarely. And if we survive today, I will always be watching over you as the Sûlrím." She smiled, stood tall again, and drew her youngest sister into her embrace.

They hugged for several seconds, but when Briganna released Donnie, she became all business again.

"As I said, you will have to provide egress for you and your ovid friend, for I will transform almost immediately and will fly toward the surface," she explained.

Donnie chewed her lip. "Will you be fast enough to get out of here?" she asked.

Briganna shrugged. "For me, that does not matter as long as the beast is destroyed. Beyond that, it is only important that you and Diana escape."

"Humph," Donnie grunted, glancing at her sister out of the corner of her eye. "Well, I'm not leaving you behind, so you'd better be able to stay close to me because I'm very fast on my broom, and that's what I'm going to use to get us away."

And she contacted Brindle and told him, as she had on occasion before, that she would need his assistance as her saddle and that he would have to attach himself to the broomstick instantly when she called for him and that he should make sure to extend his seat to fit two, because Diana would be riding behind her. The old tree assured her that he would be ready and even suggested that she materialize the broom to him now, so there would be no delay when she needed him.

She agreed to that and then she took up her sister's hand again, looked over at Briganna, and said quietly, "I'm ready whenever you are."

The two stood together, their hands clasped tightly by the other. They reached out as one and placed their clasped hands upon the last bit of the Ghérôntog that remained. Bile arose in Donnie's throat at the spongy feel of the creature and the unnatural movement below its sack of skin, but she nevertheless kept her hand firmly pressed upon it, and the united sisters let their magic rise. They began to glow with light: Donnie a brilliant, cobalt blue and Briganna a pure, blinding white.

They drew up more magic from the center of the earth and let it flow between them until the ground beneath their feet also began to glow, blue under Donnie and white under Briganna.

Watching from the edge of the high bluff above, Diana put her goggles on and was amazed that she could still see both women clearly through them, black though their lenses were. And then she looked up and realized that she could now see the entire cavern around her, the light from the two witches was increasing so fast. The cavern went on for miles, from what she could tell of it now, and it was all beginning to heave back and forth as though in panic. Diana cried out, but did not know if she was heard, for her instincts made her fall to her knees with her back to the beast and the witches. She tucked her head down and closed her eyes and still it was as though someone was shining a bright light directly into her eyes.

A piercing scream and a long hiss escaped from somewhere nearby. Diana presumed it came from the wretched thing itself, for it was behind her. Another scream sounded, and this time it cursed the daughters of Morrían to eternal damnation. She heard Briganna and Donnie banish it in their clear, raised voices, telling it coldly that not one more of Morrían's daughters would ever be sacrificed to its need again.

It screamed long and loud in pain and then it was silent for several long seconds. Once more it screamed, begging for mercy, and Diana wondered what the sisters were doing to it then, but their light got brighter and Diana had to cross her arms over her face to protect her eyes. Silence came and seemed to suck out all the oxygen and Diana gasped for breath, but then suddenly it was as though the air all around her exploded. Diana felt an overwhelming wave of power hit her skin and she was sent flying. She careened off the bluff and shot straight over its edge before she realized that the light had disappeared and it was safe for her to open her eyes. She tumbled in the air and shouted at Donnie for help, and then felt herself being pulled back through the air toward where she'd just come.

Donnie's earlier words came back to Diana, warning her to be ready for the saddle, and so Diana forced her body to curl into that position. A short moment later, she was on the broomstick behind Donnie, securely strapped in by Brindle, and they were zooming upward. Donnie threw out some more light balls and Diana could see that the cavern had indeed exploded. Great in-rushes of water were tearing at the walls and ceiling and the cavern situated above this one was already falling toward them in great chunks.

Donnie kicked her heels three times and they shot forward again. She forced her mind to clear and let her instinct take over the flying, having that guide them through the cascading debris to the cavern above. But here it was no better, for this cavern too was collapsing inward and debris was zooming around them in all directions.

Donnie looked up and saw the Sûlrím were just now entering the cavern up there. She kicked her heels again and sped after them, singular in her intent, and when she caught up to them, she passed them by, tossing back a magical netting for them to land upon. Three seconds passed while she slowed to let them all perch safely, and then the net closed up and Donnie kicked her heels three times again.

The broomstick leapt upward and soon they were in the central shaft of the prison the Ghérôntog had built. Donnie could see blue sky at the end of the shaft and figured that meant it must be morning already. They were somehow still ahead of the devastating wave that was chasing them to the surface, but only just barely for it was gaining on them with each passing second. When they shot out of the central shaft and to the fresh, clean air, Donnie shouted in surprise to see the face of Aldalis Munkinum turned up toward them at the lip of the shaft.

She had no idea what he was doing, but she knew he would die if she left him there, so she dematerialized him into the ether and waited until she found the Peaceful Glade before materializing him back to the physical plane. Even before he was fully corporeal again, he was grinning with glee and kept shouting repeatedly to the heavens, "Yes, I see! I see!" His arms were raised high and his feet could not stay still, they leapt and danced with a frantic joy, and he could not be restrained for some time.

The others were waiting in the glade, and when Donnie and Diana arrived, Falwaïn dragged Donnie from the saddle and into his arms. "We reunite like this far too often," he complained gruffly, mumbling into her hair as he nuzzled her neck, "but I will accept it because I am overjoyed to find you have returned to me safely once more."

She turned her head to smile against his lips. They kissed each other deeply and felt their bodies relaxing into the embrace.

Rex was leaning against her and even Sylvester was rubbing his head on her leg, so after her wonderfully satisfying kiss with Falwaïn, she reached down and gave them both quick caresses, scratching their ears with love. Then she stood free so she could assess the situation in the glade.

The Sûlrím were perched in the trees above, along with hundreds of other birds of various kinds. The glade was overcrowded with magical creatures who huddled together in fear, shock and sorrow at the loss of their homes. Diana was being hugged in turn by both Warren and Diego. Outside the glade, nature's chaos reigned as entire hills fell into the great gaping hole created by the death of the Ghérôntog and the subsequent subsidence of the magical lands.

Donnie shouted for quiet using her goddess voice and seconds later everyone stared at her in mute silence.

"We must leave here soon," she said, "all of us, because even the glade will fall if we remain." She tersely explained what had happened below and how that was affecting what was going on around them, most of which they could see for themselves.

She turned to Diana and said, "I need you to establish your portal to the Ganlonds. Then get everyone through who wants to go. Can you do that, please?"

Diana nodded and went off to open the *fir'mäela* at the entrance of the glade.

Donnie again used her goddess voice to give them all their choice of destinations. Those who did not wish to go to the Ganlonds, Donnie said would be dematerialized to a spot she remembered just outside Canta'Lem or to one near Anûmanétus.

Aldalis Munkinum, it turned out, had thought to somehow prove to himself that he was as powerful as any witch and had snuck away from the glade as the sun was coming up and the others were engaged in discussing how long they should wait for the Ér Ainíls to return. He had gone to the opening of the central shaft and looked down into it, apparently at the very moment Donnie and her sister had gone super nova with their magic's brilliance. He was completely blinded, likely for life, and all anyone could get out of him currently was nonsense. Brother Mire quietly said that he would take care of the bishop, so they placed the gibbering mage upon his horse and tied him to it to make sure he didn't climb or fall off it inadvertently.

Brother Mire grasped Donnie's forearm in farewell and grinned at her with a new light of respect in his eyes. "Never would I have thought to trust a witch afore, but ye I would embolden not just with me life, but with me coinage as well, knowing both would be returned in whole sum!" he joked bawdily, and Donnie found herself chuckling along with him merely because of the ridiculousness of his statement.

She had never really warmed to any of the wizards and was gladdened when all stated that they wanted to return to Anûmanétus. With a snap of her fingers, she sent those who had survived and the remaining Queen's Guards to a spot near the capital city, along with the bodies of those who had died in the battle with the Ghérôntog, heaving a sigh of relief once they were gone. She had felt so responsible for their well-being ever since agreeing to let them accompany her and her friends to the Mîrlonds and was greatly saddened that not all had made it through with their lives intact. But she knew better than to take on the burden of their deaths, for they had made their choices without coercion and therefore they all must live, or die, with the consequences of those choices whatever they may be.

Donnie turned away to find that Durreen was insisting on staying with his sister, Akanna. They argued about their plans until almost everyone else had left for the Ganlonds. Only Donnie's friends remained, and they ganged up together and ordered the two vincans to travel to the Ganlonds for now because their futures could be sorted later. They reluctantly agreed and stepped through the portal together.

Donnie didn't know what to do with the trees in and around the glade, all of whom had expressed a desire to go along to the Ganlonds, so right before she herself stepped through the portal, as the last one through, she simply dematerialized the entire glade and the ground below it and kept it all in stasis in the ether. When she reached the Ganlonds, after saying hello to Bronadulach and other council members, she was informed by the great bear that the Ganlonds wanted the Peaceful Glade from the Mîrlonds to be situated at the southern end of the new lands they'd created just before they'd set out on their journey nearly three months before.

Donnie touched the ground at her feet, took a moment to enjoy her revitalized and strengthened connection with her own magical lands, and then materialized the Peaceful Glade to the location she was shown by the Ganlonds, the image of the space clearly projected into her mind by the magical force residing deep within her magical lands.

Afterward, Donnie was exhausted and wanted nothing more than to fall into bed and sleep for days, but she was reminded that she had one more task left to accomplish by the boombox, which appeared on the ground in front of her and began to play the beautiful rock ballad, "The Promise."

So, while others were making accommodations for the new inhabitants of the magical lands and old acquaintances were being renewed all around, Donnie went to visit someone she knew reviled her with the deepest of violent passions, because she had a promise to keep with them.

***

Ixifír Bíun surveyed what could be discerned of the darkened chamber around him, a slow, burning anger seething in his chest and crackling from his long fingers in the form of blackest bolts of dark magic. His blue eyes, always so bright and brilliant in their color, were blazing with fury. His tall frame stood taut with tension and even his long blond hair felt raised from his head in frustration. There had been too many mistakes of late; errors out of his control, yes, but ones that were altering his plans all too effectively. He had been counting upon the Ghérôntog surviving all encounters with any witch or wizard looking to destroy it, but this new witch his enemies had called to arms, this damned Donemere, had managed to destroy his father's favorite beast. His own heart had fluttered and come to a momentary stop the moment the Ghérôntog had died and Ixifír had felt instinctively that she was the cause of its demise.

Understanding that her greatest weakness was those who lived on her magical lands, he had traveled immediately to Írtha to protect the one thing he knew she would seek after her success in defeating the Ghérôntog. But he was too late even for that. He glared at the broken shackles on the floor, which had been blasted apart by her magic only minutes before, probably while he was traversing the time portal.

Ixifír exhaled sharply and shook his head, shaking with restrained anger, his thoughts heavy with the need for vengeance. He strode over to the oval mirror on the wall, one of those he'd given Bréagna long ago. The glass allowed them to contact each other wherever they were. Curtailing the desire to let his anger have its way, he settled down onto the stool in front of the mirror and laid a light finger upon its mercurial surface, calling her name softly.

When she finally responded, Bréagna seemed distracted, but she smiled with real joy to see him and cried, "My love, whatever takes you to Lænemeade when you know I am not there?" She did not wait for him to answer the question, but instead chatted on happily. "I am at our latest camp about fifty miles south of Marn Dím. We have the king and his forces on the run and hope to catch them in a trap tomorrow. Since the Great Serpents owe allegiance to us," she babbled, still completely unaware of her lover's ire, "I want to make sure the royal army's passage through Bitterbend will end with us finally smiting that arrogant bastard usurper."

She prattled on a bit longer, her ice-white loveliness as arresting to Ixifír's eye as ever, for to him her perfect face was that of an avenging angel, her eyes the stormy blue of a tempestuous sea, and her curving lips as luscious and full of lustful promise as the blood red gowns with which she was typically garbed. She was beauty itself in all regards, and completely irresistible to those she turned her charms upon. But she had pledged her life to Ixifír and it gave him a thrill to know that she was his unequivocally and without restraint or reservation. She was also his greatest weapon and her dark magic was rivaled only by his own. That made their pairing even more exciting and dangerous, for they both lived to exert their power over those around them in order to subjugate and enthrall, whether it be friend or foe who found themselves the subject of the pair's maleficent desires. It was a black need that connected the two of them at the most primal level, an often wicked compunction to make others bleed, both figuratively and literally.

Ixifír had sought out Bréagna long, long ago when he had felt her break into existence as her true self, even though he had been in another universe and another time. And in that moment, with the connection between them made instantaneously, he had known with utter certainty that she was his and that their destinies were intertwined to the end of time.

When she finally stopped nattering on in order to take a breath, he interjected quietly, "The Great Serpents will not help you. They sent word to that effect, as is relayed here." He picked up a scrap of parchment from the desk on which the mirror resided and looked at it. "One of your soldiers wrote it down for all to see. It says the serpents will side with your young sister and will have no more to do with the sorceress or her icy lover from afar." The parchment in his fingers exploded into flame and turned to ash. Ixifír shrugged, wiping his hand carelessly with a filmy scarf left lying on the table by its gorgeous owner before she'd left on her trek north with most of her army. "At least, I believe that is what is written there. It was nearly unintelligible and impossible to read."

Bréagna scoffed at this news in disbelief, staring in silence at Ixifír's image for several seconds. She was thinking, as he could tell by the sudden flintiness of her eyes, which were turning their darkest blue now, and he knew she was about to go into a tirade that he would be wise to let occur. When she let loose, she railed against the serpents and against her cursed sister so freshly arisen and yet so quickly becoming her greatest enemy. Bréagna condemned magic with several venal epithets because of its determination to forestall or divert her every step, no matter how small or unimportant they were to anyone but her, and she vowed now to have her revenge in any way possible.

Ixifír listened to her a while before beginning to chuckle with no sign of mirth in his laughter. Bréagna, at first, took visible umbrage with this reaction and would have sneered back at him, but he held up a hand to ask, his voice cold and dripping with condescension, "Tell me, dear one; when you created the force field around the injured dragon you chained here for your amusement, did you make any mistakes with it, do you think?"

Bréagna was so taken aback by the oddly off-topic question, she could only shake her head after considering the query.

He looked at her skeptically and raised his eyebrows at her.

"No, it is perfect," she maintained with staunch confidence, her steely eyes flashing with defiance. "No one can reach the dragon but you and I."

He smiled faintly at her reflection, then he turned the mirror so that she could see the empty space where the dragon had been imprisoned for months. It was now empty.

Bréagna gasped and got to her feet, shoving her face toward the mirror on her end. Always volatile, she was about to begin another rant, but Ixifîr stopped her by turning the mirror back to show his face, which he let reflect fully his own wrath at her. Around his form grew a thick field of black, and his eyes and lips darkened to the color of onyx. When he spoke, his sharp words laid little cuts upon Bréagna's perfectly smooth skin and small droplets of blood oozed from these wounds until she cried out in pain and covered her face with her hands to stop their onslaught.

In that moment, Ixifîr did not care at all about her distress.

"First," he spat at her derisively, "you left the force fields around our prisoners at Gjendeben open at the top, which your clever little sister discovered and exploited so she could rescue her friends. And now she has beaten you here because, while you extended the force field overhead, you somehow did not think to do the same underfoot!"

Bréagna sat back from the looking glass in front of her, her shoulders bent and cringing. "What do you mean?" she gasped. Hesitantly, she lowered her hands to her lap so she could see her lover's chiseled countenance in the mirror.

Ixifîr hurled his words at her again, snarling, "She dug a tunnel under the field, you fool, and got the dragon out that way. Which means she has both of them with her now!" He drew himself back, his nostrils flaring as he stared at his lovely sorceress, his own cruel features fixed with determination and fury.

They stared at each other, neither moving until Ixifîr gave a little shake of his head and shot her a look filled with disdain.

When he next spoke, his voice was silky. "Because of your repeated mistakes, my dear, we have managed to lose two dragons and two Jewels of Light we might otherwise have had in our possession, and now there is nothing to stop your cunning little sister from leaving Írtha and traveling to Fûlgur!" He leaned forward to place his elbows on the desk in front of him, asking in mock earnestness, "Shall we open the portal to the time stream for her? Perhaps that could backfire upon us as well and we might, by pure chance alone, stop her at least once before she defeats us forever. Or do you still believe you can devise a plan to keep her here indefinitely?"

Bréagna's face was made white and strained by her failures. She sat quietly for a long time without speaking. But then her body slowly began to exhibit signs of recovery: her back straightened, her chin lifted on her neck, her nostrils flared, and when she finally looked at her lover it was with her usual arrogant insouciance.

"My newfound sister," she hissed, her eyes hooded heavily and her lips twisted with hatred and bitterness, "will come to regret very much the day she accepted her magical power. Her children will be the first to pay for her sins toward me, and her friends and those she protects will learn what it means to cross me. I will murder my youngest sibling just as easily as Duínagh and I did Margawse, the supposed 'all-powerful one.' Duínagh will be thrilled to assist me once again, I'm sure. And like dear Margawse, Donemere will never see us coming."

Epilogue

Gwydion's eyes were fixed upon the ground under his feet, his steps slow and measured as he traversed the forest path, belying the pace of his racing thoughts. His mind was chaotically parsing through the results of recent events and analyzing any and all failed plans, conceiving new ones he hoped would be more successful, making connections between events and histories, knowing that some of his latest ideas were fertile and should be saved for later consideration, while others were futile and only good enough to be discarded promptly. So deeply lost in his contemplations was he that he did not realize that he was not alone until Gaia's voice spoke to him.

"You are concerned," she ventured, breaking into his reverie.

Gwydion's head snapped up and his eyes swiveled to the right to meet hers. "How could I not be?" he shot back at her peevishly. The god had taken his preferred form, that of a handsome man, tall and fully bearded, with long, curly hair, light chestnut in color, which cascaded across his shoulders. His raiment showed an imposing musculature beneath them that was accented by the warrior's accoutrements he currently sported. "My plans have gone awry in every possible way, and now Duínagh is to be called into the picture again," he grouched under his breath, placing his hand casually upon the hilt of the broadsword he wore in its scabbard.

In front, behind, and to the sides of them sprang from the dirt what looked like roots that would swirl upward in a circular fashion and become the spiral figures of Artemis and her woodland hunters, with their magical arrows primed tautly in their bows. Their pebble eyes constantly searched the deep woods along the path for signs of potential enemies. These figures retracted back to the ground the farther away the two gods walked from them, disappearing on retreat, only to be called up again on advance.

Noting their protective presence around him, Gwydion chided himself for not having marked them earlier, for surely they would have heralded Gaia's arrival long before she was actually here. But he had been too intent upon his cerebral cogitations to have noticed them or anything else but his own internal dialogues.

Gaia turned to study her fellow deity as they strolled the curved path through the woods. After taking several steps together, she laid a gentle hand upon his arm to halt his frustrated footsteps. "Much progress has been made," she reminded him, arching an eyebrow at him in reproach.

She was in her guise as a young woman today, her most becoming of physical states, but also her most disconcerting. Her long hair seemed to shift color and shape as she moved, and one moment her face was lit with brilliant light and she looked dazzling and pure, and then it was shaded provocatively in shadow and she became a sultry, bewitching temptress, promising love and lust beyond compare. And all the while, her intricately woven ivy costume, with its loops and trailing fringes, served mostly to focus the observing eye upon every bountiful curve of her generous body.

Gwydion shook off her arresting hand and resumed his steps. He pursed his lips tightly in response to her comment, no longer noting her appealing appearance after having become inured to her throughout many prior millennia of fascination with her. Even though her words carried truth, he was still greatly annoyed by them.

"I was hoping to prevent Donemere having to travel to Fûlgur," he told Gaia shortly, his manner bristling, "that filthy dragon world the Ganlonds insists on maintaining. But not only has she saddled herself with two of the vile creatures, she still must fulfill her foolish promise to that *Badûran Vírat*, Ungôl." Gwydion heaved a frustrated breath and complained, "She simply will not stay on task! She is worse than her mother in that regard."

Gaia replaced the gentle hand upon his arm to again halt his footsteps and he once more turned his stormy blue eyes upon her, eyes that were dark and mysterious to others but that were not so to her.

"And you, like me, mourn Morrían still, all this long time after her sad death," Gaia whispered before smiling at her old friend with a mix of sweet reminiscence and regret in her caring expression. "I too miss her greatly, Gwydion, as you know, for she was my friend as well and I trusted no one more than she. The only soul I miss as much is Margawse, whom Morrían gave to you when she herself could not be what you needed. And dear Margawse learned to love you because of her mother's actions and the pity she felt for you."

"It was not *pity* that brought Margawse to my bed," he countered stiffly, and Gaia chuckled, conceding the correction.

"Nay, 'twas not pity Margawse felt for ye, ye spake true and fair," the Earth Goddess replied, falling for the moment into an old vernacular. "The heart of Margawse belonged to thee fully and was a grand prize ye earned from her." Gaia's fingertips ran along his forearm in a fond caress, for she knew his grief for Margawse still had the power to cut him to the quick. Giving his wrist a quick, sympathetic squeeze, she straightened and looked at him with a twinkle in her eyes. "Indeed, it seemed to me that Margawse also seldom followed your directions without changing them in both minor and major form, acts that managed to agitate you much as you are now with Donemere, if memory serves," she remarked, chuckling low again in amusement.

He nodded and smiled with her, the beloved image of his soulmate, so powerful and confident in life, rising up to expand his heart with both deep love and utter sadness, a combined sensation that had never truly left him alone at any time since her death. And for this he was grateful, for it kept Margawse close to him even though his memories of her were all that he was afforded now, making his life bittersweet but still worth living, if only for those precious moments when he would cast his mind back to the feel of her full lips upon his, the softness of her smooth skin, and the seductive scent of her flaming red hair gloriously framing her striking features. He had been enamored with some before her, certainly, and would doubtless care for others in the future, but whenever he thought of love and fullness of heart, of lust and wanton desire, of companionship and amiable conference, he thought only of her, of his wonderful Margawse.

Closing his eyes for a moment, he allowed himself those few seconds to feel his beloved and revel in her memory. Then his eyes snapped open and he resumed his march along the worn path, with an unusually quiet Gaia keeping pace beside him.

"Why is that accursed knife back to play?" he muttered gruffly, as though to himself although Gaia heard him plainly.

"We both know why it has returned and who sent it to Donemere," she replied grimly, shooting him a dark grimace. "I find it interesting that she does not choose to wield it herself this time, although she may be using Bréagna again to hide behind."

Gwydion let out a short bark of unamused laughter. "Perhaps she does not wish to kill this sister with her own hand, but rather with a spell. And a poor spell at that, which means it is likely Bréagna's," he observed tartly and his companion shrugged.

"That is possible. She is playing a game, that much we can know for certain because she always does. But perhaps she is afraid of Donemere and that is why the knife has been sent on its cursed mission rather than residing firmly in the hand that hates her sisters more than she hates breathing." Gaia sighed with undisguised grief. "Duínagh and Bréagna are disappointing in so many, many regards, aren't they?"

"Duínagh made her choice and that is to foster an even worse soul than those of either Bréagna or her Iceni lover," Gwydion reminded Gaia and the great goddess nodded.

"Yes, as painful as it is to all of us who watched her grow from laughing child to twisted woman, Duínagh makes her own choices, always."

"And that thing she reveres so much is still out there doing her bidding," Gwydion reminded his friend, shaking his head in disgust. "The stronger Donemere gets, the more surely it will be attracted to her. And then the trouble will really begin."

Gaia chuckled before pointing out to him wryly, "Don't we all feel that the stronger Donemere gets, the more we want to be in her presence?"

"Yes," admitted Gwydion, "I suppose we do, at that. Her power grows and grows all the time, and its steadfastness and morality are astounding to experience. It quickens one's heart to be near to it, as I'm sure you have felt for yourself. She has Morrían's magic, clearly, but her powers are even greater than Morrían's. Donemere is also as insightful and intelligent as her mother ever was, which is no doubt why she is so difficult to control."

He smiled momentarily at his own joke before adding, "I think she has somehow realized that she was born to be the guardian of magic, although she has yet to learn that she must fight that travesty of Duinagh's in order to succeed. Magic has certainly decided she is its savior though, hasn't it?" He shot a glance at the dubious Gaia and explained, "I mean, just look at how Donemere suddenly has three seeds at hand, even though one is not currently planted and is in its White Jewel form. That must be magic's doing, since that seed has always had the strongest call to those who would use it to further their ends. I think it will not be long before the Ganlonds make sure the White Jewel is planted as well, probably right next to what remains of the Mîrlonds."

"Which will mean that the Ganlonds, the Mîrlonds, and the Ugelonds will all be safe for now and under the guardian's protection," Gaia pointed out with satisfaction. "And that makes it the strongest haven for magical creatures anywhere. So, you see, Donemere has already succeeded at the task of setting up a magical stronghold, which I believe even you thought was to be her primary task in these early stages of the battle. Try to rejoice in that happy victory of hers, my friend, for it is more than anyone else has managed to accomplish since this terrifying threat arose and made us all scramble for cover. She has gotten us to where we are well-placed at the moment, in my opinion."

Unlike Gwydion, who had a tendency to focus mainly on the failures of himself and those working with him, Gaia was immeasurably proud of how well events had conspired of late. She was pleased that Donemere was so tightly in tune with her magical lands, for Gaia knew that they alone would provide the best guidance to her in her role as *Balmaurii*. She was also pleased that Donnie had coaxed Ghira Ma'Hai, or rather Diana as she preferred now, into her true calling once more. And she could not have engineered a better pairing of witches than Liz and Catie, nor could she have foreseen the vanquishing of two of Ixifîr Bíun's greatest sorcerers—an enormous feat effected by the two little witches' ingenuity and the love for them by their friends and family. Jesse too was a bright star, for his existence meant that the elusive Iquakawi were finally pulled into the fight against Morrían's two deviant daughters and their powerful allies.

She was further gladdened when she somehow knew without doubt that the conversation she'd just had with Gwydion was to be recorded in the books about Donnie and her friends. For a very long time now she'd been arguing with him that it was time to give up some of his secrets, for she had faith that Donemere would not fail in the task that magic had set for her and therefore not so many safeguards were needed.

Gaia pondered the whereabouts of Morrían's remaining daughters. She knew for certain where four others were, along with the two that were dead—or in Briganna's case, surprisingly transformed—and the two that insisted upon chasing evil, and finally, of course, Donemere. That made for nine sisters, which meant four more were out there hiding somewhere safe, she presumed, having disguised themselves even from her. She wondered if they had felt the ascension of their youngest sister months earlier, for she knew that Morrían's cunning daughters were all connected no matter how far in distance or time they might be from each other. She also wondered what they thought of it, and whether they would join their young sister in her fight to safeguard magic or if they would prefer to turn their backs upon the heavy responsibility of being a daughter of Morrían.

She told Gwydion nothing of these thoughts of hers and instead walked with him quietly to the Falls of Avendin, his favorite haunt in Írtha. There she would leave him, for she had an idea where she might find one of the missing daughters and she wanted to do a little investigating to confirm or disprove her theory. Only time would tell whether she was right and, if so, whether Vessica was ready to rejoin the family.

Notes from the Author

Please visit my website to learn more information about me and my writing, read my blog, find out who I'm reading, and add your name to my mailing list so you can be one of the first to know when my next project is due out or to maybe earn a little bonus read here and there of parts of my books (or maybe the whole thing). I promise to never send you spam.

My website can be found at:
https://www.cherylagross.com/

I want to thank all my readers for their support. Being an indie (independent) author means that I have to do everything myself, from the writing and storyboarding all the way through to book design, sales and marketing. While I'm pretty good at the first parts, I'm still learning the last parts and have a lot of growing to do in that regard. For instance, I am hoping to make my books available at several other venues than just Amazon by the end of 2019. I am also going to be looking to do some book readings and signings, and perhaps one day I will schedule one in your town, so please be sure to let me know who you are by joining my contact list from my website.

Also, if you would take the time to leave a review wherever you purchase my books online, that would be greatly appreciated. Search engines, especially those internal to book sites, display those titles with the highest number of reviews in their first group of results and therefore those titles get seen and purchased the most. More importantly, I just simply appreciate the feedback I get in reviews.

Lastly, I hope you enjoy reading the Donemere's Music series even half as much as I enjoy writing it. It is a positive story and one of empowerment of the mind, heart and soul, not just for the main characters, but also for those on the edges of the story who contribute so much to the telling. May we all strive to bring out the best in ourselves and each other, no matter what happens in our lives.

About the Author

Beginning when she was a very young girl in Wellsboro, Pennsylvania, Ms. Gross wrote fictional stories, sharing them with family and friends but never having quite enough confidence to attempt publishing them. By default, she fell into a career of technical writing, earning herself a niche in the technical editing market of mining study reports. She has recently returned to her hometown area, although she has previously lived in and traveled to various places throughout the world. Several years ago, she decided to take a hiatus from her professional work and focused on writing novels. The idea for Donemere's Music was born then and "Thy Path Begins" is the first of the books she wrote during this period. After some reworking, it was finally ready to take flight. The second book in the series was published in August 2017, so be on the lookout for "The Cunning Sister Arises" at the Amazon Kindle Store.

Follow Ms. Gross on Facebook:
https://www.facebook.com/DonemeresMusic1/

Titles by Cheryl A. Gross

<u>Donemere's Music</u>
Thy Path Begins (2016)
The Cunning Sister Arises (2017)
Two Stood Together (2019)

www.ingramcontent.com/pod-product-compliance
Lightning Source LLC
Chambersburg PA
CBHW030107040726
47494CB00025B/1395